READER'S DIGEST
CONDENSED BOOKS

www.readersdigest.co.uk

The Reader's Digest Association
Limited 11 Westferry Circus
Canary Wharf London E14 4HE

For information as to ownership of
copyright in the material of this
book, and acknowledgments, see
last page.

Printed in France
ISBN 0 276 42864 1

READER'S DIGEST CONDENSED BOOKS

Selected and edited by Reader's Digest

CONDENSED BOOKS DIVISION
THE READER'S DIGEST ASSOCIATION LIMITED, LONDON

CONTENTS

THE KING OF TORTS

John Grisham

John Grisham is back and on top form with this fascinating story of a young lawyer's fight against corporate greed. When he takes on the case of a man accused of a random street killing, Clay Carter assumes it is just one of the many senseless murders that hit Washington, DC every week. The reality proves very different. As Clay is drawn into the lucrative world of tort litigation, he finds there is more at stake than he imagined—including his own future.

PUBLISHED BY CENTURY

DAYS WITHOUT NUMBER

Robert Goddard

When a mystery buyer called 'Tantris' makes a ridiculously high offer for the Paleologus family home, on the grounds that it hides some priceless stained glass, Michael Paleologus refuses to sell, despite pressure from his five hard-up offspring. Then a shocking and suspicious accident breaks the stalemate, leaving Nick, the youngest son, determined to find the elusive Tantris and so discover the reason for his obsessive interest in the stained-glass window.

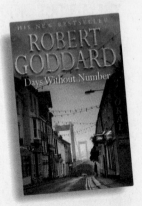

PUBLISHED BY BANTAM PRESS

THE LAST DETECTIVE   page 305

Robert Crais

This exciting thriller delivers nonstop suspense from the very first page. Private investigator Elvis Cole is looking after his girlfriend's son when the boy is snatched from outside his house. All that Cole has to go on is an anonymous phone call in which he is told that the kidnap is retribution for something he once did in Vietnam. Cole is baffled. Who could hate him so much that they would commit such a crime? Frantic, he begins a desperate hunt for the boy.

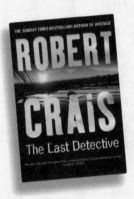

PUBLISHED BY ORION

THE CURIOUS INCIDENT OF THE DOG IN THE NIGHT-TIME   page 439

Mark Haddon

Christopher Boone suffers from a form of autism. He knows a lot about maths, but little about emotions. He loves lists, patterns and his pet rat, but hates being touched. And he's never been further than the end of the road on his own. When a neighbour's dog is killed, Christopher decides to solve the mystery; in so doing he stumbles upon a secret that turns his world upside-down. Unique, moving and funny, this book has become a surprise best seller.

PUBLISHED BY JONATHAN CAPE

THE KING
OF TORTS

JOHN GRISHAM

Clay Carter is a young lawyer stuck in an unglamorous and underpaid position at the Office of the Public Defender. Fearing that life is passing him by, he dreams of a better job in a prestigious law firm. So when the mysterious Max Pace appears, offering untold riches and a place among the legal jet set, he jumps at the chance.

Everything comes at a price, however, as Clay is soon to discover.

1

The shots that fired the bullets that entered Pumpkin's head were heard by no fewer than eight people. Three instinctively closed their windows, checked their door locks, and withdrew to the safety of their small apartments. Two others, each with experience in such matters, ran from the vicinity as fast if not faster than the gunman himself. Another, the neighbourhood recycling fanatic, was digging through some garbage in search of aluminium cans when he heard the sharp sounds of the daily skirmish, very nearby. He jumped behind a pile of cardboard boxes until the shelling stopped, then eased into the alley where he saw what was left of Pumpkin.

And two saw almost everything. They were sitting on plastic milk crates, at the corner of Georgia and Lamont in front of a liquor store. Both would tell the police they saw the boy with the gun reach into his pocket and pull it out. A second later they heard the shots. Another second, and the boy with the gun, a small black pistol, darted from the alley and ran away.

One of them opened the door to the liquor store and yelled for someone to call the police, there had been a shooting.

Minutes later, the police received a call that a young man matching the description of the one who had wasted Pumpkin had been seen on 9th Street carrying a gun in open view and acting strange.

The police found their man an hour later. His name was Tequila Watson, black male, aged twenty, with the usual drug-related police record. No family. No address. The last place he'd been sleeping was a rehab unit on W Street. He'd ditched the gun, and if he'd robbed Pumpkin then he'd also thrown away the booty. His pockets were clean, as were his eyes. The cops were certain Tequila was not under the influence of anything when he was arrested. He was handcuffed and shoved into the rear of a police car.

They drove him back to Lamont Street, where they arranged an impromptu encounter with the two witnesses. Tequila was taken into the alley where he'd left Pumpkin. 'Ever been here before?' a cop asked.

Tequila just gawked at the puddle of blood on the concrete. The two witnesses were eased into the alley, then led near Tequila.

'That's him,' both said at the same time. No doubt about it.

Tequila was taken to jail. He was booked for murder and locked away. Whether through experience or fear, Tequila never said a word to the cops as they pried and cajoled and even threatened. No indication of why he would murder Pumpkin.

No phone call was requested. Tequila seemed dazed but content to sit in a crowded cell and stare at the floor.

PUMPKIN HAD NO TRACEABLE father but his mother worked as a security guard in a large office building on New York Avenue, Washington, DC. It had taken three hours for the police to determine her son's real name—Ramón Pumphrey—to locate his address, and to find a neighbour willing to tell them if he had a mother.

Adelfa Pumphrey was sitting behind a desk, watching a bank of monitors. She was a large woman in a tight khaki uniform, a gun on her waist. The cops broke the news, then found her supervisor.

ADELFA WENT TO COURT to watch the arraignment. The police told her the punk who'd killed her son was scheduled to make his first appearance, a quick and routine matter in which he would plead not guilty and ask for a lawyer.

They herded the criminals through like cattle at an auction. All were black, all wore orange coveralls and handcuffs, all were young.

In addition to his handcuffs, Tequila was adorned with wrist and ankle chains since his crime was especially violent, though he looked fairly harmless when he was shuffled into the courtroom.

Adelfa stared at the skinny boy in the oversized coveralls and wondered why his path had crossed her boy's. The cops had told her it appeared drugs were not involved in the killing. But she knew better. Drugs were involved in every layer of street life. Adelfa knew it all too well. Pumpkin had used pot and crack and he'd been arrested once, for possession, but he had never been violent.

On one side of the courtroom was a table around which the authorities gathered. The cops whispered to the prosecutors, who flipped through files and reports and tried valiantly to keep the paperwork ahead of the criminals. On the other side was a table where the defence lawyers came and went as the assembly line sputtered along. When their names were called, the defendants were led forward to the bench, where they stood in silence.

'Tequila Watson,' a bailiff announced.

He was helped by another bailiff to stutter-step forward, chains rattling.

'Mr Watson, you are charged with murder,' the judge announced loudly. 'Can you afford a lawyer?'

'No.'

'Didn't think so,' the judge mumbled and glanced at the defence table. The fertile fields of the DC Superior Court Criminal Division, Felony Branch, were worked on a daily basis by the Office of the Public Defender, the safety net for all indigent defendants, and at any time there were usually half a dozen PDs milling around. At that moment, however, only one was present, the Honourable Clay Carter II, who had stopped by to check on two lesser felonies.

A week earlier, Mr Carter had finished a murder case, one that lasted for three years and had finally been closed with his client being sent away to a prison which he would never leave. Clay Carter was relieved that he, at that moment, had no murder files on his desk.

That, evidently, was about to change.

'Mr Carter?' the judge said. It was not an order, but an invitation to step forward to do what every PD was expected to do—defend the indigent. Mr Carter could not show weakness, especially with the cops and prosecutors watching. He swallowed hard, and walked to the bench. He took the file from the judge, skimmed its thin contents, then said, 'We'll enter a plea of not guilty, Your Honour.'

'Thank you, Mr Carter. And we'll show you as counsel of record?'

'For now, yes.' Mr Carter was already plotting excuses to unload this case on someone else at OPD.

'Thank you,' the judge said, already reaching for the next file.

Lawyer and client huddled at the defence table for a few minutes. Carter took as much information as Tequila was willing to give, which was very little. He promised to stop by the jail the next day for a longer interview.

He grabbed his briefcase and hurried away, past Adelfa Pumphrey and her little support group, into the hallway crammed with more criminals and their mommas and girlfriends and lawyers. If Clay Carter had ever been attracted to a career in OPD, he could not now remember why. In one week the fifth anniversary of his employment there would come and go, hopefully without anyone knowing it. Clay was burnt out at the age of thirty-one, stuck in an office he was ashamed to show his friends, looking for an exit with no place to go, and now saddled with another senseless murder case.

In the elevator he cursed himself for getting nailed with a murder. I'm quitting, he promised himself; the same vow he had uttered almost every day for the past year.

IN A CITY of 76,000 lawyers, many of them clustered in megafirms within rifle shot of the US Capitol, the Office of the Public Defender was far down in the minor leagues.

Some OPD lawyers were zealously committed to defending the poor and oppressed, and for them the job was not a steppingstone to another career. Regardless of how little they earned, they thrived on the satisfaction of protecting the underdog. The rest told themselves that the job was transitory, just the nitty-gritty training they needed to get launched into more promising careers. Unlimited trial experience, a knowledge of judges and clerks and cops, skill in handling the most difficult clients—these were just a few of the advantages PDs had to offer after only a few years on the job.

OPD had eighty lawyers, all working in a maze of cubbyhole offices spread over two cramped floors of the District of Columbia Public Services Building. The starting salary for an OPD lawyer was $36,000. Rises were minuscule and slow in coming. The workloads were staggering because the city was losing its own war on crime. The supply of indigent criminals was endless. Every year for the past eight the director, a woman named Glenda, had submitted a budget requesting ten more lawyers and a dozen more paralegals. In each of the last four budgets she had received less money than the year before.

Like most of the other PDs, Clay Carter had not entered law school with the plan of a career defending indigent criminals. No way. Back when Clay was in law school, his father had a law firm in DC. Clay had worked there part-time for years. The dreams had been boundless back then, father and son litigating together as the money poured in.

But the firm collapsed during Clay's last year at Georgetown, and his father left town. That was another story. Clay became a public defender because there were no other last-second jobs to grab.

It took him three years to get his own office, which was about the size of a modest suburban utility closet and had no windows. He tossed the Tequila Watson file on his desk and wondered how he might unload it on someone else. He was tired of the tough cases and all the other crap that he put up with as an underpaid PD.

There were six pink phone message slips on his desk; five related to business, one from Rebecca, his girlfriend. He called her first.

'I'm very busy,' she informed him after the initial pleasantries.

'You called me,' Clay said.

'Yes, I can only talk a minute or so.' Rebecca worked as an assistant to a low-ranking congressman who was the chairman of some useless subcommittee. But because he was the chairman he had an office he was required to staff with people like Rebecca, who was in a frenzy all day preparing for the next round of hearings that no one would attend. Her father had pulled strings to get her the job.

'I'm kinda swamped too,' Clay said. 'Just picked up another murder case.' He managed to add a measure of pride to this.

It was a game they played: Who was the busiest? Who was the most important? Who had the most pressure?

'Tomorrow is my mother's birthday,' she said, pausing slightly as if Clay was supposed to know this. He did not. He cared not. He didn't like her mother. 'They've invited us to dinner at the club.'

A bad day just got worse. The only response he could possibly give was, 'Sure.' And a quick one at that.

'Around seven. Jacket and tie.'

'Of course.'

'I gotta run,' she said. 'See you then. Love you.'

'Love you.'

He looked at her photo on his desk. Their romance came with enough complications to sink ten marriages. His father had once sued her father over a bad real-estate deal, and who won and who lost would never be clear. Her father was known as Bennett the Bulldozer for his relentless slash-and-burn development in the Northern Virginia suburbs around DC. Her mother was an aggressive social climber who wanted her daughter to marry serious money. Clay had not seen his own mother in eleven years. He had no social ambitions whatsoever. He had no money.

For almost four years, the romance had survived a monthly brawl, the majority of them engineered by her mother. It clung to life by love and lust and a determination to succeed regardless of the odds against it. But Clay sensed a fatigue on Rebecca's part, a creeping weariness brought on by constant family pressure, and age. She was twenty-eight. She did not want a career. She wanted a husband and a family and long days spent at the country club spoiling the children, playing tennis, doing lunch with her mother.

Paulette Tullos appeared from thin air and startled him. 'Got nailed, didn't you?' she said with a smirk. 'A new murder case.'

Clay would have offered her a seat, but there was no room for another chair in his office. 'What are my chances of getting rid of it?' he said.

'Slim to impossible. Who you gonna dump it on?'

'I was thinking of you.'

'Sorry. I got two murder cases already.'

Paulette was his closest friend inside the OPD. A product of a rough section of the city, she had scratched her way through college and law school at night and had seemed destined for the middle classes until she met an older Greek gentleman with a fondness for young black women. He married her and set her up comfortably in Northwest Washington, then eventually returned to Europe. Paulette suspected he had a wife or two over there, but she wasn't particularly concerned about it. She was well-off and seldom alone. After ten years, the arrangement was working fine.

AT NINE O'CLOCK the next morning, Clay Carter walked through the basement entrance to the jail and signed the register.

A surly guard led him down the hall to a long room divided by a thick sheet of Plexiglas. The guard pointed to the fourth booth from the end, and Clay took a seat.

'Your boy had a bad night,' the guard said. 'Jumped on a kid around two this morning, beat the hell out of him and put him in the hospital. Expect some additional charges.'

'Tequila? Are you sure?' Clay asked, looking over his shoulder.

'It's all on video.' End of conversation.

Tequila was brought to his seat by two guards. He was handcuffed, and though the inmates were customarily set free to chat with their lawyers through the Plexiglas, Tequila's handcuffs were not coming off. He sat down. The guards remained close.

His left eye was swollen shut, with dried blood in both corners. The right one was open and the white of the eye was bright red. There was tape and gauze in the centre of his forehead, and a butterfly

Band-Aid on his chin. Both lips and both jaws were puffy and over-sized to the point that Clay wasn't sure he had the right client.

Clay picked up the black phone receiver and motioned for Tequila to do likewise. He cradled it awkwardly with both hands.

'You are Tequila Watson?' Clay said.

He nodded yes, very slowly.

'Have you seen a doctor?'

A nod, yes.

'Did the cops do this to you?'

Without hesitation he shook his head. No.

'The other guys in the cell do it?'

A nod, yes.

'The cops tell me you beat up some kid. Is that true?'

A nod, yes.

It was hard to imagine Tequila Watson, all 150 pounds of him, bullying people in a crowded prison cell.

'Did you know the kid?'

Lateral movement. No.

'Why, exactly, did you beat up this kid?'

With great effort the swollen lips finally parted. 'I don't know.'

'Did the kid come after you? Was he trash-talking, making threats, that kind of stuff?'

'No. He was asleep.'

'Asleep?'

'Yeah.'

'Was he snoring too loud?'

On his yellow legal pad Clay scribbled the date, time, place, client's name, then ran out of important facts to take note of. He leaned in closer and lowered his voice. 'They say you killed a boy, shot him five times in the head.'

The swollen head nodded slightly.

'A Ramón Pumphrey, also known as Pumpkin. You know him?'

A nod, yes.

'What was it Tequila? A drug deal?'

'No.'

'Did you rob him?'

'No.'

'Talk to me, Tequila. I'm the only person on this planet who's working right now to help you. Give me something to work with.'

'I'll tell you the truth. I had a gun, and I wanted to shoot some-body. Anybody, it didn't matter. I left the Camp and just started walking, going nowhere, looking for somebody to shoot. I saw Pumpkin. I knew him. We talked for a minute. I said I had some rock if he wanted a hit. We went to the alley. I shot the boy. I don't know why. I just wanted to kill somebody.'

When the narrative was over, Clay asked, 'What is the Camp?'

'Deliverance Camp. A rehab place. That's where I was staying.'

'How long had you been there?'

'Hundred and fifteen days.'

'Were you clean when you shot Pumpkin?'

'Yep. Still am. Hundred and sixteen days.'

'You ever shot anybody before?'

'No.'

'Where'd you get the gun?'

'Stole it from my cousin's house.'

'So you walked out of the Camp, went to your cousin's house, stole a gun, then began walking the streets looking for someone to shoot, and you found Pumpkin?'

Tequila was nodding by the end of the sentence. 'That's what happened. Don't ask me why. I don't know. I just don't know.'

There was possibly some moisture in the red right eye of Tequila, perhaps brought on by guilt and remorse. Clay pulled some papers out of his briefcase and slid them through the opening. 'Sign these. I'll come back in a couple of days.'

'What's gonna happen to me?' Tequila asked.

'We'll talk about it later.'

'When can I get out?'

'It might be a long time.'

DELIVERANCE CAMP faced W Street in NW. Within plain sight was the empty lot of an old gas station where drug peddlers met their wholesalers and did their exchanges. According to unofficial police records, the lot had produced more bullet-laden corpses than any other piece of turf in DC.

Clay drove slowly down W Street, doors locked, hands clutching the wheel. A white boy in this ghetto was an irresistible target.

D Camp was an ancient warehouse, long abandoned, condemned, then auctioned off to a non-profit that somehow saw potential.

Clay parked his Honda Accord in front of the building. There was the usual collection of street characters loitering about: some young toughs no doubt hauling drugs and enough assault weapons to hold off the police, a couple of winos, family members waiting to visit those inside D Camp. His job had led him to most of the undesirable places in DC, and this was one of them. He had grown proficient at acting as though he had no fear. I'm a lawyer. I'm here on business. Get out of my way.

He locked the Accord and sadly admitted to himself that few if any of the thugs on this street would be attracted to his little car. It was twelve years old and pushing 200,000 miles.

He held his breath and ignored the curious stares from the sidewalk gang. He pushed a button by the doors and a voice cracked through the intercom. 'Who is it?'

'My name is Clay Carter. I'm a lawyer. I have an eleven o'clock appointment with Talmadge X.' He said the name clearly, still certain that it was a mistake. On the phone he had asked the secretary how to spell Mr X's last name, and she said, quite rudely, that it was not a last name at all. What was it? It was an X. Take it or leave it.

The door clicked open. Clay stepped inside. The reception area was a bunker with a concrete floor, cinderblock walls, metal doors, no windows, low ceiling, few lights, everything but sandbags and weapons. Behind a long government-issue table was a receptionist answering a phone. Without looking up she said, 'He'll be a minute.'

Talmadge X was a wiry, intense man of about fifty, not a hint of a smile on his wrinkled and aged face. He was very black and his clothes were very white—heavily starched cotton shirt and dungarees. Black combat boots shined to perfection. His head was shined too, not a trace of hair.

He pointed to the only chair in his makeshift office, and he closed the door. 'You got paperwork?' he asked abruptly.

Clay handed over the necessary documents, all bearing the indecipherable handcuffed scrawl of Tequila Watson.

'And you're his counsel of record?' Talmadge X asked. 'Officially?'

'Yes. Did you know about the shooting?'

'Not until you called an hour ago. We knew he left Tuesday and didn't come back. Tell me what happened.'

'This is all confidential, right?' Clay said.

'I'm his counsellor. I'm also his minister. You're his lawyer. Everything said in this room stays in this room. Deal?'

'Right.'

Clay gave the details he'd collected so far. When he finished, Talmadge X said, 'What can I do?'

'I'd like to see his file. He's given me authorisation.'

The file was lying squarely on the desk in front of Talmadge X.

'Later,' he said. 'But let's talk first. What do you want to know?'

'Let's start with Tequila. Where'd he come from?'

'The streets, same place they all come from. He was referred by Social Services, because he was a hopeless case. Never knew his father. Mother died of AIDS when he was three. Raised by an aunt or two, foster homes here and there, in and out of court. Dropped out of school. Typical case for us. Are you familiar with D Camp?'

'No.'

'We get the hard cases, the permanent junkies. We lock 'em down, give 'em a boot camp environment. There are eight of us here, eight counsellors, and we're all addicts, once an addict always an addict, but you must know that. Four of us are now ministers. I served thirteen years for drugs and robbery, then I found Jesus. Anyway, we specialise in the young crack addicts nobody else can help.'

'Tell me about his criminal record.'

Talmadge X opened the file and flipped pages. 'Bunch of petty stuff when he was a juvenile, robbery, stolen cars, the usual stuff. At eighteen he did four months for shoplifting. Got him for possession last year, three months there. Nothing violent.'

'I guess that'll help,' Clay said. 'In some way.'

'Sounds like nothing will help, sounds like life with no parole,' said Talmadge X, the voice of experience.

'You got it.'

'Sad thing is, Tequila was one of the few who could've made it.'

'Why is that?'

'Kid's got a brain. Once we got him cleaned up and healthy, he felt so good about himself. He couldn't read so we taught him. He liked to draw so we encouraged art. We never get excited around here, but Tequila made us proud.'

'You never get excited?'

'We lose sixty-six per cent, Mr Carter. Two-thirds. We get 'em in here, their bodies and brains cooked on crack, malnourished, the sickest junkies DC can produce, and we fatten 'em up, dry 'em out, lock 'em down in basic training where they're up at six o'clock scrubbing their rooms and waiting on inspection, breakfast at six thirty, then nonstop brainwashing from a tough group of counsellors who've all been exactly where they've been. After a month they're clean and they're proud. After three months we might start easing them back onto the street for an hour or two a day. Nine out of ten return, anxious to get back to their little rooms. We keep them a year, Mr Carter. We try to educate them some, maybe a little training with computers. We work hard at finding them jobs. They graduate, we all have a good cry. They leave, and within a year two-thirds of them are doing crack again and headed for the gutter.'

'Do you take them back?'

'Rarely. If they know they can come back, then they're more likely to screw up.' Talmadge X kept flipping through the file as if he had something in mind.

Clay suspected he was looking for notes or entries to be removed before it was handed over. 'When can I see that?' he asked.

'How about tomorrow? I'd like to review it first.'

Clay shrugged. If Talmadge X said tomorrow, then it would be tomorrow. 'I don't get his motive,' Clay said. 'Sounds like Tequila was the model patient. You've seen it all. You tell me why.'

'I've seen everything. But I've never seen this. We don't tolerate fighting here, but boys will be boys, and there are always little rituals of intimidation. Tequila was one of the weak ones. There's no way he would leave here, steal a gun, pick a random victim and kill him. And there's no way he would jump on a guy in jail and send him to the hospital. I just don't believe it.'

'So what do I tell the jury?'

'What jury? This is a guilty plea and you know it. He's gone, off to prison for the rest of his life.' Talmadge X closed the file and shoved it away. The meeting was over.

2

The Potomac Country Club in McLean, Virginia, was established a hundred years earlier by some wealthy people who'd been snubbed by the other country clubs. The outcasts pumped their considerable resources into Potomac and built the finest club in the DC area. They picked off a few senators from rival clubs and enticed other trophy members, and before long Potomac had bought respectability. Once it had enough members to sustain itself, like all the rest it began the obligatory practice of excluding others.

It did, however, differ in one significant way. Potomac had never denied that membership could be bought if a person had enough money. Forget waiting lists and screening committees. If you were new to DC, or you suddenly struck it rich, then status could be obtained overnight if your cheque was large enough.

As far as Clay could tell, Bennett Van Horn had written a big cheque. Bennett the Bulldozer struck gold in the late eighties when he invaded the rolling hills of the Virginia countryside. On pristine hills he built malls, apartments, condos, big houses, small houses. Ironically, though irony was lost on Bennett, he named his cookie-cutter projects after the landscape he was destroying—Rolling Meadows, Whispering Oaks, Forest Hills, et cetera. He joined other sprawl artists and lobbied the state legislature in Richmond for more money for more roads so more developments could be thrown up and more traffic created. In doing so, he became a figure in the polit-ical game, and his ego swelled.

In the early nineties, his BVH Group grew rapidly, with revenues increasing at a slightly faster rate than loan payments. He and his wife, Barb, bought a home in a prestigious area of McLean. They joined the Potomac Country Club and became fixtures. They worked hard at creating the illusion that they had always had money.

In 1994, Bennett decided to take his company public. With a blue-chip investment banker leading the way, BVHG stock roared out of the blocks at $10 a share and peaked at $16.50. In the over-the-counter market, the stock floated back to earth and landed with a thud in the $6 range. Bennett had unwisely held on to all of his 4 mil-lion shares and watched as his market value went from $66 million to almost nothing. BVHG was currently trading at $0.87 per share.

'How's your stock doing?' was the great slap-in-the-face Clay'd never had the nerve to use.

'Maybe tonight,' he mumbled to himself as he drove into the entrance of the Potomac Country Club.

To avoid the tip associated with valet parking, Clay hid his Accord in a distant lot behind some tennis courts. As he hiked to the club-house he straightened his tie and continued his mumbling. He hated the place—hated it for all the assholes who were members, hated it because he could not join, hated it because it was the Van Horns' turf and they wanted him to feel like a trespasser. For the hundredth time that day he asked himself why he'd fallen in love with a girl whose parents were so insufferable. If he had a plan, it was to elope with Rebecca to New Zealand, as far from her family as possible.

The gaze from the frosty club hostess told him, I know you are not a member, but I'll take you to your table anyway. 'Follow me,' she said with a fake smile.

Bennett was absent. Clay hugged Mrs Van Horn, a ritual both of them disliked, then offered a rather pathetic, 'Happy birthday.' He pecked Rebecca on the cheek.

'Where's Mr Van Horn?' Clay asked, hoping he was stuck out of town, or better yet, hospitalised with some grave ailment.

'He's on his way,' Rebecca said.

'He spent the day in Richmond, meeting with the Governor,' added Mrs Van Horn, for good measure. They were relentless. Clay wanted to say, 'You win! You're more important than I am!'

'What's he working on?' he asked politely, once again astounded at his ability to sound sincere.

'Political stuff,' Barb said. In truth, she probably didn't know what her husband and the Governor were discussing, or even the current price of BVHG stock. She knew how little money Clay earned, but most other details were left to Bennett.

'How was your day?' Rebecca asked, steering the conversation away from politics. Her parents were right-wing Republicans; Clay was not.

'The usual,' he said. 'And you?'

'We have hearings tomorrow, so the office was hopping today.'

'Rebecca tells me you have another murder case,' Barb said.

'Yes, that's true,' Clay said, wondering what other aspects of his job as a public defender they had been talking about.

'Who's your client?' Barb asked.

'A kid from the streets.'

'Who did he kill?'

'The victim was another kid from the streets.'

This relieved her somewhat. Blacks killing blacks. Who cared if they all killed each other? 'Did he do it?' she asked.

'It sort of looks that way.'

'How can you defend people like that? If you know they're guilty, how can you work so hard trying to get them off?'

Rebecca took a large gulp of wine and decided to sit this one out. She had been coming to his rescue less and less in recent months, he realised. A nagging thought was that, while life would be magical with her, it would be a nightmare with them. The nightmares were winning. 'Our Constitution guarantees everyone a lawyer and a fair trial,' he said condescendingly. 'I'm just doing my job.'

Barb rolled her new eyes and looked away. Many of the ladies at Potomac had been using a plastic surgeon whose speciality, evidently, was the Asian look. After the second session the eyes strained backwards at the corners, and, while wrinkle-free, were grossly artificial. Ol' Barb had been nipped and tucked and Botoxed without a long-range plan, and the transition simply wasn't working.

Rebecca took another long pull on the wine. The first time they had eaten there with her parents she had kicked off a shoe under the table and run her toes up and down his leg, as if to say, 'Let's blow this joint and hop in the sack.' But not tonight.

Bennett arrived in a rush, full of bogus apologies for being late. He slapped Clay on the back and kissed his girls on the cheeks.

'How's the Governor?' Barb asked, loud enough for the diners across the room to hear.

'Great. He sends his best. The President of Korea is in town next week. The Guv has invited us to a black-tie gala at the mansion.' This too was offered at full volume.

'Oh, really!' Barb gushed, her redone face erupting into a contortion of delight.

Should feel right at home with the Koreans, Clay thought.

'Should be a blast,' Bennett said as he lined a collection of cellphones up on the table. A few seconds behind him came a waiter with a double Scotch, Chivas with a little ice, the usual.

Clay ordered an iced tea.

'How are you, honey?' Bennett yelled across the table to Rebecca. 'You look tired, a tough day?'

'Not bad.'

The three Van Horns took a sip. Rebecca's fatigue was a favourite topic between her parents. They felt she worked too hard. They felt she shouldn't work at all. She was pushing thirty and it was time to marry a fine young man with a well-paying job so she could bear their grandchildren and spend the rest of her life at the Potomac.

Clay would not have been too concerned with whatever the hell they wanted, except that Rebecca had the same dreams. She had once talked of a career in public service, but after four years on the Hill she was fed up with bureaucracies. She wanted a husband and babies and a large home in the suburbs.

Menus were passed around. Bennett got a call and rudely handled it at the table. Once he had finished and they had ordered, he graced them with the details—a bank was not moving fast enough, he had to light a fire, blah, blah. This went on until the salads arrived.

After a few bites, Bennett said, with his mouth full, as usual, 'While I was down in Richmond, I had lunch with my close friend Ian Ludkin, Speaker of the House. You'd really like this guy, Clay, a real prince of a man. A perfect Virginia gentleman.'

Clay chewed and nodded as if he couldn't wait to meet him.

'Anyway, Ian owes me some favours, most of them do down there, and so I just popped the question.'

It took Clay a second to realise that the women had stopped eating as they watched and listened with anticipation.

'What question?' Clay asked because it seemed that they were expecting him to say something.

'Well, I told him about you, Clay. Bright young lawyer, sharp as a tack, hard worker, Georgetown Law School, handsome young man with character, and he said he was always looking for talent. Said he has an opening for a staff attorney. I said I had no idea if you'd be interested, but I'd be happy to run it by you. Whatta you think?'

I think I'm being ambushed, Clay almost blurted. Rebecca was staring at him, watching closely for the first reaction.

According to the script, Barb said, 'That sounds wonderful.'

Talented, bright, hard-working, well educated, even handsome. Clay was amazed at how fast his stock had risen. 'That's interesting,' he said, somewhat truthfully. Every aspect of it was interesting.

Bennett was ready to pounce. He, of course, held the advantage of surprise. 'It's a great position. Fascinating work. Lots of long hours, though, at least when the legislature is in session, but I told Ian that you had broad shoulders. Pile on the responsibilities.'

'Richmond's not that far away,' Barb said.

It's a helluva lot closer than New Zealand, Clay thought. Barb was already planning the wedding. He couldn't read Rebecca. At times she felt strangled by her parents, but rarely showed any desire to get away from them.

'Well, uh, thanks, I guess,' Clay said.

'Starting salary is ninety-four thousand a year,' Bennett said.

Ninety-four thousand dollars was more than twice as much as Clay was currently earning, and he assumed that everyone at the table knew it. 'That's a nice salary,' he admitted.

'Not a bad start,' Bennett said. 'Ian says you'll meet the big lawyers, all the movers and shakers down there. Contacts are everything. Do it a few years, and you'll be able to write your own ticket in corporate law. That's where the big money is, you know.'

It was not comforting to know that Bennett had suddenly taken an interest in planning Clay's life. The planning, of course, had nothing to do with Clay, and everything to do with Rebecca.

'Kick it around, sleep on it,' Bennett said. The gift had been delivered. Let's see if the boy is smart enough to take it.

23

Clay was devouring his salad with a new purpose. He nodded as if he couldn't speak. The second Scotch arrived and broke up the moment. Bennett then shared the latest gossip from Richmond. Rebecca was ignoring him and he was ignoring her.

There were stories about the Guv, a close personal friend who was putting his machine in place to run for the Senate and of course he wanted Bennett in the middle of things. There was talk of a new plane, but this had been going on for some time and Bennett just couldn't find the one he wanted. The meal seemed to last for hours, but only ninety minutes had passed when they declined dessert and started wrapping things up.

Clay thanked Bennett and Barb for the food and promised again to move quickly on the job down in Richmond.

'The chance of a lifetime,' Bennett said gravely. 'Don't screw it up.'

When they were gone, Clay asked Rebecca to step into the bar for a minute. They waited for their drinks to arrive before either spoke. When things were tense both had the tendency to wait for the other to fire first.

'I didn't know about the job in Richmond,' she began.

'I find that hard to believe. Your mother certainly knew about it.'

'My father is just concerned about you, that's all.'

Your father is an idiot, he wanted to say. 'No, he's concerned about *you*. Can't have you marrying a guy with no future, so he'll just manage the future for us. Don't you think it's presumptuous to decide he doesn't like my job so he'll find me another one?'

'Maybe he's just trying to help. He loves the favours game.'

'But why does he assume I need help?'

'Maybe you do.'

'I see. Finally the truth.'

'You can't work there for ever, Clay. You're good at what you do and you care about your clients, but maybe it's time to move on. Five years at OPD is a long time. You've said so yourself.'

'Maybe I don't want to live in Richmond. What if I don't want to work under one of your father's cronies? Suppose the idea of being surrounded by a bunch of local politicians does not appeal to me? I'm a lawyer, Rebecca, not a paper-pusher.'

'Fine. Whatever.'

'Is this job an ultimatum?'

She shrugged and sipped her drink. Marriage had been discussed on several occasions but no agreement had been reached. There was no engagement, certainly no timetable. If one wanted out, there was sufficient wiggle room, but after four years of (1) dating no one else and (2) continually reaffirming their love for each other, the relationship was headed towards permanent status.

'I'd like to go,' she said.

'Sure.' He followed her out of the club, and helped her climb into her BMW.

THE NEXT MORNING, Clay returned to the crime scene. He felt somewhat safer with Rodney, plus 9.00am was too early for the dangerous types on Lamont Street. They were still sleeping off whatever poison they had consumed the night before.

Rodney was a black paralegal with OPD. He'd been enrolled in night law school off and on for a decade and still talked of one day getting his degree and passing the Bar, but with four teenagers at home both money and time were scarce. Because he came from the streets of DC he knew them well. Part of his daily routine was a request from an OPD lawyer, usually one who was white and frightened and not very experienced, to accompany him or her into the war zones to investigate some heinous crime. He was a paralegal, not an investigator, and he declined as often as he said yes.

But he never said no to Clay. The two had worked closely together on many cases. Clay parked near the alley and they found the spot where Ramón had fallen. Having inspected the surrounding area carefully, they shot a roll of film, then went looking for witnesses.

There were none. By the time Clay and Rodney had been on the scene for fifteen minutes, word had spread. Strangers were on-site, prying into the latest killing, so lock the doors and say nothing.

After an hour, they left and headed for D Camp. As Clay drove, Rodney said, 'Jermaine got a similar case a few days ago. Kid in rehab, locked down for a few months, got out somehow, within twenty-four hours he'd picked up a gun and shot two people.'

'At random?'

'What's random round here? Two guys in cars have a fender bender and start shooting at each other. Is that random, or justified?'

'Was it drugs, robbery, self-defence?'

'Random, I think.'

Clay parked in front of D Camp and they hurried inside. Talmadge X was not in, some emergency had taken him to a hospital. A colleague named Noland introduced himself and said he was the head counsellor. In his office, he invited them to look through Tequila's file. Clay felt certain it had been cleaned up for his benefit.

'Our policy is that I stay in the room while you look at the file,' Noland explained. 'You want copies, they're twenty-five cents each.'

Clay began leafing through the file. Rodney took notes.

Tequila had been admitted in January, having been kicked out of several abuse facilities previously. He weighed 121 pounds and was five feet ten inches tall. His medical exam had been conducted at D Camp. He had a slight fever, chills, headaches, not unusual for a junkie. Other than malnourishment and a body ravaged by drugs, there was nothing remarkable. Like all patients, he had been locked down for thirty days and fed continually.

As depressing as his history was, there was a remarkable absence of violence in it. Tequila had been convicted five times for burglary, once for shoplifting, and twice for misdemeanour possession. He had never used a weapon to commit a crime. This had not gone unnoticed by TX, who, in one entry on Day 39, said, '. . . has a tendency to avoid even the slightest threat of physical conflict.'

On Day 45, he was examined by a physician. His weight was a healthy 138 pounds. There were notes about his progress in learning to read and interest in art.

Day 100: 'Tequila was awarded a two-hour pass.'

Day 104: 'Two-hour pass. He left, returned with a Popsicle.'

Day 107: 'Sent to the post office, gone almost an hour, returned.'

Day 110: 'Two-hour pass, returned, no problem.'

The final entry was Day 115: 'Two-hour pass, no return.'

Noland was watching as they neared the end of the file. 'Any questions?' he asked, as if they had consumed enough of his time.

'It's pretty sad,' Clay said, closing the file with a deep breath. He had lots of questions but none that Noland could, or would, answer.

JERMAINE VANCE shared an office with another lawyer who happened to be out, so Clay was offered his vacant chair. They compared notes on their most recent murder defendants.

Jermaine's client was a twenty-four-year-old career criminal named Washad Porter, who, unlike Tequila, had a long and frightening history of violence. Seven of his twenty-four years had been spent behind bars, and he had been convicted once of attempted murder. The only attempt at rehab had been in prison and had been clearly unsuccessful. He was accused of shooting two people four days before the Ramón Pumphrey killing. One of the two was killed instantly, the other was barely clinging to life.

Washad had spent six months at Clean Streets, a no-nonsense

abuse facility very similar to D Camp, evidently surviving the rigorous programme there. Jermaine had talked to his counsellor, and the conversation was similar to the one Clay had had with Talmadge X. Washad had cleaned up, was a model patient, was in good health, and gathering self-esteem every day.

He was released from Clean Streets in April, and the next day he shot two men with a stolen gun. His victims appeared to have been selected at random. The first was a deliveryman going about his business. There were words, some pushing and shoving, then four shots to the head, and Washad was seen running away. The delivery-man was in a coma. An hour later, Washad used his last two bullets on a petty drug dealer with whom he had a history. He was tackled by friends of the dealer, who held him for the police.

Jermaine had talked to Washad briefly, in the courtroom during his initial appearance.

'He was in denial,' Jermaine said. 'Had this blank look on his face and kept telling me he couldn't believe he'd shot anybody. He said that was the old Washad, not the new one.'

CLAY COULD THINK of only one other occasion in the past four years on which he called, or tried to call, Bennett the Bulldozer. That effort had ended dismally when he'd been unable to penetrate the layers of importance surrounding the great man.

This time it took at least five minutes to get Bennett's personal secretary on the phone. 'He's out of the office,' she said rudely. 'Leave a number and I'll put it with the rest of his messages.'

'Oh, thank you,' Clay said, and left his office number.

Thirty minutes later Bennett returned the call. He sounded indoors, perhaps in the Men's Lounge at the Potomac Country Club, double Scotch in hand, big cigar, a game of gin rummy in progress with the boys. 'Clay, how are you?'

'Fine, Mr Van Horn, and you?'

'Great. Enjoyed dinner last night. What can I do for you, son?'

'Well, I want you to understand that I really appreciate your efforts to get me that job down in Richmond.' A pause as Clay swallowed hard. 'But truthfully, Mr Van Horn, I don't see a move to Richmond in the near future. I've always seen DC as home.'

Clay had many reasons to reject the offer. Staying in DC was mid-list. The overwhelming motive was to avoid having his life planned by Bennett Van Horn and getting locked into his debt.

'You can't be serious,' Van Horn said.

'Yes, I'm very serious. Thanks, but no thanks.'

'A big mistake, son. One that could have serious consequences.'

'What kinds of consequences?'

'This could really affect your future.'

'Well, it's my future, not yours. I'll pick the next job, and the one after that. Right now I'm happy where I am.'

'We're talking about a huge increase in salary, Clay. More money, better work. Wake up, boy!'

Clay gritted his teeth and let the 'boy' pass. 'I'm not going to argue, Mr Van Horn. I called to say no.'

'You'd better reconsider.'

'I've already reconsidered. No, thanks.'

'You're a loser, Clay. You have no ambition, no guts, no vision.'

'Last night I was a hard worker—had broad shoulders, lots of talent, and I was as sharp as a tack.'

'I take it back. You're a loser.'

'And I was well educated and even handsome.'

'I was lying. You're a loser.'

Clay hung up first. He slammed the phone down with a smile. He'd sent a clear message that he would not be shoved around.

He would deal with Rebecca later, and it would not be pleasant.

CLAY'S THIRD VISIT to D Camp was more dramatic than the first two. With Jermaine in the front and Rodney in the back, Clay followed a police car and parked outside the building. Two cops, both black and bored with subpoena work, negotiated their entrance. Within minutes they were in the midst of a tense confrontation with Talmadge X and Noland, and another counsellor, a hothead named Samuel. Primarily because he was the lawyer who'd obtained the subpoena, the counsellors focused their wrath on Clay.

'You saw the file, man!' Noland yelled at him.

'I saw the file that you wanted me to see,' Clay shot back. 'Now I get the rest of it.'

'What're you talking about?' Talmadge X asked.

'I want everything here with Tequila's name written on it.'

'You can't do that.'

Clay turned to the cop holding the papers and said, 'Would you please read the subpoena?'

The cop held it high for all to see, and read: '"All files pertaining to the admission, medical evaluation, medical treatment and discharge of Tequila Watson. As ordered by the Honourable F. Floyd

Sackman, DC Superior Court Criminal Division."'

'We showed you everything,' Noland said to Clay.

'I doubt that. I can tell when a file has been rearranged.'

'We ain't fighting,' said the larger of the two cops, leaving little doubt that a good fight would be welcome. 'Where do we start?'

'His medical evaluations are confidential,' Samuel said. 'The doctor-patient privilege, I believe.'

'The doctor's files are confidential,' Clay corrected. 'But not the patient's. I have a release and waiver signed by Tequila Watson allowing me to see all of his files, including the medicals.'

They began in a windowless room with mismatched filing cabinets lining the walls. After an hour of digging, nothing useful had been found. Clay and Jermaine left Rodney to continue the search. They had more cops to meet.

The raid on Clean Streets was very similar. The two lawyers marched into the front office with two policemen behind them. The director was dragged out of a meeting. She was very irritated, but the subpoena spoke for itself: all files relating to Washad Porter.

'This was not necessary,' she said to Clay. 'We always cooperate with attorneys.'

'That's not what I hear,' Jermaine said. Indeed, Clean Streets had a reputation for contesting even the most benign requests from OPD.

When she finished reading the subpoena for the second time, one of the cops said, 'We're not going to wait all day.'

She led them to a large office and fetched an assistant who began hauling in files. 'When do we get these back?' she asked.

'When we're finished with them,' Jermaine said.

THE ROMANCE HAD BEGUN at Abe's Place. Rebecca had been in a booth with two girlfriends when Clay walked by en route to the men's room. Their eyes met, and he actually paused for a second, unsure of what to do next. The girlfriends soon got lost. Clay ditched his drinking pals. They sat at the bar for two hours and talked nonstop. The first date was the next night. Sex within a week.

Now, four years later, things were stale and she was under pressure to move on. It seemed fitting they would end things at Abe's Place.

Clay arrived first and stood at the bar. Abe's Place was nothing but a watering hole, strategically placed near Capitol Hill to catch the thirsty crowd headed for the suburbs. Great-looking women. Well dressed. Many of them on the prowl. Clay caught a few looks.

Rebecca was subdued, determined and cold. 'I talked to my

father,' she began, after their drinks had arrived.

'So did I.'

'Why didn't you tell me you were not taking the job in Richmond?'

'Why didn't you tell me your father was pulling strings to get me a job in Richmond?'

'You should've told me.'

'I made it clear.'

'Nothing is clear with you.'

'Your father called me a loser. Is that the prevailing mood in your family?'

'At the moment, yes.'

'Do you want out, Rebecca?'

'I think so,' she said, and her eyes were instantly wet.

'Is there someone else?'

'No,' she said. 'It's just that you're going nowhere, Clay. You're smart and talented, but you have no ambition.'

'Gee, it's nice to know I'm smart and talented again.'

'Are you trying to be funny?'

'Why not, Rebecca? Why not have a laugh? We love each other, but I'm a loser who's going nowhere. That's your problem. My problem is your parents. They'll chew up the poor guy you marry.'

'The poor guy I marry?' Her eyes were no longer wet. They were flashing now.

'Look, I'll make you an offer. Let's get married right now. We quit our jobs, do a quickie wedding with no one present, sell everything we own, and fly to, say, Seattle, and live on love for a while.'

'You won't go to Richmond but you'll go to Seattle?'

'Richmond is too damned close to your parents, OK?'

'Then what?'

'Then we'll find jobs.'

'What kinds of jobs? Is there a shortage of lawyers out West?'

'You're forgetting something. Remember, from last night, that I'm smart, talented, sharp as a tack. Big law firms will chase me all over the place. I'll make partner in eighteen months. We'll have babies.'

'Then my parents will come.'

'No, because we won't tell them where we are. And if they find us, we'll change our names and move to Canada.'

The light moment passed. But it reminded both of why they loved each other and of how much they enjoyed their time together. There had been much more laughter than sadness, though things were changing. Fewer laughs. More influence from her family.

Whatever she had brought to the meeting finally had to be said. She stared him directly in the eyes. 'Clay, I really need a break.'

'A month?'

'Longer than that.'

'No, I won't agree to it. Let's go thirty days without a phone call, OK? Let's meet here on June the 6th, right here at this very table, and we'll talk about an extension, or whatever you want to call it.'

'I'm calling it a breakup, Clay. The big bang. Splitsville. You go your way, I go mine. We'll chat in a month, but I don't expect a change. Things haven't changed much in the past year.'

She grabbed her bag and jumped to her feet. On the way out of the booth, she somehow managed to plant a dry kiss near his temple, but he did not acknowledge it. He did not watch her leave.

She did not look back.

3

Clay's apartment was in an ageing complex in Arlington. He leased a two-bedroom unit with Jonah, an old pal from law school who'd flunked the Bar exam four times before passing it, and now sold computers. He sold them part-time and still earned more money than Clay, a fact that was always just under the surface.

The morning after the breakup, Clay fetched the *Washington Post* from outside his door and settled down at the kitchen table with a cup of coffee.

At twenty past seven, a time when he was usually eating a bowl of cereal, the phone rang. He smiled and thought, It's her. Back already.

No one else would call so early. No one except the boyfriend or husband of whatever lady might be upstairs sleeping off a hangover with Jonah. Clay had taken several such calls over the years. Jonah adored women, especially those already committed to someone else.

But it wasn't Rebecca and it wasn't a boyfriend or a husband.

'Mr Clay Carter,' a strange male voice said.

'Speaking.'

'Mr Carter, my name is Max Pace. I'm a recruiter for law firms in Washington and New York. Your name has caught our attention, and I have two very attractive positions that might interest you. Could we have lunch today?'

Speechless, Clay would remember later that the thought of a nice lunch was, oddly, the first thing that crossed his mind.

'Uh, sure,' he managed to get out. Head-hunters were part of the legal business, same as every other profession. But they rarely spent their time bottom-feeding in the Office of the Public Defender.

'Good. Could you come to the Willard Hotel at, say, noon?'

'Noon's fine,' Clay said, his eyes focusing on a pile of dirty dishes in the sink. Yes, this was real. It was not a dream.

'Thanks, I'll see you then, Mr Carter.'

Max Pace hung up quickly, and for a moment Clay wondered who from his law school class was behind this practical joke. Or could it be Bennett the Bulldozer getting one last bit of revenge?

He had no phone number for Max Pace. He did not even have the presence of mind to get the name of his company.

Nor did he have a clean suit. He owned two, both grey, both very old and well used. His trial wardrobe. Fortunately, OPD had no office dress code, so Clay usually wore khakis and a navy blazer, unless he was going to court.

In the shower, he decided that his attire did not matter. Max Pace knew where he worked and how little he earned. If Clay showed up in frayed khakis, then he could demand more money.

Sitting in traffic on the Arlington Memorial Bridge, he decided it was his father. The old guy had been banished from DC but still had contacts. He'd finally called in one last favour, found his son a decent job. When Jarrett Carter's high-profile legal career ended in a long and colourful flameout, he pushed his son towards the Office of the Public Defender. Now that apprenticeship was over. Five years in the trenches, and it was time for a real job.

AFTER SUFFERING through the most unproductive morning of his career, Clay drove to the Willard. He asked for Pace at Reception and was directed to the Theodore Roosevelt Suite on the ninth floor. Clay knocked on the door. It opened quickly and Max Pace said hello with a businesslike smile. He was in his mid-forties, dark wavy hair, dark moustache, dark everything. Black denim jeans, black T-shirt, black pointed-toe boots. Hollywood at the Willard. Not exactly the corporate look Clay had been expecting. They shook hands.

'Thanks for coming,' Max said as they walked into an oval-shaped room laden with marble.

'Sure.' Clay was absorbing the suite; luxurious leathers and fabrics, rooms branching off in all directions. 'Nice place.'

'It's mine for a few more days. I thought we could eat up here, order room service, that way we can talk with complete privacy.'

'Fine with me.' A question came to mind, the first of many. What was a Washington head-hunter doing renting a horribly expensive hotel suite? Didn't he have an office nearby?

'Anything in particular to eat?'

'I'm easy.'

'They do a great capellini and salmon dish. I had it yesterday.'

'I'll try it.'

Max went to the phone while Clay admired the view of Pennsylvania Avenue below. When lunch was ordered, they sat and quickly got past the weather and the Orioles latest losing streak. Pace seemed at ease talking about anything for as long as Clay wanted. He was a serious weightlifter who wanted folks to know it. His T-shirt stuck to his chest and arms.

A stunt man maybe, but not a head-hunter in the big leagues.

Ten minutes into the chatter, and Clay said, 'These two firms, why don't you tell me a little about them?'

'They don't exist,' Max said. 'I admit I lied to you. And I promise it's the only time I will ever lie to you.'

'You're not a head-hunter, are you?'

'No. I'm a fireman.'

'Thanks, that really clears things up.'

'Let me talk for a moment. I have some explaining to do, and when I'm finished I promise you'll be pleased.'

'I suggest you talk real fast, Max, or I'm outta here.'

'Very well. I'm a freelancer with a speciality. I get hired by big companies to put out fires. They screw up, they realise their mistakes before the lawyers do, so they hire me to enter the picture quietly, tidy up their mess and save them a bunch of money. My services are in demand. My name may be Max Pace and it may be something else. It doesn't matter. What's important here is that I have been hired by a large company to put out a fire. Questions?'

'Too numerous to ask right now.'

'Hang on. I cannot tell you the name of my client now, perhaps never. If we reach an agreement, then I can tell you much more. Here's the story: My client is a blue-chip multinational that manufactures pharmaceuticals. About two years ago, it came up with a drug that might cure addiction to opium- and cocaine-based narcotics. Let's call this wonder drug Tarvan—that was its nickname for a while. It was discovered by mistake and quickly used on every laboratory animal available. The results were outstanding, but then it's hard to duplicate crack addiction in a bunch of rats.'

'They needed humans,' Clay said.

'Yes. The potential for Tarvan was enough to keep the big suits awake at night. Imagine, take one pill a day for ninety days and you're clean. Your craving for drugs is gone. You've kicked cocaine, heroin, crack—just like that. After you're clean, take a Tarvan every other day and you're free for life. Almost an instant cure, for millions of addicts. Think of the lives to be saved, the crimes that would not be committed, the families held together, the billions not spent trying to rehab addicts. Think of the profits. The more the suits thought about how great Tarvan could be, the faster they wanted it on the market. But, as you say, they still needed humans.'

A sip of coffee. His biceps rippled under the T-shirt.

He continued. 'So they began making mistakes. They picked three places—Mexico City, Singapore, Belgrade—places far outside the jurisdiction of the Food and Drug Administration. Under the guise of some vague international relief outfit, they built nice rehab clinics where the addicts could be completely controlled. They picked the worst junkies they could find, got 'em in, cleaned 'em up, began using Tarvan on them.'

'Human laboratories,' Clay said.

'Nothing but human laboratories. And the drug performed beautifully. After thirty days, Tarvan blunted the cravings for drugs. After sixty days, the addicts seemed quite happy to be clean, and after ninety days they had no fear of returning to the streets. Everything was monitored—diet, exercise, therapy, even conversations. After three months, the patients were turned loose, with the agreement that they would return to the clinic every other day for their Tarvan. Ninety per cent stayed on the drug, and stayed clean. Only two per cent relapsed into addiction.'

'And the other eight per cent?'

'They would become the problem, but my client didn't know how serious it would be. Anyway, they kept the beds full, and over eighteen months about a thousand addicts were treated with Tarvan. The results were off the charts. My client could smell billions in profits.'

A buzzer sounded, lunch had arrived. A waiter rolled it in on a trolley and spent five minutes fussing with the set-up. Max tipped the guy and finally got him out of the room.

'You hungry?' he asked.

'No. Keep talking. I think you're getting to the good part.'

'Good, bad, depends on how you look at it. The next mistake was to bring the show here. My client had deliberately looked at the globe and picked one spot for Caucasians, one spot for Hispanics, and one spot for Asians. Some Africans were needed.'

'We have plenty in DC.'

'So thought my client.'

Clay slowly got to his feet and walked round his chair to the window again. Max watched him closely.

Clay turned round and said, 'Tequila?'

Max nodded and said, 'Yes.'

'And Washad Porter?'

'Yes.'

A minute passed. Clay crossed his arms and leaned against the wall, facing Max. 'Go ahead,' Clay said.

'In about eight per cent of patients, something goes wrong,' Max said. 'My client has no idea what or even who might be at risk. But Tarvan makes them kill. Plain and simple. After about a hundred days, something turns somewhere in the brain, and they feel an irresistible impulse to draw blood. Makes no difference if they have a violent history. Age, race, sex, nothing distinguishes the killers.'

'That's eighty dead people?'

'At least. But information is difficult to obtain in the slums of Mexico City.'

'How many here, in DC?'

It was the first question that made Max squirm, and he dodged it. 'I'll answer that in a few minutes. Let me finish my story.'

Clay sat down again.

'The next mistake was to circumvent the FDA.'

'Of course.'

'My client has many big friends in this town. It's an old pro at buying politicians. A dirty deal was cut. It included big shots from the White House, the State Department, the Drug Enforcement Administration and the FBI, none of whom put anything in writing. No money changed hands; there were no bribes. My client did a nice job of convincing enough important people that Tarvan might save the world if it could perform in one more laboratory. These big people, names now for ever lost, found a way to smuggle Tarvan into a few, selected, federally funded rehab clinics in DC. If it worked here, then the White House and the big folks would put pressure on the FDA for quick approval.'

'When this deal was being cut, did your client know about the eight per cent?'

'I don't know. My client has not told me everything and never will. However, I suspect that my client did not know about the eight per cent. Otherwise, the risks would have been too great to experiment here. This has all happened very fast, Mr Carter.'

'You can call me Clay.'

'Thanks, Clay. I said there were no bribes. Again, this is what my client has told me. But let's be realistic. The initial estimate of profits over the next ten years from Tarvan was thirty billion dollars. Obviously, some money was going to change hands along the line.'

'But all that's history?'

'Oh, yes. The drug was pulled six days ago. Those wonderful clinics in Mexico City, Singapore and Belgrade closed up in the middle of the night and all those nice counsellors disappeared like ghosts. All experiments have been forgotten. All papers have been shredded. My client has never heard of Tarvan. We'd like to keep it that way.'

'I get the feeling that I'm entering the picture at this point.'

'Only if you want to. If you decline, then I am prepared to meet with another lawyer.'

'Decline what?'

'The deal, Clay, the deal. As of now, there have been five people in DC killed by addicts on Tarvan. One poor guy is in a coma, probably not going to make it. Washad Porter's first victim. That's a total of six. We know who they are, how they died, who killed them, everything. We want you to represent their families. You sign them up, we pay the money, everything is wrapped up quickly, quietly, with no lawsuits, no publicity, not the slightest fingerprint anywhere.'

'Why would they hire me?'

'Because they don't have a clue that they have a case. As far as they know, their loved ones were victims of random violence. You will tell them that they have a case, and that you can get them four million bucks in a very quick, very confidential settlement.'

'Four million bucks,' Clay repeated, uncertain if it was too much or too little.

'Here's our risk, Clay. If Tarvan is discovered by some lawyer, and, frankly, you're the first one who picked up even a whiff of a scent, then there could be a trial. Let's say the lawyer is a trial stud who somehow gets the right evidence. Maybe some documents that didn't get shredded. More likely from a whistle-blower. Anyway, he picks him an all-black jury and the trial plays beautifully for the family of the deceased. There could be a huge verdict. But the negative publicity for my client would be horrendous. The stock price could collapse.'

'Four million is a bargain.'

'It is, and it isn't. Take Ramón Pumphrey. Aged twenty-two, working part-time, earning six thousand a year. With a life expectancy of fifty-three more years, and assuming earnings of twice the minimum wage, the economic value of his life, discounted in today's dollars, is about half a million dollars. That's what he's worth.'

'Punitive damages would be easy.'

'Depends. This case would be hard to prove, Clay, because there's no paperwork. Those files you snatched yesterday will reveal nothing. The counsellors at D Camp and Clean Streets had no idea what kind of drugs they were dispensing. My client would spend a billion on lawyers and experts and whoever else they need to protect them.'

'Six times four is twenty-four million.'

'Add ten for the lawyer.'

'Ten million?'

'Yes, that's the deal, Clay. Ten million for you.'

'You must be kidding.'

'Dead serious. And I can write the cheques right now.'

'I need to go for a walk.'

DRIFTING NOW, on foot in front of the White House. Lost for a moment in a pack of tourists, then a stroll through Lafayette Park, all thoughts slow and confused. It was May but the air was not clear. The humidity did little to help him think.

He saw twelve black faces sitting in the box, angry folks who'd spent a week hearing the shocking history of Tarvan. He addressed them in his final summation: 'They needed black lab rats, ladies and gentlemen, so they brought their miraculous Tarvan to our city.' The twelve nodded in agreement, anxious to retire and dispense justice.

What was the largest verdict in the history of the world? Whatever it was, it would be his for the asking.

The case would never go to trial. Whoever made Tarvan would spend a helluva lot more than thirty-four million to bury the truth. And they would hire all manner of thugs to break legs and steal documents and wire phones, whatever it took to protect their secret.

He thought of Rebecca. What a different girl she would be wrapped in the luxury of his money. She would marry him in three months, or as soon as Barb could get things planned, and retire to a life of motherhood.

He thought of the Van Horns, but, oddly, not as people he still knew. He was free of those people, after four years of bondage. They would never again torment him.

He was about to be free of a lot of things.

An hour passed. He found himself at DuPont Circle. He walked along the sidewalk, sick with the thought that a respected company could prey on the weakest people it could find, then seconds later thrilled with the prospect of more money than he ever dreamed of.

Another hour passed. He was expected back at the office, a weekly staff meeting of some variety. 'Fire me,' he mumbled with a smile.

He browsed for a while in Kramer's, his favourite bookstore in DC, before walking into the café at the rear of the store. There was Max Pace, sitting alone, drinking lemonade, waiting. He was obviously pleased to see Clay again.

'Did you follow me?' Clay asked, sitting down.

'Of course. Would you like something to drink?'

'No. What if I filed suit tomorrow, on behalf of the family of Ramón Pumphrey? That one case could be worth more than what you're offering for all six.'

The question seemed to have been anticipated. 'You'd have a long list of problems. Let me give you the top three. First, you don't know who to sue. You don't know who made Tarvan, and there's a chance no one will ever know. Second, you don't have the money to fight with my client. It would take at least ten million dollars to mount a sustainable attack. Third, you'd lose the opportunity to represent all known plaintiffs. If you don't say yes quickly, I'm prepared to go to the next lawyer on my list with the same offer.'

'I could go to a big tort firm.'

'That would present more problems. First, you'd give away at least half your fee. Second, it would take five years to reach an outcome, maybe longer. Third, even the biggest tort firm in the country could easily lose this case. The truth here, Clay, may never be known.'

'It should be known.'

'Maybe, but I don't care one way or the other. My job is to silence this thing; to compensate the victims, then to bury it for ever.'

'You have a list of lawyers?'

'Yes, I have two more names, both very similar to you.'

'In other words, hungry.'

'Yes, you're hungry. But you're also bright. Today is Thursday. I need an answer by Monday. Otherwise, I'll go to the next guy.'

'How many people were treated with Tarvan in DC?'

'A hundred, give or take.'

Clay took a drink of the iced water a waiter had placed near him. 'So there are a few more killers out there?'

'Quite possibly. We're waiting and watching with great anxiety.'

'Can't you stop them?'

'Tarvan gives no clue as to who might snap, nor when they might do so. There is some evidence that after ten days without the drug a person becomes harmless again. But it's all speculative.'

'So the killings should stop in just a few days?'

'We're counting on it. I'm hoping we can survive the weekend.'

'Your client should go to jail.'

'My client is a corporation.'

'Corporations can be held criminally responsible.'

'Let's not argue that, OK? We need to focus on you and whether or not you are up to the challenge.'

'I'm sure you have a plan.'

'Yes, a very detailed one.'

'I quit my present job, then what?'

Pace pushed the lemonade aside and leaned lower. 'You establish your own law firm. Rent space, furnish it nicely, and so on. You've got to look and act like a successful trial lawyer. Your potential clients need to be impressed. You'll need a staff and other lawyers working for you. Perception is everything here. Trust me. I was a lawyer once. Clients want to see success.'

'I get the point. I grew up in a very successful law firm.'

'We know. That's one of the things we like about you.'

'How tight is office space right now?'

'We've leased some footage on Connecticut Avenue. Would you like to see it?'

They left Kramer's and ambled along the sidewalk. They stopped at an intersection. 'Right now I represent the defendant,' Clay said as they waited. 'How do I cross the street and represent his victim?'

'We've researched the ethics. Once you resign from OPD, you are free to open your own office and start accepting cases.'

'What about Tequila Watson? I know why he committed murder. I can't hide that knowledge from him, or his next lawyer.'

'Being under the influence of drugs is not a defence to a crime. He's guilty. Ramón Pumphrey is dead. You have to forget about Tequila.' They were walking again.

'I don't like that answer,' Clay said.

'It's the best I have. If you say no to me and continue to represent your client, it will be virtually impossible for you to prove he ever took a drug called Tarvan. You'll look foolish using that as a defence. Here.' They were on Connecticut Avenue, in front of a long modern building with a three-storey glass-and-bronze entrance.

Clay looked up and said, 'The high-rent district.'

'Come on. Your office is on the fourth floor.'

In the vast marble foyer, a directory listed a who's who of DC law. 'This is not exactly my turf,' Clay said, reading the names.

'It can be,' Max said.

'What if I don't want to be here?'

'It's up to you. We just happen to have some space. We'll sublease it to you at a very favourable rent.'

Carpet was being laid and walls painted in Clay's section of the fourth floor. Expensive carpet. They stood at a window and watched the traffic on Connecticut Avenue below. There were a thousand things to do to open a new firm, and he could only think of a hundred. He had a hunch that Max had all the answers.

'You can do your firm's charter online,' Max said, reading his thoughts. 'Takes about an hour. Pick a bank, open the accounts. Letterhead and such can be done overnight. The office can be complete and furnished in a matter of days. By next Wednesday you can be sitting here behind a fancy desk running your own show.'

'How do I sign up the other cases?'

'Your friends Rodney and Paulette. They know the city and its people. Hire them, triple their salaries, give them nice offices down the hall. They can talk to the families. We'll help.'

'You've thought of everything.'

'Yes. Everything. We just need a point man, Clay.'

On the way down, the elevator stopped at the third floor. Three men and a woman stepped in, all nicely tailored and carrying thick expensive leather briefcases, along with the incurable air of importance inbred in big-firm lawyers. They did not acknowledge Clay's existence. Of course, in old khakis and scuffed loafers he did not exactly project the image of a fellow member of the DC Bar.

That could change overnight, couldn't it?

He said goodbye to Max and walked back to his office. When he arrived, there were no urgent notes on his desk. The meeting he'd missed had evidently been missed by many others. No one seemed to notice that he had been absent during the afternoon.

His office was suddenly much smaller, and dingier, and the furnishings were unbearably bleak. There was a stack of files on his desk, cases he could not now bring himself to think about.

OPD policy required thirty days' notice before quitting. The rule, however, was not enforced because it could not be. People quit all the time with no notice. Glenda would write a threatening letter. He would write a pleasant one back, and the matter would end.

The best secretary in the office was Miss Glick, a seasoned warrior who might just jump at the chance to double her salary and leave behind the dreariness of OPD. His office would be a fun place to work, he had already decided.

HE MET MAX PACE for the third time that day, for dinner, at the Old Ebbitt Grille, two blocks behind the Willard. To his surprise, Max began with a martini, and this loosened him up considerably. The pressure of the situation began melting under the assault of the gin, and Max became a real person. He had once been a trial lawyer in California, before something unfortunate ended his career out there. Through contacts he found his niche in the litigation marketplace as a fireman. A fixer. A highly paid agent who sneaked in, cleaned up the mess, and sneaked out without a trace. During the steaks and after the first bottle of Bordeaux, Max said there was something else waiting for Clay after Tarvan. 'Something much bigger.'

'What?' Clay said after a long wait.

'My client has a competitor who's put a bad drug on the market. No one knows it yet. Their drug is outperforming our drug. But my client now has proof that the bad drug causes tumours. My client has been waiting for the perfect moment to attack.'

'Attack?'

'Yes, as in a class-action suit brought by a young aggressive attorney who possesses the right evidence.'

'You're offering me another case?'

'Yes. You take the Tarvan deal, wrap things up, then we'll hand you a file that will be worth much more than Tarvan.'

'Why me?' Clay asked, more to himself than to his new friend.

'That's the same question lottery winners ask. You've won the lottery, Clay. The lawyers' lottery. You were smart enough to pick up the scent of Tarvan, and at the same time we were searching for a young lawyer we could trust. Say yes, and you will become a very big lawyer. Say no, and you lose the lottery.'

'I get the message. I need some time to think, to clear my head.'

'You have the weekend.'

4

The suite was in a different hotel. Pace was moving around DC as if spies were trailing him. After a quick hello and the offer of coffee, they sat down for business. Clay could tell that the pressure of burying the secret was working on Pace. He looked tired. His movements were anxious. The smile was gone. No questions about the weekend. Pace was about to cut a deal, either with Clay Carter or the next lawyer on his list. They sat at a table, each with a legal pad, pens ready to attack.

'I think five million per death is a better figure,' Clay began. 'Sure they're street kids whose lives have little economic value, but what your client has done is worth millions in punitive damages. So we blend the actual with the punitive and we arrive at five million.'

'The guy in the coma died last night,' Pace said.

'So we have six victims.'

'Seven. We lost another one on Saturday morning.'

Clay had multiplied five million times six so many times he had trouble accepting the new figure. 'Who? Where?'

'I'll give you the dirty details later, OK? Let's say it's been a very long weekend. We were monitoring nine-one-one calls, which on a busy weekend in this city takes a small army.'

'You're sure it's a Tarvan case?'

'We're certain.'

Clay scribbled something meaningless and tried to adjust his strategy. 'Let's agree on five million per death,' he said.

'Agreed.'

Clay had convinced himself that it was a game of zeros. Don't think of it as real money. Forget the dramatic changes about to come. Ignore the sharp knife twisting in your stomach. Your opponent is weak and scared, and very rich and very wrong.

Clay swallowed hard and tried to speak in a normal tone. 'The attorneys' fees are too low,' he said.

'Oh, really?' Pace actually smiled. 'Ten million won't cut it?'

'Not for this case. Your exposure would be much greater if a big tort firm were involved.'

'You catch on quick, don't you?'

'Half will go for taxes. The overhead you have planned for me will be very expensive. Plus, I want to do something for Tequila and the other defendants who are getting shafted in all this.'

'Just give me a figure.' Pace was already scribbling something.

'Fifteen million will make the transition smoother.'

'Are you throwing darts?'

'No, just negotiating.'

'So you want fifty million—thirty-five for the families, fifteen for you. Is that it?'

'That should do it.'

'Agreed.' Pace thrust a hand over and said, 'Congratulations.'

Clay shook it. He could think of nothing to say but 'Thanks.'

'There is a contract, with some details and stipulations.' Max was reaching into a briefcase.

'What kinds of stipulations?'

'For one, you can never mention Tarvan to Tequila Watson, his new lawyer, or to any of the other defendants involved. To do so would compromise everything. As we discussed earlier, drug addiction is not a legal defence to a crime. It could be a mitigating circumstance during sentencing, but Mr Watson still committed murder.'

'I understand this better than you.'

'Then forget about the murderers. You now represent the families of their victims. Our deal will pay you five million up-front, another five in ten days, and the remaining five upon final completion of all settlements. You mention Tarvan to anyone and the deal is off.'

Clay nodded and stared at the thick contract now on the table.

'This is basically a confidentiality agreement,' Max continued, tapping the paperwork. 'It's filled with dark secrets, most of which you'll have to hide from your own secretary. For example, my client's name is never mentioned. There's a shell corporation now set up in Bermuda with a division in the Dutch Antilles that answers to a Swiss outfit headquartered in Luxembourg. The paper trail begins and ends over there and no one, not even me, can follow it without getting lost. Your new clients are getting the money; they're not supposed to ask questions. As for you, you're making a fortune. We don't expect any sermons from a higher moral ground. Just take the money, finish the job, everybody will be happier.'

'Just sell my soul.'

'As I said, skip the sermons. You're doing nothing unethical.' He filled in some blanks deep in the contract, then slid it across the table. 'This is our deal. Sign it, and I'll get us some coffee.'

Clay began reading as Max got on the phone to room service.

He would resign immediately from OPD and withdraw as counsel of record for Tequila Watson. He would charter his own law firm directly; hire sufficient staff, open bank accounts, et cetera. A proposed charter for the Law Offices of Jarrett Clay Carter II was attached, all boilerplate. He would, as soon as practicable, contact the seven families and begin the process of soliciting their cases.

Coffee arrived and Clay kept reading. Max was on a cellphone across the suite, whispering in a hushed, serious voice, no doubt relaying the latest events to his superior. For his signature, Clay would receive, by wire, $5 million, a figure that had just been neatly written in by Max. His hands shook when he signed his name, not from fear or moral uncertainty, but from shock.

When the paperwork was complete, they left the hotel and climbed into a chauffeur-driven SUV. 'I suggest we get the bank account opened first,' Max said softly. Clay was Cinderella going to the ball, just along for the ride because it was all a dream now.

'Sure, a good idea,' he managed to say.

'Any bank in particular?' Pace asked.

Clay's current bank would be shocked to see the type of activity that was coming. 'I'm sure you have one in mind,' Clay said.

'Chase Bank, on 15th,' Max said to the driver, who was already headed in that direction. Max pulled out more papers. 'Here's the lease and sublease on your office. My client used a straw company to lease it for two years at eighteen thousand a month. We can sublease it to you for the same rent.'

'That's four hundred thousand bucks, give or take.'

Max smiled and said, 'You can afford it, sir.'

At the bank, a vice-president of some strain had been reserved. Max asked for the right person and red carpets were rolled down every hallway. Clay took charge of his affairs and signed all the proper documents.

The wire would be received that afternoon, according to the veep.

Back in the SUV, Max was all business. 'As you saw from the contract, we took the liberty of preparing a corporate charter for your law firm,' he said, handing over more documents. 'You can register online from your desk at OPD.'

Clay looked out of a window. A sleek burgundy Jaguar XJ was sitting next to them at a red light, and his mind began to wander.

'Speaking of OPD,' Max was saying, 'how do you want to handle those folks?'

'Let's do it now.'

'M at 18th,' Max said to the driver. Back to Clay he said, 'Have you thought about Rodney and Paulette?'

'Yes. I'll talk to them today. But it seems as though I'll need to tell them everything.'

'Almost everything. They will be the only people in your firm who'll know what's happened. But you can never mention Tarvan.'

If anyone at OPD missed Clay it wasn't obvious. There were a dozen messages on his desk, all irrelevant now. Glenda was at a conference in New York. He quickly emailed her a letter of resignation, then filled two briefcases with his personal office junk.

Rodney's desk was in a tiny work space he shared with two other paralegals. 'Got a minute?' Clay said.

'Not really,' Rodney said, barely looking up from a pile of reports.

'There's a breakthrough in the Tequila Watson case. It'll just take a minute.'

Rodney reluctantly followed Clay back to his office, where the door was locked behind them. 'I'm leaving,' Clay began.

They talked for almost an hour, while Max Pace waited in the SUV. When Clay emerged with two bulky briefcases, Rodney was with him, also laden with a briefcase and a stuffed shopping bag. He went to his car and disappeared. Clay jumped in the SUV.

'He's in,' Clay said.

'What a surprise.'

At the office on Connecticut Avenue, they met a design consultant retained by Max. He showed Clay various designs and samples, all on the higher end of the price scale. Clay made his choices and a computer consultant arrived as the decorator left.

Shortly before 5.00pm, Max emerged from a freshly painted office and stuck his cellphone in his pocket. 'The wire is in,' he said to Clay.

'Five million?'

'That's it. You're now a multimillionaire.'

'I'm outta here,' Clay said. 'See you tomorrow.'

'Where are you going?'

'Don't ever ask that question again, OK? You are not my boss. And don't follow me. We have our deal.'

He walked along Connecticut for a few blocks, jostling with the rush-hour crowd, smiling goofily to himself, his feet never touching the concrete. Down 17th then right, past the Vietnam Memorial. Beyond it, he stopped at a kiosk, bought two cheap cigars, lit one, and continued to the steps of the Lincoln Memorial, where he sat for a long time and gazed down The Mall to the Capitol.

Clear thinking was impossible. One good thought was immediately pushed out by another. He puffed on the cigar and mentally shopped for a while, and just for the fun of it made a tally of how much he would spend if he bought everything he wanted—a new wardrobe, a really nice car, a stereo system, some travel. The total was but a small subtraction from his fortune.

And of course he would need a new address. He'd look around Georgetown for a quaint old town house. He was confident he could find something in the million-dollar range.

He thought of Rebecca, though he tried not to dwell on her. For the past four years she had been the only friend with whom he'd shared everything. Now there was no one to talk to. Their breakup was five days old, but so much had happened that he'd had little time to think about her.

'Forget the Van Horns,' he said aloud, blowing a cloud of smoke.

He lit the second cigar and called Jonah, who was at the computer store putting in a few hours. 'I have a table at Citronelle, eight o'clock,' Clay said. It was, at that moment, everybody's favourite French restaurant in DC.

'Right,' Jonah said.

'I'm serious. We're celebrating. I'm changing jobs. I'll explain later.'

IN HIS SHIRT POCKET he had brand-new business cards, the ink barely dry, declaring him to be Rodney Albritton, Chief Paralegal of the Law Offices of J. Clay Carter II.

If he'd had the time to purchase a new suit, he probably wouldn't have worn it on his first mission. The old uniform would work better—navy blazer, loosened tie, faded jeans. He found Adelfa Pumphrey at her station, staring at a wall of closed-circuit monitors but seeing nothing. Her son had been dead for ten days.

She looked at him and pointed to a clipboard where all guests were expected to sign in. He pulled out one of his cards and introduced himself. 'I work for a lawyer downtown,' he said. 'I'd like to talk to you for a couple of minutes about your son, Ramón.'

'What about him?'

'I know some things about his death that you don't.'

'Not one of my favourite subjects right now.'

'I understand that, and I'm sorry to be talking about it. But you'll like what I got to say, and I'll be quick.'

'I can take a break in twenty minutes,' she said. 'Meet me in the canteen, one floor up.'

As Rodney walked away he told himself that, yes, he was in fact worth every penny of his fat new salary. Adelfa Pumphrey would never have trusted a white guy who had approached her with such a delicate matter, at least not within the first fifteen minutes of conversation.

But Rodney was smooth and smart and black and she wanted to talk to someone.

MAX PACE'S FILE ON Ramón Pumphrey was brief but thorough; there wasn't much to cover. His father had never married his mother. The man's name was Leon Tease, and he was serving a thirty-year sentence in Pennsylvania for armed robbery and attempted murder. He and Adelfa had lived together long enough to produce two children—Ramón and a younger brother named Michael. Another brother had been sired later by a man Adelfa married and then divorced. She was currently unmarried and trying to raise, in addition to her two remaining sons, two nieces who belonged to a sister who'd been sent to prison for selling crack.

Adelfa earned $21,000 working for a company hired to guard low-risk office buildings in DC. Other than work and family, her only outside interest appeared to be the Old Salem Gospel Center not far from her apartment in Lincoln Towers, a project in the Northeast.

SINCE THEY HAD BOTH grown up in the city, they played 'Who-do-you-know?' for a few minutes. Where did you go to school? Where were your parents from? They found a couple of tenuous connections. Adelfa worked on a diet cola. Rodney had black coffee. The canteen was half-filled with low-level bureaucrats.

'You wanted to talk about my son,' she said after a few minutes of awkward chitchat. Her voice was soft and low, strained.

Rodney fidgeted and leaned in lower. 'Yes, and I'm sorry to talk about him. I got kids. I can't imagine what you're going through.'

'You're right about that.'

'I work for a smart young DC lawyer and he's onto something that can get you big money. The boy that killed Ramón had just walked out of a drug treatment facility. They'd been giving him some drugs as part of his treatment. We think one of the drugs made him crazy enough to pick a random victim and start shooting.'

Her eyes drifted away, then became moist, and for a moment Rodney could see a breakdown coming. But then she looked at him and said, 'Big money? How much?'

'More than a million bucks,' he said with a straight poker face, one he'd rehearsed a dozen times because he doubted seriously if he could deliver that punch line without going wild-eyed.

Another wayward gaze around the room. 'You jivin' me?' she said.

'There's money on the table, big money. Big corporate drug money that somebody wants you to take and keep quiet.'

'What big company?'

'Look, I've told you everything I know. My job is to meet you, tell you what's goin' on, and to invite you to come see Mr Carter, the lawyer I work for. He'll explain everything.'

The moist eyes had cleared. She shrugged and said, 'OK.'

'What time you get off?' he asked.

'Four thirty.'

'Our office is on Connecticut, fifteen minutes from here. Mr Carter will be waiting on you. You got my card.'

She looked at the card again.

'And one very important thing,' Rodney said, almost in a whisper. 'This'll work only if you keep quiet. It's a deep secret. You do what Mr Carter advises you to do, and you'll get more money than you ever dreamed of. But if word gets out, then you'll get nothing.'

Adelfa was nodding.

'And you need to start thinking about moving.'

'Moving?'

'As in a new house in a new town. You take this money back to Lincoln Towers and they'll eat you alive.'

CLAY'S RAID ON OPD had so far netted Miss Glick, the very efficient secretary who hesitated only slightly at the prospect of having her salary doubled, Paulette Tullos who, though she was well maintained by her absent Greek husband, nonetheless jumped at the chance to earn $200,000 a year, and, of course, Rodney.

To counterbalance these experienced people, he had hired his room-mate, Jonah, who, though he had never practised law—he'd passed the Bar exam on his fifth attempt—was a friend and confidant who Clay hoped might develop some legal skills. Smelling money from somewhere, Jonah had negotiated a starting salary of $90,000, which was less than that of the chief paralegal, though no one at the firm knew what the others were earning. The accountancy firm down on the third floor was handling the books and payroll.

Clay had given Paulette and Jonah the same careful explanation he had given to Rodney. To wit: He had stumbled upon a conspiracy involving a bad drug—the name of the drug and the name of the company would never be disclosed to them or to anyone else. He had made contact with the company. A quick deal was struck. Serious money was changing hands. Secrecy was crucial. Just do your jobs and don't ask a lot of questions. We're going to build a nice little law firm where we make lots of money and have some fun along the way.

Who could say no to such an offer?

MISS GLICK GREETED Adelfa Pumphrey as if she were the very first client to enter the shiny new law firm, which in fact she was. Everything smelt new—the paint, the carpet, the wallpaper, the Italian leather furniture in reception. Miss Glick brought Adelfa water in crystal that had never been used before, then returned to her task of arranging her new glass-and-chrome desk. Paulette was next. She took Adelfa into her office for the preliminary workup, making notes about family and background, the same info Max Pace had already prepared. She said the right words to a grieving mother.

So far everyone had been black, and Adelfa was reassured by this.

'You may have seen Mr Carter before,' Paulette said, working her way through the rough script she and Clay had put together. 'He was in court when you were there. He was appointed by the judge to represent Tequila Watson, but he got rid of the case. That's how he got involved with this settlement.'

Adelfa looked as confused as they'd expected her to be.

Paulette pressed on. 'He and I worked together for five years in the Office of the Public Defender. We quit a few days ago and opened this firm. You'll like him. He's a very nice guy and a good lawyer. Honest, and loyal to his clients. You're in good hands, Adelfa.'

The confusion had turned to bewilderment.

'Any questions?' Paulette asked.

'I got so many questions I don't know where to start.'

'I understand. Here's my advice. Don't ask a lot of questions. There's a big company out there that's willing to pay you a lot of money to settle a potential lawsuit you might have arising from the death of your son. If you hesitate and ask questions, you could easily end up with nothing. Just take the money, Adelfa. Take it and run.'

Paulette led her down the hall to a large office. Clay had been pacing nervously for an hour, but he greeted her calmly and welcomed her to the firm. His tie was loose, his sleeves rolled up, his desk covered with files and papers as if he were litigating on many fronts. Paulette hung around until the ice was broken, then excused herself.

Clay straddled the edge of his desk and looked down at Adelfa. He locked his arms across his chest and launched into his version of the big bad drug company narrative. Adelfa sat in a sunken leather chair, hands folded across the lap of her uniform trousers, eyes watching, never blinking, not sure what to believe.

As he wrapped up his story he said, 'They want to pay you a bunch of money, right now.'

'Who, exactly, is they?'

'You'll never know the company's identity. That's the deal. We, you and I, lawyer and client, must agree to keep everything secret.'

She finally blinked, then recrossed her hands and shifted her weight. 'How much money?' she asked softly.

'Five million dollars.'

'Good Lord,' she managed to say before she broke down. She covered her eyes and sobbed and for a long time made no effort to stop. Clay handed her a tissue from a box.

THE SETTLEMENT MONEY WAS sitting in Chase Bank, next to Clay's, just waiting to be distributed. Max's paperwork was on the desk. Clay talked her through it, explaining that the money would be transferred first thing next morning, as soon as the bank opened. He flipped pages of documents, collecting her signature where necessary. Adelfa was too stunned to say much. 'Trust me,' he said more than once. 'If you want the money, sign right there.'

'I feel like I'm doing something wrong,' she said at one point.

'No, you're the victim here, Adelfa, the victim and now the client.'

'I need to talk to someone,' she said as she signed again.

'That would be a mistake,' Clay said delicately. 'This money will improve your life if you keep it quiet. If you talk about it, then it will destroy you.'

'I'm not good at handling money.'

'We can help. If you'd like, Paulette can monitor things for you and give advice.'

'I'd like that.'

'That's what we're here for.'

Paulette drove her home. She told Clay later that when they arrived at the housing project Adelfa did not want to get out. So they sat there for thirty minutes, talking about her new life. No more welfare, no more gunshots in the night. No more gangs. No more bad schools. No more prayers to God to protect her children.

She was crying when she finally said goodbye.

THE BLACK PORSCHE CARRERA rolled to a stop under a shade tree on Dumbarton Street. Clay got out and for a few seconds was able to ignore his newest toy, but after a quick glance in all directions he turned and admired it once again. His for three days now, and he still could hardly believe he owned it.

He was eight blocks from the main campus of Georgetown University, the place he'd spent four years as a student before moving on to its law school near Capitol Hill. The town houses were historic and picturesque; the small lawns manicured; the streets covered by ancient oaks and maples. The busy shops and bars and restaurants on M Street, where he'd spent many long nights with his pals, were just two blocks to the south.

Now he was about to live here.

The town house that held his attention was on the market for $1.3 million. Four storeys, including a basement.

Clay was fifteen minutes early. The house was empty; its owners, an elderly couple, were now in warden-assisted accommodation, according to the real-estate agent. He walked through a gate beside the house and admired the small garden in the back.

He loved the house and the street, the cosiness of the neighbourhood. Sitting on the front steps, he decided he would offer one million even, then negotiate hard, bluff and walk away, and in general have a great time watching the estate agent run back and forth, but in the end he would be perfectly willing to pay the asking price.

PACE'S LIST OF VICTIMS stopped at seven. Tarvan had now been pulled for eighteen days, and from the company's experience they knew that whatever the drug did to make people start killing usually stopped working after ten days.

Number one had been a college kid, a student at George Washington who had walked out of a Starbucks coffee shop on Wisconsin Avenue in Bethesda just in time to be spotted by a man with a gun. The student was from Bluefield, West Virginia. Clay made the five-hour drive there in record time, not hurried at all but rather as a racing car driver speeding through the Shenandoah Valley. Following Pace's precise instructions, he found the home of the parents, a rather sad-looking little bungalow near downtown.

The mother was home but the father was still at work. She reluctantly let him in, but then offered some iced tea and cookies. Clay waited on a sofa in the den, pictures of the dead son everywhere. The house was a mess. What am I doing here? he thought.

The father sold insurance a few blocks away, and he was home before the ice melted in the tea glass. Clay presented his case to them. At first there were some tentative questions—How many others died because of this? Why can't we go to the authorities? Clay fielded them like a veteran. Pace had prepped him well.

They had a choice. They could get angry, make demands, want justice, or they could quietly take the money. The sum of $5 million didn't register at first, or if it did they did a wonderful job of deflecting it. They wanted to be angry and uninterested in money. They'd just buried their youngest son and the pain was immeasurable. They disliked Clay for being there, but they thanked him profusely for his concern. They distrusted him as a big-city lawyer who was obviously lying about such an outrageous settlement, but they asked him to stay for dinner.

After dinner, Clay began to press them. He was offering the only deal they would get. At 10.00pm, they signed the paperwork.

5

The final Tarvan clients to sign the documents were the parents of a twenty-year-old Howard University co-ed who'd dropped out of school one week and been murdered the next. For an hour they had sat in Clay's office. They cried at times, pouring out their unspeakable grief. At other times they were stoic, so seemingly unmoved by the money that Clay doubted they would accept the settlement.

But they did, though of all the clients he'd processed Clay was certain that the money would affect them the least. With time they might appreciate it; for now, they just wanted their daughter back.

Paulette and Miss Glick helped escort them out of the office and to the elevators, where everybody hugged everybody again. As the doors closed, the parents were fighting tears.

Clay's little team met in the conference room where they let the moment pass, thankful that no more widows and grieving parents would be visiting them. Some very expensive champagne had been iced for the occasion, and Clay began pouring.

During the second bottle, Clay rose to speak. 'I have some announcements,' he said, tapping his glass. 'First, the Tylenol cases are now complete. Congratulations and thanks to all of you.' He'd used Tylenol as a code for Tarvan, a name they would never hear. Nor would they ever know the amount of his fees.

They applauded themselves. 'Second, we begin the celebration tonight with dinner at Citronelle. Eight o'clock sharp. Could be a long evening because tomorrow the office will be closed.'

More applause, more champagne. 'Third, in two weeks we leave for Paris. All of us, plus one friend each. All expenses paid. First-class air travel, luxury hotel, the works. No exceptions. I'm the boss and I'm ordering all of you to Paris.'

Miss Glick covered her mouth with both hands. When she could finally speak, she said, 'I'll need a passport.'

'The forms are on my desk. I'll see to it. Anything else?'

'Who will you take?' Paulette asked.

'Maybe no one,' Clay said, and the room went quiet for a moment. They had whispered about Rebecca and the separation, with Jonah supplying most of the gossip. They wanted their boss happy, though they were not close enough to meddle.

'How long are we there?' asked Miss Glick.

'Seven nights,' Clay said. 'Seven nights in Paris.' And they all drifted away, swept along by the champagne. A month earlier they had been locked in the drudgery of the OPD. All but Jonah, who'd been selling computers part-time.

MAX PACE WANTED TO TALK, and since the firm was closed Clay suggested they meet there, at noon.

'You look like hell,' Pace began pleasantly.

'We celebrated last night.'

'What I have to discuss is very important. Are you up to it?'

'Fire away.'

'The Tarvan mess is over,' Pace said. 'We settled all seven cases. You did good work, Clay.'

'I'm getting paid handsomely for it.'

'I'll transfer in the last instalment today. All fifteen million will be in your account. What's left of it.'

'What do you expect me to do? You said yourself that I had to spend some money to create the right impression.'

'I'm kidding. Just be careful. Don't create too much attention.'

'Let's talk about the next case.'

Pace slid a file across. 'The drug is Dyloft, manufactured by Ackerman Labs. It's used by sufferers of acute arthritis. Dyloft is new and the doctors have gone crazy over it. It works wonders, patients love it. But it has two problems: first, it's made by a competitor of my client's; second, it's been linked to the creation of small tumours in the bladder. My client, same client as Tarvan, makes a similar drug that was popular until twelve months ago when Dyloft hit the market. The market is worth about three billion a year. My client's drug is doing a billion and a half but it's losing ground fast to Dyloft. A few months ago my client bought a small pharmaceutical company in Belgium. This outfit once had a division that was later swallowed by Ackerman Labs. A few researchers got shoved out and shafted along the way. Some lab studies disappeared then surfaced where they didn't belong. My client has the witnesses and the documents to prove that Ackerman Labs has known of the potential problems for at least the past six months. You with me?'

'Yes. How many people have taken Dyloft?'

'Probably a million, give or take.'

'What percentage get the tumours?'

'The research indicates about five per cent, enough to kill the drug.'

'You want me to sue Ackerman Labs?'

'Hang on. The truth about Dyloft will be out very shortly. As of today, there has been no litigation, no claims, no damaging studies published. Our spies tell us Ackerman is busy stashing money away to pay off the lawyers when the storm hits. But they're short of cash; they borrowed heavily to acquire other companies, most of which have not paid off, and their stock is down to around forty-two bucks from eighty a year ago.'

'What will the news about Dyloft do to the company?'

'Hammer the stock, which is exactly what my client wants. If the litigation is handled right, the news will murder Ackerman Labs. And since we have the inside proof that Dyloft is bad, the company will have no choice but to settle. They can't risk a trial, not with such a dangerous product.'

'What's the downside?'

'Ninety-five per cent of the tumours are benign, and very small. There's no real damage to the bladder.'

'So the litigation is used to shock the market?'

'Yes, and, of course, to compensate the victims. I don't want tumours in my bladder, benign or malignant. Most jurors would feel the same way. Here's the scenario: You put together a group of fifty or so plaintiffs, and file a big lawsuit on behalf of all Dyloft patients. At the same time, you launch a series of television ads soliciting more cases. You hit fast and hard, and you'll get thousands of cases. The ads run coast to coast—quickie ads that'll scare folks and make them dial your toll-free number right here in DC, where you have a warehouse full of paralegals answering the phones and doing the grunt work. It's gonna cost you some money, but if you get, say, five thousand cases, and you settle them for twenty thousand bucks each, that's one hundred million dollars. Your cut is one -third.'

'That's outrageous!'

'No, Clay, that's mass tort litigation. That's how the system works. If you don't do it, I guarantee someone else will. And very soon.'

'Where do I find fifty clients?' Clay asked.

Max thumped another file. 'We know of at least a thousand. Names, addresses, all right here.'

'You mentioned a warehouse full of paralegals?'

'Half a dozen. It'll take that many to answer the phones and keep the files organised. You could end up with five thousand clients.'

'Television ads?'

'Yep, I've got the name of a company that can put the ad together in less than three days. Nothing fancy—a voice-over, images of pills dropping onto a table, the potential evils of Dyloft, fifteen seconds of terror designed to make people call the Law Offices of J. Clay Carter II. These ads work, believe me. Run them in all major markets for a week and you'll have more clients than you can count.'

'How much will it cost?'

'Couple of million, but you can afford it.'

'What's the timetable?'

'You'll have to sign up the clients, which will take two weeks. Three days to finish the ad. A few days to buy the TV time. You'll need to hire paralegals and put them in rented space out in the suburbs; it's too expensive here. The lawsuit has to be prepared. You should be able to get it done in less than thirty days.'

'I'm taking the firm to Paris for a week, but we'll get it done.'

'My client wants the lawsuit filed in less than a month. July the 2nd, to be exact. They need to know precisely when you file the lawsuit, so they can react to the market.'

Clay stared at Pace. 'I've never handled a lawsuit like this,' he said.

Pace pulled something out of his file. 'Ever heard of the Circle of Barristers?'

'Maybe.'

'It's an old group with a new life—a bunch of trial lawyers who specialise in mass torts. They get together twice a year and talk about the latest trends in litigation. It would be a productive weekend.' He slid a brochure across to Clay. On the cover was a colour photo of the Royal Sonesta Hotel in New Orleans.

NEW ORLEANS WAS WARM and humid as always. He was alone and that was fine. Even if he and Rebecca were still together she would not have made the trip, she'd have been too busy at work. Even so, he felt the money was isolating him. Old friends were being ignored because he didn't want all the questions. Old places were no longer frequented because he could afford better. By the time Clay entered the lobby of the Royal Sonesta his shirt was wet and clinging to his back. The registration fee was $5,000, just for a few days of fraternising with a bunch of lawyers. The fee said to the legal world that only the rich who were serious about their mass torts were invited.

THE ONLY NINE O'CLOCK session on Saturday morning was a poorly attended update on class-action legislation currently being debated in Congress. The speaker was a lawyer from Washington who got off to a bad start by telling a dirty joke, which bombed. The crowd was all-white, all-male, a regular fraternity, but not in the mood for tasteless jokes. The presentation quickly went from bad humour to boredom. However, at least for Clay, the material was informative; he knew very little about class actions so everything was new.

At ten, he had to choose between a panel discussion on the latest in Skinny Ben developments and a presentation by a lawyer whose speciality was lead paint, a topic that sounded rather dull to Clay, so he went with the former. The room was full.

Skinny Ben was the nickname of an obesity pill that had been prescribed for millions. Its maker had pocketed billions and been poised to own the world when problems began developing in a significant number of users. Heart problems, traceable to the drug. Litigation exploded and the company had no desire to go to trial. Its pockets were deep and it began buying off the plaintiffs with huge settlements. For the past three years, mass tort lawyers had been scrambling to sign up Skinny Ben cases.

Four lawyers sat at a table facing the crowd. One of the panellists began talking and the entire room became still.

'That's Patton French,' the lawyer next to him whispered.

'Who's he?' Clay asked.

'Hottest mass tort lawyer in the country. Three hundred million in fees last year.'

Mr French's topic was the financial report on Healthy Living, manufacturer of Skinny Bens. He explained that approximately 300,000 Skinny Ben cases had been settled for about $7.5 billion. He estimated that there were maybe another 100,000 cases out there worth somewhere between $2 billion and $3 billion. The company was profitable and had plenty of cash to cover these lawsuits, and so it was up to those in the room to hustle on out there and find the rest of the cases. This fired up the crowd.

Clay had no desire to jump into the pit. He couldn't get past the fact that the pompous little jerk with the microphone made $300 million in fees last year and was still so motivated to earn even more. The discussion drifted into creative ways to attract new clients. One panellist had relied solely on television advertising, a topic that interested Clay for a moment but the discussion soon dissolved into a sad debate as to whether the lawyer should appear on television himself or hire some washed-up actor.

Oddly missing was any discussion about trial strategies—expert witnesses, whistle-blowers, jury selections, medical proof—the usual information lawyers exchanged at seminars. Clay was learning that these cases seldom went to trial. Courtroom skills were not important. It was all about hustling cases. And making huge fees.

At eleven, the local Porsche dealer held a Bloody Mary reception that was wildly popular. Raw oysters and Bloody Marys and non-stop chatter about how many cases one had. And how to get more. Evidently, the popular tactic was to round up as many cases as possible, then tag team with Patton French who'd be happy to include them in his own personal class action in his back yard over in Mississippi, where the juries and verdicts always went his way and the manufacturer was terrified to set foot. French worked the crowd, shamelessly talking about his 200-foot yacht, his Gulfstream jet and how he'd had to buy off his third wife with an apartment in London.

The afternoon promised to be a repeat of the morning, and Clay had had enough of the vulgar display of wealth by this organised and specialised group of lawyers, who didn't even seem to be exceptionally bright. He roamed the French Quarter, taking in the antique shops and galleries. Late in the day, he sat alone at a sidewalk café in Jackson Square. He sipped and tried to enjoy the hot chicory, but it wasn't working. Although he had not put the figures on paper, he had mentally done the maths. The Tarvan fees less 45 per cent for taxes and business expenses, minus what he'd already spent, left him with around $6.5 million. He could bury that in a bank and earn $300,000 a year in interest, which was about eight times what he'd been earning in salary at OPD. He could not imagine how he could ever spend that much money.

The only problem was a significant one. Rodney, Paulette, Jonah and Miss Glick had all left long-time jobs and put their blind faith in him. He couldn't just pull the plug now, take his money and run.

He switched to beer and made a profound decision. He would work hard for a short period of time on the Dyloft cases, which, frankly, he would be stupid to turn down since Max Pace was handing him a gold mine. When Dyloft was over, he'd give huge bonuses to his staff and close the office. He'd live the quiet life in Georgetown, travelling the world when he wanted, fishing with his father in the Caribbean, and never, under any circumstances, ever getting near another meeting of the Circle of Barristers.

HE HAD JUST ORDERED breakfast from room service when the phone rang. It was Paulette. 'Are you in a nice room?' she asked.

'Indeed I am.'

'Does it have a fax?'

'Of course.'

'Gimme the number, I'm sending something down there.'

It was from the Sunday edition of the *Post*. A wedding announcement. Rebecca Allison Van Horn and Jason Shubert Myers IV. 'Mr and Mrs Bennett Van Horn of McLean, Virginia, announce the engagement of their daughter, Rebecca, to Mr Jason Shubert Myers IV, son of Mr and Mrs D. Stephens Myers of Falls Church . . .'

D. Stephens Myers was the son of Dallas Myers, counsel to presidents beginning with Woodrow Wilson and ending with Dwight Eisenhower. According to the announcement, Jason Myers had attended Brown and Harvard Law School and was a partner in Myers & O'Malley, the youngest partner in the firm's history.

A December wedding was planned. In less than a month she had found someone she loved enough to marry.

The phone rang again and it was Paulette. 'You OK?' she asked.

'I'm fine,' he said, trying hard.

'I'm real sorry, Clay.'

'It was over, Paulette. It had been unravelling for a year. This is a good thing. Now I can forget her completely.'

'If you say so.'

'I'm OK. Thanks for calling.'

6

The office dress code had rapidly evolved into an anything-goes style. The tone was set by the boss who leaned towards jeans and expensive T-shirts, with a sports jacket nearby in case he went to lunch. He had designer suits for meetings, but for the moment those were rare events since the firm had no clients and no cases.

They met late on Monday morning in the conference room— Paulette, Rodney, and Jonah. Though she had already acquired considerable clout, Miss Glick was still just a secretary/receptionist.

'Folks, we have work to do,' Clay began the meeting. He introduced them to Dyloft, and relying on Pace's concise summaries, gave a description of the drug, as well as a quick and dirty review of Ackerman Labs—sales, profits, cash, other legal problems. Then the good stuff—the disastrous side effects of Dyloft, the bladder tumours and the company's knowledge of its problems.

'As of today, no lawsuit has been filed. But we're about to change that. On July the 2nd, we start the war by filing a class action here in DC on behalf of all patients harmed by the drug.'

'Do we have any of these clients?' Paulette asked.

'Not yet. But we have names and addresses. Today we start developing a plan for gathering clients.' Though he had reservations about television advertising, he was convinced that there was no viable alternative. Once he filed suit and exposed the drug, those vultures he'd just met in the Circle of Barristers would swarm to find the clients. The only effective way to reach large numbers of Dyloft patients quickly was by television ads.

He explained this and said, 'It'll cost at least two million bucks.'

'This firm has two million bucks?' Jonah blurted.

'It does. We start working on the ads today.'

'How many clients are we looking at?' Rodney asked.

'Thousands. It's hard to say.'

Rodney pointed at each of them, slowly counting to four. 'According to my numbers,' he said, 'there are four of us.'

'We're adding more. Jonah is in charge of expansion. We'll lease some space out in the suburbs and fill it with paralegals. They'll work the phones and organise the files.'

'Where does one find paralegals?' Jonah asked.

'In the employment sections of the Bar journals. Start working on the ads. And you've got a meeting this afternoon with a real-estate agent out in Manassas. We'll need about five thousand square feet, with plenty of wiring for phones and computers. Lease it, wire it, staff it, then organise it. The sooner the better.'

'Yes, sir.'

'How much is a Dyloft case worth?' Paulette asked.

'As much as Ackerman Labs will pay. It could range from as little as ten thousand to as much as fifty, depending on several factors, not the least of which is the extent of the damage to the bladder.'

'And how many cases might we get?'

'I don't know. Several thousand.'

'OK, let's say three thousand cases. Three thousand cases times the minimum of ten thousand dollars comes to thirty million, right?'

'That's right.'

'And how much are the attorneys' fees?' she asked.

'One-third,' he said.

'That's ten million in fees,' she said slowly. 'All to this firm?'

'Yes. And we're going to share the fees.'

The word *share* echoed around the room for a few seconds. Jonah and Rodney glanced at Paulette, as if to say, 'Go ahead, finish it off.'

'Share, in what way?' she asked, very deliberately.

'Ten per cent to each of you.'

'So in my hypothetical, my share of the fees would be one million?'

'That's correct.' They absorbed the numbers in silence for what seemed like a very long time. For Rodney, the money meant college for the kids. For Paulette, it meant a divorce from the Greek she'd seen once in the past year. For Jonah, it meant life on a sailboat.

'You're serious, aren't you, Clay?' Jonah asked.

'Dead serious. If we work our butts off for the next year, there's a good chance we'll have the option of an early retirement.'

'Who told you about this Dyloft?' Rodney asked.

'I can never answer that question, Rodney. Sorry. Just trust me.'

Jonah jumped to his feet. 'What's that agent's name?' he asked.

ON THE THIRD FLOOR of his town house, Clay had put together a small office, not that he planned to do much work there but he needed a place for his papers. It was there that he made his first tentative entry into the world of mass tort solicitation. A stiff drink for courage, and he punched the numbers.

The phone was answered by a woman, perhaps Mrs Ted Worley of

Upper Marlboro, Maryland. Clay introduced himself pleasantly, identified himself as a lawyer and asked to speak to Mr Worley.

'He's watching the Orioles,' she said. 'What's he done now?'

'Oh, nothing, nothing at all. I'd like to talk to him about his arthritis.' The first impulse to hang up and run came and went. Clay thanked God no one was watching or listening. Think of the money, he kept telling himself. Think of the fees.

'His arthritis? Thought you were a lawyer, not a doctor.'

'Yes, ma'am, I'm a lawyer, and I have reason to believe he's taking a dangerous drug for his arthritis. I just need him for a second.'

Voices in the background as she yelled something to Ted who yelled something back. Finally, he took the phone. 'Who is this?' he demanded, and Clay quickly introduced himself.

'What's the score?' Clay asked.

'Three–one Red Sox in the fifth. Do I know you?' Mr Worley was seventy years old.

'No, sir. I'm an attorney here in DC, and I specialise in lawsuits involving defective drugs.'

'OK, what do you want?'

'Through our Internet sources we found your name as a user of an arthritis drug called Dyloft. Can you tell me if you use this drug?'

'Maybe I don't want to tell you what prescriptions I'm taking.'

'Of course you don't have to, Mr Worley. But the only way to determine if you're entitled to a settlement is to tell me if you're using the drug.'

'Well, uh, I guess it's not a secret, is it?'

'No, sir.' Of course it was a secret. Why should a person's medical history be anything but confidential? The little fibs were necessary, Clay kept telling himself. Look at the big picture. Mr Worley and thousands like him might never know they're using a bad product unless they were told. Ackerman Labs certainly hadn't come clean.

'Yeah, I take Dyloft.'

'Any side effects?'

'Such as?'

'Blood in your urine. A burning sensation when you urinate.'

'No. Why?'

'We have some preliminary research that Ackerman Labs, the company that makes Dyloft, is trying to cover up. The drug has been found to cause bladder tumours in some of the folks who use it.' Clay felt rotten and wanted to apologise.

Holding the phone with one hand and rubbing his side with the other, Mr Worley said, 'You know, come to think of it, I do remember a burning sensation a couple of days ago.'

Clay charged in. 'My firm represents a lot of Dyloft users. I think you should consider getting tested. We have a doctor who can do a urinalysis for you tomorrow. Won't cost you a dime.'

'What if he finds something wrong?'

'Then we can discuss your options. When the news of Dyloft comes out, in a few days, there will be many lawsuits. My firm will lead the attack on Ackerman Labs. I'd like to have you as a client.'

'Maybe I should talk to my doctor.'

'He may have some liability too. He prescribed the drug. It might be best if you get an unbiased opinion.'

'Where do I do the test?'

Clay gave him the name and address of a doctor Max Pace had located. The $80 examination would cost Clay $300 a pop, but it was simply the price of doing business.

When the details were finished, Clay apologised for the intrusion, thanked him for his time, and hung up. Soliciting cases by phone? What kind of lawyer had he become?

TWO DAYS LATER, Clay pulled into the Worleys' driveway in Upper Marlboro and met them at the front door. The urinalysis revealed abnormal cells in the urine, a clear sign, according to Max Pace, that there were tumours in the bladder. Mr Worley had been referred to a urologist, who he would see the following week. The examination and removal of the tumours would be by cystoscopic surgery, running a tiny scope and a knife in a tube through the penis into the bladder, a procedure that was purported to be fairly routine.

Much as he wanted to, Clay could not say the tumours were probably benign. Better to let the doctors do that after the surgery.

Over coffee, Clay explained the contract for his services and answered questions about the litigation. When Ted Worley signed at the bottom, he became the first Dyloft plaintiff in the country.

And for a while it seemed as if he might be the only one. Working the phones nonstop, Clay succeeded in convincing only eleven people to show up for the urinalysis. All eleven tested negative. 'Keep pushing,' Max Pace urged.

By the end of the week, Clay had signed up three clients who tested positive for abnormal cells. Rodney and Paulette, working as a team, had seven more under contract.

The Dyloft class action was ready for war.

THE PARIS ADVENTURE cost him $95,300, according to the numbers so carefully kept by Rex Crittle, a man who was becoming more and more familiar with almost all aspects of Clay's life. Crittle was a Certified Public Accountant with a mid-sized accounting firm situated directly under the Carter suite. He too had been referred by Max Pace.

At least once a week, Clay and Crittle spent half an hour or so talking about Clay's money and how to handle it. An accounting system for the law firm was basic and easily installed. Miss Glick made all the entries and simply ran them down to Crittle's computers.

'What's this payment to East Media for half a million dollars?' Crittle asked.

'We're doing some television ads for litigation. That's the first instalment.'

'Instalment? How many more?' He gave Clay a look he'd seen before. It said, 'Son, have you lost your mind?'

'A total of two million dollars. We're filing a big lawsuit in a few days. The filing will be coordinated with an advertising blitz.'

'What about this new office out in Manassas? A lease deposit of fifteen thousand bucks?'

'Yes, we're expanding. I'm adding six paralegals in an office out there. Rent's cheaper. Trust me, Rex, the money is about to pour in.'

'It's certainly pouring out.'

'You have to spend money to make money.'

'That's what they say.'

THE ASSAULT BEGAN just after sundown on July 1. With everyone gathered in front of the television in the conference room, they waited until exactly 8.32pm, then grew quiet and still. It was a fifteen-second ad that began with a shot of a handsome young actor wearing a white coat and holding a thick book and looking sincerely at the camera. 'Attention arthritis sufferers. If you are taking the prescription drug Dyloft, you may have a claim against the manufacturer of the drug. Dyloft has been linked to several side effects, including tumours in the bladder.' On the bottom of the screen the bold words: DYLOFT HOT LINE—CALL 1-800-555-DYLO appeared. The doctor continued: 'Call this number immediately. The Dyloft Hot Line can arrange a free medical test for you. Call now!'

No one spoke when it was over. For Clay, it was a particularly harrowing moment because he had just launched a vicious attack against a mammoth corporation, one that would undoubtedly respond with a vengeance. What if Max Pace was using Clay as a pawn in a huge corporate chess match? What if Clay couldn't prove that the drug caused the tumours? He had wrestled with these questions for several weeks, and quizzed Pace a thousand times. Max had eventually handed over the ill-gotten research on the effects of Dyloft. Clay had had it reviewed by a fraternity brother from Georgetown who was now a physician in Baltimore. The research looked solid and sinister, and Clay had ultimately convinced himself that he was right and Ackerman was wrong.

The ads would run every other day for ten days in ninety markets from coast to coast. The estimated audience was 80 million.

The 800 phone number routed callers to the Sweatshop, the nickname for the shopping centre branch of the Law Offices of J. Clay Carter II. There, the six new paralegals took the calls, filled out forms, asked all the scripted questions and promised return calls from one of the staff attorneys. Within two hours of the first ads, all phones were busy. A computerised message referred callers unable to get through to the Dyloft Hot Line Web site.

At nine the next morning, Clay received a phone call from an attorney in a large firm down the street. He represented Ackerman Labs and insisted the ads be stopped immediately. He threatened all manner of legal action if Clay did not buckle immediately.

'Are you going to be in your office for a few minutes?' Clay asked.

'Yes, of course. Why?'

'I have something to send over. Should take five minutes.'

Rodney, the courier, hustled down the street with a copy of the twenty-page lawsuit. Clay left for the courthouse to file the original. Pursuant to Pace's instructions, copies were also being faxed to the *Washington Post*, *The Wall Street Journal* and the *New York Times*.

Pace had also hinted that short-selling Ackerman Labs stock would be a shrewd investment move. The stock had closed the Friday before at $42.50. When it opened on Monday morning, Clay placed a sell order for 100,000 shares. He'd buy it back in a few days, hopefully around $30, and pick up another million bucks.

HIS OFFICE WAS HECTIC when he returned. There were six incoming toll-free lines to the Sweatshop out in Manassas, and during working hours, when all six were busy, the calls were routed to the main office on Connecticut Avenue. Rodney, Paulette and Jonah were each on the phone talking to Dyloft users scattered around North America.

'Mr Pace is in your office,' Miss Glick said.

Max was holding a coffee cup and standing in front of a window.
'It's filed,' Clay said. 'We've stirred up a hornet's nest. Their
lawyers have already called. I sent them a copy of the lawsuit.'

'Good. They've been ambushed and they know they'll get slaughtered. This is a lawyer's dream, Clay, make the most of it.'

'Sit down. I have a question.'

Pace, in black as always, fell into a chair and crossed his legs. The
cowboy boots appeared to be of rattlesnake.

'If Ackerman hired you right now, what would you do?' Clay asked.

'Spin is crucial. I'd start the press releases, deny everything, blame
it on greedy trial lawyers. Defend my drug. The initial goal is to protect the stock price. I'd get the CEO on television to say all the right
things. I'd get the lawyers preparing an organised defence. I'd get the
sales people to reassure the doctors that the drug is OK.'

'But the drug is not OK.'

'I'd worry about that later. For the first few days, it's all spin. Once
the spin is in place, I would have a serious talk with the big boys. I'd
bring in the number-crunchers and figure out how much the settlements will cost. You never go to trial with a bad drug. There's no
way to control costs. One jury gives the plaintiff a million bucks. The
next jury in another state awards twenty million in punitive damages.
It's a crapshoot. So you settle. Mass tort lawyers take their percent-
ages off the top, so they're easy to settle with.'

'How much cash can Ackerman afford?'

'They're insured for at least three hundred million. Plus they have
about a half-billion in cash, most of it generated by Dyloft. They're
almost maxed out at the bank, but if I were calling the shots I'd plan
on paying a billion. And I would do it fast.'

'Will Ackerman do it fast?'

'I've watched the company for a long time, and they're not particularly sharp. Like all drugmakers, they're horrified by litigation.
Instead of using a fireman like me, they rely on their lawyers, who, of
course, have no interest in quick settlements. The principal firm is
Walker-Stearns in New York. They will put fifty associates on the
case with meters churning at full blast. Mr Worley's class action is
worth a hundred million bucks to them. Don't forget that.'

'Why don't they just pay me a hundred million bucks to go away?'

'They'll pay you even more, but first they have to pay their lawyers.
That's just the way it works.'

'But you wouldn't do it that way?'

'Of course not. With Tarvan, the client told me the truth. I found you, and wrapped up everything quietly, quickly and cheaply. Fifty million, and not a dime to my client's own lawyers.'

Miss Glick appeared in the door and said, 'A reporter from *The Wall Street Journal* is on the phone.' Clay looked at Pace who said, 'Chat him up. And remember, the other side has an entire PR unit cranking out the spin.'

THE *TIMES* AND THE *POST* ran brief stories of the Dyloft class action on the front pages of their business sections the following morning. Both mentioned Clay's name. More ink was given to the defendant's responses. The CEO called the lawsuit 'just another example of litigation abuse by the legal profession'. 'Dyloft had been thoroughly researched,' he said, with no evidence of adverse side effects.

The Wall Street Journal took another angle. In the preliminaries, the reporter had asked Clay his age. 'Only thirty-one?' he'd said, which led to a series of questions about Clay's experience, his firm, et cetera. David versus Goliath is much more readable than dry financial data or lab reports, and the story took on a life of its own. A photographer was rushed over and while Clay posed, his staff watched with great amusement.

On the front page, far left column, the headline read: THE ROOKIE TAKES ON MIGHTY ACKERMAN LABS. Beside it was a computerised caricature of a smiling Clay Carter. The first paragraph read: 'Less than two months ago, DC attorney Clay Carter was an unknown and low-paid public defender. Yesterday, as the owner of his own law firm, he filed a billion-dollar lawsuit against the third-largest pharmaceutical company in the world, claiming its newest wonder drug, Dyloft, not only relieves acute pain for arthritis sufferers but also causes tumours in their bladders.'

The article focused on Clay and his amazing rise to the forefront of mass tort litigation. It quoted the President of the National Trial Lawyers Academy as saying that he had never heard of Clay Carter, but was nonetheless 'very impressed with his work'.

'Make sure this gets on the Web site,' Clay said as he handed the article to Jonah. 'Our clients will love it.'

TEQUILA WATSON pleaded guilty to the murder of Ramón Pumphrey and was sentenced to life in prison. He would be eligible for parole in twenty years, though the story in the *Post* did not mention that. It did say that his victim had been one of several gunned down in a spate of killings that had seemed unusually random even for a city accustomed to senseless violence. The police had no explanations. Clay made a note to call Adelfa to see how her life was going.

He owed something to Tequila, but he wasn't sure what. Nor was there any way of compensating his ex-client. He rationalised that he had spent most of his life on drugs and would probably spend the rest behind bars anyway, with or without Tarvan, but this did little to make Clay feel honourable. He had sold out, plain and simple. He'd taken the cash and buried the truth.

Miss Glick came in and handed him a phone message that quickly made him forget about Tequila Watson. He punched the numbers. 'Mr Patton French,' he said into the phone. The message slip said it was urgent.

'And who's calling, please?'

'Clay Carter, from DC.'

'Oh, yes, he's been expecting you.'

Within seconds the great man himself was on the phone. 'Hello, Clay, thanks for calling me back,' he said. 'Nice story in *The Journal*, huh? Not bad for a rookie. Look, sorry I didn't get to say hello when you were down in New Orleans.'

'No problem,' Clay said. There were 200 lawyers at the Circle of Barristers gathering. There had been no reason why French should know Clay was even there. He had obviously done his research.

'I'd like to meet you, Clay. I think we can do some business together. I was on the Dyloft trail two months ago. You beat me to the punch, but there's a ton of money out there.'

Clay had no desire to crawl into bed with Patton French. On the other hand, his methods of extracting huge settlements from drug companies were legendary. 'We can talk,' Clay said.

'Look, I'm headed to New York right now. What if I pick you up in DC and take you with me? I got a new Gulfstream 5 I'd love to show off. We'll stay in Manhattan, have a wonderful dinner tonight. Talk business. Back home late tomorrow. Whatta you say?'

Other than a few phone calls and a game of racquetball that night, Clay had little to do. And he hadn't been to New York in several years. 'Sure, why not?' he said.

'Smart move, Clay. I'll meet you at Reagan National in three hours.'

The private terminal at Reagan National was packed with harried executives. Near the reception counter, a cute brunette in a short skirt held a handmade placard with his name on it. She was Julia, with no last name. 'Follow me,' she said with a perfect smile. They were cleared through an exit door and driven across the tarmac in a courtesy van.

'That's us,' Julia said as they stopped beside the largest jet there.

Patton French was, of course, on the phone. He waved Clay aboard while Julia took his jacket and his overnight bag, and asked him what he wanted to drink. Just water, with lemon. His first view inside a private jet could not have been more breathtaking.

The aroma was that of leather, very expensive leather. The seats, sofas, headrests, panels were done in various shades of blue and tan leather. The light fixtures and knobs and gadget controls were gold-plated. The trim was dark and deeply polished mahogany. It was a luxury suite in a five-star hotel, but with wings and engines.

Clay was six foot tall, and there was room to spare above his head. The cabin was long with some type of office in the rear. French was back there, still talking into a telephone, but when the plane began moving, he charged forward and attacked Clay with a violent hand-shake and toothy smile. He was probably fifty-five and a bit heavy, greying nicely with thick, wavy hair. Vigour oozed from every pore.

They sat across from each other at one of the tables.

'Julia, get me a vodka,' French said.

Julia brought their drinks and strapped herself in for takeoff.

'You want some lunch?' French asked. 'She can cook anything.'

'No, thanks. I'm fine.'

French took a long swig of the vodka, then sat back and closed his eyes as the Gulfstream sped down the runway and lifted off.

Minutes passed until they levelled off, then Julia disappeared into the kitchen. French snapped out of his meditation, took another gulp. 'Is all that stuff in *The Journal* true?' he asked.

'They got it right.'

'I gotta tell you, Clay, this Dyloft ambush of yours is a thing of beauty. And unusual. In most cases, word of a bad drug spreads slowly as more and more patients complain. Uncle Luke has sud-denly got blood in his urine for no reason, and after staring at it for a month or so he'll go to his doctor down in Podunk, Louisiana. And the doctor will eventually take him off whatever new miracle drug he had prescribed. Uncle Luke may or may not go see the family lawyer, usually a small-town ham-and-egger who in most cases wouldn't know a decent tort if one hit him. It takes time for these bad drugs to get discovered. What you've done is unique.'

Clay was content to nod and listen. This was leading somewhere.

'I have a vast network of lawyers and not a single one had heard of problems with Dyloft until a few weeks ago. I had two lawyers in my firm doing the preliminary workup on the drug, but we were nowhere close to filing suit. I know how the game is played, Clay, and I know you have some inside information.'

'I do. And I'll never tell anybody.'

'Good. That makes me feel better. I saw your ads. We monitor such things in every market. How many cases have you generated?'

'It's hard to say. They have to do the initial urinalysis. The phones have not stopped ringing.'

Julia appeared with platters of shrimp, cheeses and various cold meats. 'A bottle of that Chilean white,' Patton said. 'It should be chilled by now. Anyway, we figure there are between fifty and a hundred thousand Dyloft cases. That sound close?'

'A hundred might be on the high side,' Clay said cautiously.

'I'm a little worried about Ackerman Labs. I've sued them twice before. Ten years ago, back when they had plenty of cash. They went through a couple of CEOs who made some bad acquisitions. Now they have ten billion in debt. Anyway, Ackerman is not in danger of bankruptcy or anything like that. And they've got some insurance.'

French was fishing here and Clay decided to take the bait.

'They have at least three hundred million in insurance,' he said. 'And perhaps half a billion to spend on Dyloft.'

French smiled and almost drooled over this information. 'Great stuff, son, wonderful stuff. How good is your inside dirt?'

'Excellent. We have lab reports that we're not supposed to have. Ackerman cannot get near a jury with Dyloft.'

'Awesome,' he said, closing his eyes as he absorbed the words.

Julia was back with the wine, which she poured into two priceless goblets. French sniffed it and evaluated it and when he was satisfied he took a sip. He smacked his lips and nodded, then said, 'Let me trot out a scenario for you, Clay. And I promise you it is designed to get you more money in a shorter period of time.'

'I'm listening.'

'I'll end up with as many Dyloft cases as you. Now that you've opened the door, there will be hundreds of lawyers chasing these cases. We, you and I, can control the litigation if we move your lawsuit from DC to my back yard in Mississippi. That will terrify Ackerman Labs. They're worried now but they're also thinking, "Well, he's just a rookie, never handled a mass tort case before," and so on. But if we put your cases with mine, combine in one class action, Ackerman will have a massive corporate coronary.'

Clay was almost dizzy with doubt and with questions. 'I'm listening,' was all he could manage again.

'You keep your cases, I keep mine. We pool them, and as other cases are signed up and lawyers come on board, I'll go to the trial judge and ask him to appoint a Plaintiffs' Steering Committee. I'll be the chairman. You'll be on the committee because you filed first. I've done it dozens of times. The committee gives us control. We'll start negotiating with Ackerman pretty soon. If your inside dope is as strong as you say, we push hard for an early settlement.'

'How early?'

'Depends on several factors. How many cases are out there? How quickly can we sign them up? How many lawyers jump in the fray? And, very important, how severe are the damages to our clients?'

'Not very severe. Virtually all the tumours are benign.'

French absorbed this, frowning at first at the bad news, then seeing the good. 'Even better. Treatment is cystoscopic surgery.'

'Correct. An outpatient procedure that can be done for about a thousand dollars. Stay away from Dyloft and life returns to normal.'

'That's even better,' French said. 'Better for our clients because they're not as sick. Better for us because the settlements will come faster. The key here is getting the cases. The more cases we get, the more control we have over the class action. More cases, more fees.'

There was a noticeable reduction in power as the nose dipped slightly. 'Which airport are we heading to?' Clay asked.

'Teterboro, it's in New Jersey. All the private jets go there.'

Julia removed the trays of food and said they would be landing in five minutes. Clay became entranced by the view of the Manhattan skyline to the east. French fell asleep.

They landed and taxied past a row of private terminals, where dozens of handsome jets were either parked or being serviced.

A limo met them on the tarmac, just a few feet from where they stepped off the plane. The pilots and Julia stayed behind, tidying up and no doubt making sure the wine was chilled for the next flight.

'The Peninsula,' French said to the driver.

'Yes, sir, Mr French,' he replied.

'I'm curious about your ads,' French said, as they moved through the congestion of New Jersey. 'How are you processing the calls?'

'Nine people working the phones—seven paralegals, two lawyers. We took two thousand calls on Monday, three thousand yesterday. Our Dyloft Web site is getting eight thousand hits each day. Assuming the usual hit ratio, that's about a thousand clients already.'

'And the pool is how big?'

'Fifty to seventy-five thousand, according to my source, who so far has been pretty accurate.'

'I'd like to meet your source.'

'Forget it.'

French cracked his knuckles and tried to accept this rejection. 'We have to get these cases, Clay. My ads start tomorrow. What if we divide the country? You take the North and East, give me the South and West. It'll be easier to target smaller markets, and much easier to handle the cases. There's a guy in Miami who'll be on television within days. And there's one in California who, I promise you, is copying your ads right now. We're sharks, OK, nothing but vultures. The race is on for the courthouse, Clay. We have one helluva head start, but the stampede is coming. Give me your budget.'

What the hell, Clay thought. Sitting in the back of the limo together, they certainly seemed like partners. 'Two million for advertising, another two million for the urinalyses.'

'Here's what we'll do,' French said. 'Spend all your money on advertising. I'll front the money for the urinalyses, all of it, and we'll make Ackerman Labs reimburse us when we settle. That's a normal part of every settlement, to make the company cover all medicals.'

'The tests are three hundred dollars each.'

'You're getting screwed. I'll put some technicians together and we'll do it much cheaper.'

Clay's suite at The Peninsula had a view of Fifth Avenue. Once he was safely locked inside, away from Patton French, he grabbed the phone and began searching for Max Pace.

7

The third cellphone number found Pace at some undisclosed location. The man with no home had been in DC less and less in recent weeks. Of course he was off putting out another fire. There was no shortage of bad products out there.

Clay explained he was in New York, who he was with, and why he was there. Pace's first word sealed the deal. 'Brilliant,' he said.

'You know him?'

'Everybody in this business knows Patton French,' Pace said.

Clay gave the terms of the offer from French. Pace quickly caught up and then began thinking ahead. 'If you refile in Biloxi, Mississippi, where French is based, Ackerman's stock will take another hit,' he said. 'Do it!'

'OK. Done.'

'And watch the *New York Times* in the morning. Big story about Dyloft. The first medical report is out. It's devastating.'

'Great.'

He got a beer from the minibar and sat in front of the window and watched the frenzy on Fifth Avenue. In the past month he'd made more money than he'd ever dreamed of earning. Now, he felt as if he was spending it even faster. Be bold, he kept telling himself, take chances, roll the dice and you could get filthy rich. Another voice kept urging him to bury the money and have it for ever.

He had moved $1 million to an account offshore. He would not touch it, under any circumstances. If he made bad choices and gambled it all away, he'd still have money for the beach. He would sneak out of town like his father and never come back.

The million dollars in the secret account was his compromise.

DINNER WAS AT MONTRACHET, not for the food, which was very good, but for the wine list, which was thicker than any other in New York. French wanted to taste several red Burgundies with his veal. Five bottles were brought to the table and opened.

'I called my office,' French said. 'That lawyer in Miami is already on the air with Dyloft ads. He's set up two screening clinics and is running them through like cattle. Name's Carlos Hernández, and he's very, very good. Are we in this together?'

'Let's go over the deal.'

At which French took out a folded document. 'Here's the deal memo,' he said, handing it over while he went for the first bottle.

Clay read it carefully and signed at the bottom. French, between sips, signed as well, and the partnership was born.

'Let's file the class action in Biloxi tomorrow,' French said. 'I've got two lawyers working on it right now. As soon as it's filed, you can dismiss yours in DC. I know the in-house counsel for Ackerman Labs. I think I can talk to him. If the company will negotiate directly with us, and bypass their outside counsel, then they can save a bloody fortune and give it to us. And it will greatly expedite matters. If their outside lawyers take charge of the negotiations, it could cost us half a year in wasted time.' A phone rang somewhere in a pocket and French whipped it out with his left hand while holding a wine glass with his right. 'Excuse me,' he said to Clay.

It was a Dyloft conversation with another lawyer, somebody in Texas, obviously an old friend. The banter was polite, but French was cautious. When he slapped the phone shut he said, 'Dammit!'

'Some competition?'

'Serious competition. Name's Vic Brennan, big lawyer in Houston. He's onto Dyloft, wants to know the game plan.'

'He got nothing from you.'

'He knows. He's unleashing some ads tomorrow—radio, television, newspaper. The race is on, Clay. We have to get those cases.'

'It's about to get crazier,' Clay said. 'Big story in the *Times* tomorrow. The first bad report on Dyloft, according to my sources.'

It was the wrong thing to say, as far as dinner was concerned. For what mass tort lawyer could concentrate on food and wine when the *New York Times* was just hours away from exposing his next defendant and its dangerous drug?

THE PHONE WAS RINGING and it was still dark outside. The clock gave the time as 5.45. 'Get up!' French growled at him. 'And open the door.' By the time he unlocked it, French was pushing it open and marching past with newspapers and a cup of coffee. 'Unbelievable!' he said, flinging a copy of the *Times* on Clay's bed.

'You can't sleep all day, son. Read this!' He was dressed in hotel garb, the complimentary terry-cloth robe and white shower shoes.

The *Atlantic Journal of Medicine* was reporting that dylofedamint, known as Dyloft, had been linked to bladder tumours in about 6 per cent of those who had taken it for a year.

'Up from five per cent,' Clay said as he read.

Ackerman Labs offered a rather weak denial. The company appeared to be hunkering down. The good news, if it could be called that, was that the tumours did not appear to be malignant.

Ackerman's stock had tumbled from $42.50 on Monday morning, when the class action was filed, to $32.50 at the close on Wednesday.

'Should've shorted the damned thing,' French mumbled. Clay bit his tongue and kept a secret, one of the few he'd held on to in the past twenty-four hours.

'We can read it again on the plane,' French said. 'Let's go.'

THE STOCK WAS AT $28 by the time Clay walked into his office and tried to say hello to his weary staff.

Jonah was the first to stop by. 'We were here until midnight last night,' he said. 'It's crazy.'

'It's about to get crazier. We're doubling the TV ads.'

'We can't keep up now.'

'Hire some temporary paralegals.'

'We need computer people. We can't add the data fast enough.'

'Can you find them?'

'I know one guy, maybe two, who might be able to come in.'

'Get them.'

Jonah started to leave, then turned round and closed the door behind him. 'Clay, look, do you know what you're doing here? I mean, you're burning money faster than it's ever been burned. What if something goes wrong and it all goes belly-up?'

Clay walked round to the edge of his desk and sat on the corner. 'I'll be very honest with you, Jonah. I think I know what I'm doing, but since I've never done it before, I can't be certain. It's one huge gamble. If I win, then we all make some serious money. If I lose, then we're still in business. We just won't be rich.'

'If you get the chance, tell the others, OK?'

'I will.'

Lunch was a ten-minute sandwich break in the conference room. Jonah had the latest numbers: for the first three days, the hot line had fielded 7,100 calls and the Web site had averaged 8,000 enquiries per day. Information packets and contracts for legal services had been mailed as quickly as possible, though they were falling behind. Clay authorised Jonah to hire two part-time computer assistants. Paulette was given the task of finding three or four additional paralegals to work in the Sweatshop.

Clay described his meeting with Patton French and explained their new legal strategy. He showed them the *Times* article. 'The race is on, folks,' he said, trying his best to motivate a weary bunch. 'The sharks are coming after our clients.'

'We are the sharks,' Paulette said.

Patton French called late in the afternoon and reported that the class action had been amended to add Mississippi plaintiffs and filed in Biloxi. 'We got it right where we want it, pal,' he said.

'I'll dismiss here tomorrow,' Clay said.

Ackerman Labs closed the day at $26.25, a paper profit of $1,625,000, if Clay bought now and covered his short sale. He decided to wait. The news of the Biloxi filing would hit in the morning, and it would do nothing but hurt the stock.

BAD NEWS CONTINUED to follow the miracle drug Dyloft. Two more medical studies were published, one of which argued convincingly that Ackerman Labs cut corners on its research and pulled every string it had to get the drug approved. The FDA finally ordered Dyloft off the market.

Patton French had never seen a mass tort class come together so beautifully. Because he and Clay won the race to the courthouse in Biloxi, their class had been certified first. All other Dyloft plaintiffs wanting in on a class action would be forced to join theirs, with the Plaintiffs' Steering Committee raking off an additional fee. French's friendly judge had already appointed the five-lawyer committee— French, Clay, Carlos Hernández from Miami, and two cronies from New Orleans. In theory, the committee would handle the trial against Ackerman Labs. In reality, the five would shuffle paperwork and cover the administrative chore of keeping 50,000 or so clients and their lawyers organised.

French talked to the in-house counsel at Ackerman every day. His message was clear—let's talk settlement now, without your outside lawyers, because you know you're not going to trial with this drug.

In August, French convened a summit of the Dyloft lawyers at his ranch near Ketchum, Idaho.

Clay chartered a Lear 35, a handsome little jet about one-third the size of a Gulfstream 5, but since he was travelling alone it was quite adequate. He met the pilots in the private terminal at Reagan National, where he tried to act as if there was nothing special about hopping on board his own jet. Sure it was owned by a charter company, but for the next three days it was his.

A VAN WAS WAITING at the Ketchum–Sun Valley airport, with what appeared to be an imitation cowboy behind the wheel. Fortunately, the driver was not much of a talker, and Clay enjoyed the forty-minute ride in silence. Patton's ranch was postcard perfect and very new. The house was a lodge with enough wings and storeys to host a good-sized law firm. Another cowboy took Clay's bag. 'Mr French is on the deck out back,' he said.

The other members of the Plaintiffs' Steering Committee were there too, lounging in chairs, smoking dark cigars and working on drinks. When they realised Clay was present, they hopped to attention as if the judge had entered the courtroom. In the first three minutes of excited conversation, he was called 'brilliant', 'shrewd', 'gutsy', and, his favourite, 'a visionary'.

'You gotta tell us how you found Dyloft,' Carlos Hernández said.

'He won't tell,' French said as he mixed Clay a drink.

'Come on,' said Wes Saulsberry, one of the lawyers from New Orleans and Clay's newest friend.

'I'm sworn to silence,' Clay said.

The other lawyer from New Orleans was Damon Didier, one of the speakers at the session Clay had attended during his Circle of Barristers weekend. Didier was stone-faced and steely-eyed and Clay remembered wondering how this guy could ever connect with a jury.

A butler in a Roy Rogers-style shirt informed Mr French that dinner would be served in an hour. They moved downstairs to a games room with pool tables and big screens. A dozen or so men were drinking and talking and some were holding pool cues. 'The rest of the conspiracy,' Hernández whispered to Clay.

Patton introduced him to the group. The names, faces and home towns quickly blurred. Seattle, Houston, Topeka, Boston, and others he didn't catch. They all paid homage to this 'brilliant' young litigator who'd shocked them with his daring assault on Dyloft.

When the admiration was finally over, French said there were a few things to discuss before dinner. He began, 'As you know, I've spent a lot of time with Wicks, the in-house guy at Ackerman Labs. Bottom line is they're going to settle, and do it quickly. Their stock is so low now they're afraid of a takeover. If they know how much Dyloft will cost them, then they can restructure some debt and maybe hang on.'

'*Business Week* mentioned bankruptcy,' someone said. 'Have they used that threat?'

'Not yet. And I don't expect them to. Ackerman has far too many assets. We'll crunch the numbers in the morning—our boys think that the company has between two and three billion to settle Dyloft. We need to determine two things. First, how many potential plaintiffs are out there. Second, the value of each case.'

'Let's add 'em up,' drawled a Texan. 'I got a thousand.'

'I have eighteen hundred,' French said. 'Carlos.'

'Two thousand,' Hernández said as he began taking notes.

'Wes?'

'Nine hundred.'

The others gave their figures, but 2,000 remained the highest until French saved the best for last. 'Clay?' he said, and everyone listened intently.

'Thirty-two hundred,' Clay said, managing a grim poker face.

'Attaboy,' someone said.

'That's twenty-four thousand,' Carlos said, doing the quick maths.

'We can safely double that, which gets close to fifty, the number Ackerman has pegged. Fifty thousand into two billion is forty thousand bucks per case. Not a bad starting place.'

Clay did some quick maths of his own—$40,000 times his 3,200 cases came to something over $120 million. And one-third of that, well, his brain froze and his knees went weak.

'Does the company know how many of these cases involve malignant tumours?' asked Bernie from Boston.

'No, they don't. Their best guess is about one per cent.'

'That's five hundred cases.'

'At a minimum of a million bucks each.'

'That's another half-billion.'

'A million bucks is a joke.'

'Five million a pop in Seattle.'

Each lawyer had an opinion to offer and they did so simultaneously. When French restored order, he said, 'Gentlemen, let's eat.'

DINNER WAS A FIASCO. The dining table was a slab of polished wood that came from one tree, one grand and majestic red maple that had stood for centuries until it was needed by wealthy America. At least forty people could eat around it at one time but tonight there were eighteen for dinner.

In a room full of flamboyant egos, the most obnoxious windbag was Victor K. Brennan, a loud Texan. On the third or fourth wine, Brennan began complaining about such low expectations for each individual case. He had a forty-year-old client who made big bucks and now had malignant tumours, thanks to Dyloft. 'I can get ten million actual and twenty million punitive from any jury in Texas,' he boasted. Most of the others agreed with this. French held firm with the theory that if a few got millions then the masses would get little.

The group divided on this point, but the lines shifted so fast and the loyalties were so temporary that Clay had trouble determining where most of them stood. French challenged Brennan on his claim that punitive damages would be so easy to prove. 'You got the documents, right?' Brennan asked.

'Clay has provided some documents. Ackerman doesn't know it yet. You boys have not seen them. And maybe you won't if you don't stay in the class.'

The knives and forks stopped as all the lawyers, Clay excluded, started yelling at once. In the midst of the ruckus, Clay looked at the end of the table and saw Patton French sniff a wineglass, take a sip, close his eyes and evaluate yet another new wine.

When things settled down, Bernie from Boston told a joke about a Catholic priest and the room erupted in laughter. Food and wine were enjoyed for about five minutes until Albert from Topeka suggested the strategy of forcing Ackerman into bankruptcy. Those opposed voiced their concerns and soon there was another fight.

They fought over everything—documents, whether to press for a trial, turf, advertising, expenses, fees. Clay's stomach was in knots and he never said a word. The rest seemed to enjoy their food immensely while carrying on two or three arguments simultaneously.

After the longest dinner of Clay's life, French led them downstairs, back to the games room where the cognac and more cigars were waiting. Those who had been swearing at each other for three hours were now drinking and laughing like fraternity brothers. At the first opportunity, Clay sneaked away and found his room.

THE BARRY AND HARRY SHOW was scheduled for 10.00am on Saturday morning, time for everyone to sleep off the hangovers and choke down a heavy breakfast.

Barry and Harry had a company in New York that did nothing but analyse the finances of target companies. They had sources and spies and a reputation for peeling back the skin and finding the real truth. French had flown them in for a one-hour presentation.

Their routine was a tag team, Barry doing the graphics, Harry with the pointer. The lawyers, for once, were silent.

Ackerman Labs had insurance coverage of at least $500 million— $300 million from their liability carrier and another $200 million from a reinsurer. The cash-flow analysis was dense and took both Harry and Barry talking at once to complete.

They were also lawyers, and so were adept at assessing a company's likely response to a mass tort disaster like Dyloft. It would be wise for Ackerman to settle quickly, in stages. 'Stage one would be two billion for all level-one plaintiffs,' Harry said.

'We think they might do this within ninety days,' Barry added.

'Stage two would be half a billion for level-two plaintiffs, those with malignancy who don't die.'

'Stage three would be left open for five years to cover the death cases.'

'We think Ackerman can pay around two-point-five to three billion over the next year, then another half-billion over five years.'

'Anything beyond that, and you could be looking at a Chapter Eleven. Which is not advisable for this company. A bankruptcy would seriously choke off the flow of money. It would take from three to five years to get a decent settlement.'

Of course the lawyers wanted to argue for a while, but when all arguments had been completed French walked to the front of the room. It was time to agree on a plan, he said.

Step one was to round up the other cases. There were still plenty of Dyloft plaintiffs out there. 'Let's find them. Search out the small-time lawyers with only twenty or thirty cases, bring them into the fold. Do whatever it takes to get the cases.'

Step two would be a settlement conference with Ackerman Labs in sixty days.

Step three would be an all-out effort to keep everyone in the class. Those who 'opted out' would not have access to the deadly documents. It was as simple as that.

Every lawyer in the room objected to some part of the plan, but the alliance held. Dyloft looked as if it would be the quickest settlement in mass tort history, and the lawyers were smelling the money.

THE YOUNG FIRM'S next reorganisation occurred in the same chaotic fashion as the previous ones, and for the same reasons—too many new clients, not enough manpower. Three days after Clay returned from Ketchum, Paulette and Jonah confronted him with a list of urgent problems. Mutiny was in the air.

According to the best estimate, the firm now had 3,320 Dyloft cases, all needing immediate attention. Not counting Paulette, who was reluctantly assuming the role of office manager, and not counting Jonah, who was spending ten hours a day on a computer system to keep up with the cases, and, of course, not counting Clay because he was the boss, the firm had hired two further lawyers and now had ten young and inexperienced paralegals.

'The clients want to be talked to,' Jonah said. 'They're scared. And they want a lawyer on the other end of the phone, not some frantic paralegal. I'm afraid we'll be losing clients real soon.'

'We're drowning in paperwork,' Paulette added. 'Every preliminary medical test has got to be analysed, then verified with a follow-up. Right now, we think we have about four hundred people who need further testing. These could be the serious cases; these people could be dying, Clay. But somebody has to coordinate their medical care with the doctors. It isn't getting done, Clay, OK?'

'I'm listening,' he said. 'How many lawyers do we need?'

Paulette cast a weary look at Jonah. 'Ten,' she said.

'At least ten for now,' Jonah said. 'And maybe more later.'

A law firm down the street had just given pink slips to thirty-five associates because billings were down. It was a newsworthy story in DC because the legal job market was normally bulletproof. Paulette suggested they offer some of those associates a one-year contract. Clay volunteered to make the calls first thing next morning.

Jonah had the idea of hiring a doctor, someone to coordinate the tests and medical evidence. 'We can get one fresh out of school for a hundred grand a year,' he said. 'He wouldn't have much experience, but who cares? He's not doing surgery, just paperwork.'

'Get it done,' Clay said.

Next on Jonah's list was the matter of the Web site. The advertising had made it quite popular but they needed full-time people to respond to it. Plus it needed to be updated almost weekly with new developments on the class action.

For those who didn't use the Internet—Paulette guessed that at least half their clients fell into that group—a Dyloft newsletter was crucial. 'We need one full-time person editing and mailing the newsletter,' she said.

'Find someone,' Clay said.

PACE WANTED a late drink in a bar in Georgetown, within walking distance of Clay's house. He was in and out of the city, very vague, as always, about where he'd been and what fire he happened to be fighting. He had lightened up the wardrobe and now preferred brown—brown pointed-toe snakeskin boots, brown suede jacket.

Clay gave him a colourful description of his trip to French's ranch, and the gang of thieves he'd met there.

Into the second beer, Pace asked, 'You sold Ackerman short, right?' He glanced around, but no one was listening.

'A hundred thousand shares at forty-two fifty,' Clay said proudly.

'Ackerman closed today at twenty-three.'

'I know. I do the maths every day.'

'It's time to buy it back. Like first thing tomorrow morning. And while you're at it, buy all you can at twenty-three. It'll double.'

Six hours later, Clay was at the office, before sunrise, trying to prepare for another day of pure frenzy. And also anxious for the markets to open. His list of things to do ran for two pages, almost all of it involving the enormous task of immediately hiring ten new lawyers and finding work space to house them. At eight thirty he had a ten-minute interview with a freshly fired young lawyer named Oscar Mulrooney. The poor guy had been a star student at Yale, then highly recruited, then merged out of a job when a megafirm imploded. He'd also been married for two months and was desperate for work. Clay hired him on the spot for $75,000 a year. Mulrooney had four friends, also from Yale, who were also on the streets looking for work. Go get 'em.

At 10.00am, Clay called his broker and covered his Ackerman short sale, making a profit of $1.9 million and some change. In the same call, he took the entire profit and bought another 200,000 shares at $23, using his margin and some account credit.

Oscar Mulrooney was back at noon with his friends, all eager as Boy Scouts. Clay hired the others, then gave them the task of finding their own office space, renting furniture, hooking up phones, doing everything necessary to begin their new careers as mass tort lawyers. It was also Oscar's task to hire five more lawyers.

The Yale Branch was born.

AT 5.00PM Eastern Standard Time, Philo Products announced it would buy the outstanding common stock of Ackerman Labs for $50 a share, a merger with a price tag of $14 billion. Clay watched the drama on the big screen in his conference room, alone because everyone else was answering the damned telephones.

An endless string of experts and market analysts prattled on with all sorts of groundless opinions. Dyloft was mentioned early and often. Though Ackerman Labs had been badly managed for years, there was no doubt Dyloft had succeeded in shoving it off the cliff.

Was Philo the maker of Tarvan? Pace's client? Had Clay been manipulated to bring about a $14 billion takeover? What did it all mean for the future of Ackerman Labs and Dyloft?

Patton French called from his plane. He'd talked with Barry and Harry in New York and they were not worried about the Philo takeover. 'Ackerman owns twelve million shares of its own stock, now worth at least fifty bucks a share. The company just picked up 600 million dollars in equity alone. Plus, the government has to approve the merger, and they'll want the litigation cleaned up before saying yes. Also, Philo is notorious for avoiding courtrooms. They settle fast and quiet.'

Sounds like Tarvan, Clay thought.

'I'll keep you posted,' French said, and he was gone.

8

They met on neutral ground, in the dingy ballroom of an old hotel near Central Park, New York, the last place anyone would expect such an important gathering to take place. On one side of the table sat the Dyloft Plaintiffs' Steering Committee and behind them were all manner of associates and gofers. Across the table was the Ackerman team, headed by Cal Wicks, a distinguished veteran flanked by an equal number of supporters.

One week earlier, the government had approved the merger with Philo Products, at $53 a share, which for Clay meant another profit, somewhere around $6 million. He'd buried half of it off-shore, never to be touched.

Patton French may have had plenty of back-up, but he needed none. He took charge of the first session and soon everyone else shut up, with the exception of Wicks, who spoke only when necessary. They spent the morning nailing down the number of cases out there. The Biloxi class had 36,700 plaintiffs.

Numbers poured forth, and Clay was soon bored with it all. The only number that mattered to him was 5,380—his Dyloft share. He still had more than any single lawyer.

After three hours of nonstop statistics, they agreed on a one-hour lunch. The plaintiffs' committee went upstairs to a suite, where they ate sandwiches and drank only water. French was soon on the phone, talking and yelling at the same time. Wes Saulsberry wanted some fresh air, and invited Clay for a walk. They strolled up Fifth Avenue, across from the park. It was mid-November, the air chilly and light, the leaves blowing across the street.

'You're familiar with the lead paint cases?' Saulsberry said. 'Our clients are public buildings, all with layers of lead paint on the walls. Very dangerous stuff. We've sued the paint manufacturers, settled with a few, and it's pretty damn lucrative. Anyway, during discovery against one company I found out about another nice little mass tort you might want to look at. I can't handle it because of some conflicts.'

'I'm listening.'

'The company is in Reedsburg, Pennsylvania, and it makes the mortar used in new home construction. Seems they're having problems with a bad batch of mortar. After three years, it begins to crumble and the bricks start falling. It's confined to the Baltimore area, probably about two thousand homes.'

'What are the damages?'

'It costs roughly fifteen thousand to fix each house.'

Fifteen thousand times two thousand houses. A one-third contract and the lawyers' fees equalled $10 million.

'The proof will be easy,' Saulsberry said. 'The company knows it has exposure. Settlement should not be a problem.'

'I'd like to look at it.'

'I'll send you the file, but you have to protect my confidence.'

'You get a piece?'

'No. It's my payback for Dyloft. And, of course, if you get the chance to return the favour someday, then it will be appreciated.'

IN THE AFTERNOON, Ackerman Labs agreed an immediate settlement of a minimum of $62,000 for each Group One Dyloft plaintiff, those with benign tumours that could be removed with a fairly simple surgical procedure, the cost of which would also be borne by the company. Approximately 40,000 plaintiffs were in this class. A ferocious fight erupted when the issue of attorneys' fees was thrown on the table. Like most of the other lawyers, Clay had a contingency contract giving him one-third of any recovery, but in such settlements that percentage was normally reduced. Ackerman eventually agreed on the figure of 28 per cent for Group One fees.

Group Two plaintiffs were those with malignant tumours, and since their treatments would take months or years, the settlement was left open. No cap was placed on these damages. The attorneys would get 25 per cent in Group Two, though Clay had no idea why. French was crunching numbers too fast for anyone.

Group Three plaintiffs were those from Group Two who would die because of Dyloft. Since there had been no deaths so far, this class was also left open. The fees were capped at 22 per cent.

They adjourned at seven. In the elevator down, French handed him a print-out. 'Not a bad day's work,' he said with a smile. It was a summary of Clay's cases and anticipated fees, including a 7 per cent add-on for his role on the Plaintiffs' Steering Committee.

His expected gross fees from Group One alone were $106 million.

When he was finally alone in his room he stood in front of the window and gazed into the dusk settling over Central Park. He was numb, speechless, frozen in the window for ever as random thoughts raced in and out of his severely overloaded brain. He drank two straight whiskies from the minibar with absolutely no effect.

Still at the window, he called Paulette, who snatched the phone after half a ring. 'You just made ten million bucks,' he said, the words coming from his mouth but in a voice that belonged to someone else.

There was a pause as she began to cry. He back-pedalled and sat on the edge of the bed, and for a moment he felt like a good cry himself. 'Oh my God,' she managed to say twice.

Jonah was still at the office. When Clay told him about the settlement he began yelling into the phone, then threw it down to fetch Rodney. Clay heard them talking in the background. Rodney picked up the phone and said, 'I'm listening.'

'Your share is ten million,' Clay said, for the third time.

'Mercy, mercy, mercy,' Rodney was saying.

For a moment, Clay held the image of Rodney sitting at his old desk at OPD, files and papers everywhere, photos of his wife and kids pinned to the wall, a fine man working hard for very low pay.

What would he tell his wife when he called home in a few minutes?

When he'd finished delivering the news, he sat on the bed for a long time, sad with the realisation that there was no one else to call. He could see Rebecca, and he could suddenly hear her voice and feel her and touch her. They could buy a place in Tuscany or Maui or anywhere she wanted. They could live there quite happily with a dozen kids and no in-laws, with nannies and maids and cooks.

He clenched his jaws and dialled her number. After three rings she said, 'Hello,' and the sound of her voice made him weak.

'Hey, it's Clay,' he said, trying to sound casual. Not a word in six months, but the ice was immediately broken.

'Hello, stranger,' she said. Cordial.

'How are you?'

'Fine, busy as always. You?'

'About the same. I'm in New York, settling some cases.'

'I hear things are going well for you.'

An understatement. 'Not bad. I can't complain. How's your job?'

'I have six more days.'

'You're quitting?'

'Yes. There's a wedding, you know.'

'So I heard. When is it?'

'December 20th.'

'I haven't received an invitation.'

'Well, I didn't send you one. Didn't think you'd want to come.'

'Probably not. Are you sure you want to get married?'

'Let's talk about something else. I hear you've bought a place in Georgetown?'

'That's old news.' But he was delighted that she knew. 'Where'd you meet this guy?' he said. 'He's a worm.'

'Come on, Clay. Let's keep it nice.'

'Don't marry him, Rebecca. Your parents will eat him alive. Plus your kids will look like him. A bunch of little worms.'

The line went dead.

THE FOLLOWING MORNING, *The Wall Street Journal* ran the story under the headline: MASS TORT LAWYERS FORCE QUICK DYLOFT SETTLEMENT. Philo Products opened at $82 and quickly jumped to $85. One analyst said investors were relieved at news of the settlement. Clay monitored the news on the television in his home.

He also fielded calls from reporters. At eleven, one from *The Journal* arrived, with a photographer. He knew as much about the settlement as Clay himself.

Off the record, Clay answered all questions. Then on the record, he wouldn't comment on the settlement. He did offer some insights about himself, his rapid rise from the depths of OPD to mass tort zillionaire, and the impressive firm he was building, et cetera.

Next morning, he read the story online before sunrise. There was his face, and just above it was the headline THE KING OF TORTS, FROM $40,000 TO $100,000,000 IN SIX MONTHS.

It was a long story, and all about Clay. His background, growing up in DC, his father, Georgetown Law School, generous quotes from Glenda over at OPD, a comment from a professor he'd forgotten, a recap of the Dyloft litigation. The best part was a lengthy discussion with Patton French, in which the 'notorious mass tort lawyer' described Clay Carter as our 'brightest young star', and was quoted as saying, 'No doubt, Clay is the newest King of Torts.'

He read it twice then emailed it to Rebecca with a note at the top and bottom: 'Rebecca, Please Wait, Clay.' He sent it to her apartment and her office. The wedding was a month away.

When he finally arrived at the office, it was even more chaotic than normal. Paulette, Jonah and Rodney were still floating and completely unfocused. Every client wanted the money that day.

Fortunately, it was the Yale Branch, under the emerging brilliance of Mr Oscar Mulrooney, that stepped up to the task and put together a plan to survive until the settlement. Clay moved Mulrooney into an office down the hall, doubled his salary, and left him in charge of the mess.

Clay needed a break.

GREAT ABACO ISLAND is a long strip of land at the northern edge of the Bahamas, about 100 miles east of Florida. Clay had been there four years earlier when he'd scraped together enough money for the airfare. That trip had been one in which Clay had planned to discuss serious issues with his father. It didn't happen. Jarrett Carter was still too close to his disgrace and concerned primarily with drinking rum punch from noon on. He was willing to talk about anything but the law and lawyers. This visit would be different.

JARRETT CARTER'S reputation had been secured with a malpractice verdict against the President of the American Medical Association, a fine doctor who'd made a mistake in surgery. A pitiless jury in a conservative county had returned the verdict, and Jarrett Carter was suddenly a trial lawyer in demand. He picked the toughest cases, won most of them, and by the age of forty was a litigator with a wide reputation. Clay never doubted he would follow his father and spend his career in trials.

The wheels came off when Clay was in college. There was an ugly divorce that cost Jarrett dearly. His firm began to split with, typically, all partners suing each other. Distracted, Jarrett went two years without winning a trial, and his reputation suffered greatly. He made his biggest mistake when he and his accountant began cooking the books—hiding income, overstating expenses. They got caught, Jarrett was devastated, and prison looked likely. Luckily, an old pal from law school was the US attorney in charge of the prosecution.

The details of their agreement would for ever remain a dark secret. There was never an indictment, just an unofficial deal whereby Jarrett quietly closed his office, surrendered his licence to practise law, and left the country. So the great Jarrett Carter became a fishing boat captain in the Bahamas.

THE WINK-AND-HANDSHAKE DEAL that got Jarrett Carter out of town without an indictment had many loose ends. His passport had been confiscated by the US Department of Justice, which meant his movements were somewhat limited. 'We'd better stick to the Bahamas,' he told Clay on the phone.

They left Abaco on a Cessna Citation V, another toy from the fleet Clay had discovered. They were headed for Nassau, thirty minutes away. Jarrett waited until they were airborne before saying, 'OK, spill your guts.' He was already gulping a beer.

Clay opened a beer himself, then began with Tarvan and ended with Dyloft. Jarrett had heard rumours of his son's success, but he never read newspapers and tried to ignore any news from home.

The $100 million closed his eyes, turned him pale, or at least a slightly lighter shade of bronze, and creased his leathery forehead. He shook his head and began laughing.

'What are you doing with the money?'

'Spending it like crazy.'

Outside the Nassau airport they found a cab, a 1974 yellow Cadillac with a driver smoking pot. He got them safely to the Sunset Hotel and Casino on Paradise Island, facing Nassau Harbour.

Jarrett headed for the blackjack tables with the $5,000 in cash his son had given him. Clay headed for the pool and the tanning cream. He wanted sun and bikinis.

THE BOAT WAS A sixty-three-foot catamaran made in Fort Lauderdale. The captain/salesman was a cranky old Brit named Maltbee who snarled and fussed until they were out of the harbour and into the bay. They were headed for a half-day test drive of a boat that Jarrett said could make some real money.

According to Jarrett, the serious money was in private sailboat charters for small groups of wealthy people who wanted to work, not be pampered. Take a great boat—your own boat, preferably—and sail round the Caribbean for a month at a time. 'Ten thousand bucks a week,' Jarrett said. 'Plus you're sailing, enjoying the wind and the sun and the sea. Unlike fishing, where the work's hard and you gotta catch a big marlin every day or everybody's mad.'

They found some wind and began slicing through the smooth water. Clay had stripped down to his shorts and was covered in cream; he was about to doze when Maltbee crept up beside him.

'Your father tells me you're the one with the money.' Maltbee's eyes were hidden behind thick sunshades.

'I guess he's right,' Clay said.

'She's a four-million-dollar boat, practically new, one of our best. Built for one of those dot-commers who lost his money faster than he made it. Anyway, we're stuck with it. Market's slow. We'll move it for three million, and at that you should be charged with thievery. If you incorporate the boat under Bahamian law as a charter company, there are all sorts of tax tricks. I can't explain them, but we have a lawyer in Nassau who does the paperwork.'

Three days later, Clay signed a contract to pay $2.9 million for the boat. The Nassau lawyer chartered the Bahamian company in Jarrett's name only. The boat was a gift from son to father, an asset to be hidden away in the islands, much like Jarrett himself.

Over dinner on their last night in Nassau, in a seedy saloon packed with drug dealers and tax cheaters and alimony dodgers, Clay cracked crab legs and asked a question he'd been considering for weeks now. 'Any chance you could ever return to the States?'

'For what?'

'To practise law. To be my partner. To litigate and kick ass again.'

The question made Jarrett smile. The thought of father and son working together. The very idea that Clay wanted him to return; back to an office, back to something respectable.

'I doubt it. I surrendered my licence and promised to stay away.'

'Would you want to come back?'

'Maybe, but never to practise law again. I'm fifty-five years old, and that's a bit late to start over.'

'Where will you be in ten years?'

'I don't think like that. Plotting the future is damned ridiculous. Live for the moment, Clay. Tomorrow will take care of itself. You've got your hands full right now, seems to me.'

'The money should keep me occupied.'

'Don't blow it, son. I know that looks impossible, but you'll be surprised. New friends are about to pop up all over the place. Women will drop from the sky.'

'When?'

'Just wait.' Jarrett threw a shrimp in his mouth and changed the subject. 'Are you going to help your mother?'

'Probably not. She doesn't need help. Her husband is wealthy, remember?'

'When have you talked to her?'

'It's been eleven years, Dad. Why do you care?'

'Just curious. It's odd. You marry a woman, live with her for twenty-five years, and you sometimes wonder what she's doing.'

'Let's talk about something else.'

'Rebecca?'

'Next.'

'Let's go hit the crap tables. I'm up four thousand bucks.'

WHEN TED WORLEY received a thick envelope from the Law Offices of J. Clay Carter II, he immediately opened it. He'd seen various news reports about the Dyloft settlement. He'd watched the Dyloft Web site religiously, waiting for some sign that it was time to collect his money from Ackerman Labs.

The letter began, 'Dear Mr Worley: Congratulations. Your class-action claim against Ackerman Labs has been settled in the US District Court for the Southern District of Mississippi. As a Group One plaintiff, your portion of the settlement is $62,000. Pursuant to the Contract for Legal Services entered into by you and this law firm, a 28 per cent contingency for attorneys' fees is now applicable. In addition, a deduction of $1,400 for litigation expenses has been approved by the court. Your net settlement is $43,240. Please sign the enclosed agreement and acknowledgment forms and return them immediately in the enclosed envelope. Sincerely, Oscar Mulrooney, Attorney-at-Law.'

'A different lawyer every damned time,' Mr Worley said as he kept flipping pages that he suddenly had no desire to read.

Forty-three thousand, two hundred and forty dollars! That was the grand sum he would receive from a sleazy pharmaceutical giant that put into the marketplace a drug that caused four tumours to grow in his bladder? Just $43,240 for months of fear and stress and uncertainty about living or dying? For the ordeal of the operation, where the growths were removed one by one? He flinched at the memory.

He called six times and left six hot messages and waited for Mr Mulrooney to call him back. 'Who the hell are you?' Mr Worley began pleasantly.

Oscar Mulrooney had become an expert at handling such calls. He explained that he was the attorney in charge of Mr Worley's case.

'This settlement is a joke!' Mr Worley said. 'Forty-three thousand dollars is criminal.'

'Your settlement is sixty-two thousand, Mr Worley,' Oscar said. 'You agreed to give one-third to your attorney, without whom you would be getting nothing. It's been reduced to twenty-eight per cent by the settlement. Most lawyers charge forty-five or fifty per cent.'

'Well, aren't I a lucky bastard. I'm not accepting it.'

To which Oscar offered a well-rehearsed narrative about how Ackerman Labs could only pay so much without going bankrupt, an event that would leave Mr Worley with even less, if anything at all.

'That's nice,' Mr Worley said. 'But I'm not accepting it.'

'Look at the Contract for Legal Services, Mr Worley. It's page eleven in the packet you have. Read it, sir, and you'll see you authorised us to settle for anything above fifty thousand dollars.'

'I remember that, but it was described to me as a starting point. I was expecting much more.'

'Your settlement has already been approved by the court, sir. That's the way class actions work. If you don't sign the acceptance form, then your portion will eventually go to someone else.'

'You're a bunch of crooks, you know that?'

'Sorry you feel that way.'

'You're not sorry about a damn thing. Paper says you're getting a hundred million bucks. Thieves!' Worley slammed the phone down.

THE DECEMBER COVER of *Capitol Magazine* featured Clay Carter, looking tanned and handsome in an Armani suit, perched on the corner of his desk in his finely appointed office.

There was Clay on his patio, and Clay next to the jury box in an empty courtroom as if he'd been extracting huge verdicts from the bad guys, and, of course, Clay washing his new Porsche. He confided that his passion was sailing, and there was a new boat docked down in the Bahamas. No significant romance at the moment, and the story immediately labelled him as one of DC's most eligible bachelors.

Near the back were the announcements of forthcoming weddings. And there was Rebecca Van Horn, resplendent on a bench in a garden, a lovely photo ruined by the face of her future mate, Jason Shubert Myers IV, cuddling next to her and obviously enjoying the camera.

Bennett and Barb had pulled the right strings; Rebecca's announcement was the second largest of a dozen or so. Six pages over, Clay saw a full-page ad for BVH Group. The bribe.

Clay revelled in the misery the magazine would be causing around the Van Horn home. Rebecca's wedding, the big social bash that Bennett and Barbara could throw money at and impress the world, was being upstaged by their old nemesis.

And his upstaging was not over.

JONAH HAD ALREADY ANNOUNCED that retirement was a real possibility. He'd just spent ten days on Antigua, and when he returned to DC, in an early December snowstorm, he confided in Clay that he was mentally and psychologically unfit to practise law any longer. He'd had all he could take. He'd found a girl who, like him, loved to sail, and he was seriously looking at buying a sailboat himself.

'I need a bimbo, preferably a blonde,' Clay said as he settled into a chair across from Jonah's desk. It was after six on a Wednesday and Jonah had the first bottle of beer opened.

'The hottest bachelor in town is having trouble picking up chicks?'

'I've been out of the loop. I'm going to Rebecca's wedding, and I need a babe who'll steal the show.'

'Oh, this is beautiful,' Jonah said as he laughed and reached into a drawer in his desk. Only Jonah would keep files on women. He burrowed through some paperwork and found what he wanted. He tossed a folded newspaper across the desk. It was a lingerie ad for a department store. The gorgeous young goddess was wearing practically nothing below the waist and was barely covering her breasts with her folded arms.

Clay said, 'You know her?'

'Of course I know her. You think I keep lingerie ads for thrills? Her name is Ridley. At least that's what she goes by.'

'She lives here?' Clay was still gawking at the stunning beauty.

'She's from Georgia.'

'Oh, a Southern girl.'

'No, a Russian girl. The country of Georgia. She came over as an exchange student and never left.'

'How tall is she?'

'Five ten or so.'

Clay tossed the paper back on the desk. 'You've dated her?'

'Nope. A friend of a friend. She's on my list. I was just waiting for a confirmation. Give it a try. You don't like her, we'll find another.'

'Can you make the call?'

'Sure, no problem. It's an easy call, now that you're Mr Cover Boy, most eligible bachelor, the King of Torts.'

THEY MET FOR DINNER at a Japanese place frequented by the young and prosperous. With her blonde hair and perfect features, Ridley looked even better in person than in print. Heads jerked and necks twisted as they were led to the centre of the restaurant and placed at a powerful table. Waiters swarmed round them. Her slightly accented English was just exotic enough to add even more sex to the package, as if she needed it.

Her real name was Ridal Petashnakol. Fortunately, models could survive with only one name, so she went just by Ridley.

She had the looks and he had the money, and since they could talk about neither they thrashed about in deep water for a few minutes looking for safe ground. She cared nothing about politics or terrorism or football. Ah, the movies! She saw everything and loved them all. Even dreadful stuff that no one else went to see. Box office disasters were much beloved by Ridley, and Clay was beginning to have doubts.

She's just a bimbo, he said to himself. Dinner now, Rebecca's wedding later and she's history.

Conversation wasn't easy, but they both worked hard at it. Over dessert, a chocolate mousse, he invited her to attend a wedding reception. He confessed that the bride was his former fiancée, but lied when he said that they were now on friendly terms. Ridley shrugged as if she preferred to go to the movies. 'Why not?' she said.

As HE TURNED INTO the drive of the Potomac Country Club, Clay was hit by the moment. His last visit to this wretched place had been seven months earlier. Then he'd hidden his old Honda behind the tennis courts. Now, he was showing off a Porsche Carrera. Then, he'd avoided the valet parking to save money. Now he'd tip the kid extra. Then, he was dreading the next few hours with the Van Horns. Now he was escorting the priceless Ridley, and wherever her parents happened to be they damn sure weren't involved in his life.

They were an hour late, which was perfect timing. The ballroom was packed and a rhythm and blues band played at one end.

Heads began turning immediately. Jaws dropped. With several drinks under their belts the men did not hesitate to gawk at Ridley as she and her date inched forward. 'Hey, Clay!' someone yelled, and Clay turned to see the smiling face of Randy Spino, a law school classmate who worked in a megafirm and would never, under normal circumstances, have spoken to Clay at the Potomac.

But there he was, thrusting a hand at Clay while showing Ridley every one of his teeth. A small mob followed. Spino took charge, introducing all of his good friends to his good friend Clay Carter and Ridley with no last name. All the boys wanted to say hello.

An announcement was being made onstage and the room became quieter. The bride and groom were about to dance, to be followed by the bride and her father, then the groom and his mother, and so on. The band began playing 'Smoke Gets in Your Eyes'.

'She's very pretty,' Ridley whispered. Indeed she was. And she was dancing with Jason Myers who, though he was two inches shorter, appeared to Rebecca to be the only person in the world. She smiled and glowed as they spun slowly round the dance floor, the bride doing most of the work because her groom was as stiff as a board.

Clay wanted to attack, to bolt through the crowd and sucker

punch Myers with all the force he could muster. He would rescue his girl and take her away and shoot her mother if she found them.

'You still love her, don't you?' Ridley was whispering.

'No, it's over,' he whispered back.

The two were painful to watch, and Clay asked himself why he was there. Closure, whatever that meant. A farewell. But he wanted Rebecca to see him, and Ridley, and to know that he was faring well and not missing her.

Clay led his date to the dance floor where a mob was gyrating to some pretty good Motown. If Ridley standing still was a work of art, Ridley in full motion was a national treasure. She moved with a natural rhythm and easy grace, with the low-cut dress just barely high enough and the slit in the skirt flying open to reveal all manner of flesh. Groups of men were gathering to watch.

And watching also was Rebecca. Taking a break to chat with her guests, she noticed the commotion and looked into the crowd, where she saw Clay dancing with a knockout. She, too, was stunned by Ridley, but for other reasons. She moved back to the dance floor.

Meanwhile, Clay's eyes were working furiously to check on Rebecca without missing a movement from Ridley. The song ended, a slow number began, and Rebecca stepped between them. 'Hello, Clay,' she said, ignoring Ridley. 'How about a dance?'

'Sure,' he said. Ridley shrugged and moved away, alone for only a second before a stampede surrounded her. She picked the tallest one, threw her arms round him, and began pulsating.

'Don't remember inviting you,' Rebecca said.

'You want me to leave?' He pulled her slightly closer but the bulky wedding dress prevented the contact he wanted.

'People are watching,' she said. 'Where'd you get the bimbo?'

'Don't worry, Rebecca, she can't touch you in bed.'

'Jason's not bad.'

'I really don't want to hear about it. Just don't get pregnant, OK?'

'That's hardly any of your business.'

'It's very much my business.'

Ridley and her beau swept by them. For the first time Clay got a good look at her back, the full extent of which was on display because her dress didn't exist until just a few inches above her round and perfect cheeks. 'Is she on the payroll?' Rebecca asked.

'Not yet.'

'It might be best if you leave now, and take her with you.'

'Sure, it's your party. Didn't mean to crash it.'

'That's the only reason you're here, Clay.' She pulled away slightly.

'Hang in there for a year, OK?' he said. 'By then I'll have two hundred million. We can hop on my jet, blow this joint, spend the rest of our lives on a yacht. Your parents will never find us.'

She stopped moving and said, 'Goodbye, Clay.'

'I'll wait,' he said, then got knocked aside by a stumbling Bennett whose cheeks were already crimson from too much Chivas. 'Excuse me.' Bennett grabbed his daughter and rescued her by shuffling to the other side of the floor.

Barbara was next. She took Clay's hand and flashed an artificial smile. 'Don't make a scene,' she said without moving her lips. They began a rigid movement that no one would mistake for dancing.

'And how are you, Mrs Van Horn?' Clay said.

'Fine, until I saw you. You weren't invited to this little party.'

'I was just leaving.'

'Good. I'd hate to call security.'

'That won't be necessary.'

The music stopped and Clay jerked away from Mrs Van Horn. He grabbed Ridley and whisked her away to the bar at the back of the room. Clay ordered a beer and was planning an exit when a group of onlookers encircled them. Lawyers in the bunch wanted to talk about the joys of mass torts while pressing close to Ridley.

After a few minutes of small talk with people he detested, a thick young man in a tuxedo appeared next to Clay and whispered, 'I'm security.' He had a friendly face and seemed very professional.

'I'm leaving,' Clay whispered back.

Tossed from the Van Horn wedding reception. Ejected from the great Potomac Country Club. Driving away, with Ridley wrapped around him, he privately declared it to be one of his finest moments.

9

The announcement had said the newlyweds would honeymoon in Mexico. Clay decided to take a trip himself.

The office was filled with tension and strife. So many Dyloft clients were unhappy with their meagre settlements. The mail was brutal. Dodging the phone had become a sport. Several clients had actually found the place and presented themselves to Miss Glick with demands to see Mr Carter, who, as it happened, was always in a big trial somewhere. Usually, he was hunkering down in his office with the door locked, riding out yet another storm. After one particularly troubling day, he called Patton French for advice.

'Toughen up, ol' boy,' French said. 'You're making a fortune in mass torts, this is just the downside. It takes a thick skin.'

The thickest skin in the firm belonged to Oscar Mulrooney, who continued to amaze Clay with his organisational skills and his ambition. Mulrooney was working fifteen hours a day and pushing his Yale Branch to collect the Dyloft money as quickly as possible. With Jonah making no secret of his plans to sail round the world, Paulette dropping hints about a year in Africa to study art, and Rodney following along with some vague chatter about just plain quitting, it was obvious that the original team had lost all direction and there would soon be room at the top.

The Yale Branch now had eleven lawyers, seven of whom had actually gone to Yale. The Sweatshop had grown to twelve paralegals, all up to their ears in files and paperwork. Clay had no hesitation in leaving both units under the supervision of Mulrooney for a few weeks. He was certain that when he returned, the office would be in better shape than when he left.

IT WAS RIDLEY'S first trip on a private jet. Nonstop from Washington to St Lucia, four hours and a million miles. DC was cold and grey when they left, and when they stepped off the plane the sun and the heat hit them hard.

They boarded a commuter for the fifteen-minute flight to Mustique, the exclusive island owned by the rich and famous, an island with everything but a runway long enough for private jets.

Their house for the Christmas week had once been owned by a prince who sold it to a dot-commer who leased it when he wasn't around. Marshall, the chauffeur/butler, was waiting with a smile and an open Jeep. They threw their bags in the back and started up a winding road. No hotels, no condos, no tourists, no traffic. The house was on the side of a hill. The view was breathtaking—200 feet above the water and miles of endless ocean.

Before they could unpack in the main suite, Ridley had stripped down to virtually nothing and was in the pool. Two beers and Clay was staggering towards a hammock for a long siesta.

Rebecca was away in some tourist hotel, cuddling with little Jason. And he didn't care.

TWO DAYS AFTER CHRISTMAS, Max Pace arrived with a companion. Her name was Valeria, a rugged, outdoors type with broad shoulders, no make-up and a very reluctant smile. Max was a handsome fellow, but there was nothing attractive about his friend.

Pace was quick to change into shorts and head for the pool. Valeria pulled out some hiking boots and struck off in search of rocks to climb. Ridley disappeared into the living room of the main house, where she had a stack of videos to watch.

Because Pace had no background, there was little to talk about. At first, anyway. However, it soon became apparent that he had something important on his mind. 'Let's talk business,' he said after a nap in the sun. They moved to the bar and Marshall brought drinks.

'There's another drug out there,' Pace began. 'And it's a big one. But this time I want a piece of the action.'

'Who are you working for?'

'Me. And you. I get twenty-five per cent of the attorneys' fees.'

'What's the upside?'

'It could be bigger than Dyloft.'

'Then you get twenty-five per cent. More if you want.'

'Twenty-five is fair,' Max said, and reached across for a handshake. The deal was done.

'Let's have it.'

'There's a female hormone drug called Maxatil. Used by at least four million women aged between forty-five and seventy-five. It came out five years ago. It relieves hot flushes and other symptoms of menopause. The company is Goffman.'

'Goffman? Razor blades and mouthwash?'

'You got it. Twenty-one billion in sales last year. The bluest of all blue chips. Very little debt, sound management. But they got in a hurry with Maxatil—profits looked huge, drug looked safe, they rammed it through the FDA and for the first few years everybody was happy.'

'But?'

'But there are huge problems. A government study has been tracking twenty thousand women who've been taking the drug for four years. The report is due in a few weeks. It will be devastating. For a percentage of women, about eight per cent, the drug greatly increases the risk of breast cancer, heart attacks and strokes.'

'Who knows about the report?'

'Very few people. I have a copy of it.'

'Why am I not surprised?' Clay took a long pull on his bottle. His pulse was racing. He was suddenly bored with Mustique.

'There are some lawyers on the prowl, but they haven't seen the government report,' Pace continued. 'One lawsuit has been filed, in Arizona, but it's not a class action.'

'What is it?'

'Just an old-fashioned tort case. A one-shot deal. The lawyer is a character named Dale Mooneyham, from Tucson. He tries them one at a time, and he never loses. He's on the fast track to get the first shot at Goffman. It could set the tone for the entire settlement. The key is to file the first class action. And you can do it alone. I'll be in the background, pulling strings. I have lots of contacts with all the right shady characters. It'll be our lawsuit, and with your name on it Goffman will run for cover.'

'A quick settlement?'

'Probably not as quick as Dyloft, but that was remarkably fast.'

'The downside?' Clay asked, trying to appear cautious.

'None that I can see, except that it'll cost you millions in advertising and trial prep.'

'No problem there.'

'You seem to have the knack for spending it.'

'I've barely scratched the surface.'

'I'd like an advance of a million dollars. Against my fee.' Pace took a sip. 'I'm still cleaning up some old business back home.'

The fact that Pace wanted money struck Clay as odd. However, with so much at stake, and with their Tarvan secret, he was in no position to say no. 'Approved,' he said.

Pace and Valeria stayed for two days. Clay watched them speed away with Marshall at the wheel of the Jeep.

'Any more guests?' Ridley asked warily. Valeria had not been easy company.

'Hell no,' Clay said.

'Good.'

THE ENTIRE FLOOR above his firm became vacant at the end of the year. Clay leased half of it and consolidated his operations. He brought in the twelve paralegals and five secretaries from the Sweatshop; the Yale Branch lawyers were likewise transferred to Connecticut Avenue, where they felt more at home.

He attacked the new year with a ferocious work schedule—in the office by six with breakfast, lunch, and sometimes dinner at his desk. He was usually there until eight or nine at night, and left little doubt that he expected similar hours from those who wanted to stay.

Jonah did not. He was gone by the middle of January, his office vacated, his farewells quick. The sailboat was waiting.

The ageing Greek playboy who'd married Paulette Tullos and then left her had somehow got wind of her new money. He showed up in DC, called her at the swanky condo he'd given her and left a message on her answering machine. When Paulette heard his voice, she raced from her home and flew to London, where she'd spent the holidays and was still in hiding. She emailed Clay while he was on Mustique, telling him of her predicament and instructing him on exactly how to handle her divorce upon his return. Clay filed the necessary papers, but Paulette had decided to stay in London. 'Sorry, Clay,' she said on the phone. 'But I really don't want to work anymore.'

So Mulrooney became the confidant, the unofficial partner. He and his team had been studying the shifting landscape of class-action litigation. Now he came to Clay with a plan. With so many class actions already filed, the firm could spend its considerable resources in rounding up new clients. As with Dyloft, almost every lawsuit that had been settled was left open for a period of years to allow new participants to collect what they were entitled to. Clay's firm could simply ride the coattails of other mass tort lawyers—there were about 11,000 class actions pending in the US—sort of pick up the pieces, but for huge fees. He used the example of Skinny Bens, the diet pill fiasco.

Clay assigned two lawyers and a paralegal to the Skinny Ben front. This was less than Mulrooney asked for, but Clay had bigger plans. He laid out the war on Maxatil, a lawsuit he would direct himself. The government report, still unreleased and evidently stolen by Max Pace, was 140 pages long and filled with damning results. Clay read it twice before he gave it to Mulrooney.

On a snowy night in late January, they worked until after midnight going through it, then made detailed plans for the attack.

At two in the morning, Mulrooney said he had something unpleasant to discuss. 'We need more money.'

'How much?' Clay asked.

'There are thirteen of us now, all from big firms where we were doing quite well before we were tossed onto the streets with nothing. Ten of us are married, most have kids. You gave us one-year contracts for seventy-five thousand, and, believe me, we're happy to get them. You doubled my salary and I appreciate it. I'm getting by. But the other guys are struggling. And they're very proud men.'

'Let's do it like this, Oscar. I'll give all of you a new contract for one year, at two hundred grand. What I get in return is a ton of hours. We're on the brink here of something huge, bigger than last year. You guys deliver, and I'll do bonuses. Deal?'

'You got it, chief.'

DELIVERY ON A NEW Gulfstream 5 would be a minimum of twenty-two months, but the delay was not the biggest obstacle. The price tag was $44 million. It was simply too much. The broker explained that most new G-5s were bought by billion-dollar corporations who kept them in the air. The better deal for him, as a sole proprietor, was to lease a slightly older plane for say, six months, to make sure it was what he wanted. Then he could convert it to a sale.

The broker had just the plane. It was a G-4 that a Fortune 500 company had recently traded in. When Clay saw it sitting on the tarmac at Reagan National, his pulse took off.

The broker said, 'It's yours for thirty million.'

They sat at a small table and began the deal. The idea of a lease slowly went out of the window. With Clay's income, he would have no trouble obtaining a financing package. His mortgage note, $300,000 a month, would be only slightly more than the lease payments. And if he wanted to trade up, the broker would take it back at the highest market appraisal, and outfit him with whatever he wanted.

Two pilots would cost $200,000 a year. Clay might consider putting the plane on the certificate of a corporate air charter company. 'You could generate up to a million bucks a year in charters,' the broker said. 'That'll cover your expenses.'

A reasonable voice said to be cautious, but why wait? And who, exactly, might he turn to for advice? The only people he knew with experience in such matters were his mass tort buddies, and every one of them would say, 'You don't have your own jet yet? Buy it!'

And so he bought it.

GOFFMAN'S FOURTH-QUARTER EARNINGS were up from the year before, with record sales. Its stock was at $65, the highest in two years. In January, the company had launched an unusual ad campaign promoting not one of its many products but the company itself. 'Goffman has always been there', was the slogan and theme, and each television commercial was a montage of well-known products being used to comfort and protect America.

Mulrooney was convinced that the ad campaign, with its strong 'feel-good' message, was to brace investors and consumers for the shock of Maxatil, and this opinion was shared by Max Pace, who had taken up residence in the Hay-Adams Hotel.

Clay stopped by his suite for a late dinner. Pace was edgy and anxious to drop the bomb on Goffman. 'What's the plan?' he said.

'The ads start at eight in the morning, coast to coast,' Clay said with a mouth full of veal. 'The hot line is set up. The Web site is ready. I'll walk over to the courthouse at ten and file it myself.'

'This ain't Dyloft, remember that. There you caught a weak company at a bad moment. Goffman will be much tougher.'

'But you don't go to trial with a bad drug.'

'Not in a class action. My sources tell me that Goffman might want to litigate the case in Flagstaff since it's a single plaintiff.'

'The Mooneyham case?'

'That's it. If they win that, then this could be a long fight.'

'You said Mooneyham doesn't lose.'

'It's been twenty years or so. Juries love him. He wears cowboy hats and suede jackets and red boots and such. A throwback to when trial lawyers actually tried their cases. You should go meet him. It would be worth a trip.'

'I'll put that on my list.' The Gulfstream was just sitting in the hangar, anxious to travel.

Clay slept at the office. He had installed a small bedroom and a bath adjacent to the conference room. He was often up until after midnight, then a few hours of sleep before a quick shower, and back to the desk by six. His work habits were becoming legendary not only within his own firm but around the city as well.

Mulrooney arrived just after six, already with four cups of coffee under his belt. 'D-Day?' he asked when he barged into Clay's office.

'D-Day!'

'Let's kick some ass!'

By seven, the place was rocking with associates and paralegals watching the clocks, waiting for the invasion. Secretaries hauled coffee and bagels from office to office. At eight, they crammed into the conference room to watch the first ad:

An attractive woman in her sixties, grey hair smartly cut, designer glasses, sitting at a table, staring sadly out of a window. Voice-over: 'If you've been taking the drug Maxatil, you may have an increased risk of breast cancer, heart disease and stroke.' On the table, a close-up of a pill bottle with MAXATIL in bold. Voice-over: 'Please consult your doctor immediately. Maxatil may pose a serious threat to your health. For more information, call the Maxatil hot line.' An 800 number flashes across the bottom of the screen. The final image is the woman removing her glasses and wiping a tear from her cheek.

They clapped and cheered as if the money was about to be delivered by overnight courier. Then Clay sent them all to their posts, to sit by the phones and begin collecting clients. Within minutes, the calls started. Promptly at nine, as scheduled, copies of the lawsuit were faxed to newspapers and financial cable channels.

Goffman opened at $65¼ but by noon, the price had fallen to $61. The company hurriedly released a statement for the press in which it denied that Maxatil did the things alleged in the lawsuit. It would defend the case vigorously.

Patton French called during 'lunch'. Clay was eating a sandwich while standing behind his desk and watching the phone messages pile up. 'I hope you know what you're doing,' French said.

'Gee, I hope so too, Patton. How are you?'

'Swell. We took a long hard look at Maxatil about six months ago. Decided to pass. Causation could be a real problem. In fact, everybody passed, until you. Saulsberry, Didier, Carlos down in Miami. Guy up in Chicago has a bunch of cases, but he hasn't filed them yet. I don't know, maybe you're right. We just didn't see it, that's all.'

French was fishing. 'We got the goods on them,' Clay said.

'You'd better have your ducks in a row, Clay. These guys are good. They make Wicks and the boys at Ackerman look like Cub Scouts.'

'You sound scared, Patton, I'm surprised at you.'

'Not scared at all. But if you have a hole in your theory of liability, they'll eat you alive. Good luck.'

Clay closed his office door. He walked to his window and stood for five minutes before he felt the cool moisture of his shirt sticking to his back. Then he rubbed his forehead and found rows of sweat.

THE HEADLINE in the *Daily Profit* screamed: A LOUSY HUNDRED MILLION AIN'T ENOUGH. The story began with a quick paragraph about the 'frivolous' lawsuit filed yesterday in DC against Goffman, one of America's finest consumer products companies. Its wonderful drug Maxatil had helped countless women through the nightmare of menopause, but now it was under attack by sharks.

The story hit its stride when it went after the lead shark, a brash young DC hotshot named Clay Carter who, according to their sources, had never tried a civil lawsuit before a jury. Nonetheless, he had earned in excess of $100 million last year in the mass tort lottery.

It was difficult material to read, but Clay certainly couldn't ignore it. An editorial in *Investment Times* called upon Congress to take a serious look at litigation reform, saying that Clay Carter was nothing but a 'bully' whose ill-gotten gains would only inspire other street hustlers to sue everyone in sight.

The nickname 'bully' stuck for a few days around the office, temporarily replacing 'the King'. Clay smiled and acted as if it was an honour. But behind his locked office door he was uneasy and fretted about the haste with which he had sued Goffman. The fact that his mass tort pals were not piling on was distressing. The bad press was gnawing at him. There had not been a single defender so far.

Six days after filing the lawsuit, Pace checked in from California. 'Tomorrow is the big day,' he said.

'I need some good news,' Clay said. 'The government report?'

'Can't say,' Pace replied. 'And no more phone calls. Someone might be listening. I'll explain when I'm in town. Later.'

Someone might be listening? On which end—Clay's or Pace's? And who, please? There went another night's sleep.

The study by the American Council on Ageing was originally to test 20,000 women between the ages of forty-five and seventy-five over a seven-year period. The group was equally divided, with one getting a daily dose of Maxatil, the other getting a placebo. But after four years, the project was abandoned because the results were so bad. For those who took the drug, the risk of breast cancer jumped 33 per cent, heart attacks 21 per cent and strokes 20 per cent.

The following morning the report was published. Goffman's stock got hammered again, dropping to $51 a share. Clay and Mulrooney spent the afternoon monitoring Web sites and cable channels, waiting for some response from the company, but there was none. The reporters who'd scalded Clay when he filed the suit did not call for his reaction. He felt vindicated, but ignored. His anxiety was relieved by the deluge of phone calls from Maxatil patients.

THE GULFSTREAM FINALLY HAD to escape. Eight days in the hangar and Clay was itching to travel. He made an appointment with the great Dale Mooneyham in Tucson to talk about Maxatil.

Mott & Mooneyham had converted an old train station downtown into a pleasantly shabby suite of offices. It was a museum of sorts, a collection of products that Dale Mooneyham had taken to court and shown to juries. There was a damaged three-wheeler that had cost Honda $3 million in California, and a cheap rifle that had so enraged a Texas jury that it gave the plaintiff $11 million. Clay browsed from display to display while he waited.

An assistant finally fetched him and led him down a wide hall.

Dale Mooneyham was seated behind his desk and only half stood when Clay entered. The handshake was cold and obligatory. He was at least seventy, a big man with a thick chest and large stomach. Blue jeans, red boots, a western shirt and no necktie. He'd been dying his grey hair black, but was in need of another treatment because the sides were white, the top dark and slicked back with too much grease. Long wide face, the puffy eyes of a drinker.

'Nice office, really unique,' Clay said, trying to thaw things a bit.

'Bought it forty years ago,' Mooneyham said. 'For five thousand bucks.'

'Quite a collection of memorabilia out there.'

'I've done all right, son. I haven't lost a trial in twenty-one years.'

Clay glanced around and tried to relax in the low, ancient leather chair. The office was at least five times as big as his, with the heads of stuffed game covering the walls and watching his every move. There were no phones ringing, no faxes clattering in the distance. There was not a computer in Mooneyham's office.

'I guess I'm here to talk about Maxatil,' Clay said.

No movement except for a casual readjusting of the dark little eyes. 'It's a bad drug,' he said simply. 'I filed suit about five months ago up in Flagstaff. We should have us a trial by early fall. Unlike you, I don't file suit until my case is thoroughly researched.'

'What about your client?' Clay asked.

'I just have one. Class actions are a fraud, at least the way you and your pals handle them. Mass torts are a scam, a consumer rip-off.'

'I asked about your client.'

'Sixty-six-year-old white female, nonsmoker, took Maxatil for four years. I met her a year ago.'

Clay had intended to talk about big things, like how many potential Maxatil clients were out there, and what types of experts was Mooneyham planning to use at trial. Instead, he was looking for a quick exit. 'You're not expecting a settlement?' he asked.

'I don't settle, son. I tell the defendant up-front—"Let's not waste our time even thinking about a settlement, OK?" That's good news for you, son. I'll get first shot at Goffman, and if the jury sees things my way they'll give my client a nice verdict. All you copycats can jump on the wagon, advertise for more clients, then settle them cheap and rake yours off the top. I'll make you another fortune.'

'I'd like to go to trial,' Clay said.

'If what I read is correct, you don't know where the courthouse is.'

'I can find it.'

A shrug. 'You probably won't have to. When I get finished with Goffman they'll run from every jury.' And with that he slowly stood, reached out a limp hand, and said, 'I have work to do.'

Clay hustled from the office, down the hall, through the museum/lobby, and outside into the fierce desert heat.

THE TRIP WAS SALVAGED somewhere above Oklahoma, when the fax machine began humming. The one-page transmission was from Oscar Mulrooney, at the office. He'd pulled a story off the Internet—the annual rankings of firms and fees from *American Attorney* magazine. Making the list of the twenty highest-paid lawyers in the country was Mr Clay Carter, coming in at number eight, estimated earnings of $110 million for the previous year. There was even a photo of Clay with the caption: 'Rookie of the Year'.

Not a bad guess, Clay thought to himself. Unfortunately, $30 million of his Dyloft settlement had been paid in bonuses to Paulette, Jonah and Rodney, rewards that in hindsight seemed downright foolish. Never again. Not that Clay was complaining. No other lawyer from the DC area was in the top twenty.

Sitting in the privacy of his Gulfstream, staring at the magazine article, Clay told himself again that it was all a dream. There were 76,000 lawyers in DC, and he was number one. A year earlier his biggest dream was fleeing OPD and landing a job with a respectable firm, one that would pay him enough for some new suits and a better car. His name on a letterhead would impress Rebecca and keep her parents at bay. Such modest dreams.

Everybody in Washington would be talking about Clay's name on the list. He thought of his friends and his rivals, his law school pals and the old gang at OPD. Mostly, though, he thought of Rebecca.

THE HANNA PORTLAND CEMENT COMPANY was founded in Reedsburg, Pennsylvania, in 1946. The Hanna brothers ran the company with iron fists, but they were fair to their workers, who were their neighbours as well. When business was good, the workers received generous wages. When things were slow, everybody tightened their belts. Layoffs were rare and used only as a last resort.

The Hannas employed 4,000 of the 11,000 residents of the town and they ploughed their profits back into the plant and equipment, and into the community. They built a civic centre, a hospital, a theatre. Over the years, there was a temptation or two to sell out, but the Hanna brothers could never be sure that their factory would remain in Reedsburg. So they kept it.

The current CEO was Marcus Hanna, son of one of the founders. On the day the lawsuit arrived, Marcus was in a meeting with his cousin, Joel Hanna, the in-house lawyer. A process-server bullied his way past the receptionist and secretaries up front and presented himself to Marcus and Joel with a thick lawsuit.

It was an action filed in Howard County, Maryland, seeking unspecified damages for a class of homeowners claiming damages due to defective Portland mortar cement manufactured by Hanna.

It was no surprise that there was trouble in Howard County. A bad batch of their cement had found its way there several years earlier. It had been used by various contractors to put bricks on new homes. Both Marcus and Joel had been to Howard County and inspected several of the homes. Current thinking put the number of potential claims at 500, and the cost of repairing each unit at about $12,000. The company had product liability insurance that would cover the first $5 million in claims.

Joel left with the lawsuit. He would notify their insurance carrier, who would assign it to a litigation firm. It wouldn't be cheap.

10

On May 1, Rex Crittle left the accounting firm where he'd worked for eighteen years and became business manager of J. Clay Carter. With the offer of a huge increase in salary and benefits, he couldn't say no. The law firm was wildly successful, but it was growing so fast its business seemed out of control. Clay gave him broad authority and parked him in an office across the hall from his.

While Crittle certainly appreciated his own large salary, he was sceptical of everyone's around him. In his opinion, which he kept to himself, most of the employees were overpaid. The firm now had fourteen lawyers, twenty-one paralegals, twenty-six secretaries, a dozen or so clerks and four office gofers. A total of seventy-seven, not including Crittle and Clay. Adding in the cost of benefits, the total annual payroll was $8.4 million, and growing almost weekly.

Rent was $72,000 a month. Office expenses—computers, phones, utilities—were running at about $40,000 a month. The Gulfstream, which was the biggest waste of all and the one asset Clay said he could not live without, was costing the firm $300,000 in monthly mortgage payments and another $30,000 for pilots and hangar fees. Charter revenue had yet to show up on the books. One reason was that Clay really didn't want anyone else using his plane.

According to figures that Crittle monitored daily, the firm was burning $1.3 million a month in overheads, or $15.6 million a year. Enough to terrify any accountant, but if he questioned any expenditure Clay met it with the usual, 'You gotta spend it to make it.'

And spending they were. If the overheads made Crittle squirm, the advertising gave him ulcers. For Maxatil, the firm had spent $6.2 million in the first four months on newspaper, radio, television and online advertising. This, he had complained about. 'Full speed ahead,' had been Clay's response. 'I want twenty-five thousand cases!' The tally to date was somewhere around 18,000.

'Maxatil will be a bigger payday than Dyloft,' Clay said round the office, to fire up the troops. And he seemed to truly believe it.

The day after Crittle moved in, Rodney moved out. He was cashing in his chips and moving to the suburbs, to a very nice home on a very safe street, with a church at one end and a school at the other. With $10 million in the bank, before taxes, he had no real plans, just a determination to be a father and a husband, and a miser. He and Clay sneaked away to a deli down the street, just hours before he left the office for good, and said their goodbyes. They had worked together for six years—five at OPD, the last one at the new firm.

'Don't spend it all, Clay,' he warned his friend.

'I can't. There's too much of it.'

'Don't be foolish.'

The truth was, Rodney was secretly appalled at the way Clay was blowing through such a fortune. You pay a price for waste.

With Jonah on a boat and Paulette still in London, the original gang was now gone. Sad, but Clay was too busy to be nostalgic.

Ridley's modelling had all but ceased; she spent her time at the gym or out shopping, although she could shop for hours and spend only a modest amount.

A month earlier, after a long weekend in New York, they had

returned to DC and driven to his town house. She spent the night, not for the first time and evidently not for the last. Though nothing was said about her moving in, it just happened. Clay could not remember when he realised that her bathrobe and toothbrush and make-up and lingerie were there; they just materialised. Nothing was said. She stayed three consecutive nights, doing all the right things and not getting in the way, then she whispered that she needed a night at home. They didn't talk for two days, then she was back.

Marriage was never mentioned. Neither appeared to be looking for anything permanent. They enjoyed each other's company but both kept a roving eye. She was gorgeous and pleasant, and she did not seem to be a gold-digger. But she had secrets.

So did Clay. His biggest secret was that if Rebecca called at the right time, he'd sell everything but the Gulfstream, load her in it, and fly away to Mars.

Instead he was flying to the Caribbean with Ridley.

THEY HAD THE VILLA for a week. It was wedged into the side of a hill, overlooking the bustling harbour town of Gustavia. Ridley had found it in a catalogue of exclusive private rentals. It was a fine home—traditional Caribbean architecture, long verandahs, numerous bedrooms and bathrooms, a chef, two maids and a gardener.

Whereas Mustique was private and secluded, St Barth's was touristy and overbooked. But Ridley preferred St Barth's because of the shopping and the French food. She liked busy towns and people.

Clay was never certain how the real-estate agent materialised on the porch of the villa. She was there when he woke up one day, a charming Frenchwoman chatting with Ridley and having a coffee. She said she was in the neighbourhood, just stopped by to check on the house, which was owned by one of their clients, and how were things?

'Couldn't be better,' Clay said, taking a seat. 'A great house.'

'Isn't it wonderful?' the agent gushed. 'I was just telling Ridley that it was built only four years ago by these Canadians who've been down twice, I think. His business turned bad, and so they've put it on the market at a very reasonable price.'

A conspiratorial glance from Ridley. Clay asked the question left hanging in the air. 'How much?'

'Only three million. Started at five but, frankly, the market is a bit soft right now.'

After she left, Ridley attacked him in the bedroom. Morning sex was unheard of, but they had an impressive go at it. Dinner in a fine restaurant; she couldn't keep her hands off him. The midnight session began in the pool, went to the Jacuzzi, then to the bedroom and after an all-nighter the real-estate agent was back before lunch.

Clay was exhausted and not in the mood for more property. But Ridley really wanted the house, so he bought it. He could always sell it for a profit when the market tightened up.

'I'd like to stay for a while,' Ridley said that afternoon. Clay was planning a departure the following morning, and he'd assumed she was leaving too. 'I'd like to get this house in order,' she said. 'Meet with the decorator. Relax for a week or so.'

Why not? Clay thought. Now that I own the damned place, might as well use it. He returned to DC by himself, and for the first time in weeks enjoyed the solitude of his Georgetown home.

FOR SEVERAL DAYS Joel Hanna had considered a solo act—just him, all alone on one side of the table, facing a small army of lawyers on the other side. He would present the company's survival plan; he really needed no help with this since it was his brainchild.

But Babcock, the attorney for their insurance company, insisted on being present. His client was on the front line for $5 million, and if he wanted to be present, then Joel couldn't stop him.

Together they walked into the building on Connecticut Avenue. The elevator stopped on the fourth floor and they entered the Law Offices of J. Clay Carter II. A blonde greeted them with an efficient smile and pointed to a room just down the hall. A lawyer named Wyatt met them at the door, escorted them in, handled the introductions, and while Joel and Babcock were unpacking their briefcases another shapely young lady took their coffee orders. She served them from a silver coffee service with the JCC logo engraved on the pot and also on the fine china cups. When everyone was set, Wyatt barked at an assistant, 'Tell Clay we're all here.'

A minute passed as Mr JCC kept everyone waiting. Finally, he entered in a rush, talking to a secretary over his shoulder, a very busy man. He went straight to Joel Hanna and Babcock and introduced himself. Then he hustled round to the other side and assumed the king's throne in the middle of his team, eight feet away.

'You said you had a plan,' Mr JCC began. 'Let's hear it.'

The survival scheme was simple. The company was willing to admit, for the purposes of this meeting only, that it had manufactured a bad batch of cement, and that because of this, X number of new homes in the Baltimore area would have to be rebricked. A payment fund was needed to compensate the homeowner, while not choking the company to death, and his company was willing to borrow heavily to correct the mistake.

Babcock spoke on behalf of the insurance company. He admitted there was $5 million in coverage. His client and the Hanna company would participate in a pool.

'Do you have an accurate count of the number of homes here?' JCC asked, and every one of his minions wrote this down.

'Nine hundred and twenty-two,' Joel said. 'We've gone to the wholesalers, then to the contractors, then to the masonry subs. I think that's an accurate number, but it could be off by five per cent.'

JCC said, 'So if we assume twenty-five thousand dollars to compensate each client, we're looking at twenty-three million dollars.'

'We are quite certain that it will not cost twenty thousand to fix each house,' Joel said.

'We have statements from four masonry subs in the Howard County area,' said JCC. 'Each has seen the damage and submitted an estimate. The lowest is eighteen-nine, the highest is twenty-one-five. The average is twenty thousand bucks.'

'I'd like to see those estimates,' Joel said.

'Maybe later. Plus, there are other damages. These homeowners are entitled to compensation for their emotional distress.'

'We have estimates in the twelve-thousand-dollar range,' Joel said.

'We're not going to settle these cases for twelve thousand dollars,' JCC said, and every head shook on the other side.

Fifteen thousand dollars was a fair compromise and would get new bricks on every house. But such a settlement left only ten thousand dollars for the client after JCC lopped his one-third off the top. Ten thousand would get the old bricks off, but it wouldn't pay the brickmasons enough to put the new ones on.

Nine hundred and twenty-two cases at $5,000 each—$4.6 million in fees. JCC did the maths. After taxes it would just cover the cost of the villa on St Barth, where Ridley was still hiding out.

At $15,000 per claim, Hanna could survive. Taking the $5 million from Babcock's client, the company could add $2 million in cash currently on hand. The remaining $8 million could be borrowed.

The issue would boil down to how much Mr JCC wanted for his efforts. He could broker a fair settlement, perhaps reduce his percentage, still make several million, protect his clients, allow a fine old company to survive, and call it a victory.

Or, he could take the hard line and everybody would suffer.

MISS GLICK SOUNDED a bit rattled over the intercom. 'There are two of them, Clay,' she said, almost in a whisper. 'FBI.'

They were straight from central casting; two young clean-cut agents whipping out badges and trying to impress anyone who might be watching. The black one was Agent Spooner and the white one was Agent Lohse. They entered Clay's office and unbuttoned their jackets as they settled into chairs in the power corner of the room.

'Do you know a man named Martin Grace?' Spooner began.

'No.'

'Mike Packer?' asked Lohse.

'No.'

'Max Pace?'

'Yes.'

'They're all the same person,' Spooner said. 'Any idea where he might be?'

'No.'

'When did you see him last?'

Clay did not have to answer their questions. He could ask them to come back when he had a lawyer present. 'Not sure,' he said. 'It's been several months. Sometime in mid-February.'

'Where did you meet him?' Spooner asked.

'Dinner, in his hotel.'

'Which hotel?'

'I don't remember. Why are you interested in Max Pace?'

'This is part of a Securities and Exchange Commission investigation. Pace has a history of securities fraud, insider trading. Do you know his background?'

'Not really. He was pretty vague.'

'How and why did you meet him?'

'Let's say it was a business deal.'

'Most of his business partners go to jail. You'd better think of something else.'

'That'll do for now. Why are you here?'

'We're checking out witnesses. We know he spent some time in DC. We know he visited you on Mustique last Christmas. We know that in January he short sold a chunk of Goffman for sixty-two and a quarter a share the day before you filed your big lawsuit. Bought it back at forty-nine, made himself several million. We think he had access to a confidential government report on a certain Goffman drug called Maxatil, and he used that information to commit securities fraud.'

'Anything else?'

Lohse said, 'Did you short sell Goffman before you filed suit?'

'I did not.'

'Have you ever owned Goffman's stock?'

'No.'

Lohse put his pen in his pocket. Good cops keep their first meetings brief. Let the subject sweat and maybe do something foolish.

They stood and headed for the door. 'If you hear from Pace, we'd like to know about it,' Spooner said.

'Don't count on it,' Clay said.

'Oh, we're counting on it, Mr Carter. Next visit we'll talk about Ackerman Labs.'

THE MEETING OCCURRED late at night, just as Clay was leaving the office. Rex Crittle walked in with a sour face and announced, 'Our liability insurance carrier is cancelling coverage.'

'Why?' he asked.

'They've evaluated your practice and they don't like what they see. Twenty-four thousand Maxatil cases scare them. There's too much exposure if something goes wrong. Their ten million could be a drop in the bucket, so they're jumping ship.'

'Can they do it?'

'Of course they can. An insurance company can terminate coverage anytime it wants. We're naked on this, Clay. No coverage.'

'We won't need coverage.'

'I hear you, but I'm still worried.'

'You were worried about Dyloft too, as I recall.'

'And I was wrong.'

'Well, Rex old boy, you're wrong about Maxatil too. After Mr Mooneyham gets finished with Goffman in Flagstaff, they'll be anxious to settle. They're already setting aside billions for the class action. Any idea how much those twenty-four thousand cases could be worth? Close to a billion dollars, Rex. And Goffman can pay it.'

'I'm still worried. We've spent eight million on advertising and testing. Can we at least slow down? Why can't you take the position that twenty-four thousand cases is enough?'

'Because it's not enough.' And with that Clay smiled, picked up his jacket, patted Crittle on the shoulder and left for dinner.

HE WAS SUPPOSED to meet a former college room-mate at the Old Ebbitt Grille at eight thirty. He waited at the bar for almost an hour before his cellphone rang. The room-mate was stuck in a meeting that looked as if it would never end. He apologised.

As Clay was leaving, he glanced into the restaurant and saw Rebecca having dinner with two other ladies. He stepped back, found his bar stool and ordered another ale. He wanted desperately to talk to her, but he was determined not to interfere. A trip to the rest room would work fine.

As he walked by her table, she looked up and immediately smiled. Rebecca introduced Clay to her two friends, and he explained that he was in the bar waiting for an old college buddy for dinner. The guy was running late, it might be a while, sorry for the interruption. Oh well, gotta run. Nice seeing you.

Fifteen minutes later, Rebecca appeared in the crowded bar and stood close beside him. Very close.

'I just have a minute,' she said. 'They're waiting.'

'You look great,' Clay said, anxious to start groping.

'You too.'

'Where's Myers?'

She shrugged as if she didn't care. 'Working. He's always working.'

'How's married life?'

'Very lonely,' she said, looking away.

Clay took a drink. If not in a crowded bar, with friends waiting nearby, she would have spilled her guts.

Clay fought to suppress a smile. 'I'm still waiting,' he said.

Her eyes were wet when she leaned over and kissed him on the cheek. Then she was gone without another word.

WITH THE ORIOLES six runs down to the Devil Rays, Ted Worley debated whether to sneak to the toilet or wait until the seventh inning. But after the Dyloft nightmare he didn't push the limits of his bladder. If he needed to go, he did not hesitate. He walked to the bathroom down the hall, unzipped his trousers, and began to urinate. A very slight burning sensation caused him to glance down, and when he did he almost fainted.

His urine was dark red. He gasped and braced himself with one hand against the wall. When he finished, he took another look at the deadly calling card his body had just discharged, finally flushed, and walked back to the den. It was blood, he decided. The tumours were back, and whatever form they now had they were far more serious than before.

He told his wife the next morning. She took charge immediately, calling his urologist, lining up a visit just after lunch.

Four days later, malignant tumours were found in Mr Worley's kidneys. During five hours of surgery, the doctors removed all the tumours they could find.

The head of urology was closely monitoring the patient. A colleague at a hospital in Kansas City had reported an identical case a month earlier; a post-Dyloft appearance of kidney tumours. The patient in Kansas City was now undergoing chemotherapy and fading fast. The same could be expected for Mr Worley.

During a follow-up conversation with the colleague in Kansas City, the head of urology learned of yet another case. All three patients had been Group One Dyloft plaintiffs. Now they were dying. A lawyer's name was mentioned. The Kansas City patient was represented by a small firm in New York City.

It was a rare and rewarding experience for a doctor to be able to pass along the name of one lawyer who would sue another, and the head of urology was determined to enjoy the moment. He introduced himself to Mr Worley and explained his role in the treatment. The conversation soon turned to Dyloft, then the settlement. This fired up the old man; his face had some colour, his eyes were glaring.

The settlement was a paltry $43,000, with the lawyer taking the rest! 'I was against the settlement,' Mr Worley kept saying.

'I guess it's too late now,' Mrs Worley kept adding.

'Maybe not,' the doctor said. He told them about the Kansas City patient, a man very similar to Ted Worley. 'He's hired a lawyer to go after his lawyer,' the doctor said with great satisfaction.

'I've had a butt full of lawyers,' Mr Worley said.

'Do you have his phone number?' Mrs Worley asked. She was thinking much more clearly than her husband. Sadly, she was also looking down the road a year or two when Ted would be gone.

The urologist just happened to have the number.

THE ONLY THING mass tort lawyers feared was one of their own. A predator. A subspeciality had evolved in which a few very good trial lawyers pursued their brethren for bad settlements. Helen Warshaw was writing the training manual.

For a breed that professed so much love for the courtroom, tort lawyers fell limp with the visual of themselves sitting at the defence table, looking sheepishly at the jurors as their personal finances were kicked about in open court.

However, it rarely happened. When confronted with proof of liability, no one settled faster than a mass tort lawyer.

Warshaw had four Dyloft cases in her New York office and leads on three more when she received the call from Mrs Worley.

A few minutes on the phone with her, and Helen knew exactly what had happened. 'I'll be there by five o'clock,' she said.

She caught the shuttle to Dulles, rented a car at the airport and found the hospital in Bethesda. Mrs Worley had collected their papers, which Warshaw spent an hour with while Mr Worley took a nap. When he woke up, he did not want to talk. He was wary of lawyers, especially the pushy New York female variety. However, his wife had plenty of time and found it easy to confide in a woman. The two went to the lounge for coffee and a long discussion.

The principal culprit was and always would be Ackerman Labs. They made a bad drug. Ms Warshaw had already secured convincing medical proof that recurring tumours were linked to Dyloft.

The second culprit was the doctor who prescribed the drug.

Unfortunately, the first two culprits had been fully and completely released from all liability when Mr Worley settled his claim in the Biloxi class action.

'But Ted didn't want to settle,' Mrs Worley said more than once.

Doesn't matter. He settled. He gave his attorney the power to settle. The attorney did so, and thus became the third culprit. And the last one standing.

A WEEK LATER, Ms Warshaw filed a lawsuit against J. Clay Carter, and all other attorneys who had prematurely settled Dyloft cases. The lead plaintiff was once again Mr Ted Worley.

Borrowing a page from the defendants' own playbook, Ms Warshaw faxed copies of her lawsuit to a dozen prominent newspapers fifteen minutes after she filed it.

A brusque and burly process-server presented himself to the receptionist at Clay's office and demanded to see Mr Carter. Clay reluctantly came from his office and took possession of the paperwork that would ruin his day. Maybe his year.

The reporters were already calling by the time Clay finished reading the class action. He was stunned. He had no idea that Ted Worley was sick again. It just wasn't fair.

He went to Oscar's office and they talked about spin control—how to respond, and when. Should they put together an aggressive denial to the lawsuit and file it that day? Should Clay talk to the reporters?

Nothing was decided because they could not make a decision. The shoe was on the other foot; this was new territory.

'If I'm wrong, I'll pay the claim,' Clay said.

'Let's hope Mr Worley is the only one from this firm.'

'That's the question, Oscar. How many Ted Worleys are out there?'

SLEEP WAS IMPOSSIBLE. Ridley was in St Barth's, renovating the villa, and for that Clay was grateful. He was humiliated and embarrassed; at least she didn't know about it.

His thoughts were on Ted Worley, whose cancer was caused by a bad drug, not by a bad lawyer. But to settle a case hurriedly for $62,000 when it was ultimately worth millions smacked of malpractice and greed. Who could blame the man for striking back?

At times throughout the long night, Clay was afraid. Was this the beginning of the end? How many potential plaintiffs were out there? Each case was worth millions.

Nonsense. With twenty-five thousand Maxatil cases waiting in the wings he could withstand anything.

But all thoughts eventually came back to Mr Worley, a client who had not been protected by his lawyer. The sense of guilt was so heavy that he felt like calling the man and apologising.

Shortly after 4.00am, Clay made the first pot of coffee. At five, he went online and read the *Post*. A slow news day, so why not put the smiling face of 'The King of Torts' on the front page, bottom half? MASS TORT LAWYER SUED BY THE MASSES was the clever headline.

His buddy at *The Wall Street Journal* weighed in with the heavy artillery. Front page, left side, same hideous sketch of Clay's smug face. IS THE KING OF TORTS ABOUT TO BE DETHRONED? was the headline. The tone of the article sounded as if Clay should be indicted and imprisoned rather than simply dethroned.

The second paragraph was about Helen Warshaw. Her credentials were impressive. A certified trial advocate. Law review editor at Columbia. She was thirty-eight years old, ran marathons for fun, and was described by a former opponent as 'brilliant and tenacious'.

Mr Carter, aged thirty-two, was not available for comment.

He was at the office by seven, with a game face on, high on coffee, bouncing around the halls bantering and laughing with the early shift, making lame but sporting jokes about other process-servers on the way and reporters poking around. It was a gutsy performance, one his firm needed and appreciated. It continued until mid-morning when Miss Glick stopped it cold by stepping into his open office and saying, 'Clay, those two FBI agents are back.'

'Wonderful!' he said, rubbing his hands together.

Spooner and Lohse appeared with tight smiles and no hand-shakes. Clay closed the door and gritted his teeth.

Lohse would talk this time while Spooner took notes. Evidently, Clay's picture on the front page had reminded them that he was owed a second visit. The price of fame.

'Any sign of your buddy Pace?' Lohse began.

'No, not a peep.' And it was true. How badly he needed Pace's counsel in this time of crisis.

'You filed suit against Ackerman Labs on July 2nd of last year?'

'Yes.'

'Did you own any stock in the company before you filed?'

'No.'

'Did you sell the stock short, then buy it back at a lower price?'

Of course he had, at the suggestion of his good friend Pace. They knew the answer to the question. They had the data from the trans-actions, he was sure of that. Since their first visit, he had thoroughly researched securities fraud. He was in a grey area, a very pale one, in his opinion, but far from guilty. In retrospect, he should not have dealt in the stock. He wished a thousand times he had not.

'Am I under investigation for something?' he asked.

Spooner started nodding before Lohse said, 'Yes.'

'Then this meeting is over. My attorney will be in touch with you.' Clay was on his feet, headed for the door.

11

For the next meeting of the Dyloft Plaintiffs' Steering Committee, Defendant Patton French chose a hotel in downtown Atlanta. It was an emergency meeting. French, of course, had the Presidential Suite on the hotel's top floor, and there they met.

Carlos Hernández from Miami knew of seven of his Dyloft Group One plaintiffs who were now suffering from malignant kidney tumours. They had now joined the class action represented by Helen Warshaw. 'They're popping up everywhere,' he said.

'She's a ruthless bitch,' Wes Saulsberry said, and the others nodded in agreement. Wes had four former clients now suing him. Damon Didier had three. French had five.

Clay was relieved to have only one, but such relief was temporary.

'Actually, you have seven,' French said, handing over a print-out with Clay's name and a list of ex-clients/now plaintiffs under it.

'I'm told by Wicks at Ackerman that we can expect the list to grow,' French said.

'What's their mood?' Wes asked.

'Total shock. Philo wishes they'd never heard of Ackerman Labs.'

'I'm with them,' Didier said, shooting a nasty look at Clay.

Clay looked back at the seven names on his list. Other than Ted Worley, he did not recognise any of them. How did he come to represent these people? A ridiculous way to practise law—suing and settling for people he'd never met! And now they were suing him!

'Is it safe to assume that the medical evidence is substantial here?' Wes was asking. 'I mean, is there room to fight, to try and prove that this recurring cancer is not related to Dyloft.'

'Nope! We're screwed,' French said. 'Wicks tells me that the drug is more dangerous than a bullet to the head.'

'We have to negotiate,' Didier said. 'We're talking survival here.'

'How much is a case worth?' Clay asked, his voice still working.

'In front of a jury, two million to ten million, depending on the punitives,' French said.

'No jury will see my face in court,' Didier said. 'Not with these facts.'

'We're probably going to lose our class action,' French said. 'Everybody who's still in is trying to get out. As you know, very few of the Group Two and Three plaintiffs have settled, and, for obvious reasons, they want no part of this lawsuit. I know of at least five groups of lawyers ready to ask the court to dissolve our class and kick us out. Can't really blame them.'

Each was worried, but at different levels: Patton French probably had more money than anyone there, and he seemed confident he could withstand the financial pressures of the lawsuit. Same for Wes, who had just earned $500 million from a tobacco scam. Carlos was cocky at times, but then he couldn't stop fidgeting. It was the hard-faced Didier who was terrified.

They all had more money than Clay, and Clay had more Dyloft cases than any of them. He didn't like the maths. They agreed on a very general plan to meet with Ms Warshaw and delicately explore the possibility of negotiation. She was making it well known she did not want to settle. She wanted trials—big, tawdry, sensational spectacles in which the current and past Kings of Torts would be hauled in and stripped naked before the juries.

DURING HIS YEARS AT OPD, Clay had conducted hundreds of initial interviews, almost all at the jail. They usually started slow, with the defendant, who was almost always black, uncertain about how much he should say to his white lawyer.

It was ironic that Clay, the white defendant now, was nervously walking into his own initial interview with his black defence lawyer. And at $750 an hour, Zack Battle had better be prepared to listen fast. No ducking and weaving and shadowboxing at that rate. Battle would get the truth, as fast as he could write it down.

But Battle wanted to gossip. He and Clay's father had been drinking buddies years earlier, long before Battle sobered up and became the biggest criminal lawyer in DC. 'How is your father?' he asked. Clay quickly painted a generous, almost romantic picture of Jarrett sailing the world.

When they finally got round to it, Clay told the Dyloft story, beginning with Max Pace and ending with the FBI. He did not talk about Tarvan, but he would if it became necessary.

'This stolen research that Max Pace had,' Battle said. 'Did you have it in your possession when you sold the stock and filed suit?'

'Of course. I had to know that I could prove liability against Ackerman if we went to trial.'

'Then it's insider trading. You're guilty. Five years in the slammer. Tell me, though, how the Feds can prove it.'

Clay said, 'Max Pace can tell them, I guess.'

'Who else has the research?'

'Patton French, maybe one or two of the other guys.'

'Does French know you had this information before you filed?'

'I don't know. I never told him, or anyone else, when I got it.'

'So this Max Pace character is the only person who can nail you.'

The history was pretty clear. Clay had prepared the Dyloft class action but was unwilling to file it unless Pace could produce enough evidence. They had argued several times. Pace walked in one day with two thick briefcases filled with papers and files and said, 'There it is, and you didn't get it from me.' He left immediately. Clay reviewed the material, then asked a college friend to evaluate their reliability. The friend was a prominent doctor in Baltimore.

'Can this doctor be trusted?' Battle asked.

Before he could say anything, Battle helped him with the answer. 'Here's the bottom line, Clay. If the Feds don't know you had this secret research when you sold the stock short, they can't get you for insider trading. They have the records of the stock transactions, but those alone are not enough. They have to prove you had knowledge.'

'Should I talk to my friend in Baltimore?'

'No. If the Feds know about him, he might be wired. Then you go to prison for seven years instead of five. If I were you, I'd ditch the research, purge my files, in case they walk in with a subpoena. Go see Patton French, make sure the research cannot be traced to you. And I'd pray that Max Pace is either dead or hiding in Europe.'

THE RETURN ADDRESS was that of a prison. Though he had many former clients behind bars, Clay could not remember one named Paul Watson. He opened the envelope and pulled out a one-page letter, very neat and prepared on a word processor. It read:

Dear Mr Carter:

You may remember me as Tequila Watson. I've changed my name because the old one doesn't fit any more. I read the Bible every day and my favourite guy is the Apostle Paul, so I've borrowed his name.

I need a favour. If you could somehow get word to Pumpkin's family and tell them that I'm very sorry for what happened. I've prayed to God and he has forgiven me. I would feel so much better if Pumpkin's family could do the same. I still can't believe I killed him like that. It wasn't me doing the shooting, but the devil, I guess. But I have no excuses.

It would be great if you could write me. Sorry you had to stop being my lawyer. I thought you were a cool dude.

Best wishes,

Paul Watson

Just hang on, Paul, Clay mumbled to himself. We might be cell mates at the rate I'm going. The phone startled him. It was Ridley, down in St Barth's but wanting to come home. Could Clay please send the jet tomorrow?

No problem, dear. It only costs $3,000 an hour to fly the damned thing. That's $24,000 for the eight-hour round trip—a drop in the bucket compared to what she was spending on the villa.

THE ARTICLE WAS IN THE *Post*'s Metro section, third page, and that was a pleasant surprise after months of front-page heroics, then scandals. KING OF TORTS UNDER SEC INVESTIGATION. 'According to unnamed sources . . .' He couldn't imagine who had leaked this to the press, who would want to embarrass him even further.

He read it at home where he was, thankfully, alone because Ridley was spending a day or two at her new apartment, one Clay had signed the lease for. She wanted the freedom of living in two places, hers and his, and since her old flat was quite cramped Clay had agreed to put her up in nicer digs.

Paulette Tullos dropped in before noon. She looked great—the pounds were off, the wardrobe was expensive. She'd been bouncing around Europe for the past few months, waiting for her divorce to become final. The rumours about Clay were everywhere, and she was concerned about him. Over a long lunch, one she paid for, it slowly became apparent that she was also worried about herself. Her cut of the Dyloft loot had been slightly over $10 million, and she wanted to know if she had exposure. Clay assured her she had none. She had not been a partner in the firm during the settlement, just an associate. Clay's name was on all the pleadings and documents.

'You were the smart one,' Clay said. 'You took the money and ran.'

'I feel bad.'

'Don't. The mistakes were made by me, not you.'

Though Warshaw's class action would cost him dearly, he was still banking heavily on Maxatil. With 25,000 cases, the payday would be enormous.

THE THIRD MEETING with Hanna Portland Cement would be the last, though neither Clay nor anyone on his side of the table realised it. Joel Hanna brought his cousin Marcus, the company's CEO, with him. As usual, the two faced a small army on the other side, with Mr JCC sitting in the middle. The king.

'We have located an additional eighteen homes that should be added to the list,' Joel announced. 'That makes a total of nine hundred and forty. We feel confident there will not be any more.'

'That's good,' Clay said, rather callously. A longer list meant more clients. He represented almost 90 per cent of the class. His Team Hanna had done a superb job of convincing the homeowners to stick with his firm. They had been assured they would get more money because Mr Carter was a mass litigation expert, the new King of Torts.

During the last meeting, Clay had reduced his demands from $25,000 per claim to $22,500, a settlement that would net him fees of about $7.5 million. The Hanna company had countered with $17,000, which would stretch its borrowing capacity to breaking point. The business was on the downslope of a nasty cycle and things looked grim for the company.

At $17,000 per home, Mr JCC would earn about $5 million, if he clung to a 30 per cent contingency. If, however, he cut his share to 20 per cent, each of his clients would net $13,600, but his fees would be reduced by roughly $1.5 million. Marcus Hanna had found a reputable contractor who would repair every home for $13,500.

'Any movement on your side?' Clay asked, rather bluntly.

'No. Seventeen thousand is a stretch for us. Any movement on your side?'

'Twenty-two thousand five hundred is a fair settlement,' Clay said without flinching or blinking. 'If you're not moving, then neither are we.' His voice was hard as steel. He was convinced that if he kept pushing, Hanna would buckle.

Clay's staff was impressed by this toughness; the only doubter was Ed Wyatt, the head of Team Hanna. Before the meeting, he had explained to Clay that, in his opinion, Hanna would benefit greatly from protection and reorganisation under Chapter 11 of the bankruptcy code. Any settlement would be delayed until a trustee could decide what compensation was reasonable. Wyatt thought the plaintiffs would be lucky to get $10,000 through Chapter 11. The company had not threatened bankruptcy, a normal ploy in these situations. Clay had studied Hanna's books and felt that it had too many assets and too much pride to consider such a drastic move. He rolled the dice. The firm needed all the fees it could squeeze.

Marcus Hanna said, 'Well, then it's time to go.' He and his cousin threw their papers together and stormed out of the room.

Two hours later, in the US Bankruptcy Court for the Eastern District of Pennsylvania, the Hanna Portland Cement Company filed a Chapter 11 petition, seeking protection from its creditors, the largest of whom were those collected in a class action filed by J. Clay Carter II of Washington, DC.

A FEW DAYS LATER the *Baltimore Press* ran a long story about the bankruptcy and the reaction by the homeowners. Its details were accurate and evidence that someone very close to the settlement negotiations, possibly one of the Hannas, was whispering to the reporter. The company had offered $17,000 per plaintiff; a liberal estimate to repair each home was $15,000. The lawsuit could have been fairly settled but for the issue of attorneys' fees. Hanna admitted liability from the beginning. It had been willing to borrow heavily to correct its mistakes. And so on.

Phones began ringing nonstop at the offices of JCC as irate clients wanted someone to yell at. A security guard in the lobby just in case. Associates gossiping in small groups about the survival of the place. The boss locked in his office.

Rebecca arrived, a random visitor from the street, and gave a note to the receptionist. 'I'm an old friend,' she said, to counter the glances of the security guard, who was on high alert.

Whatever she was, she drew Mr Carter out of the back faster than anyone in the short history of the firm. They sat in the corner of his office; Rebecca on the sofa, Clay in a chair pulled as close as possible. For a long time nothing was said. Clay was too excited to utter a coherent sentence. Her presence could mean a hundred different things, none of them bad.

He wanted to lunge at her, feel her body again, smell the perfume on her neck, run his hands along her legs. Nothing had changed—same hairstyle, same make-up, same lipstick, same bracelet.

'You're staring at my legs,' she finally said.

'Yes, I am.'

'Clay, are you OK? There's so much bad press right now.'

'And that's why you're here?'

'Yes. I'm concerned.'

'To be concerned means you still care about me.'

'I do.'

'So you haven't forgotten about me?'

'No, I have not. I'm sort of sidetracked right now, with the marriage and all, but I still think about you. More and more.'

Clay closed his eyes and placed a hand on her knee, one that she immediately removed and flung away. 'I am married, Clay.'

'Then let's commit adultery.'

'No.'

'Sidetracked? Sounds like it's temporary. What's going on?'

'I'm not here to talk about my marriage. I was in the neighbourhood, thought about you, and just sort of popped in.'

'Like a lost dog? I don't believe that.'

'You shouldn't. How's your bimbo?'

'She's here and there. It's just an arrangement.'

Rebecca mulled this over, obviously not liking the arrangement.

'How's the worm?' Clay asked.

'He's OK. We get along.'

'Married less than a year and that's the best you can do?'

'Yes.' She recrossed her legs while Clay watched closely.

'Are you going to survive?' she asked.

'Let's not talk about me. Let's talk about us.'

'I'm not going to have an affair,' she said.

'But you're thinking about one, aren't you?'

'No, but I know you are.'

'It would be fun, wouldn't it?'

'It would, and it wouldn't. I'm not going to live like that.'

'I'm not either, Rebecca. I'm not sharing. I once had all of you, and I let you get away. I'll wait until you're single again.'

'That might not happen, Clay.'

'Yes, it will.'

WITH RIDLEY IN BED beside him, Clay spent the night dreaming of Rebecca. The phone rang just after 5.00am. He answered it in the bedroom, then switched to a phone in his study.

It was Mel Snelling, a college room-mate, now a physician in Baltimore. 'We gotta talk, pal,' he said. 'It's urgent.'

'All right,' Clay said, his knees buckling.

'Ten o'clock this morning, in front of the Lincoln Memorial.'

'I can do that.'

'And there's a good chance someone will be following me,' he said, then his line went dead. Dr. Snelling had reviewed the stolen Dyloft research for Clay, as a favour. Now the Feds had found him.

Clay made coffee and took a long shower. He dressed in jeans.

There was a very good chance Mel would be wired. The FBI would threaten to indict him too if he refused to snitch on his friend.

Clay arrived at the Lincoln Memorial and mixed with the few tourists who were there. A few minutes later, Mel appeared. One look at Mel's face and Clay knew that the news was bad.

They shook hands, said their hellos, tried to be cordial. 'Let's go for a walk,' Clay said, sort of pointing down The Mall.

'Sure,' Mel said, shrugging. Obviously, no trap had been planned near Mr Lincoln, then.

'Did they follow you?' Clay asked.

'I don't think so. I flew from Baltimore to Pittsburgh, Pittsburgh to Reagan National, grabbed a cab. I don't think anybody's behind me.'

'Is it Spooner and Lohse?'

'Yes, you know them?'

'They've stopped by a few times.' They were walking beside the Reflecting Pool. Clay was not going to say anything he didn't want to hear again. 'Mel, I know how the Fibbies operate. They like to pressure witnesses. Did they ask you to wear a wire?'

'Yes. But I told them, "Hell, no." '

'Thank you.'

'I have a great lawyer, Clay. I've told him everything. I did nothing wrong because I didn't trade the stock. But the pinch comes when I'm subpoenaed by the grand jury.'

'Go on,' Clay said cautiously.

They drifted to the right, away from a crowd. Mel said, almost under his breath, 'If I lie to the grand jury about the research, they'll have a hard time indicting you. But if I get caught lying, then I go to jail myself. Who else knows I reviewed the research?'

And with that, Clay realised there were no wires, no mikes, no one was listening. Mel wasn't after evidence—he just wanted to be reassured. 'Your name is nowhere, Mel,' Clay said. 'I shipped the stuff to you. You copied nothing, right?'

'Right.'

'You shipped it back to me. I reviewed it again. There was no sign of you anywhere. We talked by phone a half a dozen times. All of your thoughts and opinions about the research were verbal.'

'What about the other lawyers in the mass tort case?'

'They know I had the research before we filed suit. They know a doctor reviewed it for me, but they don't have a clue who he is.'

'Can the FBI pressure them to testify that you had the research before you filed suit?'

'No way. These guys are lawyers, big lawyers, Mel. They don't scare easily. They've done nothing wrong—they didn't trade in the stock—and they'll give the Feds nothing. I'm protected there.'

'So what do I do?'

'There's a good chance this thing won't get to a grand jury,' Clay said. 'Hold firm and it'll probably go away.'

They stopped in a crowd on a sidewalk near the Washington Monument. Mel said, 'I'm going to disappear. Goodbye. From me, no news is good news.' And with that, he darted through a group of tourists and vanished.

THE COCONINO COUNTY COURTHOUSE in Flagstaff was quiet the day before the trial. It was the second week in September, the temperature pushing 105. Clay and Oscar walked round the downtown area, then entered the courthouse in search of air conditioning.

Inside the courtroom, though, pretrial motions were being argued and things were tense. No jury sat in the box; selection would begin the following morning. Dale Mooneyham and his team covered one side of the arena. The Goffman horde, led by a fancy litigator from LA named Roger Redding, occupied the other half. Roger the Dodger, because he went all over the country, fighting the biggest trial lawyers he could find, dodging big verdicts.

Clay and Oscar took seats with the other spectators, of which there was an impressive number. Wall Street would be watching the trial closely. It would be a continuing story in the financial press. And, of course, the vultures like Clay were quite curious.

Mooneyham lumbered round the courtroom like a barroom bully, bellowing at the judge, then at Roger Redding. He was an old warrior, with a limp that came and went. Occasionally, he picked up a cane to move around with, then at times seemed to forget it.

Redding was Hollywood cool—meticulously tailored, a head full of salt-and-pepper hair, strong chin, perfect profile. He spoke in eloquent prose, beautiful sentences that rolled out with no hesitation. When he began arguing a point, he used a vocabulary that anyone could understand, and he had the talent of keeping three arguments alive at one time before tying them all beautifully together into one superbly logical point. He had no fear of Dale Mooneyham, no fear of the judge, no fear of the facts of the case.

The judge called a fifteen-minute recess so he could visit the toilet. Clay left the courtroom and went to find a soda. He was about to re-enter the courtroom when a pushy reporter stepped in front of him. He was Derek somebody with *Financial Weekly* and wanted a quick word. His newspaper was a right-wing, trial-lawyer-hating, tort-bashing, corporate mouthpiece, and Clay knew better than to give him even a 'No comment' or a 'Kiss off'.

'Can I ask what you're doing here?' Derek said.

'Same thing you're doing here.'

'And that is?'

'Enjoying the heat.'

'Is it true that you have twenty-five thousand Maxatil cases?'

'No.'

'How many?'

'Twenty-six thousand.'

'How much are they worth?'

'Somewhere between zero and a couple of billion.'

Unknown to Clay, the judge had gagged the lawyers for both sides until the end of the trial. Since he was willing to talk, he attracted a crowd. He was surprised to see himself surrounded by reporters. He answered a few more questions without saying much at all.

THE *ARIZONA LEDGER* quoted him as claiming his cases could be worth $2 billion. It ran a photo of Clay outside the courtroom, with the caption 'King of Torts in Town'. A brief summary of Clay's visit followed, along with a few paragraphs about the big trial itself. The reporter did not directly call him a greedy, opportunistic trial lawyer, but the implication was that he was a vulture, circling, waiting to attack Goffman's carcass.

The courtroom was packed with potential jurors and spectators. Nine o'clock came and went with no sign of the lawyers or the judge. They were in chambers, no doubt still arguing pretrial issues. A young man in a suit emerged from the back and headed down the centre aisle. He abruptly stopped, looked directly at Clay, then leaned down and whispered, 'Are you Mr Carter?'

Taken aback, Clay nodded.

'The judge would like to see you.'

The newspaper was in the middle of the judge's desk. Dale Mooneyham was in one corner of the large office. Roger Redding was leaning on a table by the window. The judge was rocking in his swivel chair. None of the three were happy. Awkward introductions were made. Mooneyham refused to step forward and shake Clay's hand, preferring instead to offer a slight nod and a look that conveyed hatred.

'Are you aware of the gag order I've put in place, Mr Carter?' asked the judge.

'No, sir.'

'Well, there is one. We work hard at having fair trials in Arizona, Mr Carter. Both sides want a jury as uninformed and as impartial as possible. Now, thanks to you, the potential jurors know that there are at least twenty-six thousand similar cases out there.'

Clay was not about to appear weak or apologetic, not with Roger Redding watching. 'Maybe it was unavoidable,' Clay said.

'Why don't you just leave Arizona?' Mooneyham boomed from the corner.

'I really don't have to,' Clay shot back.

'You want me to lose?'

And with that, Clay had heard enough. He wasn't sure how his presence might harm Mooneyham's case, but why run the risk?

'Very well, Your Honour, I guess I'll be seeing you.'

'An excellent idea,' the judge said.

Oscar remained in Flagstaff to monitor the trial. Clay hopped on the Gulfstream for a sombre ride home. Banished from Arizona.

12

In Reedsburg, the news that Hanna was laying off twelve hundred workers brought the town to a halt. The announcement came in a letter written by Marcus Hanna and given to all employees.

Events beyond the control of management were to blame. Flat sales were a factor, but nothing the company hadn't seen before. The crushing blow was the failure to reach a settlement in the class-action lawsuit. The company had bargained in good faith, but an overzealous and greedy law firm had made unreasonable demands.

To the 1,200 getting pink slips, Marcus promised all the help the company could provide. Unemployment benefits would last for a year. Obviously, Hanna would hire them back as soon as possible, but no promises were made. The layoffs might be permanent.

In the cafés and barbershops, in the hallways of the schools and the pews of the churches, in the beer joints and pool halls, the town talked of nothing else. Every one of the 11,000 residents knew someone who'd just lost their job at Hanna. The layoffs were the biggest disaster in the quiet history of Reedsburg.

For Clay, too, a nightmare was looming. A week earlier, a reporter from *Newsweek* had called and as usual had been stiff-armed by Miss Glick. As Clay suspected, *Newsweek* was not really interested in him, but rather, his nemesis.

It was a puff piece for Helen Warshaw. A striking photo had Ms Warshaw in a courtroom, looking tenacious and brilliant, but also very believable. Clay had never seen her before, and had hoped she would somehow resemble a 'ruthless bitch', as Saulsberry had called her. She did not. She was attractive—short, dark hair and sad brown eyes that would hold the attention of any jury.

Ms Warshaw had fifty Dyloft clients, all dying, all suing. The story gave the quick and dirty history of the class-action litigation.

Of the fifty, the reporter focused on Mr Ted Worley, of Upper Marlboro, Maryland, and ran a photo of the poor guy sitting in his back yard with his wife behind him, their arms crossed, both faces sad and frowning. Mr Worley, weak and trembling and angry, recounted his first contact with Clay Carter, a phone call from nowhere while he was trying to enjoy an Orioles game, the frightening news about Dyloft, the urinalysis, the visit from the young lawyer, the filing of the lawsuit. 'I didn't want to settle,' he said.

Mr Worley had produced all his paperwork—the medical records, the insidious contract with Carter that gave the lawyer the authority to settle for any amount over $50,000. Everything, including copies of the two letters Mr Worley had written to Mr Carter in protest of the 'sellout'. The lawyer did not answer the letters.

According to his doctors, Mr Worley had less than six months to live. Helen explained that the jury would hear from many of her clients by video, since they would not last until the trial.

Mr Carter had declined to comment.

Clay flung the magazine across his office. He wished he'd never met Ted Worley, never met Max Pace, never gone to law school.

He called Patton French, who still discounted Maxatil as a potential target, but was watching every move. All mass tort, would, sooner or later, land on his desk.

'How much cash you got left?' French asked.

'I don't know. I'm afraid to crunch the numbers.'

'Take a guess.'

'Twenty million, maybe.'

'And how much insurance?'

'Ten million. They cancelled me, but they're still on for Dyloft.'

French said, 'I'm not sure thirty million is enough for you. You have twenty-one claims now, and the number can only go up. We'll be lucky if we can settle these damned things for three mil each.'

'How many cases do you have?'

'Nineteen, as of yesterday.'

'And how much cash do you have?'

'Two hundred million. I'll be all right.'

'And the other guys?' Clay asked.

'Wes is fine. Carlos can survive if his number stays below thirty. Didier's last two wives cleaned him out. He's dead. He'll be the first one to go bankrupt, which he's done before.'

After a long silence, Clay asked, 'What happens if Goffman wins in Flagstaff? I have all these cases.'

'You're gonna be one sick puppy, that's for sure.'

'That's not what I want to hear.'

'How much have you spent on Maxatil?'

'Eight million just in advertising.'

'I'd just sit on them for a while, see what Goffman does. I doubt they'll offer anything. They're a bunch of hardasses. With time, your clients will revolt and you can tell them to get lost. But think positive.

Mooneyham hasn't lost in ages. A big verdict, and you're sitting on a gold mine, again.'

Late the next morning Clay flew to Pittsburgh, anywhere but DC. En route, he talked to Oscar, and he read the emails and news reports of the trial in Flagstaff. The plaintiff, a sixty-six-year-old woman with breast cancer, had testified. She was very sympathetic, and Mooneyham played her like a fiddle.

He rented a car and drove northeast for two hours. Finding Reedsburg on the map was almost as difficult as finding it on a highway. At the edge of town, he saw a mammoth plant in the distance. WELCOME TO REEDSBURG, a large sign said. HOME OF THE HANNA PORTLAND CEMENT COMPANY. FOUNDED IN 1946. Two large smokestacks emitted a chalky dust that drifted away with the wind.

He found a parking place on Main Street, and walked into Ethel's Coffee Shop. Ethel greeted him and took his order. Coffee and a grilled cheese sandwich.

At a table, two young men were talking about jobs. It was soon clear that neither was employed. One wore a denim cap with a Hanna Cement logo on the front. As Clay ate his grilled cheese, he listened as they fretted over unemployment benefits, mortgages, credit-card bills, part-time work.

By the front door was a table with a large plastic water bottle on it. A handmade poster urged everyone to contribute to the 'Hanna Fund'. A collection of coins and notes half filled the bottle.

'What's that for?' Clay asked Ethel when she refilled his cup.

'It's a drive to collect money for the families laid off at the plant.'

'Which plant?' Clay asked, trying to appear ignorant.

'Hanna Cement, biggest employer in town. Twelve hundred folks got laid off last week. We stick together around here. Got those things all over town—stores, cafés, churches, even the schools. Raised over six thousand so far. Money'll go for light bills and groceries if things get bad. Otherwise, it'll go to the hospital.'

Clay nodded and quickly turned back to his sandwich.

A few minutes later, he paid his bill, thanked Ethel, and dropped a $100 note into the water bottle.

If he had ever felt worse, he could not remember when.

RIDLEY CALLED EARLY on Saturday evening, quite upset. She had been unable to locate Clay for four days! No one at the office knew where he was—or just wouldn't tell her. He, on the other hand, had made no effort at all to call her. Was this any way to advance a relationship? After listening to the whining for a few minutes, Clay heard something buzz in the line and asked, 'Where are you?'

'St Barth's. In our villa.'

'How'd you get down there?' Clay had been using the Gulfstream. 'I chartered a jet.'

'Why are you down there?' he asked, a stupid question.

'I was so stressed out because I couldn't find you.'

He tried to link the two—his disappearance and her escape to St Barth's, but gave up. 'I'm sorry,' he said. 'I left town in a hurry.'

He found himself relieved that she was out of the country.

'Can you come down?' she asked perfunctorily.

'Not with the trial in Flagstaff coming to a close soon.' He doubted seriously if she had an inkling about the trial in Flagstaff.

'Will you call me tomorrow?' she asked.

'Of course. Relax, enjoy yourself down there.'

Jonah was back in town, with many adventures to report from the sailing life. They were to meet at nine at a bistro on Wisconsin Avenue for a late dinner. Around eight thirty, the phone rang, and Clay grabbed it as he was buttoning his shirt.

'Is this Clay Carter?' a male voice asked.

'Yes, who is this?' Because of the sheer number of disgruntled clients out there—Dyloft and, now, especially, those irate homeowners up in Howard County—Clay had changed numbers recently.

'I'm from Reedsburg, Pennsylvania, and I have some valuable information about the Hanna company.'

Clay sat on his bed. 'OK, I'm listening.' Someone from Reedsburg had somehow acquired his new, unlisted phone number.

'We can't talk over the phone,' the voice said.

'Why not?'

'It's a long story. There are some papers.'

'Where are you?'

'I'm in the city. I'll meet you in the lobby of the Four Seasons Hotel on M Street. We can talk there.'

Not a bad plan. There would be plenty of foot traffic in the lobby, just in case someone wanted to pull out a gun and start shooting lawyers. 'When?' Clay asked.

'Real soon. I'll be there in five minutes. How long will it take you?'

He lived only six blocks away. 'I'll be there in ten minutes,' he said.

'Good. I'm wearing jeans and a black Steelers cap.'

'I'll find you,' Clay said, then hung up. He finished dressing and hustled out. Walking rapidly, he turned south on 31st Street, lost in a world of conspiracies and payoffs and spy scenarios. A lady passed with a small dog. A young man in a black biker's jacket with a cigarette hanging from his mouth approached, though Clay barely saw him. As the two passed, under the limbs of an old red maple, the man suddenly, but with perfect precision, unloaded a short right cross that caught Clay on the chin.

Clay never saw it. He remembered a loud pop in his face, and his head crashing into a wrought-iron fence. There was a stick of some sort, and another man, two of them throwing punches and flailing away. Then the stick landed like a gunshot on the back of his skull.

He heard a woman's voice in the distance, then he passed out.

The lady walking her dog heard a commotion behind her. There was a fight, two against one, with the man on the ground getting the worst of it. She ran closer and was horrified to see two men in black jackets hammering away with large black sticks. She screamed, they ran. She whipped out her cellphone and dialled 911.

CLAY WAS TAKEN to George Washington University Hospital where a trauma team stabilised him. The initial examination revealed two large head wounds caused by something blunt, a cut on his right cheekbone, a cut in his left ear, and numerous contusions. His right fibula was cracked neatly in two. His left kneecap was in pieces and the left ankle was broken. Eighty-one stitches were required to close the two large cuts. His skull was badly bruised but not fractured. Six stitches in his cheekbone, eleven in his ear, and they rolled him into surgery to put his legs back together.

Jonah began calling after waiting impatiently for thirty minutes. He left the restaurant after an hour and headed on foot to Clay's town house. He knocked on the door, rang the bell, cursed, and was ready to throw rocks at the windows when he saw Clay's car parked down the street. He walked slowly towards it. Something was wrong there, he just wasn't sure what.

The Porsche was covered with a white dust. He called the police.

A torn and empty Hanna Portland Cement bag was found under the Porsche. Someone had evidently covered the car with cement, then thrown water at it. In spots, especially on the roof and the hood, large patches of the cement had dried and stuck to the car. As the police inspected it, Jonah told them that its owner was unaccounted for. After a long computer search, Clay's named popped up, and Jonah took off for the hospital. He called Paulette, and she was there before he arrived. Clay was in surgery.

The lady with the dog told police the assailants were white. Three college boys entering a bar on Wisconsin Avenue reported seeing two white males in black jackets hurry round the corner from N Street. They hopped into a metallic green van, where a driver was waiting for them. It was too dark to see the licence plates.

The trail grew cold quickly. It was, after all, only a beating. The same night would see two rapes in the city, two drive-by shootings, and two murders, both apparently at random.

SINCE CLAY HAD NO family in the city, Jonah and Paulette assumed the roles of spokesmen and decision-makers. At 1.30am, a doctor reported to them that the surgery had gone smoothly, all the bones were set and ready to heal. They would continue to monitor brain activity as they didn't know how serious the concussion was.

Jonah and Paulette finally saw him just after 4.00am, in his private room. Both legs were in thick, full-length casts suspended a few inches off the bed by a complex series of cables and pulleys. A sheet hid his chest and arms. Heavy gauze covered his skull and half his face. His eyes were swollen and shut; mercifully he was still unconscious. His chin was swollen, his lips puffy and blue.

They took in the full extent of his wounds, watching his chest move up and down, very slowly. Then Jonah started laughing. 'Look at that son of a bitch,' he said.

'Hush, Jonah,' Paulette hissed, ready to slap him.

'There lies the King of Torts,' Jonah said, shaking with laughter.

Then, she too saw the humour, and for a long moment they stood at the foot of Clay's bed, working hard to suppress their amusement.

An orderly wheeled in a bed. Paulette would take the first night, Jonah would get the second.

Clay finally came back from the dead around noon on Sunday. 'Who's there?' he said.

She reached out with a hand and said, 'It's me, Clay.'

Through his swollen and blurry eyes he could see a black face. It certainly wasn't Ridley. 'Who?'

'Paulette, Clay. Can't you see?'

'No. Paulette? What are you doing here?' His words were thick, slow and painful.

'Just taking care of you, boss.'

'Where am I?'

'George Washington University Hospital.'

'Why, what happened?'

'It's what they call an old-fashioned ass-kicking. You got jumped. Two guys with sticks. You need some pain pills?'

'Please.'

She raced from the room and found a nurse. Another pill, and Clay drifted away again.

The stories hit the media with a fury on Monday. Paulette muted the television and Jonah hid the newspapers.

Ridley arrived on Monday afternoon. Paulette and Jonah cleared out, happy to leave the hospital for a while. Ridley showed great affection for a few minutes and tried to interest Clay in the latest renovations to their villa. His head pounded worse and he called for a pill. She relaxed on the foldaway and tried to nap, exhausted, she said, from the flight home. On the Gulfstream. He fell asleep too, and when he awoke she was gone.

A detective stopped by for a follow-up. All suspicion pointed to some thugs from Reedsburg, but there was scant proof.

Early on Tuesday, Zack Battle stopped by and delivered some welcome news. The SEC was suspending its investigation of Clay. He had talked to Mel Snelling's lawyer in Baltimore. Mel wasn't budging, wasn't caving in to FBI pressure. And without Mel, they could not put together the necessary evidence.

'I guess the Feds saw you in the papers and figured you've been punished enough,' Zack said.

'I'm in the paper?' Clay asked.

'A couple of stories.'

'Do I want to read them?'

'I advise you not to.'

The boredom of hospital was hitting hard—the traction, the bedpans, the relentless visits by the nurses at all hours, the dreadful food, the sheer tedium of lying there, unable to move. The casts would be his for weeks, and at least two additional operations were planned, minor ones, they promised.

The aftershocks of the beating came to haunt him, and he remembered more of the sounds and sensations of being pummelled. He saw the face of the man who threw the first punch, but couldn't be sure if it was real or a dream. So he didn't tell the detective.

TO READ, HE WAS FORCED to raise half the bed and fold himself into a V—a painful one. But the swelling had begun to subside; his head was clearing. He was browsing through the newspaper articles from Arizona when Paulette answered the phone. 'It's Oscar,' she said.

'Let's hear it,' Clay said.

'Mooneyham rested on Saturday morning. The guy is brilliant, he has the jury eating out of his hand. The Goffman boys were strutting when the trial started, now they're running for the bunkers. Roger Redding put on their star expert yesterday, a researcher who testified that there is no direct link between the drug and the plaintiff's breast cancer. I thought the guy was very believable, but then Mooneyham pulled out some bad research the guy did twenty years ago. He attacked his credentials, humiliated him. The Goffman boys were sitting there like a bunch of thugs in a police line-up.'

'Beautiful, beautiful,' Clay kept saying.

'Here's the good part. I found out where the Goffman folks are staying, so I switched hotels. They know who I am, so we're like two rabid dogs circling each other. They have an in-house lawyer named Fleet who I caught in the hotel lobby yesterday after the slaughter of their expert. He said he wanted to have a drink. He had one, I had three. The reason he had only one is because he had to go back to the Goffman suite where they were going to spend the night kicking around the possibilities of a settlement.'

'Say it again,' Clay said softly.

'You heard me. Goffman is thinking about settling. They're convinced that this jury is about to nuke their company. Fleet wanted to know how many of our cases are legitimate. I said, "All twenty-six thousand." He asks if I think you would consider settling them for a hundred thousand each. That's two point six bil, Clay.'

And with that the pain immediately vanished. Clay felt like crying. 'When do you see him again?'

'It's almost eight here, the trial resumes in an hour. We agreed to meet outside the courtroom.'

'Call me as soon as you can.'

'Don't worry, chief. How are the broken bones?'

'Much better now.'

Paulette took the phone. Seconds later, it rang again. She answered, handed it back to Clay, and said, 'I'm getting out of here.'

It was Rebecca, in the hospital's lobby, on her cellphone, wondering if a quick visit would be appropriate. Minutes later, she walked into his room and was shocked at the sight of him. She kissed him on the cheek, between bruises.

'You look awful,' she said. Her eyes were moist.

'Thank you. You, on the other hand, look spectacular.'

She kissed him again, same place, and began rubbing his left arm.

'Can I ask you a question?' Clay said.

'Sure.'

'Where is your husband right now?'

'He's in either São Paulo or Hong Kong. I can't keep track.'

'What would he do if he knew you were here?'

'He would be upset. I'm sure we'd fight.'

'Would that be unusual?'

'Happens all the time. It's not working, Clay. I want out.'

In spite of his wounds, he was having an awesome day. A fortune was within his grasp, as was Rebecca. The door to Clay's room opened quietly and Ridley entered, unnoticed. 'Sorry to interrupt,' she said.

'Hi, Ridley,' Clay said weakly.

The women gave each other looks that would terrify cobras. Ridley moved to the other side of the bed, directly opposite Rebecca, who kept her hand on Clay's bruised arm.

'Ridley, this is Rebecca, Rebecca, this is Ridley,' Clay said, and then gave serious consideration to pulling the sheets over his head and pretending to be dead.

Neither smiled. Ridley began gently rubbing Clay's right arm.

Clay nodded to his left and said, 'She's an old friend,' then to his right, and said, 'She's a new friend.'

'I believe we were at your wedding reception,' Ridley said. A not too subtle reminder to Rebecca that she happened to be married.

'Uninvited as I recall,' Rebecca said.

Rebecca blinked first. She had no choice. She did, after all, have a husband. 'I guess I'll be going.' She left the room slowly, as if she didn't want to leave, to concede territory. Clay was thrilled by that.

As soon as the door closed, Ridley withdrew to the window.

'You love her, don't you?' she said, still looking out of the window.

'Naw, she's just an old friend.'

'I'm not stupid, Clay!' With that she wheeled round, grabbed her bag and stomped out of his room, heels clicking as loudly as possible.

Oscar called a few minutes later, on his cellphone outside the courtroom. A quick recess had been ordered. 'Rumour has it Mooneyham turned down ten million this morning,' he said.

'Fleet tell you this?'

'No, we didn't meet. He was tied up with some motions. I'll try to catch him during lunch and call you back.'

There were three possible outcomes in Flagstaff; two would be delightful. A verdict against Goffman would put enormous pressure on the company to settle and avoid years of litigation. A mid-trial settlement would probably mean a national compensation plan for all plaintiffs.

But a verdict in favour of Goffman would force Clay to scurry around and prepare for his own trial in DC. That prospect brought back the sharp pains in his skull and legs.

Lying motionless for hours in a hospital bed was sufficient torture in itself. Now, the silent phone made matters much worse. At any moment, Goffman could offer Mooneyham enough money to make him settle. His ego would push him all the way to a verdict, but could he ignore the interests of his client?

13

The next morning, Clay was taken back to surgery for some minor adjustments to the pins and screws in his legs. 'A bit of tweaking,' his doctor had called it. Whatever it was required a full dose of anaesthesia, which wiped out most of the day. Paulette was waiting beside the bed when he finally came round. 'Any word from Oscar?' he said, with a thick tongue.

'He called, said the trial was going well. That's about it,' Paulette reported. She adjusted his bed and his pillow and gave him water, and when he was awake for good, she left to run errands. On the way out, she handed him an overnight envelope, unopened.

From Patton French. A handwritten note passed on his best wishes for a speedy recovery. The attached memo was to the Dyloft Plaintiffs' Steering Committee (now Defendants). The Honourable Helen Warshaw had submitted her weekly additions to her class action. There were now 381 members of the class, with 24 of them ex-JCC clients who'd signed up with Ms Warshaw.

Ridley stopped by on her way home from the gym. She hauled in some magazines and tried to appear concerned. After a minute she said, 'Clay, the decorator called. I need to return to the villa.'

What an excellent idea! 'When?' he asked.

'Tomorrow, maybe. If the plane is available.'

'Sure. I'll call the pilots.' Getting her out of town would make his life easier. She was of no benefit around the hospital.

'Thanks,' she said, then sat in the chair and began flipping through a magazine. After thirty minutes her time was up. She kissed him on the forehead and disappeared.

The detective was next. Three men from Reedsburg had been arrested early on Sunday morning outside a bar in Hagerstown, Maryland. There had been a fight of some sort. They tried to leave the scene, in a dark green minivan, but the driver misjudged something and drove them into a drainage ditch. The detective produced three colour photos of the suspects—all rough-looking characters. Clay could not identify any of them.

They worked at the Hanna plant, according to the chief of police in Reedsburg. Two had recently been laid off, but that was the only information the detective had managed to extract. 'If you can't identify these guys, then I have no choice but to close the file.'

'I've never seen them before,' Clay said.

The detective placed the photos back in his file and left for ever.

OSCAR CALLED AROUND 9.30PM. The trial had just adjourned for the day. Everyone was exhausted, primarily because Dale Mooneyham had caused such carnage in the courtroom. Goffman had reluctantly hauled out its next expert, a horn-rimmed in-house lab rat who'd been in charge of the clinical trials for Maxatil, and after a wonderful and creative examination by Roger the Dodger, Mooneyham had proceeded to butcher the poor boy on cross-examination.

'Settlement?' Clay asked, drugged and sluggish and sleepy.

'No, but it should be a long night. Rumour is that Goffman might try one more expert tomorrow, then plug the dike and hunker down for the verdict. Mooneyham refuses to talk to them. He looks and acts as if he expects a record verdict.'

GOFFMAN'S CEO arrived in Flagstaff late on Wednesday night and was rushed downtown to a tall building where the lawyers were conspiring. Every discussion was centred around a doomsday scenario.

Roger Redding was adamant that the defence stick to its game plan and call its remaining witnesses, convinced the tide would turn. But Bob Mitchell, the chief in-house counsel, and Sterling Gibb, the company's long-time lawyer and golfing buddy of the CEO, had seen enough. One more witness assassination by Mooneyham and the jurors might jump up and attack the nearest Goffman executive.

Mitchell and Gibb met with the CEO alone, around 3.00am, over doughnuts. As bad as things were for the company, there remained some secrets about Maxatil that could never be revealed. If

Mooneyham had this information, or could beat it out of a witness, then the sky would indeed fall on Goffman. The CEO finally made the decision to stop the bloodletting.

When court was called to order at 9.00am, Roger Redding announced that the defence would rest.

'No further witnesses?' the judge asked. A fifteen-day trial had just been cut in half. He had a week of golf coming up!

'That's correct, Your Honour,' Redding said with a smile at the jurors, as if all was well.

'Any rebuttal, Mr Mooneyham?'

The plaintiff's lawyer slowly got to his feet. He scratched his head, scowled at Redding, and said, 'If they're done, then so are we.'

The judge explained to the jurors that in an hour they would hear the closing arguments, and by lunchtime they would have the case.

CLAY SPENT THREE HOURS on a trolley waiting in X-ray, isolated from the world. The X-rays took almost an hour, and he was back in his room, napping, when Oscar called. It was five twenty his time, three twenty in Phoenix.

'Where have you been?' Oscar demanded.

'Don't ask.'

'Goffman threw in the towel first thing this morning, tried to settle, but Mooneyham wouldn't talk. Everything happened real fast after that. Closing arguments began around ten, I guess. The jury got the case at exactly noon.'

'The jury has the case?' Clay asked, practically yelling.

'Had the case. It's over. They deliberated for three hours and found in favour of Goffman. I'm sorry, Clay. Everybody's in shock.'

'Tell me you're lying, Oscar.'

'I wish. I don't know what happened. Nobody does. Redding gave a spectacular closing argument, but I watched the jurors. I thought Mooneyham had them.'

'Dale Mooneyham lost a case?'

'Not just any case, Clay. He lost our case. And I would've bet the farm against Goffman.'

'We just did.'

'I'm sorry.'

'Look, Oscar, I'm lying here in bed, all alone. Don't leave me. Just talk to me. Tell me something.'

'After the verdict, I got cornered by Fleet, and two other guys—Bob Mitchell and Sterling Gibb. They were so happy they were about to pop. They told me that they're bringing their show on the road—Roger the Dodger and Company—and the next trial will be in DC, against Mr Clay Carter, the King of Torts, who, as we all know, has never tried a tort case. What could I say? They had just beaten a great lawyer in his own back yard.'

'Our cases are worthless, Oscar.'

'They certainly think so. Mitchell said they would not offer one cent for any Maxatil case anywhere in the country. They want trials. They want vindication. A clear name. All that crap.'

He kept Oscar on the phone for over an hour, making him replay the closing arguments and the wait for the verdict. Oscar described the shock on the plaintiff's face, a dying woman whose lawyer wouldn't take whatever Goffman was offering, supposedly $10 million. And Mooneyham, who hadn't lost in so long he had forgotten how to lose, demanding that the jury be required to fill out questionnaires and explain themselves, making a total ass of himself. And the stampede from the courtroom after the foreman uttered his majestic words as the Wall Street analysts rushed to make their calls.

Oscar ended his narrative with, 'I'm going to a bar now.'

Clay called a nurse and asked for a sleeping pill.

AFTER ELEVEN DAYS of confinement, Clay was finally set free. A lighter cast was placed on his left leg, and, though he couldn't walk, he could at least manoeuvre a little. Paulette pushed his wheelchair out of the hospital to a rented van driven by Oscar. Fifteen minutes later, they rolled him into his town house. Paulette and Miss Glick had turned the downstairs den into a temporary bedroom. His phones, fax and computer had been moved to a folding table near his bed. His clothes were stacked neatly on plastic shelves by the fireplace.

For the first two hours he was home, he read mail and financial reports and clippings, but only what Paulette had screened.

Later, after a nap, he sat at the kitchen table with Paulette and Oscar announced that it was time to start.

The unravelling began.

THE FIRST ISSUE was his law firm. Crittle had managed to trim a few costs, but the overheads were still galloping along at a million bucks a month. With no revenues, and none expected, layoffs were unavoidable. They went down a list of the employees and made the painful cuts. Though they considered the Maxatil cases worthless, it would still take work to close the files. Clay kept four lawyers and four paralegals for the job. He looked at the names of the employees who had to go, and it made him ill. 'I want to sleep on this,' he said, unable to make the final decision.

'Most of them are expecting it, Clay,' Paulette said.

Two days earlier, Oscar had reluctantly agreed to go to New York and meet with Helen Warshaw. He had presented a broad picture of Clay Carter's assets and potential liabilities, and basically begged for mercy. His boss did not want to file for bankruptcy, but if pushed too hard by Ms Warshaw he would have no choice. She had been unimpressed. She could not allow Clay to settle his cases for, say, a meagre $1 million each, when the same cases against Patton French might fetch three times that much. Plus, she was not in a settling mood. The trial would be an important one—a bold effort at reforming abuses in the system, a media-hyped spectacle.

Oscar was almost as depressed as Clay, and after a few hours of misery he left for the office. Paulette wheeled Clay outside onto the patio where they had a cup of green tea with honey. 'I got two things to say,' she said. 'First, I'm going to give you some of my money.'

'No, you're not.'

'Yes, I am. You made me rich when you didn't have to. I can't help it that you're a stupid white boy who's lost his ass, but I still love you. I'm going to help you, Clay. If you lose everything, I'll be around to make sure you're OK.'

'I don't know what to say.'

'Say nothing.'

They held hands and Clay fought back tears. A moment passed. 'Number two,' she said. 'I've been talking to Rebecca. She's afraid to see you because she might get caught. She's got a new cellphone, one her husband knows nothing about. She gave me the number. She wants you to call her this afternoon. Husband's out of town or something. I'll leave in a few minutes.'

REBECCA PARKED round the corner and hustled along to Clay's. She was not good at sneaking around; neither was he. The first thing they decided was that they would not continue it.

She and Jason Myers had decided to dissolve their marriage amicably. He preferred to work eighteen hours a day, whether in DC, New York, Palo Alto or Hong Kong. Work was more important to him than anything else. He'd simply left her, with no apologies and with no plans to change his ways. The papers would be filed in two days. She was already packing her bags.

Both had a reason to run. Clay would not, under any circumstances, remain in DC in the years to come. His humiliation was too raw and deep, and there was a big world out there where people didn't know him. He craved anonymity. For the first time in her life, Rebecca just wanted to get away—away from a bad marriage, away from her family, away from the country club, away from the pressures of making money and accumulating stuff.

Clay wanted to hold her and kiss her and make up for lost time.

She spent the night and decided not to leave. Over coffee the following morning, Clay began with Tequila Watson and Tarvan and told her everything.

PAULETTE AND OSCAR returned with more unpleasantries from the office. Oscar was finalising a settlement plan to be put before the judge in the Hanna bankruptcy. Oddly enough, the firm might be awarded a fee, though one far less than what Clay had turned down.

There was an urgent Warshaw motion to take the depositions of several of the Dyloft plaintiffs. Urgency was required because they were dying, and their video depositions would be crucial to the trial, which was expected in about a year. To employ the usual defence tactics of delay and postponement would have been enormously unfair to these plaintiffs and Clay agreed to the schedule. He also agreed, finally, to lay off ten lawyers and most of the paralegals, secretaries and clerks. He signed letters to every one of them—brief and very apologetic.

A letter to the Maxatil clients was then hammered out. In it, Clay recapped the Mooneyham trial in Phoenix. He held to the belief that the drug was dangerous, but proving causation would now be 'very difficult, if not impossible'. The company was not willing to consider an out-of-court settlement, and, given Clay's current medical problems, he was not in a position to prepare for an extended trial.

He hated to use his beating as an excuse, but Oscar prevailed. It sounded believable in the letter. At this low point in his career, he had to grab whatever advantage he could find.

He was therefore releasing each client, and doing so in sufficient time for each to hire another lawyer and pursue Goffman.

Clay couldn't help but think of Max Pace, his old pal who'd got him into the Maxatil business. Pace, one of at least five aliases, had been indicted for securities fraud, but had not been found. His indictment claimed that he used insider information to sell almost a million shares of Goffman before Clay filed suit. Later, he covered his sale and slipped out of the country with around $15 million. Run, Max, run. If he was caught and hauled back for a trial he might spill all their dirty secrets.

For the next week, Clay never left his town house. Rebecca packed Ridley's things into thirty-gallon trash bags and stuffed them in the basement. She moved in some of her own stuff, though Clay warned her that he was about to lose the house. She cooked wonderful meals and nursed him. They watched old movies until midnight, then slept late every morning. She drove him to see his doctor.

Ridley called from the island. Clay did not tell her she'd lost her place; he preferred to do that in person, when and if she returned. The renovation was coming along nicely, though Clay had seriously curtailed the budget. She seemed oblivious to his financial problems.

THE LAST LAWYER to enter Clay's life was Mark Munson, a bankruptcy expert who specialised in large, messy, individual crashes. Crittle had found him. After Clay retained him, Crittle showed him the books, the leases, the contracts, the lawsuits. Everything.

In the seventeen months since he'd left OPD, Clay had earned $121 million in fees—$30 million had been paid to Rodney, Paulette and Jonah as bonuses; $20 million had gone for office expenses and the Gulfstream; $16 million down the drain for advertising and testing for Dyloft, Maxatil and Skinny Bens; $34 million for taxes, either paid or accrued; $4 million for the villa; $3 million for the sailboat. A million here and there—the town house, the 'loan' to Max Pace, and the usual and expected extravagances of the newly rich.

Jarrett Carter's fancy new catamaran was an interesting issue. Clay had paid for it, but the Bahamian company that held its title was owned completely by his father. Munson thought the bankruptcy court might take one of two positions—either it was a gift, which would require Clay to pay gift taxes, or it was simply owned by someone else and thus not part of Clay's estate. Either way, the boat remained the property of Jarrett Carter.

Clay had also earned $7.1 million trading in Ackerman stock, and though some of this was buried offshore it was about to be hauled back. 'If you hide assets you go to jail,' Munson lectured.

The balance sheet showed a net worth of approximately $19 million. However, the liabilities were catastrophic. Twenty-six former clients were now suing for the Dyloft fiasco. That number was expected to rise, and though it was impossible to throw darts at the value of each case, Clay's exposure was significantly more than his net worth. The Hanna class-action plaintiffs were festering and getting organised. The Maxatil backlash would be nasty and prolonged. None of those expenses could be predicted either. 'Let the bankruptcy trustee deal with it,' Munson said. 'You'll walk away with the shirt on your back, but at least you won't owe anything.'

'Thanks,' Clay said, thinking about the sailboat. If they were successful in keeping it from the bankruptcy, Jarrett could sell it, buy something smaller, and Clay could have some cash to live on.

After two hours with Munson and Crittle, the kitchen table was covered with spreadsheets and print-outs, a debris-strewn testament to the greed and stupidity of the past seventeen months. It was sickening what the money had done to him.

The thought of leaving helped him to survive each day.

RIDLEY CALLED HIM from St Barth's with the alarming news that a FOR SALE sign had appeared in front of 'their' villa.

'That's because it's now for sale,' Clay said.

'I don't understand.'

'Come home and I'll explain it to you.'

'Is there trouble?'

'You might say that.'

After a long pause, she said, 'I prefer to stay here.'

'Fine. Stay in the villa until it sells. I don't care.'

'How long will that be?'

He could see her doing everything imaginable to sabotage a potential sale. At the moment he just didn't care. 'I don't know, Ridley.'

'I'm staying,' she said.

'Fine.'

RODNEY FOUND his old friend sitting on the front steps of his picturesque town house, crutches by his side, a shawl over his shoulders to knock off the autumn chill. The wind was spinning leaves in circles along Dumbarton Street.

'Need some air,' Clay said. 'I've been locked in for three weeks.'

'How are the bones?' Rodney asked, as he sat beside him.

'Healing nicely.'

Rodney had left the city and become a real suburbanite. Khakis and sneakers, a fancy SUV to haul kids around. 'How's your head?'

'No additional brain damage.'

'How's your soul?'

'Tortured, to say the least. But I'll survive.'

'Paulette says you're leaving.'

'For a while, anyway. I'll file for bankruptcy next week, and I will not be around here when it happens. Paulette has a flat in London that I can use for a few months. We'll hide there.'

'You can't avoid a bankruptcy?'

'No way. There are too many claims, and good ones. Remember our first Dyloft plaintiff, Ted Worley?'

'Sure.'

'He died yesterday. I didn't pull the trigger, but I sure didn't protect him either. His case in front of a jury is worth five million bucks. There are twenty-six of those. I'm going to London.'

'Clay, I want to help.'

'I'm not taking your money. I've already had this conversation with Paulette and with Jonah. You made your money and you were smart enough to cash out. I wasn't.'

'But we're not going to let you die, man. You didn't have to give us ten million bucks. But you did. We're giving some back.'

'No.'

'Yes. The three of us have talked about it. We'll wait until the bankruptcy is over, then each of us will do a transfer. A gift.'

'You earned that money, Rodney. Keep it.'

'Nobody earns ten million dollars in six months, Clay. You might win it, steal it, or have it drop out of the sky, but nobody earns money like that. It's ridiculous and obscene.'

'How are the kids?'

'You're changing the subject.'

'Yes, I'm changing the subject.'

So they talked about kids, and old friends at OPD, and old clients and cases there. They sat on the front steps until after dark, when Rebecca arrived and it was time for dinner.

THE *POST* REPORTER WAS Art Mariani, a young man who had documented Clay's astounding rise and his equally amazing crash with accuracy and a reasonable dose of fairness. When he arrived at Clay's house, he was greeted by Paulette and led down the hall to the kitchen. Clay hobbled to his feet and introduced himself, then went round the table—Zack Battle, his attorney; Rebecca Van Horn, his friend; and Oscar Mulrooney, his partner. Tape recorders were plugged in. Rebecca made the rounds with the coffeepot.

Clay took a swig of coffee, a deep breath and jumped into the story. He began with the shooting of Ramón 'Pumpkin' Pumphrey by his client, Tequila Watson. Dates, times, places, Clay had notes of every-thing and all the files. Then Washad Porter and his two murders. Then the other four. Deliverance Camp, Clean Streets, the amazing results of a drug called Tarvan. Without mentioning the name of Max Pace, he described the history of Tarvan in detail—the secret clinical trials in Mexico City and other cities. The drug's arrival in DC.

'Who made the drug?' Mariani asked, visibly shaken.

'I'm not completely sure,' Clay answered. 'But I think it's Philo.' He reached for a thick document and slid it over to Mariani. 'This is one of the settlement agreements. As you will see, there are two offshore companies mentioned. If you can penetrate them, pick up the trail, it will probably lead you to a shell company in Luxembourg, then to Philo.'

'OK, but why do you suspect Philo?'

'I have a source. That's all I can tell you.'

This mysterious source selected Clay from all the attorneys in DC and convinced him to sell his soul for $15 million. The details poured forth, as did the documents and settlement agreements.

'When I publish this story, what happens to your clients, the fami-lies of the victims?' Mariani asked.

'I've lost sleep worrying about that, but I think they'll be fine,' Clay said. 'The drugmaker would be insane to try and set aside those set-tlements. It's lucky to get out with a fifty-million settlement.'

'Can the families set the agreements aside when they learn the truth?' Mariani asked.

'It would be difficult.'

'What about you? You signed confidentiality agreements?'

'I'm not a factor any more. I'm about to be bankrupt. I'm about to surrender my licence to practise law. They can't touch me.' It was a sad admission that hurt Clay's friends as much as it hurt him.

'What happens to Tequila Watson, Washad Porter and the other men who were convicted of these murders?'

'First, they can probably sue the drugmaker, which won't help them much in prison. Second, there's a chance their cases could be reopened, at least the sentencing aspect.'

Zack Battle cleared his throat and everyone waited. 'Off the record, after you publish whatever you decide to publish, and after the storm dies down, I plan to take these cases and have them reviewed. I'll sue on behalf of the seven defendants, that is, if we can identify the pharmaceutical company.'

'This is very explosive,' Mariani said, stating the obvious. He studied his notes for a long time. 'What led to the Dyloft litigation?'

'That's another chapter for another day,' Clay said. 'You've documented most of it anyway. I'm not talking about it.'

'Fair enough. Is this story over?'

'For me it is,' Clay said.

PAULETTE AND ZACK drove them to the airport, to Reagan National where Clay's Gulfstream sat close to the spot he'd first seen it. Since they were leaving for at least six months, there was a lot of luggage, especially Rebecca's. Clay was getting about fine with his crutches now, but he couldn't carry anything. Zack acted as his porter.

He gamely showed them his once-beloved airplane, though they all knew this was its final voyage. Clay hugged Paulette and embraced Zack, thanked them both and promised to call within days. Once on board, Clay pulled the shades over the windows so he would see none of Washington when they lifted off.

To Rebecca, the jet was a ghastly symbol of the destructive power of greed. She longed for the tiny flat in London, where no one knew them and no one cared what they wore, drove, bought, ate, or where they worked, shopped or vacationed. She wasn't going home. She had fought with her parents for the last time.

Clay longed for two good legs and a clean slate. He was surviving one of the more infamous meltdowns in the history of American law, and it was further and further behind him. He had Rebecca all to himself, and nothing else mattered.

Somewhere over Newfoundland, they unfolded the sofa and fell asleep under the covers.

JOHN GRISHAM

As a former lawyer, John Grisham didn't find it hard to put himself in the shoes of his main character in *The King of Torts*: a young public defender whose principles are put on trial by the lure of wealth and power. Grisham understands only too well how youthful idealism can give way to the realities of life. 'We all start law school with the dream of making the world a better place, defending the poor and going after corporate wrongdoers . . . by the time we finish we're just worried about making a buck.'

However, the type of lawyers who feature in *The King of Torts* (just like their real-life counterparts, in Grisham's view), have taken the pursuit of money to extremes. 'These guys take forty per cent in fees off a settlement, which is just plain wrong. They're getting filthy rich, buying big jets and burning a lot of money'. It has to be said, though, that Grisham's success as a novelist has meant that he and his wife, Renee, have themselves become wealthy. 'I admit that I'm spoilt,' he says with a laugh. 'We give away more than we spend, and being able to help others is very gratifying, but it is admittedly also very nice to be able to go out and just indulge yourself.' So what is his greatest indulgence? Like the book's hero, Clay Carter, Grisham is the proud possessor of his own plane. 'I bought it ten years ago. It's not quite a Gulfstream, but it sure is a very nice way to travel.'

Born in Arkansas and raised in Mississippi, Grisham is very much a Southerner, and feels that his background has helped to shape his career. 'There is a strong tradition of storytelling in the South, and in my own family. In fact, the Grishams are a bunch of liars,' he jokes. 'You can't believe a word they say! It's all about who can outdo the other guy with a big story. Alongside that lies my experience as a lawyer. Lawyers see some awfully good stories in the course of their work—things you just can't believe. So the lawyering, the family tradition of tall stories, and a hyperactive imagination all came together somehow when I was thirty-five. It was then that I started writing, and it all kind of worked.'

Work it did. John Grisham has now sold over 200 million copies of his novels. Six have been adapted as Hollywood films, and *The King of Torts* has recently topped both the UK and US best-seller lists.

DAYS
WITHOUT
NUMBER

ROBERT GODDARD

The Paleologus family are said to be descendants of the last Emperor of Byzantium, a dazzling claim that Nick Paleologus has always found rather far-fetched.

But one person is convinced that the story is true, and that Nick and his siblings are in possession of an astounding secret, passed from father to son throughout the centuries.

A secret worth killing for.

PART ONE

CHAPTER ONE

He did not regret agreeing to go. He had long learned to accept the consequences of his decisions with a degree of equanimity. But consequences hatch slowly and not always sweetly, as the long drive west in his company car was reminding him. His past was a hostile country, his present a tranquil plain. By going home he was not only abandoning a refuge but proclaiming that he no longer needed one.

Heading west to reach home was also a contradiction in historical terms. However well he played the part of a middle-management Englishman, Nicholas Paleologus was, if his grandfather's claims were to be believed, something altogether more exotic: a descendant of the last Emperor of Byzantium.

He had always displayed a keen disdain for his semilegendary eastern roots. Since isolating himself from his family, he had been prepared to admit to Greek ancestry, nothing more. It scarcely seemed likely, after all, that the last of the Paleologoi should have found their way to England. Yet so their patchy history insisted.

The Paleologus dynasty ruled Byzantium for the last 200 years of its existence, until Emperor Constantine XI fell defending Constantinople in vain against the Turks in 1453. The disaster scattered those of the family it had not destroyed, to mix with humbler bearers of the name around the Mediterranean, until Constantine's great-great-great-great nephew, Theodore, fleeing an attempted murder charge in Italy, set fugitive foot on English soil. He lived out his final years as a guest of the Lower family at their mansion, Clifton, on the Cornish bank of the Tamar, opposite Plymouth, in the parish of Landulph, where he died in 1636.

It was Theodore Paleologus's memorial plaque in Landulph Church that inspired Nick's grandfather, Godfrey Paleologus, to settle in the area and devote his leisure hours to proving his descent from the imperial line. He bought a farmhouse called Trennor near the village of Cargreen and slowly transformed it into a comfortable family home. A Plymothian by birth, he never quite clinched his blood connection with Theodore, but he achieved his ambition of being buried at Landulph, though not in the Paleologus vault.

Godfrey's son Michael read archaeology at Oxford and went on to teach it there. Michael's five children, including Nick, had all been born in the city. But Michael kept Trennor as a holiday home after his parents died and ultimately retired there. Since his wife's death, he had lived alone, though four of his children were close by. Only Nick ploughed a distant furrow. And now he, too, was returning. Though not for long. And not, he suspected, for the best of reasons.

It was Friday afternoon. A dank winter darkness had outpaced him on the road. Sunday would be his eldest brother's fiftieth birthday. Andrew farmed sheep on Bodmin Moor, cutting an ever more forlorn figure—according to their sister Irene—thanks to divorce, estrangement from his only son and the dire state of British agriculture. A birthday party at Trennor—a gathering of the siblings—would do them all good, Andrew especially. But in luring Nick down, Irene had admitted that there was more to it than that. 'We need to talk about the future. I don't see how Dad can cope at Trennor on his own much longer. A possibility's cropped up and we'd like your input.' She had declined to be specific over the phone, hoping, Nick inferred, to rouse his curiosity as well as his conscience.

The rush-hour traffic was just beginning to thin as Nick reached Plymouth. He followed the A38 through the city and across the Tamar Bridge to the quayside at Saltash. Ahead he could see the warmly lit windows of the Old Ferry Inn, where Irene Viner, née Paleologus, had presided as landlady for the past twelve years. The pub had been her husband's idea, following redundancy from Devonport Dockyard. But he had soon started drinking most of the takings, a problem Irene solved only with the help of a divorce lawyer. She had gone on to make a much better job of running a pub than Nick would ever have predicted.

He pulled into the yard behind the pub, turned off the engine and climbed out. After inhaling a lungful of chill riverside air, he fetched his bag from the boot of the car and walked round to the front of the pub. He dipped his head as he stepped in through the doorway. There were two rooms, front and back, served by a double-sided bar.

Irene was perched on a stool behind the bar, sustaining a murmured conversation with the barmaid. 'Here he is,' she announced as Nick stepped into her line of sight. 'Hello, stranger.' She hopped off the stool and came out into the room to kiss him. 'You're looking well.'

'You too.'

The family resemblance was quite marked. They were of similar height and build, their sleek dark hair touched with the same amount of grey. Marginally too long in the face and aquiline in the nose to be described as conventionally good-looking, they were both striking in appearance nonetheless.

'Like the ensemble?' Irene gave a half-pirouette to show off her hip-hugging skirt, scarlet blouse and high-heeled shoes. 'Friday-night finery for the locals. There are quite a few that would defect up the road to the Boatman but for my ankles, let me tell you.'

'I can believe it.' So he could, though Irene's admirers appeared to be in short supply, a point her fading smile seemed to acknowledge.

'They'll be in soon. Fancy a drink?'

'Later, maybe. I'd like to freshen up.'

'Of course. Go straight up. I've put you in Laura's room. There's a quiche and salad in the fridge if you're hungry.'

'OK. See you in a minute.'

Nick opened the door marked PRIVATE next to the ladies' and went up the narrow staircase to the cramped living quarters. The back bedroom belonged to his niece, currently away at boarding school. He dumped his bag beside the bed, then headed for the bathroom.

Forty minutes or so had passed by the time Nick went down again and a dozen locals were now installed in the back bar, swapping jokes and gossip. Some of them he dimly recognised and they him. He did more smiling and small-talking over the next few hours than he normally spread over a month.

It was nearly midnight before the last customer had been steered out into the darkness and the barmaid sent home. Irene poured Nick and herself double Glenmorangies and joined him at a table near the fire.

'They seem a good-hearted bunch,' he remarked.

'Not too hard on you, then?' She gave him a sympathetic smile.

'No. They were all—'

'I mean the experience. You don't like crowds, do you? Especially when you're supposed to be one of them.'

'I get by.'

'Do you? I worry about you, all the way up there, alone and—'

'There's nothing to worry about. Not any more.'

Irene seemed to take the hint. 'Well, I'm glad you could make it.'

'Do you think Andrew will be?'

'Of course. Although he won't show it. You know what he's like. But it can't be a bad idea for a family to get together. Besides . . .'

'You haven't dragged me down here just for the birthday boy.'

'No.' She took a long draw on her cigarette. 'There's Dad, too.'

'Does *he* know I'm showing up on Sunday?'

'No. We thought we'd . . . surprise both of them.'

'*We?*'

'Anna and me.'

'What about Basil?'

'He knows what's going on.'

Since their brother Basil had been living with their sister Anna for some time, that, Nick assumed, was inevitable. 'Lucky him.'

Irene sighed. 'All right. Time to come clean. You haven't seen Dad in over a year. He's gone down a lot lately. He's become . . . frail.'

'He *is* eighty-four years old.'

'And showing it. If Mum was still alive, it might be different. As it is, I don't see how he can stay at Trennor on his own.'

'What about Pru?' Even as he mentioned his parents' long-serving cleaning lady, Nick calculated that she could hardly be far off eighty-four herself. 'Doesn't she keep an eye on him?'

'Yes, but she's not of much practical use any more. We have to face facts. There's a place at Tavistock that Anna reckons would be ideal for Dad. Gorton Lodge.'

As a nurse-cum-administrator at a residential home in Plymouth, Anna was, Nick supposed, qualified to judge in such matters. Still, there seemed to be an element of fence-rushing about it all. He winced at the unaccustomed sensation of sympathy for his father.

'She can tell you about it tomorrow night,' Irene continued. 'She wants you to go over there for dinner. But Gorton Lodge *is* nice, believe me. The best money can buy round here.'

A thought came to Nick, spirited up by the word money. Who was going to pay Gorton Lodge's fees? His father had always let it be known that an academic's salary left him with little to provide for his old age. The only obvious source of funds was Trennor itself. 'The house would have to be sold, Irene. What's it worth? Three hundred thousand? Three fifty at most.'

'On the open market, you're probably right.'

'What other market is there?'

'The closed kind. Someone's offered Dad half a million.'

Nick stared at his sister in astonishment. '*Half a million?*'

'That's right. Five hundred thousand pounds. Cash on the table.'

'But . . . Dad hasn't put it up for sale.'

'Hence the premium. Lodged in a lawyer's suspense account to Baskcomb's satisfaction.' Baskcomb was the family's solicitor.

'Who is this someone?'

'Name of Tantris. I know nothing about him. None of us has met him. He works through intermediaries.'

'Why does he want the place?'

'Does it matter?'

'It might. What does Dad say?'

'He says "no deal".'

'That's that, then.'

'Not if we talk him round. Show a united front.'

'So that's why I'm here.'

'Not really.' Irene looked reproachfully at him. 'I thought you had a right to know. You stand to benefit along with the rest of us. Or lose, of course, if we throw Mr Tantris's money back at him.'

'It's Dad who'd be doing the throwing. And the benefit's questionable. It would just take Gorton Lodge that bit longer to work their way through the money. As far as I can—'

'Mr Tantris will pay the fees.'

Again Nick stared at Irene in astonishment. '*What?*'

'Mr Tantris will pay. Some kind of trust fund. Legally watertight, according to Baskcomb.'

'Why would he be willing to do that?'

'To overcome our objections, of course. I imagine it's a ploy to get us on his side. I have no illusions about his motives.'

'But what *are* his motives? Why does he want Trennor so badly?'

Irene shrugged. 'Like I said, does it really matter?'

She was being evasive once too often. Nick leaned forward across the table towards her. 'Do you know, Irene?'

'Yes. It's a little . . . unusual. Surprising, even.'

'Surprise me, then.'

'Actually . . .' She smiled appeasingly at him. 'I'm going to leave that to someone much better qualified than I am.'

'Oh yes. And who might that be?'

'Mr Tantris's assistant, Elspeth Hartley, wants to meet you and explain the situation. She'll be able to answer all your questions.'

'When?'

'Tomorrow at noon. At the village church in St Neot.'

'*St Neot?*'

'It's about halfway between Liskeard and Bodmin.'

'I know where it is, for God's sake. What I don't know is why I should have to go all the way over there to meet this woman.'

'You will when you get there. Ms Hartley will explain everything.' Irene drained her glass. 'Which is why I'm going to say good night.'

ST NEOT CHURCH stood on the highest ground of the village, a weathered granite testament to the skills of its centuries-dead builders. Nick pulled up beside a small red Peugeot at the churchyard's western end. The church clock showed the time as ten minutes short of noon.

As Nick climbed out of his car, so did the driver of the Peugeot. She was a short, slim woman dressed in jeans, sweater and sheepskin coat, dark curly hair framing a pale, serious face. Nut-brown eyes regarded him solemnly through small, gold-framed glasses.

'Mr Paleologus?' she asked, with the hint of a Midlands accent.

'Yes. Ms Hartley?'

'The same.' She shook his hand. 'Glad you could make it.'

'My sister didn't leave me much choice in the matter.'

She raised her eyebrows. 'How much do you know?'

'I know your boss wants to buy Trennor. Virtually at any price, apparently. And I believe you're going to tell me why.'

'Actually, he's not my boss. More patron, really.'

'You're not his assistant?'

'I'm an art historian. Mr Tantris subsidises my researches at Bristol University. But in a sense I do seem to have turned into his assistant. The real one's too busy with high finance to come down here.'

'Down from where?'

'London. New York. Zürich.' She smiled, instantly persuading Nick that it was something she should do often. 'The location varies.'

'And Mr Tantris? What's his location?'

'Monaco, so I'm told. But I've never actually met him. I'm just grateful to him for funding my work. It's led me in some unexpected directions. I certainly never expected to come across descendants of the Byzantine emperors in the course of it, for instance.'

'Our lineage doesn't bear much scrutiny.'

'That's not what your father said. Before he showed me the door.'

'Well, it's his door.'

'I know. But it's not as if Mr Tantris wants to pull Trennor down and build twelve executive houses on the site, is it?'

'Isn't it?'

'All right.' She smiled again. 'I'd better get to why we're here. Come into the church. Then you'll understand.' She led Nick in through the churchyard gate and round to the south door.

Nick followed her into the body of the church. He stopped and looked around. The nave and aisles were well proportioned, but what took his eye were the stained-glass windows, glowing vibrantly yet delicately, seeming to magnify the thin light from the churchyard.

'Nice windows.'

'Magnificent, I think,' said Elspeth. 'And historically precious. Pre-Reformation parish church glazing schemes are extremely rare. Civil War iconoclasm's mostly to blame. Cromwellian troops were accompanied by the sound of smashing glass wherever they went.'

'Why did this survive?'

'Special pleading and elaborate planning. But we're getting ahead of ourselves. First I want you to look at the glass, I mean, *really* look.'

She led Nick along the south aisle and through the gated rood screen into a lady chapel filled with blue, red and gold light from the two corner windows on the southern and eastern sides.

'The Creation and Noah Windows, substantially unrestored and dating from the 1490s. Exquisite, I think you'll agree.'

'I do.' Nick could recognise fine craftsmanship when he saw it. The Creation story was set out in the brightly tinted panes, from God with his compasses planning the world to the green serpent coiled round the tree of the knowledge of good and evil. The last pane showed God commanding Noah to build the Ark. And there, as he turned to the next window, *was* the Ark, floating on a sea of light.

'It looks as if the plan was to tell the whole Old Testament story window by window. But we can assume money ran short, because what do we find along the aisle but local dignitaries and their pet saints. Sponsorship, by any other name.'

The five windows between Noah and the south door were indeed a sequence of haloed saints and family groups kneeling in prayer.

Nick turned to admire these humbler but no less beautiful compositions, walking slowly back along the nave. He stopped and gazed up at the east window. 'The Last Supper?' he murmured, deciphering the scene. 'But . . . different somehow from the others.'

'You're getting good at this. That's an 1820s window. There was a lot of cleaning and restoration done in the early nineteenth century, with quite a few tracery lights moved or replaced and several new windows installed. It takes some sorting out.'

'I'm sure it does.'

'But, however you look at it, there's one rather odd omission.'

'There is?'

'This is a church. The windows are lessons in glass. The Creation. The Fall. The Flood. There should be some reference to the Day of Judgment. Take it from me, a Doom Window was *de rigueur*.'

'So, why isn't there one?'

'Oh, there was. We have that from a churchwarden of the period. And talking of churchwardens, one of the present incumbents has lent me the key to the tower. This way.'

She walked back down the nave and unlocked the door to the tower. Nick followed her into the bell-ringing chamber. The ropes were tied back against the walls, allowing a clear view of the west window. But all Nick could see were illuminated saints. The Day of Judgment did not seem to have dawned in the glass.

'I think this is where the Doom Window was. The two major periods of iconoclasm were in the mid-1640s and early 1650s. St Neot came under most serious threat during the second period. There were lots of raids on neighbouring churches in the spring of 1651. But not here.'

'Why was St Neot spared?'

'It was down to the churchwardens. The vicar had been expelled from his living by then. They enlisted the help of the Rous family, who lived at Halton Barton, just a few miles north of Landulph. Strings were pulled. The windows were whitewashed, to avoid causing offence, but preserved for posterity.'

'Where's all this leading, Ms Hartley? You mentioned Landulph.'

'So I did. A letter from one of the churchwardens, Richard Bawden, has recently come to light. He refers to precautions taken before the '51 crisis. "Our finest window," he writes, "was removed five years prior thereto . . . It was immured safe in the keeping of our staunch friend Mr Mandrell, and is safe there still, I warrant." The letter dates from 1662, two years *after* the Restoration.'

'Why wasn't it brought back and reinstalled?'

'Good question. I think I have the answer. The Rous connection led me to look for Mandrell in the Halton Barton area. The Lowers of nearby Clifton were Royalist sympathisers and High Church. A neighbour of theirs turns out to be one Thomas Mandrell, who was married to a Rous. I think the window was hidden with him. But he died in 1657 and his property was made over to the Parliamentarian holder of the manor of Landulph, Sir Gregory Norton. A Norton continued to live in Mandrell's house after the Restoration. And Bawden says the window was "immured" there, which means walled up in some way. If the new occupant was a Parliamentarian, then it was probably best not to draw his attention to the Royalist treasure lying unsuspected . . . within his walls.'

'And where were these walls?'

'Can't you guess?'

Nick smiled in grudging recognition of the obvious. 'Trennor?'

She nodded. 'In one.'

THEY LEFT THE CHURCH and went into the pub, where they commandeered a fireside table, and returned to the subject of the long-lost and perhaps soon-to-be-found Doom Window of St Neot.

'You're seriously telling me this is all about antique stained glass?'

'Yes, I am. It's Mr Tantris's consuming passion, so I'm told.'

'Has he been down here?'

'Apparently. But he's a recluse. It'll have been a discreet visit.'

'And he wants to buy Trennor on the off chance of finding the missing window there—in a wall, under a floor?'

'It's a rather good chance, actually. The Bawden letter doesn't leave much room for doubt.'

'Except that Trennor's a fair-sized house.'

'Which is why vacant possession is essential. The window will have been dismantled before it was transported to Landulph. That means thirty or more separate panes of glass, wrapped and stored in a large wooden trunk for the journey, then . . . immured. We might have to pull several walls apart to find what we're looking for. That's why Mr Tantris is prepared to be so generous.'

'But he can afford to be.'

'Yes. A rich man indulging his whims. Resent him if you like. But remember Bawden said it was their finest window. It would be an extraordinary find.'

'Quite a career boost for you, I imagine.'

'Absolutely. I don't deny it. It's a wonderful opportunity for me. And not such a bad one for you and your family.'

'Because of the money?'

'Well, yes.' She grinned. 'We all need it, don't we? And from what your sister told me, it doesn't seem likely that any of you would want to hold on to Trennor after your father's death. So it makes sense to accept Mr Tantris's offer.'

'My father doesn't seem to agree. And he's the one who counts.'

'Please do your best to change his mind, Nick. That is, assuming you think he *should* change his mind. Do you?'

'Yes.' He nodded slowly in final acceptance of her argument, swayed in the end as much as anything by her sheer enthusiasm for the Doom Window project. As she had put it, there really seemed no sane alternative to going ahead. 'I rather think I do.'

FROM ST NEOT Nick drove up onto the Moor. He parked near the dam at the southern end of Colliford Reservoir and walked out along the shore, turning the situation over in his mind.

Elspeth would be in Cornwall for another week, she had told Nick. Irene had her mobile number and Elspeth hoped to hear good news before she went back to Bristol. By good news she meant his father's conversion by force of filial argument to the line of least resistance.

The oddest feature of his father's response to Tantris's offer, Nick reflected, was that in normal circumstances he would urge on the search for the window. He was an archaeologist. Excavating the past was the stuff of his professional life. If he had come up with the idea, there would have been no holding him. His intransigence was founded on resentment. Irene was trying to push him. And he did not like to be pushed.

Nor did Nick, come to that. Irene had called him down to dance to her tune and that was precisely what he was doing. He would feel better about all of it if he could rewrite at least part of that tune.

As he gazed out across the reservoir, a way of doing so came suddenly to his mind. He smiled and started back towards the car.

IT WAS ONLY a couple of miles across the Moor to Carwether Farm, but Nick would have hesitated about driving there, even if Irene had not wanted to spring his presence on their brother as a birthday surprise. Nick's relationship with Andrew had always been an edgy one.

The dog was first to detect his approach. It emerged from the shadow of a barn as he drove slowly down the potholed track and it started barking as he passed the open gate. Nick pulled up and glanced hopefully at the house as he turned off the engine.

To his relief, he heard his brother's voice. 'Quiet, Skip.' Skip instantly was. Nick looked away from the house to where the call had come from. And there was Andrew, dressed in a grease-smeared boiler suit, stepping out round the rusting rear of a Land Rover.

His hair was a good deal greyer than when they had last met, his face gaunter, and there was a hint of a stoop. The greyness went further than his hair, probably deeper too. Andrew Paleologus was one day short of fifty, but could have been taken for several years past it. He looked like a man who had been struggling for a long time to achieve something he now knew was beyond him.

Nick got out of the car. Skip growled, but made no move. The two brothers regarded each other solemnly across the yard. 'Hello, Nick,' said Andrew, just when it had begun to seem he might say nothing.

'Hello, Andrew.'

'No need to ask what brings you here.'

'Irene's got me down for your birthday.'

'Glad I could provide her with an excuse.'

'It's only partly that.'

'But the biggest part, I'd say.' He moved closer. 'Want some tea?'

'Tea would be nice.'

'Come on in. You'll have to take me as you find me.'

Nick found him rather as he had expected. The farmhouse was cold and silent, sparsely furnished and echoing to their footfalls. They went into the kitchen, where a range gave off a meagre hint of warmth.

'As soon as Irene told me she'd cook me a Sunday lunch at Trennor for my birthday, I knew it was cover for a family conference,' Andrew said as he filled the teapot. 'It stood to reason you'd be in on it. She was bound to want you down. The question was whether you'd come.'

'Well, here I am.' Nick sat down at the table. In front of him was a large-scale Ordnance Survey map of Bodmin Moor, folded open. Apparently random locations were marked on it with bright red crosses. 'Plotting something, are you?'

Andrew turned from the sink. 'What do you mean by that?'

'These crosses.' Nick smiled to defuse the moment. 'On the map.'

'Oh, those.' Andrew fetched a couple of mugs from the cupboard and plonked them and the teapot down next to the map. 'Yeah. You could say I am. They're a year's worth of recorded sightings.'

'Sightings of what?'

'Big cats.'

'You buy into that? I thought it was just . . . rural myth.'

'They're out there. If you'd seen what was done to one of my ewes last back end, you'd not doubt it.'

'Have you seen one?'

'More than one. Or the same one twice. Most recently, there.' He pointed to one of the crosses closest to Carwether. 'A panther of some kind. Large, loose-limbed and black as pitch, a field away from me.

Dusk, it was. They're nocturnal, of course. Creatures of the night.'

'Dusk can be a confusing time, visually.'

'You don't have to believe me, Nick.' Andrew gave him a half-smile that was almost contemptuous. 'I'll prove it in the end. To everyone.'

'How will you do that?'

'Infrared photography. I've been going out after dark with an image-intensifying video camera and nightscope. I'll get one on tape sooner or later.' Andrew poured the tea, then sat down at the other end of the table. 'Anyway, you're not here to discuss big cats. Fat ones, now, that's a different matter. We seem to have one by the tail.'

'You mean Tantris?'

'You know all about it?'

'I've just met Elspeth Hartley. She filled me in.'

'Persuasive woman.'

'Not as far as Dad's concerned, apparently.'

'He's bound to see it differently.'

'I'd have thought he'd want to be involved in the project. Buried treasure. Historical mystery. Irresistible, surely, to someone who's made a career out of digging up all our yesterdays.'

'You should tell him that, Nick. It might shame him into agreeing.'

'You're in favour of this, are you? Irene said you were, but—'

'Of course I'm in favour. This farm makes less and less money every year. What's the point of struggling on with nothing to show for it and no one to pass the place on to?'

'Tom not interested?'

'I wouldn't know what he's interested in. Haven't heard from him since Christmas. Just a card with his name on it. No message.'

'Is he still in Edinburgh?'

'According to the postmark. His course finished last summer. I didn't even get invited to the degree ceremony. I'm sure Kate went, though. And that Mawson slob.' The references to his ex-wife and her second husband did not suggest any lessening of hostility. But Andrew did not dwell on the point. 'Look, Nick, it'd be crazy to turn our backs on a deal like this. Irene doesn't want to be a pub landlady for the rest of her life any more than Anna wants to go on emptying bedpans. I need the money, God knows. So does Basil. And you're obviously not going to refuse your share. Dad has to be made to appreciate how much we stand to gain.'

'But what does *he* stand to gain?'

'The comfort of knowing he doesn't have to worry about us any more.' Andrew raised a smile. 'Wouldn't you think that'd be enough?'

IRENE WAS NATURALLY PLEASED that Elspeth Hartley had been able to secure Nick's support for Tantris's scheme. And she greeted with enthusiasm Nick's contention that the old man would have to go along with it eventually unless he was willing to sacrifice his scholarly integrity, which they agreed he prized above all things. Viewed in that light, it was an argument they could not lose. Though whether they would win it at Trennor the next day was a different matter.

By the time Nick set off for dinner with Anna and Basil, rain had set in. Rear lights blurred by spray trailed him across the bridge and into the centre of Plymouth. Arriving half an hour early, he parked in Citadel Road, a little way short of Anna's flat, and walked up onto the Hoe. Relishing the cold rain buffeting in from the Sound, he turned east, towards the Barbican.

There was only one other person on the Hoe: a hunched figure in a hooded anorak who was bearing down on him from the other end of the promenade. As the figure drew closer, some quality of posture and bearing suddenly struck Nick as familiar.

'Basil?'

'Nick?' It *was* Basil, his narrow, bony face peering at him from beneath the brim of the hood. 'Trust you to be the only other poor fool game for a stroll on the Hoe in this weather.'

'I got here a touch early.'

'Not a much better excuse than mine. Cooking for a guest makes Anna nervous. And a nervous Anna is a short-tempered Anna.'

'I'm hardly a guest. And since when did Anna get nervous?'

'Since I moved in. She tells me I'm enough to try the patience of a saint. Which is obviously true. I tried the patience of several and am in a position to know that their funds of it weren't inexhaustible.'

'Shall we go and see how she's getting on?'

'There's another twenty minutes yet before you're due. I think we should wait until then.'

'We'll be soaked to the skin by that time.'

'True. But I wasn't thinking of waiting here.'

The nearest pub was the Yard Arm, nestled in the lee of the towering Moat House Hotel just off the Hoe. Basil ordered a tonic water and, thinking of the drive back to Saltash, Nick did the same.

They found a table just inside the door, and only when they sat down did Nick take a serious look at his by now unhooded brother. Like Andrew, he had grown gaunt with age, but unlike Andrew there was no greyness to his features; rather, a strange, animated flush. He had shaved his head, which made his eyes look disproportionately huge. Since he had always possessed a faintly bolt-eyed gaze, the effect on strangers, Nick suspected, would be disquieting.

This was not altogether inappropriate, since Basil had led a disquieting life. More preoccupied with their Greek roots than his brothers and sisters, he had embarked on a classics degree at Oxford. Visiting Greece during the second summer of his studies, he had persuaded an Orthodox monastery near Corinth to take him on as a trainee monk. The training had stretched to more than twenty years, following which he had suddenly reappeared in his relatives' lives, beardless, unhabited and apparently bereft of his monastic vocation. He had lived at Trennor for a while, then had been taken in by Anna.

'I often come in here, you know,' he said. 'I look at the other customers—the groups, the couples, the solitaries like me. I think I'm beginning to understand society. But I've left it too late to join it.'

'Do you miss Greece?'

'Of course. But I had to leave, Nick. I was fooling myself there. And others. Here I amount to very little. But that very little *is* me.'

'See much of Dad?'

'Only under escort. To say I'm a disappointment to him would be a gross understatement.'

'I don't think he's overly impressed with any of us.'

'The record of our achievements is thin, it's true. But mine is so thin as to have disintegrated. Hence I shall take a back seat when you all explain to him tomorrow why he must accept Mr Tantris's offer.'

'You don't sound convinced that he should.'

'Oh, I'm not disputing the logic of acceptance. It's unarguable. Though I suspect Dad *will* argue.'

'So do I.'

'The question is: why?'

'I expect he thinks we're trying to steamroller him.'

'Which we are, of course.'

'For the best of reasons.'

'Really?' Basil cocked a sceptical eyebrow. 'Pardon me, Nick, but the overriding reason is greed, isn't it? Andrew, Irene and Anna want the money. So do you, I presume. It's as simple as that.'

'You seem to have left yourself off the list.'

'Ah well, I *don't* want it, you see. Wealth wouldn't agree with me. I've decided to forgo my share. You can split it between you.'

'You're not serious.'

'I'm in earnest. Don't worry, I'm not going to be holier-than-thou about it. You can all put the proceeds to good use. Dad will be royally pampered at Gorton Lodge. I don't disapprove of the arrangement.'

'You just don't want to profit from it.'

'It's not that. It's something quite pitiful, actually.'

'What?'

'Having nothing is the only knack I've perfected.' Basil shaped a grin. 'I think I'd better hang on to it.'

ANNA'S BASEMENT FLAT was full of garlic fumes when Nick and Basil entered. She emerged from the kitchen, her face as shiny as her PVC apron, greeted without comment their claim to have met in the street and gave Nick a hug and a kiss before hurrying back to the stove with a parting instruction for them to open some wine.

Anna had always been the loudest and most demonstrative of the siblings. She was now also the largest, her curvaceous figure having expanded well beyond buxomness. But she was also the most generous member of the family, which explained why she had been willing to take in an unemployed and unemployable lapsed monk.

The lounge-diner bore no trace of Basil's presence, however, dominated as it was by Anna's exuberant taste in wall-hung rugs and zigzag-patterned armchairs. There were glasses and a bottle of Chianti on the table. Nick found the corkscrew on the mantelpiece, next to a postcard of the Sydney Opera House. He turned the card round and read the message. *Hi, Anna. It's hotter than your curry here, but I'm cool. I'll email soon. Love, Z.* Z, Nick knew, was Anna's eighteen-year-old son, Zack, currently occupied in gap-year globe-trotting and the same age now as Anna had been when he was born.

'No message for his uncle, you'll notice,' said Basil, peering over Nick's shoulder.

'I wouldn't have expected one.'

'I meant for *me*. I do live here, you know.'

'And I'm sure Zack's glad of that. Must be comforting for the lad to know there's someone here to look after his mother.'

'Open the wine,' said Basil, mock-tetchily. 'It's obvious you need a drink.'

For as long as it took them to work their way through Anna's moussaka there was no discussion of the sale of Trennor and their father's future. It was only when Basil had been dispatched to the kitchen to load the dishwasher and a second bottle of Chianti had been opened that Anna decided to make her position clear.

'Irene phoned me after you left this evening and said you saw things our way, Nick. Thank God we don't have to argue about it.'

'Except with Dad.'

'He'll see reason in the end. He can't stay there much longer on his own. Pru found him on the drawing-room floor when she arrived to clean one day a few weeks back. He'd fallen over and couldn't get up. And he drinks too much. It's got steadily worse since Mum died. I don't blame him, but, well, this *is* a golden opportunity to do something about a problem we'd have to face up to sooner or later.'

'I think we should appeal to his professionalism,' Nick said. 'Stress the project's historical importance. If you let Irene emphasise Dad's supposed inability to look after himself, he'll just dig his heels in.'

'OK. I'll restrain her as best I can.'

'Basil tells me he doesn't want his share.'

'That's his vow of poverty for you. Anyway, he can't hold himself totally aloof. If I get the money together to buy a little house, he'll move with me. He'll benefit even if he doesn't profit.'

'It was good of you to take Basil in.'

'No choice, really. He *is* my brother.'

'And counsellor on the world's mysteries,' said Basil, padding in from the kitchen. 'Of which our potential benefactor is a prime example.'

Nick looked up at him. 'How do you mean?'

'Well, who is Mr Tantris exactly? We know nothing about him.'

'He's a rich man with a weakness for antique stained glass,' said Anna. 'He wants to buy Trennor for more than it's worth. What more do we need to know?'

'Aren't you even curious about him?'

'I'm curious about what I'll find to do with his money.'

'It'll be Dad's money, actually.'

'You're so picky, Basil.'

'Is it always as bad as this here?' put in Nick.

'Usually worse,' Basil replied with a cosmetically beatific smile.

CHAPTER TWO

Michael Paleologus at home among his children was as rare a spectacle as it was deceptive. He looked every inch the fond and doting parent, smiling and joking as they gathered round. He appeared both surprised and pleased when Nick arrived with Irene and emphasised how it did his heart good to see them all together.

Only the addition of the words 'here at Trennor', accompanied by a knowing smile, hinted at the argument they had come to present.

Nick's first impression was that Irene and Anna had exaggerated their father's frailty. True, he was rounder-shouldered and thinner than ever, but no more so than the general ageing process could account for. He was dressed as usual in baggy tweed and corduroy and a cardigan whose pockets sagged under the weight of pipe, matches and tobacco pouch. His hair—of which he still had a fine head—was yellowy grey, his eyes blue-green and magnified by the lenses of his glasses, on which Nick noticed a blurring galaxy of fingerprints.

Only when the old man walked any distance—such as from the drawing room to the dining room—did his unsteadiness reveal itself, as he clutched at chair-backs and door frames. Trennor suddenly ceased to seem a place where he could be safely left to live out his days. The rambling layout and inadequate heating were bad enough. But there were also rugs curling at the edges and worn stair-carpet to be taken into consideration, not to mention the treacherously steep steps down to the cellar.

A brittle conviviality prevailed before and during lunch. Andrew put up a decent show of surprise at Nick's presence and pleasure at the presents he was given. Anna talked and laughed too much, Basil too little. Irene steered the conversation between rocks and shallows with finesse. And Nick kept subtle watch on their father, who, it seemed to him, was keeping still subtler watch on all of them.

But Michael Paleologus was also drinking at a pace somewhere between steady and stiff. Whisky had been taken before the birthday champagne. He had not stinted himself on the wine with lunch. And, as the meal drew to a close, he broke out the port. By then his subtlety had faded. 'We drank a toast to Andrew before lunch,' he announced. 'Now I'd like to propose another. I loved your mother dearly and miss her sorely. It's to her memory I'd like to drink. She'd be pleased by this . . . gathering. Pleased that the family's still drawn together from time to time, here at Trennor.' If the last three words had been written down, Nick felt, they would have been italicised. 'To your mother.'

Glasses were clinked and port swallowed. The moment passed, though not all of the tension. Irene had warned Nick that she meant to raise the subject of the Doom Window project over tea, when, according to her, everyone, especially their father, would be relaxed.

After lunch their father retired to the drawing room for a snooze by the fire. Irene and Anna set to in the kitchen, assisted by Basil. Nick accompanied Andrew on a stroll down the lane.

'Before you turned up,' said Andrew, 'Dad asked me if his grandson was likely to put in an appearance. Being my birthday and all.'

'Everyone would have been pleased to see him.'

'Yeah. I'm sure they would. Me especially. No such luck, though. Dad blamed me for Tom's absence, I could tell. Something in his eyes. It's always been there . . . for me. Contempt, that's what it is.'

'Come on. That's not true. None of his grandchildren is here.'

'Laura's a girl, and Zack's illegitimate. They don't count in Dad's scheme of things. Tom's different. Dad sees him as the torchbearer. Except that he *doesn't* see him. Any more than I do. It might be different if you or Basil had married and had sons. To carry on the name.'

'I expect Tom will manage that.'

'But will I know about it?'

'Of course. He's just . . . growing up. I wasn't exactly a model citizen at his age.'

'That's a fact.' Andrew cast him a knowing look.

'I don't suppose Dad was either,' Nick said levelly.

'Maybe not. But it's not his past we have to worry about, is it? It's his future. And ours.' Andrew glanced back at the house. 'I could do with this going well. I really could.'

As NICK AND ANDREW went in through the front door, they were met by Basil emerging from the kitchen.

'Ah, there you are,' he intoned. 'I've been sent to wake Dad. Irene seems to think he'll be in need of coffee.'

'We'll do that,' said Andrew. 'I'd prefer tea, by the way.'

'Coffee for me,' said Nick.

'I'll report back.' Basil grinned and beat a retreat.

They pressed on into the drawing room. Michael was sitting where they had left him by the fire, but he was not asleep.

'Where is everybody?' he asked.

'They're just finishing up in the kitchen.'

'Good. Why don't you two sit down.'

They obeyed, perching together on one of the sofas. Michael took out his pipe and laboriously filled and lit it, studying them through the first puffs of smoke.

'Caught that big cat yet, Andrew?'

'No, Dad.'

'Think you ever will?'

'On videotape, yes. Eventually.'

'What do you think, Nicholas?'

'Me?' Nick had been hoping not to be asked for his opinion. 'Oh, I've got a pretty open mind on the subject.'

'An open mind? That's an excellent thing to have in its way. Pity you've not put it to better use, but . . . there's still time, I suppose.'

'Tell us what *you* think, Dad,' said Andrew, so abruptly that Nick suspected he had intervened for his sake. 'About big cats.'

'What I think, my boy, is that people want to believe in them. Myth can be as powerful as reality. That was one of the first lessons I learned as an archaeologist. Your grandfather and I assisted Ralegh Radford with his excavations at Tintagel in the thirties.'

Nick and Andrew had heard the tale before. The first serious archaeological investigation of Tintagel had begun in 1933, under the supervision of the subsequently celebrated director of the British School at Rome, C. A. Ralegh Radford. Godfrey Paleologus and his teenage son Michael had been among his amateur helpers.

'Those excavations revealed that the castle was constructed, probably in the 1230s, at the behest of Richard, Earl of Cornwall, brother of King Henry the Third. There wasn't a trace of King Arthur. But do you think that stopped people believing they beheld the ruins of Camelot? Of course not. They saw what they wanted to see. Well, much the same applies to your elusive big cats, I'm afraid. They—'

'Beverages and birthday cake ahoy,' announced Basil, propelling the door open with his foot and steering the tea trolley through.

Michael laid his pipe aside, nibbled at his cake and drank his coffee. And then, after Andrew had given a vaguer answer to a vague question from Anna about how it felt to be fifty, he made his move.

'Which of you has been nominated to tell me I've got to go, then?' All eyes were suddenly upon him. He smiled.

'I was going to raise the subject of Mr Tantris's offer, Dad,' said Irene. She set down her cup. 'We all agree it has to be discussed.'

'So, let's discuss it.' Michael beamed at them. 'Tantris has offered me half a million pounds plus my fees at some de luxe old fogeys' home in Tavistock to get his hands on Trennor. Correct?'

'Well, it's not—'

'The full story? No, it isn't, is it? About Tantris we know nothing, except that he has money and an interest in antique stained glass. Miss Hartley the ecclesiastical art historian theorises that the Doom Window of St Neot lies hidden in this house. To get me out, Tantris proposes to pay me about fifty per cent more than the house is worth and to bribe you five with the cost of putting me up in conscience-salving comfort at Gorton Lodge. Since I won't get the chance to spend my savings because I'll die of sheer bloody boredom within a twelvemonth, that'll leave you to share the loot between you.'

'You're painting this in the worst possible light, Dad,' Irene protested. 'We're genuinely concerned about you.'

'You're not getting any younger, Dad,' said Andrew. 'Sooner or later you'll have to move to more practical accommodation.'

'Perhaps I'd prefer that to be later.'

'So might we,' said Irene, 'if this offer hadn't been made. But it has been. We can't ignore it.'

'I'd like to know why not.'

'There's surely a compelling reason that has nothing to do with money,' said Nick, sensing his chance had come.

'And what might that be?' His father's gaze focused on him.

'The Doom Window. A historical mystery. An artistic treasure. An archaeological quest. You should be eager to lead the search, Dad, not trying to obstruct it. I can't believe sentiment is clouding your academic judgment. You'd condemn that in anyone else.'

Michael glowered at Nick. 'Judgment is the key to it, boy,' he growled. 'I don't happen to think tearing this house apart on the say-so of a dubiously qualified chit of a girl—'

'The Bawden letter links Trennor and the St Neot glass,' said Nick. 'Are you questioning Ms Hartley's interpretation of the evidence?'

'You've seen the evidence, have you, boy?'

'Well, no, but—'

'Exactly. You've accepted her word for it. You all have, because it suited you to do so. Trust nothing except primary sources in this game. And not always those. That's my motto.'

'I'm sure Ms Hartley would be delighted to show you the letter.'

'Maybe so. But why hasn't it come to light before?'

'Ask her.'

'I have. Unnoticed until she cast her eye over the archive it was part of. That was her answer.'

'But you don't believe her.'

Michael looked down. 'I'm not saying that.'

Irene sighed. 'Then what *are* you saying, Dad?'

'I'm saying I'm the only unbiased judge of what's best to do.'

'We're biased,' said Anna, 'but you're not? That's . . . ridiculous.'

'If you want to think me ridiculous, fine. But I won't be selling Trennor to a faceless millionaire to facilitate a wild-glass chase *or* to rescue any of you from the financial consequences of your own feck-lessness and there's an end to it.'

They were words uttered in anger, but they told a truth that comforted no one. He believed his children had mismanaged their lives and thereby forfeited the right to prevent him mismanaging his own.

Andrew was first to speak. 'An end to it? Yeah, Dad, it certainly sounds like it to me.' He stood up. 'Reckon I'll be on my way. Before I say something I might regret.'

'Andrew,' said Irene, 'don't go . . .'

But he was already making for the door.

'Let him go if he wants to,' said Michael, shaking his head.

'It's his birthday, Dad,' said Anna. 'Can't you lighten up a little?'

'I remember his real birthday, my girl. The day he was born, fifty years ago. I remember the hopes I had for him. And for the brothers and sisters we planned he would have. Those hopes haven't been fulfilled, not nearly. So, don't ask me to . . . "lighten up".'

Andrew was in the kitchen by now. So was Irene. The others could hear her trying to dissuade him from leaving.

'Have you any idea how hard it's been for Andrew recently, scraping by at Carwether?' asked Anna.

'Farming was his choice, not mine.'

'So what? I'm not asking you to give him careers advice. I'm asking you to sympathise with him. To *understand*. But you can't, can you? Or won't. You refuse to understand any of us.'

'I understand you only too well. As a matter of fact, my girl, I—'

The back door slammed, then Irene came back into the room. 'He's gone,' she said with a sigh. 'There was no talking him out of it.'

'It's not in his nature to take advice,' said Michael, quite neutrally.

'Any more than it's in yours,' snapped Anna.

'On the contrary. I heed the advice of those qualified to give it. I always have. It's how I made a success of my life. Whereas . . .' He smiled at them. 'Well, we demonstrate our own cases.'

'This is hopeless,' said Irene. 'I think I'd like to go home. Nick?'

He shrugged. 'Fine by me.'

'Withdraw and regroup,' said Michael. 'Yes. Quite the best tactic. Retreat to safety and prepare an alternative approach. It won't work, of course.' His smile broadened. 'But don't let me stop you trying.'

'WHY DID WE THINK it would be any different?' Irene asked rhetorically an hour later, in the back bar of the Old Ferry Inn. There were no customers to hear her words, evening opening time still being some way off. Her audience comprised Nick, Anna and Basil. They were sitting round the fire, staring glumly at each other.

'We should take Dad's advice,' Nick said softly.

'*What?*' Anna gaped at him.

'Reasoning with him won't work. He's made his mind up and there's nothing—absolutely nothing—we can do to change it. It's as simple as that.'

'That's pure defeatism,' Irene protested.

'We could change *our* minds,' said Basil. 'Urge Dad to reject the offer.'

Anna made a face. 'You mean on the basis that he'd accept it just to be contrary? You are joking, aren't you?'

Basil grinned at her. 'In the circumstances, what else can one do?'

NICK'S DEPARTURE next morning went unmarked by much in the way of a send-off. Irene was depressed and distracted by the events of the previous afternoon. Nick did not ask what she would tell Elspeth Hartley. She would think of something—in due course.

The morning was grey and mizzly, the Tamar draped in a veil of murk. Nick followed the commuter traffic over the bridge to the Devon shore, paid his toll, then put his foot down as soon as he hit the dual carriageway. It was time to leave. And he was glad of it.

Two and a half hours later he pulled into Delamere Services on the M4 to grab a coffee and stretch his legs. Before getting out of the car he checked his mobile, which he had switched off for the drive. There was a message waiting for him—from Irene.

'Something terrible's happened, Nick. Call me as soon as you can.'

He pushed the car door open, puzzling over her words as he dialled.

'Old Ferry Inn.'

'Irene? It's me. What's happened?'

'Nick. Thank God. Are you at the wheel?'

'No. I'm parked. What—'

'Dad's dead.'

'Sorry?' He could not trust himself to have heard correctly.

'Dad's dead,' Irene sobbed. 'Pru found him this morning.'

'I can't . . . What . . .'

'I know.' She swallowed hard. 'He was so very much alive yesterday. All his wits about him—too much about him, for our liking.' She sniffed. 'Sorry. It's a shock, I know. Sorry to have to inflict it on you.'

'What happened? Was it . . . his heart?'

'No. A fall. Down the cellar steps, apparently. The policeman said he seemed to have hit his head, probably on the handrail.'

Nick closed his eyes. There had been many times in his life when he had wished his father dead. Those times were behind him, buried by the overdue realisation that the mistakes he had made were not his father's fault. Michael Paleologus had been no one's idea of a perfect parent, but the older he became the more Nick had grudgingly admired his refusal to compromise. He had died as he had lived—believing he knew best.

'Nick?'

'Yes. Sorry. A fall, you say?'

'So it seems.'

'He was unsteady on his feet. You were right.'

'I know. But . . . do you think we upset him yesterday, badgering him about selling up? Do you think that might have . . . led to this?'

Nick recalled the expression on the old man's face as he had laid into them the previous afternoon. He had not been angry. He had not even been hurt. He had merely been as self-righteous as ever. 'No, Irene. I don't think so for a moment.'

NICK HAD BEEN CERTAIN he was returning that day to the life he led away and apart from his family. Instead, five hours after driving out of Plymouth, he was driving back into it.

They made a sorrowful gathering in the cramped lounge of Anna's flat. Basil doled out tea, coffee and biscuits as soon as Nick arrived.

Irene gave him a tearful hug. 'The police wanted a formal identification,' she said. 'Andrew and I went.'

'Sod of a place, that mortuary,' put in Andrew. 'Dad lying there, looking as if he might sit up any minute and tell us not to be stupid.'

'He'll be transferred to the chapel of rest tomorrow,' Irene went on. 'After the post-mortem.'

'Post-mortem? I thought you said he'd hit his head.'

'So it seems. But they need to check. There'll be an inquest.'

'Did you . . . see the wound?'

'No. It was at the back of his head, they said. We didn't ask to see it.'

'Have you talked about a date for the funeral?'

'It'll probably be next Monday,' Irene replied. 'You can stay down until then, can't you?'

'Of course.'

'We've made an appointment to see Baskcomb tomorrow.'

'Right. How's Pru?'

'Pretty upset when I saw her,' Anna replied. 'The police had fazed her with their questions. They won't let us into Trennor, you know.'

'What?'

'Just routine,' answered Irene. 'It won't be for long.'

Nick frowned, wondering what was being left unsaid. 'Routine?'

'In case it was not an accident,' said Basil softly. 'They are paid to think of such things.'

THE RAMIFICATIONS of Basil's observation were not discussed until later in the evening. Andrew had asked if anyone wanted to join him for a drink at the Yard Arm before he headed back to Carwether. Sensing there were going to be no other takers, Nick volunteered.

It was a quiet night at the pub. They settled themselves at a corner table and toasted their father's memory in Courage Best Bitter.

'A real shock, eh, Nick? Who'd have thought it, after that vintage performance he put on yesterday?'

'Perhaps it took too much out of him.'

'Less than it took out of me, I'll bet. I'd have made sure we parted on better terms if I'd . . .' He shrugged. 'Well, you know.'

'Yes. I know.'

'It'll take some getting used to. Him not being around, I mean.'

'It certainly will.'

Andrew took a deep swallow of beer. 'Some getting used to, yeah.'

'When I got Irene's message, that something terrible had happened, I thought for a moment . . . that it was you. After the way you stormed out of Trennor.'

'I was pretty upset, Nick, I don't mind admitting. But what's new? Dad's needled me for years.'

'What's new is that he won't be needling you any more.'

'No.' Andrew chuckled wryly. 'And you know what? I'll miss it.'

'Me too.'

'Yeah.' Andrew looked back at his brother. 'Be hard to explain that to anyone, though, wouldn't it?'

'It would.'

'Which is why we ought to keep quiet about yesterday's bust-up. Mention a family row, or Tantris's money, and the police could begin to wonder . . .' He lowered his voice. 'Did he fall or was he pushed?'

'Oh God. You don't think they might, do you?'

'Not if we don't give them any reason to. Obviously we'll accept Tantris's offer, but there'll be a delay. Dad's will will have to be probated, and there's the inquest. We don't need to rush into anything.'

'From what you're saying, we can't.'

'Exactly.' Andrew stared thoughtfully into his beer. 'Tantris isn't going to go away. We just have to bide our time.'

ANDREW HAD PARKED his Land Rover in one of the streets that led up from Citadel Road towards the Hoe. Nick walked to it with him after they left the Yard Arm.

'I'm hoping Tom will come down for the funeral,' said Andrew.

'He's bound to, surely.'

'Only if I succeed in contacting him. All I've reached so far is his answering machine. I could ask Kate if she's got a mobile number for him, but . . . I'd rather not.'

'Won't you tell her about Dad? They used to get on well together.'

'Suppose I'll have to. You don't think she'll want to attend, do you?'

'I don't know.'

'Can't stop her, I suppose. As long as she doesn't bring that smug bastard Mawson with her.'

They came abreast of the car. Andrew unlocked the door, climbed in, wound down the window and started up, the engine spluttering in the cold air. 'See you soon, then. I'll—' Something caught his eye. He gestured through the windscreen at a piece of paper wedged under the wiper. 'Bloody fly posters. Shift that, would you, Nick?'

Nick slid the offending item out from beneath the wiper blade. Before he could examine it, however, Andrew had clunked the Land Rover into gear and pulled away, shouting a good-night as he went.

Nick walked into the pool of light beneath the nearest street lamp and looked at what he held in his hand: a sealed blank white envelope. He tore it open and found himself staring at a condolences card. There was an artist's impression of a candle, beside the words *In Sympathy*. Inside, more words were printed. *Thinking of you at this sad time*. But there was no signature. No name. No message.

AS NICK DROVE BACK to the Old Ferry later that evening, he could not help turning the incident over in his mind. If the card had been dropped through the letterbox at Anna's flat, it would have been puzzling enough. As it was, the message seemed intended for Andrew alone—for reasons Nick could not even guess at.

Irene had closed the pub for the evening. An apologetic sign citing a family bereavement as the reason hung on the door, palely lit by the headlamps of Nick's car as he slowed for the turn into the yard.

He entered by the back door, which had been left unlocked for him, cut through the darkened bar and carried his bag up the stairs. As he reached the top, the television news cut out in the sitting room.

'Nick,' Irene called. 'Join me for a nightcap?'

'OK.'

175

Irene had left Anna's flat half an hour or so before Nick. It looked to him as if she had hit the whisky since then. The heat from the gas fire had filled the room with the smell of it. He poured himself a finger and sat down opposite her, noticing the tears in her eyes.

'Did they tell you . . . exactly when they think he died?' he asked.

'Ten hours or so before Pru found him, apparently.'

'So, late last night. And he was at the bottom of the cellar steps?'

'Yes.' She smiled. 'Maybe he'd gone to fetch a vintage claret to celebrate the defeat of his children.' More tears came.

'Did he have a bottle with him?'

Irene frowned. 'I don't know. Maybe he hadn't got that far.'

'But he must have, if he fell as he was leaving. Why would he be leaving empty-handed?'

'How do you know he fell as he was leaving?'

'Because you told me the injury was to the back of his head.'

Irene's blurred gaze snapped into focus. 'What are you getting at?'

'Nothing. Just . . . trying to understand what happened.'

'What happened was that he slipped or tripped . . . and fell. What difference can it make whether he was coming or going at the time?'

'None, I suppose. Except . . .' Nick took a sip of whisky. 'Andrew reckons we shouldn't mention Tantris's offer to the police.'

'It's none of their business.'

'No. But if they got wind of it, well, they might put two and two together and make five. Like Basil said, they're paid to be suspicious.'

'Rubbish. They're far too busy trying to solve real crimes to waste time looking for imaginary ones.'

Nick sipped some more whisky. 'Have you spoken to Laura?'

'Yes. She's coming down at the weekend. The school were happy for her to leave earlier, but I couldn't see the point.'

'She'll be needing her room. I'll move out to a hotel.'

'Wouldn't it make more sense to stay at Trennor?'

Nick could not deny it, intimidated though he was by the prospect. 'That's settled, then,' he said, before finishing his whisky.

THE NEXT DAY, after Irene had opened up the Old Ferry, Nick slipped out and drove to Landulph. The appointment with Baskcomb was not until four o'clock, which gave him an opportunity to learn what he could from the only person with any first-hand knowledge of the circumstances of his father's death.

Rain was falling and had been since dawn. Nick parked as close as he could to the door of Pru Curnow's cottage, but that was not close enough to spare him a drenching dash through the rain. Fortunately, Pru responded promptly to his yanks at the bell pull.

'Nicholas,' she announced, peering up at him. 'This is a nice surprise. You best ways come in before you drown.'

The front door led straight into the sitting room, which was crammed with bric-a-brac. Pru bustled ahead of him, a tiny figure in a floral housecoat, her white hair recently permed.

'I'm that sorry about your father, Nicholas. 'Twas a fearful shock, I don't mind telling you.'

'It must have been.'

'Will you have some tea? Or sherry? I sometimes have a glass around this time. I had to have several yesterday.'

'All right. Sherry. Thanks.'

Pru poured two glasses of Bristol Cream. 'Here's to your father,' she said, taking a generous sip. 'May he rest in peace.'

They sat down either side of the electric fire, whose glowing bars were emitting a fearsome though narrowly focused beam of heat.

'We're grateful for everything you did, Pru,' said Nick. 'Not just yesterday, I mean. Looking after Dad can't always have been easy.'

'No more it was. But we rubbed along. I'll miss him, temper and all. Have you settled on a date for the funeral?'

'Probably next Monday. We'll let you know when it's confirmed. There'll have to be a post-mortem first, of course.'

'I perfectly understand that. Though why I'm not allowed into Trennor to clear things up in the meantime is a mystery to me.'

'You don't mind going back, then? After what happened?'

'Lord bless you, no. I'm that close to the grave myself that death holds few terrors for me. 'Twas no sight for the squeamish, though.'

'How did you . . . I mean . . .'

'How did I come upon him? Well, I let myself in as usual, around ten o'clock, and there was neither sight nor sound of him. I thought he must have gone out for a walk. Then I noticed the cellar door standing open, with the light on inside. I popped my head round and looked down the steps. And there he was, sprawled on his back at the bottom. I knew he was dead, just by the way he was lying.'

'Poor old Dad.'

Pru set down her glass and stared thoughtfully at it. 'He'd got a little too fond of the liquor these last few years, which can't have helped. That'll be what took him down to the cellar, I dare say. One of those fine wines of his.'

'Did he have a bottle with him?'

'Pardon?' Pru frowned.

'Well, if he went down to fetch a bottle of wine, he'd have had it with him when he left. It would probably have smashed as he fell.'

'There was definitely no smashed bottle. Is it important?'

'Shouldn't think so.'

'Course, he'd been drinking even more just lately. A lot more. I put it down to all the argufying about selling the house.'

'Ah. You know about that, do you?'

'I was at Trennor the day Miss Hartley called round. Your father told me about the offer later. Said I had a right to know, seeing as I'd be out of a job if the sale went through.'

'Look, Pru, we'd have—'

'Oh, don't worry about me, Nicholas. Time I retired, anyhow. Why your father set his face against the sale I wouldn't know. I don't think he quite trusted Miss Hartley, though. I can say that. And I can see why. There was something, well, strange about her.'

'Was there?'

'Like her mentioning you, for one thing.'

'She mentioned *me*—specifically?'

'As she was leaving. I heard them talking at the door. Miss Hartley said, "Are you the father of Nicholas Paleologus?" Like she knew you. But when your father said yes and asked her if she knew you, she said, "No, but I've heard of him." Very peculiar, I thought.'

'What did Dad think?'

'Well, your father asked her what she meant by it, but she only said, "It doesn't matter," then took herself off smartish. I suppose it doesn't matter really, when you come down to it.'

'Probably not,' Nick said. But it mattered. Oh, it mattered all right.

CHAPTER THREE

Nick found himself with plenty to think about over a solitary lunch at the Spaniards, Cargreen's riverside pub. How had Elspeth Hartley heard of him? He had never heard of her. The only answer that came to mind was—

Nick's mobile trilled, causing him to jump with surprise. He pulled the phone out of his pocket and pressed the button. 'Hello.'

'Nick? Elspeth Hartley here.'

'Elspeth.' His heart missed a beat. 'Hi.'

'I've just been speaking to Irene. I was really sorry to hear about your father. It must have been quite a shock.'

'It certainly was.'

'Please accept my condolences.' The old-fashioned sentiment sowed a fleeting suspicion in Nick's mind that she might have already tendered her condolences—anonymously. 'Is this a bad time to talk?'

'No.'

'Good. I phoned Irene to ask if you'd been able to persuade your father to change his mind. I never expected . . . Well, it's just terrible.'

'Yeah.'

'Irene couldn't say much. There were lots of customers in. She suggested I call you and ask . . . well, where we go from here, I suppose.'

'*We* go to see our solicitor. Then we go to our father's funeral.'

'Sorry. Of course. Look, I—'

'Tell you what. Why don't we meet, later today, after the solicitor's said his piece? I should be able to answer your questions then.'

'Great.' She sounded relieved at his change of tone. 'In Plymouth?'

'If that's where you are.'

'It is, yeah. What time would suit you?'

'Six o'clock.'

'Fine with me. Do you know the Compton pub in Mannamead.'

'Can't say I do. But, don't worry, I'll find it.'

BASKCOMB AND CO shared a Georgian terraced house with a dental surgery in The Crescent, on the western fringe of the city centre. Maurice Baskcomb, Michael Paleologus's solicitor, was in his sixties now, Nick calculated, though he looked just as he had in his forties, a ruddy-cheeked, bald-pated, plain-mannered man of the law.

Baskcomb received the Paleologus siblings in his skew-ceilinged office, dressed in a suit that had seen better days. 'I've been in touch with the police and coroner as you requested, Mrs Viner,' he announced, with a nod to Irene. 'Your father's death is not being treated as suspicious, so you may proceed with funerary arrangements.'

'But there'll still have to be an inquest?' asked Andrew.

'In due course, Mr Paleologus, yes. A formality, though. Its only significance is that it will delay the settlement of your father's estate.'

'By how long?'

'That depends on the coroner's schedule.'

'What my brother is concerned about . . .' Irene began.

'Is the offer for Trennor. I quite understand, Mrs Viner. Your father's will is a straightforward document, sharing his estate equally between the five of you and appointing his sons as joint executors along with me, as you know. The estate amounts to Trennor, plus a modest amount of savings. I foresee no difficulties. Even so, it will be several months before probate is granted.'

'Well,' said Irene. 'I suppose it can't be helped.'

'Does that mean we have to wait several months—at least—before selling the house?' asked Anna in her no-nonsense fashion.

'Technically, Miss Paleologus, yes,' Baskcomb replied. 'But there would be nothing to prevent you entering into a provisional agreement to sell, which would come into effect as soon as you obtained title. Of course, you would all need to be party to such an arrangement.'

'Naturally,' said Irene.

'Now, the only other thing I should mention is that I require sight of all financial documentation kept by your father. To which end . . .' Baskcomb ferreted in the drawer of his desk. 'The police have asked me to pass these on to you.' He laid a bunch of keys on the blotter in front of him. The keys to Trennor.

When the meeting had ended they adjourned to Anna's flat. It was agreed that Nick, Irene and Basil would visit Trennor the next morning and go through their father's papers. And as soon as the funeral was out of the way, they would ask Baskcomb to open discussions with Tantris's solicitor about a provisional agreement to sell.

'We need to tell Miss Hartley something,' Irene pointed out.

'Something, but not too much,' stressed Andrew.

'Did she speak to you after phoning me, Nick?' Irene asked.

'Er, yes. Actually . . . I'm seeing her, er, well . . .' Nick glanced at his watch. 'In about half an hour.'

'You might have mentioned it,' said Andrew darkly.

'I was going to. I was just, well . . .' Nick smiled. 'Waiting for a consensus to emerge about what I should say to her.'

'And has one emerged?' Basil enquired innocently.

'Say as little as possible, right?' Nick glanced around and received consenting nods of varying emphasis. 'Well, that's what I'll do. In fact, I'll let her do all the talking.'

IT WAS STILL RAINING when Nick reached the Compton. Elspeth could not have been there long, though she was already a third of a way through a pint of beer. Nick bought himself a half and joined her at a window table. She repeated the condolences she had proffered earlier over the telephone.

'A fall,' Irene said. 'Your father fell down the stairs and hit his head?'

'The cellar steps, actually. It was on the cards, given how unsteady on his feet he'd become. At least it was quick.'

'Very quick.'

Some intonation in Elspeth's voice struck Nick as odd. He frowned at her. 'Sorry?'

'Very quick. Like you said.'

'It was certainly a shock. He was full of life on Sunday.'

'How did the party go?'

'Not very well. Dad didn't . . . see eye to eye with us. Not that it matters now.'

'No. But, Nick, you must realise I'd much rather your father was alive and you'd been able to talk him round. Nobody—including Mr Tantris—is going to take any pleasure from this turn of events.'

'I thought you'd never met Tantris.'

'I haven't. But as far as I know—'

'How far's that?'

Elspeth looked at him for a moment. 'Is something wrong?'

'Not sure.'

She drank some beer. 'What do you mean?'

'Had you and I met before Saturday?'

'No. Of course not.'

'In that case why did you ask my father about me? Specifically *me*.'

'Ah. He mentioned that, did he?' Elspeth's gaze shifted evasively.

'His housekeeper told me. She overheard your conversation.'

'I should never have asked him.' She ran a hand through her hair. 'It was a spur-of-the-moment thing.'

'And what was the spur?'

'No getting round it, is there? I was there, Nick. Cambridge, graduation day 1979.' She smiled. 'I wouldn't have recognised you. But your name stuck in my mind.'

'You were there?'

'Went with my mother to see my brother pick up his BA.'

'You were there?' Nick repeated numbly. 'Oh God.'

'It's not so bad.'

'Yes, it is. I've tried very hard to forget about it, you see.'

'Sorry to remind you.'

'Thanks. I'm sorry to *be* reminded.'

That was about as big as understatements come. Nick had fortified himself against his previous existence as the academic prodigy who had gone up to Cambridge at the age of sixteen laden with early attainment and infinite promise, only to emulate his brother Basil by failing to stay the course. Technically, he *had* graduated, thanks to the award of an aegrotat in recognition of his illness. But the university authorities might have thought twice about that had they realised he would force his way into the Senate House on graduation day and strip in the midst of the ceremony. Mercifully, Nick had no recollection of his actions that day, nor many days before and after. There were long months of separation from reality and still longer years of slow reacquaintance with it. Not that he *had* completely recovered. Like a reformed alcoholic, he carried the affliction with him. And that was what hurt him most to be reminded of.

'What did your brother read?' Nick asked irrelevantly.

'Land Economy. At the time when it happened—your graduation-day stunt, I mean—I laughed. It had been pretty boring up until then, all that ermine-hooded processional. Later, when I read a piece about you in one of the papers, I thought it was sad.'

'Sad *and* laughable. That's about spot-on.'

'What went wrong, Nick?'

'Didn't the papers tell you?'

'"Too young to handle the pressure" is more or less what they said.'

'And it's more or less true. Complicated by poor social functioning, according to one of several psychiatrists I was treated by. My intellectual overdevelopment was a camouflage for my emotional *under*-development—apparently.' Nick smiled, failing to relax the tension gripping him. 'Or you could take my father's line: I funked it.'

'What happened to you . . . afterwards?'

'Mental hospital. To tell you the truth, I'm not the right person to ask what really happened. "Out of your mind" can mean literally that.'

'But you came through it.'

'So it seems.'

'What do you do now? Irene said you work for some quango.'

'English Partnerships. You know, urban regeneration and all that.'

'Where do they hang out?'

'Milton Keynes. Excited yet?'

'Do you enjoy your work?'

'Too soon to say.'

'How long have you been there?'

'Eight years.'

Elspeth laughed. 'OK. Change of subject. How well do you know Istanbul?'

'Never been there.'

'You're a Paleologus. And you've never been to Istanbul?'

'Paleologus is my name, nothing more.'

'You're not affected by its history?'

'I try not to be.'

'A vain effort, I should have thought. History's part of us, like it or not. History is why we're sitting here talking to each other.'

'History is your profession, Elspeth. Naturally it affects you. It's nice of you to have expressed regret at my father's death, but I do understand you must be looking forward to the search for the Doom Window. This has probably brought that search a good deal closer.'

'Not for me. I've decided to bale out. I won't be doing any searching at Trennor. Tantris will have to find someone else to do it.'

'I don't understand. Why?'

'Because research is my forte and there's plenty more waiting for me elsewhere. My task was to dig out the facts and try to win your father over. The first I've done. The second . . . is sadly no longer relevant. Your solicitor can talk to Tantris's solicitor and take it from there. I'm heading back to Bristol.'

'When?'

'Tomorrow.' She grinned at him lopsidedly. 'So, this is a farewell drink. Fancy another?'

NICK WAS UNSURE which had been the greater shock: Elspeth's knowledge of his breakdown at Cambridge or her abrupt detachment from his family's dealings with Tantris. Why was she passing up the chance of all that academic kudos the Doom Window's discovery would confer? Purely in career terms, her decision made no sense.

He should have questioned her more closely. But he did not wish to confront the possibility that Elspeth was pulling out for reasons connected with his father's death. The fear of knowing too much balanced the fear of knowing too little.

Only after Basil had arrived by bus from Plymouth to join Irene and him in their document hunt at Trennor did Nick mention Elspeth's departure from their lives.

Irene, though puzzled, made little of it. 'I imagine it'll be her loss in the long run, but it's really not our concern, is it?'

Basil, on the other hand, was inclined to think it could well be. 'Do you believe that?' he asked, after Nick had reported her explanation.

To which Nick could only say, 'Why should she lie?'

Why indeed? Basil gave him an elder-brotherly look, then quietly observed, 'One object of a lie is to conceal the purpose of its telling.'

NICK, BASIL AND IRENE stood at the top of the cellar steps, looking down at the place where their father had died. There was nothing to mark the exact spot. Dusty sixty-watt light fell on the concrete treads and wooden handrail, shone back dully from the grey-painted floor and gleamed dimly on the necks of racked clarets.

'What's the name of the policeman you spoke to, Irene?' Nick asked.

'DC Wise. He's based at Crownhill.'

'Maybe I should ask him about the bottle.'

'What bottle might that be?' asked Basil.

'The one Nick thinks Dad should have dropped when he fell,' said Irene with a sigh. 'He's like a dog with a bone about it.'

'Pru says there was no bottle.'

'So, why go on about it?' Irene responded.

'Because Dad came down here to fetch a bottle of wine. That's obvious. What's not obvious is why he should leave without one.'

'Perhaps he changed his mind,' said Basil. 'Perhaps the telephone rang. Perhaps he remembered something.'

'Exactly,' said Irene. 'There's no reason for you to speak to DC Wise, Nick. He'll only be confused by you querying the circumstances.'

'Confusion is not a condition we should wish upon the constabulary,' murmured Basil. 'It can so often be transmuted into suspicion.'

Irene flashed a glare at both of them, then said, 'Why don't you two start looking for the papers Baskcomb wants while I vacuum up the worst of the dirt that the police tramped into the house? We have work to do. Remember?'

Nick and Basil set to, though with little enthusiasm. The study was their father's sanctum. In life, he would have been apoplectic to find them rifling through his desk. But they were thwarted at the outset on discovering that one of the drawers was locked. Basil began a hunt for the key, while Nick worked his way through the filing cabinet. He soon came upon bundles of bank statements and bills. These he put to one side. As far as he could see, most of the remaining space was devoted to academic correspondence from years back. Michael Paleologus had devoted too much of his life to retrieving the past to discard the records of his own.

That was one reason why Nick persisted in the search. He was looking for something more than financial records and reckoned he would find it. When Basil's hunt for the desk key took him out of the study, Nick had the room to himself.

In the bottom drawer of the cabinet, he found it: a bulging manila file with his name written on it in faded black felt-tip. He heaved the folder out onto the desk and leafed apprehensively through the contents. It was all there: letters to and from his college and the hospital he had been sent to, tracking his breakdown and five years of treatment. There were bills too, substantial ones, from his psychiatrist.

Nick pulled open one of the unlocked desk drawers in search of an envelope large enough to hold the contents of the folder. They would be leaving with him. In his haste, he yanked the drawer out as far as it would come. A slew of paperclips, pencils and assorted envelopes slid forward with the momentum, leaving the rear of the drawer empty. Except, Nick noticed, for a strip of insulating tape, stuck to the base. There was an object held beneath it. He stretched out his hand and ran his fingers over the small bulge. It felt like a key.

Nick prised the tape loose with his thumbnail, picked up the key and slid it into the keyhole of the locked drawer. The lock released at the first turn. He pulled the drawer open.

Inside there was just one object: a large white envelope, bearing the words, written in his father's hand, *Last Will and Testament*. Nick lifted the envelope and slid out the contents: a single sheet of paper. It was certainly his father's will. But it was not the one lodged with Baskcomb, and the date on it was much more recent. The document was handwritten, succinct but legalistically worded:

This is the last will and testament of me Michael Godfrey Paleologus of Trennor Landulph Cornwall which I make this fifteenth day of January 2001 and whereby I revoke all previous wills and testamentary dispositions.

I hereby appoint my cousin Demetrius Andronicus Paleologus of Palazzo Falcetto San Polo 3150 Venezia Italy to be the sole executor of this my will.

I give my house the aforementioned Trennor Landulph Cornwall and all its contents to my cousin the aforementioned Demetrius Andronicus Paleologus. I give the remainder of my property real and personal in equal shares to my children.

Nick stared at the words, transfixed. His father had written them, there was no doubt, and had signed his name beneath them. Two witnesses had also signed: Frederick Davey, retired quarryman, and Margaret Davey, housewife, of 3 Butcher's Row, Tintagel, Cornwall.

'Keyless in Trennor isn't a lot better than eyeless in Gaza,' said Basil, re-entering the study. 'But such is our—' He stopped, the stillness of Nick's posture seizing his attention. 'Is something wrong?'

'I found the key,' said Nick.

'Splendid.'

'You won't think so when you read this.' He held up the will.

Basil walked across to the desk and took the sheet of paper from his brother's hand. 'My, my,' he said when he had finished reading it.

'What do we do?' Nick asked.

'What do we do?' Basil smiled. 'We ask Irene, of course.' The vacuum cleaner was roaring somewhere in the house. 'I'll fetch her.' He dropped the document on the blotter and hurried from the room.

A moment later, Irene bustled into the room, Basil lagging a few yards behind. 'What's this about a will?' she demanded.

'See for yourself.' Nick passed her the sheet of paper.

It took no more than three seconds for Irene to grasp the significance of what she held in her hand. 'The will Baskcomb has dates from a few months after Mum died. This is dated . . . last week.'

'Quite,' said Basil.

'It's not been drawn up by a solicitor. Is it valid?'

'Signatures of the testator and two witnesses are all that's required, I believe. And there they are. It's clearly not a forgery. So, the answer to your question must be yes.'

'I've never heard of a cousin Demetrius.'

'Nor have I,' Nick joined in.

'Which makes three of us,' said Basil.

'"The remainder of my property real and personal",' Irene continued. 'What will that amount to?'

'Without Trennor, very little.'

'I don't believe it. Why would Dad do this to us?'

'To prevent us selling the house to Tantris,' said Nick.

Irene glared down at the will. 'We'll see about that.'

'What do you have in mind?' asked Nick.

'It's handwritten. So, there's no copy. And no solicitor's involved. The only living people who know of the will's existence are we three plus the Daveys. And the Daveys may not even know what's in it.'

'Are you suggesting what I think you're suggesting?' enquired Basil.

'What do you *think* I'm suggesting?'

'Something deeply criminal. Besides, how can you be sure no one else knows? Dad may have advised cousin Demetrius of his intentions.'

'But cousin Demetrius isn't here. We are. As is the will.'

'Even so—'

'Call Andrew and Anna. A family conference is in order.' Irene dropped the will onto the desk. 'There's a great deal to discuss . . . before we do anything.'

ANNA'S SHIFT DID NOT END until midafternoon and Andrew was likely to be out and about on the farm until dusk, so the family conference could not take place before early evening. Irene went back to Saltash to open up for lunchtime at the Old Ferry. Nick engineered a solitary moment in which to stuff the contents of the file about his breakdown into an envelope and take it out to his car. Then he accompanied Basil into Cargreen on foot. They were to call on Pru to tell her she could resume cleaning duties at Trennor whenever she wished, and to tap the old lady for information about their father's activities on January 15, the date he had recorded on the will, which was the Monday of the previous week.

Persuaded to review her employer's activities for that week on the grounds that they might yield signs he had been doing too much, Pru was adamant that he had had no visitors from outside the family circle and had gone out only on Monday . . . the 15th.

'He left not long after I got there and hadn't got back by the time I left. He didn't say where he was going, but there was nothing out of the ordinary about that. 'Twas no concern of mine.'

'Which means,' Basil soundly reasoned after they had adjourned to the Spaniards pub, 'that he took the will up to Tintagel for the Daveys to witness. Irene's idea that they might be unaware of the contents strikes me as even less plausible now.'

'But who are the Daveys, Basil?'

'I don't know. Could Fred Davey have been employed on the Tintagel dig, do you suppose? Quarrying's a similar line of work.'

'In the thirties, you mean? If so, he must be at least as old as Dad.'

'Yes.' Basil stared thoughtfully into his cider. 'The same generation. Like cousin Demetrius.'

'Why did Dad never tell us about Demetrius?'

'Perhaps he only found out about him recently.'

'And was so bowled over by the experience that he decided to leave him the house? It doesn't make sense.'

'It made good sense to Dad. The question, Nick, is why.'

WHEN THE TIME CAME, it was Anna who presented the clearest case.

'If we take this to Baskcomb, he'll have to abide by it. Maybe we can contest it, but we might lose and have nothing but a fat legal bill to show for it. Dad inherited this house from Granddad and we should inherit it in turn. I don't think he had the right—morally—to leave it to some cousin we've never met. We should stand by the earlier will and destroy this one. Even if the Daveys or cousin Demetrius know what's in it, they can't know for certain that Dad didn't destroy it himself. The fact that he left it here suggests he might have had second thoughts. So let's give ourselves the benefit of the doubt.'

Doubt there certainly was in Nick's mind as he listened to Anna. He suspected that the old man had deliberately bequeathed them this dilemma; that he had given them a stark but by no means simple choice; and that he had been certain of what they would choose.

'I agree with Anna,' said Irene. 'Besides, I don't think Dad meant to go through with it. I suspect he intended to threaten us with disinheritance and use this document to persuade us he meant it.'

'I don't care whether he meant it or not,' growled Andrew. 'Once the will's gone, no one can prove anything. It's obvious what we should do. I don't know what we're waiting for.'

For everyone to have their say, of course. Nick cleared his throat uneasily, struggling to find the words to replace the only ones that came into his head. '*We want the money. And we mean to take it.*' No, that would not do. Instead, all he could say was, 'I agree.'

'That we should destroy the will?' Irene's tone was insistent.

'Yes.'

'Basil?'

'Ah.' Basil leaned forward. 'My turn, is it?'

'Here we go,' muttered Andrew.

'Fear not,' said Basil, with a sidelong glance at his brother. 'I shall not attempt to dissuade you. When President Nixon's advisers came to him to report some damaging leak to the press, he was wont to ask, not whether the allegation against his administration was true or false, but whether it was deniable. Well, to apply the Nixon test, is destroying the will deniable? The answer, obviously, is yes.'

'Does that mean you agree?' asked Anna.

'It means I regard its destruction as inevitable.'

'Once we've done this,' said Irene, 'there's no turning back. We must behave as if we've never heard of a cousin Demetrius or a Mr and Mrs Davey. We must forget the will ever existed. None of us must breathe a word to anyone.' There were nods of assent, even, albeit tardily, from Basil. 'We draw a line under the whole business. All right?' There was another round of nods. 'That's settled, then.'

'Good,' said Andrew, jumping up and plucking the will from the coffee table. 'As the eldest, I think this is my prerogative.'

He tore the envelope and its contents into four, took two strides to the fireplace and tossed the fragments in among the blazing logs. The paper curled and blackened and flamed . . . and was gone.

OVER THE NEXT COUPLE OF DAYS arrangements were finalised for the funeral and a headstone was ordered. Baskcomb took delivery of the financial documentation they had assembled and set about probating what he believed was his late client's only will. Nick telephoned his father's friends and former colleagues to determine who would be attending the funeral.

He had to move out of the Old Ferry to make way for Laura and live for several days at Trennor. On Friday evening, he drove up through the rain from Saltash with his few belongings.

When he reached Trennor, the house's dark and empty present seemed to him a feeble reality to set against its teeming past. He switched on lights in every room and turned one of his mother's Maria Callas CDs up loud on the hi-fi.

Pru had made up a bed for him in his old room, and had left him a casserole to put in the oven. He set it to warm, lit the fire in the drawing room, then hunted around for a bottle of wine. He drew a blank, which supported his theory that his father had gone down to the cellar specifically to fetch some wine. Nick had not been down there since the old man's death. It was time, he decided, to cross that line.

The cellar was still and silent, the walls and floor coated with grey masonry paint that made it resemble the hull of a ship. Most of the space was taken up with wine racks. Nick and Basil had been banned from the cellar during their childhood following an incident when a bottle had been dislodged from one of the racks and broken. 'A '61 St Emilion sacrificed to the stupidity of two small boys,' as their father had raged at the time. Nick smiled at the recollection.

The breakage had happened because of his attempt to conceal himself in the narrow gap between the far wall and the last rack, which was single-sided, during a game of hide-and-seek. He walked along to the rack to remind himself just how narrow the gap really was.

But it was not there. The rack was hard against the wall. Nick was puzzled. Glancing down, he saw that some of the paint had been scraped from the floor. There were curved grooves in the surface, as if the rack had been pulled away from the wall at one end.

Nick crouched down for a closer look. Yes, that was the only possible explanation. But who had moved the rack? Surely it could only be his father. Was that why he had come down there on the night of his death? It would at least explain why he had left without a bottle.

'Nick?'

Nick started violently at the sound of Andrew's voice. He stood and turned to see his brother descending the steps.

'Not planning to drink our inheritance, are you?'

'God, you nearly gave me a heart attack,' Nick complained, aware of the thumping in his chest. 'Couldn't you have rung the doorbell?'

'I did, but I got no answer, so I let myself in. You can't hear the bell down here. I thought I'd see if you were all right. First night alone in the old place and all that. Something in the kitchen smells good.'

'One of Pru's casseroles.'

'Which you're planning to wash down with a Château Lafite before we can auction the lot off and share the proceeds?'

'That's right. You've caught me in the act.'

'Never mind. Break out one for me and we'll say no more about it.' Andrew walked up to where Nick was standing. 'Actually, though, I think it's all whites down this end.'

'What do you make of this?' Nick pointed to the marks on the floor.

Andrew looked down. 'Somebody's moved the rack.'

'Dad?'

'Who else?'

'Why would he want to?'

'Search me.' Andrew glanced around, turning the matter over in his mind. 'Shall we just forget about it?'

'I don't think I can.'

Andrew smiled. 'Me neither.'

They transferred the bottles to spare slots in the next rack. The empty rack was no great weight, and they lifted it clear of the wall without much difficulty. Nothing sinister revealed itself at first glance.

Then Nick noticed something: an unevenness in the otherwise smooth surface of the floor. Peering closer, he saw two lines of roughness, like flattened ridges, leading out at right angles from the wall, and a third linking them, running along close to the foot of the wall.

They moved the rack as far across as they could for a clearer view. This revealed a fourth line, further out and parallel to the wall, completing a rectangle about six feet by three. Nick stepped into the gap they had opened up between rack and wall and walked along to the rectangular patch of floor. Something felt different as he trod on it.

'Is there a hammer over there?' Nick pointed to a shelf behind Andrew where various tools were stored.

'Yeah.' Andrew passed him a wooden-handled ball-pein hammer.

Nick crouched down and tapped the floor either side of the line around the suspicious patch. 'This part sounds hollow.'

'It can't be. There's never been anything below here.'

'Well, it sounds like there is now. And this line round here? At a guess, I'd say somebody's dug a hole, laid a slab across it, cemented it in and painted it over. Then pushed the rack over the top to hide it.'

Andrew tried hammering for himself. 'You could be right.'

'It has to be Dad who did this. You don't remember him doing any . . . digging?'

'Nope. Anyway, why would he want to dig a hole down here?'

'To . . . hide something.'

Andrew's eyes narrowed. 'It couldn't be the window, could it? Dad couldn't have found it and hidden it down here to spite us?'

'This hole wasn't dug last week. And it must be years since Dad was physically capable of the work involved.'

'But he must have done it, or got somebody else to do it.' Andrew shook his head. 'I don't know what to make of it. But when Tantris gets his hands on this house, that hole will be opened up.'

Nick sighed. 'I doubt he'll find the Doom Window down there.'

'Me too.' Andrew smiled mischievously. 'But why wait to find out?'

They went back upstairs, and Nick turned off the oven, his appetite suddenly gone, while Andrew fetched from the barn the tools he reckoned he would need for the job: sledgehammer, chisel, crowbar, shovel. Then they lugged them down into the cellar.

Andrew peeled off his sweater and rolled up his shirtsleeves, then crouched over the slab and tapped it with the chisel, flaking off some of the paint to reveal the fine-grained granitic stone beneath.

'Looks like elvan. One good blow should do it.' With that he stood up, grasped the sledgehammer and let fly.

One good blow was not, in the event, enough. Debris sprayed up from the slab, pinging against the metalwork of the empty rack. Only at the third blow was there a loud crack. Stepping closer with the torch, Nick saw a jagged line across the centre of the slab.

'That's got it,' said Andrew. He moved back and aimed at the crack. This time the slab broke, a chunk falling into the space below, leaving a jagged hole about a foot across. 'Give me that torch.'

But as Andrew turned to take it, Nick recoiled, amazed to see a swarm of tiny flies rising from the hole. A strong smell hit him in the same instant, not just of stale air but of something much fouler.

'Bloody hell.' Andrew coughed. 'What in God's name . . .?'

Nick moved forward, batting his way through the flies. He trained the torch on the hole and saw . . . the rib cage of a skeleton.

'Christ almighty,' murmured Andrew. 'Is that what it looks like?'

'I hope not.'

'Get out of the way.' Andrew cast the sledgehammer aside and fetched the crowbar. 'Let's see for sure what's there.'

He wedged the crowbar under the slab on the far side of the hole and levered it up. Cement cracked off at the margins as the slab rose. Nick craned round him and shone the torch into the space below.

And there, beyond the rib cage, was the skull, unquestionably human, staring back at them through empty eye sockets, with flies crawling across the bone and the suety remnants of flesh.

But the flies were not what caused Nick to mutter 'My God!' An inch or so above the left eye socket there was a large, splintered hole in the bone. There was no doubt in Nick's mind: they were not looking at the remains of someone who had met a natural death.

CHAPTER FOUR

Nick and Andrew covered the broken slab with a tarpaulin their father had kept in the garage and stood the empty rack back across it. Then they left the cellar, locking the door behind them.

Andrew led the way back into the drawing room and poured large Scotches for both of them. He sipped his while leaning against the mantelpiece, on which was a photograph of their parents on their ruby-wedding anniversary in 1989. 'Think that was down there then?' he asked, tapping the frame. 'Think Mum knew about it?'

'I doubt it.'

'Bloody difficult to overlook. Burying a corpse in the cellar. Not to mention turning some poor sod into a corpse in the first place.'

'We don't know what happened.'

'We know what killed him, though. A hole in the head. And I don't reckon he got it accidentally.'

'I'm no pathologist, Andrew. Nor are you. There are human remains under the cellar. That's all we can be sure of.'

'Not quite. We can also be sure we're supposed to report a discovery like this to the police. Then they can call in the experts. Establish sex, age, cause of death, date of death—all that stuff.'

'You're right.'

'Is that what you think we should do, then?'

'I suppose so.'

'Really?' Andrew flopped down into an armchair opposite Nick. 'Just let's talk it through. It won't only be this house the police start swarming all over. It'll be our family's past. Whoever Joe Skeleton is, somebody did him in. Dad's got to be the prime suspect. And the police will give *us* the third degree in his absence. They'll look at every angle, every single dark and dirty theory they can come up with. And then there'll be the media. Journalists hanging on my gate, ringing your doorbell. Before you can say "No comment" they'll haul your five minutes of fame in Cambridge out of the archives.'

'Surely not.' But even as he said it, Nick sensed that Andrew was right. 'Well, OK. Maybe it would pan out like that. But—'

'And what about Tantris? A wealthy recluse like him might be scared off by tabloid headlines with the word murder in them.'

'Yeah. He might. But what alternative is there, Andrew?'

'We could cover it over again. Pretend we knew nothing about it.'

'And leave Tantris's people to find it? They'd call in the police.'

'All right.' Andrew thumped the arm of the chair in irritation. 'There's no easy answer. I admit it. Our father is likely to be branded a murderer. It looks as if he almost certainly *was* a murderer, though who he murdered—and why—we haven't a clue.'

'You don't know it was murder. It could have been self-defence.'

'Yeah. It could. I'm happy to believe it was. But will the law be? I doubt it.' A slow frown of realisation crossed Andrew's face. 'Hold on. Is this why Dad changed his will?'

'Maybe. It certainly explains his refusal to sell the house.'

'Yeah. He couldn't, could he? Not to someone who wanted to start checking it over for hidey-holes. And he knew we'd sell the house to Tantris after his death, which meant the body was bound to be discovered. He didn't want to be remembered as a murderer. His reputation was always important to him. So he disinherited us.'

'And that means he was confident cousin Demetrius wouldn't sell. The risk of discovery would be just as great otherwise. So Demetrius knows about the body. He may even have helped put it there.'

'Bloody hell.' Andrew sat back in his chair. 'Who *is* this Demetrius?'

Nick shook his head. 'No idea.'

'What do we do about him?'

'There's nothing we *can* do. We can't even mention him to the police without admitting we destroyed the will.' Nick sighed. 'A will that could have been a valuable piece of evidence in a murder inquiry.'

'Which we put on the fire. Well, *I* did.'

'We all agreed. We thought we could get away with it.'

'And we still can.' Andrew sat forward again, his eyes suddenly wide. 'Don't you see, Nick? It makes no difference whether we go to the police or leave it to Tantris. We're buggered either way.'

'No, no. Going to them now has to be less risky.'

'Except for the money. If Tantris took fright, where would we find another bidder for this place? Murder sells papers, not houses. I need my share, Nick. Going to the police is a risk I can't afford to take.'

'We can't ignore what's down in that cellar, Andrew.'

'I'm not suggesting we should. We could take the body out. Lose it somewhere. Cornwall's not short of old mine shafts.'

'You're not serious.'

'Why not? I reckon it's an easy two-man job. These mine shafts are dangerous places. Nobody pokes around in them.'

'Sure of that, are you?'

'Pretty sure. But would it matter if a skeleton was found down one a year or so from now? There'd be nothing to connect it with us.'

'Assuming we weren't spotted dumping it.'

'We wouldn't be. For God's sake, Nick. Out on the Moor after dark? The chances of being seen are thousands to one.'

'You're really willing to go through with this, aren't you?'

'You bet.'

'What about Basil and the girls?'

'Spare them the angst. We don't have long. Laura's due to arrive tomorrow, Tom the day after. What the others don't know about they won't worry about. You and I can solve the problem. Together.'

'Yeah, but—'

'Don't turn me down, Nick. I've never asked much of you. And I've never begged for anything. But I'm begging now. I need your help.'

ANDREW SPENT the night at Trennor. Nick knew that his brother was determined to reach a decision, but he feared that every decision was the wrong one. There was too much they did not know.

When he eventually went to bed in the small hours, Nick could not sleep, his mind racing in pursuit of an unattainable truth. Ever since arriving in Saltash one short week before, what he had most wanted was to leave again, free of family cares, unfettered by sibling woes. Now that happy state seemed like an impossible dream. Unless . . .

'I'LL DO IT.' Nick held Andrew's gaze across the kitchen, greyly filling with dawn twilight. 'I'll help you dump the body.'

He had entered to find his brother sipping from a mug of tea, staring out through the streaks of rain on the window. Then, hearing his tread, Andrew had turned to face him.

'You will?'

'Yeah. I can't face the prospect of this taking over my life. If I thought the police would take it all off our shoulders and leave us in peace, I'd happily let them. But it wouldn't be like that, would it?'

'Not a chance. My way, it's done and dusted in twenty-four hours.'

'Let's hope so.'

'Can't fail. Look, I reckon I've thought of a good site for this. Why don't we drive over there and take a look? If it seems OK, we can go back tonight and get the job done.'

'And if it doesn't seem OK?'

'We find somewhere else.'

They set off in separate cars, so that Andrew could carry on to Carwether afterwards. Their destination was the village of Minions, on the southeastern edge of Bodmin Moor. Nick knew the area from family outings to the ruins of the nearby Phoenix Mines.

The car park at Minions commanded a view of Dartmoor to the east and the sea to the south, with Caradon Hill and its giant television transmitter bulking large in the foreground. It was an exposed spot, and drifts of hail whitened the track of the long-vanished railway that had once served the district's tin and copper mines. There were a few dog-walkers about, but they were hardly likely to see anything odd in two men without a dog setting off north along the track.

'Most of the shafts round here have been capped,' said Andrew as they strode along. 'Hope they haven't got round to all of them.'

Ten minutes' brisk walking took them to a shelf of land on the highest stretch of the line. A lane wound up the valley from Minions in the direction of various farms and hamlets to the north.

'See that clump of trees down by the lane?'

'Yeah.'

'There's a shaft in there. I can remember heaving a rock down it when we were boys to see how deep it was.'

'And how deep was it?'

'Deep enough.'

'Close to a road, I see.'

'Just what I was thinking. Let's go and check it out.'

They made their way down the uneven slope through gorse and bracken and tussocky grass, and reached the clump of trees. A barbed-wire fence about five feet high, reinforced in several places, enclosed the trees and the overgrown ruin of an engine house.

Andrew prowled round the perimeter until he got a clear view of the shaft. Nick joined him and peered through the undergrowth. The open mouth of the shaft was only a few feet beyond the fence.

'Looks like we're in luck.'

'We need to be sure.' Andrew prised a large stone from the nearby turf and tossed it over the fence. They listened and counted the seconds as it vanished into the shaft. Nick had made it to six by the time it clanged against something metallic far below and came to rest.

'Like you said: deep enough.'

'This barbed wire is the only problem.' Andrew looked around. There was no one in sight. He reached into his pocket, took out a pair of pliers and stooped by the nearest fence post. 'I'll pull out a few of the staples.' Minutes later he stood up. 'That should do it.'

They walked clear of the fence and looked down the slope to the lane. It was no more than twenty feet to the verge.

'When do you want to do this?' Nick asked.

'Tonight. I'll come to Trennor around eleven.'

'There's something you ought to know before then.'

On the way back to the car park, Nick told Andrew about the condolences card left under the Land Rover's windscreen wiper in Plymouth on Monday night. 'It might not be important,' he said. 'But the card, the will, the body in the cellar: they all point to events and people that we have no knowledge of.'

'You're probably right. But one of the few pieces of good advice Dad ever gave me was "Don't worry about what you can't control." This'—he gestured back towards the shaft—'I *can* control.'

'And the rest?'

'Won't be any concern of mine or yours once we've emptied that hole under the cellar.' Andrew grinned. 'And banked Tantris's cheque.'

WHEN NICK GOT BACK to Trennor he found a strange car parked in the yard. As Pru shortly afterwards explained, in a whispered conversation in the kitchen, they had a visitor. Or rather, strictly speaking, Michael Paleologus had a visitor.

'I've put him in the drawing room, Nicholas. He was real shook up when I told him your father had passed away.'

'Who is he?'

'Says his name's David Anderson. A former student of your father's, apparently. He was expecting to see him today.'

David Anderson looked to be in his early forties, a bulky figure with a mane of greying curly hair and a ready smile.

'Mr Paleologus. Good to meet you. You're, er, Michael's son?'

'One of his sons, yes.'

'I'm sorry to hear what's happened. A fall, your housekeeper said.'

'Yes. Last Sunday. He'd been increasingly frail for quite a while. An accident was always on the cards, I'm afraid.'

'He sounded as sharp as ever when I spoke to him.'

'When did you . . . speak to him?'

'He got in touch with me about ten days ago.'

'Uh-huh. You'd stayed in contact since Oxford, had you?'

'Off and on. I teach history at Sherborne. Michael helped me get the job. So, I'd always have been happy to do him a favour. This is the first time he's actually asked.'

'What did he want you to do?'

'Just a spot of research. Straightforward, really, though fitting it in round my teaching was a bit of a bugger. But I managed to get down to Exeter Cathedral library on Wednesday and take a look at the stuff Michael was interested in. Sadly, it seems I was too late.'

'Why couldn't he go himself? I don't mean to be rude, but—'

'It's the nature of the material, Mr Paleologus. Reading seventeenth-century script isn't a simple matter. Michael knew I'd had more experience than he had in the field.'

'Seventeenth-century script?'

'Yes. To be precise, a haphazardly bound volume of correspondence from successive vicars and churchwardens of the parish of—'

'St Neot.'

Anderson looked at Nick in surprise. 'You already know.'

'Only that Dad was interested in the history of St Neot Church.'

'Yes. He'd heard about a letter written by one of the churchwardens, Richard Bawden, in 1662, concerning precautions taken during the Civil War to protect the church's evidently rather fine stained glass. He wanted me to confirm the letter's contents. It was his understanding that Bawden stated that one of the windows had been removed in 1646 and entrusted to a gentleman called Mandrell.'

'And did you confirm that?'

'Well, it's a little complicated. Let me show you this.' Anderson burrowed in his briefcase and pulled out a folder. 'It's a photocopy of the letter.' He laid the folder on the coffee table and opened it.

Nick peered down at the sheet of paper. The sloping scrawl was clearly a letter, but, as to what it said, Nick saw only a jumble of curled and tangled pen-strokes. 'Good God. You can read this?'

'With practice, yes. Bawden was answering a letter from the Bishop's secretary. He says here'—Anderson pointed to a passage—'"Mr Philpe has asked me to state my best intelligence of the precautions we took to preserve the great and particular treasure of the parish and how it so came to be spared the attentions of the Parliament's soldiery in those dark days nine years since." That takes us back to 1651, since the letter's dated the 21st of May, 1662. He goes on to say, "It was removed five years prior thereto." That means 1646. "We could not suffer it to stand at risk with Cornwall in the Parliament's hands. It was immured safe in the keeping of our staunch friend Mr Mandrell, and is safe there still, I warrant." The rest is just respectful gush.'

'Where does he actually mention the window, then?'

'That's the complication. He doesn't. "The great and particular treasure of the parish" is the phrase he uses. It's a good guess that the stained glass is what he's referring to, but that's all it can be: a guess.'

'THE GREAT AND PARTICULAR treasure of the parish'. Nick studied the phrase, legible now it had been spelt out for him, after Anderson had gone. Elspeth had quoted Bawden as referring to 'our finest window'. Nick was certain about that. Yet here, in Bawden's own hand, was something altogether more ambiguous. It might well mean the window. But it was not explicitly stated. 'Trust nothing except primary sources in this game' was one of the last things his father had said. Here was the primary source. But what was the game?

Elspeth's misrepresentation was understandable in a way. She had been asked to find the Doom Window and this was as close as she had got. After all, what could the treasure be *but* the window? To call it a guess was to undersell it. Elspeth had merely oversold it.

But was that all she had oversold? There was only one person he could ask. He rang Elspeth's mobile number.

The phone was switched off. Irritatingly, Nick had failed to ask Elspeth for her home number and he wouldn't be able to contact her via the Bristol University switchboard until Monday.

But he could not wait that long. Andrew was intent on disposing of the body that night. But what if the chain of evidence linking the Doom Window to Trennor later fell apart in their hands? What would they have achieved then by bundling a corpse down a mine shaft—other than their own incrimination?

'I'VE BROUGHT a couple of rubble bags, a roll of duct tape and a length of rope.' Andrew's announcement on arrival at Trennor late that night was severely practical. 'Two bags should be enough. Then we truss it up inside the tarpaulin and go. We can cover the slab with the rack and play dumb if anyone ever finds the hole. OK?'

'As far as it goes, yes. But there's something I have to tell you.'

'Not again.'

'It's important. It concerns . . . well, look at this.' Nick showed him the photocopy of the Bawden letter and explained its significance. 'Elspeth Hartley hasn't played fair with us. We should check—'

'Bloody hell, Nick. You can't seriously be trying to make something out of . . . out of *that*. I can't even read it. Yeah, Dad probably would have tried to quibble about it. But it doesn't sound to me like anything more than the tiniest of exaggerations.'

'Even so, I think we should ask Elspeth to explain herself.'

'Well, I don't. Are you *trying* to unravel this deal?'

'Of course not.'

'Good. Then let's concentrate on the matter in hand.'

'But that's the point. If there's really no substantial evidence that the Doom Window—'

'I'll tell you what the bloody point is.' Andrew grasped Nick by the shoulder and stared at him. 'Those bones down in the cellar are leaving. Tonight. I'll do it alone if I have to.'

SHORT OF TELEPHONING the police, Nick could not have stopped Andrew going ahead. After watching him for several minutes struggling to pull all that remained of whoever their father had buried out from beneath the slab, Nick lost patience with his own doubts and lent his assistance, which Andrew acknowledged with the faintest of smiles.

It was a struggle even for two, a mutual revulsion at handling the slimy bone and rotted flesh complicating the task. Eventually, with the rubble bags taped round the body, it became easier. They tied the tarpaulin tightly round the bundle and hauled it out to the Land Rover. Then they cleared up behind them in the cellar and set off.

Bodmin Moor was deserted and they met no traffic after leaving the B road at Upton Cross. They approached the shaft cautiously along the lane from Minions, pulled in beside it, turned off the engine and lights and waited until their eyes had adjusted to the darkness.

When they were certain there was no one about, they got out of the car and lifted the bundle out of the back. Then they stumbled up the short slope and felt their way round the fence enclosing the shaft until they reached the loosened stretch of wire. Pulling the wire up high enough for Andrew to crawl beneath it, dragging the bundle with him, made a lot of noise to Nick's ears.

'OK,' whispered Andrew. He pushed the bundle through the

undergrowth ahead of him, the tarpaulin snagging on thorns and stalks, until it was hanging over the edge of the shaft. He gave it a final shove and it tipped over. Nick heard the bundle strike the sides of the shaft several times until it finally thumped to rest far below.

Silence followed. Then Andrew said, 'Let's get out of here,' and began scrambling back beneath the fence.

A few moments later, they were on the road, the Land Rover's headlamps slicing through the darkness as they sped away.

Andrew relaxed as they left the Moor. To him it seemed clear that their problem was solved; it was plain sailing from here on.

'Tom's spending tonight with his mother. And he'll be stopping off with her on his way back. Which means she won't have an excuse to show up at the funeral. I'm picking the lad up from Bodmin Parkway tomorrow afternoon. I spoke to Irene earlier and we thought we could all get together for tea at Trennor. That OK with you?'

Nick was barely aware of what Andrew had said. In his mind's eye he could see a splintered hole in the skull of a long-dead stranger. And in his hands he could feel the weight and shape of the bone.

NICK DID NOT EXPECT to sleep well that night. Strangely, though, he plunged into nine hours of dreamless oblivion. It was midmorning when he woke. It was also the fourth Sunday of the month, which meant there was an 11.15 service at Landulph Church, according to the parish newsletter delivered earlier in the week. For reasons he did not care to analyse too closely, Nick decided to go to church. He tried Elspeth's mobile before leaving the house. It was still switched off.

The church dated from the same period as St Neot's, but was a plainer, less ambitious structure. It was not noted for much beyond the historical curiosity of Theodore Paleologus's memorial plaque.

Candlelight glimmered across the plaque's polished surface as the service unfolded. The inscription was lodged in Nick's mind: *Here lyeth the body of Theodore Paleologus of Pesaro in Italye descended from ye imperyall lyne of ye last Christian Emperors of Greece*. Above it was engraved the double-headed Byzantine eagle, symbolising the unattainable union of western and eastern Christendom.

Nick's gaze wandered often to the plaque as he sang the hymns and murmured the prayers with an agnostic's lack of practice and confidence. Yet he was aware also of something that the previous night's work had stirred in him. It amounted, he realised, to a desire for absolution. But before absolution came confession. And what he and Andrew had done they could never confess.

IRENE AND LAURA were first to arrive for tea that afternoon, bringing to a halt Nick's unavailing half-hourly calls to Elspeth. He had last seen his niece at his father's eightieth birthday party. Since then, she had grown from a slight and diffident eleven-year-old with braced teeth into a tall and self-possessed fifteen-year-old looking more like eighteen and already displaying much of her mother's elegance.

As they conversed less than sparklingly about her exam schedule, Nick had no doubt that Laura was summing him up in one word: boring. Had she known what he and her uncle Andrew had been up to the previous night, she would be unlikely to describe it as boring.

The arrival of Anna and Basil relieved the pressure on Nick to contribute conversationally. Anna possessed a sharp instinct for the preoccupations of a teenage girl and homed in on them effortlessly.

Nick's last encounter with Tom had been in London, one wet afternoon the previous October. They had met by chance outside the British Library, Nick en route for Euston station, Tom for King's Cross. Tom had looked well—soft blond floppy hair, big brown puppy-dog eyes, gym-honed physique filling out fashionable clothes.

When Tom came in with Andrew, Nick noticed a change in him. Tom's gaze had become narrower, almost wary. And he had lost a little weight. Unemployment, Nick reckoned, had taken its toll.

Tom adroitly deflected questions about life in Edinburgh, before expressing his fondness for his late grandfather and his regret at not having seen more of him in recent years.

Laura, who had clearly decided her cousin had become something of a dish since she had last set eyes on him, said suddenly, 'What do you think we ought to spend the money on, Tom?'

'We haven't gone into that yet,' put in Andrew, with an exasperated glance at Irene.

'What's this all about?' asked Tom.

'We've been made a generous offer for Trennor,' Andrew explained. 'Well, it was made to your grandfather, but it falls to us now. It seems there may be some historically important stained glass hidden—'

'*Stained glass?*' Tom sounded suitably incredulous.

'Believe it or not, yeah. It's all tied up with the Civil War. This historian thinks glass from an ancient window in St Neot Church was concealed here in the 1640s to protect it from Cromwell's troops and that it's almost certainly still here. She works for someone who's willing to pay handsomely for the chance to find out.'

'So how are they going to do that? Pull the place apart?'

'Not quite.'

'But nearly,' observed Basil.

Tom whistled. 'Don't suppose Granddad went a bundle on the idea.'

'Not at first,' Andrew cautiously admitted.

'Who's the man with the money?'

'His name's Tantris,' said Irene. 'That's about all we really—'

'*Tantris?*' Tom stared at his aunt. 'You can't be serious.'

'Why not?' asked Anna. 'It's not as unusual a name as Paleologus.'

'Yeah, but . . . He can't be called Tantris. This is a joke, right?'

'What's wrong, Tom?' Nick asked. 'Why can't he be called Tantris?'

Tom looked from one to the other of them. Then he said, 'I'm just going to get something from my bag. Can you give me the key, Dad?'

With a puzzled frown, Andrew pulled the car key out of his pocket and handed it over. Tom hurried from the room.

A few minutes later, he walked back in holding a slim paperback. It was a Penguin Classic: *The Romance of Tristan*, by Béroul. 'Granddad sent this to me a couple of weeks ago with a note attached. "You should read this." That was all. Some joke of his, I reckoned, though what the joke was . . .' He shrugged.

'What's the significance of the book, Tom?' Nick asked.

'Well, it's the oldest surviving version of the romance of Tristan and Yseult. Tristan is the nephew of King Mark of Cornwall. Yseult is the daughter of the King of Ireland. Tristan kills her uncle in fair combat, but is wounded in the process. The wound refuses to heal so Tristan casts off in a boat with neither sails nor oars, trusting to God to take him where he can be cured. He's washed up on the Irish coast, taken into the court posing as a minstrel and has his wounds tended by Yseult. Tristan's cured and returns to Cornwall. He and Yseult only become lovers later, when Yseult is sent to Cornwall under Tristan's escort to marry King Mark. But when he first meets Yseult, Tristan uses a pseudonym to avoid identifying himself as her uncle's killer. The pseudonym is an anagram of his own name. He calls himself—'

'Tantris,' said Basil softly. 'Yes, of course. The two syllables turned the other way round. I should have thought of that.'

'Yeah.' Tom nodded. 'Tristan called himself Tantris when he needed to conceal his true identity.'

'Wait a minute,' said Andrew. 'Are you saying—'

'There's no such person as Tantris.' It seemed to Nick as he spoke that he had known this for some time. 'There never has been.'

'And no Tantris,' Basil began, 'means—'

'No money.' Andrew's words were muffled by the hand he had raised to his face. 'Oh God.'

AT TEN O'CLOCK the following morning, with their father's funeral only two hours away, Andrew, Irene, Basil, Nick and Anna sat, black-suited and sombre-faced, in their solicitor's office.

Maurice Baskcomb leaned forward on his desk. 'I think it fair to say I've never experienced the like of this in my far from short legal career,' he said. 'When you telephoned me last night—'

'We're sorry to have disturbed you at home,' said Irene.

'It was an emergency, Mrs Viner, I think we can agree. As you suggested, I contacted the solicitor I've been dealing with on your behalf, Miss Palmer of Hopkins and Broadhurst, London. She could not tell me a great deal, bound as she is by rules of confidentiality, but it appears she's never met Mr Tantris. She's dealt only with his assistant, a Miss Elsmore. I gave your description of Miss Hartley to her and, though she wouldn't commit herself, I had the distinct impression that the description could have fitted Miss Elsmore. I also contacted Bristol University this morning. There is an Elspeth Hartley on their academic staff, but she's on sabbatical . . . in Boston.'

'Boston, Lincolnshire,' Basil enquired, 'or Massachusetts?'

'The latter, Mr Paleologus.'

'She set us up,' said Anna.

'She's clearly been less than open with you,' Baskcomb went on. 'And with me. And indeed with her own solicitor.'

'Her mobile phone was switched off over the weekend,' said Nick. 'Now the number's unobtainable.'

'What about the money?' asked Andrew. 'What about the half a million quid Tantris deposited with Hopkins and Broadhurst?'

'Withdrawn late Friday afternoon,' Baskcomb gloomily replied.

'How was it withdrawn?' asked Irene.

'In the form, I imagine, of a Hopkins and Broadhurst cheque.'

'Payable to whom?'

'To Miss Elsmore, presumably, or to whomsoever she nominated as payee. Miss Palmer had no authority to give me that information.'

'But it's the only way to track down the bastard behind this swindle.' Andrew glanced round at his siblings for support. 'She has to tell.'

'There's been no swindle,' Baskcomb calmly responded. 'I'm afraid it amounts to nothing more than an elaborate practical joke.'

'A *joke*?'

'I don't see the funny side of it either, Mr Paleologus.'

'But you don't lose by it, Mr Baskcomb, do you? You haven't had the prospect of quitting a farm that grows debts thicker than thistles dangled in front of you, only for it to be snatched away. My God, when I think . . .' Andrew looked away towards the window.

Then his gaze slowly drifted back to Nick. Only they knew just how far they had gone to ensure Tantris's offer remained on the table. And now they knew it had never really been there in the first place. It *was* a joke, a horribly good one. But no one was laughing. No one in Baskcomb's office anyway.

THEY EMERGED from Baskcomb's office into a damp, grey morning, each churning with anger and humiliation.

'The bitch,' hissed Anna. 'Who is she? Why did she do this?'

'It has to be some sort of con trick,' said Irene, her self-control still intact. 'But I don't understand. What did she gain from it?'

'I suspect Dad could have told us,' said Basil.

'What do you mean?'

'He saw through the Tantris pseudonym at once. He was meant to. As the book he sent to Tom demonstrates.'

'Why did he send it to Tom? Why didn't he warn us instead?'

'Again, he could have told us. Alas, it's too late to ask him now.'

'I'm not sure I can face this bloody pantomime,' said Andrew. 'You may have to get through it without me.'

'We'll get through it together, Andrew,' said Irene. 'It's time we all went back to Trennor and waited for the cortege. All this'—she glanced up at Baskcomb's office window—'will have to wait.'

CHAPTER FIVE

The hymns were sung, the prayers were said. The rector offered up some kind words and made passing mention of Michael Paleologus's celebrated lineage. Then they processed to the grave-yard and watched the coffin being lowered into the earth, while the rector made the final pronouncements. Anna sobbed and Aunt Norma, their mother's sister, dabbed her eyes. Irene merely squeezed her gloved hands together and breathed deeply.

The graveside party progressed to the churchyard gate, where Nick stepped quietly to one side while Aunt Norma embarked on a round of hugs. Her husband Archie wobbled from foot to foot. The Wellers, Michael Paleologus's closest neighbours, hovered nearby.

Julian Farnsworth, the only one of his former Oxford colleagues to show up, struck an extravagantly mournful attitude on the fringe of the group. Nick's rough calculation put Farnsworth in his mid-seventies, though he looked younger, thanks to suspiciously dark hair and an erect bearing. He dressed more smartly than most academics and was presumably the owner of the preposterously Parisian old Citroën parked further up the lane.

'Dr Farnsworth?' Nick ventured.

'Nicholas.' They shook hands. 'A pleasure to see you again, despite the occasion. A decently done service, I thought.'

'Good. I'm glad you could make it.'

'Retirement has a liberating effect on the diary, if not on the bank balance. Besides, I could hardly have stayed away in the circumstances.'

'The circumstances?' Nick felt sure he had caught something odd in Farnsworth's tone.

'Well, I'd spoken so recently to Michael . . .'

'You had?'

'Why, yes. A few days before he died.'

'Really? Do you mind my asking what—'

''Scuse me,' put in a voice. 'Mr Paleologus?'

Nick turned to meet the squinting gaze of a white-haired old man in a threadbare overcoat and a black suit, white-shirted but tieless, the shirt buttoned to the neck. He was not much above five feet tall.

'I didn't think it fitting to come to the graveside, see, not being family and all. You likely didn't spy me at the back of the church. I just wanted to make myself known before I left. I'm Frederick Davey.'

Nick covered his discomposure with a smile and shook Davey's hand. 'I'm Nicholas Paleologus. This is Dr Julian Farnsworth, an old colleague of my father's. Do you live around here, Mr Davey?'

'No, no. Tintagel. I'd not have known about this but for the notice in the paper.'

'How did you make the journey?'

'The Plymouth bus dropped me at Paynter's Cross. 'Twas shanks's pony from there.'

'How did you know Michael?' asked Farnsworth.

'Who?'

'My father, Mr Davey,' said Nick.

'Oh, sorry, I'm sure. Always thought of him as . . . Mr Paleologus. Well, young Mr Paleologus, when I first met him. He was helping his father on the dig up at the castle then.'

'The dig?' Farnsworth's archaeological senses were suddenly alert. 'You mean the Tintagel excavations of the 1930s?'

'That'll be them.'

'My, that *is* interesting. What was your involvement, Mr Davey?'

'Well, I was took off quarrying to do the spadework. Me and a good few others. 'Tweren't so very scientific, now I look back.'

'Fascinating.' The expression on Farnsworth's face suggested that he was not being sarcastic.

'I think we should be starting back for the house, Nick,' said Irene, suddenly appearing among them. 'You'll join us, Dr Farnsworth?'

'Gladly.'

'This is Mr Davey, Irene.' Nick caught her eye. 'From Tintagel.'

'What time's your bus back, Mr Davey?' asked Farnsworth.

'Quarter to five. There's only one a day, see.'

'How very inconvenient. Still, I could give you a lift some of the way . . . if we were leaving at the same time.'

AND SO FRED DAVEY was added to the party that assembled for a buffet lunch at Trennor. Once word about him had passed between Nick's siblings, a tension entered the atmosphere that only they were aware of. Davey had witnessed a will they had destroyed. It was hard for them to believe he had made the journey from Tintagel purely because he and Michael Paleologus had worked on the same dig more than sixty years before. A whispered settlement of tactics took place in the kitchen. Irene was to monopolise Baskcomb; he and Davey had to be kept apart. Anna would keep Laura and Tom out of mischief. Basil would shepherd Archie and Norma into conversation with the Wellers. Andrew would swap Cornish lore with Davey. Which left Nick to probe Farnsworth's recent contact with their father.

He started by luring Farnsworth into the study to admire Michael Paleologus's collection of archaeological books. Farnsworth had done no more than finger a few spines when Nick reminded him of what they had been discussing before Davey's arrival at the church gate.

'Why did Dad contact you?' he asked.

'Checking up on an old acquaintance. Very much my speciality. Though, as it turned out, I couldn't help him.'

'What old acquaintance was this?'

'Digby Braybourne. A contemporary of Michael's. Also an archae-ologist. Briefly a fellow at Brasenose. Oh, it must be more than forty years ago now. Let me see. Yes. Michaelmas term of '57, I'd say. An entertaining character. Left Oxford under something of a cloud.'

'What sort of cloud?'

'The sort that involves a spell in prison for fraud. Authenticating fake artefacts for one of the big auction houses. I visited him a couple of times in Reading Gaol. He asked me to stop going. So, I stopped. And that is the last I ever saw of him.'

'What happened to him?'

'Haven't the foggiest. As I told Michael. But . . . I agreed to ask around. Still turned up nothing, though. A cold trail.'

'Why did Dad want to trace him after all these years?'

'For a reunion of old army pals. They served in the war together.'

'Did they?' Nick was puzzled. His father had never once, as far as he knew, participated in regimental reunions. He had done his bit for king and country without running many personal risks, the way he had told it. Whiling away most of the war on Cyprus, bypassed by all hostilities. 'Would that have been on Cyprus, do you think?'

'Possibly. Who can say?'

'Well, Digby Braybourne, I suppose.'

'Indeed. But where is Digby?' Farnsworth smiled. 'Just like the fellow, really. Never to be found when you want him.'

THE PARTY FIZZLED to a close and the mourners left. Fred Davey never had a chance to talk last wills and testaments with Baskcomb. Though what Farnsworth meant to give him the chance to talk about en route to Tintagel was an equally disturbing thought. It was not one that Nick and his siblings were free to discuss, however, even when Pru had departed. They were constrained by the fact that Laura and Tom could know nothing about their grandfather's second will.

'It's "now you see it, now you don't" where the money's concerned, then,' Tom carelessly remarked, when discussion of the funeral had run its course.

'This Hartley woman was just having you on?' asked Laura.

'Apparently so,' said Irene.

'What are you going to do about it?'

'There's nothing we *can* do. Besides, she hasn't actually defrauded us.'

'So what was the object of the deception?' asked Tom.

'We don't know,' Irene replied.

'There has to have been one. Anyway, Granddad would have got the Tristan and Yseult reference straight off. He'd have known Tantris was a ringer. So why didn't he blow the whistle?'

'He did, Tom,' said Basil. 'He blew it to you.'

'Yeah, but what good did that do? It was you guys who needed to know. Why didn't he tell you?'

It was a good question. And one to which nobody had an answer.

IRENE AND LAURA left around dusk. It was business as usual at the Old Ferry that evening. Irene had clearly wanted to speak more freely than she could during the afternoon, but she was nothing if not self-controlled. The same could hardly be said of Anna, who fumed and fretted mutely but obviously. When Tom announced he was stepping out for a smoke and a breath of night air, nobody volunteered to go with him. The chance of unfettered discussion was welcome.

'Did Davey ask you about cousin Demetrius, Andrew?' Anna blurted out as soon as Tom had gone.

'No. But he knows. He asked me if all the family was present. Why would he do that unless he was in a position to be sure they weren't?'

'It could have been an innocent enquiry,' said Basil.

'Innocent my arse.'

'He can't prove anything,' said Anna.

'Let's hope not. If he had another copy of the will, even the pittance we stand to salvage by selling the house will slip through our fingers.'

'It's hardly a pittance,' said Nick.

Andrew shrugged. 'Easy for you to say.'

'Not so easy, actually. I've put my neck on the line just like you.' Nick could not come out and say it, but he blamed his brother for talking him out of going to the police when they discovered the body.

'We all put our necks on the line,' said Anna, deaf to the true meaning of his words. 'Squabbling like schoolboys won't help. Now, did Farnsworth say anything that implied he'd ever heard Dad mention a Venetian cousin, Nick?'

'No.' For some reason Nick felt disinclined to expand on his answer.

'Right. And my bet is we destroyed the only copy of the will.'

'What are the odds on this bet?' Andrew glumly enquired.

'The best we're going to get,' Anna replied. 'I'm as pissed off about all this as you are, Andrew, but, thanks to putting that piece of paper on the fire last week, we have this house and equal shares of what it's worth. That's all that matters now. We must put everything else behind us. I'll speak to Irene once Laura's gone back, but I'm sure she'll agree. We must go on as if we'd never heard of Elspeth Hartley.'

'What about cousin Demetrius?' asked Andrew.

'Him too. In fact, especially him. We have to draw a line under this, boys.' Anna took a large swallow of gin and tonic. 'And move on.'

MOVING ON was precisely what Nick had in mind. He could only hope the humdrum routine of his everyday life in Milton Keynes would enable him to forget the events of the previous week. Before dawn he was up and washed and packed. He wanted to be on the road, away and alone. After a hasty breakfast he went out to the car to check the tyres and top up the windscreen-washer for the journey.

As Nick opened the passenger door to fetch the tyre gauge from the glove compartment, he saw an object on the driver's seat that had not been there before: a large brown envelope, unsealed and evidently containing something bulky. On its face, in felt-penned capitals, were the words D.C. WISE, CROWNHILL POLICE STATION, PLYMOUTH.

Nick wondered how the envelope had got there. None of the windows had been forced; the car was securely locked. The key had been in the pocket of his coat, hanging in the hall since the previous morning. Someone at the funeral party must have taken it, slipped out into the yard and then slipped back again. But who would do such a thing? And why? Nick picked up the envelope and slid the contents onto the seat in front of him. It was a video cassette.

A few minutes later, he was in the drawing room, staring at the television as the video began to play. It had been shot at night, with an infrared camera. It was Bodmin Moor. The camera dwelt on the Caradon Hill transmitter long enough to fix the approximate location. Then it panned round to something closer: a fenced-off clump of trees. A vehicle, by its shape obviously a Land Rover, pulled up at the side of the road further down the slope. Its lights died. A few minutes passed, then two figures climbed out.

Identification would not be easy, though to Nick they were all too recognisable. They opened the back door of the Land Rover, lifted out a long bundle and carried it up the slope. One of them crawled under the fence, pulling the bundle after him. The bundle was pushed forward. It vanished from sight. The man inside the fence crawled back out, then he and his companion retreated down the slope.

As they climbed into the Land Rover, the camera started moving, the picture joggling as its operator hurried down the slope. The vehicle performed a three-point turn, then the lens focused on the rear number plate. And there the number suddenly was, legible for two or three seconds before the Land Rover moved forward and accelerated away down the lane, its lights coming on as it gathered speed.

'CARWETHER FARM.'

'It's me, Andrew.'

'Nick? You're up early.'

'Yeah. Look, er, when's Tom leaving?'

'His train's at eleven. Why?'

'Could I come over to see you after he's gone? It's important.'

'I suppose so. But I thought you were going home today.'

'There's something you have to see, Andrew. I can't explain on the phone. But you've got a video player, haven't you?'

'Yeah. So?'

'So expect me around noon. And say nothing to Tom.'

It was just after noon when Nick drove into the yard of Carwether Farm. Andrew was in a disgruntled mood. Nick's phone call had made him anxious and hiding his state of mind from Tom had been a strain. But that, of course, was nothing compared with the condition watching the video plunged him into.

'Oh my God,' he murmured when it had finished playing.

'Do you want to see it again?'

'What? No.' Andrew rubbed his eyes, struggling to organise his thoughts. 'I *never* want to see it again.'

'It exists, whether we like it or not. And it would be naive to imagine it's the only copy. Whoever put it in my car wants to tell us something. It's a message. They're going to send it to the police. They *might* send it. They've *already* sent it.'

'What would the police make of it?'

'Not much, as it stands. But I guess they'd have to investigate.'

'They could work out where the shaft is from the direction and distance of the Caradon Hill transmitter. Then they'd find the body.'

'Yeah.'

'And my registration number's clear to see.'

'Yeah.'

'Shit.' Andrew stood up and walked across to the television set. He stabbed at a button on the video player, releasing the cassette, and pulled it out of the machine. 'Who did this, Nick?' he asked.

'It must have been put in my car by someone at the funeral party. My coat was hanging in the hall, with the keys in the pocket.'

'That narrows the field.'

'To two, I reckon. Obviously, the family, Pru, Baskcomb and the Wellers aren't in the frame. That leaves . . .'

'Farnsworth and Davey. One or the other.'

'Or both. They left together, remember.'

'But they couldn't have shot this. Neither of them is agile enough—or technologically wised up, at a guess.'

'I agree.'

'Then it has to be Elspeth Hartley.'

'Looks that way.'

'She knew the body was there all along, didn't she? That's what it was all about. She must have followed us when we went to Minions on Saturday morning and watched us poking around the shaft. That's how she knew where to lie in wait for us.'

'She certainly seems to have been one step ahead of us all the way.'

'And she still is. What does she expect us to do about this video?'

'I'm not sure. Maybe she's giving us a chance to go to the police before she tips them off.'

'Why would she do that?'

'I don't know. But then we don't know why she's done anything. We don't really know the first thing about her.'

'Except the people she's in with.' Andrew stared down at the cassette clutched in his hands. There was a loud crack as he hooked his fingers under the plastic cover of the cassette and wrenched it off. Then he started pulling the tape out, until it snapped off at the end of the spool. He threw the empty cassette onto the floor and headed for the door, taking the jumble of tape with him.

Nick followed him into the kitchen. 'What are you doing?'

Andrew was standing by the range, dropping the tape into the fire. He replaced the lid with a thud and turned slowly round. 'You're going to tell me burning it's a waste of effort, aren't you?'

'We have to assume—'

'I know what we have to assume.' Andrew grabbed his coat and made for the door. 'The fucking worst.'

'Where are you going?'

Slamming the door behind him was Andrew's only response. Nick started after him, then stopped. What was the point? Whatever he said, Andrew would not listen. He heard a shout of 'Stay!' out in the yard, directed at the dog, followed by the noise of the Land Rover engine. Then a shadow roared past the window. Andrew was gone.

A FEW MINUTES LATER, Nick started back for Trennor, taking a circuitous route via Launceston. He did not know what to do for the best. Go to the police? Or go home and wait? Why had Elspeth given them the chance to choose? What did she want—or expect—them to do?

Strictly speaking, they did not know Elspeth was responsible for the video. Nor could they be certain either Farnsworth or Davey was involved in planting it in Nick's car, although how else could it have got there? He would have to speak to Andrew again later, when he was calmer, and try to find a way forward. Meanwhile—

A thought burst upon him. Whoever had put the video in the car would have had the run of the boot, where Nick had put the envelope holding the contents of the file on his breakdown. He pressed his foot to the floor, desperate to reach the next lay-by.

Where all, it transpired, was well. The envelope did not look as if it had been tampered with. Nick stood by the open boot, leafing through the documentary evidence of his loosened hold on reason. It was all there, every letter, every bill, and much more besides.

Including the programme for the degree ceremony he had not been supposed to attend. He pulled it out and stared at it for a moment. There was the date: Friday, June 29, 1979. And there were the names, in orderly columns. He knew he would find his own, listed as one of those proceeding to a degree *in absentia*. His father must have asked for the programme to be sent to him, a small memento of an occasion he had no doubt hoped to witness in person, whereas instead—

It was then that Nick remembered Elspeth's brother, the brother she had supposedly gone to see collect his own degree that day. He closed the boot and got back into the car, the programme clutched in his hand. He began scanning the names, unsure what he was looking for. Not Hartley, obviously. But something, someone. King's College, Trinity, St John's, Peterhouse, Clare . . .

'My God,' he heard himself say. His finger had stopped at a name in the Clare College list: *Braybourne, Jonathan Charles.*

THE TELEPHONE WAS RINGING when Nick opened the front door back at Trennor and stepped into the hall. He hurried to pick it up.

'Nicholas? Thank goodness I've caught you. It's Julian Farnsworth.'

'Dr Farnsworth? What can I do for you?'

'I'm phoning from Tintagel.'

'What are you doing there?'

'I decided to spend a few days up here before returning to Oxford. But that isn't really the point. I'm phoning about your brother.'

'Andrew?'

'Yes. He's behaving very strangely. I met him at Mr Davey's house.'

'You were with Davey?'

'Yes. I wanted to ask him some more questions about the excavations. Then your brother arrived. To say that he was overwrought is to put it mildly. He accused us of conspiring against him—and you. None of it made sense. He was ranting. We had to threaten to call the police before he would leave. I was genuinely fearful that he might become violent. I still am, as a matter of fact.'

'I don't understand.' The lie was a reflex. Nick well understood that discovering Farnsworth and Davey together must have confirmed to Andrew their suspicions about the pair. 'Where's Andrew now?'

'I've no idea. He stormed out of the house just as he had stormed into it. But he said he'd be back. Mr Davey took it as a threat and I can't say I blame him. Whether your brother knows where *I* am . . .'

'And where is that?'

'The Camelot Castle Hotel. On the headland.'

'Do you want me to come up?'

'I do. I suspect him of lurking somewhere in the neighbourhood. I could not forgive myself if some harm came to Mr Davey for lack of action on my part. I should hope you might feel the same, Nicholas.'

'I do, obviously, though—'

'I'll expect you within the hour.'

'Yes, but—'

There was no more to be said. The line was dead.

NICK DROVE FASTER than usual, north through the clearing afternoon. In less than an hour, he rounded a bend on the upland road in from the east and suddenly saw the crumpled coastline below him, and the worn stump of Tintagel Castle on its virtual island of storm-sieged rock. On a nearby platform of land, looking far more like a castle than the medieval ruins, stood the Camelot Castle Hotel.

Then Nick descended the hill, and the coast ahead was lost to view. Tintagel's main street looked drab and quiet as he drove along it. He had no reason to stop there en route to the hotel—until he saw Andrew's Land Rover, parked outside the Sword and Stone pub.

Nick pulled in on the other side of the road and got out. The Sword and Stone appeared to be open. He crossed over and went in.

The bar was sparsely decorated and cavernously chill. Two middle-aged men with big bellies and blank faces sat at one of the tables, drinking pints of lager. The only other customer, propped on a bar stool with a glass of whisky in front of him, was Andrew. He was so drunk he did not even seem surprised to see his brother.

'Hey, Nick. Want a drink?'

'What's going on, Andrew?'

'Buggered if I know.'

'Farnsworth phoned me. Said you'd been making trouble at Davey's house. Going there wasn't a very bright idea, you know.'

'Wasn't it? I caught them together, though, didn't I?' Andrew's gaze narrowed. 'The pair of them. Scheming against us.'

'You can't prove that.'

'Don't need to. I know. And now they know I know. So, what are you drinking?' Andrew nodded at the bleary-eyed barman who had shuffled out from a back room.

'I'll have a Coke.'

'You heard the man, squire. I'll have another large Bell's.'

The drinks were supplied and the money taken from a pile of change next to Andrew's elbow. The barman wandered off again.

'I don't believe in coincidence, Nick. Farnsworth wasn't round at Davey's place to catch his reminiscences of digging up old pots out at the castle. His being there is all the proof I need.'

'Look, I'll go and see Farnsworth and smooth things over. Then I'll drive you home. You obviously can't drive yourself.'

Andrew stared at him. 'Smooth things over? You must be joking.'

'It's all we can do for the present. We need to . . . take stock.'

'Take stock? Bloody hell, Nick.' Andrew shook his head in disappointment. 'What use are you, hey?' He slid off the stool and lumbered away towards a door marked GENTS. 'Go and lick Farnsworth's arse if you want to. I don't care. I'll deal with him and Davey my way. I'll have to, won't I? Should have known you'd chicken out. It's—'

Andrew's words were choked off by the slamming of the loo door behind him. The other two customers stared at Nick, their faces marginally less blank than before. Nick took an evasive swallow of Coke. Then he noticed Andrew's car keys lying on the bar.

He thought the matter over for no more than a few seconds. Then he picked up the key, drained his Coke and headed for the exit.

IT WAS A SHORT DRIVE to the Camelot Castle Hotel, out at the northern end of the village. The building was a stolid mass of castellated Victorian Gothic, cast in deep shadow by the late sun. Nick parked next to Farnsworth's Citroën and climbed out. It was colder here, he noticed. The air seemed to be chilling by the second. He hurried towards the hotel entrance.

Before he reached the door, however, Farnsworth stepped out into the porch to meet him. He was muffled up in overcoat, scarf, gloves and a deerstalker that might have looked charmingly eccentric on the streets of Oxford but here looked merely bizarre.

'Ah, Nicholas. I thought I'd take a breath of air before nightfall to calm my nerves. I had begun to despair of seeing you, I must admit. You are somewhat later than we agreed.'

'It couldn't be helped. I bumped into my brother.'

'Rather you than me. Has he calmed down?'

'Yes. As far as he needed to.'

'Have you any idea what prompted his extraordinary behaviour?'

'He was obviously surprised to find you at Davey's house.'

'Surprise I can understand, Nicholas. But not outrage. There was nothing sinister about it. Mr Davey participated in one of the most significant British digs of the twentieth century. I was interested to know what he remembered of it. Alas, I gleaned little of value, thanks to your brother's intervention.'

'I'm sorry if Andrew upset you.' Nick exerted himself to sound genuine, but he felt as suspicious as Andrew did. 'I'll take him home and make sure he causes you no further problems.'

'Where is he now, may I ask?'

'A pub in the village.'

'I suppose that will suffice, then. I'll telephone Mr Davey and let him know what's happened. It was a most disconcerting experience, Nicholas. There was no occasion for your brother to behave as he did.'

'I'll phone you in the morning, Dr Farnsworth. OK?'

Farnsworth nodded thoughtfully. 'Very well.'

WHEN NICK GOT BACK to the Sword and Stone the blank-faced pair were still nursing their lagers. But of Andrew there was no sign. The slew of change on the bar in front of his stool had vanished.

'He's gone,' said the barman, anticipating Nick's question. 'Left right after you.'

'Did he say where he was going?'

'Nope. But it can't be far. He said as you'd half-inched his car keys. He was seriously pissed off about that.'

Where had Andrew gone? Only one answer came to Nick's mind. 'Do you know a bloke called Fred Davey? He lives on Butcher's Row.'

'Butcher's Row?' The barman gave a reasonable impression of thinking. 'The row of cottages out beyond Tregatta. Isn't that called Butcher's Row?' He looked at the blank-faced pair, who responded with a slow, synchronised nod of confirmation. 'Yeah. That's it.'

NIGHT HAD FALLEN by the time Nick drove clear of the village on the Camelford road. Tregatta was a hamlet about half a mile south of Tintagel and according to the barman Butcher's Row was another half-mile further on. But this was the only road to it. If Andrew was set on revisiting Davey, Nick should be able to overtake him on the way.

But there was no sign of him. Nick was in one sense grateful for that, because beyond Tregatta there was no footpath and not much of a verge. The roadside was no place for a drunken pedestrian.

Butcher's Row was down a minor road just past the first bend after Tregatta. Nick spotted the lane and turned off along it. A terrace of four low-roofed slate cottages fronted directly onto the lane. He pulled over as far as he could opposite it under a straggling thorn hedge, jumped out and headed for the Daveys' door.

Nick gave the knocker several loud raps and heard a shuffling approach on the other side of the door.

'Who's that?' came a female voice.

'Nicholas Paleologus,' he shouted. 'Is my brother with you?'

The door was suddenly wrenched open, to reveal two figures standing in a narrow hallway. Fred Davey looked shorter than Nick remembered him from the funeral and his wife Margaret was shorter still. But there was no hint of frailty in their expressions.

'Your brother's been and gone, Mr Paleologus,' said Fred. 'A couple of hours since.'

'I thought he might have come back.'

'That he hasn't, we're glad to say,' put in Margaret. 'I thought there'd be violence done, the bait he was in.'

'I'm sorry if he caused you any trouble.'

'So Dr Farnsworth said,' Fred responded. 'We've just had him on the blower, saying you'd be taking your brother out of harm's way.'

'So I will, once I find him.'

'It'll get him into bother. Carrying on like he did.'

'I can only apologise on his behalf, Mr Davey.'

'Well . . .' Fred pushed out his bottom lip thoughtfully. 'See him home and we'll say no more about it.'

'I'll do my best.'

NICK REVERSED OUT awkwardly onto the main road and headed back towards Tintagel, reckoning Andrew must simply have gone to another pub after leaving the Sword and Stone. But as he accelerated away, he suddenly saw his brother on the roadside ahead, blundering towards him, one arm raised to shield his eyes.

Nick braked sharply to a halt, earning a horning and a flash of lights from behind. The offended driver sped past, nearly taking off the door as Nick edged it open.

'What the hell are you doing, Andrew?' Nick shouted, darting out and round to the front of the car. 'It's me. Nick.'

'Why should you care what I'm doing?' Andrew stopped and

squinted at his brother through the glare of the headlamps.

'Because we've got to stick together.'

'You stole my car keys. Funny bloody way to—' The rest was lost in the roar of a passing lorry.

'You're in no state to drive.'

'I'm in a good enough state to squeeze the truth out of Davey.'

'Don't be stupid. Get in.'

'Don't tell me I'm stupid.' Andrew stumbled forward and prodded Nick in the chest. 'I'm going there whether you like it or not.'

'Listen to me, Andrew.' Nick grabbed his brother's arm. 'We need—'

'Let go of me.' Andrew pulled Nick off him and shoved him towards the car. Nick fell back across the bonnet, while Andrew, carried off balance by his effort, reeled against the offside wing.

What happened next was compressed into a second, though to Nick, as he pulled himself upright, it seemed like a minute of slow, unfolding chance. Andrew's bearings deserted him. He took three staggering steps into the middle of the road and was lit by a clash of headlamps from both directions. A horn blared. There was a squeal of skidding tyre on tarmac. Then the dark shape of a van closed on him. There was a thump, a blur of tumbling shadows. The tyres squealed on. The wheels bounced and juddered. Something was crushed, snapped, spattered, in the mangling darkness; something that had been, until that second, Nick's brother, but was now . . .

No more.

INTERLUDE

CHAPTER SIX

T he video ended. Detective Inspector Penrose rose and removed it from the VCR. He slipped it into a large envelope, handed it to his colleague, Detective Constable Wise, then sat down heavily.

Sunlight was filtering through the windows of the drawing room, but it brought no warmth with it. A fire would have been a help, but the grate was empty. Trennor was without a permanent resident.

The audience for the video show comprised Irene Viner and Basil and Anna Paleologus, bunched awkwardly on the sofa so that all could have a good view of the television.

'What should we make of this, Inspector?' asked Irene.

'I'd hoped you might be able to tell us that,' Penrose replied, his voice gravelly and Cornish-accented. 'The registration number visible on the video corresponds with the registration number of your late brother's Land Rover. Now, a positive identification of the two figures is difficult, but we're assuming one of them is Andrew.'

'Just because it's his Land Rover.'

'It's a good reason,' said Wise.

'Granted,' said Irene. 'But where does that get us? How exactly did this video reach you?'

'It was mailed to me,' Wise replied. 'Posted in Plymouth on the 31st of January—the day after your brother's death.'

'You see a connection?'

'We see a coincidence,' said Penrose. 'Sometimes they can be meaningful.' He shifted in his seat. 'Naturally, we've shown the video to your brother Nicholas and questioned him about this, but his memory of the period leading up to the accident is still patchy.'

'Shock, according to the specialist,' said Irene. 'Seeing Andrew killed in front of him like that . . .' She shook her head. 'But I'm sure he'll tell you if he remembers anything significant.'

'Until he does,' said Wise, 'all we have to go on is this video, sent to us anonymously, apparently to alert us to the disposal of a body.'

'You don't know the . . . object . . . is a body,' said Irene.

'Right size and shape. And a couple of people going to some lengths to get rid of it. We were bound to take it seriously.'

'Yet you found no body in the shaft,' remarked Basil.

'That's true,' said Penrose. 'Which makes it all the more puzzling. The video clearly shows a large cylindrical object being dumped in the shaft. The position relative to Caradon Hill pinpoints it as Hamilton's Shaft, one of the few round there not capped.'

'We searched the shaft four days after receiving the video,' continued Wise, 'on Monday the 5th of February. We found nothing, aside from rocks and rubbish. A local farmer said he'd seen some activity around the shaft at the end of the previous week. He couldn't be specific, but we think what he saw may have been someone else searching the shaft—and removing whatever was dumped into it.'

'Maybe it was just a hoax,' said Anna. 'You know, some mischief-maker giving you the run-around.'

'Using your late brother's Land Rover,' Wise pointed out.

Penrose looked from one to the other of them. 'Can any of you recall anything your brother said or did in the weeks before his death that suggested he might be mixed up in something like this?'

'I'm afraid there's nothing,' said Irene, her glance inducing nods of confirmation from Anna and Basil. 'Nothing at all.'

'What about your nephew, Tom? Might he know something?'

'Tom's had very little contact with his father these past few years. I'm afraid we can't help you, Inspector. Much as we'd like to.'

'No. Well . . .' Penrose smiled ruefully. 'Thanks for trying.'

AFTER SEEING THE policemen out they walked back into the drawing room. Anna expressed a preference for a very large gin and tonic. Irene concurred. And Basil went along with the majority.

'What a pair,' said Anna after her first sip of gin. 'Let's hope we've seen the last of them.'

'They've no reason to take this any further,' said Irene. 'If they'd found a body in the shaft, it might have been different. As it is . . .'

'Who did you think the two people on the video were, Irene?'

'I don't know.'

'Really?'

'*I don't know.*' Irene clunked her glass down on the mantelpiece. 'Whatever this is really all about has harmed us enough. We need to draw a line under the whole dreadful business. You're not to discuss this with Nick. Is that understood? Let him recover in his own time.'

'Won't he assume they'll have shown us the video?'

'Maybe. But let him raise the subject—if he wants to. If he doesn't then let it lie. It's only for a few days. He's going up to Edinburgh to see Tom. He was in no state to explain what happened when Tom was down for Andrew's funeral, but he reckons he's equal to it now.'

'Tom seemed totally withdrawn to me,' said Anna.

'Exactly. So, the visit could be good for both of them. But Nick's still very fragile. I don't want anything to upset him before he goes.'

'Message received and understood,' murmured Basil.

'Good.'

'But remember what the inspector said. Finding nothing in the shaft is in a sense the most puzzling aspect of the whole affair.'

'You think too much, Basil,' said Anna. 'You really do.'

'Maybe you're right. Maybe I need a holiday.'

'Don't we all?'

'A complete break.' Basil nodded. 'A change of scene.'

'Not planning to don the habit again, I hope,' said Irene.

'No, no. Not that.' Basil clinked the ice thoughtfully in his glass. 'Something else altogether.'

PART TWO

CHAPTER SEVEN

Nicholas Paleologus stepped out of the door of the Old Ferry Inn into a chill, grey, salt-tanged morning. He heaved his bag onto his shoulder and gazed up at the twin spans of the Tamar road and rail bridges. He breathed deeply, wondering if the palpitations would start again. But they stayed away. He was calm and in control.

Three weeks had passed since Andrew's death. For the first of those weeks Nick had no coherent memory to draw on. His recollections—of people and places and incidents—were a jumble, detached from sequential reality. He knew it all now: what had happened and when. Yet still it lacked for him the actuality of first-hand experience. It was all at one remove from him and he from it.

The drugs were partly to blame, of course, or to thank, since the condition was both a curse and a blessing. It had certainly kept the police off Nick's back for a while. The irony was that he had pleaded memory loss for the period *prior* to the accident merely as a delaying tactic. There had been no danger of his forgetting the night he and Andrew had tipped a tarpaulined bundle into Hamilton's Shaft. Nick had assumed a moment of reckoning for it was bound to come in the end. But it never had, for the most astonishing of reasons: when the police had gone to look, the body had vanished.

Nick turned and headed towards the railway station. His car stood in the yard behind the Old Ferry, its bumper crumpled and one set of lights smashed. The vehicle was still driveable, but not by Nick. His nerves had been shredded far more drastically than his memory.

He very clearly remembered driving down to Saltash five weeks before, comfortable in the assumption that he would be staying for a couple of days. Now, at last, he was leaving, at dawn, on foot, with much lost and nothing gained.

There were a few people gathered at the station, waiting for the train to take them into Plymouth for the working day. The doctor had signed Nick off work until the end of March. He was supposed to use the period to reduce his drug dosage and ease his way back to stability. That was not what he had in mind, though. He had already halved his pill intake without suffering a recurrence of the panic attacks and he planned to halve it again. What he needed was to be sure of himself, confident that his state of mind was his own, not some pharmacological ideal of moderation.

The train came in and the passengers shuffled aboard. Nick picked up a discarded *Western Morning News* and read it aimlessly until they reached Plymouth. There, he made his way to the platform for the London train and waited, staring vacantly into space.

'Good morning, Nick.'

Nick turned to find Basil standing next to him, dressed in cagoule and walking boots, with a bulging rucksack on his back.

'Surprised to see me?'

'You could say that, yes.'

'Irene told me which train you'd be catching. I thought we could travel to London together. I'm going on holiday.'

'Holiday? This is the first I've heard of it. Where are you going?'

Basil's reply was drowned out by the Tannoy announcement of their train. Nick thought he heard him name a destination, but could not quite believe he had heard correctly.

'What?' he shouted above the recital of West Country station stops.

Then the recital abruptly ceased. And he heard Basil's answer, clear as a bell.

'WHY ARE YOU GOING to Venice?' Nick had managed to delay asking the question until they had settled in their seats and the train had pulled out of the station. 'Well? What are you up to, Basil?'

'Nothing hole-in-the-corner, I do assure you. After all, I could easily have caught another train, couldn't I?'

'In that case, why not just come out with it?'

'Because Irene has told me to tread carefully where you're concerned. As for Venice, my interest in Byzantine history can never be slaked. I've been meaning for a long time to immerse myself in a study of the treasures the Venetians looted from Constanti—'

'Demetrius Paleologus,' Nick murmured.

'Ah.' Basil smiled. 'Memory not so very fallible after all, Nick?'

'What do you hope to achieve?'

'To explain that, I need to tell you a story. But first, I'd like you to tell me what this trip of yours to Scotland is in aid of.'

'You already know. I owe Tom a better explanation of what happened to Andrew than I was able to give him at the funeral.'

'And is a better explanation . . . a complete explanation?'

'As complete as I'm capable of.'

'Then it's time we put our cards on the table. You've seen the video, Nick. So have I. Irene and Anna are all for letting sleeping dogs lie. But I fear they're failing to guard against the day when the dog wakes and comes snapping at their heels. Sorry. Too many metaphors. But I trust the point is made.'

'I'm not sure it is.'

'Then let me be specific. I've been packing up some of Dad's possessions for disposal. Irene and Anna delegated the task to me, as one with time on his hands. Naturally, they didn't like to bother you with the details and I'd be happy to spare you them myself, but for'—Basil lowered his voice—'a discovery I made in the cellar.'

Nick said nothing. There was nothing he *could* say.

'I put everything back as I found it. Of course, as one who's seen the video, I have little doubt as to what was there when you and Andrew . . . came across it. I assume removal was Andrew's idea, but I quite understand why you cooperated. It must have seemed a simple solution to a complicated problem. You might tell me: approximately how long had it been there, do you think?'

Nick forced himself to look at his brother. 'Ten years or more,' he whispered. 'At a guess.'

'Thus is Dad's reluctance to sell explained at a stroke. Poor Nick. It must have been a harrowing business. Had you and Andrew seen the video before he went up to Tintagel that day?'

Nick nodded. 'A copy was put in my car during the wake at Trennor.'

'You suspected Dr Farnsworth?'

'And/or Davey. Plus Elspeth Hartley.'

'An unholy alliance formed in pursuit of . . . what exactly?'

'Haven't a clue.'

'I spoke to Dr Farnsworth the day after the accident. He told me about an old army buddy of Dad's: Digby Braybourne. Present whereabouts unknown.'

'Like one or two others.'

'I telephoned Dr Farnsworth a few days ago. After seeing the video, I was curious to learn more about the long-lost Mr Braybourne.'

'Get anywhere?'

'Don't tease, Nick. You had the same conversation with his housekeeper as I did. She was hardly likely to have forgotten the name Paleologus. Why do you think Dr Farnsworth's gone to Edinburgh?'

'To visit an old friend, the housekeeper said.'

'But you don't believe it. Which is why you're going to Edinburgh. To find out what Dr Farnsworth is up to.'

'I'm worried about Tom.'

'With good reason, I'd say. Irene tells me you'll be seeing his mother before going up there. Is that right?'

'I'm staying with Kate and Terry tonight, yes.'

'Will you be mentioning any of this to them?'

'What do you think, Basil?'

'I think pretending the problem will go away is a fool's counsel. These people won't give up until they've got what they want.'

'And what's that?'

'I've no more idea than you. But we have to find out. Which is why I'm going to Venice. And why you're going to Edinburgh. Isn't it?'

No more was said until the train left Exeter. Nick carefully sifted his options while Basil, sensing he needed to be left to do so, contentedly leafed through a Michelin guide to Venice.

'We could both be taking a big risk,' Nick said at last, as the train gathered pace. 'You do understand that, don't you?'

'Sometimes doing nothing is the riskier choice.'

'What will you do when you reach Venice?'

'Locate our cousin's abode. If he is there, I believe I can create an opportunity to make his acquaintance.'

'And if he isn't there?'

'I shall learn what I can.'

'Be careful.'

'I will be. And I trust you'll do likewise.'

'Do you have my mobile number?'

'Of course not.' Basil grinned and handed him his train ticket. 'Write it on there.'

Nick obliged and also gave him the number of the hotel where he would be staying in Edinburgh.

'I'll call you tomorrow and let you know where I'm staying,' Basil said. 'Much of what's happened has been our own fault, Nick. If we hadn't destroyed Dad's will . . .' He shrugged. 'Who knows?'

'Clever of you to memorise Demetrius's address.'

'I thought I might have need of it.'

'If he is Tantris, you'll be stepping into the lion's den.'

'There are a lot of lions in Venice. Bronze or marble, mostly.'

'You will call tomorrow, won't you?'

'I said I would.'

'I might have some valuable information by then, you see. I'm meeting a guy I know in London.'

'From whom you may learn . . .'

'Possibly nothing. It's a stab in the dark. Let's leave it at that.'

'Very well.'

'I'd thought I might have to go to Venice myself, you know. After Edinburgh. Depending what happened.'

'You may still have to go.' Basil chuckled. 'There's just no telling what trouble I'll get into on my own.'

They parted at Paddington. A confirmed aviophobe, Basil was travelling the whole way to Venice by train. He ambled off down the steps to the Underground, pausing at the bottom for a farewell wave. As an eccentric middle-aged backpacker, he was entirely convincing. As a brother, he was the only one Nick had left. And Nick had never fully understood how fond of him he was until he saw him turn and lose himself in the Tube-bound crowd.

NICK LEFT THE STATION and headed south towards Hyde Park, reckoning he had time to walk to his rendezvous with Marty Braxton, a former colleague at English Partnerships. He was in Nick's debt, on account of the blind eye Nick had turned to his use of the office computer system for the operation of a customised number-plate mart. And the time had come to call in the debt.

When Nick arrived at the Windmill, a pub halfway between Bond Street and Regent Street, Braxton was already installed at the bar. Judging by the inroads he had made into a steak and kidney pie and a pint of beer, he had been there for quite a while.

'Hi, Nick,' came the greeting through a mouthful of pie. 'You're looking well.'

'That's a minority view at present.'

'Really? Well, dare to be different is my motto, mate. Pint?'

'OK. Thanks.'

'I can recommend the snake and pygmy.'

'I'm not hungry.'

'Suit yourself.' Braxton signalled to the barmaid and a pint was pulled. Then he piloted Nick off to a table near the stairs and toasted happy days as soon as they had settled. 'My emotional antennae tell me they aren't so happy for you, though, Nick. Is that right?'

'Family problems.'

'Can't help you there. My earliest memory's a gooseberry bush.'

'I was hoping you *could* help me, actually.'

'Ah. No time for foreplay, then. OK. You want to know if I was able to work the magic on a certain solicitor's computer system? Did I hack it, so to speak?' Braxton grinned. 'When did I ever not?' He dropped his voice. 'The things I do for an old pen-pushing pal, hey?'

'I'm grateful, Marty. Really.'

'So you should be. It shakes down like this. That cool half-million paid out by Hopkins and Broadhurst on the 26th of January? The payee was a company called Develastic. Know them?'

'I don't think so.'

'Jersey-based. Probably just a shell. Info's thin on the ground, but I managed to get the names of the directors.' Braxton handed Nick a slip of paper, on which were written three names: *Terence Mawson, Catherine Mawson, Clive Ramirez-Jones.* 'Friends of yours?'

'Not exactly.'

'But not exactly strangers either, unless you've gone pale because that pint's off.'

Nick took a swig from his glass and looked Braxton in the eye. 'There's nothing wrong with the beer. But something else'—Nick glanced back down at the slip of paper in his hand—'*is* wrong.'

He made dismal company for the rest of Braxton's lunch hour, as Braxton more than once complained. It was a relief for both of them when they parted. Nick headed south, down through Green Park and St James's Park towards Westminster Bridge, his thoughts moving faster than his feet, but with an inferior sense of direction.

Nick had warned Basil that, by going to Venice in search of their cousin Demetrius, he might be stepping into the lion's den. Ironically, Nick was now the one about to put himself in harm's way. Enemies had appeared from the least expected quarter. His brother's ex-wife and her present husband were the source of the Tantris money. Kate's invitation had suddenly acquired a sinister connotation. But he could not cancel the visit without arousing their suspicion.

ANDREW AND KATE had married while Nick was still at school and had thrown themselves into making a success of Carwether Farm. Things had only begun to go wrong after Tom was born. By then things were going wrong for Nick as well. The final breakup of their marriage passed him by. Kate married Terry Mawson in the mid-eighties, just as his building business was transforming itself into a nationwide property company. Since then he had made a fortune.

It was difficult to begrudge them their prosperity, though naturally Andrew had. Terry was a genially blunt-mannered bear of a man, fond of cigars, golf and fast cars. He was a devoted husband, despite a lack of children, which had reputedly led him to spend a lot of time and money on fertility treatments—to no avail.

Kate had preserved the unsentimental, level-headed demeanour of the farmer's wife she no longer was. She owned a riding school in Ascot and an interior design studio in Camberley. But she was not as busy as she had been. Her and Terry's concerns ticked by profitably without much involvement on their part. Leaving them free to . . .

What exactly? Nick turned the question over in his mind as the train ambled down through Hounslow and Staines. A less likely pair of conspirators than Kate and Terry he could not imagine. The Paleologus family had done them no harm. Friendly relations had been maintained. Tom was held to be a credit to his mother and by implication to his stepfather. There had been no feud.

But Kate and Terry's fingerprints were on the Tantris money. And money was one thing they were not short of.

NICK HAD PHONED KATE from Waterloo, and she was waiting for him at Sunningdale station, looking tanned and casually elegant in blue jeans, red sweater and black thigh-length coat. There were a few flecks of grey in her dark hair and laughter lines round her eyes, but otherwise she was a walking advertisement for the benefits of middle-aged affluence. She appeared carefree and wholly unconspiratorial.

'Hi, Nick,' she said, hugging and kissing him. 'It's great to see you. And looking so well. There's been quite a change since . . .'

'Andrew's funeral? I know. I was pretty well out of it then. Blame the drugs they had me dosed up with. I'd still fail an Olympic dope test, but . . . I'm getting there.'

'Glad to hear it. And to see the evidence. Now, let's go.'

Kate's Mercedes was parked outside. They climbed in and started away, Nick noticing already the anxious tightness in his stomach. He slowed his breathing and tried to relax his facial muscles.

'It's really good of you to be going up to see Tom,' Kate said. 'We're worried about him, but he wouldn't welcome me fussing around.'

'Is there any reason to worry about him? I mean, obviously, losing his father . . .'

'There's nothing specific. But, when he was down, he was so . . . tightlipped. I wish he'd talk about it. Maybe he'll open up with you.'

'I can only tell him what happened and see where we go from there.'

'And what happened was just a crazy accident. I wonder if that doesn't make it worse.'

'How do you mean?'

'I wonder if Tom doesn't want there to be someone he can blame. Only no one is to blame, are they?'

'No.' Nick looked straight ahead at the road. 'No one at all.'

A few minutes later, they turned off onto the private road through the Wentworth estate. Kate slowed to a seemly twenty miles per hour as they cruised past the security-gated properties, following a curvaceous cul-de-sac to the house that Kate and Terry called home.

Mariposa was quite possibly the biggest bungalow in Surrey. Thanks to Kate, the interior was as tastefully furnished and decorated as the extensive ground plan would permit. Mariposa was no more her natural habitat than Carwether had been, but she disguised the fact well. She was, Nick reflected, an expert at disguise.

After a brief excursion to the guest wing to dump his bag, he joined Kate for tea in the pastel vastness of the lounge. Terry, she explained, was entertaining a party of clients to an afternoon's racing at Sandown Park; he would be back in time for dinner.

'If it hadn't been arranged so long ago, I'd suspect him of deliberately engineering his absence.'

'Why would he want to do that?'

'Because he knows I want to talk to you about Andrew.'

'I wish I'd done more to stop him, Kate, but—'

'I don't mean the accident. In one of the few conversations I managed to have with my son while he was here last month, before . . . before it happened, he told me about this weird Tantris business.'

'Ah.' Nick's senses suddenly sharpened. 'Did he?'

'Was it a secret?'

'Not really. Anyway . . .' Nick sipped his tea. 'I'm glad he told you. It's better to have things . . . out in the open. Someone played a strange and rather cruel trick on us, Kate. The strangest part of it is that we don't know who—or why.'

'Terry says Andrew must have seen the deal as a lifeline.'

'I suppose he did.'

'And then the lifeline was snatched away.'

'Yes. It was.'

'Which is why we're so worried about Tom.' Kate leaned forward in her chair. 'He figured out Tantris was a fraud, didn't he? Exposed the trick for what it was. We're worried he blames himself for his father's death, Nick. He was so withdrawn at the funeral. I think he's decided he somehow tipped Andrew over the edge.'

'That's absurd. We'd have had to find out the truth sooner or later.'

'I know. Of course it doesn't make sense. Grief and guilt don't tend to. But I'm worried—*really* worried—that he's convinced himself he's in some way responsible. Which is why I'm so pleased you're going to see him. If anyone can make him understand, it's you.'

'I'll try.'

'Bless you, Nick. That's all I'm asking.'

And looking into her eyes, Nick found it hard to doubt that she meant exactly what she'd said.

LYING IN THE BATH before dinner, Nick stared up through the whorls of steam towards the shower head, focusing on a droplet of water slowly growing at its centre. With it grew his dread of the evening that stretched before him. He had almost convinced himself that Kate knew nothing about the source of the Tantris money. But, if so, then Terry had deceived her as well as the Paleologus family.

Nick climbed out of the bath, towelled himself down and pushed open the window to clear the steam. Then he heard it: the low, thrumbling engine-note of Terry's Ferrari. It growled up the drive and came to a halt with an extravagant scrunch of rubber on gravel.

'Terry's taking a shower,' Kate called to him from the kitchen as he passed the door a short while later. 'And I'm at the messy stage of a recipe. Make yourself comfortable in the lounge.'

Nick tried to do as he was told, but comfort required more than soft furnishings. He poured himself a large gin and tonic and walked to the patio door. Outside, it was raining. He could see it in the coppery glow of a floodlight on the lawn. A minute passed. Then several more.

'Nick,' came Terry's booming voice. 'Sorry we're neglecting you.'

Nick turned to meet the broad smile and sparkling eyes he remembered so well. Balding and jowly, Terry Mawson was as big as he sounded. Everyone liked him because it was so hard to dislike him. Or so, in normal circumstances, Nick would have confidently declared.

'Don't worry about it, Terry. Good to see you.'

'You too.' They shook hands and a meaty paw clapped Nick on the shoulder. 'What's that you're drinking?'

'G and T.'

'I'll join you.' Terry grabbed the bottle. 'Freshener?'

'No, thanks.'

'Very wise.' Ice rattled in a glass. Gin glugged over the cubes, followed by a fizz of tonic. 'Cheers.'

There was that impossibly broad smile again, accompanied by a wink as they touched glasses. Nick's mind reeled. Nothing made sense. Terry Mawson could not have dreamed up the Tantris scheme. Intrigue and secrecy were alien to him.

'Kate talk to you about Tom?' Terry asked.

'She did.'

'She's worried sick. So, anything you can do . . . we'll be grateful.'

'I can only try.'

''Course. Understood. It's been rough for you, I know. The way I see it, at times like this, people have to pull together. That's why I've been thinking about your . . . situation. Are you planning to go back to English Partnerships when the quack signs you off?'

'Of course.'

'Because you've got to pay the bills, right? It's not like you have a vocation for tarting up industrial wastelands.'

'Well . . . no.'

'So, if a better proposition cropped up . . .'

'What are you getting at, Terry?'

'I might be able to offer you a job. Higher salary. Flexible hours. And lots of fringe benefits. What do you say?'

'I say it sounds good. But—'

'What's the work? Undemanding, Nick, that's what. All my business interests basically look after themselves, but I still need to keep tabs on them, in case some bastard tries to rip me off. What I need is someone I can really trust to do the monitoring for me. You're a systems man and clever with it. I reckon you're just the guy I need.'

Nick could not seem to frame a response. Terry was grinning at him and his eyes were sending their own encouraging message: *Get on board and I'll see you all right*. Nick had no doubt that he would. But why? Why now? What exactly had led him into this? Generosity, for which he was undeniably noted? Or a troubled conscience?

'Don't give me an answer right out, Nick. Think it over. I haven't discussed this with Kate, so keep shtum over dinner, OK? There's no sense me mentioning it until I know where you stand. You can see that, can't you?'

'Yes.' Nick shaped a hesitant smile. 'Obviously.'

'Great. Just let it gel.' Terry squeezed Nick's shoulder. 'This is one of my better ideas, believe me.'

For Nick, dinner was a blank. Kate was a good cook and the food doubtless delicious. Certainly the wine flowed and the conversation probably did likewise, considering he could not afterwards recall any awkward silences. But his mind could only cast back to his discussion with Terry. The job offer was real. That was clear. But so was the money Hopkins & Broadhurst had repaid to one of Terry's shell companies. Everything was real. But nothing was certain.

Kate went to bed shortly before midnight, leaving Terry and Nick to their whiskies by the dying fire. Terry lit a cigar and tossed a last log on the embers.

'Maybe I should have left it till now to float the job idea,' he said, savouring his cigar. 'You were a bit distracted over dinner.'

'Well, you gave me a lot to think about. More than you may have realised, actually.'

'How d'you mean?'

'What it boils down to, Terry, is why?'

'Why the offer?'

'No.' Nick measured his moment. 'Why do you hate my family?'

Terry plucked the cigar from his mouth. 'What the bloody hell are you talking about?'

'I'm talking about the half a million pounds you lodged with Hopkins and Broadhurst to back up the fictitious Mr Tantris's offer for Trennor. The money was routed through an offshore outfit called Develastic. But you *are* Develastic, Terry. It was and is your money. And that's what makes me ask: why—why did you do it?'

Nick had expected a vehement denial, but instead Terry's shoulders were slumped and his expression crushed and guilty.

'Wait a minute,' Terry said thickly, rising to his feet. He crossed to the double doors, which stood half open, and peered out into the hall, listening for a moment. Then he quietly closed them and moved slowly back to the fireside. 'Keep your voice down, can you? Kate mustn't know. I don't like to think what it would do to her.'

'Nothing worse than it's already done to us, I imagine.'

'Yeah, but . . .' Terry sat down and hesitantly met Nick's gaze. 'I never imagined any harm would come of it. You have to believe me.'

'Do I? What's it all about, Terry?'

He shrugged. 'Not sure. You aren't the only ones taken for a ride.'

'What's that supposed to mean?'

'I just put up the dosh. I didn't know what it was going to be used for. Property speculation. That's what he said. Something to get him started in the world. Sounded kosher to me. So, why not? That's the way I saw it. Give him a leg up, treat him like my own. It's what I've always tried to think of him as, anyway.'

'You mean—'

'Tom. Yeah. He landed me in this.'

'*Tom?*'

'He said he had his eye on some property in Plymouth, ripe for conversion into flats. He reckoned he needed to buy several houses at a time to turn a good profit. The half-mill was chicken feed to me. I suppose I should have smelt a rat when he asked me not to tell Kate. It was to be our secret, he said. Well, I fell for it. I only found out what he was up to when he came to see us after your dad's funeral.'

'How did he explain himself?'

'He didn't really. He told Kate and me about the Tantris escapade, but I never tied that in with the money I'd loaned him. He had to spell that out for me later. But he wouldn't spell out what was behind it. "That's between me and Granddad," he said. Arrogant little . . .' Terry's right hand tightened into a fist, then relaxed again. 'He made it clear I was in nearly as much shit as he was if I blew the whistle on him. He said he'd tell Kate I'd gone along with his scheme for the sake of shafting Andrew. So I agreed to keep my mouth shut. Didn't have much choice. You can imagine how it would have looked to Kate.'

'Bad.'

'And then some.' Terry sighed and took a gulp of whisky. 'But what was the whole bloody charade about? Proving his family is averagely greedy isn't such a big deal, is it?'

'It proved a bit more than that.'

'Yeah. Like too much for the old fellow. The argy-bargy must have been a factor in Michael's death. Not that Tom felt responsible for it. There wasn't a lot of remorse on show. His dad's death was different. It got to him big time. Kate's right to be worried about him. He was so full of himself when he was putting the squeeze on me. But when he came down for Andrew's funeral, he was suddenly a frightened kid.'

'With good reason.' Nick was angry now, angry at the thought of how deeply and deviously Tom had plotted against them. 'He's going to have to answer for what he did.'

'He'll deny it. He'll try to put the blame on me.'

'That won't wash. You didn't come to Dad's funeral, did you?'

'So?'

'So Tom did. He was at Trennor during the wake.' Nick was thinking of the video and how it had got into his car. He and Andrew had ruled out the family as suspects. That was why they had settled on Farnsworth and Davey; there was no one else. But there was now. 'I wondered why Dad chose him as the recipient for *The Romance of Tristan*. Now I understand. He didn't. It was all a lie. Tom and Elspeth Hartley cooked it up between them. My God, it's obvious.'

'He'll still deny it.'

'Let him.' Nick was suddenly looking forward to his nephew doing precisely that. 'Let him try.'

CHAPTER EIGHT

Nick travelled up to Waterloo the next morning on a virtually empty train, proceeded to King's Cross by crowded Tube and boarded the busy noon express to Edinburgh. He fell asleep somewhere between Peterborough and York. The warble of his mobile roused him just as the train was approaching Durham.

'Hello?' The line was crackly.

'Basil here, Nick. Here as in Venice.'

'Good journey?'

'Better than my arrival. I'd failed to take the Carnival into consideration. Which means the city is full of masked revellers. A man dressed as a plague doctor is waiting to use this payphone.'

'Have you found somewhere to stay?'

'With difficulty. The Zampogna would be top of no one's list of recommended accommodation. My room does not boast a telephone, so the plague doctor and I may be seeing more of each other.'

'Is the Carnival going to interfere with your plans?'

'I can only hope not. It runs until Tuesday.'

'Well, there's a lot to be said for you lying low until I've . . . Well, I can't go into it now, Basil. There's been a development and I think it's best if you let me follow it through before you take any action.'

'How long do you need?'

'Not sure. Phone me at my hotel around six—seven, your time— and I'll explain. It'll be cheaper to use that than the mobile.'

'Very well. I'll call you then.'

'Speak to you later. Bye.'

Nick punched in Tom's number.

To his mild surprise, Tom answered straight away. 'Yuh?'

'Hi, Tom. It's Nick. I said I'd let you know when I was on my way up and here I am, on the train.'

'You're coming to Edinburgh?'

'I said I would.'

'Yeah, but somehow I . . . Anyway, that's really great. I could use a shoulder to lean on right now.' Tom sounded as if he meant it.

'Are you OK?'

'Not exactly. But best not to get into it on the phone. Where are you staying? I mean, you're welcome to slum it here, but—'

'I've booked a room at the Thistle.'

'Leith Street. I know it. OK, look, there's a place just round the corner from there. The Café Royal. It's a pub, despite the name. They'll direct you from the hotel. Six o'clock would be good for me.'

'Make it six thirty.'

'Six thirty it is. See you then.'

BLUE SKY and a tearing wind greeted Nick as he left Waverley Station and walked the short distance to the Thistle Hotel. He sat in his blandly functional room as six o'clock came and went with no call from Basil. The silence was not a worry, given his brother's reliance on Italian payphones. At six twenty, Nick left, switching off his mobile on the way; an interruption from Basil during his meeting with Tom was definitely not what was needed.

The Café Royal was just round the corner from the Thistle, in an alley off Princes Street. After-work drinkers sat in semicircular banquettes while others propped up the island bar. Nick bought a pint, installed himself in the only empty banquette and waited.

Tom arrived within five minutes, looking pale. 'Hi, Nick,' he said with a nervous smile. 'Good to see you.'

'Good to see you, Tom. Can I buy you a drink?'

'Stay where you are. It'll be quicker if I do it.' Tom's deftness at getting served seemed to confirm this. He returned with some kind of alcopop, swigging from the bottle before he had sat down. 'Never thought you'd come through with the visit,' he said.

'A promise is a promise.'

'Yeah, but I wasn't sure you'd remember. You weren't exactly in regular orbit at the time.'

'Not sure I am now.'

'No? Well, you look it. A guy fully restored, I'd say.'

Nick smiled. 'Your mother said much the same.'

'When did you see Mum?'

'I stopped overnight with Terry and her on the way up.'

Tom nodded slowly. 'Right.'

'I want to tell you, Tom, about your father and how—'

'No one's blaming you, Nick.'

'Perhaps they should be.'

'Not the way I see it. Something's going on. Something weird.' Tom dropped his voice. 'It's tied in with the Tantris deal, but I can't figure out how. Where'd the money come from? Did you ask yourself that?'

'Well, I—'

'Let me tell you the story. See what you make of it.'

The last thing Nick had expected was for Tom to mention the Tantris money. Was he going to confess before he had even been accused? All Nick could do was guard his expression—and listen.

'When I went down for Dad's funeral, Mum and Terry picked me up at Reading and we drove the rest of the way together. We couldn't face staying at Carwether, so we booked into the Moat House in Plymouth, up on the Hoe. You know it?'

'Of course.'

Tom lit a cigarette. 'The morning after the funeral I was up early. Truth is, I'd hardly slept. I went out at dawn, walked down to the Barbican and mooched about a bit. Started back round the Citadel and up the steps onto the Hoe. Where I saw Terry and Farnsworth. Standing by the War Memorial, talking. *Close* together, like they didn't want to be overheard. And grim-faced. Like it was serious.'

'Perhaps they . . . met by chance.'

'Get real, Nick. It was no chance. I turned round when I saw them and went back down the steps. I realised something was wrong. They're not even supposed to know each other. I couldn't work out what it meant, though. Still can't. But Dad went to Tintagel that day to see Farnsworth, didn't he?'

'Yes.'

'He must have rumbled them. Farnsworth and Terry.' Tom's eyes widened. 'You haven't remembered anything he said, have you?'

'I've remembered everything. But it doesn't help.'

'I was afraid it wouldn't. Shit.' Tom rubbed his forehead. 'There's worse, you see. I was pretty confident they hadn't spotted me on the Hoe. But now I reckon they must have. It's Farnsworth. He's—'

'In Edinburgh.'

Tom started. 'You know?'

'Visiting an old friend called Vernon Drysdale, his housekeeper said.'

'Drysdale was a professor at the university. Retired before my time. But I'd heard the name even before Farnsworth mentioned it.'

'You've spoken to Farnsworth?'

'Not much choice. He's stalking me, Nick. Everywhere I go, he's there, saying, "What an extraordinary coincidence, young Thomas." He's on my case. They know I saw them on the Hoe.'

'But how could they, if they were deep in conversation and you were, what, fifty yards or more away?'

'Maybe someone was watching their backs for them.'

'That's a bit—'

'Paranoid? Too fucking right. Being stalked makes you paranoid.' Tom looked away. 'Sorry. My nerves are stretched tight right now.' He looked back at Nick. 'I guess you know the feeling.'

'Not of being stalked. Are you sure about this?'

'He pops up wherever I go, Nick. What else am I supposed to think?' Tom frowned. 'You believe me, don't you?'

'Of course. But it's not possible, is it, that these . . . encounters . . . really are coincidental?'

Tom took a swig from his bottle. 'Tell you what. There's a coffee shop halfway between my flat and Princes Street. I drop in most mornings around half nine. Most mornings lately, guess who's been sipping an espresso and leafing through the *TLS* when I've gone in?'

'Farnsworth.'

'Too right. So, why don't you judge for yourself? Robusta, in Castle Street. I'll give it a miss tomorrow morning. But it's a good bet Farnsworth won't. See how he explains himself.'

THE EVENING HAD GROWN blurred at the edges by the time they left the Café Royal. Nick was finding it hard to calculate how many drinks he had consumed. Over a pasta supper and a couple of carafes of Chianti in an Italian restaurant nearby, he and Tom swapped maudlin reminiscences of Andrew, the father and the brother they had lost. Somehow, after that, they made their way to Tom's flat.

It was the ground floor of an end-of-terrace house in Circus Gardens, in the centre of the elegant Georgian New Town, affordable for an unemployed Edinburgh graduate thanks only to the generosity of his mother and, of course, his stepfather. The flat was so tastefully furnished and decorated that it hardly seemed like Tom's natural home at all. Nick would have expected clutter, bachelor grunge.

'Mum's idea of how I should live,' Tom explained. 'And Terry's idea of where I should live. If I'd just let them find me a job—career, I should say—everything would be perfect. From their point of view.'

'We all have to find our own way, Tom.'

'Yeah. But what happens if we lose our way?'

'We hope to find it again.'

'Depends, though, doesn't it? On how far you've strayed.' Tom took a deep swallow of whisky. 'Too far . . . and there's no way back.'

SOME TIME AFTER MIDNIGHT, Nick stumbled back to the Thistle, buffeted by an icy wind. He had not told Tom what Terry had said about him. He had travelled to Edinburgh intending to accuse Tom of setting in motion the events that had led to the deaths of his father and grandfather. Now, it seemed, Terry was the culprit after all.

Or was he? Nick's head would have been swimming even without the alcohol he had taken on board. Truth had never felt more elusive, certainty never seemed further from his grasp.

THE ALARM ROUSED HIM at eight the following morning. Every movement of his head induced a painful throb behind his eyes. Only when he was standing under the shower did he remember that he had still not spoken to Basil. If Basil had phoned the hotel after Nick's departure for the Café Royal, he had evidently left no message. No matter; they would talk later.

The morning was grey and cold, rain spitting in his face as he headed out along Princes Street. Robusta boasted few customers so early on such a dismal day, but Julian Farnsworth was one of them. He was at a table in the far corner, overcoat and scarf slung over a vacant chair, a half-finished double espresso in front of him.

'Nicholas,' he said, looking up with apparently genuine surprise. 'What are you doing here?'

'Same as you.' Nick bought himself a large americano from the sleepy-eyed assistant. 'Mind if I join you?'

'Not at all.'

'I'm up here visiting my nephew.'

'Ah, young Thomas. Yes. I've seen him in here a couple of times.'

'Not surprising. He lives nearby . . . But you don't.'

'I'm visiting an old friend. He has a house just outside Edinburgh.'

'Vernon Drysdale.'

'The very same. Your father's death reminded me that time is running short. Who knows at my age when a meeting with a friend may prove to be a last meeting?'

'How true.'

'They told me you were unwell, Nicholas, following your brother's tragic accident. I'm glad to find you . . . much as I recall.'

'I'm getting there.'

'Splendid. Please do accept my condolences. Andrew's death . . .' Farnsworth shook his head. 'A sad waste.'

'It was, yes.' A moment's silence intruded while Nick sipped his coffee. 'Professor Drysdale a late riser, is he?'

'Quite the reverse, since you ask. And why do you ask?'

'I simply wondered why you come into Edinburgh every morning to patronise this unremarkable establishment.'

'Oh, it's not unremarkable. The espresso is really rather good. Vernon is a man of the mind. The only coffee he keeps is instant.'

'How long are you staying with Professor Drysdale?'

'I'm not sure. Until he tires of my company, I suppose. Before he does, you should pay us a visit.' Farnsworth plucked a card from his pocket and wrote on the back with his fountain pen. 'There.'

Nick took the card and glanced down at it. *Roseburn Lodge, Manse Road, Roslin, near Edinburgh, (0131) 440 7749.*

'Do call. Vernon would be delighted to meet you. He's a medieval historian. I happen to have drawn his attention to your family's lineal descent from the last Emperor of Byzantium. He'd naturally be interested to meet any scion of the imperial dynasty.'

'Our lineal descent, as you call it, is unproven.'

'I understand differently.'

'If you don't mind my asking, how would you know?'

'One picks things up, if one knows where to look.'

'Would Terry Mawson be someone you've picked things up from?'

'Who?'

'Terry Mawson. Tom's stepfather.'

'I'm unacquainted with the gentleman.'

'I understand differently.'

'*Touché.*' Farnsworth seemed genuinely impressed to have the phrase turned against him. 'You don't trust me, do you, Nicholas?'

Nick took another sip of coffee, delaying his reply. 'No. I don't.'

'I quite understand. Blood is thicker than water. What has young Thomas told you? That I am following him, perhaps? That I am in cahoots with his evil stepfather? Some such *mélange*, no doubt. Desperation tactics, I fear. Ask yourself: is he entirely credible?'

'I'd be prepared to stand by him.'

'Naturally. But if he's lied to you, what then? If he's set out to deceive you and in the process done untold harm . . .' Farnsworth spread his palms. 'There's something I need to show you.'

'What?'

'I don't have it with me. Perhaps I could arrange for it to be delivered to you later. Are you staying with your nephew?'

'No. I'm in a hotel.'

'Excellent. I'll have it sent to you there. Which one?'

'The Thistle. In Leith Street.'

'Very well. Before the day is out, the proof will be in your hands.'

'Proof of what?'

'You'll see.' Farnsworth smiled. 'I promise.'

FARNSWORTH TURNED LEFT outside Robusta while Nick turned right and headed north to Circus Gardens, having promised Tom an immediate report on the encounter. Tom answered the door unshaven and dressed only in a thin towelling bathrobe.

'It's well gone ten,' he said huskily, as he dragged back the sitting-room curtains. 'I guess you must have found our friend.'

'He was there.'

Tom slumped down in a chair. 'How'd he explain that?'

'Implausibly, but slickly.'

'He didn't admit to dogging my footsteps, then?'

'No. But I'm sure he is.'

'Then they must know I'm onto them.' Tom rubbed his face. 'What am I going to do, Nick?'

'I'm not sure. You can't stop Farnsworth hanging around Edinburgh. And you can't prove he and Terry are up to no good.'

'Them knowing each other proves that to me.'

'Setting up the Tantris fraud involved a lot of money. Half a million pounds in ready cash. Would Terry have that amount on tap?'

'Easily.' There was a spark of alertness in the glance Tom shot at Nick. 'You think he bankrolled the operation?'

'Maybe.'

'It would fit, I suppose. I'd wondered that myself, to be honest.'

The layers of pretended knowledge and ignorance were becoming too much for Nick. He decided to cut through them. 'Farnsworth's sending me something later.'

'What?'

'Proof, he called it. Of why he's to be trusted, I think he meant.'

'But he isn't to be trusted.'

'No. So, it can't amount to much, can it?'

'The guy talks in fucking riddles.' Tom stood up and padded out. From the hall came the sound of a lighter being flicked. A few seconds later he reappeared in the doorway, dragging on a cigarette. 'Can you remember the last thing Dad said to you, Nick?'

'Very clearly. It was "Let go of me."'

'"Let go of me."' Tom repeated the words so softly and swiftly they almost sounded like an echo. 'And you did. We all did.'

'He didn't know they were going to be his last words, Tom.'

'The fact that he didn't know makes them all the more significant.'

'You've lost me.'

'Yeah.' Tom gazed at Nick through a slowly spreading haze of cigarette smoke. 'Maybe I have.'

Nick left Tom to shower and breakfast and walked back into the city centre. He had no idea what to do next, except wait on Farnsworth's promise. The man was not to be trusted. Tom was right about that. But who was to be trusted? The only name that came to mind was Basil's.

And Basil, bless him, had telephoned at last. When Nick switched his mobile back on, he found a message waiting for him.

'I've tried your hotel twice to no avail. It's Saturday morning here, and I have nothing to report. I'll try again later. *Arrivederci!*'

A gale was raging by now. Nick struggled through it to the Café Royal and saw off his hangover with rather more than the hair of the dog. It was midafternoon when he returned to the Thistle. By then he had drunk enough to have stopped caring about the uncertainties gnawing away at him. He lay down on the bed in his room and fell instantly into deep, dreamless sleep.

It was dark when he woke, and he could hear the rain still beating against the window. He peered at the luminous dial of his alarm clock: it was nearly half past eight. He switched on the bedside lamp, waited until his eyes had adjusted to the glare, then sat up.

He saw it at once: a square white envelope, lying on the floor near the door. There came a sudden, fluttering rush of palpitations. He took several long, slow breaths, waiting for the attack to pass. Then he rose, crossed the room and picked up the envelope.

It was blank, the flap unsealed. Nick carried it back to the bed and sat down again. He lifted the flap of the envelope, reached inside and pulled out an A5-sized black and white photograph.

The photograph had been taken through a café window. A couple of tables in, a man and a woman were sitting opposite each other. The woman appeared to be talking while the man was staring at her in rapt attention. They were in Robusta, Nick realised, and were clearly unaware that they were being filmed. No wonder, since the man was Tom Paleologus and he was sharing a table with Elspeth Hartley.

The ground-floor flat at 8 Circus Gardens was in darkness, the curtains open. Nick rang Tom's bell several times, more in hope than expectation. There was no response. It was nine thirty on a Saturday night, so Tom's absence was hardly suspicious. But Nick *was* suspicious. The photograph proved that Tom was the conspirator. The rendezvous between Terry and Farnsworth on Plymouth Hoe could well have been an invention. But Tom's rendezvous with Elspeth Hartley was real and undeniable.

Nick retreated to the Café Royal and sipped a pint till closing time. He was tempted to phone Farnsworth, but he felt he owed Tom a chance to explain. How could he explain, though? Tom had known of Farnsworth's promise to supply Nick with what he had called proof. And he must have realised Nick would want to discuss it with him. Was that why he had gone missing? If so, it was a futile evasion. He would have to return eventually. And Nick would be waiting.

But midnight came and went in Circus Gardens with no sign of Tom. It had stopped raining, but the temperature was plummeting, and none of the windows at number 8 was lit. In the end, Nick had no choice but to give up—until the morning.

WHEN NICK RETURNED, early on a chill New Town sabbath, and rang the bell of Tom's flat, silence was the only answer. Just as he turned away, a bustling figure rounded the corner from the next street and started up the steps to the door. Nick found himself looking down at a plump, middle-aged woman wearing a beltless white raincoat. Under one arm she held a wadge of Sunday newsprint.

'Looking for me, dear?' she enquired with a quizzical smile.

'No, er . . . Tom Paleologus.'

'It's a mite early for Tom. He's probably sleeping off last night.'

'You know what he was doing?'

'No. But he's young and it was Saturday. Tell me'—she frowned at Nick—'are you and he related?'

'I'm his uncle.'

'Yes, there's a resemblance. So you'd be . . .'

'Nick Paleologus.'

'Pleased to meet you, Nick. I'm Una Strawn, first-floor flat.'

'I'm worried about Tom . . . Una. His father died recently.'

'So I heard. Terrible, quite terrible. Tell you what. Come in with me and see if you can raise him.' Una took out a key and led the way into the communal entrance hall.

Nick went straight to Tom's door and gave it several loud knocks. 'Tom?' he called. But there was no sound from within.

'Do you want a coffee, Nick?' asked Una as she went on up the stairs. 'I set some to perk before stepping out for the papers.'

'Well . . . thanks.' Nick started after her. 'Very kind of you.'

'Not at all. I may have misled you about Tom. He could have gone away for the weekend for all I know.'

'I saw him yesterday morning. He didn't say he was going away.'

'Maybe not, but the impulsiveness of youth . . .' Una opened the door to her own flat and Nick followed her through to the kitchen.

The percolator had done its work in her absence. She filled a couple of chunky breakfast cups with the aromatic brew and invited Nick to sit down at the table. Then she took off her raincoat to reveal a voluminous pink mohair jumper and sat down opposite him.

'Have you come far, Nick?'

'From Cornwall. I *am* worried about Tom.'

'So I can tell. And it's true he's not been himself this past month or more. Not since he broke up with his girlfriend. Such a pity.'

'Do you know what went wrong?'

'There was someone else in Tom's life, I think. I've never seen her, mind, and Tom's said not a word. But Sasha—'

'Who?'

'Sasha Lovell, the girlfriend. I bumped into her recently and she was still raw about the whole thing, but quite clear that Tom had ditched her because of someone she called . . . Harriet. "She's no good for him," Sasha said, "but he just doesn't see it."'

'How could I contact Sasha?'

'She's a student at the university. They'd have an address for her, I dare say, though getting hold of it on a Sunday . . .'

'You don't know where she lives?'

'No. That is . . .' A thought seemed to strike Una. 'When I met her I was coming out of the Odeon in Clerk Street. Sasha was walking past on her way home from the university. "I live just over there," I remember she said, pointing across the road. We chatted for a few minutes. Then my bus came and I had to dash.' Seeing Nick's frown, she added, 'It's the best I can do, I'm afraid.'

'Sorry. I don't mean to seem ungrateful.'

'I'm sure there's no serious cause for concern. Tom's grieving for his father and maybe wondering if throwing Sasha over was such a good idea. That'll be all there is to it.'

'You're probably right,' Nick lied, thinking as he did so: if only.

IT WAS A LONG SHOT, but the only one Nick could take. Clerk Street was a stretch of the main road leading south from the city centre. Nick's taxi dropped him opposite a closed Odeon cinema in a neighbourhood of burger bars, kebab joints and betting shops.

Sasha Lovell's name did not appear next to any of the bell pushes in nearby doorways. Most bells lacked a name altogether, so Nick's search was beginning to look as if it was over before it had begun. 'Just over there' from the Odeon, however, could have included the

241

adjacent side street. Nick decided to check it out.

Rankeillor Street was lined with Georgian terraced houses in varying states of disrepair. Nick trudged from door to door along the northern side, with a growing conviction that he was wasting his time, although what better use he could make of it was a moot point.

And mooter still when, at the far end, he found himself staring somewhat disbelievingly at the name SASHA printed in faded capitals on a small laminated card. He pressed the bell next to it.

There was a squeal of swollen wood somewhere above him, a rattle of window and sash. He stepped back and looked up to see a round-faced young woman with orange spiky hair staring down at him from two floors above. 'What can I do you for?' she called.

'Sasha Lovell?'

'That's me.'

'I'm Nick Paleologus, Tom's uncle. Could we have a word?'

'What about?'

'Tom. I'm worried about him.'

'Well, maybe I'm not.'

'I really would be grateful for a few minutes of your time, Sasha. It's important. Can I come up?'

'No. Stay where you are. I'll come down.'

She appeared a few minutes later, clad in black from her Doc Martens to her beret, fleeced collar pulled up against the wind.

'There's a place round the corner where we can talk,' she said, leading the way. 'Are you the monk or the bureaucrat?'

'Tom told you about Basil and me, did he?'

'Sort of. Basil would be the monk, then?'

'Former monk.'

'Does that make you a former bureaucrat?'

'Could be. I've not been at my desk in quite a while.'

'Why's that?'

'Family troubles.'

'Are they why you're worried about Tom?'

'Yeah.'

'Here we are.'

Sasha turned in at the door of a muddily decorated café where one or two people were leafing through Sunday papers. They ordered from the girl behind the counter and sat down near the window.

'I can't stay long. Tell me about these family troubles of yours.'

'Tom's father and grandfather have both died recently.'

'Shit.' Sasha winced. 'That's rough.'

'I gather you and Tom broke up a while back.'

Sasha sipped her tea. 'Who told you that?'

'Una Strawn. She mentioned a woman called Harriet.'

'Harriet. That's right. The one I couldn't compete with.'

'This her?' Nick showed Sasha the photograph.

'Yeah. That *is* her. Where'd this come from?'

'It was sent anonymously . . . to Tom's mother. I think someone was trying to warn her that Harriet could be a bad influence on Tom. He's been behaving strangely. Even before the deaths in the family.'

'How did they happen? The deaths, I mean.'

'A fall, in my father's case. Not unexpected, given his age and frailty. Tom's father, my brother Andrew, died in a road accident.'

'Well, it's tough, but Tom finished with me in January. I don't—'

'Finished because of Harriet?'

'Not according to Tom. But when I saw him with her soon after, it was obvious.'

'Do you know her surname?'

'Elsmore, I think. Yeah. Harriet Elsmore.'

'What else do you know about her?'

'Nothing. It was just the one encounter. And not what you'd call a warm one. He was . . . cowed. Not the Tom I knew. She's got her claws into him somehow. And you're worried about how deep, right?'

'That's more or less the size of it.'

'Well, I don't know. She's a weird one. And not Tom's type, I'd have said. 'Course, I thought *I* was his type. He wanted me to move in with him. He was keen, right? Then Harriet comes on the scene and he's suddenly . . . ice. I mean, who is she? How does she make a living? She must be . . . what, thirty-five? It doesn't stack up.'

'Did you ask Tom about her?'

'I asked. He didn't answer.'

'He's done a bunk since I got here. I wondered if he could be with her. Does she live in Edinburgh?'

'Not sure. But I don't think so.' Sasha shook her head expressively. 'That photograph was sent to Tom's mother, right?'

'Yes.' Nick wondered if he was going to regret the instinctive lie.

'Any idea who by?'

'None.'

'Only you're not the first to ask me about Harriet Elsmore.'

'Who *was* first?'

'Some old guy. Called . . . Harmsworth. Something like that. It was about ten days ago.'

'What did he want to know?'

'Anything I could tell him about her. Which, like I've told you, isn't much. He said he was anxious to contact her and understood I might be able to help. I asked him if he knew Tom and he said yes, he was a friend of the family. That true?'

'More acquaintance than friend. His name's Julian Farnsworth. A former colleague of my father.'

Sasha thought for a moment. 'Has Tom got himself mixed up in something bad, Nick?'

'Could be.'

'Shit.' Sasha stared into her tea. 'Just when you think you're over someone . . . you have to start worrying about them.'

They left the café shortly afterwards. Nick started to take his leave, but Sasha insisted he tag along.

'There's something at the flat I want to give you,' she explained as they turned the corner into Rankeillor Street. 'I should return them to Tom, anyway. If you see him, say I asked you to pass them on. If you don't see him . . . if he stays away . . . it's up to you what you do.'

'What are we talking about?'

'Wait out here.' Sasha went ahead of him into number 56, closing the door behind her.

Nick did as he had been told, with rapidly mounting puzzlement. Then he heard the second-floor window squeak open. He looked up and Sasha met his gaze. She tossed some small object down to him. In the instant before he caught it, he realised it was a bunch of keys.

There were three keys, tied together with string. Nick stared at them, nestled in his palm. Then he heard the window close.

STANDING AT A BUS-STOP in Clerk Street, fingering the keys in his pocket, Nick promised himself he would not use them unless he had to. But the promise only begged a question: when might he have to?

The chirrup of his mobile came as a welcome distraction, as did the sound of Basil's voice when he answered.

'Good morning, Nick. How do I find you?'

'Confused. Tom's behaving oddly.'

'Bereavement can have that effect. And what of the "development" you reported when last we spoke?'

'It's kind of connected. But I can't be specific yet. Sorry.'

'No need to apologise. As it happens, I disregarded your preference in the matter and called at cousin Demetrius's residence yesterday.'

'You did what?'

'I presented my compliments at the Palazzo Falcetto, a residence sufficiently grand to suggest its owner is unlikely to be bothered about the inheritance of a modest house in Cornwall.'

'For God's sake, Basil, I asked you to—'

'You need not worry. Apparently Demetrius regularly flees Venice during the Carnival. He is expected back on Wednesday and will be informed of my visit. Seen anything of Dr Farnsworth?'

'Well, yes, we've met. He insists he's here to see an old friend.'

'You are telling me everything, aren't you, Nick?'

'As much as I can be sure of. I just need to pin things down.'

'Then you have until Wednesday. The display on this telephone indicates that my credit is draining away like sand. Goodbye, Nick.'

'Listen, Basil—' But it was too late. The line was dead.

ROSLIN SEEMED an unremarkable place: a mix of old and new housing centred on a few shops and a couple of pubs. A man walking his dog directed Nick to Roseburn Lodge, a plain greystone Georgian house, draped in ivy. A battered old estate car was parked on the short gravel drive, but there was no sign of Farnsworth's Citroën.

Nick tugged at the bell, and the door was opened by a woman wearing an apron over a threadbare dress. 'Aye?' she said.

'I'm looking for Dr Julian Farnsworth.'

'He's no here.'

'What about Professor Drysdale? Is he at home?'

'Aye, he is.'

'Could you ask him if he'll spare me a moment? Dr Farnsworth may have mentioned me. My name's Nicholas Paleologus.'

'Wait here.' She stumped off, half closing the door behind her.

Nick was left to listen to the rooks cawing in the trees. Inside, he could hear a mumble of conversation. Then the woman reappeared.

'Come away in.'

'Thanks.'

She led the way down a shadowy hall to an open doorway near the end, where she stood back to let him proceed.

The room Nick stepped into was obviously the professor's study. A vast leather-topped desk was strewn with books and papers. Two walls were lined with bookshelves, and more books were stacked on the floor and on the seat of one of the armchairs flanking the fireplace.

From the other armchair an elderly man rose stiffly to his feet and smiled in greeting. Vernon Drysdale was stout, pigeon-chested, ruddy-faced and bald as an egg. 'Mr Paleologus.' He shook Nick's hand firmly. 'It's an honour.' The Scottish burr in his voice was subdued.

'Good of you to see me, Professor. I don't know about an honour.'

'A living, breathing Paleologus. It's a wonder as well as an honour. I met your father a few times, of course. Please accept my condolences.'

'Thank you.'

'Julian tells me your elder brother also died recently. A terrible coincidence.'

'Not really a coincidence. Actually, it's Julian—Dr Farnsworth—I'm hoping to see.'

'You're out of luck, I'm afraid. He's been called away.'

'Back to Oxford?'

'I'm not sure. Julian plays his cards close to his chest, as you may be aware. He left yesterday afternoon, in something of a hurry.'

'I saw him yesterday morning. He said nothing about going away.'

'There was a phone call, then he was off, barely finding time to mention you might pop in.' Drysdale smiled. 'Won't you sit down?' He waved at the other armchair. 'Dump those books anywhere.'

'All right. Thanks.' Nick made a clearance and sat down.

'A drop of Scotch, Paleologus?'

'Thanks. Don't mind if I do.'

Drysdale moved to a section of the bookcase where a bottle of Jura malt and some tumblers were stored in front of a run of historical journals. He poured generous measures for each of them, handed Nick his glass and lowered himself stiffly into his chair. '*Slàinte.*'

'Cheers.'

'I'm sorry about Julian. One feels a measure of responsibility for one's friends, even when one shouldn't.'

'Does he visit you often?'

'Not at all. This is the first time in years.' Drysdale grinned. 'I've no doubt he had a more compelling motive for his visit than the pleasure of my company. But he's been reticent on the point. Has he intimated anything to you?'

'No. But he's been paying close attention to my nephew.'

'Ah. The last of the Paleologoi.'

'I'm sorry?'

'As the only known descendants of the Imperial family—'

'*Supposed* descendants, Professor. The lineage was a triumph of wishful thinking on the part of my grandfather.'

'Really? That's not my understanding.'

'Julian said you're something of an expert on Byzantine history.'

'A scholar, Paleologus, no more.' Drysdale frowned. 'Though in the opinion of some I've forfeited the right to call myself one.'

'How?'

'Oh, by writing on a vulgarly populist theme. A hanging offence in certain circles. But the book sells. Why should I apologise?'

'I don't suppose you should. What's it about?'

'Have you visited Rosslyn Chapel, Paleologus? We're just across the way from one of the Lothians' premier tourist attractions.'

'I've not been there.'

'Well, you should go. And there'll be some copies of *Shades of Grail* in the chapel shop. It's my humble contribution to the debate.'

'What debate is that?'

'Heard of the Knights Templar?'

'Well, I know they were a medieval order of knights, founded during the Crusades. I have the impression there's a mystery about them.'

'Indeed. I'll distil it for you as briefly as I can. For a fuller version I must refer you to my book, a bargain at six ninety-nine. But here goes. The Holy Grail is a constant in Western literature. What is it? The cup from which Christ drank at the Last Supper. Some accept it as such. Proponents of another school of thought equate the Grail with the Ark of the Covenant, the greatest treasure of the Jewish people, which was buried deep beneath King Solomon's Temple in Jerusalem to prevent it falling into Roman hands when the city fell to the legions of Titus in 70 AD. They believe the Ark contains a wondrous secret. And that the Knights Templar were formed after the capture of Jerusalem by the Crusaders in 1099 specifically to search for the Ark. The knights supposedly spent many years excavating beneath the Temple and eventually found what they were looking for. If not the Ark itself, then what it had stood as symbol for: the secret of secrets; the truth; the gnosis of man's relationship with God.'

'And what's that?'

'A good question, Paleologus. A divine question, you might say. As unknown as it's unknowable. When Jerusalem was recaptured by Saladin in 1187, the Templars moved to the fortress of Acre, along presumably with any treasure they held. When Acre fell in its turn, in 1291, they moved to Cyprus. There they remained until suppressed by fiat of Pope Clement the Fifth in 1307 on grounds of heresy, sodomy and blasphemy. The last Templar Grand Master was burned at the stake in 1314.'

'What became of the Templar treasure?'

'If it existed, you mean? Ah, well, that's what so many books have been written about. Where did it go—this great and awful secret?

Many have convinced themselves that the Templars sent their most precious possession away for safekeeping. Robert the Bruce having been excommunicated, the Templar properties in Scotland at the time were immune to the Pope's proscription of the order. The theory therefore goes that it was sent here and lies here still, somewhere beneath Rosslyn Chapel.'

'You're not serious.'

'I'm serious when I say that many believe it. Construction of the chapel did not begin until 1446, more than a hundred years after the suppression of the Templars. To my mind that constitutes a serious objection to the idea, but the true believers argue that the chapel was a permanent solution to what had been envisaged as a temporary problem. The long and short of the Templar myth is: did they find something—the Ark, the Grail, what you will—beneath the Temple? That's the question I tried to answer in *Shades of Grail*.'

'And what *is* the answer?'

'No one knows. No one *can* know for certain. There's no evidence, no proof. There's only . . .' Drysdale shrugged. 'Rumour and legend.'

'But what do you think?'

'As a historian, I think rumour and legend darken as much as they illumine. Gnosis is a concept, not an object. It's not susceptible to excavation. Such treasure is by definition . . . intangible.'

'So there's nothing hidden under the chapel?'

'The bones of a few dead knights. That's all.' Drysdale gazed into the blackness of the empty fireplace. 'That's all people ever find when they dig for gold.' He looked up at Nick with the ghost of a smile hiding beneath his whiskers. 'The secret is that there is no secret.'

CHAPTER NINE

Rosslyn Chapel was an oddly disproportionate structure, with oversized buttresses and a west wall extended to either side as if part of some larger, uncompleted building. Inside, the stone carving was remarkable. Imps, angels, knights and dragons adorned every beam, pillar and archway. The masons had worked the stone miraculously, as if it had been clay for them to squeeze and shape.

In the chapel shop, Nick bought a copy of *Shades of Grail*, then he stepped out into the open air. He walked back up the lane to the village and went into the bar of the hotel on the corner of Manse Road. As he sat by the window, drinking his beer, his mobile rang.

'Nick?' It was Terry, already sounding anxious. 'This is the first chance I've had to phone you. How have you got on with Tom?'

'Not very well. Before I could accuse him of anything, he did a moonlight flit.'

'Oh Christ. Kate'll go spare. She's phoned him a few times and got no answer. Now I know why. Where's he gone?'

'Haven't a clue. Any suggestions?'

'I haven't a clue either. He's a closed book to me. For Christ's sake, Nick, can't you . . . do something to get us out of this mess.'

'Well . . .' Nick fingered the keys in his pocket. 'I'll see what I can come up with.'

NICK ORDERED A TAXI and, as it bowled north through the Edinburgh suburbs, he settled his strategy. He would give Tom until nightfall. Then, if there was still no one at home, he would enter the flat using Sasha's keys and see what he could find. There was nothing else he could do.

He sat in his hotel room as the afternoon slowly uncoiled, reading Drysdale's book. Rosslyn Chapel was evidently only one candidate for the repository of the Templars' treasure. The old Cathar stronghold of Languedoc was another and Portugal was also in the frame. Drysdale summarised the various writings on the subject with no more than a hint of satire. *'The secret is that there is no secret.'* Nowhere did the phrase appear, but it echoed in Nick's brain as he read.

TOM HAD NOT RETURNED. That was evident to Nick as he gazed at the black, uncurtained windows on the ground floor of 8 Circus Gardens. It was nearly nine o'clock. Delay was at an end.

The first of the Yale keys he tried opened the front door. Nick hesitated in the hall, listening. He thought he could hear music, drifting down from Una Strawn's flat. He opened Tom's door and stepped inside, shutting the door smartly behind him.

To his left, an amber, rain-dappled wash of lamplight stretched across the drawing-room carpet. He headed through the open doorway to the windows on the far side of the room, where he tugged the curtains closed before moving back to the light switch.

Then he saw, lying on the coffee table, a blank white envelope, torn jaggedly open and a photograph half hidden beneath it. Nick picked up the photograph and stared at it. It was of Tom with Elspeth Hartley at Robusta, exactly the same as the one that had been slipped under Nick's door at the Thistle. There was no accompanying note.

Where should he look for clues to Tom's whereabouts? The bedroom was a good bet. Nick dropped the photograph, turned and headed back along the passage. The bedroom was at the rear of the house, overlooking the garden, so Nick felt less need to be cautious. He switched on the light as he stepped through the open doorway.

His heart jolted and he stopped in his tracks. For a shard of a crazy second he thought Tom was simply lying on the bed, watching him. But he was too still, and his eyes were staring blindly at the ceiling. His mouth was open, vomit crusted round his lips and chin. He was naked, his skin pale as marble. There were several empty pill foils and a toppled glass on the floor, close to the bed. And a drained syringe was crooked in his left arm, the needle still buried in a vein.

Tom had not run away after all.

ONCE AGAIN NICK found himself observing events as if they were somehow distant from him. It was a defence mechanism his mind had developed to hold off the demons who had once overwhelmed him. He retreated from the bedroom and dialled 999 on the telephone in the drawing room, asked for the police and told them what he had found. They said they would be with him shortly.

He could not stay in the flat. He certainly could not start the search for clues he had meant to carry out. Besides, he felt strangely certain that there would be no clues to uncover. The only evidence of Tom's involvement with Elspeth Hartley was the photograph lying on the coffee table. Nick picked it up and slid it into his coat pocket, then went upstairs to Una Strawn's flat.

THE POLICE WERE EFFICIENT and perfunctorily sympathetic. They did not challenge Nick's edited version of events. Why should they? An unemployed ex-student with a drugs habit under emotional stress was hardly a rarity in their suicide statistics. Nick explained that Tom's mother had become worried about him following his father's death. They made notes. They called for the pathologist and photographer. They did what had to be done.

Nick agreed to visit the police station next morning to make a formal statement. He went back up to Una's flat and gratefully accepted her offer of whisky and the use of her phone. She left him alone to make the call no one could make for him.

He remembered little afterwards of his conversation with Terry, apart from the relief he felt that he did not have to break the news to Kate directly. He said nothing about the syringe or the photograph and Terry asked no leading questions. Both knew there was more to be said. Both also knew that now was not the time to say it.

The police and the undertakers were still quietly going about their business downstairs an hour or so later, when Terry phoned back. Kate could not bear to stay at home any longer, he explained. They would be setting off immediately and they should reach Edinburgh by dawn. They had booked a room at the Balmoral and would contact Nick when they arrived.

Another hour passed. The photographer left, then the pathologist. Tom was loaded into an unmarked van and carried away to the mortuary. A policeman told Nick they were done. As the last car drove off into the night, 8 Circus Gardens lapsed into nocturnal stillness.

NICK REACHED HIS ROOM at the Thistle and lay on the bed with little expectation of sleep. But he must have slept because the next thing he knew was the ringing of the telephone. It was 7.38 by his watch and daylight was seeping round the curtains. He grabbed the receiver.

'Nick?'

'Terry. Where are you?'

'At the Balmoral.'

'Can you give me ten minutes?'

'Sure. I'll walk over to the Thistle and meet you in the lobby.'

TERRY WAS WAITING when Nick stepped out of the lift. He looked like the husk of his normal self, a crumpled figure with bloodshot eyes.

'This is the worst day of my life, Nick,' he said, his voice as rough as sandpaper. 'Kate's that broke up I . . . I don't know what to say or do.'

'I'm sorry, Terry. It's . . . beyond words.'

'Tell me what happened. Tell me what led up to it.'

So Nick told him everything—Tom's attempt to cast suspicion on Terry; Farnsworth's sinister comings and goings; the photograph of Tom with Elspeth, aka Harriet; the gruesome scene at 8 Circus Gardens. There was no point holding anything back.

'You've got both photographs?'

'Yes.' Nick laid them on the table.

Terry stared down at them. 'What a bloody awful business. Why did he do it? I mean, it was bad. But it didn't have to be this bad.'

'I only wish it wasn't.'

'Me too.' Terry stanched some tears. 'Sorry. It's just when I . . .' He shook his head. 'We've got to find out what Farnsworth's up to.'

'That won't be easy.' Nick leaned across the table. 'Look, Terry, there's a more immediate problem. What do you want me to say to Kate? Don't you think she's going to have to know about all this?'

Terry sighed heavily. 'I'll tell her. But now's too soon. She's still in shock. In a couple of days . . . she'll be better able to cope with it.'

'And until then?'

'Can't you just stonewall her, Nick? Say you met Tom, noticed how depressed he was, got worried, contacted his girlfriend and . . . found him? Can't you just . . . leave out the rest? I'll explain I asked you to when I tell her the whole story. I'll make sure you're in the clear.'

In the clear? Nick doubted he would ever be that. 'All right,' he said. 'It's your call.'

Nick asked Terry to drop him at the main police station so he could make his statement. Terry came in with him to find out if the post-mortem result was available. He was referred to the Procurator Fiscal's office and left Nick in the reception area with a whispered plea for him to say as little as possible.

It was a plea easily complied with. The police had pigeonholed Tom's death as a drugs-related suicide. Nick's statement was a formality. The version of events he signed his name to was the same as the one Terry wanted him to present to Kate. It was accurate. As far as it went.

When he left the police station, he realised that he was very close to Rankeillor Street. He had told Una he would break the news to Sasha without thinking through the how and the when of it. Now he could hardly pass up the opportunity. She might well have left for classes at the university, though. He walked along to number 56 with no great confidence he would find her in.

But the front door opened as he approached and Sasha smiled out wanly at him in greeting. Her eyes were moist and full. She knew.

'I saw you coming from the window. I must have been sitting up there for an hour or more staring out, just thinking about Tom.' She shook her head. 'The stupid bastard.'

'How did you hear?'

'I phoned Una. I was worried about him.'

'Did you sense something?'

'No. It's simpler than that. And worse. If only I *had* sensed something. You'd better come up.'

Sasha's flat was standard-issue student digs, complete with broken-backed furniture, Blu-Tacked posters, unwashed crockery and an atmosphere scented with joss sticks and cannabis.

'I got this in the post this morning.' Sasha passed Nick a letter written in a jagged hand. 'It's from Tom.'

'He wrote to you?'

'Yeah. He even went to the bother of finding a box with a Sunday collection. Didn't want me to hear at second hand, I suppose.'

'It's a suicide note?'

'More or less. See for yourself. There's a message for you in it.'

Nick sat down in the nearest armchair and looked at the letter.

Hi, Sash. You won't understand why I'm doing this. You'll think it's a waste. As if. Truth is, there's no other way out. Everything's fucked. I didn't know it would go down like this. I promise you that. Maybe Harriet did. Maybe she planned it this way. Total wipe-out. Could be. I've seen that side of her. But it's too late. For me, anyway. I can't deal with what I've done. It's too much.

If you see my uncle Nick, tell him to let it go. I've sent him something. He should take it as a warning. I'm getting out the only way I can. I'm sorry for hurting you. But this will be the last time. That's one promise I'll keep. I love you, Sash. If you want to do me a favour, get over me fast. Remember the laughs we had. No one can take those away. Have fun. You're better at it than me. I've got to go now. This is it. All my love, Tom.

Nick's fingers were trembling when he handed the letter back to Sasha. He tried to speak, but had to clear his throat first. 'I didn't realise he was so unhappy. If I had I'd have . . . gone easier on him.'

'What did Harriet drag him into, Nick?'

'Old family secrets. So secret I don't know what they are.'

'Will you let it go?'

'I don't think I can.'

'But you haven't seen what he's sent you yet, have you?'

'No.' Nick stood up. 'I'd better get back to the hotel. It could be waiting for me there. Whatever it is.'

'A warning, he said.'

'Yeah. Somehow, though . . . I doubt I'll heed it.'

'THIS ARRIVED FOR YOU earlier, sir,' said the receptionist at the Thistle half an hour later. She handed Nick a letter along with his key.

He recognised Tom's writing at once, but waited until he was in the privacy of his room before opening the envelope. There was no note inside, just a blown-up photocopy of a newspaper article.

Nick sat down on the bed and looked at the page of print. At the top was the newspaper title and a date: *Birmingham Post, Thursday, October 5, 2000*. Beneath that was a double-column headline: ESTATE AGENT'S MYSTERIOUS HOLIDAY DROWNING. Nick read on.

An inquest at Sutton Coldfield Magistrates' Court returned a verdict of accidental death yesterday in the case of Birmingham estate agent Jonathan Braybourne, who died while on holiday in Venice earlier this year.

Mr Braybourne, 43, a partner at Oldcorn & Co., drowned in a Venetian canal on May 30. The Italian police failed to establish how Mr Braybourne came to fall in. Bruising on his left temple suggested he may have struck his head as he fell. The incident occurred at night in a poorly lit district and Mr Braybourne's body was not discovered until the following morning.

Emily Braybourne, the deceased's sister, said in evidence that her brother had gone to Venice to visit an acquaintance, and that the Italian police had not properly questioned this acquaintance. She believed him to be implicated in her brother's murder.

The coroner, in his summing-up, said there were no grounds for suspecting the person named by Miss Braybourne. He urged her to accept that her brother's death was a tragic accident.

As Nick reread the article, its implications piled up in his mind. He reckoned he knew who Emily Braybourne was, and the 'acquaintance' of her brother's. And this, he supposed, was Tom's warning. Go on digging and Nick could end up like Jonathan Braybourne and the man in the cellar, like Andrew and his father, like Tom himself. The list of the dead was growing. The threat was not imaginary.

If that was true, Nick's position was nothing like as perilous as Basil's. He had alerted Demetrius Paleologus to his presence in Venice. He was suddenly a sitting duck. Panic seized Nick. He jabbed at his mobile, but there was no message from Basil. He rang international directory enquiries and gleaned with difficulty a telephone number for the Hotel Zampogna in Venice. He dialled it.

'*Pronto?*' The voice was female, the tone abrupt.

'Hotel Zampogna?'

'*Sì.*'

'I need to speak to Mr Paleologus. *Molto importante*. I'm his brother. I need to—'

'*Il telefono non è per i clienti.*'

'But—' But nothing. The line was dead.

What was he to do? Basil might be sipping an espresso in a café in

St Mark's Square. Or he might be at the bottom of a canal. There was no way to tell.

He dialled another number. It was a call he was due to make anyway, though he no longer felt confident of managing it sensitively.

'Old Ferry Inn.'

'Irene, this is Nick.'

'Hi. Good to hear from you. How's it going in Edinburgh?'

'Listen to me, Irene. I'm sorry to have to tell you this. Tom's dead.'

'*What?*'

'It looks like he killed himself. A drugs overdose. Kate and Terry are up here. I'm sorry I didn't tell you sooner, but—'

'When was this?'

'Over the weekend. But never mind that.'

'*Never mind?*'

'Have you heard from Basil?'

'Basil? No. But, Nick. Tom *killed himself*?'

'You can contact Kate and Terry at the Balmoral Hotel. And find out from Anna if she's heard from Basil. Will you do that for me? It's very important. I'll call you later. I have to go now.'

'Hold on, I—'

'Sorry, Irene. I *will* call later. 'Bye.'

He put the phone down and started to pack. Suddenly, what he had to do was clear to him. The only way to be sure Basil had not walked into a trap was to follow him to where the trap might be set.

THANKS TO ITS DEPARTING ten minutes late, the one o'clock train to King's Cross left with Nick on board. Before it had cleared the outskirts of Edinburgh, Terry rang him on his mobile.

'What's going on, Nick? You've checked out of your hotel. Where are you going?'

'I can't get into it now. I'm doing what I have to do to make sure this doesn't get any worse than it already is.'

'What could be worse than Tom killing himself?'

'Go see Sasha Lovell, his ex-girlfriend. Fifty-six Rankeillor Street. Tom sent her a note. That tells you about as much as I know. Before you do, though, you'd better tell Kate the truth.'

'I can't do that. Not yet.'

'We're out of time. Face her with it. That's my advice.'

'Some advice.'

'It's all I can offer. Goodbye, Terry.'

Nick was sorely tempted to turn his mobile off, but he had to keep it on in case Basil called. Basil did not call. When a call next came, as the train glided out of York station, it was from Irene.

'I've spoken to Kate, Nick. She's devastated. And your behaviour isn't helping. Where are you going?'

'Has Anna heard from Basil?'

'No. Do you know where he is?'

'He's gone to Venice to confront cousin Demetrius. And he could well be in danger.'

'You're going after him, aren't you?'

'Yes.'

'Well, you mustn't. This is no time for misguided heroics, Nick. If Basil's in trouble we don't want you getting mixed up in it as well.'

'You don't understand, Irene. I'm already mixed up in it. We all are.'

HOME WAS A BIGGER HOUSE than Nick needed in Damson Close, a prim cul-de-sac in the Walnut Tree district of Milton Keynes. It did not look neglected to Nick as he walked up the drive after paying the taxi driver. It wore his absence as lightly as it always had his presence.

He dumped his bag and the accumulated mail in the kitchen, then went round closing curtains and switching on lights. In a bedroom drawer he found the one thing he had come for: his passport. He put it in his pocket and went back down to the kitchen.

He made some tea and had just opened the freezer in search of a microwaveable supper when the doorbell rang. He looked out into the hall and saw the dark, indistinct shape of his visitor through the frosted-glass panel in the door. He had failed to switch on the porch light. The doorbell rang, lengthily, insistently. It would have to be dealt with. Nick marched to the door and opened it.

The light from the hall flooded out onto Elspeth Hartley's face. 'Hello, Nick,' she said. 'Will you come for a drive with me?'

Elspeth Hartley was not as Nick remembered. Her hair was shorter and she no longer wore glasses. She was dressed in a different style—black leather jacket and trousers and a black sweater. She looked thinner in the face and had her hands buried in her pockets.

'Well, will you? We can't talk indoors.'

'Have you any idea . . . of the damage you've done to my family?'

'Yes.'

'Yet you come here like this and calmly ask me to go for a drive?'

'Who said I was calm?'

'I just . . . don't believe it.'

'I know about Tom. I had a letter too.' She pulled a crumpled envelope from her pocket. 'He told me what he was going to do. And he said he was going to tell you about Jonty.'

'Was Jonathan Braybourne your brother?'

'Yes.'

'Which makes you Emily Braybourne.'

'Yes.'

'How did you know I'd be here?'

'Tom wanted to warn you off. But I reckoned you couldn't be warned off. You've come back for your passport, haven't you?'

'You're very clever.'

'Not really. Just a good reader of people. I've been waiting for you since this afternoon. I don't think anyone followed you and I'm pretty sure no one beat me to it. But I'll feel safer in the car. Are you coming?'

'Why should I?'

'Because you want to know the truth. And with Tom gone, I have to tell it to someone. You're the only one I can trust.'

'WHERE ARE WE GOING?' Nick asked, after they had climbed into the Peugeot and started away.

'We're not going anywhere. I'll just drive round the ring road.'

'While you tell me why you set out to destroy my family?'

'I didn't set out to destroy anyone.'

'You could have fooled me.'

'This is the deal, Nick. I talk. You listen. Are you comfortable with that? Because if not . . .'

'OK.'

'Good.' She concentrated for a moment on joining the dual carriageway that ran round the perimeter of the town, then resumed. 'How much do you know about my father?'

'Very little. According to Julian Farnsworth, my father and your father met during the war, when they were both stationed in Cyprus. But Dad never mentioned a Digby Braybourne to me. All three were archaeologists at Oxford. Your father got involved in an auction-house fraud and wound up in prison. That was in 1957. And that's it.'

'Right. Then this is the rest. My mother worked in the kitchens at Brasenose College. My father took a fancy to her and led her on with a promise of marriage. A lie, of course. It would have been unthinkable for a fellow to marry a servant. She got pregnant. Jonty was born just around the time Dad went to prison. When he came out, he was more than willing to marry Mum. He had no one else to turn to. So they got hitched. I was born in 1966. We lived out at

Cowley. Dad got a clerical job but he couldn't stick office work. He started drinking and gambling. He got the sack. Then he left us. I didn't see much of him when I was growing up, but it was more than I wanted to see of him. It was different for Jonty. He adored Dad. To do Dad justice, I think the feeling was mutual. He wanted to be a father Jonty could be proud of. But he didn't have it in him. In the end, Mum divorced him. By then, Jonty was at Cambridge and he told me later that Dad often went to see him. Mum forbade him to go to the graduation ceremony. But he heard about it later, of course.'

'You mean he heard about me?'

'Yeah. The Paleologus prodigy. According to Jonty, your fall from grace gave Dad an idea. He was over sixty and none too well. He wanted to do something for Jonty and me before it was too late. His idea involved your father. In fact, it couldn't work *without* him.'

'What was the idea?'

'I don't know. But nothing came of it. Whether your father turned him down or he bottled out of approaching him we never found out. We had no address for him. At some point in the autumn of 1980, we stopped hearing from him. Mum and I reckoned he was dead. Little by little, we forgot about him. Jonty established himself as an estate agent, got married and had children. I went to Cambridge as well, stayed on for my doctorate and started an academic career.'

'You really are an art historian, then?'

'Yeah. On sabbatical from the University of Wisconsin.'

'Do they know what you're doing with your sabbatical?'

'We had a deal, Nick. All you have to do is listen. Mum died in July '99. When we went through her affairs, we found she had a lot more money in her bank account than we'd expected. There'd been regular quarterly payments from a bank in Cyprus. It was like an extra pension. But who was paying it? The bank wouldn't say. But Jonty took Audrey and the kids to Cyprus for a holiday that autumn. While he was there, he hired a local private detective to do some digging. This guy established that the account Mum had been paid from was in the name of Demetrius Paleologus. Know him?'

'In a sense. I've never met him. He's some sort of cousin. Dad knew him. But he doesn't live in Cyprus.'

'No. Cyprus was his wartime bolt hole. He still owns several hotels there, but he lives in Venice. When our fathers were serving together in Cyprus, though, Demetrius Paleologus was there too. That has to be when they all met. And out of that, Jonty reckoned, came the moneymaking scheme Dad hatched years later. Jonty never believed

Dad had willingly lost touch with us. He believed he'd been stopped.'

'What do you mean by "stopped"?'

'Jonty meant murdered. And since we both know that you and your brother found a body under the cellar floor at Trennor, murder is what I mean too. Don't deny it, Nick. In fact, don't say a word. Just listen. Jonty looked up some old acquaintances of Dad's at Oxford, Julian Farnsworth among them. He also went to see your father, who told him to get lost. For Jonty, it all added up. The payments to Mum were conscience money. Dad's murder was what troubled those consciences, and your father and his cousin Demetrius were in the frame. When I saw Jonty last Easter he was a man obsessed. He went to Venice a few weeks later, alone. He never came back.

'I knew the moment I heard he was dead I'd have to take up where he'd left off. Wisconsin let me bring my sabbatical forward, so I had the time. Jonty had accumulated a stack of books in the months before his death. Medieval history mostly—Venice, Byzantium, the Crusades. Plus a lot of esoteric stuff about Templarism and the Holy Grail.'

'*Shades of Grail*, by Vernon Drysdale?' Nick asked.

'Yes, that was a bit of a potboiler. But Jonty had another by him. A biography of Richard, Earl of Cornwall, the man responsible for the construction of Tintagel Castle. It was called *The Left Hand of the King*. I couldn't make out what it amounted to. But the name Paleologus cropped up a lot. Jonty had a heap of literature about the archaeology and mythology of Tintagel, and just about everything printed on the subject of the St Neot glass, which put me onto the Doom Window mystery, which connected in turn with Trennor, where who should live but Michael Paleologus, Dad's old army pal.'

'Did it really connect? I know you lied about the Bawden letter.'

'It was a small misrepresentation. The "great and particular treasure of the parish" had to be the Doom Window. I'm fairly sure Mandrell, the man Bawden named as its custodian, lived at Trennor.'

'Fairly sure isn't certain.'

'All right. I'll tell you what I *am* certain of. I needed to get inside your family. I needed an ally. I chose Tom because he was the next generation on and so less likely to be a party to whatever had happened. I think he was flattered by my attentions, then genuinely attracted to me. But that was only part of the reason why he went along with it. Tom had seriously fraught relationships with his father and grandfather. He felt disapproved of. And that doesn't encourage loyalty.

'Besides, he remembered something from his childhood, when he was nine or ten. Around 1986 or '87. His grandparents had been looking after him at Trennor while his parents had a weekend away. He'd been woken up one night by the sound of them arguing. He'd gone downstairs and listened to them shouting at each other, apparently, *down in the cellar*. He crept back to bed and never breathed a word about it. But he never forgot. And one repeated phrase of his grandmother's stuck in his mind. "I want that thing removed."

'It seemed to me—and to him—that the time had come to find out what she'd been referring to. I knew what Jonty would have thought. My father's body was what she wanted removed. So, we devised a test. If Michael Paleologus had murdered my father and buried him at Trennor, he wouldn't agree to sell the house at any price, even if he could present no decent argument *not* to sell. And we wanted him to know. We wanted him to realise what it was all about.

'I borrowed the name Elspeth Hartley from an art historian at Bristol I'd worked with occasionally who I knew to be on sabbatical herself. Harriet Elsmore was a straightforward alias. Tantris was more complicated. Tom devised it as a tease *and* an additional test. He also came up with the capital we needed to give the Tantris deal wings. By then he was beginning to take pleasure in tormenting his grandfather—and, by extension, the rest of you. That wasn't what it was supposed to be about. I tried to call a halt after your father's death. But Tom was determined to go on to the end. "We can't stop now," he said. "We can't stop until it's all out in the open."

'I suspect he was at Trennor the night your father died, though he denied it. You all thought he was in Edinburgh. But he left that condolences card on Andrew's Land Rover. He followed the pair of you to Minions, guessed what you were up to and was ready and waiting when you dumped the body there late on Saturday night. He got on the train from Edinburgh at Plymouth the next day and got off at Bodmin Parkway, where Andrew was waiting to pick him up. He led you on with that story of being sent a copy of *The Romance of Tristan* by his grandfather. During the funeral party, he planted the video in your car. Then he sat back to see which way you'd jump.

'And that's when he started to lose control. Andrew's death was an accident, but Tom was substantially responsible for it. Only then did he realise, I think, that it wasn't a game. Or that it was a game with other players more powerful than either of us. Farnsworth's one of them. But there must be others. Who removed the body from the shaft? Who photographed Tom and me at Robusta? And why? That's what I've been trying to figure out. I urged Tom to leave Edinburgh. But he wouldn't. He changed so much after Andrew's death. In the end, I suppose he saw suicide as the only choice left to him.'

'And where were you, while his choices were being whittled away?'

'I was hiding. And thinking.'

'I've done a lot of thinking myself.'

'Is that why you're going to Venice?'

'I'm going to Venice because that's where Basil's gone. He's out of touch and I fear for his safety.'

'Then I suppose you must go. You should be very careful, though.'

'Do you think I might end up at the bottom of a canal?'

'Yes. I'm afraid I do.'

'You'd better hope not. If I can't settle this, they'll still be on your trail, whoever they are.'

'I'd hope not in any case. I believe your father was complicit in my father's murder, but I don't hold you responsible. You should have gone to the police when you found the body, but you've had to face the consequences of that mistake. I wish I'd done something to save Tom from himself, but it's too late. There's nothing I can do now. Except save myself—and hopefully a few others.'

'How do you propose to do that?'

'I'm going back to Milwaukee. I hope they'll leave me alone there. I hope they'll understand I'm giving up. I have to think of others as well as myself. I can't risk them targeting Jonty's children. I've told you the truth, Nick. I hope it helps. It's the only help I can offer.'

'What can you tell me about Demetrius Paleologus?'

'Nothing. I read the report on him from the private detective Jonty hired in Cyprus, but there was nothing in it beyond what you already know. An elderly absentee hotelier, resident in Venice. In possession of a valuable secret, I assume. But whatever that secret is . . .' She sighed. 'My father and my brother died because of it.'

'So did mine, in case you'd forgotten.'

'I hadn't. But what do we gain by swapping reproaches, Nick? We can't repair the past. Only the future matters. Our futures. And those of our loved ones. That's why I'm giving up. You should give up too.'

'Maybe I will. Once I know Basil's safe.'

Elspeth Hartley—or Emily Braybourne, as Nick was trying to force himself to think of her—fell silent at that.

Then Nick said, 'You reckon it's too late, don't you?'

'I reckon it's not too late for you, Nick. You still have a chance.'

'I'm going anyway.'

'I know.'

'So, perhaps you should take me home.'

NOTHING MORE WAS SAID as they completed their circuit of the ring road and headed back to Damson Close. Nick was physically tired and mentally overwhelmed. Every time he tried to piece everything together it fell apart in his mind.

There had been little traffic on the ring road and there was none at all in the residential byways of Walnut Tree. Just as they approached Damson Close, however, a dark Transit van, driving without lights, surged out from the cul-de-sac. Emily braked violently and blasted her horn, but the van swept past them and sped away.

'Christ,' said Emily. 'What a way to . . .' Then she looked at Nick. 'I don't suppose they *do* drive like that round here, do they?'

'No.'

She turned into Damson Close and drove slowly along to his house. Nothing looked amiss. She stopped and he got out.

'Wait here,' he called, starting up the drive.

The front door was ajar. The lock had been damaged. Nick stepped inside and, glancing through to the kitchen, saw the contents of his bag strewn across the floor. He instinctively patted his pocket, reminding himself that he had his passport on him. Then he looked into the office. The drawers of the desk and cabinet had been pulled open. And his computer disks were missing. He hurried back out and down the drive.

Emily was talking on her mobile, he was surprised to see. She rang off as he approached and lowered her window. 'What gives?'

'Somebody's broken in and had a look around.'

'Funny, isn't it? All this time you've been away, nothing happens. Now, straight after your return, you get turned over.'

'What do you make of that?'

'They were interested in what you might have brought with you.'

'Then they'll have been disappointed.'

'You shouldn't stay here after this. I've just been on the phone to the hotel at Heathrow I'm booked into. They have a vacancy.'

Nick considered his options. The break-in was something he could not ignore. They were onto him, whoever *they* were. And he was easy to find in his suburban isolation.

'Take it or leave it, Nick. I'd like to get moving.'

He hesitated for no more than a few seconds. 'I'll take it.'

THE HOTEL WAS ONE of a clutch of bland low-rise establishments lining the A4 on the northern side of Heathrow Airport. As a temporary refuge, it could hardly be bettered.

Emily went straight to her room, leaving Nick to down several slow Scotches in the bar. They comprehensively failed to relax him. While the pianist played, questions swirled in his mind, but answers came there none. Just as he was nearing the last sip of what he promised himself would be his last Scotch, a shadow fell across him. He looked up, to be met by Emily Braybourne's self-mocking smile.

'I couldn't sleep. Mind if I join you?'

'Feel free.'

She sat down. The waiter glided promptly alongside. Emily ordered the same malt as Nick was drinking. Nick ordered the same again. Neither spoke until the waiter returned with their drinks. He arranged the glasses on coasters and replenished the assorted nuts. Emily held Nick's gaze, her face a mask. The waiter withdrew.

'How does it stack up?' she asked. 'The damage your family has inflicted on mine—and vice versa?'

'It stacks up as too much. Far too much.'

'Time it ended, then.'

'I agree.'

'But how does it end? Tell me that.'

'I don't know.'

She took a deep breath. 'We're both frightened and lonely. But we don't have to be quite as frightened and lonely as we are. And I don't want to be. Not tonight, anyway.' Her gaze was direct, as challenging as it was somehow yielding. 'How about you?'

CHAPTER TEN

There was no farewell. That was the deal they had struck. Nick walked past her room when he left. The chambermaid was at work inside. Nick glanced at his watch and calculated that Emily was probably in the process of checking in at Terminal 4. He started walking towards the lift.

Aboard the courtesy bus to Victoria, the realisation struck him that he was already doubting his memories of the night. What they had done should not have felt so right. He was half in love with her before he ought to have finished hating her. 'There's no afterwards for us,' she had said. 'You understand that, don't you?' Only now was he beginning to. 'I'll call you when it's over,' he had said. But she had shaken her head. 'You won't.' And only now did the contradiction he had uttered ring as hollow to him as it must have done to her.

It did not have to be like that, he told himself as the Gatwick Express sped south through Surrey. He could make his future better than his past. Maybe hers too. All things were possible.

Besides, as he reminded himself when the train reached Gatwick, looking further ahead than the next couple of days was futile. He had no idea what was waiting for him in Venice. And less than none of what might be waiting for him when—and if—he came back.

As if to prove the point, bad news of a totally unexpected kind greeted him at the North Terminal check-in. Marco Polo Airport was fogbound. All flights to Venice had been cancelled. The only choice open to him was an evening flight to Milan, with no clue about when he might reach Venice. He took it.

Several times during the long afternoon, he debated whether he should phone Irene. Once he even got as far as dialling the Old Ferry's number. But then he cancelled it. He paced up and down the departure lounge. He steeled his nerves. He waited.

The 18.45 flight to Milan left on schedule. Twelve hours later, after a short and restless night in the closest hotel to Milano Centrale station, Nick boarded the first train of the day to Venice. It crossed the Venetian lagoon just before 9.00am. He was asleep at the time.

AT SANTA LUCIA Station Nick bought a map, then went into the accommodation bureau and asked for the address of the Hotel Zampogna. It was in the Cannaregio district, within walking distance.

There was no queue, so the assistant was happy to provide Nick with another location. A directory was consulted and an X marked on his map for the Palazzo Falcetto. Unless Basil was waiting for him at the Zampogna—a cheering but remote possibility—the palazzo of his mysterious cousin would be Nick's second port of call.

The route to the Zampogna was a series of uncertain zigzags along narrow alleys or beside turbid back canals. Eventually, after several wrong turnings, Nick found the alley he was looking for: Calle delle Incudine. At the corner stood a dingy-looking bar and the next building down the *calle* was the Zampogna.

The entrance was dark and discouraging, though the door was half open. Nick ventured into a narrow, dimly lit lobby. Behind a desk sat a woman clad in a shapeless brown dress and shawl.

She peered at him with no smile, her face lined and pinched. '*Sì?*'

'*Parla inglese?*'

'*Inglese?*'

'Yes. *Sì. Inglese.* 'I'm looking for my brother, Basil Paleologus. He's been staying here.'

'*Paleologus?*'

'That's right. I—'

But the name was enough. She was suddenly ranting at him, her voice echoing in the passage. Nick had no idea what she was saying, but it was not an encomium of praise for Basil, that was certain. He tried to placate her with smiles and apologies and appeasing gestures, but it did no good. In the end, all he could do was retreat.

Her imprecations followed him out into the *calle*, then subsided. With little expectation of assistance, Nick entered the bar next door. Behind a counter stood a beer-bellied *barista* with a luxuriant moustache. He exchanged a knowing look with his only other customer, a young man propped against the counter, then grinned at Nick.

'*Buongiorno.*'

'*Buongiorno. Doppio espresso, per favore.*'

'*Prego.*' The *barista* set the espresso machine hissing into action.

The young man drained his cup and dropped an empty cigarette pack on the counter. '*Ciao, Luigi,*' he said, moving out into the *calle*.

'*Ciao, Gianni,*' Luigi called over his shoulder. He kept his back to Nick as the machine slowly and noisily did its job. Then he delivered the result to the counter. '*Eccolo.*'

'Thanks.'

'You're welcome. A *doppio*'s what you need after a meeting with *la dragonessa.*' Luigi grinned. 'What was the problem?'

'I'm not sure. I'm looking for my brother. He's been staying at the Zampogna.'

'Signor Paleologus?'

'That's right. Did he come in here?'

'A couple of times. But I got the name from Carlotta—*la dragonessa*. He's your brother?'

'Yes. Basil Paleologus. I'm Nick Paleologus.'

'English Paleologoi. I didn't know they got so far.'

'What can you tell me about my brother?'

'He did the bunk. Left the Zampogna without paying his bill. Carlotta went like Etna when she found out.'

'When was this?'

'Some time Monday. He was in here early that morning for his *tè verde*. Then . . . poof! No sign. Things still in his room, Carlotta says. But no *signore*. And no money. Gone.'

'What did Carlotta do about it?'

'Shout at me. What else?'

'Didn't she contact the police?'

'*La polizia?* You're joking. They'd probably close her down.'

'But Basil might be in trouble.'

'He will be if Carlotta catches up with him. So will you, if she finds out you are family.'

'Look, I'll pay her, if that's the problem. I'm worried about my brother. He's not the type to dodge settling a bill. Surely the fact that he left his stuff behind proves he meant to return.'

Luigi shrugged. 'Maybe.'

'Could you explain that to her? You'd be doing me a big favour.'

'And that's what I'm in business for, yes? To do my customers favours.' Luigi sighed theatrically. 'OK. We give it the whirl.' He picked up the telephone and dialled. '*Carlotta? Buongiorno. Sono Luigi. Sì, sì. Si calma, Carlotta, si calma.*'

Luigi eventually replaced the telephone in its cradle with a flourish and treated Nick to a triumphant grin. 'I have a deal for you, Signor Paleologus. You can take your brother's room until he returns, or until . . . whatever. One hundred thousand lire a night from last Saturday. Plus tonight up-front. What do you say?'

Nick said yes, of course, and made a cautious return to the Zampogna. Carlotta was on her best behaviour, accepting the negotiated lire with something approximating gracious thanks, then showing Nick up to what had been Basil's room and was now his.

The room was small and minimally furnished, with a bed, a wardrobe, a cabinet, a hard chair and a framed bird's-eye view of Venice in 1500. There was a washbasin in one corner, and a tiny window commanding a vista of chimney pots and washing lines.

It was immediately apparent to Nick that Basil had left with every intention of being back in the near future. His alarm clock was on the bedside cabinet, his toiletries jumbled around the basin. And his rucksack, half filled with clothes, was stowed in the wardrobe. Nick ferreted through the rucksack, discovering nothing, before turning his attention to the rest of the room. But there was nothing to be discovered there either. The shallow drawer of the bedside cabinet contained a crumpled copy of *Corriere della Sera*. That was all.

Nick sat on the edge of the bed and picked up the paper. It was a week-old edition, folded open at an inner page. He laid it out flat on the bed. Almost at once, he noticed a circle of red ball-point round one article. He could make little of it, of course, but there was a word in the headline—*omicidio*—which he felt sure meant murder.

For the price of another espresso, Luigi supplied Nick with a rough translation. The article concerned the progress—or lack of it—of police enquiries into the murder of Valerio Nardini, a fifty-four-year-old dealer in antique maps, whose body had been found in a disused warehouse in the Arsenale district early in January; he had been shot through the head. There was speculation linking Nardini's murder to the sale at auction in Geneva two months previously of several medieval *portolani* that had allegedly been exported illegally from Italy. Luigi could not find an English word equivalent to *portolano*. 'A kind of map' was the best he could do. He remembered the case only vaguely. The Italian word for auctioneer was *banditore* and might as well be *bandito*, he joked. They were not to be trusted. He doubted the police would be making an arrest any time soon.

NICK HEADED SOUTH through the gunmetal morning, the page from the newspaper stuffed in his pocket. He was aiming for the nearest vaporetto stop, Luigi having advised him how best to reach the Palazzo Falcetto. Why Basil should be interested in a murdered map dealer he had no idea, but he also had no doubt that the reason was connected with the other deaths that had brought him to Venice.

The number 1 vaporetto crisscrossed from bank to bank down the Grand Canal. It was half filled with a subdued assortment of tourists and residents. The Carnival seemed to be over, as a drift of rain across the façades of the canalside palazzi somehow confirmed.

Nick spotted the Palazzo Falcetto while the vaporetto was nudging in towards the landing stage at the San Tomà stop, where Luigi had told him to get off. Its façade was hidden by scaffolding and thick-gauge plastic. The contractor's sign proclaimed RICOSTRUZIONE and there was clearly a lot of it going on.

Once off the vaporetto, Nick followed a devious route he had traced on his map round to the landward entrance to the palazzo, where he found a massive wrought-iron gate. He yanked at the bell.

He had yanked a second time before a heavy-lidded, unshaven young man in dusty overalls wandered into view. '*Buongiorno*,' the man mumbled as he edged open the gate.

'*Parla inglese?*'

'A little. What you want?'

'I'm looking for Signor Paleologus. He lives here, doesn't he?'

The man shrugged. 'He is not living here now. Because of . . . *la ricostruzione*. Understand? He comes to see the work. Then he goes.'

'But he's due today, isn't he?'

'*Sì*. Later.'

'Have you any idea what time?'

The man shrugged. 'Three. Four. Who knows?'

'It's vital I speak to him.' Nick took some money from his wallet and proffered a note. 'When do you think would be the best time to try?'

The man thought. 'About three forty-five.' He took hold of the note and Nick let go. 'This is when I would try.'

'Thanks.'

'You want me tell him you're coming?'

Nick hesitated, then said, 'No.'

'OK.' The man grinned and pocketed the cash. 'Our secret.' Then he closed the gate, turned on his heel and vanished.

NICK HAD MORE than three hours to kill. He took a vaporetto to the Accademia Bridge, two stops south of San Tomà. From there, he followed the signs to San Marco. He trailed slowly across the piazza, which was thick with crowds, wondering where to have lunch. He decided to walk up to the Rialto, and eat something there.

His route lay along the Calle dei Fabbri, north from San Marco. It was narrow and crowded going, past innumerable small shops. Nick paid them little attention and quite why, as he rounded a bend in front of one firmly shuttered establishment, he glanced up at the sign above the door, he could not have explained. But what he saw halted him in his tracks: VALERIO NARDINI, CARTE ANTICHE.

It was a disturbing coincidence. Nick went into a nearby bar and ordered a *grappa* and a beer. The past seemed closer in Venice than it ever had in England. He was wandering abroad in a museum-city where every exhibit might conceal a threat. Jonathan Braybourne had died here. So had Valerio Nardini. Maybe Basil too. Nick swallowed the *grappa* in two gulps, but it could not burn away the fear.

He took his mobile phone out of his pocket, intending to check for messages, but it had lost its charge, as he should have foreseen. He shoved the phone back into his pocket and started on the beer.

After a second beer and a ham roll, Nick headed on north to the Rialto Bridge. He had decided to walk to the Falcetto in order to fill the time until 3.45. The route he took was circuitous, even by Venice's standards, but he was able to stop at a bar near San Tomà for a *doppio corretto* before presenting himself at the palazzo.

The sleepy young man answered the bell, his unshaven chin a few hours darker. A flash of his eyes was the only sign of recognition.

'Is Signor Paleologus in?'

'*Sì*. You have appointment?'

'No. But can I speak to him, please? My name is Paleologus. Nicholas Paleologus.'

'Paleologus?' The man smiled, as if in recognition of a good joke. 'OK.' He held the gate open and Nick stepped through. 'Wait here.'

Nick watched the man walk away through an open doorway into a dust-fogged stairwell where two older men, one of them holding a clipboard, were deep in conversation. The conversation was interrupted. The young man gestured with his thumb. The other two glanced past him at Nick. Then one of them advanced.

He was a slim, good-looking fifty-something. Blond highlights camouflaged the grey in his hair, tinted glasses the lines round his eyes. Clearly he was not the person Nick was looking for.

'I am Paleologus,' the man nonetheless announced. 'Are we related?'

'I'm looking for Demetrius Paleologus.'

'You have found him.'

'I don't think so. There must be some mistake. He's an older man. Demetrius Andronicus Paleologus.'

'Ah. I understand. I am Demetrius Constantine. Demetrius Andronicus was my father.'

'*Was* your father?'

'Yes. I am afraid you cannot speak to him. He is close to a year dead.' Demetrius Constantine plucked off his glasses and gave Nick a concerned look. 'I am sorry. You are a long time too late.'

'I AM SORRY,' said Demetrius Constantine Paleologus for the third or fourth time since Nick's arrival. 'This is not the condition in which I would wish a Paleologus to see the Palazzo Falcetto.'

They were standing at the top of a vast if dilapidated marble staircase. To their right, through an open doorway, stretched a still vaster and yet more dilapidated ballroom. Below, drilling could be heard, growling beneath the workmen's banter.

'My father allowed the palazzo to moulder around him after my mother's death. I am restoring it to its former glory. I plan to convert it into a luxury hotel. When it is finished, it will be magnificent.'

'How long has your family lived here?'

'For more than two hundred years. But we have lived in Venice ever since the fall of Byzantium in 1453. I must tell you that I have never heard of an English branch of the family. If we are cousins, you and I, I could not say which ancestor we share.'

'I believe our fathers met in Cyprus during the war.'

'It is possible. Papa moved there in the thirties, when the Fascists started to make life difficult for him here. He was no friend of Mussolini. I was born in Cyprus. We returned here when I was a child.'

'Did your father say much about his wartime experiences?'

'No. I had the impression there was little to say. There was no fighting on Cyprus. Ah . . .' Demetrius nodded at the workman climbing the stairs towards them. 'We have news, I think.'

Demetrius had explained earlier that no one had mentioned Basil's visit to him, and it was not clear who Basil might have spoken to. The foreman had been instructed to look into the matter.

There was a conversation in rapid-fire Italian, during which the foreman did a good deal of shrugging. Then he retreated.

'Someone did call here on Saturday afternoon,' said Demetrius once the foreman had vanished from sight. 'He spoke to Bruno Stammati, my business partner. We will call him and sort it out.' Demetrius plucked a mobile from his pocket and pressed a single digit. A few seconds later, he frowned and spoke briefly in a message-leaving monotone, then rang off. 'It seems Bruno is taking his weekend today. *Tipico*. No matter. I will catch him later. Whether that will help you find out where your brother is *now*, I cannot say.'

'I'm really worried about him,' said Nick. 'Anything you can do . . .'

'Of course. It is much easier for me to make enquiries than for you. I know Venice. Who to ask. *How* to ask. So why not leave it with me? Give me twenty-four hours. If there is information, I will get it.'

'That's very kind. I—'

'Not at all. We are Paleologoi. It is my duty to help.' Demetrius smiled. 'And my pleasure.'

NICK LEFT THE PALAZZO FALCETTO in a state of shock. A wholly unconsidered possibility was now revealed as the truth. And the truth mocked all that had gone before. Michael Paleologus had bequeathed Trennor to a dead man. His late and hastily drawn will would have counted for nothing.

A chilling suspicion began to form in Nick's mind as he wandered aimlessly through the fading afternoon. Could his father have deliberately drawn up an invalid will? Had it been a last, sick joke—an elaborate dare to test how far they would go to counter a threat that did not really exist? It could not be so, Nick told himself. The old man had acted in haste, without pausing to confirm that his cousin was still alive. That was surely the truth. That *had* to be the truth.

NIGHT HAD FALLEN by the time Nick arrived back at the Zampogna. He had Demetrius's business card and a Telecom Italia phone card in his wallet, representing between them about the only practical steps he had so far succeeded in taking.

He sat in his room for twenty minutes, until it was close enough to opening time at the Old Ferry for him to be sure of speaking to Irene when he phoned. He still did not know what he was going to say to her. But he knew he had to say something.

He headed out to make the call. He had spotted a card phone in Strada Nova, and planned to use that if he did not come across another on the way. But first he needed some Dutch courage.

'Signor Paleologus,' Luigi grinningly greeted him as he stepped into the bar. 'You must have known.'

'Known what?'

'I have a package for you.' Luigi flourished a large, bulkily filled envelope, on which NICHOLAS PALEOLOGUS was written in capitals.

'What's this?'

'I don't know. It came this afternoon. I was taking a piss, while there was no one in. When I came back, it was here.' Luigi tapped the counter for emphasis. 'Right here.'

Nick picked the package up, and looked quizzically at Luigi. 'It doesn't make sense. No one knows I'm here.' He ripped up the flap of the envelope and peered inside. 'It's a book,' he announced.

'I like a good book. Mickey Spillane. That kind of thing.'

Nick slid the book out onto the counter and flinched with surprise. It was a dogeared copy of Vernon Drysdale's biography of Richard of Cornwall: *The Left Hand of the King*.

'Not Mickey Spillane,' said Luigi.

'Definitely not.' Nick opened the book and noticed, as he did so, that something was marking a place about a third of the way through. He turned to the page and focused at once on the name Paleologus, adrift in one of the paragraphs.

Then his focus shifted to the place-marker itself. It was a business card. *Valerio Nardini, Carte Antiche*. He slammed the book shut.

BACK IN THE BLEAK privacy of his room at the Zampogna, Nick reopened the book at the marked page. He stared at Nardini's card, certain that a message was being conveyed to him. But he did not even know which was the message: the card or the page.

His eye fell on the place where he had seen the name Paleologus. He began to read about secretive negotiations between Richard of

Cornwall and Andronicus Paleologus, plenipotentiary of John Vatatzes, Emperor of Byzantium, at the citadel of Limassol on Cyprus in March 1241. He read on:

> When Richard returned to England in January 1242, he was sorely downcast to learn upon his arrival at Dover that a vessel he had dispatched ahead of him from Acre the previous spring had been lost in a storm off the Scillies, its journey tantalisingly close to completion. The vessel had been under the command of Ralph Valletort, Richard's aide-de-camp in the Holy Land, who had, we can assume, been privy to the agreement reached at Limassol, though whether his voyage was connected in any way with that agreement can only be conjectured.

Nick stopped reading. For a split second, like the fugitive memory of a dream, something—some fragment—flitted across his mind. Then it was gone. His imagination was playing tricks on him, he reasoned.

It was gone eight o'clock—seven o'clock in England. He had to phone Irene. He could delay no longer. He stowed Drysdale's book in his bag in the wardrobe, then headed out.

THE NIGHT WAS COLD, still and moonless, with a dank mist rising from the canals. Nick hurried along the deserted *calles* until he reached the *campo* with the row of payphones he had passed earlier.

As he approached, card in hand, one of the phones began to ring. He stopped and stared at it, the noise magnified by the enclosing walls of the buildings round the *campo*. The ringing went on.

Nick picked up the phone. 'Yes?' he said hoarsely.

'Walk east along Strada Nova,' responded a voice he did not recognise. 'Turn right into Calle Palmarana. Follow it to the canal. There'll be a water taxi waiting for you.'

'Hold on. Who—?'

'You've got five minutes.'

The line went dead. Nick stared around him into the jumbled shadows of the *campo*. Nothing moved. A minute slowly passed as fear and curiosity wrestled within him. Then he put the phone back in its cradle and started walking—east along Strada Nova.

THE WATER TAXI was moored where Nick had been told it would be, its engine idling. The pilot looked up as Nick approached and pitched the remains of a cigarette into the Grand Canal.

'Signor Paleologus?'

'Yes.'

'*Prego.*' The man offered Nick a hand.

Nick hesitated. Was this really a good idea? No, the cautious part of his brain insisted. But what other idea did he have? He hopped aboard and stepped down into the cabin.

The pilot slipped the mooring and started back up the Grand Canal in the direction Nick had come from. A few minutes took them to the Ca' d'Oro vaporetto stop, where Nick had got off earlier. A figure stepped forward as they approached. The taxi slowed and manoeuvred alongside just long enough for him to jump aboard.

'Hi,' the newcomer said, closing the cabin doors behind him as the taxi accelerated away. He was a short, corpulent figure dressed in a thin raincoat and baggy linen suit. His eyes were sea-grey and skittering, his moist lips parted in a smile. 'Nick Paleologus?'

'Yes.'

'I'm Fergy Balaskas.' He held out a large, wavering hand that Nick somewhat reluctantly shook.

'Where are we going, Mr Balaskas?'

'The airport. Well, I'm going to the airport. You're just along for the ride. I'm not jetting off anywhere, by the way. It's just that from the airport I can take my pick of onward transport. Bus, taxi, *motoscafo*: enough options to keep you guessing.'

'Why should I care where you're going on to?'

'No reason. But what you don't know you can't tell. You're a dog with fleas, Nick. I don't want to catch any.'

'What are you talking about?'

'Precautions, old boy. You should try them yourself. I gather you got the book, incidentally. Real page-turner, isn't it?'

'Who *are* you?'

For answer, Balaskas pulled a business card from his pocket and passed it over. Nick held it up to read by the light of the cabin-lamp. *F. C. Balaskas, Private Enquiries and Debt Recovery, 217a Leoforos Archiepiskopou Leontiou, Limassol, Cyprus.*

'You're the man Jonathan Braybourne hired to investigate Demetrius Paleologus?'

'I am indeed.'

'Did you leave the parcel for me at Luigi's bar?'

'Yep. He tipped me the wink you'd shown up and I dropped the book off so we'd have a frame of reference for our *conversazione.* You're here to find your brother? Well, I met him a few days ago. I was keeping an eye on the Palazzo Falcetto when he showed up there on Saturday. I trailed him back to the Zampogna, checked him out, then the following day introduced myself. We compared notes.'

'What about?'

'Jonathan Braybourne hired me to find out who'd been paying his late mother hush money from a Cypriot bank. Well, I found out: Demetrius Andronicus Paleologus, wartime resident of Cyprus, later absentee hotelier and Venetian recluse. Since I dug into his affairs, the old boy's died. But Demetrius Constantine Paleologus, his iffy businessman son, is very much alive and kicking. I've got the bruises to prove it. Someone came after me in Limassol a while back and I had to vamoose. Seems what I found out about Demetrius the elder was a lot more than his son wanted anyone to know. Braybourne found out more still, I assume, hence the header he took into the canal.'

'You think Demetrius the younger had Jonathan Braybourne killed?'

'I think you'd be well advised to work on that assumption.'

'Did you tell Basil this?'

'Of course. The newspaper cutting about Nardini gave your brother pause for thought, but he didn't take the threat seriously enough. Don't make the same mistake. Your family's tied into all this. If you don't know how, I sure as hell don't.'

'Do you know what *portolani* are?'

Balaskas smiled. 'In English, they're called portolans. They're mariners' maps, charting coastlines and the waters between them for specific journeys. An eight-sheet Venetian portolan dated 1341, sold at auction in Geneva last November, appears to show navigational details of the North American coast more than a hundred and fifty years before Columbus sailed the ocean blue. So, it's either a fake or an authentic record of a secret chunk of history. Nardini acted as middleman for the sale on behalf of an anonymous client and there's no chance now of him putting a name to that client. But here's the strangest thing. Six months before the portolan was sold, Braybourne came to Venice with a copy of Drysdale's book. He wound up dead as well. When his wife got his possessions back, they included the book, which she passed on to me. Inside, marking the page—the same page I left it in for you—was Nardini's business card.'

'Hold on. Braybourne's *wife* gave you the book?' Doubt was refining itself in Nick's mind. Ever since discovering that Demetrius Andronicus Paleologus was dead, he had been puzzled by Emily's apparent unawareness that the Demetrius her brother had gone to see in Venice could not be the same Demetrius their father had supposedly met in wartime Cyprus. She had also referred to her discovery of *The Left Hand of the King* among Jonathan's possessions. *Her* discovery, not his wife's. Something was wrong. 'When was this?'

'Early January. Just after Nardini was killed. Which is when it got a lot too hot for me in Limassol. Coincidence? I think not.'

'What about Braybourne's sister?'

'His sister?'

'Yes. Emily Braybourne.'

Balaskas frowned. 'I've never heard of her.'

Nick fell silent as the water taxi cruised on across the flat darkness of the lagoon. It did not inevitably follow that Emily had lied to Nick. She might merely have asked her sister-in-law to make no mention of her to a third party. But he could not reason away her failure to dispel the confusion about Demetrius Paleologus's identity.

'Like I told your brother, Nick,' Fergy continued, 'we're in uncharted waters. The only way out is to take a deep breath and swim like hell. That's what I'm planning to do. I advise you to do the same.'

'I can't. I have to find Basil. When did you last see him?'

'Monday. When he returned Drysdale's book to me. We'd arranged to meet on the forty-two vaporetto. I told him as much about Demetrius as I dared. And that was as much as I knew.'

'You'd better tell me, then.'

'OK. Demetrius the elder was straight-as-a-die patrician stock. Demetrius the younger is out of a different mould. He's *persona non grata* in Cyprus because of suspected involvement in cross-border money laundering. The hotels he inherited from his father have been closed down until he answers the charges. All his Cypriot assets have been seized. There are whispers tying him in with organised crime here in Italy as well. However you slice it, the guy is bad news.'

'Oh God.'

'He's being squeezed financially, Nick. The suspect portolan wasn't the first cartographic gem Nardini marketed last year. I think Demetrius used Nardini to offload some or all of his father's archive of antique maps and atlases. He needed the money to keep his creditors at bay. And his creditors are the sort who take payment in kind if they can't get it in cash. He has a villa on the Lido guarded by the sort of goons you'd expect to see on duty outside the residence of an exiled Latin American dictator. He's in trouble and he *is* trouble. I explained that clearly to your brother.'

'What did he say?'

'He thanked me for the information. Then I got off the vaporetto. He stayed aboard. It was going on to San Michele—the cemetery island. He said he wanted to take a look at the elder Demetrius's grave. There's been neither sight nor sound of him since.'

'What do you think's happened to him?'

'I think Demetrius could answer that question for you straight off if he wanted to. I can only make an educated guess.'

'Go on, then.'

'You don't really want me to.'

'Yes, I do.'

'No.' Balaskas stared insistently at Nick. 'Believe me. You don't.'

That was almost the last thing Balaskas said to Nick before he climbed up onto the landing stage at Marco Polo airport and walked away towards the terminal building. He did not look back.

CHAPTER ELEVEN

The morning was bright, almost springlike. Nick walked east to Fondamente Nuove, where he had breakfast in a bar and gazed out across the lagoon at Isola di San Michele—the cemetery island to which Basil had carried on after his and Balaskas's parting.

Nick left the bar, walked across to the vaporetto stop and bought a ticket. As he waited, he glanced around at the other people on the landing stage and wondered if any of them might be following him. Even if they were, there was nothing he could do. Except follow Basil on the last journey he was known to have taken.

THE VAPORETTO was bound for the island of Murano. So, it transpired, were all of the passengers save Nick and an immaculately dressed old woman carrying a large bunch of flowers. At the Cimitero stop, they were the only two to get off.

Nick followed the old woman through an archway into the cemetery. The graves stretched away into the walled distance, separated by avenues of raked gravel, beside which cypresses stood at measured intervals. The old woman hurried on ahead.

Spotting a sign to the cemetery office, Nick headed back into the cloisters flanking the church of San Michele. The office was open.

The attendant spoke decent English and, to Nick's surprise, recognised the name of Paleologus. He handed Nick a map showing the cemetery layout and prodded at a section labelled *Rec. Greco*. 'He was

Orthodox, yes? You will find him there. The stone is quite recent.'

Of course. Old Demetrius had kept the faith of his Byzantine fore-fathers. Glancing at the map as he went, Nick headed past the crematorium building towards two walled compounds. One was reserved for Protestants, the other for Greek and Russian Orthodox.

Nick wandered between the graves, looking for the brightness of new stone. It was warm now, the high walls trapping the heat of the sun. A dove was cooing somewhere.

Then he saw the name, spelt in the Greek style. PALAIOLOGOS. A lizard scurried from the stone as Nick's shadow fell across it.

> QUI RIPOSANO DIMITRIOS ANDRONIKOS PALAIOLOGOS
> NATO IL 2 FEBB 1908   MORTO IL 24 MAR 2000
> E LA CONSORTE GIULIA AGOSTINI PALAIOLOGOS
> NATA IL 11 LUG 1914   MORTA IL 22 AGOS 1986

Carved above the inscription was the double-headed eagle of Byzantium. No Paleologus, it seemed, was permitted to renounce his past.

Nick was suddenly struck by a thought. Reading Balaskas's report, which she must have come across among her brother's possessions, Emily would not have known its subject was already dead. Jonathan Braybourne had probably only learned as much shortly before his own death. It was possible that Emily still did not realise there was a younger and potentially more dangerous Demetrius Paleologus to be borne in mind. She had not necessarily deceived Nick after all.

Suddenly his shadow seemed to stretch, blotting the sunlight from the inscribed words and dates. He turned and started with surprise at the sight of the very man he had just been thinking of.

Demetrius Paleologus smiled. 'This is a big coincidence, cousin.'

'Yes. It is.'

'When we spoke yesterday, I remembered I had not been here for too long. What brought you?'

'Curiosity, I suppose.'

'Perhaps you needed to see with your own eyes in order to believe. It is sometimes hard for me to believe he is really dead . . . I spoke with Bruno this morning. He remembers meeting your brother. But that is all. And that is no help to you, is it?'

'Not really.'

'My other enquiries will take longer. You will have to be patient.'

'I'll try.'

'Good. You came by vaporetto?'

'Yes. I'd better be off now. You'll want to be alone.'

'There's no need to leave. You can ride back with me on my launch. Just give me a few moments. Take a look at the family vault while you wait.' Demetrius pointed towards an ivy-hung greystone mausoleum near the rear wall of the compound. 'My mother did not want to be buried there. So, my father rests with her here. His father and many fathers before his father are in the Paleologus vault.'

Nick walked slowly away, leaving Demetrius to stand, head bowed, by his parents' grave.

The name Paleologus was inscribed in Greek capitals within the pediment above the vault's padlocked steel door: ΠΑΛΑΙΟΛΟΓΟΣ. Nick had never felt so close to the departed ranks of his ancestors. The dust they had been brought to seemed to float in the air around him.

'Where are you, Basil?' he murmured. 'What happened to you?'

'Shall we go?'

Nick turned to see Demetrius walking towards him, his teeth gleaming white in the sunlight.

They walked round to the main part of the cemetery and headed down the cypress-lined central avenue, away from the church. At the far end the boundary wall was broken by a high, ornamental gateway. Nick could see a man leaning against the bars of the gate.

Demetrius signalled with his hand to the man, who pushed himself upright and swung the gate open as they started up the steps towards him. 'I'm going to my villa on the Lido. Why don't you accompany me? Bruno is coming there straight from the airport later this morning. I thought maybe you would like to speak to him in person.'

They stepped through the gate and out onto a landing stage. Demetrius's launch, a sleek-hulled lagoon limousine, stood ready for them, its engine purring. The pilot glanced up at them through reflective sunglasses. He was tanned and muscular, like his crewmate, and Nick wondered if they were representative of the 'goons' Balaskas had claimed Demetrius employed. He heard the gate clang shut behind him and realised that the invitation to visit the villa was both an opportunity too good to miss and a risk too grave to run.

'A handsome craft, no? Step aboard. We will show you what she is capable of.'

Nick hesitated for a fraction of a second, then went ahead.

THE TRIP TO THE LIDO was a high-octane surge. The blast of chill air soon forced Nick down into the cabin with Demetrius, who gazed back proudly at the sparklingly chevroned wake. As they approached the long, low western shore of the Lido, the pilot throttled back and steered in towards the narrow mouth of a canal.

Demetrius ushered Nick out of the cabin and pointed to the villa on the left-hand corner of the canal. 'Mine,' he announced. It was larger and starker than most of its neighbours, a cream-stuccoed edifice of simple lines and little obvious pretension.

A short distance down the canal was a landing-stage. The pilot hove to and tied up. Nick and Demetrius disembarked, Demetrius leading the way through a wrought-iron gate and along a gravel path to the drive on the landward side of the house.

The main door of the villa opened as they approached. A fellow looking like a close relation of the pilot and his crewmate, though more smartly dressed, held it back for them.

They entered a cool, empty hall and moved on into a large draw-ing room, expensively furnished in Art Deco style that was elegantly at odds with a state-of-the-art wide-screen TV and hi-fi.

'Make yourself comfortable,' said Demetrius. 'Coffee, perhaps? Or something stronger?'

'Coffee would be fine.'

'I'll join you.' Demetrius stepped back into the hallway and spoke briefly to the man who had let them in, addressing him as Mario. When he returned to the drawing room, he sat down in a pastel leather armchair and gestured for Nick to sit opposite him.

'I must thank you for coming here, Nicholas.'

'It was no problem.'

'Indeed it was not. But you might have made it so much more dif-ficult. As it is . . .' Demetrius smiled. 'Here we are. Here *you* are.'

'Why should I have made it difficult? Am I missing something?'

'Perhaps.'

A silence fell as Mario entered, carrying a lacquer tray with two cups of black coffee, a small jug of cream and a sugar bowl on it. He set the tray down and left without a word. Demetrius leaned for-ward, spooned some sugar into his coffee and stirred it slowly.

'I have had you followed, Nicholas. You should understand that. We did not meet on San Michele this morning by chance.'

'You've . . . had me followed? Why?'

'To make sure you did not stray too far.'

'Now, look here—' Nick started up from his chair.

'Sit down, Nicholas. I want to show you something.' Demetrius plucked a remote control from the low table between them, pointed it at the television and pressed a button. A picture flashed into view.

Nick stared at the image on the screen. Basil was sitting on a chair in the middle of a featureless room. His feet were tied to the legs of the chair and his arms were pinioned behind him. He was wearing a T-shirt, jeans and espadrilles. His expression was blank, neither fearful nor defiant. There was no sign that he had been maltreated. But he was a prisoner. Of that there was no doubt.

'What you're watching, Nicholas, is a closed-circuit link with the place where Basil is held. The people holding him will not hesitate to kill him if I give the word. Allow me to demonstrate the peril of his situation.' Demetrius took his mobile out of his pocket, pressed a button and conveyed some *sotto voce* instructions. A balaclava-clad figure appeared on the screen. He stepped into position beside Basil and pulled out a gun, holding it in front of Basil's face. Basil pulled his head back slightly, but otherwise did not react.

'You've made your point,' said Nick, forcing himself to speak in a measured tone.

'Good.' Demetrius murmured into the phone and Nick watched as balaclava man lowered the gun and walked away. 'Now, do sit down.'

Nick lowered himself slowly back into his chair and swallowed hard. His mouth was dry, his palms damp, his brain a chaos of competing thoughts. Yet he was still in control of himself. And he knew that for Basil's sake he had to stay that way. 'What do you want?'

'Your full cooperation.'

'And if I give you that?'

'Basil goes free.'

'Then you've got it.'

'You should hear what it involves first.'

'Tell me.'

'My associate will be arriving shortly. All will be explained then.' He flicked the remote at the television. The screen blanked out.

'Is it Bruno Stammati we're waiting for?'

'No.' Demetrius looked round, as if he had heard something. 'Ah. A car on the drive, I think.' He glanced at his watch. 'On schedule.'

Nick had heard nothing. Then the sound of a slamming car door reached him, followed by footsteps. The front door of the villa opened and the footsteps clacked along the marbled hall towards them. Nick looked up, cursing his foolishness for hoping even at this late, desperate stage that he would not see the face of the woman he had come to think of as Emily Braybourne.

Then he saw. And it was her.

'Hello, Nick,' she said, meeting his gaze directly. There was no hint of shame or regret in her expression. She seemed utterly calm.

'What should I call you now?' Nick asked, not troubling to conceal the bitterness in his voice.

'Call her Emily,' said Demetrius. 'Yes. She *is* Emily Braybourne.'

'Is that true?' Nick threw the question at her.

'Yes.' As she walked across to the coffee table, Nick noticed that she was carrying a slim silver-grey briefcase. She laid it on the table, then stepped back and sat down facing him, one hip propped on the arm of Demetrius's chair. 'A lot else I told you was true too.'

'You never mentioned getting into bed with your brother's murderer.'

'An interesting choice of metaphor, Nicholas,' said Demetrius, idly running his hand along Emily's black-trousered thigh. 'You speak in the business sense, of course. Which is appropriate, since Emily has long learned to view the loss of her brother as a sad necessity of business. Isn't that so, *cara*?'

'Yes.' She did not flinch as she said the word.

'She has a theory, you see. An elegant theory that fits the facts. We shall soon find out if it's correct. Either way, I'll get what I want.'

'And what's that?'

Demetrius glanced up at Emily. 'Tell him.'

'Jonty found out about the portolans Demetrius was smuggling through Switzerland,' she neutrally began. 'He tried to pressurise Demetrius into letting him in on the deal, hoping that would enable him to crack the secret. But the secret has nothing to do with the portolans. And pressurising Demetrius was a fatal mistake. When I thought it through, I realised he could be a better ally than a foe. So, we joined forces. Revenge doesn't make you rich or happy, Nick. But maybe becoming rich and happy is a kind of revenge. It's the one I've opted for. Demetrius's father left a lot of valuable stuff behind. But there was something far more valuable he had a stake in.'

'Papa used to hint to me when I was growing up that there was some great secret he would reveal to me one day,' said Demetrius. '*Il segreto favoloso*, he called it. But he said later I had proved myself unworthy. So he kept the secret from me. It was safe with another, he said. I could not be trusted. When your father tried to contact him recently, I knew why, so I made sure he did not learn of his old friend's death. Papa had died with the secret. But it had not died with him.'

'The knowledge was passed down from generation to generation,' Emily resumed. 'Your ancestor, Theodore Paleologus, didn't settle in Landulph by chance. He went there in quest of something *his* ancestor, Emperor Michael the Eighth, had heard discussed at Limassol in the spring of 1241. A relic of some kind, an artefact preserving sacred information. It had been discovered in Jerusalem by the Knights Templar and could no longer be safely left in the Holy Land. A secure repository was required. That's why Richard of Cornwall built his castle at Tintagel. He'd been commissioned to provide a safe hiding place that would draw no one's attention to its true purpose.

'He travelled to the Holy Land in 1240 to report that all was ready. He met a delegate from the Byzantine Emperor and informed him of what was intended, to ensure that both branches of Christendom were party to the decision. Shortly afterwards, Ralph Valletort, who owned the manor of Lewarne, in the parish of St Neot, set sail from Acre, bound for Tintagel, carrying the artefact with him.

'The ship foundered off the Scillies. The artefact was lost. But Valletort survived. I think the reason for the elusive nature of the artefact is that even those who decided its fate did not actually see it. An inner cadre of the Knights Templar guarded its secret. Several such knights doubtless accompanied Valletort on the voyage. Perhaps they confided in him. Perhaps he inspected the artefact for himself. I'm certain that he *knew*—and was responsible for incorporating a reference to the secret in the Doom Window at St Neot.

'The point is that the Doom Window predates and transcends the fifteenth-century glazing scheme. That's why it was removed in 1646. The churchwardens knew it had to be preserved at all costs. Hence its concealment at Trennor. And hence, I believe, your grandfather's purchase of Trennor in 1921.'

'Hold on,' Nick interrupted. 'What would my grandfather have known about all this?'

'More than you think. Remember what I said. From generation to generation. When the excavations began at Tintagel in 1933, your grandfather and your father were on the scene. But were they there to help—or to hinder? Fred Davey worked with his father on that dig. And his grandfather had worked on the last lead-mining venture at Tintagel, in the 1870s. There have always been rumours that something came to light back then—an underground chamber beneath the great hall of Tintagel Castle. Such a chamber could easily be a repository, for an article of great worth. The article had never arrived, of course. It had ended up on the seabed. Even so, the discovery of the chamber would have raised a lot of questions. I suspect the Daveys, father and son, conspired with the Paleologoi, father and son, to ensure it remained undiscovered.

'Later, serving on Cyprus during the war, your father met a long-lost cousin who knew as much, if not more, about the nature and meaning of the artefact destined for but never delivered to Tintagel in 1241. They became friends and confidants. Your father also confided in an army pal, who was left in no doubt that something hugely significant—and therefore hugely lucrative to those who uncovered it—was concealed at Trennor.'

'You can't prove any of this,' Nick objected.

'Oh, but we can,' said Demetrius. 'That's the beauty of it. Your father would not have let the knowledge perish from his branch of the family. He would have passed it on to the next generation.'

'It must be so,' said Emily. She looked at Nick, something like guilt or pity darkening her face for the first time. 'One of you knows.'

Demetrius smirked. 'But which one?'

'It wasn't Andrew,' said Emily. 'He was too keen to sell to the mythical Mr Tantris. Your sisters are ruled out for the same reason. Which leaves you and Basil as the only possible candidates. You were both lukewarm at best about the sale.'

'But if it was Basil,' said Demetrius, 'why would he come here in such evident innocence? Why would he take such a risk?'

'He wouldn't,' said Emily.

'Exactly.' Demetrius and Emily were rehearsing for Nick's benefit a debate they had already had several times over. 'Besides, I have held a gun to the man's head with every appearance of being willing to pull the trigger. And he has revealed nothing.'

'You bastard.' Nick stared at Demetrius, willing him to understand what he could not afford to say: that if he could ever contrive a way to strike back at him he would not hesitate.

'It's you, Nick,' Emily said quietly. 'You're the one.'

Nick looked straight at her. 'You're wrong.'

'Won't you tell us *il segreto favoloso*, Nicholas?' Demetrius sarcastically enquired.

'I don't know it.'

'Disclose the secret and Basil goes free.'

'I don't have it to disclose.'

'We think you do.'

'For God's sake—'

'You've had your chance.' Demetrius took out his mobile again.

'*Stop!*' Nick was out of his chair, lunging towards Demetrius.

'It's all right.' Emily clasped Nick's shoulders, her face close to his. 'It's OK, Nick. He isn't going to make the call.'

Nick looked past her at Demetrius, who fixed him with his gaze and ostentatiously tossed the phone into an empty chair to his right.

'No call,' said Demetrius softly.

'Sit down, Nick.' Emily's eyes pleaded with him.

He pushed her away and stood where he was for a moment, swaying slightly. The tension eased by a degree. He sat down.

Emily crossed to the chair where Demetrius had tossed the phone, put it on the table next to the briefcase and sat down herself. 'Listen, Nick. We believe you know, but you may not know you know.'

'What the hell's that supposed to mean?'

'I'm talking about your breakdown and what may have caused it. I think your father told you the secret. You were the prodigy, the budding genius—the obvious choice, really. But it was too much for you. You couldn't cope with the knowledge. You rejected it. You put it out of your mind. But the subconscious doesn't take orders. It's still there, locked away. All you have to do is turn the key.'

He stared at her. Could it be true? Could she be right?

'I need to hypnotise you, Nick. Don't worry. I know how it's done. With your cooperation, we can unlock the memory you've suppressed for so long. We can learn the truth.'

'The patient has to trust the hypnotist. Otherwise it doesn't work.'

'It'll work,' said Emily with quiet insistence. 'You just have to let me take control. This will help.' She released the catches on the briefcase and raised the lid. From inside she took a slim plastic holder, snapped it open and laid it on the table. Inside was a syringe and a small bottle of fluid. 'It's a simple tranquilliser. It'll take effect more quickly if I administer it intravenously. We need you to be relaxed.'

'Full cooperation was our agreement,' said Demetrius. 'This is the only way you're going to see your brother again.'

'What guarantee do I have that I'll see him again if I do go through with this?'

'None. But killing Basil would draw the police's attention to the name Paleologus. Since I plan to buy Trennor from your family in order to exploit what's hidden there, I'd be foolish to make such a connection for them. So give me what I want and you and Basil can have a happy reunion at the Zampogna later today.'

'What do you say, Nick?' Emily's eyes had not left him.

Nick sighed. 'Get on with it.'

'Yes.' Emily took a deep breath. 'All right. Roll up your sleeve.'

As Nick did so, she loaded the syringe, then sat on the table and leaned forward to inject him. He looked away from the needle, his focus blurring slightly, aware of her perfume tingling in his nostrils.

'OK. You can relax now.'

He sat back, feeling certain that relaxation was, in the circumstances, impossible. 'What if you're wrong? What if I don't know?'

'I'm not wrong. This is the answer. I'm sure of it.'

Nick's eyes were trained on Emily. 'Those other players in the game you told me about. There aren't any, are there? You arranged with Demetrius here for your father's body to be removed from the shaft.'

'We can't have the police digging around at Trennor, Nicholas,' said Demetrius. 'There's no telling what they might find.'

'But you sent the video to the police in the first place.'

'I had to make Tom believe we were serious,' said Emily.

'How did you dispose of your father's body, Emily?'

'Cremation,' she murmured. 'It was decently done.'

'That's all right, then.'

'Try to relax. Try not to think.'

'I wish I couldn't.'

'I'm going to record what you say under hypnosis, OK? Your words might be slurred. We need to be able to go over it later.'

'Be my guest.'

Emily took a pocket recorder out of the case and set it up on the edge of the table closest to Nick. 'How are you feeling now?'

'Great.' Nick had intended to be sarcastic, but actually a strange euphoria was beginning to creep over him. 'Where does Farnsworth come into all this, by the way? Is he working for you?'

'Forget Farnsworth.'

'You're getting ahead of yourself, Emily. It's only when the patient's in a trance that you can tell him what to forget.'

'I think we're ready. Could you close the curtains, Demetrius?'

Demetrius stood up and walked away towards the windows. The light dimmed. Emily took a pen-torch out of the case, laid it on the table and switched it on, with the light shining towards her. Then she switched the tape recorder on as well.

'Look at the torch, Nick. And listen to me. Relax as much as you can. Breathe slowly. Slow everything down. Keep looking at the torch. Keep listening to me. Forget everything else. Let it fall away. As you do, start counting in your mind, backwards from one hundred.'

Nick started counting. And Emily's voice seemed to keep pace with him, slowing as he slowed, falling almost to a murmur as the numbers wound lethargically down in his head.

'Your eyelids are beginning to feel heavy. Give way to the drowsiness. Close your eyes. Let yourself drift away. Keep counting. Slowly. Very slowly. Let yourself go. Let yourself go completely.'

Her voice was all he could hear. He realised that her voice was one of the things that had most attracted him to her. It reminded him of another voice from deep in his past. It had belonged to a guide at Buckland Abbey, Sir Francis Drake's old home near Plymouth. Nick had gone there with his father during one of his summer vacations from Cambridge and been entranced by the woman's particular tone and timbre. He had stood listening to her telling visitors much the same thing about the history of the house several times over.

Something else had happened that day. There had been a painting on display of Drake's burial at sea off the Panamanian coast in 1596. Something about the name of the Spanish settlement the ship had been lying off, mentioned on the caption, had struck Nick as reminiscent of a phrase firmly lodged in his mind at the time. Nombre de Dios. That was it. That was the place. Nombre de Dios. The Name of God. It resembled the Spanish rendering of another English phrase. He had said it under his breath, his father standing beside him. If he let his mind dwell on the moment, far off though it was, he would retrieve the words. He felt sure of it. All he had to do . . .

'TEN. YOU REMEMBER NOTHING except that you remember nothing. You haven't forgotten. It simply hasn't happened. Nine. You aren't so deeply asleep now. Your limbs are lighter. Eight. The world is returning to you and you to it. Seven. You are beginning to sense your surroundings, to hear other things than my voice. Six. You're aware of yourself and where you are. Five. You feel comfortable. Refreshed. Happy. Four. You're beginning to wake up. Light is seeping through your eyelids. Three. You're nearly awake. You have only to open your eyes. Two. You are awake. One. You open your eyes.'

Nick blinked and looked around. He was alone. The room was empty. There was a click as the tape recorder switched itself off. He stared at the machine, wondering how long it was since Emily had gone, leaving him to obey her recorded instructions. It felt as if only a few minutes had passed since he had entered the trance, as if she had asked him nothing, had hypnotised him and then immediately reversed the effect. But he knew that was not true. He knew she must have asked him many questions and he must have answered them.

The briefcase had gone, along with the syringe and the pen-torch. The house was filled with silence. Nick felt woozy, as if the tranquilliser was still affecting him. He looked down at the tape recorder. Emily had said she would record what he said under hypnosis. But they must have taken that tape with them.

What about Basil? The urgency of the question burst suddenly on Nick's mind. Had he given them what they wanted? Had he done enough to save his brother? He stumbled towards the door.

That was when he noticed the blood—bright blotches of it in a meandering arc across the pale carpet, from the table to the door. He moved to the door and pulled it open. Light flooded into the room, dazzling him. As his eyes adjusted, he saw a man lying on the floor about halfway along the hall, close to the wall. There was a pool of blood around him, wine-red against the polished white marble. A gun was cradled in the upturned palm of his right hand.

Nick took the few steps it needed for him to see the man's face. It was Mario. Nick looked to his left, through an open doorway, into a room kitted out as a study, with desk, filing cabinet and computer. Something on the desk caught his attention.

Edging clear of the pool of blood, he stepped cautiously into the room. Demetrius Constantine Paleologus was lying dead across the desk. His head was turned towards Nick, his right cheek flattened against the desk. There was blood beneath and around him, a dark meniscus of it pooled across the wood.

Nick began to tremble. How could so much have happened without his being aware of it? Two men were dead. But where was Emily?

He moved back into the hall, averting his gaze from Mario's body. There were drops of blood on the floor at intervals between him and the front door. He walked carefully between them, his senses straining. As he reached the door, his ears detected a sound from outside. A low, thrumbling note. He eased the door open.

It was a car engine, in idling mode. He could smell its exhaust fumes. He peered round the edge of the door.

A small white Fiat was parked on the drive, its bonnet pointing away from the villa, a haze of exhaust rising behind it. The driver's door was wide open. And Emily was sitting at the wheel.

Nick rushed out and down the steps. He rounded the car and met Emily's gaze as she looked up at him. Her face was grey, her hair streaked with sweat. Her left hand was on the steering wheel, her right clutched to her stomach. Blood was oozing through her fingers and dripping down from the seat to the door sill and the gravel below. The briefcase lay on the passenger seat, blood smeared round its handle. A gun was wedged between the case and the back of the seat.

'Hello, Nick,' Emily murmured. 'It's . . . strangely good to see you.'

'What happened?' He knelt beside her.

'Things didn't quite . . . work out.'

'I'll phone for an ambulance.'

'Don't.' She clasped his arm. 'Please don't.'

'We've got to get you to a hospital.'

'I don't think so.'

'For God's sake, Emily—'

'Listen to me. While you still can. Demetrius sent the launch to pick up Basil. He'll be free by now. I waited until I was sure of that . . . before I made my move. Demetrius never saw the double-cross coming. He thought I really had sold out to him.' She laughed, inducing a grimace of pain. 'He underestimated me. But I underestimated him too. He had a knife. And I simply wasn't quick enough. Nearly. But not quite. Clever. But not clever enough. Story of my life.' She smiled through gritted teeth. 'And my death.'

'You're not going to die.'

'Clean away or nothing: that's the deal. I'm not prepared to spend the next couple of decades in prison. Let me go, Nick.' She tried to smile again. 'You're better off without me. Everyone is.'

'Where's your phone?'

'Didn't bring one.'

Nick stretched across her to reach the case. Her rapid breaths fanned his cheek as he prised at the catches. They would not budge.

'It's combination-locked.'

He looked round at her. She shook her head. She would not tell.

'Better this way. Believe me.'

'I'll phone from the house.' He ducked as he moved back out of the car. Her grip on his arm tightened.

'It was some secret, Nick. Quite some secret.'

'What?'

'You told me. There was no tape. Except the one I prerecorded . . . to bring you out of the trance . . . after I'd gone. So, with Demetrius dead, I'm the only one who knows. I'm the only one who can tell you . . . what it is.' She winced. 'Don't you want to stay . . . and find out?'

'We can talk later.'

'There won't be a later.'

'Yes, there will.' He lifted her hand off his arm as gently as he could and laid it in her lap. 'I'll be back in a few minutes.'

'OK.' She closed her eyes. 'Have it your way.'

He ran towards the villa, his feet crunching on the gravel. Two strides carried him to the top of the steps. He flung the door open and rushed into the hall.

And then he heard the shot.

CHAPTER TWELVE

The vaporetto was halfway across the lagoon on its run from the Lido to the Grand Canal when Nick saw the police launch heading fast in the opposite direction. He had dialled the emergency number on the first payphone he had come to after leaving the villa and repeated the same message through a jabber of questions. '*Tre morti. Villa Margherita. Via Cornaro, il Lido.*' It was all he could say and all he could risk saying. Emily was dead. Nothing could alter that. And nothing could wipe from his mind's eye the sight of how she had died. Nick swallowed hard and gripped the rail tightly as he watched the bouncing shape of the launch diminish as it sped on.

He closed his eyes and rewound the sequence of events that had led to the moment of Emily's death. He could have acted differently. But he could not have chosen to save her. She had already chosen not to be saved. He could only have chosen to stay and to listen and to learn at last the secret locked in his memory.

Instead, he had turned away. Part of him was glad of that. What secret could matter in the face of so much death? He no longer cared what it might be, nor whether he would ever find out. Curiosity had been burned out of him. All he cared about now was Basil.

BY THE TIME the vaporetto reached Ca' d'Oro, more than an hour had passed since Nick's phone call to the emergency services. He hurried north by a route he now knew well to the Zampogna, praying he would find Basil waiting for him.

Carlotta greeted him with an incomprehensible announcement that Nick desperately wanted to believe meant Basil had turned up.

'Signor Paleologus? My brother? Is he here?'

'*C'è qualcuno qui per lei.*'

'What?'

'*Con Luigi.*'

The last word he understood. He rushed straight out and into the bar next door.

'Signor Paleologus,' boomed Luigi. 'You have more relatives in Venice than me. Here is another.'

But the bulky figure propped at the counter was not technically a relative. Nor did he seem pleased to see Nick.

'Terry?'

'Surprised to see me?'

'Yes. I mean . . . what . . .'

Terry stood upright and glared at Nick. 'I want to know what the bloody hell you're up to. You can start with telling me where I can find Harriet Elsmore.' The glare hardened. 'Well?'

With some difficulty, Nick persuaded Terry to put his questions on hold until they had reached the spartan privacy of Basil's old room in the Zampogna.

'Is this dump the best you can do?' Terry asked as he recovered his breath from the short climb up Carlotta's steepling stairs.

'It's where Basil was staying.'

'Where is he now?'

'Never mind. Why are you here, Terry?'

'Irene said you'd come here to find Basil. But I don't buy it. You're here because Harriet Elsmore's here. That's it, isn't it?'

'No. That isn't it.'

'Tell Kate the truth. That was your brilliant advice, wasn't it? Well, I told her. And now she blames me for Tom's death. She won't speak to me. She won't listen to me. She's cut me off.'

'I'm sorry.'

'Not as sorry as I am. I figure the only way I can repair the damage I've done—yeah, I admit it, the damage *I've* done—is to get the people who pushed Tom over the top. I caught up with Farnsworth. I applied some pressure. It didn't take much.'

'You beat up an old man?'

'I threatened to. That's all it took. He told me everything.'

'I doubt that.' Nick was certain that Farnsworth had played a more central role in events than he was likely to have admitted. But Nick was also certain that he no longer cared.

'Your father and grandfather uncovered some secret at Tintagel in the thirties. Digby Braybourne knew what it was, but Farnsworth only ever heard hints and whispers. It's to do with Trennor. Something valuable's hidden there. Farnsworth reckoned your father's death gave him the chance to find out what, so he started digging. He claims Harriet Elsmore is Braybourne's daughter, out for revenge *and* the secret. She sucked Tom into her plans and, as far as I'm concerned, she's responsible for what happened to him.'

'She probably is.'

'Right. So, where is she hiding? You know, don't you, Nick?'

'It's too late, Terry. For her, for you, for me. For everyone.'

'I'm not leaving until I find out where she is.'

'No. I don't suppose you are.' Nick stepped across to the basin, ran some cold water onto his hands and wiped his face. 'Well, OK, then. Here's how it is. Earlier this morning, Harriet Elsmore, real name Emily Braybourne, murdered Demetrius Constantine Paleologus, the man she blamed—correctly—for her brother's death. She murdered one of his bodyguards too. Then she killed herself. With a bullet through the head. I saw her die. The police are cleaning up the mess even as we speak. If you go looking for her now, all you'll do is implicate yourself—and me. Go home, Terry. Make your peace with Kate. You'll find a way. I'm sorry, I really am. But there's no revenge to be had. It's all been used up. There's nothing left.'

Terry's bluster was suddenly spent. He had been sustained by the belief that he could bludgeon his way to justice and a reconciliation with Kate. Now he knew better. He was out of his depth. He had been foolish to come. But he was not so foolish as to remain.

Terry's hangdog departure settled nothing for Nick, however. He could only wait for Basil to show up at the Zampogna, telling himself all the while that he would show up. Soon. Or later. Or eventually.

An hour passed. Then two. Fears and fantasies began to swarm in Nick's head. Perhaps Demetrius had never meant to release Basil. Perhaps the CCTV pictures had been faked. Perhaps Basil was dead, his body lying undiscovered in a disused warehouse like Nardini's.

He had waited long enough. There was nothing else for it. He was done with evasion. All he could do for Basil was go to the police and tell them as much as he knew in the hope that it would be enough. He threw on some clean clothes and set out.

IT WAS A HALF-HOUR ride on the vaporetto from Ca' d'Oro to San Zaccaria, the nearest stop to the Questura. Nick stood in the stern as the boat chugged past the Palazzo Falcetto, and on round the curve of the Grand Canal, while a grey shroud stretched itself slowly across the sky. The afternoon grew rapidly cold and dank.

As Nick gazed blankly ashore, the mouldering palazzi gave way to the stately flank of the Doge's Palace. A view of the Piazzetta and the Basilica was briefly framed by the columns of San Marco and San Teodoro. Glancing up at the winged lion atop the right-hand column, Nick suddenly remembered his attempt to warn Basil against coming to Venice. '*You'll be stepping into the lion's den.*' But Basil had brushed the warning aside. '*There are a lot of lions in Venice. Bronze or marble, mostly.*' Nick smiled, despite himself.

And then he saw, standing near the foot of the lion's column, a figure he took at first for a hallucination—a figment of his own wishful thinking. It could not be Basil, he told himself. It simply could not be. He blinked. But the figure did not vanish. He blinked again. And still it was there. And this time he knew for sure. It *was* Basil.

THE NEXT FOUR or five minutes were an agony for Nick. The vaporetto slowed as it approached San Zaccaria, and slowed again. Basil was out of sight now and Nick could only hope he had not strayed far. He leapt off onto the landing stage while the boatman was still pushing back the rail, ran down the ramp, then sprinted towards the bridge leading to the Piazzetta. As he crested the hump of the bridge, the area around the columns came into view. There was no sign of Basil. His heart jolted. But he kept running.

Then, as he rounded the corner of the Doge's Palace and glanced to his right, he saw him. Basil was sitting on one of the flood platforms in front of the Basilica, staring into space. He had lost weight, which, combined with the white stubble round his head and chin, made him appear old and haggard, almost pitiful.

Nick slowed to a walk, daring himself to believe it. The distance shrank between them. Then he called his brother's name. Basil looked round. And the smile that lit his face was anything but pitiful.

'Nick! Thank God.' Basil jumped up and threw a hug round Nick. 'I'd nearly given up waiting.'

Nick unwrapped himself and gazed into Basil's smiling face, slowly realising that he too was smiling, just as broadly. 'I've been at the Zampogna. Expecting you at any moment. For three hours.'

'They said they'd bring you here, Nick. Some time this afternoon. They said I was to stay here until you arrived and that it would be the worse for you if I didn't.'

'When did they let you go?'

'It must have been around noon. They've been holding me in a derelict house on some abandoned island out in the lagoon. I was brought here by launch and told very clearly that I'd only see you again if I obeyed their instructions to the letter.'

It had to have been part of some devious ploy. But the ploy was now irrelevant. 'Listen, Basil. We need to get out of Venice. In a hurry.'

'I wouldn't argue with that. My visit's hardly been a happy one.'

'Have you got your passport? I couldn't find it in your room.'

'It's in my pocket.'

'Same here. So, what's stopping us?'

'I ought to settle my bill at the Zampogna.'

'Already done. All we need to do is grab our things from the room.'

'I have the impression there's something you're not telling me.'

'I'll tell you everything once we're on our way.' Not quite, Nick reflected. He would tell Basil *almost* everything.

'You're not going to try to force me onto an aeroplane, are you?'

'Not if you can find us a train to catch pdq.'

'How about the overnight express to Paris? It leaves at seven forty-five. That's how I'd planned to depart. Though not necessarily tonight.'

'But tonight it is. Let's go.'

THEY TOOK a water taxi up to the Fondamenta dell'Abbazia, as close to the Zampogna as it could get. Basil related how he had been set upon while walking back to the Zampogna after his visit to San Michele on Monday morning. Heavies had shoved him, bound, gagged and blindfolded, into a launch, and taken him to a room in a crumbling old house on a deserted island. Demetrius had shown up later, demanding to be told the secret that his father and Basil's father had apparently shared. But Basil could not tell him.

'It is surprisingly easy to refuse to disclose what one genuinely does not know, Nick. And the threat of death only confirmed the equanimity with which I regard the prospect. I was not really frightened at all until I realised that you too were in Demetrius's clutches. Doubtless he had you abducted for the same reason.'

'Yes. The same.'

'Why have we been released, then? Because he came to understand that neither of us could help him? Or . . . because one of us could?'

But there Nick called a halt. He wanted to be out of Venice before he told Basil what had happened. He wanted to be sure they had made good their escape before he revealed what they were escaping from.

BASIL'S GRASP of basic Italian got them in and out of the Zampogna within minutes, leaving Carlotta bemused but content, given that Nick had already paid her for the night's stay. Denying themselves a final visit to Luigi's bar, they headed west towards Santa Lucia. Night had fallen, but time was on their side.

It was still on their side after they had bought their tickets, so Basil proposed telephoning Irene to reassure her that they were both well. Nick insisted on being the first to speak to her.

'Old Ferry Inn.'

'Irene, this is Nick.'

'Nick? Where in God's name have you been?'

'I've found Basil. He's fine. So am I. We're at the railway station in Venice, waiting for a train out.'

'Where did you find him?'

'A monastery. He'd booked himself in for a retreat.'

'*Without telling anyone*?'

'You know Basil.'

'Put him on.'

'I will in a minute. The thing is, Irene, I only caught up with him an hour ago. There hasn't been time . . . to go into everything.'

'Have you told him about Tom?'

'Not yet. I'll do it later.'

'All right. Have you contacted this cousin of ours—Demetrius?'

'Demetrius Andronicus Paleologus died a year ago, Irene. Dad's will meant nothing.'

'What?'

'I'll explain when we get back.'

'When's that going to be?'

'Oh . . .' Nick contemplated the wilderness of his short-term future for a moment. 'Soon enough.'

While Basil spoke to Irene, Nick cast his eye around the station concourse. There was no sign of pursuit in any form. Their train was up on the departures board. They were going to make it.

THE RIALTO EXPRESS to Paris pulled out dead on time. They had paid for a sleeping compartment, but made no early move to occupy it. There was a virtually empty seating carriage just beyond the restaurant car. The train gathered speed across the night-blanked flatness of the Veneto Plain. Somewhere between Padua and Vicenza the whiskies Nick was drinking started to take effect. He began to talk.

NICK WOKE TO THE SWAY of the train and the snores of his brother on the bottom bunk. They had gone to bed in sombre spirits. Basil had taken the news of Tom's death as a judgment on the whole family's folly in pursuing the Tantris offer. 'We failed him,' he had said several times the previous night. And so they had, Nick supposed, although it was equally true to say that Tom had failed them. But Nick was done with apportioning blame. Lying there in the dark, he sensed a change within himself. Where he should have felt overwhelmed by all that had happened, he felt instead released. He still flinched at the memory of how Emily had chosen to die, but he glimpsed now the essence of her act. She had controlled her destiny to the last, whereas Nick had never controlled his from the start. Or maybe he had simply not started *yet*. To him beginning seemed more possible than continuing. And the time to begin had arrived.

THREE HOURS LATER, after a meagre breakfast and a walk beside the Seine, Nick and Basil were sitting on a bench in the square behind Notre-Dame as a cool, clear Parisian morning cast its spell.

'I'm not coming back with you, Basil.'

'There's a surprise,' said Basil.

'You don't *sound* surprised.'

'That's because I knew you weren't.'

'How?'

'The explanation can wait. Though not as long as the one you will eventually proffer to Irene and Anna. There's no reason, as far as I can see, why they should hear about this.' Basil held up a folded copy of *Corriere della Sera*, which he had bought at the Gare de Lyon. The lower front-page headline LIDO DI VENEZIA: STRAGE SAN-GUINOSA IN UNA VILLA DI LUSSO—helpfully if loosely translated by Basil as MURDER MOST FOUL AT LIDO VILLA—was printed above an article that made no mention of an English cousin of the deceased Demetrius Paleologus being sought by the police, although it did imply a connection between Demetrius's murder and the supposedly accidental death nine months before of an Englishman by the name of Jonathan Braybourne. 'I hardly think the *Western Morning News* is likely to devote even the briefest of paragraphs to such an event. For the rest, what is there to say? You found me and all is well. Or, if not well, then not as bad as it might be.'

'I need to go away. To think. To put my life back together.'

'I quite understand. Although, if you'll take my advice, you'll not think too much. Thinking is what makes people unhappy. I never do more than the bare minimum myself.'

'What's the minimum in this case?'

'The modest amount necessary to reveal that Irene and Anna can-not sell Trennor without our consent. We risk nothing by delaying our return.'

'*We?*'

'I'm not going back either. Which is how I could be so certain you weren't going back with me.' Basil smiled. 'I for one would welcome a travelling companion.'

'So would I.' Nick returned his brother's smile, appreciating as he did so just how welcome the company would be. 'Where were you thinking of going?'

Basil grinned. 'New Orleans, perhaps. Or Las Vegas.'

'You must be joking. For one thing we'd have to fly.'

'Not necessarily. I believe you can hitch passage on a container ship. Antwerp would be the place to try. Or Marseilles.'

'Now you *are* joking.'

'About the container ship, yes. But not about the trip. Demetrius succeeded in reminding me that I am perversely unafraid of death. So, flying really should be no problem. I may experience the odd panic attack while we're airborne, but the worst that can happen is that I embarrass my kid brother.'

'I'm old enough to cope with a little embarrassment.'

'You're game, then?'

'Yeah.' Nick nodded. 'I am. When shall we go?'

'When can you be ready?'

'I *am* ready. But we'd have to organise tickets. So . . .' Nick suddenly realised how much he was relishing the prospect. 'Tomorrow?'

'Tomorrow it is.'

'We'd better find a travel agent.'

Basil raised a thoughtful finger. 'Actually, there's something I need to show you first. And to tell you. It's not far. And it won't take long.'

'Can't it wait?'

'No.' Basil gazed up at the flying buttresses. 'Now is the time.'

THE CHAPEL OF SAINTE-CHAPELLE, in the Palais de Justice, near the other end of the Île de la Cité, was their destination. Its soaring spire and slender buttresses lacked the massive Gothic presence of Notre-Dame but, as Basil seemed anxious to point out, the chapel was only eighty years younger than Notre-Dame.

'It was built for Louis the Ninth in the 1240s to house the holy relics he'd brought from the Latin Emperor of Constantinople,' he whispered as they moved from window to window. 'He'd paid several times more for them than it cost to build this. A pious dupe, I fear. What would he not have paid, I wonder, for the artefact entrusted to Richard of Cornwall? He bought the relics in the same year as the conference at Limassol, 1241. It occurs to me that Richard may have met Andronicus Paleologus specifically to reassure the Byzantine Emperor that the artefact wasn't destined for a rich monarch's collection. A generous touch on Richard's part, especially if it was the genuine article. Which prompts the question: what was the article?'

'I'm not holding out on you, Basil. I don't know.'

'Ah, but you *did* know. That day at Buckland Abbey you told me about last night. You knew then.'

'Yes. I think I did.'

'Had you come here at the time, the comparison with Louis the Ninth and his expensive relics might have lodged in your mind rather than the echo of that Spanish place name, Nombre de Dios.'

'What are you getting at, Basil?'

'The truth. I think I know the other phrase you can't call to mind.'

Nick stopped and stared at his brother. 'You do?'

'Yes. In fact, I'm sure of it.'

'What is it?'

'*Número de Días.*' Basil's voice dropped still further. 'The Number of Days.'

Nick could not speak. For the moment, he could not even move. Basil was right. *Número de Días* was the phrase.

'Dad took me to Buckland Abbey one day not long after I came back from Greece,' Basil went on. 'I'd forgotten the visit until you mentioned your own trip there with him. He spent a long time in the gallery, studying that picture of Drake's burial at sea. Then he used the same phrase it had put you in mind of. He must have heard you say it all those years before. "*Número de Días.*" He was remembering what you no longer could. He turned to me and said, "Do you know the legend of the Number of Days, Basil?" As it happened, I did, prompting him to make some crack about my years as a monk not being entirely wasted. Then he said, "When I'm dead and gone, tell Nick the legend. Bring him here and tell him. Will you do that?" I said I would, but I'm afraid it was rather a vague undertaking on my part. The point of his request escaped me, as it was bound to. Only now do I understand. He said one more thing, you see, before we left the gallery: "He'll remember." He meant you, of course. And he may well have been right. I'd have called our visit—and my promise—to mind eventually. I'm certain of that. So, sooner or later, you and I would have gone to Buckland Abbey together and looked at the picture. And then, at long last . . .'

'I'd have remembered.' Nick let his unfocused gaze drift across the river. They had left Sainte-Chapelle and walked to the Square du Vert-Galant, the tree-bowered western prow of the Île de la Cité. 'We're a long way from Buckland Abbey. You'll have to remember for me. What is the legend of the Number of Days?'

'I first heard about it from an old monk named Brother Philemon, on his deathbed. During the forty days between the Resurrection and the Ascension, the risen Christ was several times asked by the apostles when he would return in glory; when the Kingdom of God would be inaugurated on Earth. He replied that it was not for men to know. But some believe he relented in the case of James, his blood brother, and an ambivalent figure in the history of the Church, since to the Catholics the existence of siblings of Christ is literally inconceivable, by reason of Mary's perpetual virginity. Some believe Jesus told James how many years would elapse before he came again.'

'The Number of Days.'

'Exactly so. If James made a record of the divine intelligence entrusted to him and arranged with his Pharisee friends to have it secreted in some vault beneath the Temple prior to his death, it may have lain there, undiscovered, until the Knights Templar began their excavations in the twelfth century. We should envisage an inscribed stone tablet, I think. Papyrus would not have been durable enough. The inscription would be in Greek, of course, rendering it unintelligible to the average medieval man.

'The Greek numbering system used letters: alpha for one, beta for two, gamma for three and so on up to ten, except that the extinct letter digamma stood for six; then kappa for twenty, lamda for thirty and so on up to a hundred, except that another extinct letter, koppa, stood for ninety; then sigma for two hundred, tau for three hundred and so on up to a thousand, except that yet another extinct letter, sampi, stood for nine hundred. A thousand was alpha with an accent, and the sequence started over again. Bear in mind that a number—a date—would look like just another word to the uninitiated. And a Greek word depicted in a stained-glass window in medieval Cornwall would have eluded the subtlest of interpreters.'

'I remember the phrase—the Number of Days,' Nick said dreamily. 'But not the rest. Not any of it.'

'I dare say you will, in time.'

'And I don't believe it anyway. There is no Day of Judgment. No set date. No preordained apocalypse.'

'For our purposes, Nick, the ultimate reality of Doomsday is neither here nor there. The discovery of an inscribed tablet beneath the Temple of Jerusalem seeming to confirm the legend of James's unique foreknowledge of the Second Coming was a remarkable, astonishing, awe-inspiring event, and a revelation that could not be countenanced in Rome. It makes not a jot of difference what we think about it. The people who found it believed it. As many still would. Unless the time recorded has already passed, of course. That would be a crack of doom of an entirely different order.'

'You think the Doom Window of St Neot held the secret?'

'Yes. I do.'

'And you think the glass from the window—with the secret in it—is walled up at Trennor?'

'Yes. Don't you?'

Nick thought for several long moments, then sighed and gave a nod of resignation. 'Yes. Of course I do.'

Nick felt confounded by his own certainty. Whether he believed the legend or not was irrelevant. Others had believed it—and acted accordingly. In that sense, the legend was bound to be true. The secret was that there was a double secret: one of finding; one of knowing. What the walls of Trennor held they could be made to give up. Nick and Basil could will it to be so. But they could also will it not to be so. The choice rested with them. And it was really no choice at all. Nick understood that with the sharp and sparkling clarity of finely cut glass. The secret was a secret they could never allow to be known.

A FEW MINUTES LATER, the brothers Paleologus could be seen crossing the Pont Neuf linking the Île de la Cité with the right bank of the Seine. They were walking fast and confidently, almost jauntily. They were walking, in fact, like two men who knew where they were going.

'AXMΣ

*I*t was a chill winter morning, chiller inside St Neot Church than out. Richard Bawden's breath clouded in the air as he opened the tower door and gazed up at the west window. It appeared to his eye no older than the Noah and Creation Windows at the other end of the church, which had been there for nigh on 150 years. But the Doom Window dated from much further back, according to local lore, which also ascribed to it an importance beyond estimation.

The window was made up of twelve panes arranged in three panels. The images within—of flood and fire, of sinners and demons, of the ladder from hell to heaven and the scales of judgment—had been familiar to Bawden since childhood. Those who would destroy such a work of art and faith could not be in the right. And its destruction could not be permitted. It had to be made safe, without delay. Fairfax was already reported to have taken Launceston and the havoc his troops might wreak did not bear contemplation.

Bawden closed his eyes and uttered a prayer, begging God's pardon for the sacrilege of what they meant to do. Soon the sexton would arrive and they would set about dismantling the window, prising back the leads and lifting out the panes, wrapping them in sackcloth and carrying them to the cart, where they would be placed in a crate and swathed in straw for their journey to Landulph. Bawden's prayer became a plea for God's blessing. 'Let the day go well, Lord,' he murmured.

Opening his eyes, he looked from one light to another. It was idle to suppose that he would live to see their restoration. He pondered then the abiding mystery of the window: the green-garlanded gold letters at the base of each light. It was generally believed that they stood as symbols for some matter of deep significancy, but, if so, the symbols were too abstruse to comprehend. He had heard the vicar express the opinion that the letters and pictures together formed what he called a rebus—a visual riddle, which he confessed to find unfathomable. The truth of it might never be known. Certain it was, however, that the mystery could only be solved if the glass was preserved.

The rattle of the latch on the south door drew his thoughts back to the task at hand. He retreated into the nave as the door creaked open just far enough for the sexton to make a sidelong entrance. He was carrying in his right hand a heavy leather bag, in which he transported his tools. Pushing the door shut behind him, he advanced into the church.

'Good morrow, Master Davey,' said Bawden.

John Davey nodded and moved past him into the tower, where he lowered the bag to the floor. He opened a cupboard next to the gathered bell ropes, lifted out a ladder and propped it against the wall beneath the Doom Window. Then he turned and stared at Bawden in solemn scrutiny. 'Have you heard from Mandrell?' he asked.

'I have,' Bawden replied. 'He will ride out to meet us on the road.'

'You trust him?'

'I would trust him with my life.'

'Reckon you're a-doing that. And mine along of yours.'

'I know.'

'But there's nothing else for it.'

'Truly there is not.'

'Shall us begin, then?'

'Yes.' Bawden looked up at the window. 'Let us begin.'

ROBERT GODDARD

Robert Goddard is renowned for producing mysteries within a mystery, and is a master at fooling the reader into thinking that he has all the pieces to the puzzle. In fact, so addictively challenging are Goddard's novels that he now has a sizable following of loyal fans, including former Prime Minister John Major, who once invited him to lunch at Chequers.

Set in Cornwall and Venice, *Days Without Number* took fifteen months to write. Deceptively simple at first, the plot develops into a mind-boggling conundrum that keeps the reader, and Goddard's beleaguered hero, guessing till the end. 'I like to set my central characters a series of problems that they have to solve,' Goddard explains. 'For me, it's always better when the main character is an ordinary person, not a police inspector or someone used to dealing with these situations, but someone entangled in the plot and who has something to lose.' So is his hero usually the kind of person he would like to be? 'For the duration of the writing, I probably am that character. Writing is a solitary activity . . . you're left sharing your life with characters who are given the time and space to do what they want to do.'

Robert Goddard read history at Cambridge and worked as an educational administrator in local government before concentrating fulltime on writing. In this, his fifteenth novel, he used legend, historical fact and local Cornish tales to paint an authentic backdrop to the plot. 'Researching the past involves a lot of research. But once it has been done you have to forget about it. Just absorb it and be confident that it is there in your mind. If you remain hyperconscious of the research, there's a danger you will fill your narrative with too much boring detail.' In fact, it was as a result of frustration with the offerings of other novelists that Goddard first set pen to paper. 'I'd just got married and my wife was fed up with me complaining how bad some books were,' he admits. 'She said I should have a try and I finally did.'

THE LAST DETECTIVE

DETECTIVE

ROBERT CRAIS

When Ben Chenier is kidnapped, private investigator Elvis Cole is shocked to the core. Ben is his girlfriend's ten-year-old son and he cares deeply for the boy.

As the police churn their way slowly through standard investigative procedures, Elvis knows that time is running out. It is up to him to find Ben, and he is prepared to go to any lengths to do so.

When extreme measures are required, who better to call on than his trusted friend, ex-Marine Joe Pike . . .

CHAPTER ONE

A silence filled the canyon below my house that fall; no hawks
floated overhead, the coyotes did not sing, the owl that lived in
the tall pine outside my door no longer asked my name. A smarter
person would have taken these things as a warning, but the air was
chill and clear in that magnified way it can be in the winter, letting
me see beyond the houses sprinkled on the hillsides below and out
into the great basin city of Los Angeles. On days like those, when
you can see so far, you often forget to look at what is right in front of
you, what is so close that it is a part of you. I should have seen the
silence as a warning, but I did not.

'How many people has she killed?' I called out.

Grunts, curses, and the snap of punches came from the next room.
Ben Chenier shouted, '*What?*'

'How many people has she killed?' We were twenty feet apart, me
in the kitchen and Ben in the living room, shouting at the tops of our
lungs—Ben Chenier, also known as my girlfriend's ten-year-old son,
and me, also known as Elvis Cole, the World's Greatest Detective
and Ben's caretaker while his mother, Lucy Chenier, was away on
business. This was our fifth and final day together.

I went to the door. 'Is there a volume control on that thing?'

Ben was so involved with something called a Game Freak that he
did not look up. You held the Game Freak with one hand and worked
the controls with the other while the action unfolded on a built-in
computer screen. Ben had been playing the game since I had given it

to him the day before, but I knew he wasn't enjoying himself, and that bothered me. He had hiked with me in the hills and had let me teach him some of the things I knew about martial arts. He'd come to the office where I work as a private investigator. I had brought him to school in the mornings and home in the afternoons, and between those times we had cooked Thai food, watched Bruce Willis movies and laughed a lot together. But now he used the game to hide from me. I knew why, and seeing him like that left me feeling bad.

I dropped onto the couch next to him. 'We could go for a hike.'

He ignored me.

I said, 'You want to talk about me and your mom?'

My work brings me into contact with dangerous people, and last summer that danger rolled over my shores when a murderer named Laurence Sobek threatened Lucy and Ben. Lucy was having a tough time with that, and Ben had heard our words. Lucy and Ben's father had divorced when Ben was six, and now he worried that it was happening again. We had tried to talk to him, but boys—like men—find it hard to open their hearts.

Ben nodded towards the action on the screen. 'Check it out. This is the Queen of Blame.'

A young Asian woman with spiky hair and an angry snarl faced three muscle-bound steroid-juicers in what appeared to be a devastated urban landscape. Her voice growled electronically from the Game Freak's little speaker. '*Eat fist, scum!*'

I said, 'Some woman.'

'Uh-huh. A bad guy named Modus sold her sister into slavery, and now the Queen is going to make him pay the ultimate price.'

The Queen of Blame punched a man so fast that her hands blurred. Blood and teeth flew everywhere.

I spotted a pause button on the controls, and stopped the game. 'I know that what's going on between me and your mom is scary. I just want you to know that we're going to get through this. Your mom and I love each other. We're going to be fine.'

'I know.'

'She loves you. I love you, too.'

Ben looked up at me. His little-boy face was smooth and thoughtful. He wasn't stupid; his mom and dad loved him, too, but that hadn't stopped them from getting divorced.

'Elvis?'

'What?'

'I had a really good time staying with you. Wish I didn't have to go.'

'Me too, pal. I'm glad you were here.'

Ben smiled, and I smiled back. Funny how a moment like that could fill a man with hope. I patted his leg. 'Mom's going to get back soon. We should get the grill ready so we're good to go with dinner when she gets home. Burgers OK?'

'Can I finish the game first? The Queen is about to find Modus.'

'How about you take her out onto the deck? She's pretty loud.'

'OK.'

I went back into the kitchen, and Ben took the Queen outside. Even that far away, I heard her clearly. '*Your face is pizza!*' Then her victim shrieked in pain.

I should have heard more. I should have listened even harder.

Less than three minutes later, Lucy rang from her car. 'I'm in Long Beach. Traffic's good so I'm making great time. How are you guys holding up?'

Lucy Chenier was a legal commentator for a local television station. Before that, she had practised civil law in Baton Rouge, Louisiana, which is where we met. Her voice still held the hint of a French-Louisiana accent.

'We're good. I'm getting hamburgers together.'

'How's Ben?'

'He was feeling low today, but he's better now. He misses you.'

We fell into a silence that lasted too long. Lucy had phoned every night but our exchanges felt incomplete. It wasn't easy being hooked up with the World's Greatest Detective.

Finally, I said, 'I missed you.'

'I missed you, too. Hamburgers sound really good.'

She sounded tired. But she also sounded as if she was smiling.

'You want to speak with Ben? He just went outside.'

'That's all right. Tell him that I'm on my way and that I love him, and then you can tell yourself that I love you, too.'

We hung up and I went out onto the deck to pass along the good word, but the deck was empty. I went to the rail. Ben liked to play on the slope below my house, and climb in the black walnut trees that grow further down the hill. The deepest cuts in the canyon were just beginning to purple, but the light was still good. I didn't see him.

'*Ben?*'

He didn't answer.

'*Hey, buddy! Mom called!*'

He still didn't answer.

I checked the side of the house, then went back inside. I looked in the guest room where Ben slept, and the downstairs bathroom, then went out of the front door into the street. I live on a narrow private road along the top of the canyon. Cars rarely pass so it's a safe street.

I didn't see him. I went back inside. 'Ben! That was Mom on the phone!' I thought that might get an answer. The Mom Threat.

Nothing.

'BEN!'

My nearest neighbour, Grace Gonzalez, had two little boys, but Ben never went over to see them without first telling me. He never went down the slope or out into the street or even into the carport without first letting me know. It wasn't his way to just disappear. I went back inside and phoned next door. I could see Grace's house from my kitchen window.

'Grace? It's Elvis next door.' Like there might be another Elvis further up the block. 'Is Ben over there?'

'Nope. Was he supposed to be?'

'I don't know. He was here a few minutes ago, but now he's not.'

Grace hesitated. 'Let me ask the boys. They could have gone downstairs without me seeing.'

I checked the time. Lucy had called at 4.22; it was now 4.38. I took the phone out onto my deck, hoping to see Ben trudging up the hill, but the hill was empty.

Grace came back on the line. 'My guys haven't seen him. Let me look out front.'

'Thanks, Grace.'

Her voice carried clearly across the canyon that separated our homes when she called him, and then she came back on the line. 'I don't see him. You want me to come over there and help you look?'

'You've got your hands full with your boys. But if he shows up, will you call me?'

'Right away.'

I turned off the phone and stared down into the canyon. The slope was not steep, but he could have taken a tumble or fallen from a tree, so I worked my way down it. My feet sank into the loose soil, and footing was poor.

'*Ben! Where in hell are you?*'

Walnut trees twisted from the hillside like gnarled fingers, their trunks grey and rough. The largest pushed out of the ground with five heavy trunks that spread like an opening hand. I had climbed it with Ben, and we had talked about building a tree house there.

'*Ben!*'

I listened hard and held my breath as I heard a faraway voice.

'BEN!'

I imagined him further down the slope with a broken leg. Or worse.

'I'm coming.'

I followed the voice through the trees, certain that I would find him, but as I heard the voice more clearly I knew it wasn't his. The Game Freak was waiting for me in a nest of stringy autumn grass. Ben was gone.

I called as loudly as I could. '*BEN!!!*'

No answer came except for the sound of my own thundering heart and the Queen's tinny voice. '*Now you die! Now you die!*'

I hurried back up the hill.

I LEFT A NOTE in the middle of the kitchen floor: STAY HERE—I'M LOOKING FOR U. Then I drove down through the canyon, trying to find him. The sun was dropping. Shadows pooled between the ridges as if the canyon was filling with ink.

If Ben had sprained an ankle, he might have hobbled downhill instead of making the climb back to my house; he might have knocked on someone's door for help; he might be limping home on his own. Sure, that had to be it. Ten-year-old boys don't simply vanish.

When I reached the street below my house, I parked and got out. The light was fading faster and the murk made it difficult to see.

'Ben?'

If Ben had come downhill, he would have passed beside one of three houses. No one was in at the first two, but a housekeeper answered at the third. She let me look in their back yard. Nothing. I looked over a wall into the neighbouring yards, but he wasn't there, either.

I went back to my car. It was all too likely that we would miss each other; as I drove along one street, Ben might turn down another. But I didn't know what else to do. Twice I waved down passing security patrols to ask if they had seen a boy matching Ben's description. Neither had. I drove faster, trying to cover as much ground as possible before the sun set. The streets were brighter the higher I climbed, but a chill haunted the shadows. Ben was wearing a sweatshirt over jeans. It didn't seem enough.

When I reached home, I called out again as I let myself in, but still got no answer. The note was untouched, and the message counter read zero.

I phoned the private security firms whose cars prowl the canyons every day around the clock. I explained that a child was missing and gave them Ben's description. Even though I wasn't a subscriber, they were happy to help.

When I put down the phone, I heard the front door open.

'Ben?'

'It's me.'

Lucy came into the living room. She was wearing a black business suit that was wrinkled from so long in the car. She was clearly tired, but she made a weak smile. 'Hey. I don't smell hamburgers.'

It was two minutes after six. It had taken Lucy exactly one hundred minutes to get home after we last spoke. It had taken me one hundred minutes to lose her son.

Lucy saw the fear in my face. 'What's wrong?'

'Ben's missing.'

She glanced around as if Ben might be hiding behind the couch. 'What do you mean, missing?'

'He went outside around the time you called, and now I can't find him. I drove all over the canyon, looking for him, but I didn't see him. He isn't next door. I don't know where he is.'

'He just *left*?'

I showed her the Game Freak as if it was evidence. 'I don't know. He was playing with this when he went out. I found it on the slope.'

Lucy stalked outside onto the deck. 'Ben! *Ben*!'

'Luce, I've been calling him. I called the security patrols. I was just going to call the police.'

'Dammit, Ben, you'd better answer me!'

I stepped out behind her and took her arms. She was shaking. She turned into me, and we held each other.

'Do you think he ran away?' Her voice was small against my chest.

'No, he was fine, Luce. He was OK after we talked. He was laughing at this stupid game.'

I told her that I thought he had probably hurt himself when he was playing on the slope, then got lost trying to find his way back.

'Those streets are confusing down there, the way they snake and twist. He was probably too scared to ask for help; he's been warned about strangers enough. If he got on the wrong street and kept walking, he probably got more lost. We should call the police.'

Lucy nodded, wanting to believe, and then she looked at the canyon. 'It's getting dark.'

That single word: dark. It summoned every parent's greatest dread.

I said, 'Let's call. The cops will light up every house in the canyon until we find him.'

As Lucy and I stepped back into the house, the phone rang.

Lucy jumped even more than me. 'That's Ben.'

I answered the phone, but the voice on the other end didn't belong to Ben or Grace Gonzalez or the security patrols.

A man said, 'Is this Elvis Cole?'

'Yes. Who's this?'

The voice was cold and low. He said, 'Five-two.'

'Who is this?'

'Five-two. You remember Five-two?'

I gripped the phone with both hands. I didn't understand, but the sharp fear of bad memories was already cutting deep. 'Who is this?'

'This is payback, you bastard. This is for what you did.'

I heard myself shout. 'What did I do? *What are you talking about?*'

'You know what you did. I have the boy.'

The line went dead.

Lucy plucked my arm. 'Who was it? What did they say?'

I barely heard her. I was caught in a yellowed photo album from my own past, flipping through pictures of another me, of young men with painted faces, hollow eyes and the sour smell of fear.

Lucy pulled harder. 'Stop it! You're scaring me.'

'It was a man, I don't know who. He says he has Ben.'

Lucy grabbed my arm with both hands. 'Ben was *kidnapped*? What did the man say? What does he *want*?'

My mouth was dry. My neck cramped with painful knots.

'He wants to punish me. For something that happened a long time ago.'

ON THE SECOND DAY of his visit, Ben waited until Elvis was washing his car before sneaking upstairs. He had been planning his assault on Elvis's personal belongings for many weeks. Elvis was a private investigator, which was a pretty cool thing to be, and he had some neat stuff: a great video and DVD collection of old science-fiction and horror movies that Ben could watch any time he wanted and a bulletproof vest hanging in his front entry closet. You didn't see that every day.

Ben was convinced that Elvis had other cool stuff stashed in his upstairs closet. He knew, for instance, that Elvis kept guns up there, locked in a special safe that Ben could not open. Ben didn't know what he would find, but he might luck out with a couple of issues of Playboy *or some neat police stuff like handcuffs.*

So when Elvis went outside to wash his car, Ben knew that his chance was at hand and raced through the house to the stairs.

Elvis and his cat slept upstairs in an open loft that looked down over the living room. The cat didn't like Ben, but then it didn't like anyone except for Elvis and his partner, Joe Pike. Every time Ben walked into a room the cat would lower its ears and growl. Ben was scared of it.

He worked his way to the head of the stairs, then peered over the top riser to make sure the cat wasn't sleeping on the bed.

The coast was clear.

Ben went to Elvis's closet. He had already been in it a couple of times when Elvis showed him and his mom the gun safe, so he knew that the little room contained Tupperware containers filled with pictures, stacks of old magazines, and other stuff. Ben riffled through the magazines first, but was disappointed by their content: mostly boring issues of Newsweek. *He hoisted himself up to see what was on top of the gun safe, a tall steel box, but all he found were a few old baseball caps.*

A high shelf stretched across the closet above Elvis's shirts. He saw boots, boxes, a sleeping-bag and a black nylon gym bag. He thought that the gym bag might be worth checking out, but he would need to grow a couple of feet to reach it. He placed his hands on top of the safe, heaved himself up, then hooked a knee on top and pushed himself onto the safe. He stretched for the gym bag, holding onto the shelf with one hand, but he lost his balance. He tumbled sideways into the shirts, pulling the gym bag with him as he hit the floor.

Ben scooped up the shirts, and that's when he found the cigar box. It must have been sitting on top of the gym bag. A few faded snapshots and five blue plastic cases had spilled out.

Ben sat cross-legged to examine his discovery.

The pictures showed soldiers in army uniform. One showed some guy sitting on a bunk, laughing. He had a tattoo high on his left arm. Ben had to look close to read it: RANGER. *He figured it was the man's name. Another picture showed five soldiers loaded with rucksacks, rocket launchers and black rifles standing in front of a helicopter. The second soldier from the left was holding a sign with numbers on it. The soldier on the far right looked like Elvis. Wow.*

Ben opened a blue case. A red, white and blue ribbon about an inch and a half long was pinned to grey felt. Beneath it was a medal: a gold five-pointed star. In the centre of the gold star was a tiny silver star. Ben closed the case, then opened the others. Each contained a medal.

He looked through the rest of the pictures. One showed a bunch of guys outside a tent, drinking beer; another showed Elvis sitting on sandbags with a rifle across his knees. Ben had hit the mother lode! This was exactly the kind of cool stuff he had hoped to find! He concentrated so hard on the pictures that he never heard Elvis approach.

Elvis said, 'Busted.'

Ben jerked with surprise and felt himself flush.

Elvis stood in the door, his raised eyebrows saying, What do we have here, sport?

Ben was mortified. 'I'm sorry I snooped in your stuff.'

Elvis made a little faraway smile and rubbed Ben's head. 'It's OK, bud. I said you could look around while you were here. But you don't have to sneak. All you have to do is ask. OK?'

It was hard to look Elvis in the eye, but Ben burned with curiosity. He showed Elvis the picture of the five soldiers by the helicopter. 'Is that you, second from the end?'

Elvis stared at the picture, but did not touch it.

Ben showed him the picture of the guy on the bunk. 'Who's Ranger?'

'His name was Ted Fields, not Ranger. A Ranger is a kind of soldier.'

'What do Rangers do?'

'Pushups.'

Elvis took the photo from Ben and put it back into the cigar box. Ben grew worried that Elvis would stop answering his questions, so he snatched up one of the blue cases and opened it.

'What's this?'

'They call it a Silver Star.'

'You have two.'

'The army had a sale.'

Ben saw that Elvis was uncomfortable but this was the coolest stuff he had ever seen. He snatched up a third medal case. 'Why is this one purple and shaped like a heart?'

'Let's get this stuff away and finish with the car.' Elvis put away the medal cases, then picked up the pictures.

Ben knew that Elvis must have done something pretty darned brave to win all these medals, but Elvis never talked about any of that. How could a guy have all this neat stuff and keep it hidden? Ben would wear his medals every day!

'How did you get that Silver Star medal? Were you a hero?'

Elvis kept his eyes down as he put the pictures in the cigar box and closed the lid. 'No, bud. No one else was around to get them, so they gave them to me.'

'I hope I get a Silver Star medal one day.'

Elvis got such a hard expression that Ben grew scared. But then the hard eyes softened. Ben was relieved.

Elvis took one of the Silver Stars from its case and held it out. 'Tell *you what, bud—I'd rather you take one of mine.' And just like that, Elvis gave Ben one of his Silver Stars.*

Ben held the medal like a treasure. The ribbon was shiny and smooth; the medallion was a lot heavier than it looked and its points were really sharp.

'I can keep it?'

'Sure. They gave it to me, and now I'm giving it to you.'

'Wow. Thank you! Could I be a Ranger, too?'

Elvis seemed a lot more relaxed now. He made a big deal out of placing his hand on Ben's head like Ben was being knighted.

'Sure. You are officially a US Army Ranger. This is the best way to become a Ranger. Now you don't have to do all those pushups.'

Ben laughed.

Elvis closed the cigar box and put it back high on the shelf. 'Anything else you want to see? I have some real smelly boots up here.'

'Ewww. Gross.'

They both were smiling and Ben felt better. All was right with the world.

Elvis gently squeezed the back of Ben's neck and steered him towards the stairs. 'Let's go finish washing the car, and then we can pick out a movie.'

Ben put the Silver Star in his pocket, but every few minutes he fingered the star's five sharp points through his trousers and thought that it was pretty darned cool.

That night Ben wanted to see the pictures again, but Elvis had acted so upset that Ben didn't want to ask. When Elvis was taking a shower, Ben heaved himself back atop the safe, but the cigar box was gone.

CHAPTER TWO
time missing: 3 hours, 56 minutes

The police arrived at twenty minutes past eight that night. Lucy stood sharply when the doorbell rang.

I said, 'I've got it. That's Lou.'

Adult missing persons were handled by the Missing Persons Unit downtown but children were dealt with by Juvenile Section detectives. Calling my friend Lou Poitras, a homicide lieutenant, saved time. He rolled out a Juvie team as soon as we got off the phone.

Poitras was a wide man with a face like boiled ham. His black leather coat was stretched tight across a chest and arms that were swollen from a lifetime of lifting weights. He looked grim as he kissed Lucy's cheek. 'How you guys doing?'

'Not so good.'

Two Juvenile Section detectives got out of a car behind him. The lead detective was an older man with loose skin and freckles. His driver was a younger woman with a long face and smart eyes. Poitras introduced them as they came into the house.

'This is Dave Gittamon. He's been a sergeant on the Juvie desk longer than anyone I know. This is—ah, sorry, I forgot your name.'

'Carol Starkey.'

Starkey's name sounded familiar but I couldn't place it. She smelt like cigarettes.

Poitras said, 'Have you gotten another call since we spoke?'

'No. We had the one call, and that was it.'

'I'll have a backtrace done through the phone company.'

We took them into the living room. I described the call I'd received and how I had searched for Ben. If he had been abducted from the slope beneath my house, then the spot where I found the Game Freak was a crime scene. Gittamon glanced at the canyon through the glass doors.

Starkey said, 'If he's still missing in the morning, I'll take a look.'

I didn't want to wait. 'Why don't we go now? We can use flashlights.'

Starkey said, 'We can't light this type of environment well enough at night, what with all the brush and the uneven terrain. We'd as likely destroy any evidence as find it. Better if I look in the morning.'

Gittamon nodded. 'Carol has a lot of experience, Mr Cole.'

Lucy joined us at the doors. 'Shouldn't we call the FBI? Doesn't the FBI handle kidnappings?'

Gittamon answered with the gentle voice of a man who had spent years dealing with frightened parents and children. 'We'll call the FBI if it's necessary, but first we need to establish what happened.'

'We know what happened: someone stole my son.'

Gittamon turned and went to the couch. Starkey sat with him, taking out a small spiral notebook.

'I know that you're frightened, Ms Chenier; I would be frightened too. But it's important for us to understand Ben and whatever led up to this.'

I said, 'Nothing led up to this, Gittamon. Someone just grabbed him.'

Lucy said, 'I understand, Sergeant, but this is my child.'

'I know, so let's talk.'

Gittamon asked Lucy a few general questions that didn't have anything to do with her son being grabbed off a hill. While they spoke, I wrote down everything the caller had said to me, then went upstairs for a picture of Ben and one of the snapshots he had found of me in my army days. I had not looked at that picture or any of the others for years until Ben found them. I hadn't wanted to.

Poitras was sitting on a chair in the corner when I got back. He said, 'We'll have that phone number traced in a couple of hours.'

I gave the pictures to Gittamon. 'This is Ben. The other picture is me in Vietnam. I wrote down what the man said.'

Gittamon glanced at the pictures, then passed them to Starkey. 'Why the picture of you?'

'The man who called said "five-two". You see in the picture, the man next to me is holding a sign that shows a number? Five-two was our patrol number. I don't know what else this guy could have meant.'

Starkey glanced up. 'You don't look old enough for Vietnam.'

'I wasn't.'

Gittamon said, 'All right, what else did he say?'

I pointed at the sheet. 'I wrote it down for you word for word.'

Gittamon glanced over the sheet, then passed it to Starkey, too.

Poitras said, 'You recognise his voice?'

'I've been racking my brain, but no, I didn't recognise it.'

Gittamon took back the picture from Starkey and frowned. 'Do you believe him to be one of the men in this picture?'

'No, that's not possible. A few minutes after this picture was taken, we went out on a mission, and everyone was killed but me. That makes it stand out, the five-two; that's why I remember.'

Lucy sighed softly. Starkey's mouth tightened as if she wanted a cigarette. Gittamon squirmed, as if he didn't want to talk about something so uncomfortable. I didn't want to talk about it, either.

'Well, ah, was there some kind of incident?'

'No, not if you're asking if it was my fault. It just went bad. I didn't do anything except survive.'

Starkey shifted towards Gittamon. 'We should get Ben's description out to patrol.'

Poitras nodded. 'Talk to the phone company, too. Have them set up a line trap on Elvis's phone.'

Starkey took her cellphone into the hallway. While she was making the calls, Gittamon asked about my past few days with Ben. When I told him I had found Ben looking through my closet, Gittamon raised his eyebrows.

'So Ben knew about this five-two business?'

'Not about the others getting killed, but he saw the pictures.'

'And this was when?'

'Earlier in the week. Three days ago, maybe. What does that have to do with anything?'

Gittamon glanced at Lucy, then looked back at me. 'I'm just trying to see how this fits. The implication is that this man on the phone took Ms Chenier's son as revenge for something that you did—not Ms Chenier, but you. Ben isn't your son or stepson, and hasn't lived with you except for these past few days. I understand that correctly, don't I? You and Ms Chenier maintain separate residences?'

'Yes, that's right.'

'Then why would he take Ms Chenier's son if it's you he hates so much? Why wouldn't he burn down your house or shoot you or even just sue you? You see what I'm getting at?'

I saw, and didn't much like it. 'Look, that's not it. Ben wouldn't do that. He's only ten.'

Lucy glanced from Gittamon to me, then back. 'Are you saying that Ben staged his own abduction?'

'No, ma'am, it's too early to say, but I've seen children stage abductions for all manner of reasons, especially when they're feeling insecure. A friend's older brother could have made the call to Mr Cole.'

I was angry. I went to the doors. A part of me hoped that Ben would be on the deck, watching us, but he wasn't. I said, 'If you don't want to raise false hopes, then stop. I spent the past five days with Ben. He wasn't feeling insecure, and he wouldn't do that.'

Lucy's voice snapped behind me. 'Would you rather someone had kidnapped him?'

I turned. Hope glowed in her eyes like hot sparks.

Gittamon gestured to Starkey that she could close her notebook, then he stood. 'Ms Chenier, please, I'm not saying Ben staged his own abduction but it's something we have to consider. I'd like a list of Ben's friends and their phone numbers.'

Lucy stood with them, as intent and focused as I had ever seen her. 'I'll have to get them from home. I can go do that right now.'

I said, 'Gittamon, you going to ignore the call?'

'No, Mr Cole, we're going to treat this as an abduction until we know otherwise. Can you put together a list of the people involved in whatever happened to you in the army?'

'They're dead.'

'Well, their families. We might want to speak with them. Carol, would you get together with Mr Cole on that?'

Starkey handed me her card and then she and Poitras stood. The four of us went to the door.

Starkey said, 'I'll come by tomorrow morning to see where you found the Game Freak. I can get the names then. What's a good time?'

'Sunrise.'

If Starkey heard the anger in my answer she didn't show it. 'Better light around seven.'

'Fine.'

Gittamon said, 'If he calls again, let us know. Call any time.'

That was it. Lucy and I did not speak as we watched them drive away, but once they were gone Ben's absence was a physical force in the house. Three of us present, not just two.

Lucy picked up her briefcase. 'I want to get those names for Sergeant Gittamon.'

'Call me when you get home, OK?'

Lucy glanced at the time, then closed her eyes. 'I have to call Richard. God, that's going to be awful, telling him about this.'

Richard Chenier was Lucy's ex-husband and Ben's father. He lived in New Orleans. Richard and Lucy had argued often about me. I guessed they would argue more.

Lucy fumbled with her briefcase and her keys and all at once she started crying. I cried, too. We held each other tight, the two of us crying, my face in her hair.

I said, 'I'm sorry. I don't know what happened or who would do this or why, but I'm sorry.'

'Don't.'

I didn't know what else to say.

I walked her out to her car, then stood in the street as she drove away. The cold night air felt good, and the darkness felt good, too. Lucy had been kind. She had not blamed me, but Ben had been with me, and now he was gone. The weight of the moment was mine.

I went back inside and stared at the picture of me with Roy Abbott and the others. Abbott looked like a twelve-year-old. I didn't look much older. I had been eighteen. Eight years older than Ben. I didn't know where Ben was, but I would bring him home.

I stared at the men in the picture. 'I'll find him. I'm going to bring him home. I swear to God I will.'

The men in the picture knew I would do it.

Rangers don't leave Rangers behind.

ONE MOMENT Ben was with the Queen of Blame on the hillside below Elvis Cole's house; the next, unseen hands covered his eyes and mouth and carried him away so quickly he didn't know what was happening. After the initial surprise of being jerked off his feet, Ben thought that Elvis was playing a trick on him, but the trick did not end.

Ben struggled and tried to kick, but someone held him so tightly he could neither move nor scream for help. He floated soundlessly across the slope and into a waiting vehicle. A heavy door slammed. Tape was pressed over his mouth, then a hood was pushed over his head, covering him with blackness. His arms and legs were taped together. He fought against the taping, but now more than one person held him. They were in a van. Ben smelt gasoline and the pine-scented stuff his mother used when she cleaned the kitchen.

The vehicle moved. They were driving.

The man who now held him said, 'Anyone see you?'

A rough voice answered from the front of the vehicle. 'It couldn't have gone any better. Make sure he's OK.'

Ben figured that the second voice belonged to the man who took him and was now driving. The man holding him squeezed Ben's arm.

'Can you breath? Grunt or nod to let me know.'

Ben was too scared to do either, but the first man answered as if he had. 'He's fine. Christ, you should feel his heart. Hey, you were supposed to leave his shoe. He still has his shoes.'

'He was playing one of those Game Boy things. I left the game instead. That's better than a shoe.'

They drove downhill, then up. Ben worked his jaws against the tape but couldn't open his mouth. His eyes filled and he strained against the tape that held his legs.

The man patted Ben's leg. 'Take it easy.'

They drove for a few minutes, then stopped. Ben thought they would get out, but they didn't. He heard another man climb into the van and say. 'He's out on heez deck.'

Ben had heard Cajun French and French accents for much of his life, and this was familiar, though somehow different. A French man speaking English, but with some other accent beneath the French. That made three of them; three total strangers had taken him.

The first man said, 'Roger that. I see him.'

The second man said, 'What's he doing?'

'He's moving down the slope.'

Ben realised that they were talking about Elvis. The three men were watching Elvis Cole. Elvis was looking for him.

The rough voice said, 'He found the kid's toy. He's running back to his house.'

'I wish I could see.'

'There's nothing to see, Eric. Stop bitching and settle down. Now we wait for the mother.'

When they mentioned his mother, Ben felt an intense jolt of fear, terrified they would hurt her. He tried to pull his arms free of the tape. He wanted to warn his mom and get the police and kick these men until they cried like babies.

Eric held tight. 'Jesus, stop flopping around. You're going to hurt yourself.'

They waited for what seemed like hours, then the rough voice said, 'I'll make the call.'

Ben heard the door open and somebody get out. After a minute, the door opened again and whoever it was got back in.

The rough voice said, 'That's it.'

They drove downhill, then back up again on winding streets. After a while, the van braked. Ben heard the mechanical clatter of a garage door opening. They eased forward, then the engine shut off and the garage door closed behind them.

Eric said, 'C'mon, kid.' He cut the tape holding Ben's legs, then jerked him to his feet.

'Ow!'

'C'mon, you can walk. I'll tell you where.'

Ben was in a garage. The hood had accidentally been pushed up enough for him to glimpse the van—white and dirty, with dark blue writing on the side. Eric turned him away before he could read what was written.

'We're coming to a step. C'mon, lift your feet!'

Ben felt for the step with his toe.

'Forget it. This is taking too long.' Eric carried Ben into the house like a baby, then dropped his legs. 'I'm putting you down. Stand up.'

As Ben stood, he glimpsed a dim room empty of furniture.

'OK, I've put a chair behind you. Siddown. I've got you. You won't fall.'

Ben lowered himself until the chair took his weight. It was hard to sit with his arms taped to his sides; the tape pinched his skin.

'OK, we're good to go. Is Mike outside?'

Mike. The rough-voiced man. Now Ben knew two of their names.

The third man said, 'I want to see his face.' *I-wahnt-tu-see-heez-fehss.* His voice, only inches away, was eerie and soft.

320

'Mike won't like it.'

'Stand behind the boy if you are afraid.' *Stand-beehind-dee-boy.*

'Oh, what the hell.'

Ben was scared again. He knew that he was about to see the men and he didn't want to.

The hood was pulled off from behind. An enormously tall man stood in front of him, so tall that his head seemed to brush the ceiling, and so black that his skin drank the room's dim light and glowed like gold. A row of round purple scars lined the man's forehead above his eyebrows. Three more scars followed the line of his cheeks below each eye, like something had been pushed under the skin.

Ben tried to twist away but Eric held tight. 'He's an African, kid. He won't eat ya until he cooks ya.'

The African carefully peeled the tape from Ben's mouth. Ben was so afraid that he trembled. It was dark outside: full-on night.

'I want to go home.'

Eric made a soft laugh. Eric had short red hair, milky skin and a gap between his front teeth like an open gate.

A door opened behind them and a third man came into the room. He had to be Mike. Mike looked like GI Joe in a black T-shirt that was tight across his chest and biceps. He stared down at Ben.

'How you doing?'

'What did you do to my mother?'

'Nothing. We just waited for her to get back so that I could call. I wanted her to know you're gone.'

'I don't want to be gone. I want to go home.'

'I know. We'll take care of that as soon as we can. You want something to eat?'

'I want to go home.'

'You need a pee?'

'Take me home. I want to see my mom.'

Mike patted Ben's head. 'I'm Mike. He's Mazi. That's Eric. You're going to be with us for a while, so be cool. That's just the way it is.' Mike glanced at Mazi and Eric. 'Put'm in the box.'

It happened just as fast as when they had plucked him from the hill. They scooped him up, retaped his legs and carried him outside into the cold night air. Ben struggled as they pushed him into a large plastic box like a coffin. He tried to sit up, but they pushed him down. A heavy lid slammed closed over him. The box suddenly moved and then fell away beneath him as if they had dropped him down a well. He hit the ground *hard*.

Something rained down onto the box with a scratchy roar only inches over his face. Then it happened again.

Ben realised, with an explosion of horror, what they were doing. He slammed into the sides of his plastic prison, but he couldn't get out. The sounds that rained down on him grew further and further away as Ben Chenier was buried in the earth.

CHAPTER THREE
time missing: 6 hours, 16 minutes

Ted Fields, Luis Rodriguez, Cromwell Johnson and Roy Abbott had died less than three hours after our team picture was taken. Team photographs had been taken before every mission. Crom Johnson used to joke that it was so the army could identify our bodies. I turned the picture face down so I wouldn't have to see them.

I listed the people in the remaining pictures, then tried to remember the other men who had served in my company. I couldn't. After a while the idea of making a list seemed silly. No one in my company had reason to hate me or steal a ten-year-old boy. No one I had known in Vietnam would. Still, I wrote the list.

Lucy called just before eleven. The house was so quiet that the sudden ring was as loud as a gunshot. My pen tore the page.

She said, 'I couldn't stand not knowing. Did he call back?'

'No, not yet. I would have called. I'll call you right away.'

'God, this is a nightmare. I just got off the phone with Richard. He's flying out tonight.'

'How was he?'

'Furious, frightened, belligerent—nothing I didn't expect.'

Richard hadn't wanted Lucy to move to Los Angeles, and he had never liked me. They fought often about it, and now they would fight even more. I guess she was calling for moral support.

'You want me to come by tomorrow after Starkey leaves?'

Richard could shout at me instead of her.

'I don't know. Maybe. I'd better get off the line. I'm worried that man will try to call you again about Ben. I'll talk to you tomorrow.'

The phone rang a second time almost as soon as I put it down. I let it ring twice, taking the time to ready myself.

'This is Detective Starkey. I hope I didn't wake you.'

'Sleep isn't an option, Starkey. I thought you were him.'

'Sorry. He hasn't called again, has he?'

'Not yet. It's late; I didn't think you'd still be on the job.'

'I waited to hear from the phone company. They show you received a call at six fifty-two this evening from a cell number registered to a Louise Escalante in Diamond Bar.'

'I don't know her.'

'I figured you wouldn't. She says her purse was stolen this afternoon, along with her phone. I'm sorry, but I think she's a dead end.'

Stealing a phone meant the man who took Ben had criminal experience. He had anticipated the line trace, which meant he had planned his action. Smart crooks are harder to catch than stupid crooks. They are also more dangerous.

'Mr Cole, are you getting those names together for me?'

'I'm doing that now, but I'm thinking about another possibility, too. Doing what I do, I've helped put some people in jail or out of business, and they're the kind of people who would hold a grudge. If I make a list, would you be willing to run their names, too?'

'Sure. Not a problem.'

'Thanks. I appreciate this.'

'I'll see you in the morning. Try to get some sleep.'

The darkest part of the night stretched through the hours until, little by little, the eastern sky lightened. I barely noticed. By the time Starkey arrived, I had filled twelve legal-sized pages with names and notes. It was 6.42 when I answered the door. She was early.

Starkey held up a cardboard tray with two cups from Starbucks. She passed one of them to me.

'That's nice of you, Starkey. Thanks.'

She glanced at the Game Freak on the dining table with the pages. 'How far down the hill did you find the toy?'

'Fifty, sixty yards. You want to get going down there now?'

'When the sun is higher, we'll get direct light. It'll be easier to see small objects and reconstruct what happened.'

'You sound like you know what you're talking about.'

'I've worked a few scenes. Let's see what you have with the names.'

I showed her the list of people from my civilian cases first. Beside each name I had written the crimes they had committed, whether or not they had been sentenced to prison, and whether or not I had killed anyone close to them.

Starkey said, 'Jesus, Cole, it's all mobsters and murderers. I thought you private guys did nothing but divorce work.'

'I pick the wrong cases.'

'No shit. You have reason to believe that any of these people are familiar with your military history?'

'So far as I know, none of them knows anything about me, but I guess they could find out.'

'I'll run them through the system to see if anyone's been released. Now let's talk about these other four men, the guys who died. Could their families blame you because their kid died and you didn't?'

'I wrote to their parents after it happened. Luis Rodriguez's mother and I corresponded until she died. Ted Fields's family sends me Christmas cards. When I mustered out, I went to see the Johnsons and Ted's family. Everyone was upset but no one blamed me.'

Starkey watched me as if she were convinced there had to be more, but she couldn't imagine what. I stared back at her, and once more thought she looked familiar.

I said, 'Have we met?'

Starkey glanced away. She took a foil packet from her jacket and swallowed a white tablet and pulled a packet of cigarettes from her jacket. 'Can I smoke in here?'

'You can smoke on the deck. You sure we haven't met?'

Starkey sighed. 'OK, Cole, here's how you know me. The Bomb Squad lost a tech in Silver Lake a couple of months ago.'

'That was *you*?'

Starkey broke for the deck. I followed her.

Carol Starkey had bagged a serial killer who murdered bomb technicians. Mr Red had been headline news, but most of the stories were about Starkey. Three years before, when Starkey herself had been a bomb tech, she had been trying to de-arm a bomb in a trailer park when an earthquake triggered the initiator. Both Starkey and her partner had apparently been killed, but Starkey was resuscitated at the scene. She had literally risen from the dead.

Maybe she read what I was thinking. 'Don't even dream about asking, Cole. Don't ask if I saw white lights or pearly gates.'

'I don't care about that. All I care about is finding Ben.'

'Good. That's all I care about, too. The bomb squad stuff, that's behind me. Now I do this.'

'I'm glad, but do you know anything about finding a missing boy?'

Starkey blew a geyser of smoke, angry. 'What are you asking? If I'm up to the job?'

I was angry too. I had been angry since last night and I was getting angrier by the second. 'Yeah, that's exactly what I'm asking.'

'I reconstructed bombs and bomb scenes, and traced explosives. I made cases against the assholes who built bombs. *And* I nailed Mr Red. So you don't have to worry, Cole. I know how to detect, and you can bet your private-eye ass that I'm going to find this boy.'

The sun was high now. The slope was bright. Starkey snapped her cigarette over the rail, then turned to face me. 'We got plenty of light. Show me where you found the toy.'

STARKEY CHANGED SHOES outside her car, then met me at the side of my house wearing a pair of beat-up cross-trainers with her trousers rolled to her knees. She stared warily down at the slope. 'It's steep.'

'Are you scared of heights?'

'I was just saying. The soil here is loose and you've already been tramping around down there. That's going to make it harder. I want you to show me where you found the Game Freak, then get the hell out of my way. We clear?'

'Look, I'm good at this too, Starkey. I can help.'

'That remains to be seen. Show me.'

I led Starkey down the slope, staying alongside the narrow paths that Ben had used so that we wouldn't disturb his footprints. Ben's trail was easy to follow until we reached the trees, then the soil grew rocky. It didn't matter; I knew the way from yesterday. We cut across the slope. Starkey slipped twice and cursed both times.

I pointed out the patch of grass where I had found the Game Freak and several of Ben's footprints. Starkey squatted and looked as if she was trying to memorise every rock.

She glanced at my feet. 'You wearing those shoes yesterday?'

'Yeah. New Balance. You can see the prints I left yesterday.'

I pointed my prints out to her, then lifted a foot so that she could see the sole of my shoe. She studied the pattern then frowned at me.

'OK, Cole, you seem to know what you're doing down here, so I'm going to let you help. We just wanna figure out what happened. After that, we'll bring in SID.'

Criminalists from Los Angeles Police Department's Scientific Investigation Division would be responsible for identifying and securing any evidence of the crime.

Starkey divided the area into a rough grid of squares, which we searched one at a time. Ben's prints were jumbled and could have meant anything, but finally they headed downhill.

She said, 'Where are you going?'

'I'm following Ben's trail.'

'I can barely see the scuffs. You a hunter, or what?'

'I used to do this in the army.'

Ben's footprints led through the grass for another eight feet, but then I lost his trail. I found no other sign of his passing. It was as if he had sprouted wings.

'If someone grabbed Ben, we should see signs of a struggle or at least the other person's footprints, but I don't see anything.'

'You're just missing it, Cole.'

'There's nothing to miss. Ben's prints just stop, and the soil here bears none of the scuffs you'd expect to find if he struggled.'

Starkey squinted at the ground. 'Maybe Gittamon was right. Maybe you can't find a struggle because he ran away.'

'If Ben had run away from this point, he would have left prints, but he didn't. Someone carried him.'

'Then where are the other person's prints?'

I stared at the ground, shaking my head. 'I don't know.'

'That's stupid, Cole. We'll find something. Keep looking.'

Starkey paralleled my move downhill. She was three or four yards to my side when she stopped to study the ground. 'Hey, is this the boy's shoe or yours?'

A faint line marked the heel of a shoe that was too large to be Ben's. The impression was crisp without being weathered, and was free of debris. I got behind it and sighted forward to see which way the print was headed. It pointed to the place where Ben's trail ended.

'It's him, Starkey. You got him.'

Starkey pushed a sprig of rosemary into the soil to mark the print's location, and then we widened our circle but found nothing more. Additional shoe prints should have been salted through Ben's like the overlapping pieces of a puzzle, but all we had was the partial heel print of a single shoe. This frightened me. I considered the slope and the dead winter leaves spread over the ground. A man had worked his way uphill through heavy brush and brittle leaves so quietly that Ben did not hear him. The man would not have been able to see him through the thick brush, which meant that he had located Ben by the sound of the Game Freak. Then he took a healthy ten-year-old boy so quickly that Ben had no chance to call out.

I said, 'Starkey, forget the names I gave you from my old cases. None of those people is good enough to do this. Just run the people who served with me.'

I stared at the thick brush, thinking hard about the people I had known and what the best of them could do. The skin on my back prickled. The leaves and branches that surrounded us became the broken pieces of an indistinct puzzle. A man with the right skills could be ten feet away, watching us, and we would never see him.

I lowered my voice. 'The man who did this has combat experience, Starkey. He was trained to hunt humans and he's good at it.'

'Look, Cole, don't get spooky. We don't know what we're dealing with, so why don't we wait until SID gets here?'

I walked back up the hill and Starkey trailed slowly after me. I didn't wait for her to catch up. Shadows from a past that should have been buried lined the path back up to my house. The shadows outnumbered me, and I knew I would need help with them. When I reached my house, I went into the kitchen and phoned a gun shop I know in Culver City.

'Let me have Joe.'

'He isn't here.'

'It's important you find him. Tell him to meet me at Lucy's right away. Tell him that Ben Chenier is missing.'

I hung up and went out to my car. I started the engine, but sat with my hands on the steering wheel, trying to stop their shaking.

The man who took Ben had probably stalked us for days. He had studied when we came and when we left. He knew my home and the canyon, and how Ben went down the slope to play, and he had done it all so well that I did not notice. It took special training and skills to hunt humans. I had known men with those skills, and they scared me. I had been one of them.

CHAPTER FOUR
time missing: 17 hours, 41 minutes

Beverly Hills makes people think of mansions, but the flats south of Wilshire are lined with modest homes. Lucy and Ben shared an apartment in a two-storey building shaped like a U, with the arms embracing a courtyard filled with towering palms. It was not a limousine street, but a black presidential stretch limo was waiting by the fire hydrant outside the building.

I wedged my car into a parking spot half a block down and walked up the sidewalk. The limo driver had the windows raised and the engine running. Parked across the street, in front of Gittamon's car, were two men in a Mercury Marquis. They had flat expressions that said they were used to being in the wrong place at the wrong time and not much bothered by it. They watched me like cops.

A man I had never met before answered the door. 'May I help you?'

It must be Richard, I thought. I put out my hand. 'Elvis Cole. I wish we weren't meeting like this.'

Richard's face darkened. He ignored my hand. 'I wish we weren't meeting at all.'

Lucy stepped in front of him, looking uncomfortable. 'Don't start.'

Something sour flickered in Richard's eyes, but he turned back into her apartment. Richard was Lucy's age, but his hair was silver on the sides and thinning. He wore a black shirt, khaki slacks that were wrinkled from the plane, and Bruno Magli moccasins that cost more than I made in a week. Even wrinkled and sleepless, Richard looked rich. He owned a natural gas company with international holdings.

Lucy lowered her voice as I followed her inside. 'They just got here.'

In Lucy's small living room, Richard joined a solidly built man in a dark business suit. He had short, steel-grey hair and eyes that looked like the wrong end of gun sights. He put out his hand.

'Leland Myers. I run security for Richard's company.'

Richard said, 'I brought Lee to help find Ben since you people managed to lose him.'

As Myers and I shook hands, Gittamon came out of the hall with Ben's orange iMac, which he put on a table by the door. 'We'll have his email by the end of the day. You'd be surprised what children tell their friends.'

I was annoyed that Gittamon was still chasing the staged abduction theory. 'You're not going to find anything in his email. Starkey and I searched the slope this morning. We found a shoe print where Ben dropped his Game Freak. It was probably left by the man who took Ben, and he was likely someone who served with me in Vietnam.'

Lucy shook her head. 'I thought the others were dead.'

'They are, but this could be someone else from my company with a certain type of combat experience. I gave Starkey a list of names, and I'll try to remember more. You don't learn how to move the way this man moved by hunting deer on the weekends. He knows how to move without leaving a trail, and he knows how to hunt people, because Ben never saw him coming.'

I told them how Ben's footprints ended abruptly and that we had found only the one other print. Richard listened with increasing agitation. By the time I finished he was pacing in tight circles.

'This is great, Cole. You're saying some kind of murdering Green Beret commando like Rambo took my son?'

Gittamon checked his pager. 'We don't know that, Mr Chenier. Once SID reaches the scene, we'll investigate more thoroughly. Mr Cole might be jumping to conclusions.'

Richard glanced at Gittamon, then stared at Lucy. 'No, I'm sure that Mr Cole has it right. Cole has a history of attracting dangerous people. I tried to tell my ex-wife that associating with Cole puts her and Ben in danger, but would she listen? No.' His voice grew louder. 'She never listened because our son's safety wasn't as important to her as getting what she wants.'

Lucy slapped him with a single hard shot that snapped on his cheek like a firecracker. 'Stop it. You don't always have to be such an asshole, Richard.'

Gittamon squirmed as if he wished he were anywhere else.

Myers touched Richard's arm. 'Richard, we need to get started.'

Richard's jaw knotted as if he wanted to say more but was chewing the words to keep them inside. He glanced at Lucy, then averted his eyes as if he suddenly felt embarrassed by his outburst. 'I promised myself I wouldn't do that, Lucille. I'm sorry.'

Lucy didn't answer. Her left nostril pulsed as she breathed. I could hear her breathing from across the room.

Richard wet his lips awkwardly, then moved away from her. He shrugged at Gittamon. 'She's right, Sergeant—I'm an asshole, but I love my son and I'll do whatever I can to find him. That's why I'm here, and that's why I brought Lee.'

Leland Myers cleared his throat. 'We should see this hill Cole described. Debbie's good with a crime scene. He should be in on this.'

Gittamon said, 'Who's Debbie?'

Richard sat on a chair and rubbed his face with both hands. 'Debbie DeNice: it's short for Debulon or something. He's a retired New Orleans detective. Homicide—right, Lee?'

'Phenomenal case-clearance rate. He's here with Ray Fontenot.'

Richard pushed to his feet again. 'They're both ex-New Orleans PD. The best in the city. Everyone I brought is the best.'

Myers glanced at Gittamon, then me. 'I'd like to get my people up to your house, Cole. I'd also like a copy of those names.' He glanced at Gittamon. 'If SID is on the way, we'd better get going, but I'd also like a quick brief on what we know and what's being done, Sergeant. Can I count on you for that?'

'Oh, yes, absolutely.'

I gave them directions to my house, and Myers offered to carry Ben's computer down to Gittamon's car. They left together. Richard followed after them, but hesitated when he reached Lucy and looked at me. His mouth tightened. 'Are you coming?'

'In a minute.'

Richard looked at Lucy, and the hardness around his mouth softened. He touched her arm. 'I'm staying at the Beverly Hills on Sunset. I shouldn't have said those things, Lucille. I regret them and I apologise, but they're true.'

He glanced at me again, then left.

Lucy raised a hand to her forehead. 'This is a nightmare.'

THE SUN HAD RISEN like a flare, so intense that it washed the colour from the sky. When I reached the street, Richard was waiting by the black limo with Myers and the two men from the Mercury Marquis. They were probably his people from New Orleans.

They stopped talking and Richard stepped out in front of the others to meet me. He didn't bother hiding his feelings now; his face was angry. 'This is your fault. It's only a matter of time before one of them gets killed because of you, and I'm not going to let that happen.'

Myers touched Richard's arm. 'We don't have time for this.'

Richard brushed away his hand. 'I want to say it.'

I said, 'Take his advice, Richard. Please.'

Debbie DeNice, tall and angular, and Ray Fontenot, a large man with eyes the colour of dishwater, moved to Richard's other side.

DeNice said, 'Take his advice—or what?'

It had been a long night. Pressure built in my head, but I answered him calmly. 'It's still morning. We're going to see a lot of each other.'

Richard said, 'Not if I can help it. I don't like you, Cole. I want you to stay away from my family.'

I made myself breathe. This man was Ben's father and Lucy's former husband. I told myself that if I said or did anything to him it would hurt them. We didn't have time for this. We had to find Ben.

'I'll see you up at the house.' I tried to go round them, but DeNice stepped sideways to block my path.

'You don't know what you're dealing with, partner.'

Myers said, 'Debbie . . .'

Richard stared up at Lucy's apartment. He seemed more confused than angry. 'She was stupid and selfish to move to Los Angeles. She was stupid to be involved with someone like you, and selfish to take Ben away. I hope she comes to her senses before one of them dies.'

New Orleans was probably a tough beat, and De Nice, who had scars on the bridge of his nose, looked like the kind who enjoyed it tough. I could have tried again to step round him, but I didn't.

'Get out of my way.'

DeNice opened his coat to flash his gun, 'You don't get the picture.'

Something flickered at the edges of light; an arm roped with thick veins looped round DeNice's neck; a heavy blue .357 Colt Python appeared under his right arm. DeNice floundered off balance as Joe Pike, my partner of many years, appeared out of nowhere and lifted him backwards.

Fontenot clawed under his own jacket. Pike snapped the .357 across Fontenot's face. Fontenot staggered.

I said, 'Richard, we don't have time for this. We have to find Ben.'

Pike wore a sleeveless grey sweatshirt, jeans, and dark glasses that glittered in the sun. The muscles in his arm were bunched like cobblestones around DeNice's neck.

Leland Myers watched Pike the way a lizard watches, not really seeing, more like he was waiting for something that would trigger his own preordained reaction: attack, retreat, fight. He spoke calmly. 'That was stupid, Debbie, unprofessional. You see, Richard? You can't play with people like this.'

Richard seemed to wake, as if he was coming out of a fog. He shook his head. 'Jesus, Lee, what does DeNice think he's doing? I just wanted to talk to Cole. I can't have something like this.'

Myers never looked away from Joe. He took DeNice's arm even though Pike still held him. 'We're good now. Let go.'

Pike's arm tightened.

I said, 'Richard, listen. I know you're upset, but I'm upset, too. We have to focus on Ben. Finding Ben comes first. You have to remember that. Go get in your car. I don't want to have this conversation again.'

Richard's jaw muscle flexed, but he went to his car.

Myers was still watching Pike. 'You going to let go?'

I said, 'It's OK now, Joe. Let him go.'

Pike said, 'Whatever.'

DeNice could have played it smart, but didn't. When Pike released him, DeNice spun and threw a hard, straight punch. He moved a lot faster than a thick man should and had probably surprised a lot of men with his speed. Pike dodged the punch, trapped DeNice's arm in a joint lock, and hooked DeNice's legs from under him. The detective hit the sidewalk on his back, his head bouncing on the concrete.

Myers pulled DeNice to his feet and pushed him towards the Marquis. Fontenot was already behind the wheel, holding a bloody handkerchief to his face.

Myers joined Richard at the limo, and then both cars drove away.

When I turned to Joe, I saw a dark glimmer at the edge of his lip. 'You're bleeding. Did that guy tag you?'

Pike never got tagged. Pike was way too fast ever to get tagged. He touched away the blood, then climbed into my car.

'Tell me about Ben.'

A LIGHT HAD APPEARED over Ben's head that morning, shining like a faraway star. An air hole had been cut into the box. Ben put his eye to the hole and saw a tiny disk of blue at the end of a tube.

He cupped his mouth to the hole. *'I'm down here! Help me! Help!'*

No one answered.

'HELP!'

Ben had freaked out during the night. He'd managed to work his arms out of the tape and then free his legs. He kicked the walls like a baby having a tantrum, and tried to push off the top by getting on all fours. Ben was absolutely certain that Mike and Eric and the African had been T-boned by a speeding bus and now no one knew that he was trapped in this awful box. He would starve to death and die of thirst. Eventually he lost track of time and drifted at the edges of sleep.

'Help! I'm down here! Please let me out!'

No one answered.

'Ma-maaaaaaaa!'

Something kicked his foot and he jumped as if 10,000 volts had amped through his body.

'Jesus, kid! Stop whining!'

The Queen of Blame leaned on her elbow at the far end of the box. She didn't look happy.

Ben shrieked. 'You're not real! You're only a game!'

'Then this won't hurt.' She twisted his foot. *Hard.*

'Ow!'

She couldn't be real! He was trapped in a nightmare!

The Queen grinned nastily, then touched him with the toe of a gleaming boot. 'You don't think I'm real, big guy? Go ahead. Feel it.'

Ben reached out. The boot was as slick as a polished car and as solid as the box around him. He jerked back his hand.

The Queen laughed. 'You wouldn't last two seconds against Modus!'

'I'm only ten! I'm scared and I want to go home!'

The Queen examined her nails as if she was bored. Each nail was a glistening razor-sharp emerald. 'So go.'

'I've been *trying* to go. We're *trapped!*'

The Queen raised her eyebrows again. 'Are we?' She watched him without expression. 'You can leave any time you want.'

Ben's eyes welled with tears. 'That isn't funny! I've been calling for help all night and no one can hear me!'

The Queen's eyes blazed and her hand raked the air. 'Claw your way out, you idiot! See how *sharp!*' Her nails were glittering knives.

Ben cowered back, terrified. 'Get away from me.'

She leaned closer. '*Feel how they cut!*'

'Go away!'

She lunged at him.

Ben screamed as the razor-sharp points dug into his leg.

Then he woke up. He blinked into the darkness. The box was silent and empty. It had all been a nightmare, except that Ben could still feel the sharp pain of her nails in his thigh.

He rolled onto his side, and the sharp thing bit deeper.

'Ouch!' He felt to see what was sticking into him. Elvis Cole's Silver Star was in his pocket. He took it out and traced the medal's five points with his fingers. They were hard and sharp, just like a knife. He pressed a point into the plastic overhead, then sawed the medal back and forth. He felt the plastic with his fingers. A thin line was scribed in his sky.

Ben worked the medal some more, and the line grew deeper. He pushed faster and harder, his arms pumping like pistons. Tiny bits of plastic fell through the darkness like rain.

WITH THE WINDOWS covered and the air conditioning off so that the neighbours wouldn't hear it running, the house felt like an oven. Mike Fallon didn't mind. He had been in plenty of Third World shit-holes where heat like this was a breath of cool air.

Eric Schilling and Mazi Ibo had gone out to steal a car, so Fallon stripped down to exercise. Sweat glazed his skin as he did 200 press-ups, 200 crunches, 200 leg lifts, and 200 back bends without pausing between sets, and then repeated the cycle twice more.

Fallon was towelling off when the garage door rumbled open. That would be Eric and Mazi, but he picked up his .45 just in case.

They came through the kitchen with two bags, Eric calling out 'Mike? Yo, Mike?'

Fallon stepped out behind them and tapped Eric with the gun.

He jumped. 'Jesus! You scared me.'

'Pay more attention next time. If I was the wrong guy, you wouldn't have a next time.'

Eric and Mazi put down the bags. Mazi tossed a green apple to Fallon, then took a bottle of Orangina for himself.

Fallon said, 'You get the car OK?'

'Mazi got it.'

Mazi said, 'Eets good cahr. Nice seats.'

Eric took two cellphones from a bag and tossed them to Fallon. They needed the phones and the car for what they had planned.

Fallen watched as they put out the food, then said, 'Listen up.'

Eric and Mazi looked over. They had been planning this for a long time, but now they were getting close to the edge. It would be go or no-go in just a few hours.

'Once we double-cross this guy, there's no going back. Are we all good on this?'

Eric said, 'Hell, yes. I want the money. So does Mazi.'

Fallon had known how they would answer, but he was glad he had asked. He dropped to the floor to pull on his socks and shoes. He wanted a shower, but the shower could wait. 'I'm gonna go find an AO. Stow the chow, then check the kid. Make sure he's tight.'

The AO was the 'area of operation' that they would secure and maintain for the double-cross.

'He's tight. He's under three feet of dirt.'

'Check him anyway, Eric. We'll probably have to put him on the phone to convince these guys.'

Fallon slipped his gun into his trousers, then started for the garage. Eric called after him. 'What are we going to do with the kid if we don't get the money?'

Fallon didn't even break stride. 'Put him back in the box and plug up the hole.'

CHAPTER FIVE
time missing: 18 hours, 38 minutes

I told Joe Pike about Ben and the call as we drove to my house.

Pike said, 'The man on the phone didn't make any demands?'

'He told me it was payback. That's all he said. Payback for what happened in Vietnam.'

Pike grunted. He knew what happened to me that day in Vietnam. He was the only person I'd told outside of army personnel and the families of the other four men.

When we reached my house, a pale blue SID van was parked across my drive, where Starkey was helping a tall, gangly criminalist named John Chen to unload his equipment. Gittamon was changing shoes in the back seat of his car. Richard and his people had gathered at the side of my house with their jackets off and sleeves rolled. A nasty purple bruise had risen under Fontenot's eye. DeNice openly glared at us.

Pike and I parked off the road, past my house, then walked back to the van.

Starkey was still smoking. 'You see all those people? Gittamon is letting them come down the hill.'

'This is my partner, Joe Pike. He's coming, too.'

'Jesus, Cole, this is a crime scene, not a safari.'

John Chen emerged from the van with a day pack and an evidence kit. He bobbed his head when he saw us. 'I know these guys. Hi, Elvis. Hiya, Joe. We've worked together.'

Starkey blew out a huge bloom of smoke, and Pike moved to stand with Chen. Upwind.

Myers walked over and asked Starkey for the list of names.

She said, 'Any luck, we'll hear back later today.'

'Cole said I could have the list. We'll run our own check.'

Starkey took out the list. She gave it to me. I handed it to Myers.

He said, 'What are we waiting for?'

Starkey glanced at Gittamon, clearly irritated that he was taking so long, and called out to prod him. 'Any time, Sergeant.'

'Almost ready.' He was red-faced from bending over.

Myers went back to the others, and Starkey had more of her cigarette. The black cat who shares the house with me came round the corner. He probably came because he smelt Pike, but when he saw other people standing in front of the house, he arched his back and growled. Even DeNice looked over.

Starkey said, 'What's wrong with that thing?'

'He doesn't like people. Don't take it personally. He doesn't like anyone except for me and Joe.'

Pike went over to the cat and stroked its fur. The cat flopped onto its side and rolled onto its back. That cat worships Joe Pike.

Gittamon finished with his shoes and climbed out of his car. 'All right, Carol. Let's see what you found.'

Starkey said, 'Go first, Cole. Take us down.'

Pike and I went over the edge first, paralleling Ben's path like I had done that morning. Starkey kept up better this time, even though she helped Chen with his equipment, but Gittamon and DeNice had trouble with the footing.

We passed through the walnut trees, then circled the rise to come out above the area where I had found the Game Freak. I pointed out where Ben's footprints ended, then showed them the partial. I squatted at its heel again, and showed them how it was headed towards Ben. Chen marked the location with an orange flag. Pike bent next to me to study the print, then moved downhill without a word.

Starkey said, 'Hey, be careful. We don't want to disturb anything.'

Gittamon and Richard crowded between Chen and Starkey to see the print, with DeNice and Fontenot behind them.

Myers considered it without expression. 'You haven't found any other evidence?'

Starkey said, 'Not yet.'

Richard stared at the partial print, so still that he might have been numb. He touched the dry soil beside it, then glanced around at the brush as if to fix the place in his mind. 'Is this where my son was taken, Cole? Is this where you lost him?'

I didn't answer. I stared at the print, and once more followed its line towards Ben. I had searched the ground between the partial and the terminus of Ben's prints at least three times. It was soft and dusty and should have been covered with prints.

I pointed out what I saw, talking more to myself than the others. 'Ben was over there, facing away from us, playing the Game Freak.'

Ben's ghost walked past on the path, its feet leaving Ben's prints. A darker ghost stepped through me, moving towards him. Its right foot kissed the impression into the dust in front of me.

'Ben didn't know he was here until he reached this spot. The other person moved slow until he reached this spot, then maybe Ben heard him or turned for no reason . . .'

The dark ghost suddenly accelerated towards Ben, pushing off in the soft soil and leaving the partial print. I watched it happen.

'Ben still didn't know what was happening or we'd see scuffs in his footprints. The stranger grabbed Ben from behind and lifted him off his feet. He covered Ben's mouth so he couldn't scream.'

The dark ghost carried a struggling boy into the brush. When the ghosts faded, I was shaking. 'That's what happened.'

Myers was staring at me. So were Starkey and Chen. Myers shook his head. 'So where are his other prints?'

'That's how good he was, Myers. He didn't leave any other prints. This one was a mistake.'

Richard shook his head, disgusted. 'I can't believe this is all you have, one crappy hole in the dirt, and your only explanation is that Rambo stole my son.'

DeNice glanced around. 'Maybe he didn't look hard enough.'

Myers nodded, and Fontenot and DeNice set out over the hill.

Gittamon leaned closer to the print. 'Can you make a cast of this, John?'

Chen pinched a bit of soil and let it dribble through his fingers. He frowned. 'You see how fine and dry the soil is? It won't hold its structure. You got soil like this, you can lose a lot of detail when you make the pour. The weight of the plastic deforms the impression.'

Starkey said, 'Start working, John. You'll get a cast.'

Richard watched DeNice and Fontenot searching through the brush, and checked the time. He shook his head. 'Lee, this is going to take for ever at this rate. Hire more people if we have to and bring in whoever we need. I don't care what it costs.'

Starkey watched Gittamon like she was hoping he would say something, and she spoke up when he didn't. 'If more people come out it'll end up like a zoo down here.'

Richard slipped his hands into his pockets. 'That isn't my problem, Detective. My problem is finding my son. If you want to arrest me for obstruction, I'm sure that'll make a good story in the local news.'

Gittamon said, 'No one's talking about anything like that. We just have to be concerned with preserving the crime scene.'

Myers touched Richard's arm. The two of them had a low conversation, then Myers turned back to Gittamon. 'You're right, Sergeant. We need to worry about preserving the evidence and also the case against whoever took Ben. Cole shouldn't be here.'

I stared at him, but Myers had the same unreadable expression.

I said, 'I don't get your point, Myers. I've already been here. I was all over this slope searching for Ben.'

Richard shifted his shoulders impatiently. 'What's not to understand, Cole? I'm enough of a lawyer to know you'll be a material witness in whatever case arises. You might even be named as a party. Either way, your presence creates a problem.'

Starkey said, 'Why would he be a party?'

'He was the last person to see my son alive.'

The canyon grew hot. Sweat leaked from my pores. Chen was the only one who moved. He tapped a sheet of rigid white plastic into the soil a few inches from the shoe print. He would frame the print like that to support the sole, then spray a thin sealant to bind the surface.

I said, 'What are you saying, Richard?'

Myers touched Richard's arm. 'He's not accusing you, Cole, but it's clear that the man on the phone bears a grudge against you. Maybe it will turn out that you used to know him and didn't like him any more than he likes you.'

Richard said, 'Myers is right. If his lawyer can establish that the grudge goes both ways, he'll argue that you purposefully contaminated the evidence against him. He might even claim that you planted evidence. Look at O.J.'

Gittamon squirmed. 'No one is doing anything improper here.'

'Sergeant, I'm on your side, but we have a problem with this,' Richard insisted. 'Ask the prosecutor's office what they think.'

Gittamon watched Pike and Richard's detectives moving through the brush. He glanced at Starkey, but all she did was shrug.

He said, 'Ah, Mr Cole, maybe you should wait up at your house.'

'What good would it do, Gittamon? I've already been all over this slope, so it won't make any difference if I keep looking.'

Gittamon shuffled nervously. 'I'll see what the chief thinks.'

Richard and Myers turned away and joined Fontenot and DeNice. Gittamon hunkered down beside Chen so that he wouldn't have to look at me.

Starkey watched all of them for a moment, then shrugged at me. 'Look, if we get a bounce on one of those names you gave us, we'll have something to work with. Just wait upstairs and I'll let you know.'

I shook my head. 'You're crazy if you think I'm going to wait.'

'What else can you do?'

'Think like him.'

I waved Pike over, and we climbed the hill to my house.

CHAPTER SIX
time missing: 19 hours, 08 minutes

When people look at Joe Pike, they see an ex-cop, ex-Marine, the muscles and the dark glasses riding a secret face. Pike grew up at the edge of a small town where he spent his childhood hiding in the woods from his father, who liked to beat Pike bloody with his fists. Marines weren't frightened of brutal alcoholics, so Pike made himself into a Marine. The Marines saw Pike move well in the woods, so they taught him to track and stalk. Now Pike was the best that I had ever seen at those things, all because he once used to be a scared little boy in the woods. But when you see someone, all you see is what they let you see.

Pike and I studied the canyon from my deck. I said, 'He couldn't know when Ben would leave my house or be alone, so he needed a safe place to watch and wait.'

Pike nodded at the ridge across the canyon, a crooked finger of knobbly peaks that rose and fell as they stepped down into the basin. 'He had to be over there with a scope or glasses.'

'That's the way I see it.'

'From where he was, he would have been able to see us here on your deck. That means we can see his hiding place.'

I went inside for my binoculars and a map, then came back out on the deck. I said, 'OK. If it was you, where would you be?'

Pike studied the map and considered the residential streets that threaded along the canyon's sides. 'I'd pick a spot where the locals couldn't see me. That means I'd park where people wouldn't wonder about my car—on a fire trail or in the brush—but I'd still want fast access to my vehicle. When I saw Ben, I wouldn't have much time to get to my car, drive here, park, then look for him.'

'What about two men? One keeping watch, the other waiting on this side with a cellphone?'

Pike shrugged. 'Either way, someone had to be on the far side, watching. If we're going to find anything, that's where we'll find it.'

We picked out obvious reference points like an orange house and a row of six bearded palms, and marked their locations on the map. Once we had reference points, we took turns to scan the far hillside for houses being remodelled, clumps of trees, and other places where a man could wait without being seen. We located them on the map relative to our reference points.

We did this for almost two hours, then Joe Pike said, 'Let's hunt.'

I thought about telling Starkey what we were doing, but decided that it was better if she didn't know. She might feel obligated to remind us that Gittamon had told us not to jeopardise their case. All I cared about was finding a boy.

We snaked our way across the canyon to the opposite ridge. Everything had looked different from a thousand yards away. Close up, the trees and houses were unrecognisable. We checked our map against the landmarks we had noted and tried to find our way.

The first place we considered was an undeveloped area at the end of a fire road. Unpaved fire roads wrap through the Santa Monica

Mountains like veins through a body, mostly so that county work crews can cut back brush before the fire season. We parked between two driveways at the end of the road and squeezed round the gate.

Pike said, 'He wasn't here. Parking between these houses is asking to be seen.'

Seven spots that had seemed likely from my deck were too exposed to the neighbours. We scratched them off the map. Four more locations could be reached only by parking in front of houses. We scratched them, too.

The sun seemed to sprint across the sky. Finding likely spots took for ever; searching them, even longer. Traffic picked up as moms delivered children from school; kids with skateboards and spiky hair watched us from drives. Adults on their way home from work eyed us suspiciously from their SUVs.

I said, 'Look at all these people. Somebody has to have seen something. Someone had to.'

Pike said, 'Slow down. I know you're scared, but if you hurry you'll miss something. We'll do what we can, then come back tomorrow. You know the drill.'

On most of the streets, houses were shoehorned in, but a few held stretches that were too steep to carry foundations. Three of those stretches had unobstructed views of my home.

The first two were nearly vertical troughs on the inside of sharp curves. The third was more promising: a shoulder on the point of an outside curve that sloped downhill near the foot of the ridge. We pulled off the street and got out of my car. Starkey and Chen were tiny dots of colour climbing up to my house. I couldn't tell who was who, but it would have been easy with binoculars.

Pike said, 'Good view.'

Two small cars and a dusty pick-up were parked off the road near us. They probably belonged to the men who were remodelling a house nearby. One more car wouldn't stand out.

I said, 'It'll be faster if we split up. You take this side of the shoulder. I'll cross the top, then move down the far side.'

Pike set off without a word. I worked my way across the top of the shoulder, trying to find a footprint or scuff mark. I didn't.

Grey knots of brush sprouted over the slope like mould, thinning around stunted oaks and ragged pine trees. I moved downhill in a zigzag pattern, following erosion cuts and natural paths between great stiff balls of sagebrush. Twice I saw marks that might have been made by someone passing, but they were too faint to be sure.

The shoulder dropped away. I looked across the canyon. The windows in Grace Gonzalez's house glowed with light. My A-frame hung from the slope with its deck jutting out like a diving board. If I were surveilling my house, this would be a fine place for it.

Pike appeared silently through the sagebrush. 'It's too steep on that side for anyone to use.'

'Then help me with this side.'

We searched the ground beneath two pines, then worked our way further down the slope towards a single scrub oak. We moved parallel to each other, covering more ground that way. The sun kissed the ridge. Purple shadows pooled around us. Time was everything.

Pike knelt and touched the ground. 'Here.'

'What is it?'

'Got a partial print here, then another partial. Moving your way.'

The sun settled even faster, like a sinking heart. Ben had been missing for more than twenty-seven hours.

I said, 'Do they match with the print we found at my place?'

'I couldn't see that one clearly enough to know.'

Pike stepped over the prints. I told myself that they could have been made by anyone, but I knew it was the man who had stolen Ben. A dampness prickled my hands.

I stepped between two balls of sagebrush and saw a fresh footprint in the dust. It pointed uphill.

'Joe.'

'Got it.'

We moved closer to the tree. Thin grass had sprouted in the fractured light under the branches. The grass on the uphill side was flat, as if someone had sat on it.

'Joe.'

'I see it. I've got footprints in the dirt to the left. I can get closer.'

Behind us, the sun was swallowed by the ridge. The shadows around us deepened and lights came on in the houses.

'Not now. Let's tell Starkey. Chen can try to match the prints, and then we start knocking on doors. This is it, Joe. He was here. He waited for Ben here.'

We backed away, followed our own footprints up the hill, then drove to my house. Starkey must have left over an hour ago, but when we tooled around the curve she was parked outside my front door.

We swung into the carport, then hurried out to tell her.

I said, 'I think we found where he waited, Starkey. We found prints and crushed grass. We've gotta get Chen out to see if the prints match, and then we have to go door-to-door. The people who live over there might've seen a car or even a licence tag.'

It came out of me in a torrent as if I expected her to cheer, but she didn't. She seemed unhappy, her face dark like a gathering storm.

'I think we have something here, Starkey. What's the matter?'

She sucked at her cigarette. 'He called again.'

I knew there was more to it, but I was scared she would tell me that Ben was dead.

Maybe she guessed what I was thinking. 'He didn't call you. He called your girlfriend.'

'What did he say?'

Starkey's eyes were careful. 'You can hear it yourself. She hit the record button on her message machine and got most of the call. C'mon, we want you to see if it's the same man.'

I didn't move. 'Did he say something about Ben?'

'Not about Ben. C'mon, everybody's down at the station now.'

'Starkey, did he hurt Ben? Goddammit, tell me what he said.'

'He said you killed twenty-six civilians, then you murdered your buddies to get rid of the witnesses. That's what he said, Cole. You wanted to know. Follow me down. We want you to hear it.'

Starkey drove away, and I was swallowed by darkness.

CHAPTER SEVEN
time missing: 27 hours, 31 minutes

The Hollywood Division Police Station was a flat red-brick build-ing a block south of Hollywood Boulevard, midway between Paramount Studios and the Hollywood Bowl. The evening streets were choked with traffic going nowhere at a glacial pace. Tour buses cruised the Walk of Fame and lined the kerb outside the Chinese Theatre, filled with tourists who had paid thirty-five dollars to sit in traffic. It was full-on dark when I turned into the parking lot behind the station. Richard's limo was parked by a fence. Starkey was wait-ing by her car.

'Are you carrying a weapon?' she asked me.

'It's at home. You think I want to murder some witnesses?'

'Don't be so testy. Where's Pike?'

'I dropped him off at Lucy's. If this asshole has her phone number, he probably knows where she lives.'

We went inside through double glass doors, then along a tiled hall into a room marked DETECTIVES. Chest-high partitions cut the room into cubicles but most of the chairs were empty. Gittamon and Myers were speaking quietly across the room, Myers holding a slim leather briefcase. Gittamon excused himself and came over.

'Did Carol explain what happened?'

'She told me about the call. Where's Lucy?'

'We're set up in an interview room. I'm going to warn you that the tape is disturbing. He says some things.'

Starkey interrupted him. 'Before we get to that, Cole should tell you what he found. They might have something, Dave.'

I described the prints and the crushed grass that Pike and I had found, and what I thought they meant. Gittamon listened like he wasn't sure what to make of it, but Starkey explained.

'Cole's making sense about someone having to be across the canyon. I'll check it out with Chen tomorrow as soon as we have enough light. Maybe we'll get a match on the shoes.'

Gittamon and Myers led me to an interview room, where Lucy and Richard were waiting at a clean grey table. The room was painted beige because an LAPD psychologist had determined that beige was soothing, but nobody looked soothed.

Richard said, 'Finally. The sonofabitch called Lucy, Cole.' He put his hand on her back, but she shrugged it away.

I pulled a chair beside her and lowered my voice. 'How are you?'

She softened for a moment, but then a fierceness came to her face. 'I want to make sure that Ben is safe and then I want to do things to this man.'

'I know. Me, too.'

She glanced at me with her fierce eyes, then shook her head and stared at the tape recorder. Gittamon took a seat opposite her; Starkey and Myers stood in the doorway.

'Ms Chenier, you don't have to hear this again. There's really no need,' Gittamon said.

'I want to hear it. I'll be hearing it all night.'

'All right, then. Mr Cole, just so you know, Ms Chenier received the call at five forty this evening. She was able to record most of the conversation, but not the beginning.'

'Did you trace back to the same number?'

'The phone company is working on it now. This recording is a duplicate. We've sent the original to SID. They might be able to pull something off the background, but it isn't likely.'

Gittamon pressed the play button. The cheap speaker filled with a hiss, then a male voice began in mid-sentence:

> The Voice: *. . . know you had nothing to do with this, but he's gotta pay for what he did.*
> Lucy: *Please don't hurt him! Let him go!*
> The Voice: *Shut up and listen! You listen! Cole killed them! I know what happened and you don't, so LISTEN!*

Gittamon stopped the tape.

'Is this the man who called you last night?'

'Yes, that's him.'

Everyone in the room watched me. Lucy was leaning forward, poised at the edge of the table, the tendons taut on her hands.

Gittamon noted my answer in his pad. 'Now that you're hearing the voice a second time, do you recognise him?'

'No. I don't know who it is.'

Lucy said, 'Are you sure?'

'I don't know him, Luce.'

Gittamon touched the button again. 'All right, then. We'll go on.'

When he pressed the button, the two voices overlapped, each shouting to be heard over the other.

> Lucy: *Please, I'm begging you—*
> The Voice: *I was there, lady. I know! They slaughtered twenty-six people—*
> Lucy: *Ben is a child! He never hurt anyone! Please!*
> The Voice: *They were in the bush, off on their own, so they figured, no one will know if we don't tell them, so they swore each other to secrecy, but Cole didn't trust them—*
> Lucy: *Tell me what you want! Please, just let my son go—*
> The Voice: *Abbott, Rodriguez, the others—he murdered them to get rid of the witnesses! He fired on his own team!*
> Lucy: *He's a baby—!*
> The Voice: *Sorry it had to be your son, but Cole's gonna pay. This is his fault. He made my life hell.*

The message stopped.

The tape recorder hissed quietly for several seconds then Gittamon rewound the tape. He cleared his throat.

I said, 'That's so absurd. What do you want me to say to something like this? None of that happened. He's making it up.'

Richard tapped the table. 'How do we know?'

'We're not here to make accusations, Mr Chenier,' said Gittamon.

'This asshole on the tape is making the accusations, not me. What I care about is Ben, and that *this* sonofabitch'—he jabbed at the tape recorder—'hates Cole so much that he's taking it out on my son.'

Lucy said, 'Just calm down, Richard. You're making it worse.'

'How totally blind about Cole can you be, Lucille? You don't know anything about him.'

'I know that I believe him.'

'Of course, you would say that.' Richard glared at me then looked back at Lucy. 'Let's see how much you really know.' He waved at Myers. 'Lee, let me have that.'

Myers passed him the briefcase. Richard took out a manila folder and slapped it on the table. 'Cole joined the army because a judge gave him a choice: jail or Vietnam. Did you know that, Lucille? You've exposed yourself and our son to dangerous low-life trash since you've been with this man and you act like it's none of my business. Well, my son is my business.'

Lucy stared at the folder without touching it. Richard stared at me, but he was still talking to her. 'I had him looked into. Your boyfriend has been a magnet for trouble ever since he was a kid—assault, assault and battery, grand theft auto. Go on, read it.'

A hot wash of blood flooded my face. I felt like a child who had been caught in a lie because the other me was so far in the past that I had put him away. I tried to remember whether or not I had told Lucy, and knew by the tight expression in her eyes that I hadn't.

'Did he tell you, Lucille? Did you ask him before you left your son with him? Or were you so caught up in your own self-centred needs that you couldn't be bothered? Wake up, Lucille'

Richard stalked round the table without waiting for Lucy or anyone else to speak, and left. Myers stood in the door for a moment, staring at me with his expressionless lizard eyes. Then he followed Richard out.

Starkey finally broke the silence. 'I'm sorry, Ms Chenier. That must have been embarrassing.'

Lucy nodded. 'Yes. Very.'

I said, 'I got into some trouble when I was sixteen years old. What do you want me to say?'

No one looked at me.

Gittamon reached across the table to pat Lucy's arm. 'It's hard when a child is missing. Would you like someone to take you home?'

I said, 'I'll take her.'

'We'd like to ask you a few more questions, Mr Cole.'

Lucy stood. 'I have the car. I'll be fine.'

I touched her arm. 'He made it seem more than it was. I was a kid.'

Lucy nodded. She touched me back, but still didn't look at me. 'I'll be fine. Are we finished here, Sergeant?'

'You are, yes, ma'am. Are you going to be all right tonight? You might want to stay at a hotel or with a friend.'

'No, I want to be home if he calls again.' Lucy squeezed round the table, then stopped in the doorway. She looked at me. 'I'm sorry. That was shameful.'

'I'll come by later.'

She left without answering.

Gittamon cleared his throat. 'Why don't we get a little coffee?'

He left, and Starkey gave me one of those weak smiles people make when they feel bad for you. 'Rough, huh?' She pulled the folder across the table and read whatever was inside. 'Man, Cole, you were a real mess when you were a kid.'

I nodded. Neither of us spoke again until Gittamon returned.

I told them about Abbott, Rodriguez, Johnson and Fields, and how they died. I had not described those events since the day I told Pike. You have to let go of the dead or the dead will carry you down.

Gittamon said, 'All right, this man on the tape knows your team number, the names of at least two of these men, and that everyone died except you. Who would know these things?'

'Their families. The guys in my company at the time. The army.'

Starkey said, 'Cole gave me a list of names earlier. I had Hurwitz run checks on them, including the dead guys. We got zip.'

'One of them might have a younger brother. Or a son. He says on the tape, "He made my life hell." He's telling us that he suffered.'

I said, 'He told us that he was there, too, but only five people went out and the other four are dead. Call the army and ask them. The citation and after-action reports will tell you what happened.'

Starkey said, 'I already called. I'm gonna read that stuff tonight.'

Gittamon glanced at his watch. 'All right. We'll talk to the families tomorrow. Anything else?'

I said, 'Can I have a copy of the tape? I want to hear it again.'

Starkey said, 'Go home, Dave. I'll get his tape.'

Gittamon got up. He hesitated, then looked at me. 'If I had any idea he was going to do that, I wouldn't have allowed it.'

'I know. Thanks.'

Gittamon went home. Starkey left with the tape and did not come back. A few minutes later, a detective I had not met before brought a copy of the tape, then walked me outside.

I stood on the sidewalk wishing that I had taken the folder. I wanted to see what Richard knew, but I didn't want to go back inside. I had never felt so helpless and alone.

BEN WIPED THE SWEAT from his eyes. In the depthless black of the box, he tried to work with them closed, but all of his instincts drove them open. His clothes were soaked, his shoulders ached and his hands were cramped into claws, but Ben felt ecstatic.

'I'm gonna get out. *I'm getting OUT!*'

A cut opened across his plastic sky. Ben had worked furiously throughout the night and through the day. The Silver Star bit through the plastic again and again, and loose soil fell like rain.

'Yeah, that's it! *YEAH!*'

He had dulled three of the star's five points, but by the afternoon of the first day the cut stretched across the width of the box. Ben worked his fingers into the gap and pulled as hard as he could, but the plastic was strong and did not bend easily.

Ben heard a mumble and a thump, and he wondered if he was dreaming again. He stopped working, and listened.

'Answer me, kid. I can hear you down there.'

It was Eric! His voice sounded hollow coming down the pipe.

'Answer me, goddammit.'

The light from the pipe was gone; Eric must be so close that he blocked the sun. Ben held his breath. A few hours ago he had prayed for them to return, but if they discovered him trying to escape they would take away the medal and bury him again—then he would be trapped for ever!

The light returned, and then Eric's voice sounded farther away.

'The little prick won't answer. You think he's OK?'

Ben heard Mazi clearly. 'Eet weel not mahter.'

Eric tried once more. 'Kid? You want some water?'

Here in the darkness of the box, Ben hid from them. They wouldn't know if he was alive or dead unless they dug him up.

'Kid?'

Ben held perfectly still.

'You little shit!'

The light reappeared as Eric moved away. Ben counted to a hundred, then resumed work with a fury. He was in a race with them now; he had to get out before they came back to dig him up. The

African's words echoed in the darkness: *Eet weel not mahter*.

Ben felt along the split until he found its centre, then set to work carving a tiny notch. The star's point cut through the plastic, and the notch grew. He gripped the split again and pulled. A shower of soil fell all at once. Ben brushed dirt from his eyes. The split had opened into a narrow triangular hole.

'*Yes!*'

He put the Silver Star in his pocket, pulled his T-shirt over his face like a mask, then scooped away more soil. He worked his hand through the split up to his elbow then gripped the plastic on either side of the T-shaped hole and hung with all his weight as if he was doing a chin-up. He had the door; all he had to do was open it.

Ben scrunched into a ball, pulling his knees to his chest. He propped a knee onto the left side of the T and gripped the right with both hands. He strained so hard that his body arched from the floor.

The plastic tore.

Ben's grip slipped and he fell. '*Yes! Yes Yes Yes!*'

Ben wiped his hands as best he could, then took another grip. He pulled so hard that his head buzzed, and the roof abruptly split as if the plastic had simply surrendered. A landslide of dirt poured through, but Ben didn't care—the box was open.

He wiggled onto his side, and worked his arm and then his head up into the hole. The freshly turned soil moved easily. He twisted his shoulders through the hole and clawed dirt down past his sides. He reached higher, clawing for the surface, but the earth pressed in on him from all sides, pushing him under. He was being crushed!

He was filled with panic, and the absolute certainty that he was going to die—then he broke through the surface and cool night air washed his face. A canvas of stars filled the sky. He was free.

Ben got his bearings. It was night, and he was in the back yard of a house in the hills. He was in a flowerbed at the edge of a patio. Neighbouring houses sat behind walls that were hidden by ivy.

Ben ran to the side of the house, then slipped into the shadows of a walkway that ran along the side of the building to the front. He crept along, moving so quietly that he could not hear his own footsteps. When he reached a chain-link gate, he wanted to throw it open and run, but he was scared that the men would hear him. He eased the gate open. The hinges made a low squeal, but then swung free.

Ben crept through. He was close to the front of the house and could see a brightly lit home across the street. All he had to do was run to the neighbour's door. His face split into a grin—he had escaped! He stepped into the drive just as steel hands clamped over his mouth and jerked him backwards.

Ben tried to scream, but couldn't. He kicked and fought, but more steel wrapped his arms and legs. They had come from nowhere.

'Stop kicking,' Eric whispered in Ben's ear.

Tears blurred Ben's eyes. *Don't put me back in the box*, he tried to say; *don't bury me!* But his words could not get past Eric's hand.

Mike stepped forward and gripped Eric's arm. 'A ten-year-old kid, and he beat you. I should beat you myself.'

'At least we got him. It saves us the trouble of diggin' him up.'

Mike searched Ben's pockets and came out with the Silver Star. He held it up by the ribbon. 'Did Cole give you this?'

The best Ben could do was nod.

Mike dangled the medal in front of Eric. 'He cut his way out with this. See how the points are dull? You should've searched him.'

'It's a fuckin' medal, not a knife.'

Mike grabbed Eric's throat with such speed that Ben didn't see his hand move. 'Mess up again, I'll put you down.'

Eric tried to answer again, but couldn't.

Mike let go. He considered the Silver Star again, then pushed it into Ben's pocket. 'You earned it.'

Ben's eyes filled. He had come so close.

CHAPTER EIGHT
time missing: 28 hours, 02 minutes

Pike sat unmoving within the stiff branches and leathery leaves of a rubber tree across from Lucy Chenier's apartment. Small gaps between the leaves afforded him a clean view of the stairs leading up to her apartment. Pike carried a Colt Python .357 Magnum in a clip holster on his right hip, a six-inch SOG double-edged fighting knife, a .25-calibre Beretta palm gun strapped to his right ankle, and a leather sap. He rarely needed them. Lucy was safe.

Pike's bad shoulder ached. He had been shot twice almost eight months ago. The bullets had shattered his shoulder blade, spraying bone fragments like shrapnel through his left lung and the surrounding muscles. He had almost died. Even now his shoulder was slow, his movements awkward. He was less than he had been.

When Cole had dropped Pike off earlier that evening, Pike had approached Lucy's apartment on foot from three blocks away. The man who took Ben could have been watching the apartment, so Pike checked nearby buildings, roofs and cars at the kerb, then slipped into the trees. He became a shadow within other shadows.

Lucy's white Lexus had appeared an hour later. She parked, then hurried upstairs. From the stiff way she carried herself, Pike sensed that she was upset.

Richard's black limo rolled up ten minutes after Lucy got home. Richard got out and climbed the stairs. When Lucy opened the door she was framed by gold light. The two of them spoke for a moment, then Richard went in. The door closed.

The Mercury Marquis arrived from the opposite direction, Fontenot driving with DeNice along for the ride. Myers jumped out of the limo to speak with them. He was angry and slapped the roof of the Marquis. *'Get your shit together and find that kid!'* Then he climbed the stairs. DeNice got out of the Marquis and into the limo. Fontenot accelerated away, but swung into a driveway one block up and parked. Richard and Myers hurried down, got into the limo, and sped away. Pike waited for Fontenot to follow them, but he didn't. Now two of them watched Lucy.

Pike was good at waiting. He could wait for days without moving and without being bored, because he could allow his mind to be empty. If your moments were empty, time had no meaning.

Cole's yellow Corvette pulled up to the kerb. As always, it needed a wash. Pike kept his own red Jeep Cherokee spotless, as well as his condo, his weapons, his clothes and his person. He found peace in order and did not understand how anyone could tolerate less. Cleanliness was order, and order was control. Pike had spent most his life trying to maintain control.

THE JACARANDA TREES that lined Lucy's street were lit by lamps that were yellow with age. The air was colder than in Hollywood itself, and rich with the scent of jasmine. I knew Pike was watching, but I could not see him and did not try. Fontenot was easy to make out, hunched in a car up the block like Sam Spade. I guess Richard wanted someone watching out for Lucy, too.

I climbed the stairs and knocked softly at her door. I could have used my key, but that seemed more confident than I felt. 'It's me.'

The deadbolt turned with a quiet slap. Lucy opened the door wearing a white terry robe, her hair combed back. She looked good, even with her face closed and unsmiling.

She said, 'They kept you a long time.'

'We had a lot to talk about.'

Lucy stepped back to let me in, then closed and locked the door. She was holding her cordless phone. She led the way to the dining room without looking at me.

I said, 'I want to talk to you about this.'

'I know.' She put the phone on the table, but kept her hand on it. 'I've been sitting here with this phone. Ever since I got home I've been scared to put it down. They set up one of those trap things on it in case he rings again. They said I could make calls like normal, not to worry about it. Ha. Like normal.'

I guess staring at the phone was easier than looking at me. I covered her hand with mine. 'Luce, what he said, those things aren't true.'

'I know. You couldn't do anything like that.'

'We didn't murder people. We weren't criminals.'

'I know. I know that. You don't have to say this.'

'What Richard said—'

'*Shh!*' Her eyes flashed hard and the shh was a command. 'I don't want you to explain. I've never asked before, and you've never told me, so don't tell me now.'

'Lucy—'

'I've heard you and Joe talk. I've seen what you keep in that cigar box. Those are your things to know, not mine, like old lovers and the stupid things we do when we're kids. I thought, he'll tell me if he needs to, but now it all seems so much more important than that—'

'I wasn't hiding anything. I wasn't keeping secrets. Some things are better left behind, that's all.'

She slipped her hand from under mine, and sat back. 'What Richard did, having you investigated, was unforgivable. I apologise.'

'I got into some trouble when I was a kid. It wasn't horrendous.'

She shook her head to silence me and lifted the phone on both hands as if it were an object of study. 'I've been holding this phone so tight, wondering whether I'll ever see my baby again. I thought if only I could force myself into the mouthpiece through these little holes and come out on the other end of the line—' She stiffened with a terrible tension that made her seem brittle.

I leaned towards her, wanting to touch her, but she drew back.

'I saw myself doing it the way you see yourself in a dream, and when I squeezed out of the phone at the other end, Ben was in a warm bed, safe and sleeping, so peaceful I didn't want to wake him. I watched his beautiful face and tried to imagine what you looked like when you were his age . . .' She looked up with a sadness that seemed painful. 'But I couldn't. I've never seen a childhood picture of you. You never mention your family, or where you're from. I tease you about Joe, how he never talks, but you don't say any more than him, not about the things that matter, and I find that so strange.'

'My family wasn't exactly normal. My grandpa raised me, mostly, my grandfather and my aunt, and sometimes I didn't have anyone—'

'Your secrets are your own.'

'They're not *secrets*. When I was with my mother, we moved a lot. I needed rules, and there weren't any rules. I wanted friends, so I made some bad choices and got in with bad kids—'

'Shh. Shh.'

'I needed someone to be there, and they were what I had. They came around with a stolen car, and I went along for a ride.'

She touched my lips, my chest over my heart.

'I'll find Ben, Luce. I swear to God I'll bring him home.'

She shook her head so gently that I almost did not see. 'No.'

'Yes, I will. I'll find him. I'm going to bring him home.'

Her sadness grew to an ache so clear that it broke my heart. 'I don't blame you for this happening. All that matters is that Ben is gone, and I should have known it would happen.'

'What are you talking about? How could you know?'

'Richard is right, Elvis. I shouldn't be with you. I shouldn't have let my child stay with you.'

My belly cramped with a sour heat. I wanted her to stop. 'Luce—'

'I really and truly don't blame you, but things like this—and what happened last summer—I can't have those things in my life. My son had a normal childhood before I knew you. I had a normal life. I let my love for you blind me, and now my son is gone.'

Tears gathered on her lashes, then fell down her cheeks. She didn't blame me; she blamed herself.

'Luce, don't talk like that.'

'That man on the tape hates you and he has my son. He hates you so much that you can only make it worse. Leave it to the police.'

'I can't walk away; I have to find him.'

She gripped my arm and her nails cut into my skin. 'You'll get him killed! You're not the only one who can do this, Elvis; you're not the last detective in Los Angeles! Let the others find him. Promise me.'

I wanted to pull her close and hold her and feel her hold me, but my own eyes filled and I shook my head. 'I'm going to bring him home, Luce. I can't do anything else.'

She let go of my arm, then wiped her eyes. Her face was as dark and hard as a death mask. 'Get out.'

'You and Ben are my family.'

'No. We're not your family.'

I felt impossibly heavy, like I was made of lead. 'You're my family.'

'*Get out!*'

'I'll find him.'

'*You'll get him killed!*'

I left her like that and went down to my car. I couldn't feel the chill any more. The sweet scent of the jasmine was gone.

HIS NAME HAD BEEN James Cole until he was six years old. Then his mother announced, 'I'm going to change your name to Elvis.'

Jimmie didn't know if his mother was playing a game. Maybe it was the uncertainty that made him so scared. 'I'm Jimmie.'

'No, now you're Elvis. That's your new name. Isn't it exciting? We'll tell everyone tomorrow.'

Jimmie started crying. 'I'm Jimmie.*'*

She smiled at him with all the love in the world, cupped his face in her hands and kissed his forehead with warm, sweet lips.

She had been gone for twelve days. She did that sometimes, just up and left without saying a word because that was the way she was. A free spirit, she called it; a crazy head case, he had heard his grandfather say. Every time she left he was angry with himself for having driven her away. Every day while she was gone he promised God he would be a better boy if only she'd come back.

The next day she took Jimmie to school, marched him to the head of his first-grade class, and made the announcement. 'We want everyone to know that Jimmie has a new name. I want you to meet Elvis Cole.'

All of the kids laughed. Jimmie bit his tongue so he would not cry.

That evening, Jimmie and his mom were eating hamburgers in their kitchen. Jimmie had spent most of the past twelve days thinking about something his Aunt Lynn had told him—that his mom was searching for his daddy when she went away. He wanted it to be true. He wanted her to find him and make him come home so that they could be a family. Then she wouldn't go away any more. He worked up his courage to ask. 'Were you trying to find my daddy? Is that where you went?'

His mother stopped with the hamburger halfway to her mouth. She stared at him for the longest time, then put down her hamburger. 'Of course not, Elvis. Why ever would I do something like that?'

'Who's my daddy?'

She leaned back, her face playful. 'I can't ever tell anyone your daddy's name and I won't.'

'Was his name Elvis?'

His mother laughed. 'No, you silly.'

'Was it Jimmie?'

'No, and if you ask me every other name that ever was I'll tell you no, no, no. But I will tell you one special thing.'

Jimmie grew scared. She had never told him anything about his father, and he suddenly wasn't sure he wanted to know. 'What?'

She leaned close, her face as bright as an electric bulb. 'Your father is a human cannonball.'

Jimmie stared at her. 'What's a human cannonball?'

'A man so brave that he fires himself from a cannon so he can fly through the air. Think about that, Elvis—flying through the air, up above everyone else.' His mother's eyes grew sad. 'People want you to be ordinary. They don't like it when people are different. They don't like it when a man soars over their heads while they stand in the dirt. Just remember that he loves you, Elvis, and that I love you, too. Remember that always, no matter how bad times get. Will you remember that?'

'Yes, Mama.'

Her crying woke him later that night. He crept to her door where he watched his mother thrash beneath her sheets, speaking in voices he did not understand.

Elvis Cole said, 'I love you too, Mama.'

Four days later she vanished again.

His Aunt Lynn took Elvis to his grandfather. That night, the old man made them potted meat sandwiches with lots of mayonnaise.

The old man had been distant all afternoon, so Elvis was scared to say anything, but he wanted to tell someone about his father so badly that he thought he would choke.

'I asked her about my daddy,' he said eventually.

The old man chewed his sandwich.

'He's a human cannonball.'

'Is that what she told you?'

'He gets shot out of a gun so that he can fly through the air. He loves me very much. He loves Mommy, too. He loves us both.'

The old man stared at Elvis as he finished eating. He looked sad. When the sandwich was gone, the old man murmured, 'She made that up. She's out of her mind.'

The next day, his grandfather called the Child Welfare Division of the Department of Social Services. They came for Elvis that afternoon.

PIKE WATCHED Elvis Cole get into his car and sit there without moving. He pushed a leaf out of the way, to see better. When Cole's cheek caught the light, Pike saw that his friend was crying.

After Cole drove away, Pike left the rubber tree and slipped through the shadows to Lucy's door. He passed within fifteen feet of Fontenot's car, but Fontenot did not see him.

Pike stood well back from the peephole. Lucy had been uneasy with him since the Sobek business, so he wanted her to see him before she opened the door. He knocked.

The door opened.

Pike said, 'I'm sorry about Ben.'

She glanced past him at the street. 'Where's Elvis?'

'Gone. May I come in?'

She let him enter. After she closed the door, she waited with her hand on the knob. Pike saw that she was uncomfortable. He wouldn't be staying.

'I'm across the street. I thought you should know that.'

She shook her head. 'I don't want either of you involved. Richard has someone outside.'

'I know about him. He doesn't know about me.'

She closed her eyes and leaned against the door as if she wanted to sleep until this was over. Pike thought he understood. It must be terrible for her with Ben missing.

He wasn't clear why he had come or what he wanted to say. He was unclear about too many things these days. Finally he said, 'I saw Elvis leave. He's hurting.'

'Jesus, I'm hurting, too, and it's not your business. I know he's hurt. I know that. I'm sorry.'

Pike tried to find the words. 'I want to tell you something.'

'What?'

He didn't know how to say it. 'I want to tell you.'

She grew irritated. 'Jesus, Joe, you never say anything but here you are. If you want to say something, say it.'

'He loves you.'

'Oh, that's too perfect. God knows what's happening to Ben but, to you, it's all about him.'

Pike considered her. 'You don't like me.'

'I don't like the way violence follows you, you and him. I've known police officers all my life. I know prosecutors who've spent *years* building cases against murderers and mob bosses, and none of them has had their children stolen. None of them draws violence like you!'

Pike shrugged. 'I haven't heard the tape. All I know is what Starkey told us. Do you believe it?'

'Of course not. I told him so.'

She blinked, then crossed her arms, holding tight. 'Goddammit, I hate to cry.'

Pike said, 'Me, too.'

She rubbed hard at her face. 'I can't tell if that's a joke. I never can tell if you're joking.'

'If you don't believe those things, then trust him.'

She shouted now. 'It's about *Ben*. It's not about me or him or you. I have to protect myself and my son. I cannot have this insanity in my life. I am *normal*! I want to be *normal*! Are you so perverted that you think this is normal? It isn't. It is insane!'

Pike didn't know what else to say. He reached past her and turned off the lights. 'Turn them on after I'm gone.'

He let himself out. He slipped down the stairs, thinking about what she had said, until he was alongside the Marquis. The windows were down. Fontenot was still behind the wheel. There was Pike, ten feet away, and Fontenot didn't know. Pike hated him for it, hated him for having seen his friend come out of Lucy's apartment in such pain. He moved closer to the Marquis and slapped the roof, the sound as loud as a gunshot. Fontenot made a startled grunt and scrambled under his jacket for his gun.

Pike aimed his .357 at Fontenot's head and the cop went completely still. He relaxed a bit when he recognised Pike.

'Jesus Christ, what are you doing?'

'Watching you.'

Fontenot glanced up and down the sidewalk like he expected to see someone else. 'You scared the shit out of me. Where'd you come from? What in hell are you doing?'

Pike fought back a wave of emotion. 'I want to tell you.'

'What?'

The moment passed. Pike had control. He lowered the gun.

Fontenot said, 'What is it you wanna say, goddammit?'

Pike didn't answer. He melted into the darkness. A few minutes later he was back in the rubber tree, and Fontenot still didn't know.

Pike thought about what Lucy had said about his partner. Cole had never told him much, either, but you didn't need to ask if you looked closely. The worlds that people build for themselves are an open book—people build what they never had, but always wanted.

Pike waited. Pike watched. The empty moments rolled past.

time missing: 31 hours, 22 minutes

I brought the tape home, and played it. I already knew that I didn't recognise the voice, so I listened to get a sense of the man.

'They slaughtered twenty-six people . . .'

He had no accent, which meant he probably wasn't from the South or New England. Rodriguez had been from Brownsville, Texas, and Cromwell Johnson from Alabama; they both had thick accents, so their friends and families probably had accents, too. Roy Abbott had been from upstate New York and Ted Fields from Michigan. Neither had accents that I could remember, though Abbott spoke with the careful pronunciation of a Yankee farmer.

'They were in the bush, off on their own . . .'

The man on the tape sounded younger than me; not a kid, but too young to have been in Vietnam. Crom Johnson and Luis Rodriguez both had younger brothers, but I had spoken with them when I got back from the war and I didn't believe that they would be involved. Abbott had sisters, and Fields was an only.

'. . . they swore each other to secrecy, but Cole didn't trust them . . . Abbott, Rodriguez, the others—he murdered them to get rid of the witnesses! He fired on his own team!'

His language was melodramatic, as if he had chosen his words to amplify the drama.

I played the tape again.

'I know what happened and you don't, so LISTEN!'

He sounded angry, but also as if he was saying the words without truly feeling them. The false quality in his tone convinced me that he did not know me or the others. He was faking.

I was there, lady!'

But he wasn't. Only five of us were in the jungle that day, and the other four died.

I had spent all evening unsuccessfully trying to figure out who he was, but maybe the answer was to figure out how he knew what he knew. If he hadn't served with me, then how did he know about Rodriguez and Abbott? How did he know our team number, and that I was the only one who survived?

The house creaked like a beast shifting in its sleep. The stairs to my loft grew threatening; the hall to Ben's room ended in darkness. The

357

man on the tape had watched me and my house, so he had known when we were home and when we weren't. I went upstairs for the cigar box, and sat with it on the floor, looking through the contents.

When a soldier mustered out of the army, he was given what was known as a Form 214. The 214 showed the soldier's dates of service, a summary of his career. Details were few. But whenever a soldier was awarded a medal or commendation, he or she was also given a copy of the orders accompanying the medal, which described why the army saw fit to make its presentation. Rod, Teddy and the others had died, and I had been given a five-pointed star with a red, white and blue ribbon. I had never worn it, but I kept the orders. I reread them. The description of the events that day was slight, and included the name of only one other man involved: Roy Abbott. The man who took Ben could have got some of his information from my house, but not all of it.

I hadn't slept in almost fifty hours. I brushed my teeth, took a shower, then put on fresh clothes. At exactly 6.00am, I called the army's department of personnel in St Louis. It was 8.00am in St Louis; the army was open for business.

I asked to speak with someone in the records department. An older man picked up the call. 'Records. This is Stivic.'

I identified myself as a veteran, then gave him my date of separation and social security number. 'I want to find out if anyone has requested my 201 file. Would you guys have a record of that?'

Where the 214 was the skeleton of a military record, a soldier's 201 file contained the detailed history of his career. Maybe my 201 showed the other names. Maybe the man on the tape had been able to get a copy.

'We'd have a record if it was sent.'

'How can I find out?'

'You'd know. Anyone can get your 214, but we don't give out the 201 without permission unless it's by court order.'

I said, 'What if someone pretended to be me?'

'Like you could be someone else pretending to be you right now?'

'Yeah. Like that.'

Now Stivic sounded pissed off. 'Is this a joke?'

'No. My house was robbed. Someone stole my 214, and I think he might've got hold of my 201.'

'The 201 doesn't work that way. If you wanted a copy of your 201, you'd have to file the request in writing, along with your thumb print. If someone else wanted your 201, say for a job application, you'd still have to give your permission. The only way someone gets that 201 without you knowing about it is by court order.'

'I still want to know if someone requested it, and I don't have eight weeks to wait for the answer.'

'We have thirty-two people in our department. We ship two thousand pieces of mail every day. You want me to holler if anyone remembers your name?'

I said, 'Were you a Marine?'

'Master Sergeant, retired. If you want to know who requested what, gimme your fax number and I'll see what I can do.'

I gave him my fax number just to keep him going.

'One more question, Master Sergeant. My 201, can you pull it up there on your computer?'

'I'm not telling you anything that's on anyone's 201.'

'I just want to know if it contains an account of a certain action and whether or not the account contains two names. If it does, I'll request the file, and you can have all the thumb prints you want.'

He hesitated. 'Is this a combat action?'

'Yes, sir.'

He hesitated again, thinking about it. 'What's that name?'

I heard him punching keys as I told him, then the soft whistle of his breath.

'Are the names Cromwell Johnson and Luis Rodriguez in the report?'

His voice came back hoarse. 'Yes, they are. Ah, you still want to know if anyone requested this file?'

'I do, Master Sergeant.'

'Gimme your phone number and I'll check this through myself. It might take a few days, but I'll do that much for you.'

'Thanks, Master Sergeant. I really appreciate this.'

I gave him my number, then started to hang up. He stopped me.

'Mr Cole, ah, listen . . . you would've made a good Marine. I woulda been proud to serve with ya.'

'They made it sound better than it was.'

His voice grew soft. 'No. They don't do that. I spent thirty-two years in the Marine Corps, and now I'm on this phone 'cause I lost my foot in the Gulf. I know how they make it sound. I'll walk this through for you, Mr Cole; that's the goddamned least I can do.'

He hung up before I could thank him again.

If the man on the tape didn't scam a copy of my 201, then the only other name he had to work with was Roy Abbott. I had written to the Abbotts about Roy's death, and spoken with them once. I didn't remember Mr Abbott's first name, but the New York Information operator showed only seven Abbotts in Middletown, and she was happy to run through the list. I remembered his name when I heard it. She read off the number, then I hung up. I thought about what I would say if I called them and how I would say it. *Hi, this is Elvis Cole. Does anyone in your family want to kill me?* Nothing seemed right and everything seemed awkward. *Remember the day Roy came home in a box?* I made myself a cup of coffee, then forced myself back to the phone. I called.

An older woman answered.

'Mrs Abbott?'

'Yes. Who is this?'

'My name is Elvis Cole. I served with Roy. I spoke with you a long time ago. Do you remember?'

She spoke to someone in the background, and Mr Abbott came on the line. 'This is Dale Abbott. Who is this, please?'

He sounded the way Roy had described him: plain-spoken and honest, with the nasal twang of an upstate farmer.

My hands shook. 'Elvis Cole. I was with Roy in Vietnam. I wrote to you about what happened a long time ago, and then we spoke.'

'Oh, sure, I remember. How are you, son? We still have that letter of yours. That meant a lot to us.'

I said, 'Mr Abbott, has anyone called recently, asking about Roy?'

'No. No, let me ask Mama. Has anyone called about Roy?'

He didn't cover the phone. He spoke to her as clearly as to me, as if the two conversations were one.

He said, 'No, she says no one called. Should they have?'

I hadn't wanted to tell them why I was calling or about Ben, but I found myself telling him all of it. Words poured out of me as if I were giving confession.

Dale Abbott was quiet and encouraging. We spoke for the better part of an hour about Ben, Roy and many things: Roy's four younger sisters were married with families. Three had sons named after Roy, and one a son named after me. I had never known that.

At one point, Mr Abbott put Roy's mom back on the line, and, while she spoke with me, he found the letter I had written. He came back on the line.

'I want to read something you wrote. I don't know if you'll remember. This is you, writing: "I don't have a family, so I liked hearing about Roy's. I told him he was lucky to come from people like you and he agreed. I want you to know he fought to the end. He was a Ranger all the way, and he did not quit. I am so sorry I could not bring him home to you. I am so sorry I failed." ' Mr Abbott's voice grew thick and he stopped reading. 'You didn't fail, son. You brought Roy home.'

My eyes burned. 'I tried, Mr Abbott. I tried so hard.'

'You brought my boy back to us, and you did not fail. Now you go find this other little boy, and you bring him home, too. No one here blames you, son, and never did.'

I tried to say something, but couldn't.

Mr Abbott cleared his throat, and then his voice was strong. 'I have one more thing to say. What you wrote, that part about you not having a family, that's the only part that isn't true. You've been part of our family since the day Mama opened that letter.'

I told Mr Abbott that I had to go, then brought the coffee out onto my deck.

The cat was crouched there, his legs tucked tight underneath him as he stared at something beyond the deck.

I sat by him and touched his back. 'What do you see, buddy?'

His great black eyes were intent. His fur was cool in the early-morning chill, but his heart beat strong in the warmth beneath.

The first week after I moved into this house, and began the process of making someone else's home into mine, I decided to rebuild the rail around the deck so I could sit with my feet dangling in space. I was outside one day, working away, when the cat hopped onto the corner of my deck. He didn't look happy to see me. The side of his face was swollen with a dripping red wound. I remember saying, 'Hey, what happened to you?' He growled and his hair stood on end, but he didn't seem scared; he was probably cranky because he didn't like finding a stranger in his house. I brought out a cup of water, then went back to work. He ignored the cup at first, but after a while he drank. Drinking looked hard for him, so eating was probably worse. He was very thin, and probably hadn't eaten in days. I took apart the tuna sandwich I was saving for lunch, and made a paste with the tuna and mayonnaise and a little water. He arched his back when I put the tuna paste near the cup.

The two of us watched each other. After a while, he edged towards the fish, then lapped at it without taking his eyes from me. The wound in the side of his head was yellow with infection, and appeared to be a bullet wound. I held out my hand. He growled. I did not move. He sniffed, then crept closer. My scent had been mixed with the tuna that was still on my fingers. He tasted my finger with a tiny cat kiss, then turned to show me his side. That's a big step for cats. I touched the soft fur. He allowed it. Since that day we have been friends, and he has been the most constant living creature in my life. Apart from Joe Pike.

I stroked his back. 'I am so sorry I lost Ben. I won't lose him again.'

The cat head-bumped my arm, then peered at me with his black mirror eyes. He purred.

Forgiveness is everything.

THE FIVE MEMBERS of team 5-2 sat on the steel floor of the helicopter, the big rotor overhead spooling up clouds of red dust as the pilots readied for launch. Cole grinned at their new teammate, Abbott, a short, sturdy kid from Middletown, New York.

Their sergeant, Luis Rodriguez, a twenty-year-old from Texas, winked at Cole. 'You think he's nervous?'

Abbott's face tightened. 'I'm not nervous.'

Cole thought that Abbott looked like he was about to puke. This was his first Long Range Patrol mission. He patted Abbott's leg and grinned at Rodriguez. 'No way, Sergeant. This is Clark Kent with a Ranger scroll. He drinks danger for breakfast and wants more for lunch; he catches bullets in his teeth and juggles hand grenades for fun—'

Ted Fields, eighteen years old and from East Lansing, Michigan, encouraged Cole's rap. 'Hoo!'

Rodriguez and Cromwell Johnson, the nineteen-year-old radio operator from Mobile, Alabama, echoed the cry. It was a Ranger thing.

They were all grinning at Abbott now, the whites of their eyes brilliant against the mottled paint that covered their faces. There they were, five young men wearing camouflage fatigues, packing M16s, as much ammo, hand grenades and claymore mines as they could carry, and the bare minimum of gear necessary to survive a one-week reconnaissance patrol in the heart of Indian Country.

They were all trying to take the edge off the new guy's fear, and, as the helicopter lifted off, Cole leaned close to Abbott's ear, so that his voice wouldn't blow away.

'You're going to be fine. Stay calm and stay silent.'

Abbott nodded, serious.

Roy Abbott had come into the Ranger company three weeks earlier and had been assigned a bunk in Cole's hootch. Cole liked Abbott as soon as he saw the pictures the new guy pinned up: pictures of his mom and dad and four younger sisters, the old man ruddy-faced, Abbott's mother heavy and plain, and the four little girls all neat and normal with tucked skirts and pimples.

Cole watched the pictures go up and asked about them.

Abbott eyed Cole suspiciously, as if one sharpy too many had made fun of him. 'You really wanna know?'

He described how everyone worked the farm and lived in the same little community where their families had lived for almost two hundred years. Abbott's father had served in Europe during World War II. Now Abbott was following in his footsteps.

When Abbott was done with his own history, he asked Cole, 'How about your family?'

'My mother's crazy.'

Abbott finally asked another question because he didn't know what else to say. 'Was your dad in the army, too?'

'Never met him. I don't know who he is.'

'Oh.'

Abbott grew quiet. He finished putting away his gear, then went off.

Cole swung out of his bunk to look closely at the pictures. Mrs Abbott probably baked biscuits. Mr Abbott probably took his son hunting. Their family probably said grace and ate dinner together at a great long table. Cole spent the rest of the afternoon wishing Roy Abbott's family was his.

The helicopter banked hard over a ridge, dived for a shabby over-grown clearing as if it were landing, then bounced into the sky.

Abbott clutched his M16, eyes wide in surprise as the Huey climbed above the ridge line. 'Why didn't we land? Was it gooks?'

'We'll make two or three false inserts first. That way Charlie doesn't know where we get off.'

The Huey made two more false insertions. The next would be for real.

'Lock and load.'

All five Rangers charged their rifles and set the safeties. Cole figured that Abbott would be scared, so he leaned close. 'Keep your eye on Rodriguez. He's gonna run for the tree line as soon as we get down there. You watch the trees, but don't shoot unless one of us shoots first.'

The helicopter cut power and flared two feet off a dry creek in the bottom of a ravine. Cole pulled Abbott's arm to make sure he jumped, and the five of them thudded into the grass. The Huey powered away even as they hit the ground. They ran for the trees, Rodriguez first, Cole at the rear. As soon as the jungle swallowed them, team 5-2 flopped to the ground in a five-pointed star, their feet at its centre, the

Rangers facing out. That way they could see and fight in a 360-degree perimeter. They waited, watching for movement.

Five minutes.

Ten minutes.

The jungle came to life. Birds chittered. Monkeys barked. Rain dripped through the triple canopy overhead, soaking their uniforms.

Cole heard the low rumble of an air strike far to the west, then realised it was thunder. A storm was coming.

Rodriguez eased to his feet. Cole tapped Abbott's leg. Time to get up. They stood. No one spoke. Discipline was everything.

They set off up the hill. Cole knew the mission inside out. They would crest the ridge, then follow a well-worn NVA trail, looking for a bunker complex where army spooks believed a battalion of North Vietnamese Army regulars was massing. A battalion was a thousand people. The five members of team 5-2 were sneaking into an area where the odds would be two hundred to one against them.

Rodriguez walked point. Ted Fields walked slack behind him, meaning that, as Rod looked down to pick a path, Fields would pick up his slack by watching the jungle ahead. Johnson carried the radio. Abbott followed Johnson, and Cole followed Abbott, covering their rear.

They moved quietly uphill. Cole watched Abbott, cringing every time the new guy caught a vine on his gear, but overall he thought the kid was a pretty good woodsman.

Thunder rolled over the ridge, closer than before, and the air grew misty They climbed into a cloud.

It took thirty minutes of hard work to crest the hill, then Rodriguez gave them a rest. Darkness had fallen. Rod glanced at the sky, his expression saying that the crappy weather was screwing them. If they needed air cover, they wouldn't get it.

They slipped a few yards down the opposite side of the ridge, then Rod suddenly raised a closed fist. All five of them automatically dropped to a knee, rifles out left and right, to cover both flanks. Rod signalled Cole, the last man. He made a V sign, then cupped his fingers into a C. He pointed at the overlapping footprints on the ground, then opened and closed his fist three times—five, ten, fifteen. Rod was estimating fifteen Vietcong soldiers.

Abbott glanced back at Cole. His face was streaked with rain, and his eyes were wide. Cole was scared too, but he forced a smile.

Team 5-2 had been in the jungle for fifty-six minutes. They had less than twelve minutes left to live.

They continued along the ridge for less than a hundred yards when *they found the main trail. It was laced by VC and NVA prints. Rod made a circle with his upraised hand, telling the others that the enemy was all around them. Cole's mouth was dry even with the rain.*

Exactly three seconds later, all hell would break loose.

Rod stepped alongside a tall banyan tree just as a gnarled finger of lightning arced down the tree, jumped, and detonated the claymore mine strapped to the top of his pack. The upper half of Ted Fields vaporised in a red mist. The concussion hit Cole like a tidal wave and knocked him down. His ears rang and a great writhing snake of light twisted wherever he looked. The lightning's flash had blinded him.

Johnson screamed into his radio. 'Contact! We have contact!'

Cole scrambled forward and covered Johnson's mouth. 'Be quiet! There's Charlie all around us. That lightning set off Rod's claymore.'

What could be the odds? A million to one? Here they were on the side of a mountain surrounded by Vietcong and a lightning bolt had fired them up.

Johnson said, 'I'm fuckin' blind. I can't see.'

'That's the afterburn, man, like a flashbulb. I got that, too. Just take it easy. Fields and Rod are down.'

Cole's vision slowly cleared, and he saw that Johnson's head was bleeding. He twisted round to see Abbott. 'Abbott?'

'I'm good.'

Cole pushed the radio phone into Johnson's hands. 'Get the base. Tell 'em to get us the hell out of here.'

Cole crawled past Johnson. Rodriguez was alive, but one side of his head was gone.

'Sergeant? Rod?'

Rodriguez did not respond.

Cole knew that the VC would arrive soon to investigate the explosion. They had to leave immediately. He went back to Johnson. 'Tell 'em we have one KIA and one head wound. We're going to have to drag back over the ridge to where we came in.'

Johnson repeated Cole's report in a low murmur.

Cole motioned Abbott forward. 'Watch the trail.'

Abbott didn't move. He stared at what was left of Ted Fields, opening and closing his mouth like a fish. Cole jerked him away.

'Goddammit, Abbott, watch for Charlie! We don't have time for this.'

Cole wrapped a pressure bandage round Rodriguez's head, working as fast as he could. Rod thrashed and tried to push him away. Cole lay on him to pin him down, then wrapped his head with a second bandage. The rain pounded down. Thunder made the forest shudder.

Johnson crawled up beside him. 'Thunderstorm has 'em grounded, man. The helicopters can't get in. We're on our own.'

Cole finished tying off the bandage, then pulled out two Syrettes of morphine and popped both into Rodriguez's thigh. 'You think the three of us can carry Rod and Fields?'

'Are you crazy? Fields ain't nothing but hamburger.'

'Rangers don't leave Rangers behind.'

'Didn't you hear what I just said? They can't get the helicopter in here. The thunderhead's gotta move out before anybody's goin' anywhere.'

Maybe Johnson was right about Fields—they could come back for him later. But right now they had to evacuate the area and it would take two of them to carry Rodriguez.

'OK, we'll leave Ted here. Abbott, you're gonna help me carry Rodriguez. Crom, get the rear and tell 'em what we're doing.'

'I'm on it.'

Johnson transmitted their intentions as Cole and Abbott lifted Rodriguez between them. That's when a bright red geyser erupted from Abbott, followed by the chunking snap of an AK-47.

Johnson screamed, 'Gooks!' and sprayed the jungle with bullets.

Abbott dropped Rodriguez and fell.

The jungle erupted in noise and flashes of light.

Cole fired past Johnson even though he couldn't see the enemy. He swung his M16 in a tight arc, emptying his magazine in two short bursts. Bullets snapped past him and kicked up leaves and dirt all around. The noise was deafening, but Cole barely heard it. It was that way in every firefight.

Johnson rattled off short bursts while Cole ejected a second magazine, then rammed home a third. He crawled over Rodriguez to check Abbott. The guy was pressing on his stomach to cover his wound.

Cole pulled Abbott's hand away and saw a grey coil of intestine. He pushed Abbott's hand back on the wound. 'Press on it! Press hard!*'*

Cole fired at shadows, and shouted at Johnson. 'Where are they? I don't see them!'

Johnson didn't answer. He reloaded and fired with determination.

Cole watched Johnson's bullets chew up a heavy thatch of jungle, then saw muzzle flashes to the right. He tore a hand grenade from his harness, shouted to warn Johnson, then threw it. The grenade went off with a loud CRACK! Cole threw a second and Johnson lobbed a grenade of his own.

'Fall back! Johnson, let's go!'

Johnson scuttled backwards, firing as he withdrew.

Cole shook Abbott. 'Can you get to your feet? We gotta get out of here, Ranger!'

Abbott rolled over and pushed to his knees. He kept his left hand pressed hard to his stomach, and moaned with the effort.

Johnson didn't need to be told what to do. Fields might be dead, but Rodriguez was alive. They would carry him out.

Johnson and Cole lifted Rodriguez by his harness.

Cole shouted, 'Go, Abbott. Uphill the way we came.'

Abbott stumbled away.

Cole and Johnson dragged Rodriguez, firing awkwardly with their free hands. The shooting had died down when they threw the grenades, but now it built steadily again. Cole felt bullets snap past. Johnson grunted and stumbled, then caught himself.

'I'm OK.'

Johnson had been hit in the calf.

Then Cole felt two hard thuds shudder through Rodriguez and knew that their team leader had been hit again. Rodriguez belched a huge gout of his blood and his body convulsed.

They put Rodriguez down behind a tree. Johnson fired down the hill, chewing up two magazines as Cole checked Rodriguez for a pulse. There was none.

Cole's eyes burned hot and angry; first Fields, now Rodriguez. He pulled the grenades from Rod's harness, threw one, then another— CRACK! CRACK! They fell back, Cole firing as Johnson ran, then Johnson firing to cover Cole. Cole had still not seen a single enemy soldier.

They caught up with Abbott at the top of the hill and took cover.

'Johnson, get on the radio. Tell 'em we've got to get out of here.'

Cole stripped off Abbott's gear, then pulled open his shirt. 'Don't look! Keep your eyes on the trees.'

Abbott was crying. 'It burns! It hurts like the dickens! It really hurts!'

Cole loved Roy Abbott in that moment, loved him and hated him both, loved him for his innocence and fear, and hated him for taking a round that slowed them down and might get them killed.

He held Abbott's hand. 'Rangers lead the way. Say it, Roy. Rangers lead the way.'

Abbott struggled to echo, fighting back tears. 'Rangers lead the way.'

The bandages that Cole applied were soaked through with red even before he had finished wrapping them round Abbott—a sure sign of arterial bleeding. Cole wanted to run away, leaving Abbott, the blood and the Vietcong behind, but he grabbed a morphine Syrette and pushed it into Abbott's thigh.

'*Wrap him again, Johnson. Pull it tight, then hook him up.*'

Cole snatched up the radio as Johnson wrapped Abbott with more bandages. '*Five-two, Five-two, Five-two. We have heavy contact. We have two KIA and one critical wounded, over.*'

The crackle of static was his only answer.

'*We are pulling back. Do you copy?*'

Static. No radio. No extraction. Nothing. They were on their own.

They helped Abbott to his feet.

Johnson stepped out front to walk point when a shot cracked dully under the rain and his head blew apart.

Abbott screamed.

Cole spun round and fired blindly. He dumped his magazine, then picked up Johnson's rifle and emptied that magazine, too.

'*Shoot, Abbott! Fire your weapon!*'

Abbott fired blindly, too.

Cole shot at everything. He fired because something was trying to kill him and he had to kill it first. He threw his last hand grenade, CRACK! then stripped off Johnson's ammo packs and the radio.

He pushed Abbott down the hill, then fired another magazine into the rain. He reloaded, fired, then hoisted the radio. Bullets slammed into the deadfall in front of him.

Cole ran. He caught up with Abbott, hooked an arm under his shoulders and pulled him forward. They tumbled down the side of the mountain, stumbling through glistening green leaves as thick as leather. Vines ripped at their legs and clawed at their rifles. The pop of gunfire stayed close at their heels.

Cole led them down a steep incline into a drainage overflowing with rain. He stayed in the water so they wouldn't leave tracks, pulling Abbott along the rushing stream.

Somewhere to their left, an AK ripped on full automatic.

Abbott ploughed headlong into a tree and crashed into the weeds. His face was white where the camouflage paint had washed away.

Cole pulled him to his knees. '*Get up, Ranger. Keep going.*'

'*My stomach hurts.*' The entire front of his uniform and the thighs of his trousers were saturated with blood.

Cole pulled Abbott onto his shoulders in a fireman's lift and staggered under the weight. The jungle thinned. They were getting close to the clearing where the helicopter had dropped them.

Cole wrestled the radio free as he stumbled along the creek. '*Five-two, five-two, five-two, over.*'

The captain's broken voice came back. '*Copy, Five-two.*'

'*Three KIA, one wounded critical. Charlie's on our ass. You hear me? We're dying out here.*'

Cole was crying. He sucked breath like a steam engine, and he was so scared that his heart seemed in flames.

The captain's voice came back. '*Cole, is that you?*'

'*Everyone is gone. Abbott's bleeding to death.*'

'*A First Cavalry pilot thinks he can get to you from the south. He's low on fuel, but he wants to try.*'

Shouts came from behind Cole, and then an AK opened up. Cole didn't have the strength to look round. He staggered on.

'*He's flying up the ravine under the clouds. You have to pop a smoke for him, son. We cannot vector to your position, over.*'

'*Roger smoke.*'

Cole broke out of the jungle into the clearing. The dry creek was now filled with rushing water. Cole sloshed in up to his waist and waded across, fighting the current. His arms and legs felt dead, but then he was out of the water and on the other side. He rolled Abbott onto the high grass and looked for the helicopter. He thought he saw it, a black speck blurred by the rain. He pulled a smoke marker. Bright purple smoke swirled behind him.

The black speck tilted on its side and grew.

Cole sobbed. They were coming to save him.

He dropped to his knees beside Abbott. '*Hang on, Roy; they're coming.*'

Abbott opened his mouth and spat up blood.

Something flashed past Cole with a sharp whip-crack as the rattling hammer of an AK sounded in the tree line. Muzzle flashes danced in the green wall like fireflies.

Cole emptied his magazine at the flashes, jammed in another.

'*Abbott!*'

Abbott slowly rolled onto his belly. He dragged his weapon into the firing position and fired a single round.

The jungle sparkled. More flashes joined the first until the jungle was lit by twinkling lights. The tall stringy grass fell around Cole as if it was being mowed by invisible blades. He burned through his magazine in a single burst, packed in another and burned through that one.

'*Fire your weapon, Abbott! FIRE!*'

Abbott fired once more.

Cole heard the blurring thump of the helicopter now.

He reloaded and fired. He was down to his last four-pack of magazines but the trees were alive with enemy soldiers.

'Shoot, dammit!'

Abbott rolled onto his side. His voice soft. 'I didn't think it would be like this.'

The helicopter was suddenly loud and the grass around them swirled. As the heavy machine wobbled to the earth, pocked with bullet holes and trailing smoke, First Cavalry troops jammed the cargo bay like refugees. Their gunner opened up, his big .30 calibre weapon chewing at the jungle, and they added their fire. The helicopter had been shot to hell, but still the pilot was bringing his ship through a thunderstorm and into a wall of gunfire.

'C'mon, Roy, let's go.'

Abbott did not move.

'Let's go!' Cole slung his rifle, lifted Abbott and lurched to his feet. Something hot ripped through his trouser leg and a bullet shattered the radio. Cole stumbled to the helicopter and heaved Abbott into the bay. Cavalry troopers piled onto each other to make room. Cole clambered aboard.

AK fire popped and pinged into the bulkhead.

The crew chief screamed at him. 'They told us it was only one guy!'

Cole's ears rang so loudly that he could not hear. 'What?'

'We're too heavy. We can't take off!'

The turbine howled as the pilot tried to climb. The helicopter wallowed like a whale.

The crew chief grabbed Abbott's harness. 'Push him off! We can't fly!'

Cole levelled his M16 at the man's chest. The crew chief let go.

'He's dead, Ranger, push him off! You're going to get us killed!'

'He's coming with me.'

'We're too heavy! We can't fly! Push him out!'

Cole wrapped his finger over the trigger. Abbott was going home. Families take care of their own. 'He's coming with me.'

Rage and fear burned off the young Ranger like steam. He would do anything and kill anyone to complete his mission. The Cavalry troops understood. They pushed off ammo cans and rucksacks, anything they could shed to lighten the load.

The turbine shrieked. The rotor found hold in the thick humid air, and the helicopter lumbered into the sky.

THE THUNDERHEAD PASSED from the mountains four hours later. A reaction force comprised of Rangers from Cole's company assaulted the area to reclaim the bodies. Specialist Fourth Class Elvis Cole was among them.

For his actions that day, he was awarded the nation's third-highest decoration for bravery and valour, the Silver Star.

It was Cole's first decoration. He would earn more.

Rangers don't leave Rangers behind.

CHAPTER TEN

time missing: 41 hours, 00 minutes

After I spoke with the Abbotts, I phoned the other families to let them know that the police would be calling, and why. I was on the phone for almost three hours.

Starkey rang my bell at 8.45. When I opened the door, John Chen was waiting behind her in his van.

I said, 'I spoke with the families. None of them had anything to do with this or knows anyone who would. You get any hits on the other names I gave you?'

Starkey squinted at me. 'Are you drunk?'

'I've been up all night. I listened to that damned tape a dozen times. Did you get any hits or not?'

'I told you last night, Cole. We got nothing.'

I felt irritated with myself for forgetting. I grabbed my keys and stepped outside. 'C'mon. I'll show you what we found. Maybe John can match the prints.'

'Lay off the coffee. You look like a meth freak about to implode.'

'You're no beauty yourself.'

'That might be because Gittamon and I got hauled up at six o'clock this morning by the Bureau commander because of you.'

'Did Richard complain?'

'Rich assholes *always* complain. Here's the order of the day: you're gonna take us to whatever you've found, then you're gonna stay out of our business. Never mind that you seem to be the only guy around here besides me who knows how to detect. You're out.'

'If I didn't know better, I'd think you just paid me a compliment.'

'Don't let it go to your head. It turns out Richard was right about you being a material witness. It just feels like kicking a guy when he's down, is all, shutting you out like this, and I don't like it.'

I felt bad for snapping at her.

She said, 'I guess you didn't suddenly recognise the voice on the tape or remember something that would help?'

'No, I've never heard his voice in my life. I played it over the phone to the families, and they didn't recognise it, either.'

Starkey cocked her head as if she were surprised. 'That was a good idea, Cole, playing the tape for them. I hope none of them lied to you.'

'Why'd you have Hurwitz bring me the tape last night instead of doing it yourself?'

Starkey went to her car without answering. Then she said, 'Drive yourself. You'll need to get back on your own.'

I got into my car and led them across the canyon to the shoulder where Pike and I had parked the day before. Once there, Starkey changed into her running shoes while Chen unloaded his evidence kit. They followed me down through the brush. As we got closer to the prints, I felt anxious. Being here was like being closer to Ben, but not if the shoe prints didn't match. If they didn't match, we had nothing.

We reached the first print, a clean clear sole pressed into the dust.

Chen got down on his hands and knees for a closer look. Then he glanced up and grinned. 'It's the same shoe, Starkey. I can see it even without the cast. Size eleven Rockports showing the same pebbled sole and traction lines.'

My heart thudded hard in my chest. Starkey punched my arm.

Chen flagged eight more prints, and then we reached the tree. The depression behind the tree was still clear.

'That's it, just this side of the oak. See where the grass is crushed?'

Starkey touched my arm. 'You wait here.'

She moved closer, stooped to look at my house from under the oak's limbs, then considered the surrounding hillside. 'All right, Cole. I don't know how you found this place, but you figured this bastard good. John, I want a full area map.'

'I'll need help. We've got a lot more physicals than yesterday.'

Starkey squatted at the edge of the crushed grass, then bent to look at something in the dirt. She said, 'John, gimme the tweezers.'

Chen handed her a Ziploc bag and tweezers from his evidence kit. Starkey picked up a small brown ball with the tweezers and put it into the bag. She looked up into the tree, then at the ground again.

I said, 'What is it?'

'They look like mouse turds, but they're not. They're all over.'

Starkey picked one from a leaf of grass and put it onto her palm.

I moved closer. A dozen more brown flecks stood out clearly on the ground or clung to the grass. I knew what they were because I had seen them when I was in the army. 'It's tobacco.'

Chen said, 'How do you know?'

'A smoker on patrol chews tobacco to get his fix. You chew, there's no smoke to give you away. That's what this guy did. He chewed, then spit out the bits of the tobacco when they were used up.'

Starkey glanced at me, and I knew what she was thinking. Another connection to Vietnam. She handed the bag to Chen, dry-swallowed a white pill, then studied me for a moment. 'I want to try out something on you. Over by your house, this guy doesn't leave anything, one measly little partial that we could barely see. Here, he leaves crap all over the place.'

'He felt safe here.'

'Yeah. He had a good spot down here where no one could see him. I'm thinking that if he got careless down here, maybe he got careless up on the street, too. I oughta phone Gittamon and have him organise a door-to-door this side of the canyon, but there aren't many houses on this stretch, and we got that construction site right around the curve . . . By the time Gittamon and the uniforms get out here, you and I could have done the door-to-door.'

'I thought I wasn't supposed to be involved?'

'I didn't ask for conversation. You want to do it or you want to waste time?'

'Of course I want to do it.'

Starkey glanced at Chen. 'You tell anyone, I'll kick your ass.'

We left Chen calling SID for another criminalist, and walked back along the curve to the construction site. A single-storey house had been ripped apart to expand the ground floor and add a second storey. A long blue Dumpster sat in the street in front of the house, already half-filled with lumber and debris.

An older man was bent over a set of plans in the garage, explaining something to a sleepy young guy wearing electrician's tools.

Starkey didn't wait for them to notice us or excuse the interruption. She badged the older guy. 'LAPD. I'm Starkey, he's Cole. Are you the boss here?'

The older man identified himself as Darryl Cauley, the general contractor. His face closed with suspicion. The younger guy started away, but Starkey stopped him.

'Yo, stay put. We want to talk to everyone.'

Cauley darkened even more. 'What is this?'

Talking to people wasn't one of Starkey's strengths, so I answered before he decided to call his attorney.

'We believe that a kidnapper was in the area, Mr Cauley. He parked or drove on this street every day for the past week or so. We want to know if you noticed any vehicles or people who seemed out of place.'

The electrician hooked his thumbs on his tools and perked up. 'Was someone kidnapped?'

Starkey said, 'A ten-year-old boy. The day before yesterday.'

'Wow.'

Mr Cauley tried to be helpful, but explained that he divided his time between three different sites. 'I got subcontractors coming and going, I got the different crews. Do you have a picture, a mugshot?'

'No, sir. We don't know who he is or what he looks like. We don't know what he was driving, either, but we believe he spent a lot of time around the curve where your crew is parked.'

The electrician glanced towards the curve. 'Oh, man, that is so creepy.'

Cauley said, 'I'd like to help, but I don't know. These guys here, their friends drop by, their girlfriends. There's always someone new . . .'

Starkey said, 'Can we talk to your crew?'

'Sure. James, you wanna call your guys? And tell the framers to come down.'

Cauley had nine men working that day. Everyone cooperated when they heard that a child was missing, but no one remembered anyone out of the ordinary.

Starkey lit a cigarette. 'Let's do the houses.'

'OK. I suggest we split up. It'll be faster. You take the houses on this side.'

Starkey agreed. I trotted back, past our cars, to the houses on the far side. An Ecuadorean housekeeper answered at the first, but she hadn't seen anything. No one answered at the next house. At the third I spoke with another housekeeper, then I reached a couple of houses where no one was home. It was a weekday and people were working.

I thought about trying the houses further up the street but Starkey was leaning against her Crown Vic when I got back to our cars.

I said, 'You get anything?'

'Do I look like it? I've talked to so many people who haven't seen anything that I asked one broad if she ever went outside.'

'People skills aren't your strong point, are they?'

'Look, I've gotta call Gittamon to get some help out here. I want to run down the garbage men, the mailman, the security cars that work this street, anyone who might've seen something. You and I have taken it as far as we can. You gotta split.'

'C'mon, Starkey, I can't walk away now.'

She spoke carefully, with a soft voice. 'It's scut work, Cole. You need to get some rest. I'll call you if we get something.'

'I can call the security companies from my house.'

My voice sounded desperate even to me. She shook her head. 'You know that movie they make you watch before the plane takes off, when they're telling you what to do in an emergency?'

My head was filled with a faraway buzz as if I were drunk and hungry at the same time. 'What does that have to do with anything?'

'They tell you that if the plane loses pressure, you're supposed to put on your own oxygen mask before you put on your kid's. The first time I saw that I thought, bullshit, if I had a kid I'd put on her mask first. But the more I thought about it, the more it made sense. You have to save yourself first because, if you're not alive, you can't help your child. That's you, Cole. You have to put on your mask if you want to help Ben. Go home. I'll call you if something pops.'

I climbed into my car. I didn't know if I would go home, or not. I didn't know if I *could* sleep. I drove around the curve and saw a catering van parked by the Dumpster. It had just arrived. Maybe if I hadn't been so tired I would have thought of it sooner: construction crews have to eat, and catering vans feed them, twice a day every day, breakfast and lunch. It was eleven fifty. Ben had been missing almost forty-four hours..

I left my car in the street and ran to a narrow door at the back of the van that had been propped open. Inside, two young men in white T-shirts were bent over a grill. A short, round woman barked orders at them in a mixture of Spanish and English as they dished up grilled chicken sandwiches and paper plates spilling over with tacos and salsa verde to the line at the window.

The woman glanced over and nodded towards the open wall of the van. 'You got to stand in line over here.'

'A little boy has been kidnapped. We think the man who took him spent a lot of time on this street. You might have seen him.'

She came to the door, wiping her hands on a pink towel.

'Wha' you mean, a little boy? You the police?'

The electrician from earlier was in line at the window. He said, 'Yeah, he's with the cops. Some guy stole a kid, can ya believe that, right around here? They're trying to find him.'

The woman stepped out of the van to join me. Her name was Marisol Luna and she owned the catering business. I asked if she had noticed any vehicles parked in the area during the past two weeks, or anyone who didn't seem to fit.

'I don' think so.'

'What about when no one else was parked there? One vehicle by itself?'

'I see the plumber. We finish the breakfast here and we goin' that way'—she pointed towards the curve—'an' I see the plumber go down the hill.'

I glanced towards the work crew. 'How do you know he was the plumber?'

'It say on the van. Emilio's Plumbing. My husband, his name is Emilio. That's why I remember. But he no look like my Emilio. He black. He have things on his face like bumps.'

I called out to the construction workers. 'Where's Cauley? Can someone get Cauley?' Then I turned back to Mrs Luna. 'The man who went down the hill was black?'

'No. The man in the van, he black. The man on the hill, he Anglo.'

'Two men?'

The buzzing in my head grew more frantic. The electrician came round the end of the van with Mr Cauley who asked, 'You guys have any luck?'

'Have you had a plumber or plumbing contractor working here named Emilio or Emilio's Plumbing, anything like that?'

Cauley shook his head. 'Nope. I use the same sub over and over, a man named Donnelly.'

Mrs Luna said, 'The van, it say Emilio's Plumbing.'

The electrician said, 'Hey, I've seen that van.'

The buzz in my head suddenly vanished. I felt light and alive with a clarity that was perfect. It was the same feeling I had when we were hidden on a VC trail and heard them approaching and knew the whole bloody thing was about to go down.

I said, 'I need you to come with me, Mrs Luna. I need you to talk to the police right now. They're just around the curve.'

Marisol Luna got into my car without complaint. I didn't take the time to turn round. We drove to Starkey in reverse.

THE SUN GLARED ANGRILY from low in the southern sky, heating the great bowl of air in the canyon. Starkey held her hand to shield her eyes. 'OK, Mrs Luna, tell me what you saw.'

Marisol Luna, Starkey and I stood in the street at the top of the curve. Mrs Luna pointed back towards the construction site, telling us how she remembered it.

'We come aroun' the curve, and the plumber truck is right here.'

She indicated that the plumber's van had been pretty much where we were standing. It could not have been seen from the construction site or the surrounding houses.

'My van is big, you know? Very wide. I say to Ramón, "Look at this, this guy is taking up all of the street."'

I said, 'Ramón is one of the guys who works for her.'

'Let her tell it, Cole.'

Mrs Luna continued. 'I have to stop because I cannot get around' the van unless he move. Then I see the name, and it make me smile like I tell Mr Cole. I tell my husband that night, I say, "Hey, I saw you today."'

Starkey said, 'When did this happen?'

'That would be three days. I see it three days ago.'

The day before Ben was stolen. Starkey took out her notebook.

Mrs Luna described the van as white and dirty, but she couldn't recall anything else except the name on its side—Emilio's Plumbing.

Starkey said, 'So you came around the curve here and the van was blocking the road. Which way was it facing?'

'This way, facing me. The black man was driving. The Anglo man was on the other side. They were talking through the window.'

Mrs Luna stepped onto the shoulder and turned, showing us their positions. 'The black man, he have these things on his face. They look like sores. He big, too. A really big man.' Mrs Luna raised her arms high and wide over her head. 'He fill the windshield like thees.'

'What about the white guy?' I asked. 'Anything you remember about him?'

'I sorry, no. I lookin' at the black man and the van. We tryin' to get by, you see? The other man, he step back 'cause his friend have to make room for us, it so narrow here.'

'So the other guy went down the hill, and the black guy waited for him to come back?'

'No, no, he go too.'

'Did you see where the white guy went or see him come back?'

'No. We had another breakfast before we get ready for lunch.'

Starkey took down Mrs Luna's details and gave her a card. Her pager went off, but she ignored it. She said, 'You've been a big help, Mrs Luna. I'll probably want to talk to you some more this evening or tomorrow. Would that be OK?'

'I happy to help.'

'If you remember anything, don't wait to hear from me. It might seem small, but whatever you remember could help us.'

Starkey took out her phone and went to the edge of the shoulder to call her office for a wants-and-warrants search and to register a BOLO—Be On the Look Out—for a van with Emilio's Plumbing written on its side.

Mrs Luna watched Starkey with her brow furrowed. 'I remembering now. The white man have a cigar. He was standing like that—like the lady—and he take out a cigar.'

The tobacco.

'That's right. He have a cigar. He didn't smoke it, but he chewed it. He bite off little pieces, then spit them out.'

I tried to encourage her. I wanted the memories to come and the picture to build. We walked over to join Starkey. I touched her arm, the touch saying *listen*.

Mrs Luna stared down the street as if she could see her catering van pinched against the hill and the plumber's van driving away.

'I got the van away from the rocks an' I look back at him. He was looking down. He was doing something with his hands, and I watch him to see. He unwrap the cigar and put it in his mouth and then he went down there.' She pointed downhill. 'He have dark hair. It was short. He wear a green T-shirt. I remember now. It dark green and look dirty.'

Starkey glanced at me. 'He unwrapped the cigar?'

'He do something with it, I don't know what, then he put it in his mouth.'

I realised what Starkey was asking. I said, 'If he tossed the wrapper, we might get a print.'

I started searching the edge of the shoulder, but Starkey shouted at me. '*Stop it*, Cole! Get back! Do not disturb this scene!'

Starkey took Mrs Luna's arm. 'Don't think too hard, Mrs Luna. Just let it come. Show me where he was standing?'

Mrs Luna crossed the street then looked back at us. She moved one way and then the other, trying hard to remember. She pointed. 'Go right a little bit. A little more. He was there.'

Starkey squatted to look more closely at the ground. She touched the earth for balance, then eyeballed a wide area.

I spoke quietly to Mrs Luna. 'What time were you here?'

'Nine thirty, maybe. We got to get the van ready for lunch.'

By nine thirty the heat would have been climbing, and, with it, the air. A breeze would have been coming up the canyon.

'Starkey, the breeze would have been blowing uphill to your left.'

Starkey looked to her left. She crept forward a step, touched aside rosemary sprigs and weeds, then crept again, her movements slow. She dribbled a handful of dirt through her fingers and watched the dust float on the breeze. She followed its trail, more to the left and further out, and then she slowly stood.

Mrs Luna and I both hurried over. A clear plastic cigar wrapper was hooked in dead weeds. It was dusty and yellow with a red and gold band inside. It could have blown here from anywhere. It might have been here before him or come after, but maybe he left it behind.

We stood over the wrapper as if even the weight of light might make it vanish, and then we shouted for John Chen.

THE PREVIOUS NIGHT, when they brought Ben inside after they caught him, Eric and Mazi had made him sit on the floor in the living room while Mike made a call on a cellphone from another part of the house. When Mike came back, he held the phone a few inches from Ben's mouth. 'Say your name and address.'

Ben shouted as loud as he could. '*Help! Help me—!*'

Eric clamped a hand over his mouth. Ben was terrified that they would hurt him, but Mike only turned off the phone and laughed.

'Man, that was perfect.'

Eric squeezed Ben's face hard. He was still pissed off because Ben had got him in trouble by almost getting away, so his face was flushed as red as his hair. 'Stop shouting or I'll cut off your head.'

Mike said, 'Hey, he did great, yelling for help like that. Stop squeezing his face.' Mike tucked the phone back into a green duffle, then took out a cigar. He peeled off the wrapper.

'He won't yell any more, will you, Ben?'

Ben was scared, but he shook his head, no. Eric let go.

Ben said, 'Who was on the phone?'

Mike glanced at Eric, ignoring him. 'Put him in the room. If he starts screaming, put him back in the box.'

Ben said, 'I won't scream. Who was that? Was that my mama?'

Mike didn't answer any of his questions.

Eric locked him in an empty bedroom with giant sheets of plywood nailed over the windows, and told him to get some sleep, but Ben couldn't. He spent the night huddled at the door, trying to hear them through the crack, hoping to find out what they were going to do with him. He heard Eric and Mazi laughing, but they never once mentioned him.

Late the next morning, Eric opened the door. 'Let's go. We're taking you home.'

Ben didn't trust Eric, but he wanted to go home so badly that he pretended it was real.

Eric marched him through the house to the garage. When he reached to open the door to the garage, his plaid baggy shirt pulled tight and Ben saw a pistol outlined at the small of his back. Eric hadn't been wearing the gun yesterday.

The garage was heavy with the smell of paint. They had painted the van brown and covered the writing on its sides. Mazi was waiting behind the wheel. Mike was already gone.

Eric led Ben to the rear of the van. 'Me and you are gonna ride in back. Here's the deal: I won't tie you up if you sit still and keep your mouth shut. If we stop at a red light or something and you start screaming, I'll shut you up good, then it's the bag. We clear on that?'

'Yes, sir.'

'Something happens like we get pulled over by the cops, you pretend like you're having a great time. Come through on that, we'll take you home. Got it?'

'Yes, sir.'

Eric lifted Ben into the back of the van and shut the doors. The garage door rumbled open as Mazi started the engine. Eric spoke into a cellphone, 'We're go.'

They drove out onto the street and down the hill. The van was a big, windowless cavern with two seats up front and nothing in the back except a spare tyre, a roll of duct tape and some rags. Eric sat on the tyre with the phone in his lap, and made Ben sit next to him.

Ben could see the street past Mazi and Eric, but not much else. 'Where are we going?'

'We're taking you home. We gotta see a man first, but then you'll go home.'

Ben sensed that Eric was telling him that he was going home so that he would behave. He glanced at the van's doors, deciding that he would run if he got the chance. When he turned forward again, Mazi was watching him through the mirror.

Mazi's eyes went to Eric. 'He go-eeng to run.'

'He's cool.'

Mazi's eyes lingered on Ben a moment, then returned to the road.

They wound their way out of the hills along a residential street that Ben didn't recognise, then climbed onto the freeway. He saw the Capitol Records Building and then the Hollywood Sign.

'This isn't the way to my house.'

'Told you. We gotta see someone first.'

Ben sneaked another glance at the doors. Handles were set into each door, but he didn't see anything that looked like a lock. He checked to see if Mazi was watching him, but Mazi was watching the road. The downtown skyscrapers were growing in the windshield.

They left the freeway, slowing as they curved down the ramp. Ben looked at the doors again. They would probably stop at a traffic light or stop sign at the bottom of the ramp. If Ben made it out of the van, the people in the other cars would see him. He didn't think that Eric would shoot him. Eric would chase him, but even if Eric caught him, the other people would call the police. Ben was scared, but he told himself to do it. All he had to do was pull the handle and shove open one of the doors.

As the van reached the bottom of the ramp. Ben edged towards the doors.

Eric and Mazi were watching him. Eric took Ben's arm.

'We're not stupid, kid. That African there can read your mind.'

They turned between a row of faded warehouses, then over a bridge and past more buildings that looked abandoned. The van stopped.

Eric spoke into the phone. 'The Eagle has landed.' He listened for a moment, then put away the phone and pulled Ben towards the doors. 'I'm gonna open the doors, but we're not getting out, so don't go nuts.'

'You said I was going home.'

Eric's grip tightened. 'First we're gonna do this. When I open the doors, you're gonna see a couple of cars. Mike's here with another guy. Don't start screaming or anything. If you're cool, we'll give you to him and he'll take you home. You good with that?'

'Yes! I wanna go home!'

'OK, here we go.'

Eric pushed open the doors.

Ben squinted at the sudden bright light, but stayed quiet and didn't move. In front of two parked cars less than ten feet away, Mike stood with a large, thickset man Ben didn't know. The man looked into Ben's eyes and nodded, the nod saying, You're going to be OK.

Mike was talking to someone else on his phone. Then he said, 'OK, here he is,' and held the phone to the other man's ear so that he could talk while Mike still held the phone.

The other man said, 'I see him. He looks OK.'

Mike took back the phone. 'You heard that?' He listened, then spoke into the phone again. 'Now I want you to hear something else.'

Mike moved so quickly that Ben didn't understand what was happening. Mike put a gun to the big man's head and fired one time. The big man crumpled sideways. Ben jumped at the unexpected explosion, and Eric held him close.

Mike spoke into the phone again. 'You hear that? That was me killing the asshole you sent. No negotiations—the clock is running.'

He turned off his phone, slipped it into his pocket and came to the van. Ben tried to twist away, but Eric held tight.

'Dude, that was harsh. You mean business.'

'They understand that now.'

Ben stared at the body as it sank in a growing red pool, and Mike stroked his head with an unexpected kindness.

'You're OK, son.'

He pulled off Ben's left shoe. Eric carried the boy out of the van and put him into Mike's seat. Eric got in with him. Mazi was already behind the wheel. They drove away, leaving Mike with the body.

CHAPTER ELEVEN
time missing: 44 hours, 17 minutes

We got our second break when we took Mrs Luna back to her catering truck. Though Ramón was unable to add to what she had told us, her grill cook, Hector Delarossa, remembered the van.

'It was a sixty-seven Ford four-door Econoline. Crack in the left front windshield and spot rust on the lamps.'

I asked him to describe the two men, but he didn't remember either of them.

I said, 'You saw the van had rust spots around the headlights, but you can't describe the men?'

'It's a classic, yo? Me and my bro we're Econoheads. We're rebuilding a sixty-six. We even got a website. You should check it out.'

Starkey called in the information and then I followed her to Glendale. The Scientific Investigations Department shares its space with LAPD's Bomb Squad in a sprawling facility north of the freeway.

We parked next to each other in the parking lot, then Starkey led me to a two-storey white building that belonged to SID. Chen's van was outside. Starkey waved our way past the reception desk, then led me to a laboratory where four or five workstations were grouped together but separated by glass walls. Criminalists and lab techs were perched on stools or swivel chairs, one in each glass space.

Starkey swaggered in like she owned the place. The techs smiled and called out when they saw her. Starkey gibed with them and seemed more relaxed than at any time since I had met her.

Chen had put on a white lab coat and vinyl gloves and was working near a large glass chamber. He had split the cigar wrapper along its length and pinned it flat to a white sheet of paper. One end of the wrapper was smudged with white powder and little brown stains. The outline of a fingerprint was obvious, but the pattern was blurred. Starkey made a face. 'This looks like shit.'

Chen hunched over the bench. 'I've only been at it fifteen minutes. I wanted to see if I could get anything with the powder or ninhydrin.'

The white smear was aluminium powder. The brown stains were a chemical called ninhydrin, which reacted with the amino acids left whenever you touch something.

Starkey frowned at him as if he was stupid. 'This thing's too old to pick up latents with powder.'

'It's the fastest way to get an image into the system. I figured it was worth a shot.'

Starkey grunted. She was OK with whatever might be faster.

'The nin doesn't look much better.'

'Too much dust, and the sunlight probably broke down the aminos. I was hoping we'd get lucky but I'm gonna have to glue it.'

I said, 'What does that mean, you have to glue it?'

Now Chen looked at me as if I was the one who was stupid. But he didn't want to miss out on the chance to show off. He explained while he worked: every time you touch something, you leave an invisible deposit of sweat. Sweat is mostly water, but also contains amino acids, glucose, lactic acid and peptides—what Chen called the organics. As long as some moisture remained in the organics, techniques like dusting worked, because the powder would stick to the water, revealing the swirls and patterns of the fingerprint. But when the water evaporated, all you had left was an organic residue.

Chen used forceps to place the wrapper on a glass dish. He put the dish into the glass chamber. 'We boil a little Super Glue in the chamber so the fumes saturate the sample. The fumes react with the organics and leave a sticky white residue along the ridges of the print.'

Starkey told me, 'The fumes are poisonous as hell. That's why he's gotta do it in the box.'

I didn't care what he did or how he did it, so long as we got results. 'How long is this going to take?'

'An hour. Maybe more,' Chen replied. 'I've gotta watch it. So much reactant will build up that you can ruin the prints.'

We had nothing to do but wait, and we weren't even sure if anything would be found. I bought a Diet Coke from a machine in the reception area, and Starkey bought a Mountain Dew. We took our drinks outside so that she could smoke. It was quiet and still in Glendale, with the low wall of the Verdugo Mountains above us and the tip of the Santa Monicas below.

Starkey sat on the kerb. I sat beside her. I tried to conjure a picture of Ben alive and safe, but all I saw were flashes of shadow and terrified eyes.

'Did you call Gittamon?' I asked.

'And tell him that I bailed on a crime scene to come over here with a guy that I was specifically ordered to keep off the case? That would be you, by the way.' Starkey flicked ash from her cigarette. 'I'll call him when we know what John finds.'

I said, 'Listen. I want to thank you.'

'You don't have to thank me. I'm doing my job.'

'A lot of people have the job, but not everyone busts their ass to get it done. I owe you.'

Starkey grinned. 'That sounds pretty good, Cole.' She ate another white tablet.

I decided to change the subject. 'Starkey, are those breath mints or are you a drug addict?'

'It's an antacid. I have stomach problems from when I was hurt'.

Hurt. Being blown apart in a trailer park was 'hurt'.

'I'm sorry. That wasn't my business.'

She shrugged, then flicked her cigarette into the parking lot. 'This morning you asked why I didn't bring you the tape.'

'I just wondered. You said you'd be back.'

'Your military records were waiting in the fax machine, the 201 and the 214. I started reading while I was waiting for the tape. I saw that you were wounded.'

'Not when I was out with five-two. That was another time.'

'Yeah, I know. But I saw you got hit by mortar fire and I was just curious about what happened to you. You don't have to tell me if you don't want. I know it doesn't have anything to do with this case.'

She struck up a fresh cigarette to hide behind the movement, as if she was suddenly embarrassed that I knew why she was asking. A mortar shell was a bomb. In a way, bombs had got both of us.

'It wasn't anything like with you, Starkey, not even close. Something exploded behind me and then I woke up under some leaves. I got a few stitches, that's all.'

'The report says they took twenty-six pieces of frag out of your back and you almost bled to death.'

I wiggled my eyebrows up and down like Groucho Marx. 'Wanna see the scars, little girl?'

Starkey laughed. 'Your Groucho sucks.'

'My Bogart's even worse. Want to hear that?'

'You want to talk scars? I could show you scars.'

We smiled at each other, and I think both of us felt awkward. It wasn't banter any more and it somehow felt wrong. I guess my expression changed. Now both of us looked away.

She said, 'I can't have kids.'

'I'm sorry.'

'Jesus, I can't believe I told you that.'

Now neither of us was smiling. We sat in the parking lot, drinking our caffeine as Starkey smoked.

I glanced at her. 'Is that why you're on the Juvenile desk?'

She nodded.

Neither of us said very much after that until John Chen came out. He had the prints.

WHITE CONCENTRIC CIRCLES covered the wrapper in overlapping smudges. People don't touch anything with a single clean grip. Their fingers shuffle and slide; they adjust and readjust their grip, laying fingerprint on top of fingerprint in confused and inseparable layers.

Starkey and I stood on either side of Chen as he inspected the wrapper through a magnifying glass attached to a flexible arm.

'Most of this stuff is garbage, but we've got a couple of clean patterns we can work with.'

He brushed dark blue powder on two sections of the wrapper, then used a can of pressurised air to blow off the excess. Two dark blue fingerprint patterns now stood in sharp contrast to the white smudges. Chen hunched more closely over the magnifying glass.

'Got a nice double-loop core here. Got a clean tentarch on this one. Couple of isles.' He nodded at Starkey. 'If he's in the system, we can find him.'

Starkey squeezed his shoulder. 'Excellent, John.'

Chen photographed each print and fed the images into his computer. He filled out an FBI fingerprint identification form that was basically a description of the two fingerprints with their identifying characteristics listed by type and location—what Chen called 'characteristic points'.

He spent almost twenty minutes logging the architecture of the two prints into the appropriate forms, then hit the SEND button.

I said, 'How long does it take?'

'It's computers, man. It's fast.'

Starkey's pager buzzed. She glanced at it. 'Gittamon. Too bad. I gotta have a cigarette.'

Starkey was turning away when Chen's computer chimed with an incoming email.

He said, 'Let's see.'

The file downloaded automatically when Chen opened the email. An NCIC/Interpol logo flashed over a set of photos showing a man with deep-set eyes and a strong neck. His name was Michael Fallon.

'We've got a ninety-nine point nine-nine per cent positive match on all twelve characteristic points. It's his cigar wrapper.'

Starkey nudged me. 'So? Do you know him?'

'I've never seen him before in my life.'

Chen scrolled the file so that we could read Fallon's personal data. His last known residence was in Amsterdam, but his current whereabouts were unknown. He was wanted for two unrelated murders in Colombia and two more in El Salvador, and had been indicted under the International War Crimes Act by the UN for participating in mass murder, genocide and torture in Sierra Leone. Interpol cautioned that he was to be considered extremely dangerous.

Fallon had extensive military experience. He had served in the United States army for nine years, first as a paratrooper, then as a Ranger. He had served an additional four years, but whatever he had done during those years was described only as 'classified'.

Starkey said, 'What does that mean?'

I knew what it meant, and felt a sharp tightness in my chest that was more than fear. I knew how he had come by the skills to watch and move and leave no sign when he stole Ben. I had been a soldier, and I had been good at it. Mike Fallon was better.

'He was in Delta Force.'

Chen said, 'The terrorist guys? No shit.'

Delta. D-boys. The Operators. Delta trained for hard, hot insertions against terrorist targets, and membership was by invitation only. They were the best killers in the business.

'He doesn't know me,' I said eventually. 'He's too young for Vietnam.'

'Then why?'

I didn't know.

We kept reading. After Fallon left the service, he had used his skills to work as a professional soldier in Nicaragua, Lebanon, Somalia, Afghanistan, Colombia, El Salvador, Bosnia and Sierra Leone. Michael Fallon was a mercenary.

Starkey said, 'This is just great, Cole. You couldn't have a garden-variety lunatic after you. You gotta have a professional killer.'

'I don't know him, Starkey. I've never heard of him. I've never known anyone named Fallon, let alone someone like this.'

'*Someone* knows him, buddy, and he sure as hell knows you. John, can we get a hard copy of this?'

'Sure. I can print the file.'

I said, 'Print one for me, too. I want to show Lucy, then talk to the people in her neighbourhood. After that, we can go back to the construction site. It's easier when you show people a picture. One memory leads to another.'

Starkey smiled at me. 'We? Are we partners now?'

Somewhere in the minutes between the parking lot and our waiting for the file, it had become 'we'. As if she wasn't on LAPD and I wasn't a man desperate to find a lost boy. As if we were a team.

'You know what I meant. We finally have something to work with. We can build on it. We can keep going.'

Starkey smiled wider, then patted my back. 'Relax, Cole. We're going to do all that stuff. Play your cards right and I might let you tag along. I'm going to put this on the BOLO.'

Starkey added the photo to the BOLO on the van, then phoned a request for information about Fallon to the LA offices of the FBI, the US Secret Service and the Sheriffs. After that, we rolled back to Lucy's. We.

The street outside Lucy's apartment was jammed with Richard's limo, Gittamon's black and white, and a second black and white with MISSING PERSONS UNIT emblazoned on the side. Gittamon answered the door when we knocked. He seemed surprised to see us, then angry. He glanced back inside, then lowered his voice. He kept the door pulled like he was hiding.

'Where have you been? I've been calling you all morning.'

Starkey said, 'I was working. We found something, Dave. We know who took the boy.'

'You should have told me. You should have answered my calls.'

'What's going on? Why is Missing Persons here?'

Gittamon glanced back inside again, then opened the door.

'They fired us, Carol. Missing Persons is taking the case.'

CHAPTER TWELVE
time missing: 47 hours, 38 minutes

Richard rubbed his hand nervously through his hair. His clothes were wrinkled worse than yesterday, as if he had slept in them. Lucy sat cross-legged on the couch and Myers was leaning against the far wall. He was the only one of them who looked rested and fresh. They were listening to an immaculately groomed woman in a dark business suit and her male clone, who were seated on chairs from the dining room. Lucy stared at me. She didn't want me involved, yet here I was. Making it worse.

Gittamon cleared his throat to interrupt. He stood at the edge of the living room like a child reprimanded before the class. 'Ah, Lieutenant, excuse me. This is Detective Starkey and Mr Cole. Carol, this is Detective-Lieutenant Nora Lucas and Detective-Sergeant Ray Alvarez, from the Missing Persons Unit.'

Lucas had one of those shrunken, porcelain faces with absolutely no lines—probably because she never smiled.

Alvarez held my hand too long when we shook. 'I thought we understood that Mr Cole wasn't going to be involved, Sergeant.'

Richard paced to the window. He looked at Lucas and Alvarez. 'What can you people do that's any different from what's already being done?'

Myers said, 'More horsepower.'

Lucas nodded. 'That's right. We'll bring the full authority of the Missing Persons Unit to finding your son, not to mention our experience. Finding people is what we do.'

Alvarez leaned forward. 'We're the A-team, Mr Chenier. We'll get the case organised, review what's been done and find your son. We'll also cooperate with you and Mr Myers in your own efforts.'

Richard turned impatiently. 'That's great. Now I want to get back to finding my son instead of just talking about it. Come on, Lee.'

I said, 'We know who took him.'

Everyone looked at me as if they weren't sure what I had said.

Lucy opened her mouth, then stood. 'What did you say?'

'We know who took Ben. We have a description on the vehicle and two men, and an ID on one of them.'

Myers peeled himself from the wall. 'You're full of shit, Cole.'

Starkey held out the Interpol file so Lucy could see Fallon's picture.

'Look at this man, Ms Chenier. Try to remember if you've seen him before. Maybe at a park when you were with Ben, or after school.'

Lucy studied Fallon as if she was falling into his picture.

Richard hurried across the room so he could see. 'Who is that? What did you find out?'

I ignored Richard and the rest. I was totally focused on Lucy.

'Think hard, Luce—maybe you thought you were being followed; maybe you got a weird vibe from someone and this was him.'

'I don't know. I don't think so.'

Lucas said, 'Who is that?'

Starkey glanced at Lucas and Alvarez, then handed the sheet to Gittamon. 'His name is Michael Fallon. I've put out a BOLO. At least one other man was involved—a black male with distinctive marks on his face, but we don't have an ID for him yet. Probably because we're not the A-team.'

Richard stared at Fallon's picture. He breathed hard and rubbed his hair again. He shoved the picture at Myers. 'You see this? You see what they have? They've got a suspect.'

Myers nodded with little roach eyes. 'I can see that, Richard.' The roach eyes came to me. 'How do you know it's him?'

'We found a cigar wrapper on the ridge opposite my house. We found it near footprints that match the footprint where Ben was taken.'

Richard's eyes were bright. 'That footprint we saw? The one you showed us yesterday?'

Starkey said, 'Yeah. And we got a hit on fingerprints from the wrapper on twelve out of twelve points. It doesn't get more positive than that.'

Both Lucas and Alvarez got up so they could see the picture, too.

Lucas glanced at Gittamon. 'You didn't tell me about this.'

'I didn't know. I called her, but she didn't call back.'

Starkey said, 'We found the wrapper this morning. We only got the ID a few minutes ago. That's what Cole and I were doing while you people were figuring out how to steal our case.'

'Take it easy, Detective.'

'Read his warrants. Fallon is a professional killer. He's got a war-crimes indictment. He's murdered people all over the world.'

Lucas said, '*Detective!*' She glanced at Lucy as she said it, and her voice snapped across Starkey like a slap.

Starkey flushed deep when she realised what she had said. *This guy is a professional killer. He's murdered people all over the world.* And now he has your son.

'I'm sorry, Ms Chenier. That was insensitive.'

Richard went to the door, anxious to leave. 'Let's get on this, Lee. Lee. We can't waste any more time with this.'

Myers didn't move. He said, 'I'm not wasting time. I'm investigating how Cole knows this man. Everything I've heard so far fits with the tape. Cole and Fallon have a lot in common. How do you know each other, Cole? What does this guy want from you?'

'He doesn't want anything from me. I don't know him, never met him, and don't have any idea why he's doing this.'

'That isn't what he says on the tape.'

Lucy's forehead was lined in concentration. 'This doesn't make sense. He has to have some connection with you.'

'He doesn't. There isn't.'

Lucas whispered to Alvarez, then spoke loudly to interrupt. 'Let's not get sidetracked. This is a good start, Detective. Ray, call SID to confirm the identification, then have Central distribute the picture.'

Lucas had assumed command of the case, and she wanted everyone to know that she was still running the show.

'Mr Chenier, Ms Chenier—what we want to do now is bring the elements of the investigation together. This won't take long, then we can get on with developing this lead.'

Starkey said, 'It's already developed. We just have to find the sonofabitch.'

Gittamon touched her arm. 'Carol. Please.'

Richard muttered something, then opened the door. 'You people can do what you want, but I'm going to find my son. Lee, let's go. Do you need a copy of that?'

'I have what I need.'

'Then let's get the hell out of here.'

They left.

Alvarez turned towards Gittamon. 'Sergeant, you and Starkey wait outside. We'll review what you've done so far when we're finished with Ms Chenier.'

Starkey said, 'Have you people been asleep? We made a major breakthrough here. We don't need a meeting about it.'

Alvarez raised his voice. 'Wait outside until we're finished. You too, Gittamon. Stop wasting time and get on with it.'

Starkey stalked out, and Gittamon followed, so humiliated that he shuffled.

Alvarez said, 'You stick around, too, Cole. We want to know why this guy has it in for you.'

'No, I'm not wasting more time with that. I'm going to find Ben.' I looked at Lucy. 'I know you don't want me involved, but I'm not going to leave it alone. I'm going to find him, Luce.'

'You'd better be downstairs, Cole. I'm not asking; I'm telling.' Alvarez added something else, but I had already shut the door.

Starkey and Gittamon were on the sidewalk, arguing. I ignored them. I went to my car but I didn't know where to go. I looked at Michael Fallon's picture and tried to figure out what to do.

This doesn't make sense. He has to have some connection with you.

All investigations run the same course: you follow the trail of a person's life to see where it crosses with another. Fallon and I had both been in the army, but we had been in the army at different times, and, so far as I knew, our lives had never crossed.

I glanced up and down the street to see if I could spot Joe. He would be here, watching, and I needed him. *'Joe!'*

Men like Michael Fallon lived and worked in a shadow world that I knew nothing about; they paid cash and were paid in cash, lived under other names and moved in circles so clannish that they were known in their true lives by very few others.

'*Joe!*'

Pike touched my shoulder. He might have stepped out of a tight thatch of plants at the corner of the building. The sun glinted off his dark glasses like polished armour in the sun.

My hands shook when I gave him the file. 'This man took Ben. He's fought and done things everywhere. I don't have any idea how to find him.'

Pike had lived and worked in dark places, too. He read through the file without speaking until he had finished.

'Men like this don't fight for free. People hire him, so somebody knows how to reach him. All we have to do is find that person.'

'I want to talk to them.'

He shook his head. 'They won't talk to you, Elvis. People like this won't even let you get close.'

Pike stared, but he didn't seem to be staring at me. I wondered what he was thinking.

'I can't go home. I can't just wait.'

'It's out of your hands.'

PIKE THOUGHT that Cole's eyes looked like tunnels the colour of bruises. Pike had seen the same eyes on combat soldiers with too much trigger time. Cole was in The Zone: amped up and wrung out.

You get in The Zone, Pike knew, and your thinking grew fuzzy. You could get yourself killed.

Pike ran the three blocks to his Jeep. His back hurt from having been still for so long, and the jogging hurt his shoulder.

Mercenaries were recruited by private military outfits, security firms with international contracts, and 'consultants'. The talent pool was small. The same people hired the same people over and over, just like software engineers jumping from job to job in Silicon Valley. Only with shorter life expectancies.

Pike once knew a few consultants, but he didn't know if they were still in the business, or if any of them would be willing to help. He had been out of that life for a long time. He drove to his condo in Culver City. The phone numbers for the men he had known were in a safe in his bedroom. They weren't written as digits but as a coded list of words. He got them, then made the calls.

The first seven numbers were no longer in use. War was a business with a high casualty rate. Pike scored on the eighth.

'Yeah?'

Pike recognised the voice as soon as he heard it. Even though they had not spoken for ten years.

'This is Joe Pike. Remember?'

'Hell, yeah. How ya been?'

'I'm trying to find a professional named Michael Fallon.'

The man hesitated, and the easy familiarity was gone. 'I thought you left the game.'

'That's right. I'm out.'

Pike sensed that the man was suspicious. He was wondering if Pike was now working with the Feds.

'I don't know what you got in mind, Pike, but I'm a security consultant. I don't do business with terrorists, drug dealers or dictators.'

He was saying all that for the Feds, who might be eavesdropping, but Pike happened to know that it was also true.

'I understand. That's not why I'm calling.'

'OK. So what you want is a consultation, right?'

'That's right. Fallon was with Delta, but then he went freelance. Two years ago he was in Amsterdam. Today, he's in Los Angeles.'

'Delta, huh?'

'Yes.'

'Those boys bring top dollar.'

'I want to see him face-to-face. That's the important part.'

'Uh-huh. Tell me something that might ring a bell.'

Pike cited the countries where Fallon was known to have worked: Sierra Leone, Colombia, El Salvador, the others.

The man said, 'I know some people who worked in those places. You really out of the game?'

'Yes.'

'That's a shame, man. What's in this for me?'

Pike was prepared to pay. 'A thousand dollars.'

The man laughed. 'I'd rather book you into a job.'

'Two thousand.'

'I can probably find someone who knows this guy, but I might have to call all over the goddamn world. I'm going to have costs.'

'Five thousand.'

It was an outrageous amount, but Pike hoped that the figure would be persuasive.

'You have to see it from my side—if something happens to this guy, your Fed buddies will use this little transaction between us to hammer me as an accessory.'

'No one is listening.'

'Yeah, right.'

Pike didn't respond. Pike had learned that if he didn't say anything, people often told themselves what they wanted to hear.

'Tell you what, I'll ask around, but you gotta let me book a job for you. I don't know what or when, but one day I'll call. If I find someone who can help you, you gotta go. That's my price.'

Pike regretted calling this number. He considered trying to find someone else, but the first seven numbers had given him nothing. Ben was waiting. Elvis was waiting. The weight of their need kept him on the phone.

'C'mon, Pike, it isn't just the calls. I haven't heard from you in years. If I find somebody who's dealt with him, I'll have to vouch for you.'

A Zen fountain sat on a polished black table in the corner of Pike's living room: a small bowl filled with stones, and water burbling between the stones. Pike listened to the burble. It sounded like peace.

'All right.'

'Give me your number. I'll call back when I have something.'

Pike gave the man his number, then stripped off his clothes. He brought the phone into his bathroom so he could hear it from the shower. He let hot water beat into his back and shoulder, and tried his best to think about nothing.

Forty-six minutes later, the phone rang. The man gave him a name and an address, and told him that it had been arranged.

Two messages were waiting on my answering machine when I got home. One was Grace Gonzalez from next door, asking if she could do anything to help, and the other was Crom Johnson's mother, returning my call. I didn't feel strong enough to talk to either.

Normal people bring in their mail after they get home from work, so that's what I did. Normal people take a shower, then change into fresh clothes. I did that, too. It felt like pretending.

I was eating a sandwich in front of the television when my phone rang. I grabbed it, thinking that it would be Joe.

'This is Bill Stivic from the army's department of personnel in St Louis. I'm calling for Elvis Cole, please.'

Master Sergeant Bill Stivic, USMC, retired. It felt like weeks since I had spoken with him. It had only been that morning.

'Hi, Master Sergeant. Thanks for getting back to me.'

'No problem. Here's what we have—first, like I told you this morning, we never send the 201 to anyone except you unless it's by court order or we get a request from a law enforcement agency.'

'I remember.'

'The records here show that yesterday we telefaxed your file to a Detective Carol Starkey out where you live in Los Angeles.'

'That's right. I spoke with Starkey today.'

'The only other request we've had was eleven weeks ago. We were served with a court order by a judge named Rulon Lester. Both your 201 and 214 were sent to his office at the State Superior Court building in New Orleans.'

Another dead end. I thought of Richard waving the manila folder. The bastard had gone all out to check up on me.

'Those are the only two times my files have been sent? You're sure they couldn't have been sent to anyone else?'

'Just the two. The records section keeps track for eight years.'

'You have a phone number for the judge, Master Sergeant?'

'They don't keep a copy of the order, just that your files were sent and why, along with the court's filing number. You want that?'

He read off the details. I thanked him, then put the phone down. New Orleans was in the central time zone, so the courts would be closed, but their offices might still be open. I called Information and got numbers for the State Superior Court and Judge Lester's office. The coincidence between Richard living in New Orleans and a judge there ordering my files was obvious, but I wanted to be sure.

A woman with a clipped Southern accent answered on the first ring. 'Judge Lester's office.'

I tried to sound older and Southern. 'This is Bill Stivic with the army's department of personnel in St Louis. I'm trying to track down a file we sent to the judge.'

'The judge has left for the day.'

'Then I'm in a world of hurt, sugar. I pulled a whammy of a mistake when I sent the file down to y'all. I sent the original, and that was our only copy.' Sounding desperate was easy.

'I'm not sure I can help you, Mr Stivic. If the file is admitted evidence or case documentation, it can't be returned.'

'I don't want it returned. I should've made a copy first. If you could find it, maybe I could get you to overnight a copy to me up here. I'd pay for it out of my own pocket.' Sounding pathetic was easy, too.

She said, 'Well, let me take a look.'

'You're a lifesaver, you truly are.'

I gave her the date and the file number from Lester's court order, then held on. She came back a few minutes later.

'I'm sorry, Mr Stivic, but we don't have those records any longer. The judge sent them on to a Mr Leland Myers as part of the requested action. Perhaps you could get a copy from his office?'

I let her give me Myers's number, and then I hung up. I thought about the folder that Richard had slapped on the table when we were listening to the tape. Myers had probably handled the investigation. It felt like a dead end. Fallon could have got most of what he knew by breaking into my house, and could have learned the rest a thousand other ways. All I had learned from Stivic was what I already knew—Richard hated my guts.

I went back to the sandwich but I no longer wanted it. My body ached and my eyes burned from the lack of sleep. The past two days were catching up with me. The phone rang again but I wanted to let it ring, and never move again. I answered. It was Starkey.

'Cole! We found the van downtown! They just called it in!'

She shouted out the location and her voice was strained as if the news wasn't good.

The aches were suddenly gone, as if they had never been. 'Did they find Ben?'

'I don't know. I'm on my way now. The others are on the way, too. Get down there, Cole, right away.'

'Goddammit, Starkey, what is it?'

'They found a body.'

The phone fell out of my hands. It floated end over end, taking forever to fall. By the time it hit the floor, I was gone.

THE LOS ANGELES RIVER is small, but mean. People who don't know the truth of it just see a tortured trickle that snakes along a concrete gutter like some junkie's vein. They don't know that we put that river in concrete to save ourselves; they don't know the river is small because it's sleeping, and that every year and sometimes more it wakes. Before we put the river in that concrete plain at the bottom of those tall concrete walls, it flashed to life with the rain to wash away trees and houses and bridges, and cut its banks to breed new channels almost as if it were looking for people to kill. It found what it looked for too many times. The concrete is a prison. The prison works, most of the time.

The van had been left in the river's channel under an overpass. Starkey was waiting in her car at a chain-link gate, and rolled forward when she saw me coming. I got in the car and we squealed down a ramp and parked behind three radio cars and two vehicles from Parker Center. The patrol officers were at the base of the overpass with two kids. The detectives had just arrived; two were with the kids and a third was peering into the van.

Starkey said, 'Cole, you wait until I see what's what.'

The van had been painted to change its appearance, but it was a four-door '67 Econoline with rust around the headlights. The new paint was thin, letting the *Em* from *Emilio's* show through like a shadow. The driver's door and the left rear door were open. A bald detective was staring into the back. Starkey badged him.

'Carol Starkey. I put out the BOLO. We heard you got a vic.'

The detective said, 'Oh, man, this one's nasty.'

I moved past him to see inside, and Starkey grabbed my arm. I shook her off, and there it was: a thick-bodied Caucasian man in a sports jacket and slacks, spread on his stomach with one leg crossed over the other as if he had been rolled into the back of the van. His clothes and the floor around him were heavy with blood. His head had been cut from his body at the top of his neck and was tipped against a spare tyre just behind the front seat. His face was hidden. Fat desert flies covered the body.

Ben was not in the van.

The detective muttered, 'The things some people will do.'

'You get an ID?'

'Not yet. I'm Tims, Robbery-Homicide. The CI's on the way.'

The Coroner Investigator was responsible for determining the cause and time of death, so the police weren't supposed to do anything but preserve the evidence until the CI cleared the scene.

I said, 'We're looking for a boy.'

'What you see is what we got—one corpse and no blood trails. Why'd you ask about a boy?'

'Men driving this van kidnapped a ten-year-old boy two days ago.'

'No shit. Well, if you have suspects here, I want their names.'

Starkey gave him Fallon's name and description, along with a description of the black guy. While he was writing it down, I asked him who opened the van. He nodded towards the kids.

'They came down here to ride on the ramps. They saw the blood dripping and opened it up. Way the blood's still leaking, I'd say this couldn't have happened more than three or four hours ago.'

Starkey said, 'Did you check them for his wallet?'

'Didn't have to. See on his butt where the jacket's pushed up? You can see the bulge. Wallet's still in his pocket.'

'Tims, listen,' Starkey said. 'If we can put this van to a location, we'll be closer to finding the boy. The vic might have had a hand in it. We need an ID.'

Tims shook his head. He knew what she was asking. 'You know better than that. The CI's on his way. It won't be long.'

I went to the driver's door. Tims and Starkey were still at the rear. The other detectives and the patrol officers were with the kids. I climbed up into the front seat and squeezed into the van's bay. It smelt like a butcher shop.

When Tims saw me, he lurched towards the rear doors.

'Hey! Get outta there! Starkey, get your partner outta there!'

Starkey stepped in front of Tims and braced her arms across the door as if she was peering inside at me. She was also blocking the door to keep him from pulling me out. One of the detectives and two of the uniforms ran over to see why Tims was shouting.

'Cole. Would you please do this fast?'

Flies swarmed around me in an angry cloud. I took the dead man's wallet, then went through his pockets. I found a handkerchief, two quarters and a hotel card key. An empty shoulder holster was strapped under his arm. I tossed the wallet and other things onto the front seat, then turned back to the head. It was obscene and awful, and I didn't want to touch it. Tims was shouting, but his voice receded until it was just another fly buzzing in the heat. I balled the handkerchief and used it to shift the head. I saw that it had been placed on a black training shoe. A boy's shoe.

'Cole, who is it?'

'It's DeNice. Starkey, they left Ben's shoe in here.'

'Did they leave a note? Is there anything else?'

'I don't see anything. Just the shoe.'

The Missing Persons car rolled down the ramp with its blue dash lights popping, and Richard's limo brought up the rear.

Starkey said, 'Get out of there. Bring his things with you.'

She trotted away to intercept Lucas and Alvarez. I climbed out of the van and put everything on the ground. My hands were gloved in blood. The wallet and Ben's shoe and the other things were smeared with it. One of the officers said, 'Dude, you're a mess.'

Lucas stepped round Starkey and rushed over to the van. She looked inside, then staggered backwards. 'Oh, my God.'

DeNice's wallet contained sixty-two dollars and a driving licence, but nothing that indicated how he had found Fallon or had come to be dead in the van.

Richard and Myers pushed past Alvarez, and Richard turned white when he saw the blood.

'What's in there? Is it—? Is—?'

'It's DeNice. They left his head in Ben's shoe.'

Richard and Myers looked into the van before Alvarez could stop them, and Richard made a deep gasping sound.

'Holy God!' He grabbed Myers to steady himself, then turned away.

Myers stared into the van. His jaw flexed and knotted, but the rest of him was still. One of the big flies lit on his cheek, but he didn't seem to feel it.

I said, 'They left Ben's shoe. Ben's shoe was in that.'

I thought about what Pike had said about men like Fallon doing whatever they did for money. I thought about DeNice in the van with the blood and the gore and Ben's shoe, and I knew that they hadn't done this for me. They had done it for Richard.

'They didn't just kill him, Richard—*They cut off his head!*'

Richard threw up.

Starkey looked worried, maybe because I was screaming. 'Take it easy, Cole.'

Richard was bent over and heaving. He looked frantic and sick.

I said, 'They hit you for ransom, didn't they? They're jamming you for ransom and you got cute with DeNice.'

Starkey and Lucas looked at me.

Richard straightened up, his face blotched with fury. 'You don't know what you're talking about! None of that's true!'

'These guys are using DeNice to scare somebody and they weren't trying to scare me.'

Lucas said, 'How can you say that?'

'Fallon's a mercenary. He doesn't do anything unless he's going to make money, and Richard has money. They're working the ransom.'

Richard lurched forward like he was going to hit me, but Myers took his arm. Richard trembled. 'This is all your fault, you bastard. I'm not going to stand here listening to this while my son is missing.'

He stumbled to his limo, leaned against the side of it and threw up again. Myers walked over and joined him.

I said, 'He's lying. They're both lying.'

Starkey watched Richard and Myers. 'We're talking about the man's son here, Cole. If these guys were grinding him for ransom, why wouldn't he tell us?'

'I don't know. He's scared. Look what they did to DeNice.'

'Then why all that stuff with you?'

'Maybe it started with me about something else, but when Richard got here they saw the money.'

Starkey didn't look convinced. 'Maybe DeNice got too close to them.'

'DeNice wasn't good enough to find them. They arranged some kind of meet because they're chasing Richard for ransom, and they used DeNice to make sure he pays.'

It was the only way the pieces fitted.

Lucas wet her lips, as if the notion of it disturbed her. 'I'd better speak with Mr Chenier.'

Starkey said, 'Maybe we can trace DeNice's moves from last night to see how he got here. Maybe Fontenot knows something.'

Lucas looked at the van as if it held secrets we might never know. 'This isn't a simple missing person case any more.'

Starkey said, 'No. If it ever was.'

Lucas considered me. 'I have some Handiwipes and alcohol in my car. You need to take care of yourself.'

Starkey stayed with Lucas and Alvarez to question Richard and Myers. I took the Handiwipes and alcohol to my car. I got off as much of the blood as I could, put on a T-shirt and an old pair of running shoes that I kept behind my front seat, then sat in my car watching the cops. The detectives were bunched around Richard and Myers. Richard was freaking out, but Myers was as calm as a spider waiting at the edge of its web. I stared at the van and saw what they had left in it even though I was a hundred feet away. I would always see it. They had cut off his head, and the men who did it had Ben.

My cellphone rang. It was Pike. I told him about DeNice, about going inside the van. My voice sounded strange.

He said, 'I found someone who can help.'

ERIC AND MAZI treated Ben differently after Mike shot the man. They stopped to pick up In-N-Out burgers on the way back. When they reached the house, they let him sit with them while they ate and played cards. They were a lot more relaxed. Even Mazi laughed and made jokes. It was as if killing that man had freed them.

They sat in a circle on the floor. Ben sneaked glances at the gun that bulged under Eric's shirt. All he thought about was getting the weapon, shooting them, then running to the house across the street. When Mike came back, he would shoot him, too.

When Ben looked up from the gun, he saw Mazi staring at him. It creeped Ben out, the way he did that.

Mazi said, 'He theenkeeng ah-bout your gun.'

'Big deal. He did all right out there. He's a natural-born killer.'

Ben said, 'I can shoot.'

Eric glanced up from his cards. 'What kinda shooting you do?'

'I have a twenty-gauge shotgun and a .22. I've been duck hunting with my uncles and my grandpa. I've shot my mom's pistol.'

Eric liked talking about guns. He reached under his shirt and took out his own, which was big and black with a checked grip.

Mazi said, 'Stop eet. Put dee gun ah-way.'

Eric ignored him and turned the pistol from side to side so Ben could see. 'This is a Colt .45. It used to be standard issue until the army went pussy with this 9 millimetre shit. A 9mm holds more bullets, but you don't need more bullets if you hit your target with this. You wanna hold it?'

Ben said, 'Yeah.'

Eric pressed something and the magazine fell out. He pulled the slide. The gun coughed up a bullet and Eric caught it in the air. He handed the gun to Ben.

Ben took it. It was heavy, and too big for his hands. Eric showed him how to work the safety and the slide, then handed back the gun so that Ben could do it himself. The slide was hard to pull.

Ben held the gun tightly. He pulled back the slide and locked it in place. All he had to do was shove in the magazine, release the slide, and it would be loaded and cocked. The magazine was by his knee.

Eric took back the gun. 'That's enough.'

He jammed in the magazine, jacked the slide, then returned the loose bullet to the magazine. 'You gotta keep a round in the chamber. One in the box and good to go. If you need it, you won't have time to dick around.'

They played cards all afternoon. Ben sat close to Eric, thinking about the gun being loaded and cocked with one in the box. All he had to do was release the safety. He rehearsed doing it in his mind. If he got his chance, he wouldn't have time to dick around.

Eric went to the bathroom, but took the gun with him. When he returned, he had tucked it back in his trousers on his far side. Ben told them that he had to go to the bathroom too. Mazi took him. When they came back to the cards, Ben sat at Eric's side, near the gun.

Mike didn't return until almost dark.

'OK, we're set.'

'You find dee plaze?'

'Everything's rigged and ready to rock. They won't see it coming.'

Eric said, 'Fuck all that. I wanna know if we're getting the money.'

'After they see what's in the van, I'd say yes.'

Eric laughed. 'This is so sweet.'

'I'm gonna grab a shower. Get your shit together. Once we leave here, we won't come back.'

Ben stayed close to Eric. If they worked it the same as before, Mike would leave by himself and Ben would go with Eric and Mazi. Ben planned to sit as close to Eric's gun as possible, in case he got a chance to grab it.

Ben's mom had told him about something called 'visualisation' which all the best tennis players did to help their game. The mental rehearsal helped you do the real thing. He imagined every possible scenario: Eric getting into the car ahead of him, Eric getting out, Eric bending over to pick up a quarter—Ben only needed one brief moment when Eric's back was turned. He would lift Eric's shirt with his left hand and grab the gun with his right; he would jump back as Eric turned, and release the safety; he would pull the trigger. He would keep pulling the trigger until they were dead.

Suddenly, Mike came from the back of the house with a pump-action shotgun and a pair of binoculars. 'This is it. Showtime.'

Eric shoved up from the floor like it couldn't come too soon, pulling Ben with him. 'Let's get it on.'

They slung their duffle bags over their shoulders and trooped through the house. Ben was so scared that his ears buzzed, but he stayed close to Eric. A battered blue compact that Ben hadn't seen before was waiting next to the sedan in the garage.

Eric steered him towards it. 'OK, troop, step lively.'

Behind them, Mike said, 'The kid's coming with me.'

Mike took Ben's arm and turned him towards the sedan, while Eric climbed into Mazi's blue compact.

Ben pulled back from Mike. 'I don't want to go with you. I want to go with Eric.'

'Get in the car.'

Mike pushed him into the passenger side, then got in behind the wheel with his shotgun. The garage door opened, and Mazi and Eric drove away. Ben watched Eric's pistol go with them, cocked, good to go, with one in the box. It was like seeing a life preserver drift out of reach while he drowned.

Mike put the shotgun on the floor so that it rested between his legs. Ben looked at it. He had a 20-gauge Ithaca shotgun at home and had once killed a mallard.

Ben stared hard at Mike. 'I know how to shoot.'

Mike said, 'So do I.'

PIKE WAS WAITING for me at one of those anonymous office buildings that were clustered just south of Los Angeles Airport. When I got out of my car, he studied me in that motionless way he has.

'I said, 'What?'

'They have a bathroom in here.'

He brought me into the lobby. I went into the men's room, turned on the hot water and let it run until steam fogged the mirror. DeNice's blood was still speckled around my nails and in the creases of my skin. I washed my hands and arms under the running hot water. I cupped my hands and drank some cold water, then went back to the lobby.

We walked up three flights of stairs and into a waiting room that smelt of new carpet. Polished steel letters on the wall identified the company: THE RESNICK RESOURCE GROUP—*Problem Resolution and Consultation*.

A young woman smiled at us from a desk. 'May I help you?'

Pike said, 'Joe Pike for Mr Resnick. This is Elvis Cole.'

'Ah, yes. We're expecting you.'

A young man in a three-piece suit came out of a door behind the receptionist and held it for us. He was carrying a black leather bag. 'Afternoon, gentlemen. You can come with me.'

As soon as we were out of the waiting room, he opened the bag. 'I'm Dale Rudolph, Mr Resnick's assistant. The weapons go in here and will be returned when you leave.'

I said, 'I'm not armed.'

Pike put his .357, a .25, the sap, and the double-edge knife into the bag. Rudolph's expression never changed, as if men de-arming themselves were an everyday occurrence. Welcome to life in the Other World.

Rudolph passed a security wand over us, then put the wand into the bag. 'Okey-doke. Mr Resnick is expecting you.'

He led us into a bright airy office that could have belonged to someone who sold life insurance, except for the pictures of rocket batteries and armoured vehicles. A man in his late fifties with crew-cut grey hair came round his desk. He was probably a retired general with connections to the Pentagon; most of these guys were.

'John Resnick. That's all, Dale. Please wait outside.' He sat on the edge of his desk, but didn't offer us a seat. 'Which one's Pike?'

Pike said, 'Me.'

Resnick looked at him. 'Our mutual friend speaks well of you. The only reason I agreed to see you is because he vouched for you. He didn't mention anyone else.'

Pike said, 'If our mutual friend spoke well of me, then that should cover it. Either I'm good or I'm not.'

Resnick seemed to like that answer. 'Fair enough.' He knew what we wanted and got to the point. 'I used to work with a private military outfit in London. We used Fallon once, but I would never use him again. If you're trying to hire him, I would recommend against it.'

I said, 'We don't want to hire him; we want to find him. Fallon and at least one accomplice abducted my girlfriend's son.'

Resnick's left eye flickered with an unexpected tension. 'Mike Fallon is in Los Angeles?'

I told him again. 'Yes. He took my girlfriend's son.

'I can't believe that he's in Los Angeles or any place in this country. But if he is, and if he did what you said, you should go to the police.'

'We have. The police are trying to find him too.'

Pike said, 'But you know him. The thought is that you know how to reach him, or know someone who does.'

Resnick considered Pike, then slid off his desk and went to his seat. The sun was beginning to lower, and jets arced out of the airport heading west over the sea. Resnick watched them.

'That was years ago. Michael Fallon is under a war-crimes indictment for atrocities he committed in Sierra Leone. Last I heard, he was living in South America. If I knew how to find him, I would have told the Justice Department.' Resnick glanced at Pike. 'If you find him, will you kill him?'

He asked it as simply as if he wanted to know whether or not Pike enjoyed football.

Pike didn't answer, so I answered for him. 'If you want him dead, he's dead. All I care about is the boy. I'll do anything to get the boy.'

Resnick said, 'I believe in rules, Mr Cole. In a business like mine, rules are all we have to keep us from becoming animals.' He watched the jets wistfully. 'When I was in London, we sent Mike Fallon to Sierra Leone. He was supposed to guard the diamond mines under a contract we had with the government, but he went over to the rebels. They did things you can't imagine. You would think I'm making it up.'

I told him what I saw in the van at the edge of the Los Angeles River. I guess it sounded familiar.

Resnick shook his head. 'An animal. He can't work as a mercenary any more, not with the indictments. No one will hire him. You think he kidnapped this child for ransom?'

'I think so, yes. The boy's father has money.'

'The last I heard Fallon was in Rio, but I'm not even sure of that. There must be a lot of money at stake for him to come back.'

Pike said, 'He has an accomplice. A large black man with sores on his face.'

Resnick frowned. 'On his forehead and cheeks?'

'That's right.'

He leaned forward with his forearms on the desk. It was clear that he recognised the description. 'Those are tribal scars. One of the men Fallon used in Sierra, Mazi Ibo, had scars like that.' Resnick grew excited. 'Is a third man involved?'

'We don't know. It's possible.'

'All right, listen. Ibo was tight with another merc named Eric Schilling. A year ago, something like that, Schilling contacted us looking for security work. He's local, from LA, so Ibo might have contacted him. We might have kept something.' Resnick went to work on his computer, punching keys.

I said, 'Was he involved in Sierra Leone?'

'Probably, but he wasn't listed in the indictments. That's why he can still work. He was one of Fallon's people. That's why it stood out when he contacted us. I won't hire any of Fallon's people even if they weren't involved. Yeah, here it is.' Resnick copied an address, then handed it to me. 'He had a mail drop in San Gabriel under the name Gene Jeanie. They always use these fake names. I don't know if it's still good.'

'Do you have a phone for him?'

'They never give a phone. It's a way to stay insulated.' Resnick stood and came round his desk. 'Don't mistake these men for your basic criminals. Fallon was as good as it gets, and he trained these people. No one is better at killing.'

Resnick gripped my hand and held it. He looked into my eyes as if he was searching for something. 'Do you believe in God, Mr Cole?'

'When I'm scared.'

'I pray every night. I pray because I sent Fallon to Sierra Leone, so I've always felt that part of his sin must be mine. I hope you find him. I hope the boy is safe.'

CHAPTER FOURTEEN
time missing: 49 hours, 58 minutes

I called Starkey from the parking lot while Pike phoned the San Gabriel Information operator. Starkey answered on the sixth ring. I said, 'I have two more names. The man Mrs Luna saw with Fallon is named Mazi Ibo, M-A-Z-I, I-B-O. He worked for Fallon in Africa.'

'Hang on, Cole, slow down. How do you know that?'

'Pike found someone who recognised the description. You'll be able to get his picture from the FBI for a positive identification from Mrs Luna. Did Richard confess to the ransom?'

'He still denies it. They tore outta here an hour ago, but I think you're onto it, Cole.'

Pike lowered his phone and shook his head. Schilling wasn't listed.

'OK, here's the other name. I don't know whether he's involved, but he might be in contact.' I gave her Schilling's name. 'He keeps a mail drop in San Gabriel. We just checked with Information, but they don't show a listing. Can you get it?'

'Hang on. I gotta get to my radio.'

Pike shook his head. 'He won't be listed.'

'We don't know that. We might get lucky.'

Starkey came back on the line. 'They got squat for Eric Schilling. What's that mail drop address?'

I gestured for the address, but Pike slipped it into his pocket. He took my phone and turned it off.

I said, 'What are you doing?'

'They'll have a rental agreement, but she'll have to get a warrant. They'll have to find the owner, wait for him to come down, it'll take for ever. We can get it faster.'

I understood what Pike meant and agreed to it without hesitation. I was beyond hesitation. I had to find Ben.

Pike went to his Jeep and I went to my car, my head filled with the atrocities that Resnick had told us about. I realised that I didn't have my gun. Suddenly I wanted a weapon badly.

I said, 'Joe. My gun's at the house.'

Pike opened his passenger door and reached under the dash. He found a black shape and passed it to me. It was a Sig Sauer 9mm in a black clip holster. I thought it would make me feel safer, but it didn't.

We drove hard, following the I-10 freeway that stretched the width of Los Angeles.

Eric Schilling's mail drop was a private postal service called Stars & Stripes Mail Boxes in a strip mall in a part of San Gabriel where most of the people were of Chinese descent. The mall held three Chinese restaurants, a pharmacy, a pet store and the postal business. The parking lot was crowded, and Pike and I parked on a side street, then walked back to the mail drop. It was closed.

Stars & Stripes was a storefront business with a pet store on one side and a pharmacy on the other. An alarm strip ran along its glass front and door. Inside, mailboxes were set into the walls in the front part of the store, divided from the back office by a sales counter with a heavy steel curtain. Customers could let themselves into the front after hours to get their mail, but couldn't get into the office. The curtain looked strong enough to cage a rhino.

Schilling's box number was 205. We wouldn't know if the box still belonged to Schilling until we were inside.

Pike said, 'The rental agreements will be in the office. It might be easier to get in through the back.'

We walked round to the alley that ran behind the mall. Two men in white aprons sat on crates in the open door of one of the restaurants, peeling potatoes and carrots into a large metal bowl.

We found the service door for Stars & Stripes Mail Boxes. It was faced with steel and set with two industrial-strength deadbolt locks.

Pike said, 'Can you pick the locks?'

'Yeah, but not fast. These locks are made to resist picks, and we have those guys over there.'

Pike and I looked at the men, who were trying their best to ignore us. It would be faster to go through the front.

We walked back to the parking lot. A Chinese family with three little boys was standing outside the pet store, watching the puppies and kittens inside. Their mother smiled at me as we passed and I smiled back, everything so civil and peaceful, everything so fine.

Pike and I went to the glass door. We could wait for someone to come for their mail and walk in with them, but hanging around for a couple of hours was not an option.

I said, 'When we break the door, the alarm is going to ring. We have to pop the face off his mailbox, get past the curtain, then go through the office. All these people here in the parking lot will see us, and someone will call the police.'

'Are you trying to talk me out of this?'

The evening sky had turned a rich dark blue, but the streetlights had not yet flicked on. Families walked along the narrow walk. An old man hobbled out of the pharmacy. Here we were, about to break into some honest citizen's place of business. We would destroy property and scare the hell out of all these people who would end up witnesses against us if and when we were brought to trial.

'Yes, I guess I am. Let me do this part by myself. Why don't you wait in your car?'

Pike said, 'Anyone can wait in the car. That isn't me.'

'I guess not. We'll go in the front but leave through the back.'

We moved our cars and parked in the alley outside the service door, then walked around to the front again. Pike brought a crowbar. I brought a flathead screwdriver and my jack handle.

The family from the pet store was standing directly in front of Stars & Stripes Mail Boxes.

I said, 'You're too close to the door. Please step aside.'

The woman said, 'I'm sorry. What?'

I pointed at the door with my jack handle. 'There's going to be glass. You need to move.'

Pike stepped close to her husband like a towering shadow. 'Go.'

They suddenly understood what was going to happen and pulled their children away, speaking fast in Chinese.

I hit the door with my jack handle and shattered the glass. The alarm went off with a loud, steady buzz that echoed like an air-raid siren. The people in the parking lot looked towards the sound. I knocked the remaining glass out of the door frame and stepped in. Pike came in after me.

Pike went for the curtain and I went for the mailbox. The boxes were built sturdy, with doors set flush to a metal frame. I worked the screwdriver's blade under the door, then hammered it open with the jack handle. The box was packed with mail. None of it was addressed to Eric Schilling or Gene Jeanie; it was addressed to Eric Shear.

I shoved the letters into my pockets, then ran to help Pike.

The metal curtain was stretched between pipes anchored into the walls. We used the crowbar and the jack handle to prise the pipe from the wall. It bent at a crazy angle and we pushed it aside.

People were gathering in the parking lot, pointing at the shop. I didn't know how long Pike and I had been inside, but it couldn't have been long: forty seconds, a minute.

We shoved through into the office. Stacks of packages crowded the floor and a filing cabinet stood in the corner beside a cluttered desk.

Pike checked the service door as I went to the files. He shouted over the alarm that the way was clear. 'The deadbolts open with levers.'

I opened the filing drawers, expecting to see folders filled with paperwork, but they only held office supplies. Pike peeked out of the back door. Our time was running out.

'Faster,' said Pike

'I'm looking.' I scattered papers and envelopes from the desk, then opened the last drawer. All I found were ordering records for supplies; nothing referred to the boxes or the clients who rented them.

Pike tapped my back. 'We got a problem.'

An overweight man in a yellow shirt was surrounded by people in the parking lot, all of them pointing our way. The word SECURITY was stencilled on the shirt, and he wore a pistol in a black nylon holster clipped to his right hip. He crept forward with his hand on his gun. He looked scared.

Pike slipped past me with his pistol out.

I caught his arm. 'Joe, don't.'

'I'm not going to hurt him. Keep looking.'

The guard knelt behind a car and peered over the trunk. Pike moved into the door so that the guard saw him. That was enough. The guard threw himself to the ground. Discretion is the better part of valour when all you get is minimum wage.

Pike and I heard the sirens at the same time. We had run out of time. He glanced back at me. 'Did you find it?'

'No.'

Pike fell back past the counter to the service door. 'Keep looking. We have a few seconds.'

That's when I saw the brown cardboard box under the desk. It was just the right size and shape for storing file folders. I pulled it out and pushed off the top. It was filled with folders numbered from 1 to 600. I pulled the folder marked 205.

'We're out. *Go!*'

Pike jerked open the door. Outside, the air was cool and the alarm wasn't so loud. The two men with their potatoes shouted into their kitchen when they saw us, and others came out as we left. Eight blocks away, we turned our cars onto a service street and stopped to look through the file. It contained a rental agreement for Eric Shear that showed a phone number and his address.

ERIC SHEAR LIVED in a four-storey apartment building less than ten minutes from the mail drop. It was a large building, the kind that packed a hundred apartments around a central atrium and billed itself as 'secure luxury living'. Places like that are easy to enter.

We parked in a red zone across the street, then Pike got into my car. I dialled Schilling's number. An answering machine with a male voice picked up on the second ring.

I hung up and told Pike that it was a machine.

He said, 'Let's go see.'

Pike brought the crowbar. We walked along the side of the building until we found an outside stairwell enclosed in a cagelike door. The door required a key, but Pike wedged the crowbar into it and popped the lock. We climbed to the second floor. Eric Shear's apartment number was listed as 313.

It was early evening, just after dark. Cooking smells and music came from the apartments along with an occasional voice. Number 313 was at the end of the hall past a set of elevators. Two folded sheets of paper were wedged into Schilling's door a few inches above the knob.

Pike and I went to either side of the door. We listened. Schilling's apartment was silent. The wedged papers were notices reminding all tenants that rent was due on the first of the month and that the building's water would be turned off for two hours last Thursday.

Pike said, 'He hasn't been home in a while.'

I put my finger over the peephole, and knocked. No one answered.

I knocked again, then took out the gun. 'Open it.'

Pike wedged the crowbar between the door and the jamb, and the frame splintered with a loud crack. I shoved through the door with the gun up. A kitchen and dining area were across the living room. A hall opened to our left, showing three doorways. Pike followed me down the hall, gun first through each door.

'Joe?'

'Clear.'

We went back to the entry to shut the door, then turned on more lights. The living room had almost nothing in it, just a leather couch, a card table and an enormous television. It was more like a camp than a home. A small cordless phone sat on the counter that divided the kitchen from the living room, but there was no answering machine. It was the first thing I looked for, thinking we might find a message.

I said, 'His answering machine must be in the back.'

Pike moved back to the hall. 'Saw it when I cleared the bedroom. I'll take the bedroom, you check out here.'

Orangina bottles cluttered the kitchen counters. Dirty dishes were piled in the sink, and take-out food containers spilled out of a waste basket. I emptied the basket onto the floor and looked for receipts. The most recent date was six days ago. The orders were way too much for a man living alone and easily enough for three.

I said, 'They were here, Joe.'

He called back. 'I know. Come see this.'

I moved back to the bedroom. Pike was kneeling by a rumpled futon, all that passed for furniture in the room. A radio/alarm clock sat on the floor by the futon, along with a second cordless digital phone with a message machine built into its base.

'Did you hear something on his machine?'

'No messages. He has some mail here, but I called you for this.'

Pike turned towards a row of snapshots that had been pinned to the wall above the futon. They were pictures of dead people of various races. A grinning red-haired man posed with the bodies. At his side in two of the pictures was a tall black man with marks on his face.

Pike tapped a picture. 'Ibo. The red hair would be Schilling. These pictures aren't just from Sierra Leone, either. Look at the vics. This could be Central America. This one could be in Bosnia.'

One of the pictures showed the red-haired man holding a human arm as if it were a trophy. I felt sick.

'They lost their minds.'

Pike nodded. 'It's like Resnick said.'

'I don't see anyone who looks like Fallon.'

'Fallon would be too smart to let his picture be taken.'

I turned away. 'Let's see his mail.'

Pike had found a stack of mail addressed to Eric Shear, including his phone bills for the past two months. Almost all of his calls were to area codes around Los Angeles, but six calls stood out. Three weeks ago, Eric Schilling had phoned an international number in San Miguel, El Salvador, six times over a four-day period.

'I glanced at Pike. You think it's Fallon? Resnick thought South America.'

'Dial it and see.'

I dialled the El Salvador number. The connection made a faraway hiss as it bounced off the satellite. The number rang twice, then was answered by a recording: 'You know the drill. Talk to me.'

I felt the same cold prickle I had felt that first day on the slope, but now anger boiled around it like mist. I hung up. It was the same man who had called me the night Ben was stolen and whose voice was recorded on Lucy's tape.

'It has to be him. I recognise his voice.'

Pike's mouth twitched. 'Starkey's going to love this. She's going to bag a war criminal.'

I studied the pictures again. I had never met Schilling or Fallon— they had no reason to know anything about me. Thousands of children came from families with more money than Richard, but they had kidnapped Ben. They had tried to make it seem as if their motive was vengeance against me, but they were almost certainly holding up Richard for ransom money; yet he was denying it. All kidnappers tell their victims not to go to the police, and I could understand Richard was scared, which was perhaps why he was denying it. But the pieces of the rest of the puzzle did not fit.

I went into the bathroom. Magazines were stacked beside the toilet. The waste basket overflowed with wads of tissue and Q-tips, but several white pages jutted up through the trash. I upended the basket. A photocopy of my 201 Form fell to the floor.

I said, 'Joe. Schilling has my file.'

Pike stepped through the door behind me. I flipped through the files with a slow sense of numbness, then handed the pages to Joe.

'The only two people who had copies of this were Starkey and Myers. Myers had a judge in New Orleans get a copy of my file for Richard. No one else could have had it.'

The pieces of the puzzle came together like leaves settling to the bottom of a pool. The picture they built was hazy, but it began to take shape.

Pike stared at the pages. 'Myers had this?'

'Yeah. Myers and Starkey.'

Pike cocked his head. His face grew dark. 'How would Myers know them?'

'Myers handles security for Richard's company. Schilling called Resnick for security work; maybe Myers hired him. Schilling could have brought in the others.'

Pike glanced at the pages again, then shook his head, still trying to see it. 'But why would Myers give them your file?'

'Maybe it was Myers's idea to steal Ben.'

Pike said, 'Jesus.'

'Myers had a window into Richard's life. He knew that Lucy and Ben were out here, and he knew that Richard was worried about them. Richard probably did nothing but bitch about how much danger they were in because of me, so maybe Myers started thinking he could use Richard's paranoia to get some of Richard's money.'

'Set up a kidnapping, then control the play from inside.'

'Yeah.'

Pike shook his head. 'It's thin.'

'Why else would they get my file? Why target Ben as the victim and try to make me look like the reason it's happening?'

'You going to call Starkey?'

'What would I tell her and what could she do? Myers isn't going to admit it unless we have proof.'

We went through the entire apartment again. We searched every place we could think of to find something that would connect Schilling to Myers and still we had nothing.

Then I thought of another place we could look. 'We have to get inside Myers's office. Come on.'

Pike stared at me as if I had lost my mind. 'What's wrong with you? Myers's office is in New Orleans.'

'Lucy can do it. She can search his office from here.'

I explained as we ran to our cars.

LUCY STARED AT ME past the edge of the door as if she were hiding. Her face was masked in a darkness that went beyond the absence of light; as soon as I saw her I knew they had told her about DeNice.

'I know. Let me in, Luce. I need to talk to you. Joe's downstairs.'

I eased the door open and stepped in without waiting for her to ask. She was holding her phone. I doubt that she had put it down since last night. She seemed dazed, as if the weight of the nightmare had drained all her strength.

She walked to the couch. 'They decapitated one of Richard's detectives. They left Ben's shoe in the blood.'

'We're going to get him, Luce. We're going to find him. Did you speak with Lucas or Starkey?'

'They were here a little while ago. The two of them and a detective from downtown.'

'Tims.'

'They said it was going to be on the news, and they didn't want me to see it like that. They asked me about Fallon again, and two other men, an African and someone named Schilling. They had pictures.'

'Did they mention Richard? Did you speak with him this evening?'

'I've called him, but he hasn't returned my calls.' She frowned at me. 'Why would they mention Richard?'

'We think that Fallon might have contacted Richard to ask for ransom money. That's probably why Fallon did what he did to DeNice, to scare Richard into paying.'

She frowned deeper. 'Richard didn't say anything about that.'

'If Fallon scared him badly enough, he wouldn't. Lucy, listen, I think that Myers is involved. That's why they took Ben, and that's how they knew about me. Through Myers.'

I put the copy of my 201 in her hands. She looked at it without understanding.

'This is my military record. You can't get it from the army unless you have a court order. The army sent out two copies of this thing, one to Starkey because of this investigation, and one to a judge in New Orleans three months ago. That judge sent it to Myers.'

Lucy looked at the pages. 'Richard had you investigated.'

'Myers would have handled that. Myers also handles security at Richard's overseas facilities. Schilling was looking for security work in Central America.'

'Richard has holdings in El Salvador.' She glanced up again, and now she didn't seem so hazy. Her anger showed in the way she held her head. 'The judge in New Orleans, who was he?'

'Rulon Lester. Do you know him?'

She thought about it, trying to place the name, then shook her head. 'No, I don't think so.'

'I spoke with his assistant. He sent my file to Myers, so Myers had one of only two copies that the army released. Joe and I found this copy in an apartment in San Gabriel that belongs to Eric Schilling. He made at least six phone calls to a number in San Miguel, El Salvador, that belongs to Michael Fallon. It's Fallon on your tape, Lucy. I called the number. I recognised his voice.'

I opened Schilling's phone bills and pointed out the calls to El Salvador. She stared at the number, then dialled it into her phone. I watched her as it rang. Her face darkened as she listened to his voice, then she jabbed hard at the phone to end the call. She smashed the phone down onto the arm of the couch. I didn't stop her. I waited.

'The only way they could have got my 201 file is through Myers. Myers probably set up the entire thing. They nabbed Ben with me as the smoke screen because Richard would buy into that. Myers probably even talked him into coming out here to try to find Ben. That way, Myers could control how Richard reacted. He could feed Richard the ransom demand and encourage him to go along.'

Lucy stood. 'Richard's at the Beverly Hills Hotel. Let's go see him.'

'And tell him what? We have the file, but we can't prove Myers knows them. If we don't have something definite, he'll deny everything and then we're stuck. He'll know that we know, and then the only thing left for him is to get rid of the evidence.'

Get rid of Ben.

Lucy lowered herself onto the couch. 'So what can we do?'

'If Myers hired these people, Richard's company would have a record of it. We have Fallon's phone number and Schilling's. If Myers called either of them from a company phone, those records will exist.'

Lucy slumped back, thinking. She glanced at her watch. 'It's almost ten in Louisiana. Everyone from the office should be home.'

She went into her bedroom and returned with a battered leather address book. 'I had friends at Richard's company before we were divorced. I was close to some of these people.'

She settled back with her phone, pulled her legs up so that she was sitting cross-legged and dialled a number.

'Hello, Sondra? It's Lucy. Yeah, here in LA. How are you?'

Sondra Burkhardt had been Richard's comptroller for sixteen years and she oversaw the accounting department. She had played tennis with Lucy at LSU. Lucy had got her the job. Sondra had three children. The youngest was six, and Lucy was her godmother.

'Sondra, I need a favour that's going to sound strange and I don't have time to—' Lucy paused, listening, then nodded. 'Thanks, babe. I'm going to give you three names, and I need to know whether or not they were ever on the payroll. Can you do that from home?'

I interrupted. 'Central America. Any time in the past year.'

Lucy nodded. 'They would have been foreign hires, probably in Central America sometime in the past year. Myers would have been the one to hire them.'

Lucy gave her the names, then asked if we could get a list of all the calls that Myers had made to Schilling's phone number in Los Angeles and Fallon's number in San Miguel. After that, Lucy settled back with the phone to her ear. 'She's looking.'

'OK.'

She made a small smile, and I smiled back. The awkwardness between us had somehow vanished in the mutual effort of searching for Ben. But then her brow knotted. 'I'm sorry, Sondra, say that again.'

Lucy shook her head as if she didn't understand what she was hearing. Then I realised that she was resisting what she was hearing.

I said, 'What is it?'

'She found eleven calls to the San Miguel number. Myers only made four of the calls. Richard made the other seven.'

'That can't be right. It had to be Myers. Myers must have used his phone.'

Lucy shook her head. 'They weren't made from Richard's office. The company pays for the phones at his house, too. Richard called San Miguel from home.'

'Have her print out the call list and fax it to us.'

Lucy gave Sondra her fax number. Her voice was distant.

The list of calls printed out a few minutes later. We stood over the fax as if it were a crystal ball and we were waiting to see the future.

Lucy read the list, holding my hand so tightly that her nails cut into my skin. She saw that the calls were indeed from Richard's number. 'What did he do? Oh, my God, what did he do?'

I had been wrong about everything. Richard had been so frightened that something bad would happen to Ben and Lucy because of me that he had decided to make it happen himself. He arranged for the fake kidnapping of his own son to drive us apart. Through Myers, he had hired people willing to do anything. He probably hadn't known who they were or what they had done until Starkey and I pulled the Interpol file. But Fallon had double-crossed him, and now Richard was caught.

'Oh my God, what did he do?'

Richard had lost Ben.

I took Lucy's hand. 'Now it's time to see Richard. Let's get Joe.'

THE BEVERLY HILLS HOTEL was a great pink beast that sprawled along Sunset Boulevard. Movie stars and oil sheiks felt comfortable staying behind the manicured walls; I guess Richard felt comfortable there, too. He was in a bungalow that cost $2,000 a night.

Lucy was the only one of the three of us who looked like she belonged. We crossed the lobby, then followed a winding path through verdant grounds that smelt of night-blooming jasmine.

Richard was home; Myers had answered his phone. That meant Fallon still had Ben, and Richard was still trying to buy him back.

The private bungalows that dotted the path were separated from each other, hidden by landscaping. It was like walking through a tailored jungle.

Ahead of us, we saw Fontenot standing outside a door at a fork in the path. Myers came out, spoke to him, then went up the path. Fontenot went into the bungalow that Myers had left.

'Is that Richard's?' I asked Lucy.

'No, Myers has that one. It's not a full bungalow; it's just a room. Richard has the bungalow across.'

'Wait here. I want to get Fontenot first. He might know something that will help us, and it'll be faster if you wait.'

Pike said, 'Fontenot will help. I promise.'

Lucy nodded. She knew that speed was everything.

Joe and I didn't bother with knocking. We hit the door so hard that the doorknob caught in the wall.

Fontenot was watching television with his feet up on the bed. A pistol sat on the floor beside him, but he hesitated, seeing our guns.

I said, 'Did you see DeNice? Did you see what they did to him?'

Fontenot was shaky getting to his feet. He had the twitchy eyes of someone who had been nervous for most of the day.

'What the fuck are you doing?'

I kicked his gun under the bed. 'Is Richard in his room?'

'I don't know where Richard is. Get out of here.'

Pike snapped his pistol across Fontenot's face and Fontenot fell sideways onto the bed. Pike cocked his pistol and pressed the muzzle into Fontenot's ear.

I said, 'We know. We know that Richard hired them, that this was all about destroying me, but that it turned upside-down. Is Richard in contact with these people? Has he made a deal for Ben?'

Fontenot closed his eyes.

'Is Ben still alive?'

Fontenot tried to say something, but his lower lip trembled. He closed his eyes tighter, like he was trying not to see. 'They cut off Debbie's head.'

I shouted into his face. *'IS BEN STILL ALIVE?'*

'Richard doesn't have enough money. They want it in cash, and they only gave him a few hours. We got some of it, but not all. That's why DeNice went to see them, and look what they did.'

Lucy came to the door. 'How much do they want for my son?'

'Five million. Richard couldn't put it together. He's been trying all day, but that was all he could get.' Fontenot waved at the closet, and cried even more.

A large black duffle was in the closet. It was heavy with packs of $100 bills, but it wasn't heavy enough.

WHEN MYERS OPENED the door to the bungalow opposite, I pushed Fontenot hard into the room.

Richard was haggard, his hair sticking out as if he'd been running his hands over his head all afternoon. Even Myers looked beaten.

Richard was holding his cellphone with both hands, like a Bible. 'Get out. Get them out of here, Lee.'

Pike heaved the bag into the middle of the floor. 'Look familiar?'

A smile flickered at the corner of Myers's mouth. He was probably relieved. 'I'd say they know what we're doing.'

Lucy came in behind Joe.

Richard's eyes widened and he raked his hand across his head. 'They don't know anything. Keep your mouth shut.'

Myers stared at him. 'Richard, stop. It's time to stop before this mess gets worse. The wheels are coming off, Richard. Wake up.'

Lucy was as rigid as a statue, her face impassive. 'You self-absorbed sonofabitch. Where is my son?'

Richard's eyes fluttered like two trapped moths. His mouth hung loose, as if he had aged a thousand years since yesterday. I didn't feel angry any more. I felt empty and worried for Ben.

I turned to Myers. 'What's Fallon doing? How're they playing this?'

Richard screamed. *'Shut up!'*

Myers moved faster than I thought he could; he grabbed Richard by the shirt and bent him backwards towards the bed. 'Get your head around it, Richard—*they know*. Now let's get back to business. Your son is waiting.' He shoved Richard away then turned back to the black duffle bag. 'That's three point two million dollars, but they want five million. We tried to tell them, but, you know, no one ever believes you with something like this. DeNice was their answer.'

Myers looked at me. 'Fallon's been jamming us all day, pushing it forward to keep us off balance. All of it started this morning.'

'Where are you with it?'

'He gave us today to get the money. Just the one day. Richard has to call them by nine o'clock. That's in eight minutes. Fallon told us not to bother calling after that. You know what he'll do after that.'

Pike said, 'You should have told the police.'

Myers glanced at Richard, then shrugged.

Richard said, 'They were supposed to take him away for a few days. He was supposed to watch videos and eat pizza until we came out; that's all it was supposed to be.'

Lucy took a step towards him. 'You had your son *kidnapped!*'

'I'm sorry. It wasn't supposed to be this way. I'm sorry.'

Lucy slapped him, then hit him with her fist over and over again. He didn't try to protect himself.

'Luce.' I caught her arms gently and eased her away.

Richard blubbered like a baby and slumped onto the edge of the bed. 'I can't get the money in time. It wasn't supposed to be like this.'

Myers said, 'We have four minutes.'

Fontenot shook his head. 'He wants the money this bad, he'll wait.'

Pike spoke softly. 'No, he won't. He's pressing because that's how he controls the situation. He won't give you time to think. He wants the money, but he also wants to survive the mission, and that means he will not let you stall. He planned the operation, and now he's working the plan. He'll do what he said he would do.'

Fontenot said, 'Jesus Christ, you make it sound like he's in a war.'

Richard rubbed his face. His fingers went through his hair. He looked calmer now, but still nervous. 'I don't know what to do.'

I looked at Myers. 'What's supposed to happen?'

'He tells us where to meet, then we trade the money for Ben.'

I looked at the bag. It was big because three million took up a lot of room, but five million would take up a lot more.

I went over to the bed and sat beside Richard. We stared at each other for a moment, and then he glanced away.

I said, 'Do you love him?'

Richard nodded.

'I love him, too.'

Richard blinked. You can't know how much I hate you.

'I know, but now we're going to save Ben together.'

'Haven't you been listening? I already offered them the three million, but they wouldn't take it. They said it's five or nothing, and I don't have that much. I can't get it. I don't know what to tell them.'

I put the cellphone back into his hands. 'Do what you do best, Richard. Lie. Tell them that you have all five million and that you're ready to trade for your son.'

Richard stared at the phone, and then he dialled.

CHAPTER FIFTEEN

time missing: 52 hours, 38 minutes

Richard made the call at exactly nine o'clock and he sounded convincing. Myers and I listened as he repeated Fallon's instructions. He was to bring the money to the west end of Santa Monica Airport. He was to bring it alone.

Myers and I both shook our heads.

Richard's voice shook when he answered. 'No way. Myers is coming. It'll be just us, and you'd better have Ben. Yes, I'll call you when I see you. Fifteen minutes.'

Richard put down his phone and looked at me. 'What do we do?'

'Exactly what he told you to do. We'll do the rest.'

Pike and I left at a run. We knew that Fallon was probably already at the airport, set up so he could see Richard approach and watch for the police. We had to get to the airport before Richard, and stay out of sight. We had to come at Fallon in a way he didn't expect.

I drove fast, and so did Pike, the two of us rat-racing across the city.

Sunset Boulevard glowed with violet light that shimmered on the hood of my Corvette. The cars we raced past were frozen in place, their taillights stretched in front of us like liquid red streaks. We roared across Westwood, into Brentwood, and then towards the sea.

Santa Monica Airport was a nice little place. You could get a good hamburger there and sit on benches across from the tower to watch the airplanes take off and land. Ben and I had done that more than once.

Old hangars lined the south side of the airfield, many of them empty; I guess they were cheaper to abandon than repair.

I called Myers as we got close. 'We're almost there. Where are you?'

'We just left the hotel. I'd say twelve or fifteen minutes.'

'You're driving?'

'Yeah. Richard's in the back.'

'When you reach the airport, slow down so that Pike and I have enough time.'

'We can't be too late, Cole.'

'They'll see your limo turn into the airport. They'll know you're here. That's what matters. They know you're from out of town, so just drive like you're confused.'

'Shit, man, I'm doing that now.'

I had to smile, even then.

I leaned on the horn, slowing for red lights but never once stopping. All four tyres smoked as I turned towards the sea.

I picked up the phone. 'Myers?'

'I'm here.'

'Two minutes.'

We blew west two blocks north of the airport. The tower stood silently in the distance, asleep for the night.

Pike stopped at the embankment by the end of the runway, but I kept going. Office buildings gave way to residential streets. I left my car a block away and ran on foot to the dark hangars that lined the south side of the field like overgrown shadows.

Fallon would probably have a man on the roof and maybe another on the little service road that Richard would be using. A few cars were parked along the road, but I couldn't see if anyone was in them.

I edged past the last hangar, then peeked round the corner. A few small airplanes were on the ramp with a row of fuel trucks parked by them. There was no way to get to them without being seen.

I whispered into the phone. 'Myers?'

'We're at the east side. Do you see them?'

'Not yet. Go slow. I'm moving.'

A trailer set up as a temporary office jutted out between the hangars. I slipped out to its end for a better view. I scanned the roof lines, then the shadows along the base of the hangars, and then the trucks. Nothing moved. I looked for shadows and shapes that were out of place, but everything seemed normal. No other cars were present. The hangar doors were closed. Fallon was probably waiting nearby if he was waiting anywhere at all.

I whispered into the phone again. 'I don't see anything, Myers.'

'OK, I'm at the place where he said to turn.'

Light swept between two hangars, and then the limousine emerged and turned towards me. They were fifty yards away. Maybe sixty.

The limo stopped.

I said, 'I'm right in front of you.'

'Copy. We're getting out. I'm putting in my earpiece so I can hear you. You see something, you tell me, goddammit.'

The passenger door opened and Myers stepped out.

I checked the roof line and service road again, looking for the tell-tale bump of a human head, but saw nothing. I watched the shadows at the base of the ramp, and still saw nothing.

The third fuel truck from the end of the row flicked its lights.

I said, 'Myers.'

His voice came back low. 'I got it. Richard's calling the number.'

I strained hard to see inside the truck but it was too far away. I trained my gun on the truck's grill. I would put down the phone as soon as I saw Ben. My aim was better with both hands.

I said, 'Tell him to get out with Ben. Make him show Ben.'

Pike would have moved up on the far side. He would be closer than me and have a better position. He was a better shot.

Myers's soft voice came through again. 'Richard's getting out to show the money. He wants to see the bags.'

'Don't do that, Myers. Make him show Ben.'

'Richard's scared.'

'Myers, make him show Ben. I don't see Ben.'

'Ben's on the phone.'

'That's not good enough. You have to see him.'

'Keep your eyes on that truck. Richard's flashing the money.'

The limo's back door opened. Myers helped Richard out with two bags, and then they looked at the truck. Three million dollars is heavy, and five had to look still heavier.

The truck lights flicked again. All of us stared at it.

Twenty feet behind Richard and Myers, a shadow moved between the oil drums that were stacked at the mouth of the hangar. I caught the movement as Myers turned. Schilling and Mazi surged out of the shadows with their pistols up and ready.

I yelled, '*Myers!*'

Their hands exploded like tiny suns, flashbulbing their faces with red light. Myers went down. They kept shooting him until they reached the money, and then they fired at Richard. He fell backwards into the car.

I fired two fast shots, then turned for the truck. I expected it to rumble to life or shots to come from the darkness, but none of that happened. I sprinted as hard as I could, shouting Ben's name.

Behind me, Schilling and Mazi heaved the money into the limo and got in with it.

Pike ran up onto the ramp from the far side and fired as the limo squealed away. All of us had thought that they would leave in their own vehicle, but the limo was their planned getaway.

I ran hard all the way to the truck, but I knew that it was empty and always had been. Fallon had rigged the lights with a remote. He was someplace else, and Ben was still with him.

I spun back round, but the limo was gone.

PIKE THOUGHT: These people are so damned good they're beating us.

Schilling and Ibo stepped out from between the oil drums as if they had come through an invisible door. Pike had studied those drums, but seen nothing. It happened so quickly that he was nothing more than a witness to the execution.

Pike ran forward, trying to get into range, as Cole shouted. Pike and Cole fired at almost the same instant, but Pike knew they were too late; the limo's left headlight shattered and a bullet careened off its hood. The limo ripped away as Cole raced towards the truck.

Pike searched for movement; someone had controlled the truck's lights, and that would be Fallon. Now that Schilling and Ibo had the money, Fallon would also run, and might give himself away.

Then a shot boomed. Not a handgun but something heavy. Light flashed in one of the parked cars, followed by a second boom.

Pike saw shadows in the car. A man and a boy.

Pike shouted at Cole as the car pulled away, then ran hard for his Jeep, his shoulder sending sharp lightning through his arm as he ran.

Pike thought, I'm scared.

MIKE WASN'T LIKE Eric or Mazi. Mike didn't bullshit or play the radio. He spoke only to give commands. That was it.

They turned into a parking lot at the airport, then sat with the engine running. After a while, Mike lifted the binoculars to watch something across the field. Ben couldn't tell what was happening.

The shotgun was resting with the muzzle on the floor and the stock leaning against Mike's knee. The safety was off. Ben thought, I'll bet he's got one in the box and good to go just like Eric.

Mike scared him. If it had been Eric sitting here, Ben thought he would go for the gun. All he had to do was grab the trigger and the gun would go off. But Mike reminded him of a sleeping cobra. You might think it was sleeping but you never knew.

Mike took what looked like a small walkie-talkie from the dashboard. He keyed the walkie-talkie, and lights flickered across the runway. Mike spoke on his phone, and then put it to Ben's ear.

'It's your dad. Say something.'

Ben grabbed the phone. 'Daddy?'

His father sobbed, and just like that Ben cried like a baby, gushing tears and hiccuping. 'I wanna go home.'

Mike took back the phone, then peered through the binoculars again. He keyed the walkie-talkie once more, and now the far lights flashed and stayed on. Overlapping erratic pops came from the far side of the airport and Mike straightened, focused so completely on whatever was happening that Ben thought: *Now!*

He lunged across the seat. His fingers wrapped round the trigger guard just as Mike grabbed his arm. The shotgun went off like a bomb. Ben jerked the trigger again and the shotgun thundered, blowing a second hole in the floor.

Mike pulled Ben's hand off the gun as easy as tearing paper, and shoved Ben back into his seat. Ben threw his arms over his head, certain that Mike would beat him, but Mike put the shotgun back in its place, and started manoeuvring out of the parking lot.

Once they were going, Mike glanced over at him. 'You're a tough little bastard.'

Ben thought, Too bad I missed.

FALLON'S CAR SPED towards the exit. He would have to drive past a soccer field, then between the office buildings, before he came out onto Ocean Boulevard. Once he reached Ocean, he would be gone.

I punched Pike's number on speed dial. 'C'mon, Joe—answer.'

Fallon's car picked up speed. He would be on his way to meet Schilling and Ibo. The limo was big and obvious, and now it was missing a headlight. They would abandon it soon.

Pike suddenly answered. 'I'm moving.'

'Eastbound at the end of the soccer field, white two-door coupé. He'll come out on Ocean. I lost him.'

I ran for my car as hard as I could, phone in one hand, gun in the other, past the hangars and the houses. Pike would be racing north towards Ocean Boulevard. I got in the car and jammed away from the kerb so hard that the tachometer needle was swallowed in red.

'Joe? *Where is he?*'

'Stop screaming. He's eastbound on Ocean, wait, turning south on Centinela. I have him. Six cars ahead.'

Centinela was behind me. I spun the car, smoking the tyres out of a one-eighty. Horns all around me blew, but they sounded far away.

I kept screaming. 'Myers is dead. They shot Richard, too, and he fell back into the limo. I don't know whether they killed him or not.'

'Just take it easy. Fallon doesn't know we're still in the game.'

Fallon drove with a low profile so he wouldn't get stopped by a cop, but all I cared about was catching him. I hit eighty on the side streets, turned parallel to Centinela, then jammed it to a hundred.

Pike called out the cross streets they were passing. I caught up to them one street at a time, and then I pulled ahead. I turned towards Centinela with all four tyres sliding and my engine clattered.

I was close to Centinela and getting closer, three blocks away and then two. I snapped off my lights and jerked to the kerb just as Fallon's car rolled through the intersection and turned towards the freeway. Ben sat in the passenger seat. He stared out of the window.

'I'm on him, Joe. I see him.'

Pike said, 'Fall in behind after I make the turn.'

Fallon wouldn't go far. They would change cars and then get rid of Ben and Richard. No kidnapping ends any other way.

Pike said, 'He's slowing.'

Fallon's car slipped under the freeway, then turned.

Pike pulled to the kerb. I did the same. After a bit, Pike's Jeep crept forward and turned past a row of small houses. He eased into a parking lot and got out. I followed.

Pike nodded towards a house across the street with a FOR SALE sign in its front yard. 'That one.'

The limo was mostly hidden behind the house and the white car was as far up the drive as it could go. A dark blue sedan was parked in front, probably their escape vehicle. Lights moved in the house.

I started across the street, but Pike stopped me. 'You have a plan or you just going to kick down the door?'

'You know what's going to happen. We don't have any time.'

Pike grabbed the back of my neck and pulled me eye to eye. 'Don't die on me.'

'Ben's inside.'

'They were right in front of us at the airport, and we didn't see them. They beat us. You know what happens if they beat us now.'

I took a deep breath. Pike was right. Pike was almost always right. Shadows moved across the windows.

I said, 'Check the windows on the far side. I'll go down the drive. We'll meet at the back. They probably entered the house through the back door. They're in a hurry, so maybe they left it unlocked.'

Pike said, 'Just keep it tight. Maybe we can get shots through the windows, but if we have to go in, we go in together.'

We split apart as we crossed the street. Pike went to the far side of the house as I moved down the drive. The first two windows showed a dark living room, but the other two were brightly lit. I moved away from the house so the glow wouldn't illuminate me, and looked in the windows from the dark shadow of a bush in the neighbour's yard. Mazi Ibo and Eric Schilling were in the kitchen. Ibo walked into another part of the house, but Schilling came out of the back door. He had two large duffle bags slung over his shoulders.

An old saying is that no battle plan survives first contact with the enemy.

Schilling stopped by the limo, letting his eyes adjust to the dark. He was less than twenty feet away. I didn't move. I held myself absolutely still. My heart hammered but I didn't let myself breathe.

Schilling stepped past the white car into the driveway and went towards the blue sedan. I moved softly at first but picked up speed. He heard me when he was halfway down the drive. He turned fast, but it was too late by then. I hit him hard between the eyes with my pistol, then grabbed him and hit him twice more.

I eased Schilling down, found his gun and hurried to the back door. It was open and the kitchen was empty. Nothing moved in the house. Ibo and Fallon might come back at any moment, but the stillness frightened me far more than that. Maybe they were already tending to business. All kidnappings end the same way for the victim.

I should have waited for Pike, but I stepped into the kitchen and moved towards the hall. My head was buzzing. Maybe that was why I didn't hear Fallon behind me until it was way too late.

MIKE TURNED into a narrow drive alongside a small dark house.

Ben said, 'Where are we?'

'End of the line.'

Mike pulled him across the seat and into the house. Eric was waiting for them in a dingy pink kitchen. Two green duffle bags were heaped on the floor.

'We got a problem back here,' Eric said.

They followed him out of the kitchen and into a small bedroom. Ben saw Mazi shoving money into two more green duffles, but then he saw his father. Richard was sprawled on the floor against the wall, holding his stomach, with blood all over his trousers and arm.

Ben shouted, '*Daddy!*' and ran to his father, hugged him and started crying. None of them stopped him.

'Hey, pal. Hey.' His dad stroked the side of his face and started crying, too. 'I'm so sorry, bud. I am so sorry. This is all my fault.'

His daddy's eyes were so sad that Ben sobbed even louder.

His father said, 'I love you so much. You know that, don't you?'

Ben's words choked in his chest.

Then Mike squatted next to them and examined Richard. 'Let me see. Looks like you got one in the liver.'

Eric came over. 'He fell back into the car. What was I going to do? We had to get out of there.'

Mike stood. 'Let's keep the ball rolling. Get the money repacked and put it in the car. They're OK right now. We'll take care of it before we leave.'

'Someone else was at the airport.'

'Forget it. That was Cole. He's still back there, beating off.'

Mike and Eric left Mazi packing the money and went into another part of the house.

Ben snuggled close to his father and whispered. 'Elvis will save us.'

His dad pushed himself up to sit a little straighter, wincing with the pain. Mazi glanced over, then went back to the money.

Richard stared at the blood on his hand. 'This is my fault. Everything that's happened is my fault. I'm the stupidest man in the world.'

Ben didn't understand. He didn't know why his father was saying these things, but hearing them scared him, and he cried even more. 'No, you're not. You're not stupid.'

His father touched his head. 'You're never going to understand and neither is anyone else, but I want you to remember that I loved you.'

'Don't die!'

'I'm not. And neither are you.'

His father stroked Ben's head, then pulled his face close and kissed him on the cheek. He whispered in Ben's ear. 'I love you, boy. Now you run. Run, and don't stop.'

The sadness in his father's voice terrified him. Ben hugged him and held on tight. His father kissed him again just as something heavy thumped in another room. Mazi jerked erect with his hands still filled with money, and then Mike pushed Elvis Cole through the door. Elvis fell to one knee, and his eyes fluttered vaguely. His head was bleeding. Mike pressed the shotgun into his neck.

Mike looked at Mazi. 'Put him in the bathtub and use your knife. The shotgun's too noisy. Then take care of them.'

A long slim knife appeared in Mazi's hand.

Ben's dad said it again and this time his voice was strong. 'Run.'

Then Richard pushed himself up from the floor and charged towards Mazi with a fury that Ben had never seen in his dad. His father caught Ibo in the back and slammed him full-tilt into Elvis and Mike, even as Mike's shotgun erupted and thunder echoed through the house.

Ben ran.

PIKE CREPT ALONGSIDE the house as quietly as air. He reached an empty bedroom, dark except for an open doorway framed in light. He heard the low voices of men inside the house, but couldn't tell who was speaking or what they were saying.

Schilling appeared in the hall, carrying two duffles, moving towards the rear. Then Schilling was gone. Pike cocked the .357.

The next two windows glowed with light. Pike eased closer. Mazi was with Richard and Ben. Pike was surprised to find them still alive, but Fallon was probably keeping them to use as hostages until the very last moment. In a perfect world, Fallon, Schilling and Ibo would have been in the room together. Pike would have shot them through the window to end this mess. Now, if Pike shot Ibo, he would lose the advantage of surprise.

Pike knew that Cole was probably at the back of the house, but he decided to wait. Schilling and Fallon might step back into the room at any moment, and then Pike could finish it. He braced his gun against an acacia tree to steady his aim. He settled in to wait.

Then Fallon pushed Cole into the room, and Pike couldn't wait any longer. He ran to the back, searching for a way into the house.

THE BACK OF MY HEAD pulsed where Fallon hit me. I tried to stay on my feet, but the room tilted and I hit the vinyl floor hard.

A faraway voice said, 'Come on, asshole.'

The kitchen blurred, and when I looked up I wasn't in the kitchen any more. A dark tower swayed over me and two blurs huddled against the far wall. I tipped forward, but stopped myself with my hand as the world focused. I think I smiled, but maybe it only seemed that way.

'I found you.'

Ben was ten feet in front of me.

Behind me, Fallon tossed two pistols into the pile of money, then spoke to Ibo. 'He had Eric's gun. I've gotta go see what happened.'

Ibo stared at me. 'He keel Eric?'

'I don't know. Put him in the bathtub and use your knife. The shotgun's too noisy. Then take care of them.'

Ibo pulled out a long knife and stepped towards me, just as

Richard heaved up from the floor. Richard did not move fast or well, but he charged across the room with the commitment of a father desperate to save his child. The shotgun exploded over my head. Richard hit Ibo from behind as the first shot punched into his side. He drove Ibo into me and me into Fallon as the second blast wrecked his thigh. I reared up into the shotgun as Ibo spun towards Richard with the knife. The shotgun exploded into the ceiling as Ben ran for the door.

I threw an elbow, but Fallon snapped the shotgun down across my face. I hooked my arm over the barrel but Fallon hung on. We bounced off the wall, locked together. I butted him, and his nose shattered. He pulled hard on the shotgun, then suddenly let go, and I lost my balance. I fell backwards with the shotgun as Fallon grabbed Schilling's pistol from the money. All of it happened in milliseconds; maybe even faster. Ben screamed.

PIKE SWUNG ROUND the corner of the house with his gun in a two-hand combat grip, cocked and ready to fire. The back yard was clear. Pike slipped to the back door and glanced into the kitchen. He expected to see Schilling, but the room was empty. He stepped inside and moved towards the hall, gun up, though his shoulder burned and his grip on the pistol was not firm. He glanced at the back door to check for Schilling just as Fallon's shotgun went off twice— *BOOM BOOM*—so loud and heavy that the shots rattled the house.

Pike moved even faster, crossing the hall to enter the bedroom.

Fallon and Cole were twisted together in a tight embrace, then Cole tumbled backwards with the shotgun. Pike drew down on Fallon in that same moment, finger tightening to drop the hammer for a head shot even as Ibo screamed—'*I hahv dee boy.*' He held Ben as a shield, with a knife to Ben's throat.

Pike jerked the .357 around at Ibo, but the shot wasn't clean and his hand wasn't steady. Fallon saw Pike in that same heartbeat and brought up his own handgun, inhumanly fast, and Pike swung his .357 back onto Fallon, knowing that Fallon had him cold, but Fallon hesitated because Cole brought up the shotgun, screaming to pull Fallon's attention, and then all of them were caught in that instant between beats when the human heart is still.

THE GUNFIRE and screams jolted Schilling awake. His head cleared, but he felt drunk and woozy. Then he remembered what was happening. They were in the house with the money.

He crawled towards it.

THE THREE GUNS poised like snakes to strike. I covered Fallon, then swung back to Ibo. Fallon's gun jumped from Pike to me, then back to Pike, and Pike shifted between Fallon and Ibo. Ibo held Ben high to protect his head and chest. If anyone shot, everyone would shoot, and all of us would be consumed by gunfire.

Ibo shouted again, making himself small behind Ben's struggling body. '*I hahv dee boy!*'

Pike and Fallon were locked on each other, holding their pistols with two-hand grips, arms tight.

Fallon said, 'Look at the knife. Shoot me, and he'll bleed out the kid.'

'*I do eet! I keel heem!*'

I swung the shotgun to Fallon, then back to Ibo. Pike was on one wall, me on the other, Ibo between us. The little room was humid with sweat. I shouted at Ibo. 'Put him down and walk out!'

Fallon edged towards the money, and Pike moved closer to Ibo. Ben struggled, seemed to be reaching towards his pocket.

I swung the shotgun back towards Fallon. 'You and Ibo put down your weapons, then we'll put down ours.'

Fallon shifted his aim back to Pike. 'You first.'

Richard tried to pull his legs under him but he slid in his own blood. I didn't know how much longer he would last.

Ben screamed then, his scream wailing and strange. '*Daddy!*'

I edged closer to Ibo.

'*Stay bahk!*'

Ben struggled harder, and his hand slipped from his pocket. I saw what he held, and knew what he was planning to do.

Fallon shifted his aim from Pike to me. 'He'll do it. We'll both do it. Give us the goddamn money and we'll give you the kid!'

'You'd kill him anyway.'

They had us and we had them, but Ben was caught in the middle, his eyes white with fear.

I said, 'Ben, I'm taking you home. You hear me, buddy? I'm going to bring you home. Joe. You on Fallon?'

'Yo.'

I lowered the shotgun.

Fallon shifted his gun back to Joe, then came to me again. He didn't know what I was doing, and the not knowing scared him.

I placed the shotgun on the floor. I straightened, watching Mazi, then took one step towards him. Fallon shifted his gun again.

Fallon shouted, 'We'll kill him, Cole! We'll kill you, too!'

I moved closer to Ben.

Ibo screamed, *'I keel heem! I do eet.'*

'I know. You and Fallon would both do it. You're animals.'

My voice was quiet and conversational, like I was making an everyday observation. I stopped an arm's length from Ben. Fallon was behind me with the gun, so I couldn't see him, but Pike was behind me too. I smiled at Ben, telling him he would be fine.

I said, 'Any time you're ready, bud. Let's go home.' Giving him permission. Saying, Do the thing you're thinking and I will back you.

Ben brought the Silver Star up like a claw and raked the medal into Ibo's eyes. Ibo flinched, ducking his head, and that's when I moved. I jammed my fingers behind the blade and twisted the knife from Ben's throat as gunshots exploded behind me. The knife cut deep into my fingers, but I held tight and rolled Ibo's hand backwards over his wrist, turning the knife towards him. Ben tumbled free. Another shot rang out, then another. I didn't know what was happening across the room. I couldn't look.

PIKE DECIDED that if he got a clean shot on Ibo, he would take it, even though Fallon would kill him. But Ibo wasn't stupid, and kept Ben high like a shield with Ben's head protecting his own. Pike had no target. He shifted his aim back to Fallon. He watched Fallon's eyes flick back and forth as he weighed his own options. Fallon would be thinking that with Cole hurt he had a free shot to put down Pike, then he could still beat Cole.

Pike thought, *He's going to shoot first.*

Pike's gun wobbled. His heart pounded, and sweat leaked down the sides of his face. Fallon had his gun up, too, aimed at Pike as Pike was aimed at him, but Fallon's gun was rock steady.

Pike glanced at Elvis. He glanced at Ben. He braced himself for Fallon's bullet, then glanced again at Ibo, hoping for a shot, but Ibo still hid behind Ben. He glanced back at Fallon.

Pike thought, *I'll kill you before I die.*

Then Ibo grunted in a way that neither man expected. Pike glimpsed a sudden movement as Cole and Ibo grappled. Fallon glanced to see, and Pike had his chance. He squeezed the trigger just as Eric Schilling charged out of the hall. Schilling slammed into Pike's back, driving Pike into Fallon. The .357 boomed harmlessly past Fallon's ear. Fallon trapped Pike's gun arm, then whipped his pistol towards Pike's head. Pike slipped to the side, but Schilling hooked Pike's bad arm. More pain flashed in Pike's shoulder and made him gasp. He dropped to his knees to slip Schilling's grip, wrapped Schilling's legs with his bad arm, and lifted. His arm screamed again, but Schilling upended. In the same moment, Fallon cracked his pistol down hard on Pike's face, then pushed the gun into Pike's shoulder. Fallon was fast, but Pike was fast too. He trapped Fallon's wrist as the gun fired. Pike held on. He had Fallon's wrist, but his bad arm was weak.

Across the room, Cole and Ibo were locked in a death struggle, but Ben had gone to his father. Schilling scrambled for a gun that was lying in the money. Fallon kneed Pike, but Pike caught his leg and pushed him over. They crashed to the floor. Fallon's gun flew free with the impact. Two feet away, Schilling came up with the pistol and wheeled towards Pike. Pike rolled off Fallon, came up with his gun, and blew out the side of Schilling's head. Pike rolled back towards Fallon, but Fallon caught the pistol in both hands. Both of them had the gun, and the gun was between them, Fallon's two good arms against Pike's one. Sweat and blood ran from their faces as both men tried to turn the gun. The burning in Pike's arm grew as his shoulder slowly failed. Pike strained harder, but the gun slowly came towards his chest.

Pike went into the deepest part of himself, a world of quiet. It was the only place where he could truly be at peace with himself. Pike went to that place now and drew strength.

Pike stared into Fallon's animal eyes. Fallon sensed that something had changed. Fear played over his face.

The gun moved towards Fallon.

THE SCARS ON Ibo's face glowed violet as he tried to turn the knife. He was a large, strong man, but I pushed so hard that the room darkened around me. Ibo's arm broke with a crack. He moaned. More shots rang out behind me, but they seemed a part of someone else's world. The knife touched the hollow at the base of Ibo's throat. He hissed as I pushed. The knife slid deep. Ibo's eyes grew wider. His mouth opened and closed. I pushed until the knife wouldn't go further, then Ibo made a long sigh and his eyes lost focus.

I let go. He took forever to hit the floor. I turned, barely able to stand. Pike and Fallon were struggling on the floor. I pointed the gun at Fallon's head. 'That's it, you sonofabitch. It's over.'

Fallon studied the end of the shotgun, then stared at me. They had a pistol between them. They were fighting for it.

'Let go of it, Fallon. Let go.'

Fallon glanced at Pike, then nodded.

The pistol between them fired—*BOOM!*—and Fallon slumped back against the wall. Pike came up with the pistol, ready in case

Fallon made a move, but Fallon only blinked down at the hole in his chest. He seemed surprised to see it even though he had made it himself. He looked up at us. Then he was dead.

I said, 'Ben?'

I staggered sideways and fell to a knee. It hurt. My hand was bleeding badly. It hurt, too.

Ben was trying to make Richard stand up. Richard moaned, so I guessed he was still hanging on. Pike kept me from falling onto my face and pushed a handkerchief into my hand.

'Wrap your hand and see about Ben. I'll get an ambulance.'

I tried to stand again, but couldn't, so I crawled to Ben. I put my arms round him. 'I found you, Ben. I'm going to bring you home.'

Ben shuddered like he was freezing, and sobbed words that I did not understand. Pike called for an ambulance, then eased us aside. He tied off Richard's leg with his belt to stop the bleeding, then used Schilling's shirt as a compress on the belly wound. I held Ben tight through it all, and never once let go. 'I have you,' I said. 'I have you.'

The sirens came as Ben's tears soaked my chest.

BEN WANTED TO GO with his father to the hospital, but the paramedics would not allow it. More sirens were coming. That would be the police.

Pike said, 'I'll wait. You take Ben.'

Ben and I crossed the street and got into my car.

I said, 'Let's call your mom.'

When Lucy realised it was me, she said, 'Is Ben all right? Please God tell me he's all right.' Her voice shook.

'He's as right as he could be. It was bad, Luce. It was awful.'

Ben sat quietly while I told Lucy what happened. I was careful in what I said; I didn't know if Ben knew about Richard's involvement, and I didn't want him to hear it from me. If she wanted me to pretend that none of this happened, I would. If she wanted me to keep it from Ben, I would. If she wanted me to lie to the police and in court to cover for Ben's father, I would do that, too.

She said she would meet us at the hospital, then I passed the phone to Ben.

Ben didn't say anything as we drove to the hospital, but he held on to my arm. We reached the hospital first and sat on a bench in the ER waiting room while the doctors did their work. Before it was done, Richard would have been in surgery for eighteen hours.

I leaned towards Ben. He looked so small, so young.

I said, 'How're you doing?'

'I'm OK.'

'You saw some awful stuff today. You had some really bad things happen. It's OK to be scared. It's OK to talk about it.'

'I wasn't scared.'

'I was scared. I was really, really scared. I'm scared right now.'

Ben's face frowned. 'Maybe I was a little scared.'

We were looking for the soft-drink machine when Lucy came striding fast through the sliding doors.

Ben took off running. 'Mommy!'

Lucy crumbled into tears. She hugged Ben so tight that she might have been trying to crush him into her body. She covered him with kisses and smeared him with tears, but that was all right. Every boy wants that from his mother.

Lucy saw me. She cried harder, and then she opened her arms.

I said, 'I brought him home.'

'Yes. Yes, you did.'

I held them as hard as I could, but even that wasn't enough.

SIXTEEN DAYS LATER, Lucy came to my house to tell me goodbye. She and Ben had given up their apartment in Beverly Hills. Lucy had left her job. They were moving back to Baton Rouge, Louisiana. Ben was already there with his grandparents. I understood; really, I did. These things don't happen to normal people, and shouldn't.

We stood on the deck, side by side at the rail. We had spoken often these past sixteen days. We had talked over what she would do, and here we were, saying goodbye. She would be seeing me soon enough. Richard had been indicted.

The two of us didn't say very much that afternoon; most of it had already been said. We had been way too good to end it on bad feelings. I didn't want that.

I gave her my best smile. Mr Playful. Mr Brave. 'Luce, I understand. I think it's right for Ben.'

She nodded, but still looked awkward. Maybe it had to be awkward.

I said, 'I'm going to miss you. I'm going to miss Ben. I miss you guys already.'

Lucy blinked hard and stared at the canyon. 'God, I hate this part.'

'You're doing this for Ben and for you. I'm good with that.'

She came close to me. It was all I could do not to cry.

Lucy turned and ran into my house. After a time I heard the front door open and shut. Her car started, then pulled away.

MY PHONE RANG two days after Lucy left. It was Starkey.

She said, 'You gotta be the luckiest asshole I know.'

Joe Pike and I were painting my deck. After the deck, we were going to paint my house. I might even wash my car.

I said, 'No offence, but I'm expecting my lawyer to call. We have this little matter of felony burglary.'

Pike looked over from the end of the deck. His hands and arms were grey from sanding dried filler. The postal service that we destroyed was owned by a man named Fadhim Gerella. We had repaid Mr Gerella for the damage we had done, as well as additional money for lost business. Mr Gerella was happy with that, and had refused to press charges, though the San Gabriel District Attorney was being tough about it.

Starkey said, 'Your lawyer's going to call, all right, but I'm going to tell you first.'

'Tell me what?'

Pike glanced over.

'You're in the clear, Cole. You and Pike. The governments of Sierra Leone, Angola and El Salvador—three *governments*, Cole—interceded in your behalf. They'll probably give you a medal.'

I sat on the deck.

'I don't hear anything, Cole. You still with me?'

'Hang on.' I cupped the phone and told Pike. He never looked up from the sanding.

Starkey said, 'Does this call for a celebration or what? How about I buy you some sushi and eight or ten drinks?'

'You want to take us out?'

'Not Pike, moron. Just you.'

'Starkey, are you asking me out?'

'Don't be so full of yourself.'

I wiped the sweat and the dust from my eyes.

'Cole? Did you faint from the excitement?'

'Don't take this wrong, Starkey. I like it that you asked, but this isn't a good time for me.'

'I understand, Cole. Forget it. Listen, I'll call you another time.'

Starkey hung up. I put down my phone and stared at the canyon.

Pike said, 'Call her.'

I took the phone inside, and, after a while, I did.

ROBERT CRAIS

'Books are my Disneyland, my personal amusement park,' says American author Robert Crais, who clearly relishes the creative freedom that becoming a successful novelist has brought him. He started his career as a writer for television during 1980s—which was a much more restrictive environment. 'I wrote for so many television series during that time that I sometimes feel like the answer to a Trivial Pursuit question,' he says. '*Miami Vice, Hill Street Blues, Cagney and Lacey*—these were exciting series to work on and I learned an enormous amount. But I wanted the freedom to write about whatever interested me, in any way I wanted. For me writing is about freedom,' he says. 'And novels were always the dream.'

His first, *The Monkey's Raincoat*, was published in 1987 and introduced private eye Elvis Cole and his enigmatic partner Joe Pike. The pair have appeared in eight subsequent novels. Crais admits that while Elvis Cole, and to a lesser extent Joe Pike, share elements of his own personality, there are also differences. 'Norman Mailer says something interesting about this in his new book on writing, *The Spooky Art*. He says that if your characters are kept down to your own level, then you can't take on large themes. You need to write about people who are larger than yourself. That's what I do.

'*The Last Detective* started with a notion I had of Elvis Cole taking care of his girlfriend's son, Ben Chenier, and the fear and guilt he would feel if Ben disappeared. There is no more horrifying feeling than that of losing a child. I'm a father and it was something to which I could relate. I also wanted to explore a child's need for a family and how what we experience as children informs our lives as adults. In the novel, Elvis is searching for Ben, but he's also searching for himself. The theme of abandonment between Elvis and Ben seemed to resonate.'

Elvis Cole is clearly a character close to Robert Crais's heart and this is underlined by the fact that while he has sold film rights to his two stand-alone novels, *Demolition Angel* and *Hostage*, he has no intention of doing so for the Elvis Cole novels. 'Elvis and Joe aren't for sale,' he states firmly.

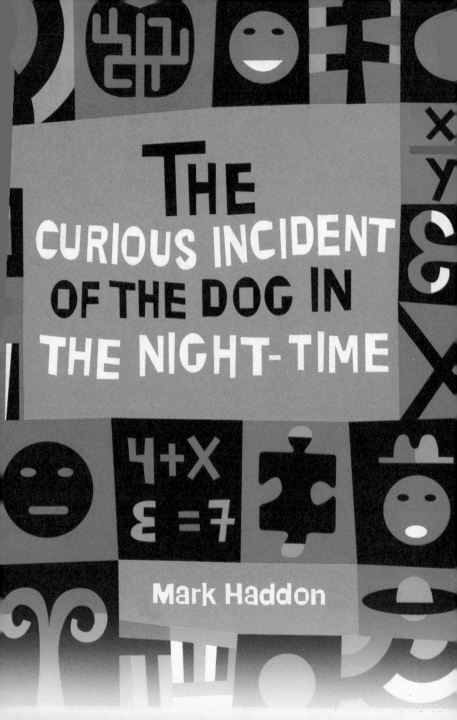

THE
CURIOUS INCIDENT
OF THE DOG IN
THE NIGHT-TIME

Mark Haddon

'Siobhan said that the book should begin with something to grab people's attention. That is why I started with the dog. I also started with the dog because it happened to me and I find it hard to imagine things which did not happen to me.'

Christopher Boone, 15

ONE

It was 7 minutes after midnight. The dog was lying on the grass in the middle of the lawn in front of Mrs Shears's house. Its eyes were closed. It looked as if it was running on its side, the way dogs run when they think they are chasing a cat in a dream. But the dog was not running or asleep. The dog was dead. There was a garden fork sticking out of the dog. I decided that the dog was probably killed with the fork because I could not see any other wounds in the dog and I do not think you would stick a garden fork into a dog after it had died for some other reason, like a road accident, for example. But I could not be certain about this.

I went through Mrs Shears's gate, closing it behind me. I walked onto her lawn and put my hand on the muzzle of the dog. It was still warm.

The dog was called Wellington. It belonged to Mrs Shears who was our friend. She lived on the opposite side of the road, two houses to the left.

Wellington was a poodle. Not one of the small poodles that have hairstyles, but a big poodle with curly black fur.

I stroked Wellington and wondered who had killed him, and why.

MY NAME IS Christopher John Francis Boone. I know all the countries of the world and their capital cities and every prime number up to 7,507. Eight years ago, when I first met Siobhan, she showed me this picture and I knew that it meant 'sad', which is what I felt when I found the dead dog.

Then she showed me this picture

and I knew that it meant 'happy', like when I'm reading about the Apollo space missions, or when I am still awake at three or four in the morning and I can walk up and down the street and pretend that I am the only person in the whole world.

Then she drew some other pictures

but I was unable to say what these meant.

I got Siobhan to draw lots of these faces and then write down next to them exactly what they meant. I kept the piece of paper in my pocket and took it out when I didn't understand what someone was saying. But it was very difficult to decide which of the diagrams was most like the face they were making because people's faces move very quickly.

When I told Siobhan that I was doing this, she got out a pencil and another piece of paper and said it probably made people feel very and then she laughed. So I tore the original piece of paper up and threw it away. And Siobhan apologised. And now if I don't know what someone is saying I ask them what they mean or I walk away.

I PULLED THE FORK out of the dog and lifted him into my arms and hugged him. I like dogs. You always know what a dog is thinking. It has four moods. Happy, sad, cross and concentrating. Also, dogs are faithful and they do not tell lies because they cannot talk.

I had been hugging the dog for 4 minutes when I heard screaming. I looked up and saw Mrs Shears running towards me from the patio. She was wearing pyjamas and a housecoat and she had no shoes on. She was shouting, 'What have you done to my dog?'

I do not like people shouting at me. It makes me scared that they are going to hit me or touch me and I do not know what is going to happen.

'Let go of the dog!' she shouted.

I put the dog down on the lawn and moved back 2 metres.

She bent down. I thought she was going to pick the dog up herself, but she didn't. Perhaps she noticed how much blood there was and didn't want to get dirty. Instead, she started screaming.

I put my hands over my ears and closed my eyes and rolled forward till I was hunched up with my forehead pressed onto the grass. The grass was wet and cold. It was nice.

TWO

This is a murder mystery novel.

Siobhan said that I should write something I would want to read myself. Mostly I read books about science and maths. I do not like proper novels. In proper novels people say things like, 'I am veined with iron, with silver and with streaks of common mud. I cannot contract into the firm fist which those clench who do not depend on stimulus.' (I found this book in the library when Mother took me into town once.) What does this mean? I do not know. Nor does Father. Nor do Siobhan or Mr Jeavons. I have asked them.

Siobhan has long blonde hair and wears glasses that are made of green plastic. And Mr Jeavons smells of soap and wears brown shoes that have approximately 60 tiny circular holes in each of them.

But I do like murder mystery novels. So I am writing a murder mystery novel.

In a murder mystery novel someone has to work out who the murderer is and then catch them. It is a puzzle. If it is a good puzzle you can sometimes work out the answer before the end of the book.

Siobhan said that the book should begin with something to grab people's attention. That is why I started with the dog. I also started with the dog because it happened to me and I find it hard to imagine things which did not happen to me.

Siobhan read the first page and said that it was different. She put this word into inverted commas by making the wiggly quotation sign with her first and second fingers. She said that it was usually people who were killed in murder mystery novels. I said that two dogs were killed in *The Hound of the Baskervilles*, the hound itself and James Mortimer's spaniel, but Siobhan said they weren't the victims of the murder, Sir Charles Baskerville was. She said that this was because readers cared more about people than dogs, so if a person was killed in the book readers would want to carry on reading.

I said that I wanted to write about something real and I did not know any people who had been killed, except Edward's father from school, Mr Paulson, and that was a gliding accident, not murder, and I didn't really know him. I also said that I cared about dogs because they were faithful and honest, and some dogs were cleverer and more interesting than some people.

THEN THE POLICE ARRIVED. I like the police. They have uniforms and numbers and you know what they are meant to be doing. There was a policewoman and a policeman. The policewoman had a hole in her tights on her left ankle and a red scratch in the middle of the hole. The policeman had a big leaf stuck to the bottom of his shoe.

The policewoman put her arms round Mrs Shears and led her back towards the house.

I lifted my head off the grass. The policeman squatted down beside me and said, 'Would you like to tell me what's going on here, young man?'

I sat up and said, 'The dog is dead.'

'I'd got that far,' he said.

I said, 'I think someone killed the dog.'

'How old are you?' he asked.

I replied, 'I am 15 years and 3 months and 2 days.'

'And what, precisely, were you doing in the garden?' he asked.

'I was holding the dog,' I replied.

'And why were you holding the dog?' he asked.

This was a difficult question. It was something I wanted to do. I like dogs. It made me sad to see that the dog was dead.

I wanted to answer the question properly, but the policeman did not give me enough time to work out the correct answer.

'Why were you holding the dog?' he asked again.

'I like dogs,' I said.

'Did you kill the dog?' he asked.

I said, 'I did not kill the dog.'

'Is this your fork?' he asked.

I said, 'No.'

'You seem very upset about this,' he said.

He was asking too many questions and he was asking them too quickly. They were stacking up in my head like loaves in the factory where Uncle Terry works. The factory is a bakery and he operates the slicing machines. And sometimes the slicer is not working fast enough but the bread keeps coming and there is a blockage. I sometimes think of my mind as a machine. It makes it easier to explain to other people what is going on inside it.

The policeman said, 'I am going to ask you once again . . .'

I rolled back onto the lawn and pressed my forehead to the ground again and made the noise that Father calls groaning. I make this noise when there is too much information coming into my head from the outside world. It is like when you are upset and you hold the radio against your ear and you tune it halfway between two stations so that all you get is white noise and then you turn the volume right up so that this is all you can hear and then you know you are safe because you cannot hear anything else.

The policeman took hold of my arm and lifted me onto my feet.

I didn't like him touching me like this.

And this is when I hit him.

The policeman looked at me for a while without speaking. Then he said, 'I am arresting you for assaulting a police officer.'

This made me feel a lot calmer because it is what policemen say on television and in films.

Then he said, 'I strongly advise you to get into the back of the police car because if you try any of that monkey business again, I will seriously lose my rag. Is that understood?'

I walked over to the police car, which was parked just outside the gate. He opened the back door and I got inside. He climbed into the driver's seat and made a call on his radio to the policewoman who was still inside the house. He said, 'The little bugger just had a pop at me, Kate. Can you hang on with Mrs S while I drop him off at the station? I'll get Tony to swing by and pick you up.'

And she said, 'Sure. I'll catch you later.'

We drove off. The police car smelt of hot plastic and aftershave and takeaway chips.

I watched the sky as we drove towards the town centre. It was a clear night and you could see the Milky Way. Some people think the Milky Way is a long line of stars, but it isn't. Our galaxy is a huge disc of stars millions of light years across and the solar system is somewhere near the outside edge of the disc.

And then I thought about how, for a long time, scientists were puzzled by the fact that the sky is dark at night, even though there are billions of stars in the universe and there must be stars in every direction you look, so that the sky should be full of starlight because there is very little in the way to stop the light reaching earth.

Then they worked out that the universe was expanding, that the stars were all rushing away from one another after the Big Bang, and the further the stars were away from us the faster they were moving, some of them nearly as fast as the speed of light, which was why their light never reached us.

I like this fact. It is something you can work out in your own mind just by looking at the sky above your head at night and thinking without having to ask anyone.

WHEN I GOT to the police station they made me take the laces out of my shoes and empty my pockets at the front desk in case I had anything in them that I could use to kill myself or escape or attack a policeman with.

The sergeant behind the desk had very hairy hands and he had bitten his nails so much that they had bled.

This is what I had in my pockets

1. A Swiss Army Knife with 13 attachments including a wire-stripper and a saw and a toothpick and tweezers.

2. A piece of string.

3. 3 pellets of rat food for Toby, my rat.

4. £1.47 (this was made up of a £1 coin, a 20p coin, two 10p coins, a 5p coin and a 2p coin).

5. A piece of a wooden puzzle which looked like this

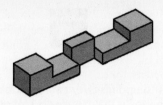

6. A red paperclip.
7. A key for the front door.

I was also wearing my watch and they wanted me to leave this at the desk as well but I said that I needed to keep my watch on because I needed to know exactly what time it was. And when they tried to take it off me I screamed, so they let me keep it on.

They asked me if I had any family. I said I did. They asked me who my family was. I said it was Father, but Mother was dead. And I said it was also Uncle Terry but he was in Sunderland and he was Father's brother, and it was my grandparents, too, but three of them were dead and Grandma Burton was in a home because she had senile dementia and thought that I was someone on television.

Then they asked me for Father's phone number.

I told them that he had two numbers, one for at home and one which was a mobile phone and I said both of them.

It was nice in the police cell. It was almost a perfect cube, 2 metres long by 2 metres wide by 2 metres high. It contained approximately 8 cubic metres of air. It had a small window with bars and, on the opposite side, a metal door with a long, thin hatch near the floor for sliding trays of food into the cell and a sliding hatch higher up so that policemen could look in and check that prisoners hadn't escaped or committed suicide. There was also a padded bench.

I wondered how I would escape if I was in a story. I decided that my best plan would be to wait for a really sunny day and then use my glasses to focus the sunlight on a piece of my clothing and start a fire. I would then make my escape when they saw the smoke and took me out of the cell. And if they didn't notice I would be able to wee on the clothes and put them out.

I wondered whether Mrs Shears had told the police that I had killed Wellington and whether, when the police found out that she had lied, she would go to prison. Because telling lies about people is called *Slander*.

THREE

I find people confusing. This is for two main reasons.

The first main reason is that people do a lot of talking without using any words. Siobhan says that if you raise one eyebrow it can mean lots of different things. It can mean 'I want to do sex with you' and it can also mean 'I think that what you just said was very stupid.'

Siobhan also says that if you close your mouth and breathe out loudly through your nose it can mean that you are relaxed, or that you are bored, or that you are angry, and it all depends on how much air comes out of your nose and how fast and what shape your mouth is when you do it and how you are sitting and what you said just before and hundreds of other things which are too complicated to work out in a few seconds.

The second main reason is that people often talk using metaphors. These are examples of metaphors

I laughed my socks off.
He was the apple of her eye.
They had a skeleton in the cupboard.
We had a real pig of a day.
The dog was stone dead.

The word metaphor means carrying something from one place to another, and it comes from the Greek words μετα (which means *from one place to another*) and φερειν (which means *to carry*) and it is when you describe something by using a word for something that it isn't. This means that the word metaphor is a metaphor.

I think it should be called a lie because a pig is not like a day and people do not have skeletons in their cupboards. And when I try to make a picture of the phrase in my head it just confuses me because imagining an apple in someone's eye doesn't have anything to do with liking someone a lot and it makes you forget what the person was talking about.

My name is a metaphor. It means *carrying Christ* and it comes from the Greek words χριστος (which means *Jesus Christ*) and φερειν and it was the name given to St Christopher because he carried Jesus Christ across a river. Mother used to say that it meant Christopher was a nice name because it was a story about being kind and helpful, but I do not want my name to mean a story about being kind and helpful. I want my name to mean me.

IT WAS 1.12AM when Father arrived at the police station. I did not see him until 1.28am but I knew he was there because I could hear him.

He was shouting, 'I want to see my son,' and 'Why the hell is he locked up?'

Then I heard a policeman telling him to calm down. Then I heard nothing for a long while.

At 1.28am a policeman opened the door of the cell and told me that there was someone to see me.

I stepped outside. Father was standing in the corridor. He held up his right hand and spread his fingers out in a fan. I held up my left hand and spread my fingers out in a fan and we made our fingers and thumbs touch each other. We do this because sometimes Father wants to give me a hug, but I do not like hugging people, so we do this instead, and it means that he loves me.

Then the policeman told us to follow him down the corridor to another room. In the room was a table and three chairs. He told us to sit down on the far side of the table and he sat down on the other side. There was a tape recorder on the table and I asked whether I was going to be interviewed and he was going to record the interview.

He said, 'I don't think there will be any need for that.'

He was an inspector. I could tell because he wasn't wearing a uniform. He also had a very hairy nose. It looked as if there were two very small mice hiding in his nostrils.

He said, 'I have spoken to your father and he says that you didn't mean to hit the policeman.'

I didn't say anything because this wasn't a question.

He said, 'Did you mean to hit the policeman?'

I said, 'Yes.'

He squeezed his face and said, 'But you didn't mean to hurt the policeman?'

I thought about this and said, 'No. I didn't mean to hurt the policeman. I just wanted him to stop touching me.'

Then he said, 'You know it is wrong to hit a policeman, don't you?'

I said, 'I do.'

He was quiet for a few seconds, then he asked, 'Did you kill the dog, Christopher?'

I said, 'I didn't kill the dog.'

He said, 'Do you know that it is wrong to lie to a policeman and that you can get into a very great deal of trouble if you do?'

I said, 'Yes.'

He said, 'So, do you know who killed the dog?'

I said, 'No.'

He said, 'Are you telling the truth?'

I said, 'Yes. I always tell the truth.'

And he said, 'Right. I am going to give you a caution.'

I asked, 'Is that going to be on a piece of paper like a certificate I can keep?'

He replied, 'No, a caution means that we are going to keep a record of what you did, that you hit a policeman but that it was an accident and that you didn't mean to hurt the policeman.'

I said, 'But it wasn't an accident.'

And Father said, 'Christopher, please.'

The policeman closed his mouth and breathed out loudly through his nose and said, 'If you get into any more trouble we will take out this record and see that you have been given a caution and we will take things much more seriously. Do you understand what I'm saying?'

I said that I understood.

Then he said that we could go and he stood up and opened the door and we walked out into the corridor and back to the front desk where I picked up my Swiss Army Knife and my piece of string and the 3 pellets of rat food for Toby and my £1.47 and the piece of the wooden puzzle and the paperclip and my front door key which were all in a little plastic bag and we went out to Father's car which was parked outside and we drove home.

FOUR

I do not tell lies. Mother used to say that this was because I was a good person. But it is not because I am a good person. It is because I can't tell lies.

Mother was a small person who smelt nice. And she sometimes wore a fleece with a zip down the front which was pink and it had a tiny label which said *Berghaus* on the left bosom.

A lie is when you say something happened which didn't happen. But there is only ever one thing which happened at a particular time and a particular place. And there are an infinite number of things which didn't happen at that time and that place. And if I think about something which didn't happen I start thinking about all the other things which didn't happen.

For example, this morning for breakfast I had Ready Brek and some hot raspberry milkshake. But if I say that I actually had Shreddies and a mug of tea, I start thinking about Coco Pops and lemonade and porridge and Dr Pepper and how I wasn't eating my breakfast in Egypt and there wasn't a rhinoceros in the room and Father wasn't wearing a diving suit and so on and even writing this makes me feel shaky and scared, like I do when I'm standing on the top of a very tall building and there are thousands of houses and cars and people below me and my head is so full of these things that I'm afraid that I'm going to forget to stand up straight and hang on to the rail and I'm going to fall over and be killed.

This is another reason why I don't like proper novels, because they are lies about things which didn't happen and they make me feel shaky and scared.

And this is why everything I have written here is true.

THERE WERE CLOUDS in the sky on the way home, so I couldn't see the Milky Way.

I said, 'I'm sorry,' because Father had had to come to the police station, which was a bad thing.

He said, 'It's OK.'

I said, 'I didn't kill the dog.'

And he said, 'I know.'

Then he said, 'Christopher, you have to stay out of trouble, OK?'

I said, 'I didn't know I was going to get into trouble. I like Wellington and I went to say hello to him, but I didn't know that someone had killed him.'

Father said, 'Just try and keep your nose out of other people's business.'

I thought for a little and I said, 'I am going to find out who killed Wellington.'

And Father said, 'Were you listening to what I was saying, Christopher?'

I said, 'Yes, I was listening to what you were saying, but when someone gets murdered you have to find out who did it so that they can be punished.'

And he said, 'It's a bloody dog, Christopher, a bloody dog.'

I replied, 'I think dogs are important, too.'

He said, 'Leave it.'

And I said, 'I wonder if the police will find out who killed him and punish the person.'

Then Father banged the steering wheel with his fist and the car weaved a little bit across the dotted line in the middle of the road and he shouted, 'I said leave it, for God's sake.'

I could tell he was angry because he was shouting, and I didn't want to make him angry so I didn't say anything else until we got home.

When we came in through the front door I went into the kitchen and got a carrot for Toby, my rat, and I went upstairs and I shut the door of my room and I let Toby out and gave him the carrot. Then I turned my computer on and played 76 games of **Minesweeper** and did the **Expert Version** in 102 seconds, which was only 3 seconds off my best time which was 99 seconds.

At 2.07am I decided that I wanted a drink of orange squash before I brushed my teeth and got into bed so I went downstairs to the kitchen. Father was sitting on the sofa watching snooker on the television and drinking whisky. There were tears coming out of his eyes.

I asked, 'Are you sad about Wellington?'

He looked at me and sucked air in through his nose. Then he said, 'Yes, Christopher, you could say that. You could very well say that.'

I decided to leave him alone because when I am sad I want to be left alone. So I just went into the kitchen and made my orange squash and took it back upstairs to my room.

MOTHER DIED 2 years ago.

I came home from school one day and no one answered the door, so I went and found the secret key that we keep under a flowerpot behind the kitchen door. I let myself into the house and carried on making the Airfix Sherman Tank model I was building.

An hour and a half later Father came home from work. He runs a business and he does heating maintenance and boiler repair with a man called Rhodri who is his employee. He knocked on the door of my room and opened it and asked whether I had seen Mother.

I said that I hadn't seen her and he went downstairs and started making some phone calls. I did not hear what he said.

Then he came up to my room and said he had to go out for a while and he wasn't sure how long he would be. He said that if I needed anything I should call him on his mobile phone.

He was away for 2½ hours. When he came back I went downstairs.

He was sitting in the kitchen staring out of the back window down the garden to the pond.

Father said, 'I'm afraid you won't be seeing your mother for a while.' He didn't look at me when he said this. He kept on looking through the window.

Usually people look at you when they're talking to you. I know that they're working out what I'm thinking, but I can't tell what they're thinking. It is like being in a room with a one-way mirror in a spy film. But this was nice, having Father speak to me but not look at me.

I said, 'Why not?'

He waited for a very long time, then he said, 'Your mother has had to go into hospital.'

'Can we visit her?' I asked, because I like hospitals. I like the uniforms and the machines.

Father said, 'No. She needs rest. She needs to be on her own. She has a problem . . . a problem with her heart.'

I said, 'We will need to take food to her,' because I knew that food in hospital was not very good. David from school, he went into hospital to have an operation and he hated the food, so his mother used to take meals in every day.

Father said, 'I'll take some in to her while you're at school and I'll give it to the doctors and they can give it to your mum, OK?'

I said, 'But you can't cook.'

Father put his hands over his face and said, 'Christopher. Look. I'll buy some ready-made stuff from Marks and Spencer's and take those in. She likes those.'

I said I would make her a Get Well card, because that is what you do for people when they are in hospital.

Father said he would take it in the next day.

FIVE

In the bus on the way to school next morning we passed 4 red cars in a row which meant that it was a **Good Day**, so I decided not to be sad about Wellington.

Mr Jeavons, the psychologist at the school, once asked me why 4 red cars in a row made it a **Good Day**, and 3 red cars in a row made it a **Quite Good Day**, and 5 red cars in a row made it a **Super Good**

Day, and why 4 yellow cars in a row made it a **Black Day**, which is a day when I don't speak to anyone and don't eat my lunch and *Take No Risks*. He said that I was clearly a very logical person, so he was surprised that I should think like this because it wasn't very logical.

I said that I liked things to be in a nice order. And one way of things being in a nice order was to be logical. Especially if those things were numbers or an argument. But there were other ways of putting things in a nice order. And that was why I had **Good Days** and **Black Days**. And I said that some people who worked in an office came out of their house in the morning and saw that the sun was shining and it made them feel happy, or they saw that it was raining and it made them feel sad, but the only difference was the weather and if they worked in an office the weather didn't have anything to do with whether they had a good day or a bad day.

I said that when Father got up in the morning he always put his trousers on before he put his socks on and it wasn't logical but he always did it that way, because he liked things in a nice order, too.

Mr Jeavons said that I was a very clever boy.

I said that I wasn't clever. I was just noticing how things were. That was just being observant. Being clever was when you looked at how things were and used the evidence to work out something new. Like the universe expanding, or who committed a murder.

Mr Jeavons asked me whether this made me feel safe, having things always in a nice order and I said it did.

Then he asked if I didn't like things changing. And I said I wouldn't mind things changing if I became an astronaut, for example, which is one of the biggest changes you can imagine, apart from becoming a girl or dying.

He asked whether I wanted to become an astronaut and I said I did. He said that it was very difficult to become an astronaut. I said that I knew. You had to become an officer in the air force and you had to take lots of orders and be prepared to kill other human beings, and I couldn't take orders. Also I didn't have 20/20 vision. But I said that you could still want something that is very unlikely to happen.

Terry, who is the older brother of Francis, who is at the school, said I would only ever get a job collecting supermarket trolleys or cleaning out donkeys at an animal sanctuary and they didn't let spazzers drive rockets that cost billions of pounds. When I told this to Father he said that Terry was jealous of my being cleverer than him. Which was a stupid thing to think because we weren't in a competition. But Terry is stupid, so *quod erat demonstrandum* which is

Latin for *Which is the thing that was going to be proved*, which means *Thus it is proved*.

I'm not a spazzer, which means spastic, and even though I probably won't become an astronaut I am going to go to university and study mathematics, because I like mathematics and physics and I'm very good at them. Father says Terry is most likely to end up in prison. Terry has a tattoo on his arm of a heart-shape with a knife through the middle of it.

But this is what is called a digression, and now I am going to go back to the fact that it was a Good Day. Because it was a Good Day I decided that I would try to find out who killed Wellington because a Good Day is a day for projects and planning things.

When I said this to Siobhan she said, 'Well, we're meant to be writing stories today, so why don't you write about finding Wellington and going to the police station.'

And that is when I started writing this.

MOTHER DIED 2 weeks after she went into hospital.

I had not been into hospital to see her but Father had taken in lots of food from Marks and Spencer's. He said that she had been looking OK and seemed to be getting better. She had sent me lots of love and had my Get Well card on the table beside her bed. Father said that she liked it very much.

The card had pictures of cars on the front. I did it with Mrs Peters at school who does art, and it was a linocut, which is when you draw a picture on a piece of lino and Mrs Peters cuts round the picture with a Stanley knife and then you put ink on the lino and press it onto the paper, which is why all the cars looked the same because I did one car and pressed it onto the paper 9 times. And I coloured all the cars in with red paint to make it a **Super Super Good Day** for Mother.

Father said that she died of a heart attack and it wasn't expected.

I said, 'What kind of heart attack?' because I was surprised. Mother was only 38 years old and heart attacks usually happen to older people, and Mother was very active and rode a bicycle and ate food which was healthy and high in fibre and low in saturated fat like chicken and vegetables and muesli.

Father said that he didn't know what kind of heart attack she had had and now wasn't the moment to be asking questions like that.

Then he said, 'I'm sorry, Christopher, I'm really sorry.'

But it wasn't his fault.

Then Mrs Shears came over and cooked supper for us. And she

was wearing sandals and jeans and a T-shirt which had the words **WINDSURF** and **CORFU** and a picture of a windsurfer on it.

And father was sitting down and she stood next to him and held his head against her bosoms and said, 'Come on, Ed. We're going to get you through this.'

And then she made us spaghetti and tomato sauce.

After dinner we played Scrabble and I beat her 247 points to 134.

SIX

I decided that I was going to find out who killed Wellington even though Father had told me to stay out of other people's business.

This is because I do not always do what I am told. And this is because when people tell you what to do it is usually confusing and does not make sense.

For example, people often say 'Be quiet,' but they don't tell you how long to be quiet for. Or you see a sign which says **KEEP OFF THE GRASS** but it should say **KEEP OFF THE GRASS AROUND THIS SIGN** because there is lots of grass you are allowed to walk on.

Also people break rules all the time. For example, Father often drives at over 30mph in a 30mph zone and sometimes he drives when he has been drinking and often he doesn't wear his seat belt. And in the Bible it says *Thou shalt not kill* but there were the Crusades and two World Wars and the Gulf War and there were Christians killing people in all of them.

Also I don't know what Father means when he says 'Stay out of other people's business' because I do lots of things with other people, at school and in the shop and on the bus, and his job is going into other people's houses and fixing their boilers and their heating. And all of these things are other people's business.

Siobhan understands. When she tells me not to do something she tells me exactly what it is that I am not allowed to do. And I like this. But when other people tell you what you can't do they don't do it clearly, so I decide for myself what I am going to do and what I am not going to do.

That evening I went round to Mrs Shears's house and knocked on the door and waited for her to answer it.

When she opened the door she was holding a mug of tea and she was wearing sheepskin slippers and she had been watching a quiz programme on the television because I could hear someone saying, 'The capital city of Venezuela is . . . a) Maracas, b) Caracas, c) Bogotá or d) Georgetown.' And I knew that it was Caracas.

She said, 'Christopher, I really don't think I want to see you right now. What are you doing here?'

I said, 'I wanted to come and tell you that I didn't kill Wellington. And also I want to find out who killed him.'

Some of her tea spilled onto the carpet.

I said, 'Do you know who killed Wellington?'

She didn't answer my question. She just said, 'Goodbye, Christopher,' and closed the door.

Then I decided to do some detective work.

I could see that she was watching me and waiting for me to leave because I could see her standing on the other side of the frosted glass in her front door. So I walked down the path and out of the garden. Then I turned round and saw that she wasn't standing in her hall any longer. I climbed over the wall and walked down the side of the house into her back garden to the shed where she kept her gardening tools.

The shed was locked with a padlock so I walked round to the window in the side. Then I had some good luck. When I looked through the window I could see a fork that looked exactly the same as the fork that had been sticking out of Wellington. It had been cleaned because there was no blood on the spikes. I could see some other tools: a spade and a rake and one of those long clippers people use for cutting high branches. And they all had the same green plastic handles like the fork. This meant that the fork belonged to Mrs Shears. Either that or it was a *Red Herring*, which is a clue that makes you come to a wrong conclusion or something which looks like a clue but isn't.

I wondered if Mrs Shears had killed Wellington herself. But if she had killed Wellington, why did she come out of the house shouting, 'What have you done to my dog?'

I thought that Mrs Shears probably didn't kill Wellington. But whoever had killed him had probably killed him with Mrs Shears's fork. And the shed was locked. This meant that it was someone who had the key to Mrs Shears's shed, or that she had left it unlocked, or that she had left her fork lying around in the garden.

I heard a noise and turned round and saw Mrs Shears standing on the lawn looking at me.

I said, 'I came to see if the fork was in the shed.'

And she said, 'If you don't go now I will call the police again.'

So I went home.

When I got home I said hello to Father and went upstairs and fed Toby and felt happy, because I was being a detective and finding things out.

MRS FORBES AT SCHOOL said that when Mother died she had gone to heaven. That was because Mrs Forbes is very old and she believes in heaven. But when Mother died she didn't go to heaven because heaven doesn't exist.

Mrs Peters's husband is a vicar called the Reverend Peters, and he comes to our school sometimes to talk to us, and I asked him where heaven was and he said, 'It's not in our universe. It's another kind of place altogether.'

I said that there wasn't anything outside the universe and there wasn't another kind of place altogether. Except that there might be if you went through a black hole, but a black hole is what is called a *Singularity*, which means it is impossible to find out what is on the other side because the gravity of a black hole is so big that even electromagnetic waves like light can't get out of it, and electromagnetic waves are how we get information about things that are far away. And if heaven was on the other side of a black hole dead people would have to be fired into space on rockets to get there, and they aren't.

I think people believe in heaven because they don't like the idea of dying, because they want to carry on living and they don't like the idea that other people will move into their house and put their things into the rubbish.

The Reverend Peters said, 'Well, when I say that heaven is outside the universe it's really just a manner of speaking. I suppose what it really means is that they are with God.'

And I replied, 'But where is God?'

And the Reverend Peters said that we should talk about this on another day when he had more time.

What actually happens when you die is that your brain stops working and your body rots, like Rabbit did when he died and we buried him at the bottom of the garden. And all his molecules were broken down into other molecules and they went into the earth and were eaten by worms and went into the plants and if we go and dig in the same place in 10 years there will be nothing except his skeleton left. And in 1,000 years even his skeleton will be gone. But that is all right because he is a part of the flowers and the apple tree and the hawthorn bush now.

Mother was cremated. This means that she was burnt and ground up and turned into ash and smoke. I do not know what happens to the ash and I couldn't ask at the crematorium because I didn't go to the funeral. But the smoke goes out of the chimney and into the air and sometimes I look up into the sky and I think that there are molecules of Mother up there, or in clouds over Africa or the Antarctic, or coming down as rain in the rain forests in Brazil.

SEVEN

The next day was Saturday and there is not much to do on a Saturday unless Father takes me on an outing to the boating lake or to the garden centre, but on this Saturday England were playing Romania at football which meant that we weren't going to go on an outing because Father wanted to watch the match on the television.

So I decided to do some more detection on my own. I decided that I would go and ask some of the other people who lived in our street, which is called Randolph Street, if they had seen anyone killing Wellington or whether they had seen anything strange happening in the street on Thursday night.

Usually I do not like talking to strangers. This is because I do not like people I have never met before. They are hard to understand. It is like being in France, which is where we went on holiday sometimes when Mother was alive, to camp. And I hated it because if you went into a shop or a restaurant you couldn't understand what anyone was saying which was frightening.

It takes me a long time to get used to people I do not know. For example, when there is a new member of staff at school I do not talk to them for weeks and weeks. I just watch them until I know that they are safe. Then I ask them questions, like whether they have pets and what is their favourite colour and what do they know about the Apollo space missions and I get them to draw a plan of their house and I ask them what kind of car they drive, so I get to know them.

So talking to the other people in our street was brave. But if you are going to do detective work you have to be brave, so I had no choice.

First of all I went out and I knocked on the door of number 40 which is opposite Mrs Shears's house which means that they were most likely to have seen something. The people who live at number 40 are called Thompson.

Mr Thompson answered the door. He said, 'Can I help you?'

I said, 'Do you know who killed Wellington?'

I did not look at his face. I do not like looking at people's faces, especially if they are strangers. He did not say anything for a few seconds. Then he said, 'Who are you?'

I said, 'I'm Christopher Boone from number 36 and I know you. You're Mr Thompson.'

He said, 'I'm Mr Thompson's brother.'

And I said, 'Do you know who killed Wellington?'

He said, 'Who the fuck is Wellington?'

I said, 'Mrs Shears's dog. Mrs Shears is from number 41.'

He said, 'Someone killed her dog?'

I said, 'With a garden fork. Do you know who killed him?'

He said, 'I haven't a bloody clue.'

I said, 'Did you see anything suspicious on Thursday evening?'

He said, 'Look, son, do you really think you should be going around asking questions like this?'

And I said, 'Yes, because I want to find out who killed Wellington, and I am writing a book about it.'

And he said, 'Well, I was in Colchester on Thursday, so you're asking the wrong bloke.'

I said, 'Thank you,' and I walked away.

There was no answer at house number 42.

I had seen the people who lived at number 44, but I did not know what their names were. They were black people and they were a man and a lady with two children, a boy and a girl. The lady answered the door. There were 5 bracelets made out of a silver-coloured metal on her wrist and they made a jangling noise. She said, 'It's Christopher, isn't it?'

I said that it was, and I asked her if she knew who killed Wellington. She knew who Wellington was so I didn't have to explain, and she had heard about him being killed.

I asked if she had seen anything suspicious on Thursday evening. But she said she hadn't.

And then I decided to do what is called *Trying a Different Tack*, and I asked her whether she knew of anyone who might want to make Mrs Shears sad.

And she said, 'Perhaps you should talk to your father about this.'

And I explained that I couldn't ask my father because the investigation was a secret because he had told me to stay out of other people's business.

She said, 'Well, maybe he has a point, Christopher.'

And I said, 'So, you don't know anything which might be a clue?'

And she said, 'No. And you be careful, young man.'

I said that I would be careful and then I said thank you to her for helping me with my questions and I went to number 43 which is the house next to Mrs Shears's house.

The people who live at number 43 are Mr Wise and Mr Wise's mother who is in a wheelchair, which is why he lives with her so he can take her to the shops and drive her around.

It was Mr Wise who answered the door. He smelt of body odour and old biscuits and off popcorn which is what you smell of if you haven't washed for a very long time. I asked Mr Wise if he knew who had killed Wellington on Thursday night.

He said, 'Bloody hell, policemen really are getting younger, aren't they?' Then he laughed.

I do not like people laughing at me, so I turned and walked away.

I did not knock at the door of number 38 which is the house next to our house because the people there take drugs and Father says that I should never talk to them, so I don't. They play loud music at night and they make me scared when I see them in the street.

Then I noticed that the old lady who lives at number 39, which is on the other side of Mrs Shears's house, was in her front garden, cutting her hedge. Her name is Mrs Alexander. She has a dachshund, so she is probably a good person because she likes dogs. But the dog wasn't in the garden with her. It was inside the house.

Mrs Alexander was wearing jeans and training shoes which old people don't normally wear. There was mud on the jeans and the trainers were New Balance trainers. I went up to Mrs Alexander and said, 'Do you know anything about Wellington being killed?'

She turned the electric hedge-trimmer off and said, 'I'm afraid you're going to have to say that again. I'm a little deaf.'

So I said, 'Do you know anything about Wellington being killed?'

And she said, 'I heard about it yesterday. Dreadful. Dreadful.'

I said, 'Do you know who killed him?'

And she said, 'No, I don't.'

And I said, 'Thank you for helping me with my investigation.'

And she said, 'You're Christopher, aren't you?'

I said, 'Yes. I live at number 36.'

And she said, 'We haven't talked before, have we?'

I said, 'No. I don't like talking to strangers. But I'm doing detective work.'

And she said, 'It's very nice of you to come and say hello.'

I didn't reply to this because Mrs Alexander was doing what is called chatting, where people say things to each other which aren't questions and answers and aren't connected.

Then she said, 'Even if it's only because you're doing detective work.'

And I said, 'Thank you,' again.

I was about to turn and walk away when she said, 'I have a grandson your age.'

I tried to do chatting by saying, 'My age is 15 years and 3 months and 3 days.'

And she said, 'Well, almost your age.'

Then we said nothing for a little while until she said, 'You don't have a dog, do you?'

And I said, 'No, but I have a rat. He's called Toby.'

And she said, 'Oh.'

Then I said, 'Most people don't like rats because they think they carry diseases like bubonic plague. But that's only because they lived in sewers and stowed away on ships coming from countries where there were strange diseases. But rats are very clean. Toby is always washing himself. And you don't have to take him out for walks. I just let him run around my room so that he gets some exercise.'

Mrs Alexander said, 'Do you want to come in for tea?'

And I said, 'I don't go into other people's houses.'

And she said, 'Well, maybe I could bring some out here. Do you like lemon squash?'

I replied, 'I only like orange squash.'

And she said, 'Luckily I have some of that. And what about Battenberg?'

I said, 'I don't know because I don't know what Battenberg is.'

She said, 'It's a kind of cake. It has four pink and yellow squares in the middle and it has marzipan icing round the edge.'

And I said, 'Is it a long cake with a square cross-section which is divided into equally sized, alternately coloured squares?'

And she said, 'Yes, I think you could describe it like that.'

I said, 'I think I'd like the pink squares but not the yellow squares because I don't like yellow. And I don't know what marzipan is so I don't know whether I'd like that.'

And she said, 'I'm afraid marzipan is yellow, too. Perhaps I should bring out some biscuits instead. Do you like biscuits?'

And I said, 'Yes. Some sorts of biscuits.'

And she said, 'I'll get a selection.'

Then she turned and went into the house. She moved very slowly because she was an old lady and she was inside the house for more than 6 minutes and I began to get nervous because I didn't know what she was doing. I didn't know her well enough to know whether she was telling the truth. I thought she might be ringing the police and then I'd get into much more serious trouble because of the caution. So I walked away. And as I was crossing the street I had a stroke of inspiration about who might have killed Wellington. I was imagining a **Chain of Reasoning** inside my head which was like this

1. Why would you kill a dog?
   a) Because you hated the dog.
   b) Because you were mad.
   c) Because you wanted to make Mrs Shears upset.
2. I didn't know anyone who hated Wellington, so if it was **a)** it was probably a stranger.
3. I didn't know any mad people, so if it was **b)** it was also probably a stranger.
4. Most murders are committed by someone who is known to the victim. In fact, you are most likely to be murdered by a member of your own family. This is a fact. Wellington was therefore most likely to have been killed by someone known to him.
5. If it was **c)** I only knew one person who didn't like Mrs Shears, and that was Mr Shears who knew Wellington very well indeed.

This meant that Mr Shears was my **Prime Suspect**.

Mr Shears used to be married to Mrs Shears and they lived together until two years ago. Then Mr Shears left and didn't come back. This was why Mrs Shears came over and did lots of cooking for us after Mother died, because she didn't have to cook for Mr Shears any more. And also Father said that she didn't want to be on her own.

And sometimes Mrs Shears stayed overnight at our house and I liked it when she did because she made things tidy and she arranged the jars in order of their height on the shelves in the kitchen and she put the knives, forks and spoons in the correct compartments in the cutlery drawer. But she smoked cigarettes and she said lots of things I didn't understand, for example, 'I'm going to hit the hay,' and, 'It's brass monkeys out there.' And I didn't like it when she said things like that because I didn't know what she meant.

And I don't know why Mr Shears left Mrs Shears, but if Mr Shears didn't want to live in the same house as Mrs Shears any more, he probably hated her and he might have come back and killed her dog to make her sad.

I decided to try to find out more about Mr Shears.

ALL THE OTHER CHILDREN at my school are stupid. Except I'm not meant to call them stupid, even though this is what they are. I'm meant to say that they have learning difficulties or that they have special needs. But this is stupid because everyone has learning difficulties because learning to speak French or understanding Relativity is difficult, and also everyone has special needs, like Father who has to carry a little packet of artificial sweetening tablets around with him to put in his coffee to stop him getting fat, or Siobhan who has glasses so thick that they give you a headache if you borrow them, and none of these people are Special Needs, even if they have special needs.

I am going to prove that I'm not stupid. Next month I'm going to take my A level in Maths and I'm going to get an A grade. No one has ever taken an A level at our school before and the headmistress, Mrs Gascoyne, didn't want me to take it at first. She said they didn't have the facilities to let us sit A levels. She said they didn't want to treat me differently from everyone else because it would set a precedent. And I could always do my A levels later, at 18.

I was sitting in Mrs Gascoyne's office with Father when she said these things. And Father got really cross. He said, 'Christopher is getting a crap enough deal already without you shitting on him from a great height as well. This is the one thing he is really good at.'

Then Mrs Gascoyne said that she and Father should talk about this at some later point on their own. But Father asked her whether she wanted to say things she was embarrassed to say in front of me, and she said no, so he said, 'Say them now, then.'

And she said that if I sat an A level I would have to have a member of staff looking after me on my own. And Father said he would pay someone £50 to do it after school and he wasn't going to take no for an answer. And she said she'd go away and think about it. And the next week she rang Father and told him that I could take the A level and the Reverend Peters would be what is called the invigilator.

After I've taken A level Maths I am going to take A level Further Maths and Physics and then I can go to university. There is not a university in our town, which is Swindon, so we will have to move to another town where there is a university because I don't want to live on my own or in a house with other students.

Then, when I've got a degree in Maths, or Physics, or Maths and Physics, I will be able to get a job and earn lots of money and I will be able to pay someone who can look after me and cook my meals and wash my clothes, or I will get a lady to marry me and be my wife and she can look after me so I have company and am not on my own.

I USED TO THINK that Mother and Father might get divorced. That was because they had lots of arguments and sometimes they hated each other. This was because of the stress of looking after someone who has Behavioural Problems like I have. I used to have lots of Behavioural Problems, but I don't have so many now because I'm more grown up and I can take decisions for myself and do things on my own like buying things at the shop at the end of the road.

One of my Behavioural Problems is getting cross when someone has moved the furniture. It makes me feel dizzy and sick if someone has moved the sofa and the chairs around in the living room or the dining room. Mother used to do this when she did the hoovering, so I made a special plan of where all the furniture was meant to be and I put everything back in its proper place afterwards.

Sometimes I would make Mother and Father really angry and they would shout at me or they would shout at each other. Sometimes Father would say, 'Christopher, if you do not behave I swear I shall knock the living daylights out of you,' or Mother would say, 'Christopher, you are going to drive me into an early grave.'

EIGHT

When I got home Father was sitting at the table in the kitchen and he had made my supper. He was wearing a lumberjack shirt. The supper was baked beans and broccoli and two slices of ham and they were laid out on the plate so that they were not touching. I don't eat food if different sorts of food are touching each other.

Father said, 'Where have you been?'

And I said, 'I have been out.' This is called a white lie. A white lie is not a lie at all. It is where you tell the truth but you do not tell all of the truth. And I said a white lie because I knew that Father didn't want me to be a detective.

Father said, 'I have just had a phone call from Mrs Shears.'

I started eating my supper.

Then Father asked, 'What the hell were you doing poking round her garden?'

I said, 'I was doing detective work trying to find out who killed Wellington.'

Father replied, 'How many times do I have to tell you, Christopher? Keep your nose out of other people's business.'

I said, 'I think Mr Shears probably killed Wellington. He is my Prime Suspect. Because I think someone might have killed Wellington to make Mrs Shears sad. And a murder is usually committed by someone known—'

Father banged the table with his fist so that the plates and his knife and fork jumped around and my ham jumped so that it touched the broccoli so I couldn't eat the ham or the broccoli any more.

Then he shouted, 'I will not have that man's name mentioned in my house.'

I asked, 'Why not?'

And he said, 'That man is evil.'

And I said, 'Does that mean he might have killed Wellington?'

Father put his head in his hands and said, 'Jesus wept.'

I could see that Father was angry with me, so I said, 'I know you told me not to get involved in other people's business but Mrs Shears is a friend of ours.'

And Father said, 'Well, she's not a friend any more.'

And I asked, 'Why not?'

And Father said, 'OK, Christopher. I am going to say this for the last and final time. Look at me when I'm talking to you. Look at me. You are not to go asking Mrs Shears about who killed that bloody dog. You are not to go asking anyone about who killed that bloody dog. You are not to go trespassing in other people's gardens. You are to stop this ridiculous bloody detective game right now.'

I didn't say anything.

Father said, 'I am going to make you promise, Christopher. And you know what it means when I make you promise.'

I did know what it meant when you say you promise something. You have to say that you will never do something again and then you must never do it because that would make the promise a lie.

I said, 'I know.'

Father said, 'Promise me that you will give up this ridiculous game.'

I said, 'I promise.'

I THINK I WOULD make a very good astronaut.

To be a good astronaut you have to be intelligent and I'm intelligent. You also have to understand how machines work and I'm good at understanding how machines work. You also have to be someone who would like being on their own in a tiny spacecraft thousands and thousands of miles away from the surface of the earth and not panic or get claustrophobia or be homesick or insane. And I like really little spaces, so long as there is no one else in them with me. Sometimes when I want to be on my own I get into the airing cupboard in the bathroom and pull the door closed behind me and sit there and think for hours and it makes me feel very calm.

So I would have to be an astronaut on my own, or have my own part of the spacecraft that no one else could come into. I wouldn't be homesick because I'd be surrounded by lots of the things I like, which are machines and computers and outer space. And I would be able to look out of a little window in the spacecraft and know that there was no one else near me for thousands of miles, which is what I sometimes pretend at night in the summer when I go and lie on the lawn and look up at the sky and put my hands round the sides of my face so that I can't see the chimney and the washing line and I can pretend I'm in space. And all I could see would be stars. And stars are the places where the molecules that life is made of were constructed billions of years ago.

And I would like it if I could take Toby with me into space, and that might be allowed because they sometimes do take animals into space for experiments, so if I could think of a good experiment you could do with a rat that didn't hurt the rat, I could make them let me take Toby. If they didn't let me I would still go because it would be a Dream Come True.

THE NEXT TIME I went to school I told Siobhan that Father had told me I couldn't do any more detecting which meant that the book was finished. I showed her the pages I had written so far, and she said that it didn't matter. She said the book was really good as it was and that I should be very proud of having written a book at all, even if it was quite short. But I said that it wasn't a proper book because it didn't have a proper ending because I never found out who killed Wellington so the murderer was still At Large.

And she said that was like life, and not all murders were solved and not all murderers were caught. Like Jack the Ripper.

I said I didn't like the idea that the person who killed Wellington was still At Large and could be living somewhere nearby. Then I said, 'Father said I was never to mention Mr Shears's name in our house again and that he was an evil man and maybe that meant he was the person who killed Wellington.'

And she said, 'Perhaps your father just doesn't like Mr Shears.'

And I asked, 'Why?'

And she said, 'I don't know, Christopher. I don't know because I don't know anything about Mr Shears.'

I said, 'Mr Shears used to be married to Mrs Shears and he left her, like in a divorce. But I don't know if they were actually divorced.'

And Siobhan said, 'Well, Mrs Shears is a friend of yours, isn't she? Perhaps your father doesn't like Mr Shears because he left Mrs Shears. Because he did something bad to someone who is a friend.'

And I said, 'But Father says Mrs Shears isn't a friend of ours any more.'

And Siobhan said, 'I'm sorry, Christopher. I wish I could answer all these questions, but I simply don't know.'

Then the bell went for the end of school.

The next day I saw 4 yellow cars in a row on the way to school which made it a **Black Day** so I didn't eat anything at lunch and I sat in the corner of the room all day and read my A level Maths course book. And the next day, too, I saw 4 yellow cars in a row on the way to school, which made it another **Black Day**, so I didn't speak to anyone and for the whole afternoon I sat in the corner of the Library groaning with my head pressed into the join between the two walls and this made me feel calm and safe. But on the third day I kept my eyes closed all the way to school until we got off the bus because after I have had 2 **Black Days** in a row I'm allowed to do that.

IT WASN'T THE END of the book because 5 days later I saw 5 red cars in a row which made it a **Super Good Day** and I knew that something special was going to happen. When I got home I went down to the shop at the end of our road to buy some liquorice laces and a Milky Bar with my pocket money. And when I had bought them I turned round and saw Mrs Alexander, the old lady from number 39, in the shop as well. She wasn't wearing jeans now. She was wearing a dress like a normal old lady. And she smelt of cooking.

She said, 'What happened to you the other day? I came out again and you'd gone. I had to eat all the biscuits myself.'

I said, 'I went away.'

And she said, 'I gathered that.'

I said, 'I thought you might ring the police.'

And she said, 'Why on earth would I do that?'

And I said, 'Because I was poking my nose into other people's business and Father said I shouldn't investigate who killed Wellington. And a policeman gave me a caution and if I get into trouble again it will be a lot worse because of the caution.'

Then the Indian lady behind the counter said to Mrs Alexander, 'Can I help you?' and Mrs Alexander said she'd like a pint of milk and a packet of Jaffa Cakes, so I went out of the shop.

When I was outside I saw that Mrs Alexander's dachshund was sitting on the pavement. It was wearing a little coat made out of tartan material which is Scottish and check. She had tied its lead to the drainpipe next to the door. I like dogs, so I bent down and I said hello to her dog and it licked my hand. Its tongue was rough and wet and it liked the smell on my trousers and started sniffing them.

Then Mrs Alexander came outside and said, 'His name is Ivor.'

I didn't say anything.

Mrs Alexander said, 'You're very shy, aren't you, Christopher?'

And I said, 'I'm not allowed to talk to you.'

And she said, 'Don't worry. I'm not going to tell the police and I'm not going to tell your father because there's nothing wrong with having a chat. Having a chat is just being friendly, isn't it?'

I said, 'I can't do chatting.'

Then she said, 'Do you like computers?'

And I said, 'Yes. I like computers. I have a computer at home in my bedroom.'

And she said, 'I know. I can see you sitting at your computer in your bedroom sometimes when I look across the street.'

Then she untied Ivor's lead from the drainpipe.

I wasn't going to say anything because I didn't want to get into trouble. But then I thought that this was a **Super Good Day** and something special hadn't happened yet so it was possible that talking to Mrs Alexander was the special thing. She might tell me something about Wellington or about Mr Shears without me asking her, and that wouldn't be breaking my promise.

So I said, 'And I like maths and looking after Toby. And also I like outer space and I like being on my own.'

And she said, 'I bet you're very good at maths, aren't you?'

And I said, 'I am. I'm going to do my A level Maths next month. And I'm going to get an A grade.'

And Mrs Alexander said, 'Really?'

I replied, 'Yes. I don't tell lies. I'm the first person to do an A level from my school because it's a special school.'

And she said, 'Well, I am very impressed. I hope you do get an A.'

And I said, 'I will.'

And then I did some reasoning. I reasoned that Father had only made me do a promise about five things which were

1. Not to mention Mr Shears's name in our house.

2. Not to go asking Mrs Shears about who killed that bloody dog.

3. Not to go asking anyone about who killed that bloody dog.

4. Not to go trespassing in other people's gardens.

5. To stop this ridiculous bloody detective game.

And asking about Mr Shears wasn't any of these things. And if you are a detective you have to *Take Risks* and this was a **Super Good Day** which meant it was a good day for *Taking Risks*, so I said, 'Do you know Mr Shears?' which was like chatting.

And Mrs Alexander said, 'Not really, no. I mean, I knew him well enough to say hello and talk to a little in the street, but I didn't know much about him. I think he worked in a bank.'

And I said, 'Father says that he is an evil man. Do you know why he said that? Is Mr Shears an evil man?'

And Mrs Alexander said, 'Why are you asking me about Mr Shears, Christopher? Is this about Wellington?'

And I nodded because that didn't count as being a detective.

Mrs Alexander sucked in a big breath and said, 'Perhaps it would be best not to talk about these things, Christopher.'

And I asked, 'Why not?'

And she said, 'Because . . .' Then she stopped and decided to start saying a different sentence. 'Because maybe your father is right and you shouldn't go around asking questions about this.'

And I asked, 'Why?'

And she said, 'Because he is going to find it quite upsetting.'

And I said, 'Why is he going to find it upsetting?'

Then she sucked in another big breath and said, 'Because . . . because I think you know why your father doesn't like Mr Shears very much.'

Then I asked, 'Did Mr Shears kill Mother?'

And Mrs Alexander said, 'Kill her? No. No. Of course he didn't kill your mother.'

And I said, 'Did he hurt her so that she had to go into hospital?'

And Mrs Alexander said, 'Did she have to go into hospital?'

And I said, 'Yes. And it wasn't very serious at first, but she had a heart attack when she was in hospital. And she died.'

And Mrs Alexander said, 'Oh my goodness,' and then she said, 'Oh, Christopher, I am so, so sorry. I never realised.'

Then I asked her, 'Why did you say, "I think you know why your father doesn't like Mr Shears very much"?'

Mrs Alexander put her hand over her mouth and said, 'Oh dear, dear, dear.' But she didn't answer my question.

Instead she asked me a question. She said, 'So you don't know?'

And I said, 'Don't know what?'

She replied, 'Christopher, look, I probably shouldn't be telling you this.' Then she said, 'Perhaps we should take a little walk in the park together. This is not the place to be talking about this kind of thing.'

I was nervous. I knew that Mrs Alexander was an old lady and that she liked dogs. But she was a stranger.

But I was excited, too. Because I thought she might tell me a secret. And the secret might be about who killed Wellington. Or about Mr Shears. And if she did that I might have more evidence against him, or be able to *Exclude Him From My Investigations*.

So because it was a **Super Good Day** I decided to walk into the park with Mrs Alexander even though it scared me.

When we were inside the park Mrs Alexander stopped walking and said, 'I am going to say something to you because if I don't explain, you'll carry on wondering what I meant. And you might ask your father. And I don't want you to do that because I don't want you to upset him. So I'm going to explain why I said what I said. But you have to promise not to tell anyone I said this to you.'

And I said, 'I promise.' Because if Mrs Alexander told me who killed Wellington, or she told me that Mr Shears had really killed Mother, I could still go to the police and tell them because you are allowed to break a promise if someone has committed a crime.

And Mrs Alexander said, 'Your mother, before she died, was very good friends with Mr Shears.'

And I said, 'I know.'

And she said, 'No, Christopher. I'm not sure that you do. I mean that they were very good friends. Very, very good friends.'

I thought about this for a while and said, 'Do you mean that they were doing sex?'

And Mrs Alexander said, 'Yes, Christopher. That is what I mean.'

Then she said, 'I'm sorry, Christopher. I really didn't mean to say anything that was going to upset you. But you see, I thought you knew. That's why your father thinks that Mr Shears is an evil man. And that will be why he doesn't want you going around talking to people about Mr Shears. Because it will bring back bad memories.'

And I said, 'Was that why Mr Shears left Mrs Shears, because he was doing sex with someone else when he was married to Mrs Shears?'

And Mrs Alexander said, 'Yes, I expect so.' Then she said, 'I'm sorry, Christopher. I really am. Are you OK?'

And I said, 'I think I should go now. I'm scared of being in the park with you because you're a stranger.'

And she said, 'I'm not a stranger, Christopher, I'm a friend. And if you want to talk about this you can come and see me any time you want. You only have to knock on my door.'

And I said, 'OK.'

And she said, 'Christopher, you won't tell your father about this conversation, will you?'

And I said, 'No. I promised.'

Then I went home.

NINE

When I got home, Rhodri was there. Rhodri is the man who works for Father, helping him do heating maintenance and boiler repair. And he sometimes comes round to the house in the evening to drink beer with Father and watch the television and have a conversation.

Rhodri was wearing a pair of white dungarees which had dirty marks all over them and he had a gold ring on the middle finger of his left hand and he smelt of something I do not know the name of which Father often smells of when he comes home from work.

I put my liquorice laces and my Milky Bar in my special food box on the shelf which Father is not allowed to touch because it is mine.

Then Father said, 'And what have you been up to, young man?'

And I said, 'I went to the shop to get some liquorice laces and a Milky Bar.'

And he said, 'You were a long time.'

I said, 'I talked to Mrs Alexander's dog outside the shop. And I stroked him and he sniffed my trousers.' Which was another white lie.

Then Rhodri said to me, 'So, how are you doing, Captain?'

And I said, 'I'm doing very well, thank you,' which is what you're meant to say.

And he said, 'What's 251 times 864?'

And I thought about this and I said, '216,864.' Because it was a really easy sum because you just multiply **864 x 1,000** which is **864,000**. Then you divide it by **4** which is **216,000** and that's **250 x 864**. Then you just add another **864** on to it to get **251 x 864**. And that's **216,864**.

And I said, 'Is that right?'

And Rhodri said, 'I haven't got a bloody clue,' and he laughed.

I don't like it when Rhodri laughs at me. Rhodri laughs at me a lot. Father says it is being friendly.

Then Father said, 'I'll stick one of those Gobi Aloo Sag things in the oven for you, OK?'

This is because I like Indian food because it has a strong taste. But Gobi Aloo Sag is yellow so I put red food colouring into it before I eat it. And I keep a little plastic bottle of this in my special food box.

And I said, 'OK.'

Then I went into the garden.

Siobhan said that when you are writing a book you have to include some descriptions of things and she said it was best to describe things that were interesting or different. I said that I could take photographs and put them in the book. But she said the idea of a book was to describe things using words so that people could read them and make a picture in their own head.

She also said that I should describe people in the story by mentioning one or two details about them. Which is why I wrote about Mr Jeavons's shoes with all the holes in them and the policeman who looked as if he had two mice in his nose and the thing Rhodri smelt of but I didn't know the name for.

So I decided to do a description of the garden. But the garden wasn't very interesting or different. It was just a garden, with grass and a shed and a clothes line. But the sky was interesting and different because usually skies look boring because they are all blue or all grey or all covered in one pattern of clouds and they don't look like they are hundreds of miles above your head. But this sky had lots of different types of clouds in it at different heights so you could see how enormous it was.

Furthest away in the sky were lots of little white clouds which looked liked fish scales or sand dunes that had a very regular pattern. Then, next furthest away and to the west were some big clouds which were coloured slightly orange because it was nearly evening and the sun was going down. Closest to the ground was a huge cloud which was coloured grey because it was a rain cloud. And it was a big pointy shape and it looked like this

And when I looked at it for a long time I could see it moving very slowly and it was like an alien spaceship hundreds of kilometres long, like in *Blake's 7* or *Close Encounters of the Third Kind*, except that it wasn't made of solid material, it was made of droplets of condensed water vapour, which is what clouds are made of.

People think that alien spaceships would be solid and made of metal and have lights all over them and move slowly through the sky because that is how we would build a spaceship if we were able to build one that big. But aliens, if they exist, would probably be very different from us. They might look like big slugs, or be flat like reflections. Or they might be bigger than planets. Or they might not have bodies at all. They might just be information, like in a computer. And their spaceships might look like clouds, or be made up of unconnected objects like dust or leaves.

THE HOUND OF THE BASKERVILLES is my favourite book. I like it because I like Sherlock Holmes and I think that if I were a proper detective he is the kind of detective I would be. He is very intelligent and he solves the mystery and he says *The world is full of obvious things which nobody by any chance ever observes.*

But he notices them, like I do. Also it says in the book *Sherlock Holmes had, in a very remarkable degree, the power of detaching his mind at will.*

And this is like me, too, because if I get really interested in something, like practising maths, or reading a book about the Apollo missions, or Great White sharks, I don't notice anything else and Father can be calling me and I won't hear him. And this is why I am very good at playing chess, because I detach my mind at will and concentrate on the board and after a while the person I am playing will stop concentrating and start scratching their nose or staring out of the window and then they will make a mistake and I will win.

Also Dr Watson says about Sherlock Holmes . . . *his mind . . . was busy in endeavouring to frame some scheme into which all these strange and apparently disconnected episodes could be fitted.*

And that is what I am trying to do by writing this book. And I am going to include two interesting facts about Sherlock Holmes. **1.** In the original Sherlock Holmes stories Sherlock Holmes is never described as wearing a deerstalker hat, which is what he is always wearing in pictures. The deerstalker hat was invented by a man called Sidney Paget who did the illustrations for the original books. **2.** In the original Sherlock Holmes stories Sherlock Holmes never says, 'Elementary, my dear Watson.' He only ever says this in films.

THAT NIGHT I WROTE some more of my book and the next day I took it into school so that Siobhan could read it during morning break and tell me if I had made mistakes with the spelling and the grammar.

Later she said she had read the bit about my conversation with Mrs Alexander. She said, 'Are you going to tell your father about this?'

And I replied, 'No.'

And she said, 'Good. I think that's a good idea, Christopher.' And then she said, 'Did it make you sad to find out that your mother and Mr Shears had an affair?'

And I said, 'No.'

And she said, 'Are you telling the truth, Christopher?'

And then I said, 'I always tell the truth.'

And she said, 'I know you do, Christopher. But sometimes we get sad about things and we don't like to tell other people that we are sad about them. We like to keep it a secret. Or sometimes we are sad but we don't really know we are sad. So we say we aren't sad. But we are.'

And I said, 'I'm not sad.'

And she said, 'If you do start to feel sad about this, I want you to know that you can come and talk to me about it. Because I think talking to me will help you feel less sad. And if you don't feel sad but you just want to talk to me about it, that would be OK, too. Do you understand?'

And I said, 'I understand.'

And she said, 'Good.'

And I replied, 'But I don't feel sad about it. Because Mother is dead. And because Mr Shears isn't around any more. So I would be feeling sad about something that isn't real and doesn't exist. And that would be stupid.'

And then I practised maths for the rest of the morning and at lunch I didn't have the quiche because it was yellow, but I did have the carrots and the peas and tomato ketchup. And for afters I had some blackberry and apple crumble, but not the crumble bit because that was yellow too, and I got Mrs Davis to take it off for me.

MY MEMORY IS LIKE A FILM. That is why I am really good at remembering things, like the conversations I have written down in this book, and what people were wearing, and what they smelt like, because my memory has a smelltrack which is like a soundtrack.

And when people ask me to remember something I can simply press **Rewind** and **Fast Forward** and **Pause** like on a video recorder, but more like a DVD because I don't have to Rewind through everything in between to get to a memory of something a long time ago.

If someone says to me, 'Christopher, tell me what your mother was like,' I can Rewind to lots of different scenes and say what she was like in those scenes. For example I could Rewind to July 4, 1992 when I was 9 years old, which was a Saturday, and we were on holiday in Cornwall and in the afternoon we were on the beach in a place called Polperro. Mother was wearing a pair of shorts made out of denim and a light blue bikini top and she was smoking cigarettes called Consulate which were mint flavour. And she wasn't swimming.

Mother was sunbathing on a towel which had red and purple stripes and she was reading a book by Georgette Heyer called *The Masqueraders*. And then she finished sunbathing and went into the water to swim and she said, 'Bloody Nora, it's cold.' And she said I should come and swim, too, but I don't like swimming because I don't like taking my clothes off. And she said I should just roll up my trousers and walk into the water a little way, so I did. And Mother said, 'Look. It's lovely.' And she jumped backwards and disappeared under the water and I thought a shark had eaten her and I screamed and she stood up out of the water again and came over to where I was standing and held up her right hand and spread her fingers out in a fan and said, 'Come on, Christopher, touch my hand. Come on now. Stop screaming. Touch my hand. Listen to me, Christopher. You can do it.' And after a while I stopped screaming and I held up my left hand and spread my fingers out in a fan and we made our fingers and thumbs touch. And Mother said, 'It's OK, Christopher. It's OK. There aren't any sharks in Cornwall,' and then I felt better.

I can't remember anything before I was about 4 because I wasn't looking at things in the right way before then, so they didn't get recorded properly.

And this is how I recognise someone if I don't know who they are. I see what they are wearing, or if they have funny hair, or a certain type of glasses, or they have a particular way of moving their arms and I do a **Search** through my memories to see if I have met them before.

And this is also how I know how to act in difficult situations when I don't know what to do. For example, if people say things that don't make sense, like, 'See you later, alligator,' or 'You'll catch your death in that,' I do a **Search** and see if I have ever heard someone say this before.

Other people have pictures in their heads, too. But they are different because they are sometimes of things that aren't real and didn't happen. For example, sometimes Mother used to say, 'If I hadn't married your father I think I'd be living in a little farmhouse in the South of France with someone called Jean. And he'd be, ooh, a local handyman. You know, painting and decorating for people, gardening, building fences. And we'd have a verandah with figs growing over it and there would be a field of sunflowers at the bottom of the garden and a little town on the hill in the distance and we'd sit outside in the evening and drink red wine and watch the sun go down.'

And sometimes, when someone has died, like Mother died, people say, 'What would you want to say to your mother if she was here now?' or 'What would your mother think about that?', which is stupid because Mother is dead and you can't say anything to people who are dead and dead people can't think.

And Grandmother has pictures in her head, too, but her pictures are all confused, like someone has muddled the film up and she can't tell what happened in what order, so she thinks that dead people are still alive and she doesn't know whether something happened in real life or whether it happened on television.

TEN

When I got home from school Father was still out at work, so I unlocked the front door and went inside and took my coat off. I went into the kitchen and put my things on the table. And one of the things was this book. I made myself a raspberry milkshake and then went through to the living room to watch one of my *Blue Planet* videos about life in the deepest parts of the ocean, about sulphur chimneys, which are underwater volcanoes where gases are ejected from the earth's crust into the water. Scientists never expected there to be any living organisms there because it was so hot and so poisonous, but there are whole ecosystems there.

I like this bit because it shows you that there is always something new that science can discover, and all the facts that you take for granted can be completely wrong. And also I like the fact that they are filming in a place which is harder to get to than the top of Mount Everest but is only a few miles away from sea level. And it is one of the quietest and darkest and most secret places on the earth. And I like imagining that I am there sometimes, in a spherical metal submersible with windows that are 30cm thick to stop them imploding under the pressure. And I imagine that I can control the motors and move anywhere I want to on the seabed and never be found.

Father came home at 5.48pm. I heard him come through the front door and into the living room. He was wearing a lime-green and sky-blue check shirt and there was a double knot on one of his shoes but not on the other.

He said, 'Howdy, Pardner,' which is a joke he does.

And I said, 'Hello.'

I carried on watching the video and Father went into the kitchen.

I had forgotten that I had left my book on the kitchen table because I was interested in the ***Blue Planet*** video. This is what is called *Relaxing Your Guard*, and it is what you must never do if you are a detective.

Father came back into the living room. He said, 'What is this?', but he said it very quietly and I didn't realise that he was angry because he wasn't shouting. He was holding the book in his right hand.

I said, 'It's a book I'm writing.'

And he said, 'Is this true? Did you talk to Mrs Alexander?' He said this very quietly as well, so I still didn't realise that he was angry.

And I said, 'Yes.'

Then he said, 'Jesus, Christopher. How stupid are you?'

This is what Siobhan says is called a rhetorical question. It has a question mark at the end, but you are not meant to answer it because the person who is asking it already knows the answer. It is difficult to spot a rhetorical question.

Then Father said, 'What the fuck did I tell you, Christopher?' This was much louder.

And I replied, 'Not to mention Mr Shears's name in our house. And not to go asking Mrs Shears, or anyone, about who killed that bloody dog. And not to go trespassing in other people's gardens. And to stop this ridiculous bloody detective game. Except I haven't done any of those things. I just asked Mrs Alexander about Mr Shears because—'

But Father interrupted me and said, 'Don't give me that. You knew exactly what you were bloody doing. I've read the book, remember?' And when he said this he held up the book and shook it. 'What else did I say, Christopher?'

I thought that this might be another rhetorical question, but I wasn't sure. I found it hard to work out what to say because I was starting to get scared and confused.

I said, 'I don't know.'

And he said, 'Come on. You're the memory man.'

But I couldn't think.

And Father said, 'Not to go around sticking your nose into other people's business. And what do you do? You go around raking up the past and sharing it with every Tom, Dick and Harry you bump into. What am I going to do with you, Christopher? What the fuck am I going to do with you?'

I said, 'I was just doing chatting with Mrs Alexander. I wasn't doing investigating.'

And he said, 'I ask you to do one thing for me, Christopher. One.'

And I said, 'I didn't want to talk to Mrs Alexander. It was Mrs Alexander who—'

But Father interrupted me and grabbed hold of my arm really hard.

Father had never grabbed hold of me like that before. Mother had hit me sometimes because she was a very hot-tempered person, which means that she got angry more quickly than other people and she shouted more often. But Father is levelheaded, which means he doesn't get angry as quickly and he doesn't shout often. So I was very surprised when he grabbed me.

I don't like it when people grab me. And I don't like being surprised either. So I hit him, like I hit the policeman when he took hold of my arms and lifted me onto my feet. But Father didn't let go, and he was shouting. And I hit him again. And then I didn't know what I was doing any more.

I had no memories for a short while. I know it was a short while because I checked my watch afterwards. It was like someone had switched me off and then switched me on again. And when they switched me on again I was sitting on the carpet with my back against the wall and there was blood on my right hand and the side of my head was hurting.

And Father was standing on the carpet looking down at me and he was still holding my book in his right hand, but it was bent in half and all the corners were messed up, and there was a scratch on his neck and a big rip in the sleeve of his green and blue check shirt and he was breathing really deeply.

After about a minute he turned and he walked through to the kitchen. Then he unlocked the back door into the garden and went outside. I heard him lift the lid of the dustbin and drop something into it. Then he came into the kitchen again, but he wasn't carrying the book any more. Then he locked the back door and put the key into the little china jug that is shaped like a fat nun and he stood in the middle of the kitchen and closed his eyes.

Then he opened his eyes and said, 'I need a fucking drink.'

And he got himself a can of beer.

THE NEXT DAY Father said he was sorry that he had hit me and he didn't mean to. He made me wash the cut on my cheek with Dettol to make sure that it wasn't infected, then he got me to put a plaster on it so it didn't bleed.

Then, because it was a Saturday he said he was going to take me on an expedition to show me that he was properly sorry, and we were going to Twycross Zoo. He said there wouldn't be too many people because it was forecast to rain, and I was glad about that because I don't like crowds of people and I like it when it is raining. So I went and got my waterproof, which is orange.

I had never been to Twycross Zoo before so I didn't have a picture of it in my mind before we got there, so we bought a guidebook from the information centre and then we walked round the whole zoo and I decided that my favourite animals were

1. RANDYMAN, which is the name of the oldest **Red-Faced Black Spider Monkey** (*Ateles paniscus paniscus*) ever kept in captivity. Randyman is 44 years old which is the same age as Father.
2. The **PATAGONIAN SEA LIONS** called Miracle and Star.
3. MALIKU, which is an **Orang-Utan**. I liked it especially because it was lying in a kind of hammock made out of a pair of stripy green pyjama bottoms and on the blue plastic notice next to the cage it said it made the hammock itself.

Then we went to the café and Father had plaice and chips and apple pie and ice cream and a pot of Earl Grey tea and I had sandwiches and I read the guidebook to the zoo.

And Father said, 'I love you very much, Christopher. Don't ever forget that. And I know I lose my rag occasionally. I know I shout. And I know I shouldn't. But I only do it because I worry about you, because I don't want to see you getting into trouble and I don't want you to get hurt. Do you understand?'

I didn't know whether I understood. So I said, 'I don't know.'

And Father said, 'Christopher, do you understand that I love you?'

And I said, 'Yes,' because loving someone is helping them when they get into trouble, and looking after them, and telling them the truth, and Father looks after me when I get into trouble, like coming to the police station, and he looks after me by cooking meals for me, and he always tells me the truth, which means that he loves me.

And then he held up his right hand and spread his fingers out in a fan, and I held up my left hand and spread my fingers out in a fan and we made our fingers and thumbs touch each other.

Then we went and looked at the giraffes. And the smell of their poo was like the smell in the gerbil cage at school, and when they ran their legs were so long it looked like they were running in slow motion.

Then Father said we had to get home before the roads got busy.

ELEVEN

When I got home from school on Monday, Father was still at work, so I went into the kitchen and took the key out of the little china jug shaped like a nun and opened the back door and went outside and looked inside the dustbin to find my book.

I wanted to get my book back because I liked writing it. I liked having a project to do and I liked it especially if it was a difficult project like a book. Also I still didn't know who had killed Wellington and my book was where I had kept all the clues that I had discovered and I did not want them to be thrown away.

But my book wasn't in the dustbin.

I put the lid back on the dustbin and walked down the garden to have a look in the bin where Father keeps the garden waste, but my book wasn't in there either.

One other possibility was that Father had hidden my book somewhere in the house. So I decided to do some detecting and see if I could find it. Except I had to keep listening really hard all the time so I would hear his van when he pulled up outside the house so he wouldn't catch me being a detective.

I started by looking in the kitchen. My book was approximately **25cm x 35cm x 1cm** so it couldn't be hidden in a very small place. I looked on top of the cupboards and down the back of drawers and under the oven and I used my special Maglite torch and a piece of mirror from the utility room to help me see into dark spaces.

Then I detected in the utility room.

Then I detected in the dining room.

Then I detected in the living room where I found the missing wheel from my Airfix Messerschmitt Bf 109 G-6 model under the sofa.

Then I went upstairs, but I didn't do any detecting in my own room because I reasoned that Father wouldn't hide something from me in my own room unless he was being very clever and doing what is called a *Double Bluff* like in a real murder mystery novel, so I decided to look there only if I couldn't find the book anywhere else.

I detected in the bathroom, but the only place to look was in the airing cupboard and there was nothing in there.

Which meant that the only room left to detect in was Father's bedroom. I didn't know whether I should look in there because he had told me before not to mess with anything in his room. But if he was going to hide something from me the best place to hide it would be in his room. So I told myself I would not mess with things in his room. I would move them and then I would move them back. And he would never know I had done it so he wouldn't be angry.

I started by looking under the bed. There were 7 shoes and a comb and a piece of copper pipe and a chocolate biscuit and a dead bee and a Homer Simpson pattern tie, but not my book.

I looked in the drawers on either side of the dressing table, but these only contained aspirin and nail clippers and dental floss.

Then I looked in his clothes cupboard. In the bottom of the cupboard was a large plastic toolbox that was full of tools for doing do-it-yourself, like a drill and some screws and a hammer, but I could see these without opening the box because it was made of transparent grey plastic. Then I saw that there was another box underneath the toolbox so I lifted the toolbox out of the cupboard. The other box was an old cardboard box that is called a shirt box because people used to buy shirts in them. And when I opened the shirt box I saw my book.

Then I didn't know what to do.

I was happy because Father hadn't thrown my book away. But if I took the book he would know I had been messing with things in his room and he would be very angry and I had promised not to mess with things in his room.

Then I heard his van pulling up outside the house and I knew that I had to think fast and be clever. So I decided that I would leave the book where it was because I reasoned that Father wasn't going to throw it away if he had put it into the shirt box and I could carry on writing in another book that I would keep secret and then, maybe later, he might change his mind and let me have the first book back again and I could copy the new book into it. And if he never gave it back to me I would be able to remember most of what I had written so I would put it all into the second secret book.

Then I heard Father shutting the door of the van.

And that was when I saw the envelope.

It was addressed to me and it was lying under my book in the shirt box with some other envelopes. I picked it up. It said

Christopher Boone
36 Randolph Street
Swindon
Wiltshire

Then I noticed that there were lots of other envelopes and they were all addressed to me. And this was interesting and confusing.

And then I noticed how the words Christopher and Swindon were written. They were like this

Christopher

Swindon

I only know 3 people who do little circles instead of dots over the letter *i*. And one of them is Siobhan, one of them was Mr Loxely who used to teach at the school, and one of them was Mother.

And then I heard Father opening the front door so I took one envelope from under the book and I put the lid back on the shirt box and I put the toolbox back on top of it and I closed the cupboard door really carefully.

Then Father called out, 'Christopher?'

I said nothing because he might be able to hear where I was calling from. I stood up and walked round the bed to the door, holding the envelope, trying to make as little noise as possible.

Father was standing at the bottom of the stairs and I thought he might see me, but he was flicking through the post which had come that morning so his head was pointing downwards. Then he walked away from the foot of the stairs towards the kitchen and I closed the door of his room very quietly and went into my own room where I hid the envelope underneath my mattress. Then I walked downstairs and said hello to Father.

And he said, 'So, what have you been up to today, young man?'

And I said, 'Today we did *Life Skills* with Mrs Gray. Which was *Using Money* and *Public Transport*. And I had tomato soup for lunch, and 3 apples. And I practised some maths in the afternoon and we went for a walk in the park with Mrs Peters and collected leaves for making collages.'

And Father said, 'Excellent. What do you fancy for chow tonight?'

Chow is food.

I said I wanted baked beans and broccoli.

And Father said, 'I think that can be very easily arranged.'

Then I sat on the sofa and I read a book.

Then I went into the kitchen and had my baked beans and broccoli while Father had sausages and eggs and a mug of tea.

Then he said, 'I'm going to put those shelves up in the living room, if that's all right with you. I'll make a bit of a racket, I'm afraid, so if you want to watch television we're going to have to shift it upstairs.'

And I said, 'I'll go and be on my own in my room.'

And he said, 'Good man.'

And I said, 'Thank you for supper,' because that is being polite.

And he said, 'No problem, kiddo.'

And I went up to my room.

And when I was in my room I shut the door and I took out the envelope from underneath my mattress. I held the letter up to the light to see if I could detect what was inside the envelope but the paper of the envelope was too thick. I wondered whether I should open the envelope because it was something I had taken from Father's room. But then I reasoned that because the envelope was addressed to me, it belonged to me so it was OK to open it.

Inside there was a letter. And this is what was written in the letter

451c Chapter Road
Willesden
London NW2 5NG
0208 887 8907

Dear Christopher,

I'm sorry it's been such a very long time since I wrote my last letter to you. I've been very busy. I've got a new job working as a secretery for a factory that makes things out of steel. You'd like it a lot. The factory is full of huge machines that make the steel and cut it and bend it into watever shapes they need. This week they're making a roof for a cafe in a shopping centre in Birmingham.

Also we've moved into the new flat, as you can see from the address. It's not as nice as the old one and I don't like Willesden very much, but it's easier for Roger to get to work and he's bought it (he only rented the other one), so we can get our own furnature and paint the walls the colour we want to.

And that's why it's such a long time since I wrote my last letter to you because it's been hard work packing up all our things and then unpacking them and getting used to this new job.

I'm very tired now and I must go to sleep and I want to put this

*into the letterbox tomorrow morning, so I'll sign off now and write
you another letter soon.*

*You haven't written to me yet, so I know that you are probably
still angry with me. I'm sorry Christopher. But I still love you. I
hope you don't stay angry with me for ever. And I'd love it if you
were able to write me a letter.*

I think about you all the time.

Lots of Love,

Your Mum x x x x x x

Then I was really confused because Mother had never worked as a
secretary for a firm that made things out of steel. Mother had
worked as a secretary for a big garage in the centre of town. And
Mother had never lived in London. Mother had always lived with us.
And Mother had never written a letter to me before.

There was no date on the letter so I couldn't work out when
Mother had written the letter and I wondered whether someone else
had written the letter and pretended to be Mother.

And then I looked at the front of the envelope and I saw that there
was a postmark with a date on it and it said

Which meant that the letter was posted on October 16, 1997,
which was 18 months after Mother had died.

And then the door of my bedroom opened and Father said, 'What
are you doing?'

I said, 'I'm reading a letter.'

And he said, 'I've finished the drilling. That David Attenborough
nature programme's on telly if you're interested.'

I said, 'OK.'

Then he went downstairs again.

I looked at the letter and thought really hard. It was a mystery and I couldn't work it out. Perhaps the letter was in the wrong envelope and it had been written before Mother had died. But why was she writing from London? But the longest she had been away was a week when she went to visit her cousin Ruth, who had cancer, and Ruth lived in Manchester.

And then I thought that perhaps it was a letter to another person called Christopher, from that Christopher's mother.

I was excited. When I started writing my book there was only one mystery I had to solve. Now there were two.

I decided that I would not think about it any more that night because I didn't have enough information and could easily *Leap to the Wrong Conclusions* which is a dangerous thing to do because you should make sure you have all the available clues before you start deducing things. That way you are less likely to make a mistake.

I decided that I would wait until Father was out of the house. Then I would go into the cupboard in his bedroom and look at the other letters and see who they were from and what they said.

I folded the letter and hid it under my mattress. Then I went downstairs and watched the television.

TWELVE

It was 6 days before I could go back into Father's room to look in the shirt box in the cupboard.

On the fifth day, which was a Sunday, it rained very hard. I like it when it rains hard. It sounds like white noise everywhere, which is like silence but not empty.

I went upstairs and sat in my room and watched the water falling in the street. It was falling so hard that it looked like white sparks. And there was no one around because everyone was staying indoors. And it made me think how all the water in the world was connected, and this water had evaporated from the oceans somewhere in the middle of the Gulf of Mexico or Baffin Bay, and now it was falling in front of the house and it would drain away into the gutters and flow to a sewage station where it would be cleaned and then it would go into a river and go back into the ocean again.

And in the evening on Monday Father got a phone call from a

lady whose cellar had flooded and he had to go out and fix it in an emergency. So he told me to behave and to ring him on his mobile phone if there was a problem, and then he went out in the van.

I went into his bedroom and opened up the cupboard and lifted the toolbox off the top of the shirt box and opened the shirt box.

I counted the letters. There were 43 of them. They were all addressed to me in the same handwriting.

I took one out and opened it. Inside was this letter

3rd May

> *451c Chapter Road*
> *London NW2 5NG*
> *0208 887 8907*

Dear Christopher,

We have a new fridge and cooker at last! Roger and I drove to the tip at the weekend to throw the old ones away. Then we went to a secondhand shop and bought a new cooker and a new fridge. Now the house feels a little bit more like home.

I was looking through some old photos last night, which made me sad. Then I found a photo of you playing with the train set we bought for you. And that made me happy because it was one of the really good times we had together.

Do you remember how you played with it all day and you refused to go to bed at night because you were still playing with it? And do you remember how we told you about train timetabels and you had a clock and you made the trains run on time. And there was a little woodden station, too, and we showed you how people who wanted to go on the train went to the station and bought a ticket and then got on the train? And then we got out a map and we showed you the little lines which were the trains lines connecting all the stations. You played with it for weeks and weeks and we bought you more trains and you knew where they were all going. I liked remembering that a lot.

I have to go now. It's half past three in the afternoon.

I know you always like to know exactly what time it is. And I have to go to the Co-op and buy some ham to make Roger's tea with. I'll put this letter in the postbox on the way to the shop.

Love,
Your Mum x x x x x x

Then I opened another envelope. This was the letter that was inside

Flat 1, 312 Lausanne Rd
London N8 5BV
0208 756 4321

Dear Christopher,

I said that I wanted to explain to you why I went away when I had the time to do it properly. Now I have lots of time. So I'm sitting on the sofa with this letter and the radio on and I'm going to try to explain.

I was not a very good mother, Christopher. Maybe if things had been differant, maybe if you'd been differant, I might have been better at it. But that's just the way things turned out.

I'm not like your father. Your father is much more pacient. He just gets on with things and if things upset him he doesn't let it show. But that's not the way I am and there's nothing I can do to change that.

Do you remember once when we were shopping in town together? And we went into Bentalls and it was really crowded and we had to get a Christmas present for Grandma? You were frightened because of all the people in the shop. And I was talking to Mr Land who works on the kichen floor and went to school with me. And you crouched down on the floor and put your hands over your ears and you were in the way of everyone. So I got cross, because I don't like shopping at Christmas, either, and I told you to behave and I tried to pick you up and move you. But you shouted and you knocked those mixers off the shelf and there was a big crash. And everyone turned round to see what was going on. And Mr Land was realy nice about it but there were boxes and bits of broken bowl on the floor and everyone was staring and I saw that you had wet yourself and I was so cross and I wanted to take you out of the shop but you wouldn't let me touch you and you just lay on the floor and screamed. The maniger came and asked what the problem was and I was at the end of my tether and I had to pay for two broken mixers and we just had to wait until you stoped screaming. I had to walk you all the way home which took hours because I knew you wouldn't go on the bus again.

I remember that night I just cried and cried and your father was really nice about it at first and he made you supper and he put you to bed and he said these things happen and it would be OK. But I said I couldn't take it any more and eventually he got really cross and he told me I was being stupid and should pull myself together.

We had a lot of argumants like that. Because I often thought I couldn't take any more. By the end we stopped talking to each other very much because we knew it would always end up in an argumant and it would go nowere. And I felt realy lonley.

That was when I started spending lots of time with Roger. I mean obviously we had always spent lots of time with Roger and Eileen. But I started seeing Roger on his own because I could talk to him. He was the only person I could really talk to. And I know you might not understand any of this, but I wanted to explain, so that you knew. And even if you don't understand now, you can keep this letter and read it later and maybe you might understand then.

Roger told me that he and Eileen weren't in love with one another any more and that they hadn't been in love for a long time, which meant that he was feeling lonely too. So we had a lot in common. And then we realised that we were in love with one another. He suggested that we should move into a house together. But I said that I couldn't leave you, and he was sad about that but he understood that you were realy important to me.

And then you and me had that argumant. Do you remember? It was about your supper one evening. I'd cooked you something and you wouldn't eat it. You hadn't eaten for days and you were look-ing so thin. You started to shout and I got cross and I threw the food across the room. Which I know I shouldn't have done. And you grabbed the chopping board and you threw it and it hit my foot and broke my toes. Then, of course, we had to go to the hospital and I had that plaster put on my foot. And afterwards, at home, your father blamed me for getting cross with you. He said that if he could keep his temper then I should bloody well keep my temper.

I couldn't walk properly for a month, do you remember? And your father had to look after you. And I remember looking at the two of you and seeing you together and thinking how you were really differant with him. Much calmer. And you didn't shout at one another. And it made me so sad because it was like you didn't really need me at all. It was like I was invisible. And I think that was when I realised you and your father were probably better off if I wasn't living in the house. Then he would only have one person to look after instead of two.

Then Roger said that he had asked the bank for a transfer to London, and he was leaving. He asked me if I wanted to come with him. I thought about it for a long time, Christopher. Honestly, I did. And it broke my heart, but eventualy I decided it would be better for all of us if I went. So I said yes.

I meant to say goodbye. I was going to come back and pick up some clothes when you were back from school. And that was when I was going to explain and say that I would come back and see you as often as I could and you could come down to London to stay with us. But when I rang your father he said I couldn't come back. He was really angry. He said I couldn't talk to you. I didn't know what to do. He said that I was being selfish and that I was never to set foot inside the house again. So I haven't. But I have written you these letters instead.

I wonder if you can understand any of this. I know it will be very difficult for you. But I hope you can understand a little. Christopher, I never meant to hurt you. I thought that what I was doing was the best for all of us. I hope it is. And I want you to know that this is not your fault.

I used to have dreams that everything would get better. Do you remember, you used to say that you wanted to be an astranaut? Well, I used to have dreams where you were an astranaut and you were on the television and I thought that's my son. I wonder what it is that you want to be now. Has it changed? Are you still doing maths? I hope you are.

Please, Christopher, write to me sometime, or ring me on the telephone. The numbers at the top of the letter.

Love and Kisses,
Your Mother x x x x x x

Then I opened a third envelope. This was the letter that was inside

18th September

> *Flat 1, 312 Lausanne Road*
> *London N8 5BV*
> *0208 756 4321*

Dear Christopher,

Well, I said I'd write you every week, and I have. In fact, this is the second letter this week, so I'm doing even better than I said.

I have got a job! I'm working in Camden, at Perkin and Rashid, which is a Chartered Survayors.

It's a nice office. I don't know how long I'll stay here, though. I have to do a lot of adding up of numbers for when we send bills out to clients and I'm not very good at doing this (you'd be better at it than I am!). The pay is not very good, either. So I shall be looking for something better as soon as I get the chance.

I went up to Alexandra Palace the other day. It's a big park just round the corner from our flat, and the park is a huge hill with a big conference centre on the top and it made me think of you because if you came here we could go there and fly kites or watch the planes coming into Heathrow airport and I know you'd like that.

I have to go now, Christopher. I'm writing this in my lunch hour. Please write to me sometime and tell me about how you are and what your doing at school.

Loads and loads of love,
Your Mother x x x x

And there was a fourth letter, but I stopped reading because I felt sick. Mother had not had a heart attack. Mother had not died. Mother had been alive all the time. And Father had lied about this.

I tried really hard to think if there was any other explanation but I couldn't think of one. And then I couldn't think of anything at all because my brain wasn't working properly. I rolled onto the bed and curled up in a ball. My stomach hurt.

I don't know what happened then because there is a gap in my memory, like a bit of the tape had been erased. But I know that a lot of time must have passed because later on, when I opened my eyes again, I could see that it was dark outside the window. And I had been sick because there was sick all over the bed.

I heard Father coming into the house and calling out my name, which is another reason why I know a lot of time had passed. And then I heard him come up the stairs and walk into the room. He said, 'Christopher, what the hell are you doing?' and his voice sounded tiny and far away, like people's voices sometimes do when I am groaning and I don't want them to be near me.

And he said, 'What the fuck are you . . .? That's my cupboard, Christopher. Those are . . . Oh shit . . . Shit, shit, shit.'

He said nothing for a while. Then he put his hand on my shoulder and moved me onto my side and he said, 'Oh Christ.' But it didn't hurt when he touched me, like it normally does. I could see him touching me, like I was watching a film of what was happening in the room, but I could hardly feel his hand at all. It was just like the wind blowing against me. And he was silent again for a while.

Then he said, 'I'm sorry, Christopher. I'm so, so sorry. You read the letters.'

Then I could hear that he was crying because his breath sounded all bubbly and wet. He said, 'I did it for your good, Christopher. Honestly I did. I never meant to lie. I just thought . . . it was better if you didn't know . . . that . . . that . . . I didn't mean to . . . I was going to show them to you when you were older. I didn't know what to say . . . I was in such a mess . . . She left a note and . . . Then she rang and . . . I said she was in hospital because . . . because I didn't know how to explain. It was so complicated. So difficult. And I . . . I said she was in hospital. And I know it wasn't true. But once I'd said that . . . I couldn't . . . I couldn't change it. Do you understand . . . Christopher . . .? It just . . . It got out of control and I wish . . .'

Then he was silent for a really long time.

Then he touched me on the shoulder again and said, 'Christopher, we have to get you cleaned up, OK?'

He shook my shoulder a little bit but I didn't move.

And he said, 'Christopher, I'm going to go to the bathroom and I'm going to run you a hot bath. Then I'm going to come back and take you to the bathroom, OK? Then I can put the sheets into the washing machine.'

I heard him get up and go to the bathroom and turn the taps on. I listened to the water running into the bath. Then he came back and touched my shoulder again and said, 'Let's do this really gently, Christopher. Let's sit you up and get your clothes off and get you into the bath, OK? I'm going to have to touch you, but it's going to be all right.'

Then he lifted me up and made me sit on the side of the bed. He took my jumper and my shirt off and put them on the bed. Then he made me stand up and walk through to the bathroom. And I didn't scream. And I didn't fight. And I didn't hit him.

WHEN I WAS LITTLE and I first went to school, my main teacher was called Julie, because Siobhan hadn't started working at the school then. She only started working at the school when I was twelve.

And one day Julie sat down at a desk next to me and put a tube of Smarties on the desk, and she said, 'Christopher, what do you think is in here?'

And I said, 'Smarties.'

Then she took the top off the Smarties tube and turned it upside-down and a little red pencil came out and she laughed and I said, 'It's not Smarties, it's a pencil.'

Then she put the little red pencil back inside the Smarties tube and put the top back on. She said, 'If your mummy came in now, and we asked her what was inside the Smarties tube, what do you think she would say?'

And I said, 'A pencil.'

That was because when I was little I didn't understand about other people having minds. And Julie said to Mother and Father that I would always find this very difficult. But I don't find this difficult now. Because I decided that it was a kind of puzzle, and if something is a puzzle there is always a way of solving it.

It's like computers. People think computers are different from people because they don't have minds, even though, in the Turing test, computers can have conversations with people about the weather and wine and what Italy is like, and they can even tell jokes.

But the mind is just a complicated machine. And when we look at things we think we're just looking out of our eyes like we're looking out of little windows and there's a person inside our head, but we're not. We're looking at a screen inside our heads, like a computer screen.

And people think they're not computers because they have feelings and computers don't have feelings. But feelings are just having a picture on the screen in your head of what is going to happen tomorrow or next year, or what might have happened instead of what did happen, and if it is a happy picture they smile and if it is a sad picture they cry.

THIRTEEN

After Father had given me a bath and dried me off with a towel, he took me to my bedroom and put some clean clothes on me.

Then he said, 'Have you had anything to eat yet this evening?'

But I didn't say anything.

So he said, 'OK. Look. I'm going to put your clothes and the bedsheets into the washing machine and then I'll come back, OK?'

I sat on the bed and looked at my knees.

So Father went out of the room and then I heard him start the washing machine and I heard the boiler starting up and the water in the water pipes going into the washing machine.

I doubled 2s in my head because it made me feel calmer. I got to **33,554,432** which is 2^{25}, which was not very much because I've got to 2^{45} before, but my brain wasn't working very well.

Then Father came back into the room again and said, 'How are you feeling? Can I get you anything?'

I didn't say anything. I carried on looking at my knees.

And Father didn't say anything either. He just sat down on the bed next to me and put his elbows on his knees and looked down at the carpet between his legs where there was a little red piece of Lego.

Then I heard Toby waking up, because he is nocturnal, and I heard him rustling in his cage.

And Father said, 'Look, maybe I shouldn't say this, but . . . I want you to know that you can trust me. And . . . OK, maybe I don't tell the truth all the time. God knows, I try, Christopher, God knows I do, but . . . Life is difficult, you know. It's bloody hard telling the truth all the time. Sometimes it's impossible. And I want you to know that I'm trying, I really am. And perhaps this is not a very good time to say this, and I know you're not going to like it, but . . . You have to know that I am going to tell you the truth from now on. About everything. Because . . . if you don't tell the truth now, then later on . . . later on it hurts even more. So . . .'

Father rubbed his face with his hands and pulled his chin down with his fingers and stared at the wall. I could see him out of the corner of my eye.

And he said, 'I killed Wellington, Christopher.'

I wondered if this was a joke, because I don't understand jokes, and when people tell jokes they don't mean what they say.

But then Father said, 'Please. Christopher. Just . . . let me explain.' Then he sucked in some air and said, 'When your mum left, Eileen . . . Mrs Shears . . . was very good to us. Very good to me. She helped me through a very difficult time. And I'm not sure I would have made it without her. You know how she was round here most days. Helping out with the cooking and cleaning. Popping over to see if we needed anything . . . I thought . . . Well . . . I thought she might . . . eventually . . . want to move in here. Or that we might move into her house. We got on really, really well. I thought we were friends. And I guess I thought wrong . . . We argued and . . . she said some things I'm not going to say to you because they're not nice, but they hurt . . . I think she cared more for that bloody dog than for me, for us. And maybe that's not so stupid, looking back. Maybe we are a bloody handful. Anyway, we had quite a few rows. After this particularly nasty little blowout, she chucked me out of the house. And you know what that bloody dog was like after the operation . . . Nice as pie one moment, roll over, tickle its stomach. Sink its teeth into your leg the next.

Anyway, we're yelling at each other and it's in the garden relieving itself. So when she slams the door behind me the bugger's waiting for me. And . . . I know, I know. Maybe if I'd just given it a kick it would probably have backed off. But all I could think was that she cared more about this bloody dog than she did about you or me.'

Then Father said, 'I'm sorry, Christopher. I promise you, I never meant for it to turn out like this.' And then I knew that it wasn't a joke and I was really frightened.

Then he held up his right hand and spread his fingers out in a fan.

But I screamed and pushed him backwards so that he fell off the bed and onto the floor.

He sat up and said, 'OK. Look. Christopher. I'm sorry. Let's leave it for tonight, OK? I'm going to go downstairs and you get some sleep and we'll talk in the morning. It's going to be all right. Honestly. Trust me.'

Then he stood up and took a deep breath and went out of the room.

I sat on the bed for a long time looking at the floor. Then I heard Toby scratching in his cage. I looked up and saw him staring through the bars at me.

I had to get out of the house. Father had murdered Wellington. That meant he could murder me, because I couldn't trust him, even though he had said, 'Trust me,' because he had told a lie about a big thing. But I couldn't get out of the house straight away because he would see me, so I would have to wait until he was asleep.

The time was 11.16pm.

I tried doubling 2s again, but I couldn't get past 2^{15} which was **32,768**. So I groaned to make the time pass quicker and not think.

Then it was 1.20am, but I hadn't heard Father come upstairs to bed. I wondered if he was asleep downstairs or whether he was waiting to come in and kill me. So I got out my Swiss Army Knife and opened the saw blade so that I could defend myself. Then I went out of my bedroom and listened. I couldn't hear anything, so I started going downstairs really quietly. And when I got downstairs I could see Father's foot through the door of the living room. I waited for 4 minutes to see if it moved, but it didn't. So I carried on walking till I got to the hallway. Then I looked round the door of the living room.

Father was lying on the sofa with his eyes closed. He was asleep.

I took both my coats and my scarf from the hooks next to the front door and I put them all on because it would be cold outside at night. Then I went upstairs again really quietly, but it was difficult because my legs were shaking. I went into my room and I picked up

Toby's cage. He was making scratching noises, so I took off one of the coats and put it over the cage to make the noise quieter. Then I carried him downstairs again.

I went into the kitchen and I picked up my special food box. I unlocked the back door and stepped outside. Then I held the handle of the door down as I shut it again so that the click wasn't too loud. Then I walked down to the shed at the bottom of the garden.

It would be a bit warmer in the shed but I knew that Father might look for me there, so I went round the back and squeezed into the gap between the wall of the shed and the fence, behind the big, black, plastic tub for collecting rainwater. Then I sat down.

I decided to leave my other coat over Toby's cage because I didn't want him to get cold and die. I opened up my special food box. Inside was the Milky Bar and two liquorice laces and three clementines and a pink wafer biscuit and my red food colouring. I didn't feel hungry but I knew that I should eat something because if you don't eat something you can get cold, so I ate two clementines and the Milky Bar.

Then I wondered what I would do next.

BETWEEN THE ROOF of the shed and the big plant that hangs over the fence from the house next door I could see the constellation **Orion**. People say that **Orion** is called Orion because Orion was a hunter and the constellation looks like a hunter with a club and a bow and arrow, like this

But this is really silly because it is just stars, and you could join up the dots in any way you wanted and make it look like a lady with an umbrella who is waving, or the coffee maker which Mrs Shears has, which is from Italy, with a handle and steam coming out, or like a dinosaur

And there aren't any lines in space, so you could join bits of **Orion** to bits of **Lepus** or **Taurus** or **Gemini** and say that they were a constellation called **The Bunch of Grapes** or **The Bicycle** (except that they didn't have bicycles in Roman and Greek times which was when they called **Orion** Orion).

And anyway, **Orion** is not a hunter or a coffee maker or a dinosaur. It is just Betelgeuse and Bellatrix and Alnilam and Rigel and 17 other stars I don't know the names of. And they are nuclear explosions billions of miles away. And that is the truth.

I STAYED AWAKE UNTIL 3.47. That was the last time I looked at my watch before I fell asleep. It has a luminous face and lights up if you press a button so I could read it in the dark.

I looked at the sky a lot. I like looking up at the sky in the garden at night. In summer I sometimes come outside at night with my torch and my planisphere, which is two circles of plastic with a pin through the middle. On the bottom is a map of the sky and on top is an aperture which is shaped in a parabola and you turn it round to see a map of the sky that you can see on that day of the year from the latitude 51.5° North which is the latitude that Swindon is on.

And when you look at the sky you know you are looking at stars which are hundreds and thousands of light-years away from you. And some of the stars don't even exist any more because their light has taken so long to get to us that they are already dead, or they have exploded and collapsed into red dwarfs. And that makes you seem very small, and if you have difficult things in your life it is nice to think that they are what is called *negligible* which means that they are so small you don't have to take them into account when you are calculating something.

I didn't sleep very well because of the cold and because the ground was very bumpy underneath me and because Toby was scratching in his cage a lot. But when I woke up properly it was dawn and the sky was all orange and blue and purple and I could hear birds singing. And I stayed where I was for another 2 hours and 32 minutes, and then I heard Father come into the garden and call out, 'Christopher?'

So I turned round and I found an old plastic sack that used to have fertiliser in it and I covered myself and Toby's cage and my special food box with it. And then I heard Father coming down the garden and I took my Swiss Army Knife out of my pocket and got out the saw blade and held it in case he found us. And I heard him open the door of the shed and look inside. And then I heard his footsteps in the bushes round the side of the shed and my heart was beating really fast but he didn't see me because I heard him walking back up the garden again.

Then I looked at my watch and I stayed still for 27 minutes. And then I heard Father start the engine of his van. I knew it was his van because I heard it often and the neighbours' cars all sound different.

And when I heard him drive away from the house I knew it would be safe to come out.

And then I had to work out what to do.

And I did this by thinking of all the things I could do and deciding whether they were the right decision or not.

I decided that I couldn't go home again.

And I decided that I couldn't go and live with Siobhan because she couldn't look after me when school was closed because she was a teacher and not a friend or a member of my family.

And I decided that I couldn't go and live with Uncle Terry because he lived in Sunderland and I didn't know how to get to Sunderland and I didn't like Uncle Terry because he smoked cigarettes and stroked my hair.

And I decided I couldn't go and live with Mrs Alexander because even if she had a dog, she was a stranger.

And then I thought that I could go and live with Mother because I knew where she lived because I could remember the address from the letters. Except that she lived in London and I'd never been to London before. I'd only been to France, and to Sunderland to visit Uncle Terry and to Manchester to visit Aunt Ruth. I had never been anywhere apart from the shop at the end of the road on my own. And the thought of going somewhere on my own was frightening.

But then I thought about going home again, or staying where I was, or hiding in the garden every night and Father finding me and that made me feel even more frightened. And I felt like I was going to be sick again.

And then I realised that there was nothing I could do which felt safe. And I made a picture of all the possibilities in my head, and imagined crossing out all the possibilities which were impossible, which is like in a maths exam, when you look at all the questions and decide which ones you are going to do, and you cross out all the ones which you are not going to do because then your decision is final and you can't change your mind. And the picture in my mind was like this

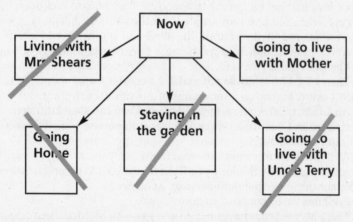

Which meant that I had to go London to live with Mother. And I could do it by going on a train because I knew all about trains from the train set, how you looked at the timetable and went to the station and bought a ticket and looked at the departure board to see if your train was on time and then you went to the right platform and got on board. And I would go from Swindon station where Sherlock Holmes and Dr Watson stop for lunch when they are on their way to Ross from Paddington in **The Boscombe Valley Mystery**.

And then I thought that I had to be like Sherlock Holmes and I had to *detach my mind at will to a remarkable degree* so that I did not notice how much it was hurting inside my head.

I thought I would need money if I was going to go to London. And I would need food to eat because it was a long journey and I wouldn't know where to get food from. And then I thought I would need someone to look after Toby when I went to London because I couldn't take him with me.

And then I *Formulated a Plan*. And that made me feel better. I took the liquorice laces and the pink wafer biscuit and the last clementine and the red food colouring out of my special food box and put them in my pocket and hid the special food box under the fertiliser bag. Then I picked up Toby's cage and my extra coat and I climbed out from behind the shed. I walked up the garden and down the side of the house to the front. I made sure there was no one in the street. Then I went to Mrs Alexander's house which is next door to Mrs Shears's house, and I knocked on the door.

Then Mrs Alexander opened the door, and she said, 'Christopher, what on earth has happened to you?'

And I said, 'Can you look after Toby for me?'

And she said, 'Who's Toby?'

And I said, 'Toby's my pet rat.'

Then Mrs Alexander said, 'Oh . . . Oh, yes. I remember. You told me.'

Then I held Toby's cage up and said, 'This is him.'

Mrs Alexander took a step backwards into her hallway.

And I said, 'He eats special pellets and you can buy them from a pet shop. But he can also eat biscuits and carrots and bread and chicken bones. But you mustn't give him chocolate because it's got caffeine and theobromine in, which are methylxanthines, and it's poisonous for rats in large quantities. And he needs new water in his bottle every day, too. And he likes to come out of his cage, but it doesn't matter if you don't take him out.'

Then Mrs Alexander said, 'Why do you need someone to look after Toby, Christopher?'

And I said, 'I'm going to London.'

And she said, 'How long are you going for?'

And I said, 'Until I go to university.'

And Mrs Alexander said, 'Right. Are you and your father moving house?'

And I said, 'No.'

And she said, 'So, why are you going to London?'

And I said, 'I'm going to live with Mother.'

And she said, 'I thought you told me your mother was dead.'

And I said, 'I thought she was dead, but she was still alive. And Father lied to me. And also he said he killed Wellington.'

And Mrs Alexander said, 'Oh, my goodness.'

And I said, 'I'm going to live with my mother because Father killed Wellington and he lied and I'm frightened of being in the house with him.'

And Mrs Alexander said, 'Is your mother here?'

And I said, 'No. Mother is in London.'

And she said, 'So you're going to London on your own?'

And I said, 'Yes.'

And she said, 'Look, Christopher, why don't you come inside and we can talk about this and work out what is the best thing to do.'

And I said, 'I can't come inside. Will you look after Toby for me?'

And she said, 'I really don't think that would be a good idea, Christopher. Where's your father at the moment?'

And I said, 'I don't know.'

And she said, 'Well, perhaps we should try and give him a ring. I'm sure he's worried about you. And I'm sure that there's been some dreadful misunderstanding.'

So I turned round and I ran across the road back to our house. And I didn't look before I crossed the road and a yellow Mini had to stop and the tyres squealed on the road. And I ran down the side of the house and back through the garden gate.

I tried to open the kitchen door but it was locked. So I picked up a brick that was lying on the ground and I smashed it through the window and the glass shattered everywhere. Then I put my arm through the broken glass and I opened the door from the inside.

I went into the house and I put Toby down on the kitchen table. Then I ran upstairs and I grabbed my schoolbag and I put some food for Toby in it and some of my maths books and some clean pants and a vest and a clean shirt. Then I came downstairs and I opened the fridge and I put a carton of orange juice into my bag, and a bottle of milk that hadn't been opened. And I took two more clementines and two tins of baked beans and a packet of custard creams from the cupboard and I put them in my bag as well, because I could open them with the can opener on my Swiss Army Knife.

Then I looked on the surface next to the sink and I saw Father's mobile phone and his wallet. He must have left them when he left the house. And I picked up his wallet and I took his bank card out because that was how I could get money because the card has a PIN number which is the secret code which you put into the machine at the bank. And Father hadn't written it down in a safe place, which is what you're meant to do, but he had told me because he said I'd never forget it. And it was 3558. I put the card into my pocket.

Then I took Toby out of his cage and put him into the pocket of one of my coats because the cage was very heavy to carry all the way to London. And then I went out of the kitchen door into the garden again. I went out through the garden gate and I started walking towards the school because that was a direction I knew, and when I got to school I could ask Siobhan where the train station was.

It takes 19 minutes for the bus to get to school from our house, but it took me 47 minutes to walk the same distance so I was very tired when I got there and I hoped that I could stay at school for a little while and have some biscuits and some orange juice before I went to the train station. But I couldn't, because when I got to the school I saw that Father's van was parked outside in the car park. And I knew it was his van because it said **Ed Boone Heating Maintenance & Boiler Repair** on the side with a crossed spanners sign.

And when I saw the van I wanted to curl up on the ground and do groaning. But I knew that if I did then Father would come out of the school and he would see me and he would catch me and take me home. So I took lots of deep breaths like Siobhan says I have to do if someone hits me at school, and I counted 50 breaths and I concentrated very hard on the numbers and did their cubes as I said them. And that made the hurt less painful.

And then I made a decision that I would have to find out how to get to the train station and I would do this by asking someone, and it would be a lady because when they talked to us about Stranger Danger at school they say that if a man comes up to you and talks to you and you feel frightened you should call out and find a lady to run to because ladies are safer.

So I got out my Swiss Army Knife and I flicked out the saw blade and I held it tightly in the pocket that Toby wasn't in so that I could stab someone if they grabbed hold of me, and then I saw a lady on the other side of the street with a baby in a pushchair and a little boy with a toy elephant, so I decided to ask her. And I crossed the road.

And I said to the lady, 'Where can I buy a map?' And I could feel the hand that was holding the knife shaking.

And she said, 'Patrick, put that down, it's dirty. A map of where?'

And I said, 'A map of here.'

And she said, 'I don't know. Where do you want to get to?'

And I said, 'I'm going to the train station.'

And she laughed and she said, 'You don't need a map to get to the train station.'

And I said, 'I do, because I don't know where the train station is.'

And she said, 'You can see it from here.'

And I said, 'No, I can't. And also I need to know where there is a cash machine.'

And she pointed and said, 'There. That building. Says *Signal Point* on the top. There's a British Rail sign on the other end. The station's at the bottom of that. Patrick, I've told you a thousand times . . .'

And I looked and I could see a building with writing at the top but it was a long way away so it was hard to read, and I said, 'Do you mean the stripy building with the horizontal windows?'

And she said, 'That's the one.'

And I said, 'How do I get to that building?'

And she said, 'Gordon Bennett.' And then she said, 'Follow that bus,' and she pointed to a bus that was going past.

So I started to run. But buses go really fast and I had to make sure that Toby didn't fall out of my pocket. But I managed to keep running after the bus for a long way and I crossed 6 side roads before it turned down another street and I couldn't see it any more. I stopped running because I was breathing really hard and my legs hurt. And I was in a street with lots of people. And I walked at the edge of the road because I didn't like all the people being near me and all the noise because it was too much information in my head and it made it hard to think, like there was shouting in my head. So I put my hands over my ears and I groaned very quietly.

And then I noticed that I could still see the ⇌ sign that the lady had pointed at, so I kept on walking towards it.

And then I couldn't see the ⇌ sign any more. And I had forgotten to remember where it was, and this was frightening because I was lost and because I do not forget things. Normally I would make a map in my head and I would follow the map but there was too much interference and this had made me confused. So I made a plan.

I knew that the train station was near. And if something is nearby you can find it by moving in a spiral, walking clockwise and taking every right turn until you come back to a road you've already walked on, then taking the next left, then taking every right turn and so on.

And that was how I found the train station. And I went inside.

I SEE EVERYTHING. That is why I don't like new places. If I am in a place I know, like home, or school, or the bus, or the shop, or the street, I have seen almost everything in it beforehand and all I have to do is to look at the things that have changed or moved.

Most people are lazy. They never look at everything. They do what is called *glancing*, and the information in their head is really simple. For example, if they are in the countryside, it might be

1. I am standing in a field that is full of grass.
2. There are some cows in the fields.
3. It is sunny with a few clouds.
4. There is a village in the distance.

And then they would stop noticing anything because they would be thinking something else like, 'Oh, it is very beautiful here,' or, 'I'm worried that I might have left the gas cooker on.' (This is really true because I asked Siobhan what people thought about when they looked at things, and this is what she said.)

But if I am standing in a field in the countryside I notice everything. For example, I remember standing in a field on Thursday, June 15, 1994, because Father and Mother and I were driving to Dover to get a ferry to France and we did what Father called *Taking the scenic route* which means going by little roads and stopping for lunch in a pub garden, and I had to stop to go for a wee, and I went into a field with cows in and I stopped and looked and I noticed these things

1. There are 19 cows in the field, 15 of which are black and white and 4 of which are brown and white.
2. There is a village in the distance which has 31 visible houses and a church with a square tower and not a spire.
3. There are ridges in the field which means that in medieval times it was what is called a *ridge and furrow* field and people who lived in the village would have a ridge each to do farming on.
4. There is an old plastic bag from Asda in the hedge, and a squashed Coca-Cola can with a snail on.
5. I can see three different types of grass and two colours of flowers in the grass.

And there were 31 more things in this list of things I noticed but Siobhan said I didn't need to write them all down. And it means that it is very tiring if I am in a new place because I see all these things, and if someone asked me afterwards what the cows looked like, I could ask which one, and I could do a drawing of them at home and say that a particular cow had patterns on it like this

When I am in a new place, because I see everything, it is like when a computer is doing too many things at the same time and the central processor unit is blocked up. And when I am in a new place and there are lots of people it is even harder because people are not like cows and flowers and grass and they can talk to you and do things that you don't expect, so you have to notice everything that is in the place, and also you have to notice things that might happen as well. And sometimes, when I am in a new place and there are lots of people there it is like a computer crashing and I have to close my eyes and put my hands over my ears and groan, which is like pressing **CTRL + ALT + DEL** and shutting down programs and turning the computer off and rebooting so that I can remember what I am doing and where I am meant to be going.

FOURTEEN

My train set had a little building that was two rooms with a corridor between them, and one was the ticket office where you bought tickets, and one was a waiting room where you waited for the train. But the train station in Swindon wasn't like that. It was a tunnel and some stairs, and a shop and café and a waiting room.

And it was like standing on a cliff in a really strong wind because it made me feel giddy and sick because there were lots of people and it was really echoey and there was only one way to go and that was down the tunnel, and it smelt of toilets and cigarettes. So I stood against the wall to make sure that I didn't fall over and go into a crouch on the ground. And I wanted to go home. But I was frightened of going home and I tried to make a plan of what I should do in my head but there were too many things to look at and too many things to hear.

So I put my hands over my ears to block out the noise and think. And I thought that I had to stay in the station to get on a train and I had to sit down somewhere and there was nowhere to sit down near the door of the station so I had to walk down the tunnel. So I said to myself, in my head: 'I will walk down the tunnel and there might be somewhere I can sit down and then I can shut my eyes and I can think,' and I walked down the tunnel trying to concentrate on the sign at the end that said **WARNING CCTV in operation**. And it was like stepping off the cliff onto a tightrope.

And eventually I got to the end of the tunnel and there were some stairs and I went up them and there were still lots of people and I groaned. There were signs saying **Great Western** and **cold beers and lagers** and **CAUTION WET FLOOR** and **Your 50p will keep a premature baby alive for 1.8 seconds** and **transforming travel** and **Refreshingly Different** and **No Smoking** and there were some little tables with chairs next to them and no one was sitting at one of the tables and it was in a corner and I sat down on one of the chairs next to it and I closed my eyes. And I put my hands in my pockets and Toby climbed into my hand and I gave him two pellets of rat food from my bag and I gripped the Swiss Army Knife in the other hand, and I groaned to cover up the noise, but not so loud that other people would hear me and come talk to me.

And then I tried to think about what I had to do, but I couldn't think because there were too many other things in my head, so I did a maths problem to make my head clearer.

When I looked up I saw that there was a policeman standing in front of me and he was saying, 'Anyone at home?' but I didn't know what that meant.

And then he said, 'Are you all right, young man?'

I looked at him and I thought for a bit so that I would answer the question correctly and I said, 'No.'

And he said, 'You're looking a bit worse for wear.'

He had a gold ring on one of his fingers and it had curly letters on it but I couldn't see what the letters were.

Then he said, 'The lady at the café says you've been here

for 2½ hours and when she tried talking to you, you were in a complete trance.' Then he said, 'What's your name?'

And I said, 'Christopher Boone.'

And he said, 'Where do you live?'

And I said, '36 Randolph Street' and I started feeling better because I like policemen and it was an easy question, and I wondered whether I should tell him that Father killed Wellington and whether he would arrest Father.

And he said, 'What are you doing here?'

And I said, 'I needed to sit down and be quiet and think.'

And he said, 'OK, let's keep it simple. What are you doing at the railway station?'

And I said, 'I'm going to see Mother. She lives in London.'

And he said, 'So, you don't live with your mother?'

And I said, 'No. But I'm going to.'

And then he sat down next to me and said, 'So, where in London does your mother live?'

And I said, '451c Chapter Road, London NW2 5NG.'

And he said, 'Jesus. What is that?'

And I looked down and I said, 'That's my pet rat, Toby,' because he was looking out of my pocket at the policeman.

And the policeman said, 'A pet rat?'

And I said, 'Yes, a pet rat. He's very clean and he hasn't got bubonic plague.'

And the policeman said, 'Well, that's reassuring. Have you got a ticket?'

And I said, 'No.'

And he said, 'Have you got any money to get a ticket?'

And I said, 'No.'

And he said, 'So, how precisely were you going to get to London?'

And then I didn't know what to say because I had Father's cashpoint card in my pocket and it was illegal to steal things, but he was a policeman so I had to tell the truth, so I said, 'I have a cashpoint card,' and I took it out and showed it to him. And this was a white lie.

But the policeman said, 'Is this your card?'

And then I thought he might arrest me, and I said, 'No, it's Father's.'

And he said, 'OK,' but he said it really slowly and he squeezed his nose between his thumb and his forefinger.

And I said, 'He told me the number,' which was another white lie.

And he said, 'Why don't you and I take a stroll to the cashpoint machine, eh?'

And I said, 'You mustn't touch me.'

And he said, 'Why would I want to touch you?'

And I said, 'I don't know. But I got a caution for hitting a policeman. I didn't mean to hurt him and if I do it again I'll get into even bigger trouble.'

Then he looked at me and he said, 'You're serious, aren't you?'

And I said, 'Yes.'

And he said, 'You lead the way.'

And I said, 'Where?'

And he said, 'Back by the ticket office' and pointed with his thumb.

And then we walked back through the tunnel, but it wasn't so frightening this time because there was a policeman with me.

And I put the cashpoint card into the machine like Father had let me do sometimes and it said **ENTER YOUR PERSONAL NUMBER** and I typed in **3558** and pressed the **ENTER** button and the machine said **PLEASE ENTER AMOUNT**.

And I asked the policeman, 'How much does it cost to get a ticket for a train to London?'

And he said, 'About 20 quid.'

And I said, 'Is that pounds?'

And he said, 'Christ alive' and laughed. But I didn't laugh because I don't like people laughing at me, even if they are policemen. And he stopped laughing, and said, 'Yep. It's 20 pounds.'

So I pressed **£50** and five £10 notes came out of the machine, and I put the notes and the receipt and the card into my pocket.

And the policeman said, 'Well, I guess I shouldn't keep you chatting.'

And I said, 'Where do I get a ticket for the train from?' because if you are lost and you need directions you can ask a policeman.

And he said, 'You are a prize specimen, aren't you?'

And I said, 'Where do I get a ticket for the train from?' because he hadn't answered my question.

And he said, 'In there,' and he pointed to a big room with a glass window on the other side of the train station door, and then he said, 'Now, are you sure you know what you're doing?'

And I said, 'Yes. I'm going to London to live with my mother.'

And he said, 'Has your mother got a telephone number?'

And I said, 'Yes. It's 0208 887 8907.'

And he said, 'And you'll ring her if you get into any trouble, OK?'

And I said, 'Yes' because I knew you could ring people from phone boxes if you had money, and I had money now.

And he said, 'Good.'

I walked into the ticket office and I turned round and I could see that the policeman was still watching me so I felt safe. And there was a long desk at the other side of the big room and a window on the desk and there was a man standing in front of the window and a man behind the window, and I said to the man behind the window, 'I want to go to London.'

And the man in front of the window said, 'If you don't mind' and he turned round so that his back was towards me and the man behind the window gave him a bit of paper to sign and he signed it and pushed it back under the window and then he picked up his ticket and turned round and looked at me.

I kept my hand on my Swiss Army Knife in case he touched me. And then he walked away and there was no one else in front of the window and I said to the man behind the window, 'I want to go to London.' I turned round and I saw that the policeman had gone now and I was scared again, so I tried to pretend I was playing a game on my computer and it was called **Train to London** and it was like **Myst** or **The Eleventh Hour**, and you had to solve lots of different problems to get to the next level, and I could turn it off at any time.

And the man said, 'Single or return?'

And I said, 'What does *single or return* mean?'

And he said, 'Do you want to go one way, or do you want to go and come back?'

And I said, 'I want to stay there when I get there.'

And he said, 'For how long?'

And I said, 'Until I go to university.'

And he said, 'Single, then. That'll be £17.'

And I gave him the £50 and he gave me £30 back and a little yellow and orange ticket and £3 in coins and I put it all in my pocket with my knife. And I didn't like the ticket being half yellow but I had to keep it because it was my train ticket.

And then he said, 'If you could move away from the counter.'

And I said, 'When is the train to London?'

And he looked at his watch and said, 'Platform 1, 5 minutes.'

And I said, 'Where is Platform 1?'

And he pointed and said, 'Through the underpass and up the stairs. You'll see the signs.'

And *underpass* meant *tunnel* because I could see where he was pointing, so I went out of the ticket office, but it wasn't like a computer game because I was in the middle of it and it was like all the signs were shouting in my head and someone bumped into me as they walked past and I made a noise like a dog barking to scare them off.

I pictured in my head a big red line across the floor which started at my feet and went through the tunnel and I started walking along the red line, saying 'Left, right, left, right, left, right,' because sometimes when I am frightened or angry it helps if I do something that has a rhythm to it, like music or drumming, which is something Siobhan taught me to do.

And I went up the stairs and I saw a sign saying: ← **Platform 1** and the ← was pointing at a glass door so I went through it, and someone bumped into me again with a suitcase and I made another noise like a dog barking, and they said, 'Watch where you're going,' but I pretended that they were just one of the Guarding Demons in **Train to London** and there was a train. And I saw a man with a newspaper and a bag of golf clubs go up to one of the doors of the train and press a big button next to it and the doors were electronic and they slid open and I liked that. And then the doors closed behind him.

I looked at my watch and 3 minutes had gone past since I was at the ticket office which meant that the train would be going in 2 minutes. I went up to the door and I pressed the big button and the doors slid open and I stepped through the doors.

And I was on the train to London.

THERE WERE LOTS of people on the train, and I didn't like that, so I stood very still in the train carriage and didn't move.

And then I heard someone say, 'Christopher.'

It was the policeman again. And he said, 'Caught you just in time' and he was breathing really loudly and holding his knees. And he said, 'We've got your father at the police station.'

And I thought he was going to say that they had arrested Father for killing Wellington, but he didn't. He said, 'He's looking for you.'

And then I thought that he was going to take me back to Father and that was frightening because he was a policeman and policemen are meant to be good, so I started to run away, but he grabbed me and I screamed. And then he let go.

And he said, 'OK, let's not get overexcited here.' And then he said, 'I'm going to take you back to the police station and you and me and your dad can sit down and have a little chat about who's going where.'

And I said, 'I'm going to live with Mother, in London.'

And he said, 'Not just yet, you're not.'

And I said, 'Have you arrested Father?'

And he said, 'Arrested him? What for?'

And I said, 'He killed a dog. With a garden fork. The dog was called Wellington.'

And the policeman said, 'Did he now?'

And I said, 'Yes, he did.'

And he said, 'Well, we can talk about that as well.' And then he said, 'Right, young man, I think you've done enough adventuring for one day.'

And then he reached out to touch me again and I started to scream again, and he said, 'Now listen, you little monkey. You can either do what I say, or I am going to have to make . . .'

And then the train jiggled and it began to move.

And then the policeman said, 'Fuck.' And he looked at the ceiling of the train and he put his hands together in front of his mouth like people do when they are praying to God in heaven and he breathed really loudly into his hands and made a whistling noise. Then he stopped because the train jiggled again and he had to grab hold of one of the straps hanging from the ceiling.

And then he said, 'Don't move.' He took out his walkie-talkie and pressed a button and said, 'Rob . . .? Yeah, it's Nigel. I'm stuck on the bloody train. Yeah. Don't even . . . It stops at Didcot Parkway. So, if you can get someone to meet me with a car . . . Cheers. Tell his old man we've got him but it's going to take a while, OK? Great.' And then he clicked his walkie-talkie off and he said, 'Let's get ourselves a seat,' and he pointed to two seats nearby which faced each other, and he said, 'Park yourself. And no monkey business.'

And we sat down facing one another.

And he said, 'You are a bloody handful, you are.'

And I wondered whether the policeman would help me find 451c Chapter Road, London NW2 5NG.

I looked out of the window and we were going past factories and scrapyards and there were 4 caravans in a muddy field with 2 dogs and some clothes hanging up to dry. There were so many things it made my head hurt, so I closed my eyes, but then I opened them again because it was like flying, but nearer to the ground, and I think flying is good.

And then I wanted to go for a wee, but I was on a train. And I didn't know how long it would take us to get to London and I felt a panic starting, and I started to tap a rhythm on the glass with my knuckles to help me wait and not think about wanting to go for a wee. I looked at my watch and waited for 17 minutes, but when I want to go for a wee I have to go really quickly and so I leaked a bit and wet my trousers.

And the policeman looked across at me and put his newspaper down and said, 'Oh, for God's sake go to the toilet, will you?'

And I said, 'But I'm on a train.'

And he said, 'They do have toilets on trains, you know.'

And I said, 'Where is the toilet on the train?'

And he pointed and said, 'Through those doors, there. But I'll be keeping an eye on you.'

I got up out of my seat and I closed my eyes so that my eyelids were just little slits so I couldn't see the other people on the train and I walked to the door, and when I got through the door there was another door on the right and it was half open and it said **TOILET** on it, so I went inside. And it was horrible because it smelt of poo, and I didn't want to use it but I had to because I really wanted to wee. I flushed the toilet and then I tried to use the sink but the tap didn't work, so I put spit on my hands and wiped them with a paper tissue and put it into the toilet.

Then I went out and I saw that opposite the toilet there were two shelves with cases and a rucksack on them and it made me think of the airing cupboard at home and how I climb in there sometimes and it makes me feel safe. So I climbed onto the middle shelf and I pulled one of the cases across like a door so that I was shut in, and it was dark and there was no one in there with me and I couldn't hear people talking so I felt much calmer and it was nice.

And I did some quadratic equations like $0 = 437x^2 + 103x + 11$ and $0 = 79x^2 + 43x + 2089$ and I made some of the coefficients large so that they were hard to solve.

And then the train started to slow down and someone came and stood near the shelf and knocked on the door of the toilet, and it was the policeman and he said, 'Christopher . . .?' He opened the door of the toilet and said, 'Bloody hell' and he was so close that I could see his walkie-talkie and his truncheon on his belt and I could smell his aftershave, but he didn't see me.

And then he went away again, running.

And then the train stopped and I wondered if it was London, but I didn't move because I didn't want the policeman to find me.

And then a lady with a jumper that had bees and flowers made of wool on it came and took the rucksack off the shelf over my head and she said, 'You scared the living daylights out of me.'

But I didn't say anything.

And then she said, 'I think someone's out there on the platform looking for you.'

But I carried on not saying anything.

And she said, 'Well, it's your lookout,' and she went away.

Three other people walked past and one of them put a big parcel on the shelf above my head but he didn't see me. And then the train started going again.

I WONDERED WHETHER I should have got off the train because it had just stopped at London, and I was scared because if the train went anywhere else it would be somewhere where I didn't know anybody.

And then I closed my eyes and did some more maths puzzles so I didn't think about where I was going.

And then the train stopped again, and I thought about getting off the shelf and going to get my bag and get off the train. But I didn't want to be found by the policeman and be taken to Father, so I stayed on the shelf and didn't move, and no one saw me.

And then I remembered that there was a map of England and Scotland and Wales on the wall of one of the classrooms at school, and it showed you where all the towns were and I pictured it in my head with Swindon and London on, and it was like this

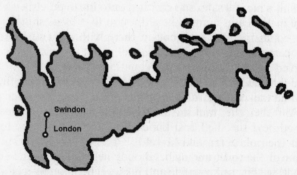

And I had been looking at my watch since the train had started at **12.59pm**. And the first stop had been at **1.16pm** which was 17 minutes later. And it was now **1.39pm** which was 23 minutes after the stop, which meant that we would be at the sea if the train didn't go in a big curve. But I didn't know if it went in a big curve.

And then there were another 4 stops and 4 people came and took bags away from the shelves and 2 people put bags on the shelves, but no one moved the big suitcase that was in front of me.

And then the train stopped and a lady with a yellow waterproof coat came and took the big suitcase away.

And then the train was really quiet and it didn't move again and I couldn't hear anyone. So I decided to get off the shelf and go and get my bag and see if the policeman was still sitting in his seat.

So I got off the shelf and I looked through the door, but the policeman wasn't there. And my bag had gone as well.

And then I heard the sound of feet and I turned round and it was another policeman, not the one who was on the train before, and I could see him through the door, in the next carriage, and he was looking under the seats. And I decided that I didn't like policemen so much any more, so I got off the train.

And when I saw how big the room was that the train was in and I heard how noisy and echoey it was I had to kneel down on the ground for a bit because I thought I was going to fall over. And then I worked out which way to walk, and I decided to walk in the direction the train was going when it came into the station because if this was the last stop, that was the direction London was in.

So I stood up and I imagined that there was a big red line on the ground which ran parallel to the train to the gate at the far end and I walked along it and I said 'Left, right, left, right . . .'

And when I got to the gate a man said to me, 'I think someone's looking for you, sonny.'

And I said, 'I know,' because I thought it might be Mother and the policeman in Swindon had phoned her up with the phone number I had told him.

But he said, 'Oh, right. You wait here, then, and I'll go and tell him,' and he walked back down the side of the train to find the policeman.

So I carried on walking. And I covered my ears with my hands and I went and stood against the wall of a little shop which said **Hotel and Theatre Reservations Tel: 0207 402 5164** in the middle of the big room and then I took my hands away from my ears and I groaned to block out the noise and I looked round the big room at all the signs to see if this was London. And the signs said

Sweet Pastries **Heathrow Airport Check-In Here** *Bagel Factory* **Stationlink** Buses W H Smith MEZZANINE **Heathrow Express** First Class Lounge **easyCar.com** *The Mad Bishop* **and Bear Public House** Fuller's London Pride Dixons **Our Price** Paddington Bear at Paddington Station **Tickets** Taxis ♦**Toilets** First Aid Way Out **Praed Street**

The Lawn Q Here Please Upper Crust Sainsbury's **Local**
ⓘ**Information** GREAT WESTERN FIRST ⓟ Position Closed
Closed Position Closed Fast Ticket Point

There were too many and my brain wasn't working properly and
this frightened me so I closed my eyes again and counted slowly to
50 but without doing the cubes. And I stood there and I opened my
Swiss Army Knife in my pocket and held on to it tight.

And then I made my hand into a little tube with my fingers and I
opened my eyes and I looked through the tube so that I was only
looking at one sign at a time and after a long time I saw a sign that
said ⓘ **Information** and it was above a window on a little shop.

And a man came up to me and he was wearing a blue jacket and
blue trousers and he had brown shoes and he was carrying a book in
his hand and he said, 'You look lost.'

So I took out my Swiss Army Knife.

And he said, 'Whoa. Whoa. Whoa. Whoa. Whoa,' and held up
both his hands. And then he walked away backwards.

So I went to the shop that said ⓘ **Information** and I could feel my
heart beating very hard and I could hear a noise like the sea in my
ears. And when I got to the window I said, 'Is this London?' but
there was no one behind the window.

And then someone sat behind the window and she was a lady and
she was black and she had long fingernails which were painted pink.
And she said, 'Indeed it is.'

And I said, 'How do I get to 451c Chapter Road, London NW2
5NG?'

And she said, 'Where is that?'

And I said, 'It's 451c Chapter Road, London NW2 5NG. Sometimes
you can write it *451c Chapter Road, Willesden, London NW2 5NG.*'

And the lady said to me, 'Take the tube to Willesden Junction,
honey. Or Willesden Green. Got to be near there somewhere.'

And I said, 'What sort of tube?'

And she said, 'Are you for real?'

And I didn't say anything.

And she said, 'See that big staircase with the escalators? See the
sign? Says *Underground.* Take the Bakerloo Line to Willesden
Junction or the Jubilee to Willesden Green. You OK, honey?'

And I looked where she was pointing and there was a big staircase
going down into the ground and there was a big sign over the top of
it like this

And I thought *I can do this* because I was doing really well and I was in London and I would find my mother. And I had to think to myself *the people are like cows in a field*, and I just had to look in front of me all the time and make a red line along the floor in the picture of the big room in my head and follow it.

And I walked across the big room to the escalators. It was a staircase but it was moving and people stepped onto it and it carried them down and up and it made me laugh because I hadn't been on one before and it was like something in a science fiction film about the future. But I didn't want to use it so I went down the stairs instead.

And then I was in a smaller room underground and there were lots of people and there were pillars which had blue lights in the ground around the bottom of them and I liked these, but I didn't like the people, so I saw a photobooth like one I went into on March 25, 1994, to have my passport photo done, and I went into the photobooth because it was like a cupboard and it felt safer and I could look out through the curtain. And I did detecting by watching and I saw that people were putting tickets into grey gates and walking through. And some of the people were buying tickets at big black machines on the wall.

And I watched 47 people do this and I memorised what to do. Then I imagined a red line on the floor and I walked over to the wall where there was a poster which was a list of places to go and it was alphabetical and I saw Willesden Green and it said £2.20 and then I went to one of the machines and there was a little screen which said **PRESS TICKET TYPE** and I pressed the button that most people had pressed which was **ADULT SINGLE** and **£2.20** and the screen said **INSERT £2.20** and I put 3 £1 coins into the slot and there was a clinking noise and the screen said **TAKE TICKET AND CHANGE** and there was a ticket in a little hole at the bottom of the machine, and a 50p coin and a 20p coin and a 10p coin and I put the coins in my pocket and I went up to one of the grey gates and I put my ticket into the slot and it sucked it in and it came out on the other side of the gate. And someone said, 'Get a move on,' and I made a noise like a dog barking and I walked forward and the gate opened this time and I took my ticket like other people did and I liked the grey gate because that was like something in a science fiction film, too.

And then I had to work out which way to go, so I stood against a wall so people didn't touch me, and there was a sign for **Bakerloo Line** and **District and Circle Line** but not one for **Jubilee Line** like the lady had said, so I made a plan and it was to go to *Willesden Junction on the Bakerloo Line*.

And there was another sign for the Bakerloo Line, and a list of place names. And I read them all and I found **Willesden Junction** and followed the arrow beside it and I went through the left-hand tunnel and there was a fence down the middle of the tunnel and the people were walking straight ahead on the left and coming the other way on the right like on a road, so I walked along the left and the tunnel curved left and then there were more gates and a sign said **Bakerloo Line** and it pointed down an escalator, so I had to go down the escalator and people were standing close to me and I wanted to hit them to make them go away but I didn't hit them because of the caution.

And then I was at the bottom of the escalator and there were two ways to go and one said **Northbound** and I went that way because **Willesden** was on the top half of the map and the top is always north on maps.

And then I was in another train station but it was tiny and it was in a tunnel and there was only one track and the walls were curved and they were covered in big adverts and they said **WAY OUT** and **London's Transport Museum** and **Take time out to regret your career choice** and **JAMAICA** and **For Stations beyond Queen's Park take the first train and change at Queen's Park if necessary** and **Hammersmith and City Line**. And there were lots of people standing in the little station and it was underground so there weren't any windows and I didn't like that, so I found a bench and I sat at the end of it.

And then there was a sound like people fighting with swords and I could feel a strong wind and a roaring started and I closed my eyes and the roaring got louder and I groaned really loudly and I thought the little station was going to collapse or there was a big fire somewhere and I was going to die. And then the roaring turned into a clattering and a squealing and it got slowly quieter and then it stopped and I kept my eyes closed because I felt safer not seeing what was happening. And then I could hear people moving again and I opened my eyes and saw that the people were getting onto a train that wasn't there before and it was the train that was roaring. And there was sweat running down my face from under my hair and I was moaning like a dog when it has hurt its paw and I heard the sound but I didn't realise it was me at first.

And then the train doors closed and the train started moving and it roared again but not as loud this time and it went into the tunnel at the end of the little station and it was quiet again and the people were all walking into the tunnels that went out of the little station.

I was shaking and I wanted to be back at home, and then I realised I couldn't be at home because Father was there and he told a lie and he killed Wellington which meant that it wasn't my home any more. My home was 451c Chapter Road, London NW2 5NG and it scared me, having a wrong thought like *I wish I was back at home again*, because it meant my mind wasn't working properly.

And then more people came into the little station and it became fuller and then the roaring began again and I closed my eyes and felt sick and I felt the feeling like a balloon inside my chest and it was so big I found it hard to breathe. And then the people went away on the train and the little station was empty again. And I just wanted to go to sleep so that I wouldn't have to think, but I couldn't go to sleep and I just had to sit there and wait and hurt.

AND THIS IS ANOTHER description because Siobhan said I should do descriptions and it is a description of the advert that was on the wall of the little train station opposite me, but I can't remember all of it.

The advert said

Dream holiday,

think Kuoni

in Malaysia

and behind the writing there was a big photograph of 2 orang-utans swinging on branches and there were trees behind them but the leaves were blurred because the camera was focusing on the orang-utans and not the leaves and the orang-utans were moving.

And *orang-utan* comes from the Malaysian word *ōranghūtan* which means *man of the woods*.

And adverts are pictures or television programmes to make you buy things like cars or Snickers. But this was an advert to make you go to Malaysia on a holiday. And Malaysia is in Southeast Asia and it is made up of Peninsular Malaysia and Sabah and Sarawak and Labuan and the capital is Kuala Lumpur and the highest mountain is Mount Kinabalu which is 4,101 metres high, but that wasn't on the advert.

And Siobhan says people go on holidays to see new things and relax, but it wouldn't make me relaxed and you can see new things by looking at earth under a microscope or drawing the shape of the solid made when 3 circular rods of equal thickness intersect at right angles. And I think that there are so many things just in one house that it would take years to think about all of them properly. And, also, a thing is interesting because of thinking about it and not because of it being new.

FIFTEEN

The trains coming in and out of the station were in a rhythm, like music or drumming. And it was like counting and saying 'Left, right, left, right, left, right . . .' which Siobhan taught me to do to make myself calm. And I was saying in my head, 'Train coming. Train stopped. Train going. Silence. Train coming. Train stopped. Train going . . .' as if the trains were only in my mind. Normally I don't imagine things that aren't happening because it is a lie and it makes me feel scared, but it was better than watching the trains coming in and out of the station.

And I didn't open my eyes and I didn't look at my watch. And it was like being in a dark room with the curtains closed so I couldn't see anything, like when you wake up at night, and the only sounds you hear are the sounds inside your head. And that made it better because it was like I was in bed and I was safe.

And then the silences between the trains coming and going got longer and longer. And I could hear that there were fewer people in the little station so I opened my eyes and I looked at my watch and it said 8.07pm and I had been sitting on the bench for approximately 5 hours but it hadn't seemed like approximately 5 hours, except that my bottom hurt and I was hungry and thirsty.

And then I realised that Toby was missing because he was not in my pocket. I didn't want him to be missing because we weren't in Father's house or Mother's house and there wasn't anyone to feed him in the little station and he would die and he might get run over by a train.

And then I looked up at the ceiling and I saw that there was a long black box which was a sign and it said

```
1   Harrow  &  Wealdstone      2  min
3   Queens  Park               7  min
```

And then the bottom line scrolled up and disappeared and a different line scrolled up into its place and the sign said

```
1   Harrow  &  Wealdstone      1  min
2   Willesden  Junction        4  min
```

And then it changed again and it said

```
1   Harrow  &  Wealdstone
**  STAND BACK TRAIN APPROACHING  **
```

And then I heard the roaring of a train coming into the station and I worked out that there was a big computer somewhere and it knew where all the trains were and it sent messages to the black boxes in the little stations to say when the trains were coming, and that made me feel better because everything had an order and a plan.

And the train came into the little station and it stopped and 5 people got onto the train and 7 people got off and then the doors closed automatically and the train went away. And when the next train came I wasn't so scared any more because the sign said TRAIN APPROACHING so I knew it was going to happen.

And then I decided that I would look for Toby. So I stood up and I looked up and down the little station and in the doorways that went into tunnels but I couldn't see him anywhere. And then I looked down into the black, lower-down bit where the rails were, and then I saw two mice and they were black because they were covered in dirt. And I liked that because I like mice and rats. But they weren't Toby, so I carried on looking.

And I saw Toby. I knew he was Toby because he was white and he had a brown egg shape on his back. So I climbed down off the concrete. And he was eating a bit of rubbish that was an old sweet paper. And someone shouted, 'Jesus. What are you doing?'

And I bent down to catch Toby but he ran off. And I walked after him and I bent down again and I said, 'Toby . . . Toby' and I held out my hand so that he could smell that it was me.

And someone said, 'Get out of there, for fuck's sake,' and I looked up and it was a man wearing a green raincoat and he had black shoes and his socks were showing and they were grey with diamond patterns on them. And he tried to grab my shoulder, so I screamed. And then I heard the sound like swordfighting and Toby started running again, and I grabbed at him and I caught him by the tail.

And the man with the diamond patterns on his socks said, 'Oh Christ. Oh Christ.'

And then I heard the roaring and I lifted Toby up and grabbed him with both hands and he bit me on my thumb and there was blood coming out and I shouted and Toby tried to jump out of my hands.

The roaring got louder and I turned round and I saw the train coming and I was going to be run over and killed so I tried to climb up onto the concrete but it was high and I was holding Toby in both my hands.

And then the man with the diamond patterns on his socks grabbed hold of me and pulled me and I screamed, but he kept pulling me up onto the concrete and we fell over and I carried on screaming. And then the train came into the station and I stood up and I put Toby into the pocket inside my jacket and he went very quiet and he didn't move.

And the man with the diamond patterns on his socks was standing next to me and he said, 'What do you think you were playing at?'

But I didn't say anything.

And he said, 'What were you doing?'

And the doors of the train opened and people got off and there was a lady standing behind the man with the diamond patterns on his socks and she was carrying a guitar case like Siobhan has.

And I said, 'I was finding Toby. He's my pet rat.'

And the man said, 'Fucking Nora.'

And the lady with the guitar case said, 'Is he OK?'

And the man said, 'Him? Mad as a fucking hatter,' and he was pressing a handkerchief against his face and there was blood on the handkerchief.

And the lady said, 'Are you OK?' and she touched my arm so I screamed again.

And she said, 'OK. OK. OK.'

And I was sitting on the ground and the woman knelt down on one knee and she said, 'Is there anything I can do to help you?'

And if she was a teacher at school I could have said, 'Where is 451c Chapter Road, Willesden, London NW2 5NG?' but she was a stranger, so I said, 'Stand further away' because I didn't like her being so close. And I said, 'I've got a Swiss Army Knife and it has a saw blade and it could cut someone's fingers off.'

And she said, 'OK, buddy. I'm going to take that as a no,' and she stood up and walked away.

Another train came and the man with the diamond patterns on his socks and the lady with the guitar case got on and it went away again.

And then 8 more trains came and I decided that I would get onto a train and then I would work out what to do.

So I got on the next train.

And there were 11 people in the carriage and I didn't like being in a room with 11 people so I concentrated on things in the carriage. And there were signs saying **There are 53,963 holiday cottages in Scandinavia and Germany** and **Penalty £10 if you fail to show a valid ticket for your entire journey** and **Discover Gold, Then Bronze** and **TVIC** and **EPBIC** and **Obstructing the doors can be dangerous**.

The train wobbled a lot and I had to hang onto a rail and we went into a tunnel and it was noisy and I closed my eyes and I could feel the blood pumping in the sides of my neck.

And then we came out of the tunnel and went into another little station and it was called **Warwick Avenue** and it said it in big letters on the wall and I liked that because you knew where you were.

And I timed the distance between stations all the way to Willesden Junction and all the times between stations were multiples of 15 seconds like this

Paddington	**0:00**
Warwick Avenue	**1:30**
Maida Vale	**3:15**
Kilburn Park	**5:00**
Queen's Park	**7:00**
Kensal Green	**10:30**
Willesden Junction	**11:45**

And when the train stopped at **Willesden Junction** and the doors opened automatically I walked out of the train. And then the doors closed and the train went away. And everyone who got off the train walked up a staircase and over a bridge except me, and then there were only two people that I could see and one was an Indian man in a shop which was a little window in a wall. I didn't want to talk to him because I had already talked to lots of strangers, which is dangerous, and the more you do something dangerous the more likely it is that something bad happens. But I didn't know how to get to 451c Chapter Road, London NW2 5NG so I had to ask somebody.

So I went up to the man in the little shop and I said, 'Where is 451c Chapter Road, London NW2 5NG?'

And he picked up a little book and handed it to me and said, 'Two ninety-five.' And the book was called *LONDON AZ Street Atlas and Index* and I opened it up and it was lots of maps.

And the man in the little shop said, 'Are you going to buy it or not?'

And I said, 'I don't know.'

And he said, 'Well, you can get your dirty fingers off it if you don't mind,' and he took it back from me.

And I said, 'Where is 451c Chapter Road, London NW2 5NG?'

And he said, 'You can either buy the A to Z or you can hop it. I'm not a walking encyclopedia.'

And I said, 'Is that the A to Z?' and I pointed at the book.

And he said, 'No, it's a sodding crocodile.'

And I said, 'Is that the A to Z?' because it wasn't a crocodile and I thought I had heard wrongly because of his accent.

And he said, 'Yes, it's the A to Z.'

And I said, 'Can I buy it?'

And he said, 'Two pounds ninety-five, but you're giving me the money first. I'm not having you scarpering,' and then I realised that he meant £2.95 when he said *Two ninety-five*.

And I paid him £2.95 and he gave me change just like in the shop at home and I went and sat down on the floor against the wall and I opened up the book.

And inside the front cover there was a big map of London with places on it like **Abbey Wood** and **Poplar** and **Acton** and **Stanmore**. And it said **KEY TO MAP PAGES**. And the map was covered with a grid and each square of the grid had two numbers on it. And **Willesden** was in the square which said **42** and **43**. And I worked out that the numbers were the numbers of the pages where you could see a bigger scale map of that square of London. And the whole book was a big map of London, but it had been chopped up so it could be made into a book, and I liked that.

Willesden Junction wasn't on pages 42 and 43. I found it on page 58 which was directly under page 42 on the **KEY TO MAP PAGES** and which joined up with page 42. And I looked round Willesden Junction in a spiral, like when I was looking for the train station in Swindon, but on the map with my finger.

And it took me a long time to find Chapter Road because it wasn't on page 58. It was back on page 42, and it was in square 5C.

And this was the shape of the roads between Willesden Junction and Chapter Road and this was my route

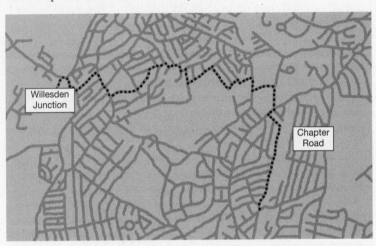

So I went up the staircase and over the bridge and I put my ticket in the little grey gate and went into the street and looked around and it was dark and there were lots of bright lights and I hadn't been outside for a long time and it made me feel sick. I kept my eyelids very close together and I just looked at the shape of the roads and then I knew which roads were **Station Approach** and **Oak Lane**, the roads I had to go along, and I started walking.

I got to 451c Chapter Road, London NW2 5NG and it took me 27 minutes and there was no one in when I pressed the button that said **Flat C.** So I decided to wait and I hoped that Mother was not on holiday because that would mean she could be away for more than a whole week, but I tried not to think about this because I couldn't go back to Swindon.

I sat down on the ground behind the dustbins in the little garden that was in front of 451c Chapter Road, London NW2 5NG. And then it started to rain and I got wet and I started shivering because I was cold.

And then it was 11.32pm and I heard voices of people walking along the street.

And a voice said, 'I don't care whether you thought it was funny or not,' and it was a lady's voice.

And another voice said, 'Judy, look. I'm sorry, OK,' and it was a man's voice.

And the other voice, which was the lady's voice, said, 'Well, perhaps you should have thought about that before you made me look like a complete idiot.'

And the lady's voice was Mother's voice.

Mother came into the garden and Mr Shears was with her, and the other voice was his.

So I stood up and I said, 'You weren't in, so I waited for you.'

And Mother said, 'Christopher.'

And Mr Shears said, 'What?'

And Mother put her arms round me and said, 'Christopher, Christopher, Christopher.'

And I pushed her away because she was grabbing me and I didn't like it, and I pushed really hard and I fell over.

And Mr Shears said, 'What the hell is going on?'

And Mother said, 'I'm so sorry, Christopher. I forgot.'

And I was lying on the ground and Mother held up her right hand and spread her fingers out in a fan so that I could touch her fingers, but then I saw that Toby had escaped out of my pocket so I had to catch him.

And Mr Shears said, 'I suppose this mean Ed's here.'

There was a wall round the garden so Toby couldn't get out and I grabbed him and put him back in my pocket and said, 'He's hungry. Have you got any food I can give him, and some water?'

And Mother said, 'Where's your father, Christopher?'

And I said, 'I think he's in Swindon.'

And Mr Shears said, 'Thank God for that.'

And Mother said, 'But how did you get here?'

And my teeth were clicking against each other because of the cold and I couldn't stop them, and I said, 'I came on the train. And it was really frightening. And I took Father's cashpoint card so I could get money out and a policeman helped me. But then he wanted to take me back to Father. And he was on the train with me. But then he wasn't.'

And Mother said, 'Christopher, you're soaking. Roger, don't just stand there. And then she said, 'Oh my God. Christopher. I didn't . . . I didn't think I'd ever . . . Why are you here on your own?'

And Mr Shears said, 'Are you going to come in or are you going to stay out here all night?'

And I said, 'I'm going to live with you because Father killed Wellington with a garden fork and I'm frightened of him.'

And Mr Shears said, 'Jesus Christ.'

And Mother said, 'Roger, please. Come on, Christopher, let's go inside and get you dried off.'

So I stood up and I went into the house and Mother said, 'You follow Roger,' and I followed Mr Shears up the stairs and there was a landing and a door which said **Flat C** and I was scared of going inside.

And Mother said, 'Go on, or you'll catch your death,' but I didn't know what *you'll catch your death* meant, and I went inside.

And then she said, 'I'll run you a bath,' and I walked round the flat to make a map of it in my head so I felt safer.

And then Mother made me take my clothes off and get into the bath and she said I could use her towel which was purple with green flowers on the end. And she gave Toby a saucer of water and some Bran Flakes and I let him run around the bathroom.

Then Mother came into the bathroom and she sat on the toilet and she said, 'Are you OK, Christopher?'

And I said, 'I'm very tired.'

And she said, 'I know, love.' And then she said, 'You're very brave.'

And I said, 'Yes.'

And she said, 'Why didn't you write to me, Christopher? I wrote you all those letters. I kept thinking something dreadful had happened, or you'd moved away and I'd never find out where you were.'

And I said, 'Father said you were dead.'

And she said, 'What?'

And I said, 'He said you went into hospital because you had something wrong with your heart. And then you had a heart attack and died and he kept all the letters in a shirt box in the cupboard in his bedroom and I found them because I was looking for a book I was writing about Wellington being killed and he'd taken it away from me and hidden it in the shirt box.'

And then Mother said, 'Oh my God.'

And then she didn't say anything for a long while. And then she made a loud wailing noise like an animal.

And I didn't like her doing this because it was a loud noise, and I said, 'Why are you doing that?'

And she didn't say anything for a while, and then she said, 'Oh, Christopher, I'm so sorry.'

And I said, 'It's not your fault.'

And then she said, 'Bastard. The bastard. Christopher, let me hold your hand. Just for once. Just for me. Will you? I won't hold it hard,' and she held out her hand.

And I said, 'I don't like people holding my hand.'

And she took her hand back and she said, 'No. OK. That's OK. Let's get you out of the bath and dried off.'

And I got out of the bath and dried myself with the purple towel. But I didn't have any pyjamas so I put on a white T-shirt and a pair of yellow shorts, which were Mother's, but I didn't mind because I was so tired. And while I was doing this Mother went into the kitchen and heated up some tomato soup because it was red.

And then I heard someone opening the door of the flat and there was a strange man's voice outside, so I locked the bathroom door. And there was an argument outside and a man said, 'I need to speak to him,' and Mother said, 'He's been through enough today already,' and the man said, 'I know. But I still need to speak to him.'

And Mother knocked on the door and said a policeman wanted to talk to me and I had to open the door. And she said she wouldn't let him take me away and she promised. So I picked Toby up and opened the door.

And there was a policeman outside the door and he said, 'Are you Christopher Boone?'

And I said I was.

And he said, 'Your father says you've run away. Is that right?'

And I said, 'Yes.'

And he said, 'Is this your mother?' and he pointed at Mother.

And I said, 'Yes.'

And he said, 'Why did you run away?'

And I said, 'Because Father killed Wellington who is a dog, and I was frightened of him.'

And he said, 'So I've been told.' And then he said, 'Do you want to go back to Swindon to your Father or do you want to stay here?'

And I said, 'I want to stay here.'

And he said, 'And how do you feel about that?'

And I said, 'I want to stay here.'

And the policeman said, 'Hang on. I'm asking your mother.'

And Mother said, 'He told Christopher I was dead.'

And the policeman said, 'OK. Now. Let's . . . let's not get into an argument about who said what here. I just want to know whether . . .'

And Mother said, 'Of course he can stay.'

And then the policeman said, 'Well, I think that probably settles it as far as I'm concerned.'

And I said, 'Are you going to take me back to Swindon?'

And he said, 'No.'

And then I was happy because I could live with Mother.

And the policeman said, 'If your husband turns up and causes any trouble, just give us a ring. Otherwise, you're going to have to sort this out between yourselves.'

And then the policeman went away and I had my tomato soup and Mr Shears stacked up some boxes in the spare room so he could put a blow-up mattress on the floor for me to sleep on.

And I went to sleep and then I woke up because there were people shouting in the flat and it was 2.31am. And one of the people was Father and I was frightened. He was shouting, 'I'm talking to her. And I am not going to be told what to do by you of all people.'

And Mother shouted, 'Roger. Don't. Just . . .'

And Mr Shears shouted, 'I'm not being spoken to like that in my own home.'

And Father shouted, 'I'll talk to you how I damn well like.'

And Mother shouted, 'You have no right to be here.'

And Father shouted, 'No right? No right? He's my son, in case you've forgotten.'

And Mother shouted, 'What in God's name did you think you were playing at, saying those things to him?'

And Father shouted, 'What was I playing at? You were the one that bloody left.'

And Mother shouted, 'So you decided to just wipe me out of his life altogether?'

And Mr Shears shouted, 'Let's all just calm down here, shall we?'

And Father shouted, 'Well, isn't that what you wanted?'

And Mother shouted, 'I wrote to him every week. Every week.'

And Father shouted, 'Wrote to him? What the fuck use is writing to him? I cooked his meals. I cleaned his clothes. I looked after him every weekend. I looked after him when he was ill. I worried myself sick every time he wandered off somewhere at night. I went to school every time he got into a fight. And you? What? You wrote him some letters.'

And Mother shouted, 'So you thought it was OK to tell him his mother was dead?'

And Mr Shears shouted, 'Whoa, whoa, whoa.'

And Father said, 'I'm going to see him. If you try to stop me . . .'

And then Father came into my room. But I was holding my Swiss Army Knife with the saw blade out in case he grabbed me. And Mother came into the room as well, and she said, 'It's OK, Christopher. I won't let him do anything. You're all right.'

And Father bent down on his knees near the bed and he said, 'Christopher? I'm really, really sorry. About Wellington. About the letters. About making you run away. I never meant . . . I promise I will never do anything like that again. Hey. Come on, kiddo.'

And then he held up his right hand and spread his fingers in a fan so that I could touch his fingers, but I didn't because I was frightened.

And Father said, 'Christopher, please.'

And there were tears dripping off his face.

And no one said anything for a while.

And then Mother said, 'I think you should go now,' but she was talking to Father, not me.

And then the policeman came back because Mr Shears had rung the police station, and he told Father to calm down and he took him out of the flat.

And Mother said, 'You go back to sleep now. Everything is going to be all right. I promise.'

And then I went back to sleep.

sixTEEN

The next morning I had fried tomatoes for breakfast and a tin of green beans which Mother heated up in a saucepan. In the middle of breakfast, Mr Shears said, 'OK. He can stay for a few days.'

And Mother said, 'He can stay as long as he needs to stay.'

And Mr Shears said, 'What's he going to do? There's no school for him to go to. We've both got jobs. It's bloody ridiculous.'

And Mother said, 'Roger. That's enough.'

After Mr Shears had gone to work she made a telephone call to the office and took what is called *Compassionate Leave*, which is when someone in your family dies or is ill.

Then she said we had to go and buy some clothes for me to wear and some pyjamas and a toothbrush and a flannel. So we went out of the flat and we walked to the main road which was Hill Lane and it was really crowded and we caught a No. 266 bus to Brent Cross Shopping Centre. Except there were too many people in John Lewis and I was frightened and I lay down on the floor next to the wrist-watches and I screamed and Mother had to take me home in a taxi.

Then she had to go back to the shopping centre to buy me some clothes and some pyjamas and a toothbrush and a flannel, so I stayed in the spare room while she was gone.

And when Mother got home she brought me a glass of strawberry milkshake and showed me my new pyjamas, and the pattern on them was 5-pointed blue stars on a purple background.

And I said, 'I have to go back to Swindon.'

And Mother said, 'Christopher, you've only just got here.'

And I said, 'I have to go back because I have to sit my Maths A level.'

And Mother said, 'You're doing Maths A level?'

And I said, 'Yes. I'm taking it on Wednesday and Thursday and Friday next week.'

And Mother said, 'God.'

And I said, 'The Reverend Peters is going to be the invigilator.'

And Mother said, 'I mean, that's really good.'

And I said, 'I'm going to get an A grade. And that's why I have to go back to Swindon. Except I don't want to see Father. So I have to go to Swindon with you.'

Then Mother put her hands over her face and breathed out hard, and she said, 'I don't know whether that's going to be possible.'

And I said, 'But I have to go.'

And Mother said, 'Let's talk about this some other time, OK?'

And I said, 'OK. But I have to go to Swindon.'

And she said, 'Christopher, please.'

And I drank some of my milkshake.

And, later on, at 10.31pm, I went out onto the balcony to find out whether I could see any stars, but there weren't any because of all the clouds and what is called *Light Pollution* which is light from street-lights and car headlights and lights in buildings reflecting off tiny particles in the atmosphere and getting in the way of light from the stars. So I went back inside.

SHE MADE ME PROMISE never to leave the flat on my own because it was dangerous and because you couldn't trust people in London because they were strangers. And the next day she had to go to the shops again and she made me promise not to answer the door if anyone rang the bell. And when she came back she brought some food pellets for Toby and three *Star Trek* videos and I watched them in the living room until Mr Shears came home and then I went into the spare room again.

And the day after that the office where Mother worked rang and told her she couldn't come back to work because they had got someone else to do her job for her, and she was really angry and she said that it was illegal and she was going to complain, but Mr Shears said, 'Don't be a bloody fool. It was a temporary job.'

And when Mother came into the spare room before I went to sleep I said, 'I have to go to Swindon to take my A level.'

And she said, 'Christopher, not now. I'm getting phone calls from your father threatening to take me to court. I'm getting it in the neck from Roger. It's not a good time.'

And I said, 'But I have to go because it's been arranged and the Reverend Peters is going to invigilate.'

And she said, 'Look. It's only an exam. I can ring the school. We can get it postponed. You can take it some other time.'

And I said, 'I can't take it another time. It's been arranged. And I've done lots of revision. And Mrs Gascoyne said we could use a room at school.'

And Mother said, 'Christopher, I am just about holding this together. But I am this close to losing it, all right? So just give me some . . .' Then she stopped talking and she put her hand over her mouth and she stood up and went out of the room. And I started feeling a pain in my chest like I did on the underground because I thought I wasn't going to be able to go back to Swindon and take my A level.

And the next morning I looked out of the window in the dining room to count the cars in the street to see whether it was going to be a **Quite Good Day** or a **Good Day** or a **Super Good Day** or a **Black Day**, and I looked out of the window for 3 hours and I saw 5 red cars in a row and 4 yellow cars in a row which meant it was both a **Good Day** and a **Black Day** so the system didn't work any more. But if I concentrated on counting the cars it stopped me thinking about my A level and the pain in my chest.

And in the afternoon Mother took me to Hampstead Heath in a taxi and we sat on the top of a hill and looked at the planes coming in to Heathrow airport in the distance. And I had a red ice lolly from an ice-cream van. And Mother said she had rung Mrs Gascoyne and told her that I was going to take my Maths A level next year so I threw my red ice lolly away and I screamed for a long time and the pain in my chest hurt so much that it was hard to breathe and a man came up and asked if I was OK and Mother said, 'Well, what does it look like to you?' and he went away.

And then I was tired from screaming and Mother took me back to the flat in another taxi and the next morning was Saturday and she told Mr Shears to go out and get me some books about science and maths from the library, and they were called *100 Number Puzzles* and *The Origins of the Universe* and *Nuclear Power*, but they were for children and not very good so I didn't read them, and Mr Shears said, 'Well, it's nice to know my contribution is appreciated.'

And when Mother and Mr Shears argued I took the little radio from the kitchen and I went and sat in the spare room and I tuned it halfway between two stations so that all I could hear was white noise, and I turned the volume up really loud and I held it against my ear and the sound filled my head and it hurt so that I couldn't feel any other sort of hurt, like the hurt in my chest, and I couldn't think about not doing my A level or the fact that there wasn't a garden at 451c Chapter Road and I couldn't see the stars.

And then it was Monday. And it was very late at night and Mr Shears came into my room and woke me up and he had been drinking beer because he smelt like Father did when he had been drinking beer with Rhodri. And he said, 'You think you're so fucking clever, don't you? Don't you ever, ever think about other people for one second, eh? Well, I bet you're really pleased with yourself now, aren't you?'

And then Mother came in and pulled him out of the room and said, 'Christopher, I'm sorry. I'm really, really sorry.'

The next morning, after Mr Shears had gone to work, Mother packed lots of her clothes into two suitcases and told me to come downstairs and bring Toby and get into the car. And she put the suitcases into the boot and we drove off. But it was Mr Shears's car and I said, 'Are you stealing the car?'

And she said, 'I'm just borrowing it.'

And I said, 'Where are we going?'

And she said, 'We're going home.'

And I said, 'Do you mean home in Swindon?'

And she said, 'Yes.'

And I said, 'Is Father going to be there?'

And she said, 'Please, Christopher. Don't give me any hassle right now, OK? Just . . . Just . . . It's going to be all right, Christopher, OK? It's going to be all right.'

And I said, 'Are we going back to Swindon so I can do my Maths A level?'

And Mother said, 'What?'

And I said, 'I'm meant to be doing my Maths A level tomorrow.'

And Mother spoke very slowly and she said, 'We are going back to Swindon because if we stayed in London any longer . . . someone was going to get hurt. And I don't necessarily mean you.'

And I said, 'What do you mean?'

And she said, 'Now I need you to be quiet for a while.'

And I said, 'How long do you want me to be quiet for?'

And she said, 'Half an hour, Christopher. I need you to be quiet for half an hour.'

And we drove all the way to Swindon and it took 3 hours 12 minutes and we had to stop for petrol and Mother bought me a Milky Bar but I didn't eat it. Then we got caught in a long traffic jam and I fell asleep.

When we got to Swindon Mother had keys to the house and we went in and she said, 'Hello?' but there was no one there because it was 1.23pm. And I was frightened but Mother said I would be safe, so I went up to my room and closed the door. I took Toby out of my pocket and I let him run around and I played **Minesweeper** and I did the **Expert Version** in 174 seconds, which was 75 seconds longer than my best time.

And then it was 6.35pm and I heard Father come home in his van and I moved the bed up against the door so he couldn't get in and he came into the house and he and Mother shouted at each other.

Father shouted, 'How the fuck did you get in here?'

And Mother shouted, 'This is my house, too.'

And Father shouted, 'Is your fancy man here, as well?'

And then I picked up the bongo drums that Uncle Terry had bought me and I knelt down in the corner of the room and I pressed my head into the join between the two walls and I banged the drums and I groaned and I carried on doing this for an hour. Then Mother came into the room and said Father had gone to stay with Rhodri for a while and we would get a place to live of our own in the next few weeks.

Then I went into the garden and I found Toby's cage behind the shed and I brought it inside and I cleaned it and put Toby back in it.

And I asked Mother if I could do my Maths A level the next day.

And she said, 'You're not listening to me, are you, Christopher?

I told you. I rang your headmistress. I told her you were in London. I told her you'd do it next year.'

And I said, 'But I'm here now and I can take it.'

And Mother said, 'I'm sorry, Christopher. I was trying to do things properly. I didn't know we'd be coming back.'

And my chest began hurting again and I folded my arms and I rocked backwards and forwards and groaned.

And Mother said, 'Come on. This isn't going to solve anything.' Then she asked if I wanted to watch one of my *Blue Planet* videos, but I didn't say anything because I knew I wasn't going to be able to do my Maths A level and it was like pressing your thumbnail against a radiator when it's really hot and the pain starts and it makes you want to cry.

Then Mother made me some carrots and broccoli and ketchup, but I didn't eat them.

And I didn't sleep that night either.

The next day Mother drove me to school in Mr Shears's car because we missed the bus. And when we were getting into the car, Mrs Shears came across the road and said to Mother, 'You've got a fucking nerve.'

And Mother said, 'Get into the car, Christopher.'

But I couldn't get into the car because the door was locked.

And Mrs Shears said, 'So, has he finally dumped you, too?'

Then Mother opened her door and got into the car and unlocked my door and I got in and we drove away.

And when we got to school Siobhan said, 'So you're Christopher's mother.' And Siobhan said that she was glad to see me again and she asked if I was OK and I said I was tired. And Mother explained that I was upset because I couldn't do my Maths A level so I hadn't been eating properly or sleeping properly.

And then Mother went away and I drew a picture of a bus using perspective so that I didn't think about the pain in my chest.

And after lunch Siobhan said that she had spoken to Mrs Gascoyne and she still had my A level papers in sealed envelopes in her desk.

So I asked if I could still do my A level.

And Siobhan said, 'I think so. We're going to ring the Reverend Peters this afternoon to make sure he can still be your invigilator. And Mrs Gascoyne is going to write a letter to the examination board to say that you're going to take the exam after all. And hopefully they'll say that that's OK. But we can't know that for sure.' She stopped talking for a few seconds. And then she said, 'Is this what you want to do, Christopher? You don't have to do it. If you say you don't want to do it no one is going to be angry with you.'

And I said, 'I want to do it' because I don't like it when I put things in my timetable and I have to take them out again, because when I do that it makes me feel sick.

And Siobhan said, 'OK.'

And she rang the Reverend Peters and he came into school at 3.27pm and he said, 'So, young man, are we ready to roll?'

And I did **Paper 1** of my Maths A level sitting in the Art Room. And Reverend Peters was the invigilator and he sat at a desk while I did the exam and he read a book called *The Cost of Discipleship* by Dietrich Bonhoeffer and ate a sandwich. And in the middle of the exam he went and smoked a cigarette outside the window, but he watched me through the window in case I cheated.

And when I opened the paper and read through it I couldn't think how to answer any of the questions and also I couldn't breathe properly. So I took deep breaths like Siobhan said I should do when I want to hit someone in school and I counted fifty breaths and did cubes of the cardinal numbers as I counted, like this: **1**, **8**, **27**, **64**, **125**, **216**, **343**, **512**, **729**, **1,000**, **1,331**, **1,728**, **2,197**, **2,744**, **3,375**, **4,096**, **4,913** . . . etc. And that made me feel a little calmer. But the exam was 2 hours long and 20 minutes had already gone so I had to work really fast and I didn't have time to check my answers properly.

And that night, just after I got home, Father came back to the house and I screamed but Mother said she wouldn't let anything bad happen to me and I went into the garden and lay down and looked at the stars in the sky and made myself negligible. And when Father came out of the house he looked at me for a long time and then he punched the fence and made a hole in it and went away.

And I slept a little bit that night because I was doing my Maths A level. And I had some spinach soup for supper.

And the next day I did **Paper 2** and the Reverend Peters read *The Cost of Discipleship* but this time he didn't smoke a cigarette and Siobhan made me go into the toilets before the exam and sit on my own and do breathing and counting.

And I was playing *The Eleventh Hour* on my computer that evening when a taxi stopped outside the house. Mr Shears was in the taxi and he got out of the taxi and threw a big cardboard box of things belonging to Mother onto the lawn. Then he got some keys out of his pocket and got into his car and drove away and Mother ran out of the house and into the street and she threw the box and it hit the boot of his car as he drove away and Mrs Shears was looking out of her window when Mother did this.

The next day I did **Paper 3** and the Reverend Peters read the *Daily Mail* and smoked 3 cigarettes.

And this was my favourite question

> Prove the following result:
> 'A triangle with sides that can be written in the form
> $n^2 + 1$, $n^2 - 1$ and $2n$ (where $n > 1$) is right-angled.'
> And show, by means of a counterexample, that the converse is false.

And I was going to write out how I answered the question except Siobhan said it wasn't very interesting, but I said it was. And she said people wouldn't want to read the answers to a maths question in a book, and she said I could put the answer in an *Appendix*, which is an extra chapter at the end of a book that people can read if they want to.

And then my chest didn't hurt so much and it was easier to breathe. But I still felt sick because I didn't know if I'd done well in the exam.

It's best if you know a good thing is going to happen, like an eclipse or getting a microscope for Christmas. And it's bad if you know a bad thing is going to happen, like having a filling or going to France. But I think it is worst if you don't know whether it is a good thing or a bad thing which is going to happen.

And Father came round to the house that night and I was sitting on the sofa watching *University Challenge* and just answering the science questions. And he stood in the doorway of the living room and he said, 'Don't scream, OK, Christopher. I'm not going to hurt you.'

And Mother was standing behind him so I didn't scream.

Then he came a bit closer to me and he crouched down and he said, 'I wanted to ask you how the exam went.'

But I didn't say anything.

And Mother said, 'Tell him, Christopher. Please.'

So I said, 'I don't know if I got all the questions right because I was really tired and I hadn't eaten so I couldn't think properly.'

And then Father nodded and he didn't say anything for a short while. Then he said, 'Thank you.'

And I said, 'What for?'

And he said, 'Just . . . thank you.' Then he said, 'I'm very proud of you, Christopher. Very proud. I'm sure you did really well.'

And then he went away and I watched the rest of *University Challenge*.

And the next week Father told Mother she had to move out of the house, but she couldn't because she didn't have any money to pay rent for a flat. And I asked if Father would be arrested and go to prison for killing Wellington because we could live in the house if he was in prison. But Mother said the police would only arrest Father if Mrs Shears did what is called *pressing charges*, because the police don't arrest people for little crimes unless you ask them and Mother said that killing a dog was only a little crime.

But then everything was OK because Mother got a job on the till in a garden centre and the doctor gave her pills to take every morning to stop her feeling sad, except that sometimes they made her dizzy and she fell over if she stood up too fast. So we moved into a room in a big house that was made of red bricks. And the bed was in the same room as the kitchen and I didn't like it because it was small and the corridor was painted brown and there was a toilet and a bathroom that other people used.

And I didn't like waiting to find out about my Maths A level. And whenever I thought about the future I couldn't see anything clearly in my head and that made a panic start. So Siobhan said I shouldn't think about the future. She said, 'Just think about today. Think about things that have happened. Especially about good things.'

One good thing was that I helped Mother paint her room **White With A Hint Of Wheat**, except I got paint in my hair and she wanted to wash it out by rubbing shampoo on my head when I was in the bath, but I wouldn't let her, so there was paint in my hair for 5 days and then I cut it out with a pair of scissors.

There were more bad things than good things. And one of them was that Mother didn't get back from work till 5.30pm so I had to go to Father's house between 3.49pm and 5.30pm because I wasn't allowed to be on my own and Mother said I didn't have a choice so I pushed the bed against the door in case Father tried to come in. And sometimes he tried to talk to me through the door, but I didn't answer him. And sometimes I heard him sitting on the floor outside the door quietly for a long time.

And another bad thing was that Toby died because he was 2 years and 7 months old which is very old for a rat, and I said I wanted to bury him, but Mother didn't have a garden, so I buried him in a big plastic pot of earth like a pot you put a plant in. And I said I wanted another rat but Mother said I couldn't have one because the room was too small.

Mother picked me up from Father's house one day after she had finished work and Father said, 'Christopher, can I have a talk with you?'

And I said, 'No.'

And Mother said, 'It's OK. I'll be here.'

And I said, 'I don't want to talk to Father.'

And Father said, 'I'll do you a deal.' And he was holding the kitchen timer which is a big plastic tomato sliced through the middle and he twisted it and it started ticking. And he said, 'Five minutes, OK? That's all. Then you can go.'

So I sat on the sofa and he sat on the armchair and Mother was in the hallway and Father said, 'Christopher, look . . . Things can't go on like this. I don't know about you, but this . . . this just hurts too much. You being in the house but refusing to talk to me . . . You have to learn to trust me . . . And I don't care how long it takes . . . If it's a minute one day and two minutes the next and it takes years I don't care. Because this is important. This is more important than anything else. Let's call it . . . let's call it a project. A project we have to do together. You have to spend more time with me. And I . . . I have to show you that you can trust me. And it will be difficult at first because . . . because it's a difficult project. But it will get better. I promise.' Then he rubbed the sides of his forehead with his fingertips, and he said, 'You don't have to say anything, not right now. You just have to think about it. And, um . . . I've got you a present. To show you that I really mean what I say. And to say sorry. And because . . . well, you'll see what I mean.'

Then he got out of the armchair and he walked over to the kitchen door and opened it and there was a big cardboard box on the floor and there was a blanket in it and he bent down and put his hands inside the box and he took out a little sandy-coloured dog.

He came back through and gave me the dog and he said, 'He's two months old. And he's a golden retriever.'

And the dog sat in my lap and I stroked it.

And no one said anything for a while.

Then Mother said, 'You won't be able to take him away with you, I'm afraid. The bedsit's too small. But your father's going to look after him here. And you can come and take him out for walks whenever you want.'

And I said, 'Does he have a name?'

And Father said, 'No. You can decide what to call him.'

And the dog chewed my finger.

And then it was 5 minutes and the tomato alarm went. So Mother and I drove back to her room.

And the next week I got the results of my Maths A level and I got an A grade which is the best result and it made me feel like this

And I called the dog Sandy. And Father bought him a collar and a lead and I was allowed to take him for walks to the shop and back. And I played with him with a rubber bone.

And Mother got flu and I had to spend three days with Father and stay in his house. But it was OK because Sandy slept on my bed so he would bark if anyone came into the room during the night. And Father made a vegetable patch in the garden and I helped him. And we planted carrots and peas and spinach and I'm going to pick them and eat them when they're ready.

And I went to a bookshop with Mother and I bought a book called *Further Maths for A Level* and Father told Mrs Gascoyne that I was going to take A level Further Maths next year and she said, 'OK.' And I am going to pass it and get an A grade. And in two years' time I am going to take A level Physics and get an A grade. And then, when I've done that, I am going to go to university in another town. And it doesn't have to be in London because I don't like London and there are universities in lots of places and not all of them are in big cities. And I can live in a flat with a garden and a proper toilet. And I can take Sandy and my books and my computer.

And then I will get a First Class Honours Degree and I will become a scientist. And I know I can do this because I went to London on my own, and because I solved the mystery of Who Killed Wellington? and I found my mother and I was brave and I wrote a book and that means I can do anything.

MARK HADDON

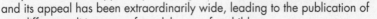

A book about a fifteen-year-old boy with Asperger's Syndrome who decides to write a mystery story about a dead dog that he finds in a neighbour's garden, hardly sounds like the stuff a best seller is made of. Yet *The Curious Incident of the Dog in the Night-Time* has become just that. It has been sold in twenty-four languages, Hollywood has snapped up film rights, and its appeal has been extraordinarily wide, leading to the publication of two different editions: one for adults, one for children.

Asperger's Syndrome is a form of autism, of which Haddon says, 'The thing about the condition is that it's a continuum. At one end of the scale you've got individuals who can't fit in to society at all; at the other end there are perfectly normal people who just happen to like alphabetising their record collections. I think that's why people recognise Christopher. I deliberately didn't use the word Asperger's anywhere in the book. I don't want Christopher to be seen as a case study. I wanted him to be a character.'

When he graduated from Oxford with a degree in English, Haddon went to Scotland to spend a year as a voluntary live-in carer to a disabled man. Then, in London, he worked part-time for Mencap and Hackney Social Services, while eking out a living as a cartoonist and illustrator. 'I worked as an illustrator for quite a while, but didn't want to go into advertising, which was the logical next step. Advertising is a world to be avoided at all costs, so I thought it would be a good idea to start doing books.' One of them, *The Real Porky Philips*, saw him short-listed for a Nestlé Smarties book prize in 1994. When he later became involved in television he created a series called *Microsoap* and was awarded two BAFTAs.

It may be Haddon's experience of writing for children that has helped him to portray Christopher's world view with such accuracy. The boy's 'voice' is one of the things that makes the book so strikingly unique. 'It's wonderful to write in,' says Haddon, 'because it makes you simply paint a picture, very concretely, and leave the readers to make up their own minds about absolutely everything. I also like the fact that the novel puts you instantly inside the mind of someone that you would probably never get into in real life at all.'

ACKNOWLEDGMENTS AND PICTURE CREDITS: The King of Torts: pages 6–8: skyscraper: Getty Images/Photodisc; man in office: Getty Images/Stone; photomontage: Rick Lecoat @ Shark Attatck; page 147: © Jare Roul Burdine. Days Without Number: pages 148–150: © Jonathan Ring; page 301: © Jane Brown. The Last Detective: pages 302–304: sunset: Getty Images/Stone; helicopter: Getty Images/The Image Bank; photomontage: Curtis Cozier; page 435 © Patrik Giardino. The Curious Incident of the Dog in the Night-time: pages 436–438: illustration: Lasse Skarbovik/The Organisation; page 539: © Claire McNamee.

DUSTJACKET CREDITS: Spine from top: Spine from top: skyscraper: Getty Images/Photodisc; man in office: Getty Images/Stone; photomontage: Rick Lecoat @ Shark Attack; © Jonathan Ring; sunset: Getty Images/Stone; helicopter: Getty Images/The Image Bank; photomontage: Curtis Cozier; illustration: Lasse Skarbovik/The Organisation.

Printed by Maury Imprimeur SA, Malesherbes, France
Bound by Reliures Brun SA, Malesherbes, France